Pamela Belle lives in Wiltshire with her husband, Steve, and two sons, Hugh and Patrick. She is the author of eight historical novels including *Wintercombe*, *Herald of Joy*, *A Falling Star* and *Treason's Gift*. *The Silver City* is her first fantasy novel and is the first of a trilogy.

THE
SILVER
CITY

PAMELA BELLE

PAN BOOKS
LONDON, SYDNEY AND AUCKLAND

First published 1994 by Pan Books

a division of Pan Macmillan Publishers Limited
Cavaye Place London SW10 9PG
and Basingstoke

Associated companies throughout the world

ISBN 0 330 32876 X

Copyright © Pamela Belle 1994

The right of Pamela Belle to be identified as the
author of this work has been asserted by her in accordance
with the Copyright, Designs and Patents Act 1988.

1 3 5 7 9 8 6 4 2

A CIP catalogue record for this book is available from
the British Library

Typeset by CentraCet Limited, Cambridge
Printed by Mackays of Chatham PLC, Kent

FOR PATRICK, MY SECOND SON –
WELCOME TO THE WORLD

ACKNOWLEDGEMENTS

I would like to thank all those who have helped me with this book, and with its rather different predecessors. In particular, I owe a great debt to my mother, who as always read the whole manuscript and offered many helpful corrections and suggestions; to my husband, Steve, whose encouragement has never failed and whose assistance with various recalcitrant wonders of modern technology has been vital so many times; and last, but not least, to my agent, Vivienne Schuster, who has helped and guided me for twelve years, and without whom I would probably have given up writing long ago!

Pamela Belle

GLOSSARY,
AND
NOTE ON PRONUNCIATION

Brek	(Toktel'yan)	'No'
Charsh	(Toktel'yan)	Tropical reed growing along the Kefirinn in Toktel'yi, used to make paper
Djarlck	(Toktel'yan)	Musical instrument with eight strings and a curved neck
Engren	(Tanathi)	Contraceptive herb only found growing around Lake Raiyis
Gellin	(Zithiriani)	Alcoholic drink made from fermented honey
Issir	(Tanathi)	The sunset star
Iyal	(Tanathi)	The morning star
Kal-Gan	(Toktel'yan)	Puzzle of differing geometric shapes arranged to form a whole
Katchek	(Toktel'yan)	Salad dish with oil and citrus dressing
Kedrin	(Zithiriani)	Warm, dry summer wind from the steppe
K'tenn	(Toktel'yan)	'Enter'
Kuldi	(Zithiriani and Tanathi)	Refreshing beverage made by infusing dried leaves of the kuldi plant in hot water
Marek	(Tanathi)	A tent
Ral	(Zithiriani)	Potent spirit made from distilled grain
Sith	(Zithiriani)	Musical instrument with sixteen pairs of strings
Skrath	(Zithiriani)	Simpler version of 'tek' (see below)
Tek	(Tanathi)	Complicated game played with counters on a specially woven carpet

NOTES ON PRONUNCIATION

Most names are spelt as pronounced. As a general rule, stress is laid evenly on both syllables of two-syllable words, and on the second syllable of words of three syllables or more (e.g. ZiTHIRian, AnSARyon, TanATHi).

An apostrophe indicates missing letters and should technically be pronounced as a brief pause, but in practice many speakers omit this altogether. Exceptions include Ska'i and D'thliss.

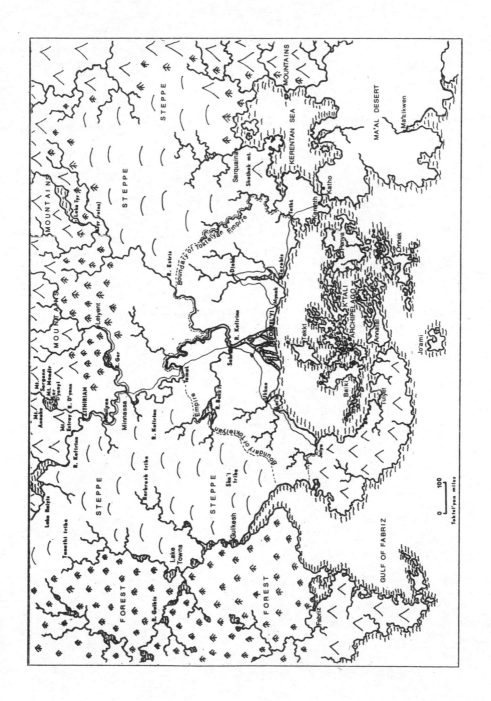

PART
ONE

ONE

They had flushed the deer from a scrub-filled gully on the side of a gentle slope, and it leapt up and away with a flash of its white rump, and half-a-dozen members of the Tanathi tribe in urgent pursuit.

The stag ran for its life, with the wonderful flying grace of its kind, but the wide rolling grassland of the steppe could offer it no shelter, no chance to hide, or rest, or double back. The hunters slackened their speed a little. Despite their youth, they were too experienced to exhaust the horses to no good purpose.

Halthris rode beside her brother, Abreth, leading the chase. This was what she loved above all: the wind streaming her braided hair; the vast wild space of the steppe all around her, seeming so empty yet so full of teeming and secret life; the feel of her horse Ennim beneath her, strong and warm and eager, friend as well as servant; and the company of the other hunters, her brother, her cousin, the men with whom she had grown up, and shared so much laughter.

She had all this, and it was her life: how much longer would she be able to resist the clamour of voices, led by her father and her mother and her sister, urging her to marry that nice man Vinnath, and settle down by the Hearth?

Abreth shouted something, and she followed his pointing hand. The white-rumped stag, leaping over the grass in huge tireless bounds, seemed to be in danger of escaping them altogether.

Abreth gestured, and shouted again. 'Fess – use Fess, or we'll all go to bed hungry tonight!'

Fess. She had run alongside them, a swift dappled shadow in the grass, silent, beautiful, deadly, waiting on the signal that would unleash her attack. Halthris turned in the saddle and made a swift, sweeping movement of her arm. And Fess, loosed from her invisible bond, began to accelerate away from them.

She had watched the cat run so often, but still the astonishing speed, the power and the savagery freed at her command, could fill Halthris with a vast, choking, inexpressible joy. She shouted with delight as Fess streaked down the hill, eating up the ground with that enormous bounding stride, and swept on, across the shallow valley towards the long slope of the next low, rocky hill, where the deer, unaware of the spotted, feline death behind it, was springing towards safety.

The huge muscles on the cat's haunches propelled her into the air. One sweep of her paw, and the stag crashed down in the dust, the great bulk of the hunting cat clinging to its back: and then only the thrashing stems of the grass showed where the final struggle was taking place.

Full stomachs tonight. Halthris, grinning, held out her right hand, palm upwards, and her brother slapped his own hand across it in the universal Tanathi gesture of triumph. They slowed their horses and trotted towards the kill, half-way up the next slope.

As was customary, and only fair, Fess was taking her share of the meat, and they must wait until she had finished. At last replete, she stalked off into the grass, with her aloof, delicate stride, to wash and clean herself. Later, when they had returned to the camp, she might slip away during the night to catch herself one of the hares or rabbits that abounded in this part of the steppe. Fess was a free agent, owing loyalty only to Halthris, who had reared her from a small cub, and taught her to hunt and to kill for the tribe.

Abreth and his cousin Kettan were dealing with the deer: they would each carry a piece back with them to the camp, where their companions waited with the horse herd. The other members of the hunting party took the opportunity to rest, and to check their mounts' legs. And Halthris, still filled with the exultation of a successful chase, dismounted, leaving Ennim to graze, and went in search of Fess.

No one else in all the Tanathi had a hunting-cat, although they were not unknown of in the tribe. In the wild, they were rare indeed, and seldom seen. She had found Fess more than two years ago, a tiny mewing cub, sole survivor of a spring flash flood which had swept away the rest of the litter, and left her stranded on a boulder, cold and drenched and close to death. Halthris had warmed her inside her tunic, carried her everywhere, and fed her mares' milk from a leather bottle: and Fess had lived, and grown strong, and repaid the love and care which had saved her life by becoming Halthris's companion and friend. One day, perhaps next spring, she would slip back to the wild, to find a mate and rear cubs of her own, but Halthris accepted this inevitable future parting. To have the assistance of a hunting-cat showed the especial favour of the gods: and like all such favours, the arrival of the gift, and its eventual departure, were matters entirely beyond her control.

Halthris walked through the long grass. Here, on the exposed western side of the hill, it grew only knee-high: in the valleys, it sometimes reached her shoulder. At this time of year, with autumn approaching, there were no flowers, but the dry rustling heads of a stand of steppe poppies scattered their seeds as she brushed past them, to rise again next year in splashes of brilliant crimson and scarlet.

She could not see Fess, whose spotted hide, brown and gold, blended perfectly with the dappled, flickering shadows crossing the grass, but there was rustling and movement just ahead of her, below the rocky crest of the hill. She whistled softly. 'Fess?'

And a man stood up right in front of her.

He was short, ugly, clad in a jerkin of the badly cured leather worn by the southern tribes: and he brandished a double-headed axe, and grinned at her through a greasy moustache.

Halthris yelled a warning and whipped her knife out of its scabbard, cursing the bad luck that had left her other weapons, her bow and arrows and spear, with her horse. She waved the knife threateningly, her eyes narrowed and intent, her brain working feverishly. Had Abreth heard her? More to the point, had Fess? Urgently, she whistled the two-toned signal that should bring the cat to her side.

The man moved forward, still with that terrible, bloodthirsty grin splitting his broad, dun-coloured face. He spoke through brown, gapped teeth. 'No good, Tanathi woman. You dead soon. Friends too.' He swept the axe through the air with a swish, chopping at the grass. 'Nice head. No run.'

She backed away, and yelled again. Surely she had not strayed beyond earshot? Behind her, she could visualize the slope sinking downwards, the tall poppies, the tussocks and rocks waiting to trip her up, and if she fell she was surely dead.

She changed her grip on the knife and threw it, in one fluid, desperate movement. The man's reactions were too quick: he dodged sideways and the blade flicked past him to vanish in the grass, leaving her defenceless. She could only run, and pray to Emmesar the Hare that she would reach the others before he caught her, or threw the axe . . .

Down the hill, someone shouted. And as the man's glance shifted briefly to the source of the sound, Fess sprang silently out of the grass behind him, and struck him down.

When Abreth, panting, arrived at his sister's side a moment later, it was all over. The man lay prone in the grass, with Fess sitting watchfully by his side, one paw placed on his chest. A single, raking blow had ripped down his unprotected head, neck and arm, and he was bleeding heavily.

Halthris, the double axe in one hand and the man's iron-bladed knife in the other, did not take her eyes off her captive. She said caustically to her brother, 'What kept you? If it hadn't been for Fess, I'd certainly be dead, and so might you.'

Abreth ignored her: he was staring in astonished bewilderment at Fess's prey. 'A Ska'i tribesman! What in Hegeden's name is he doing here? Their lands are a month's ride away.'

'I don't know – but he's here, as you can see.' Halthris rammed the knife into her scabbard, which was too small for it. 'And much more to the point, where are the rest of them? The Ska'i are like wolves – they always hunt in packs.'

Kettan came loping up the hill, wiping his bloodstained hands on a hank of grass, his amber-coloured braids leaping with each stride. Like Abreth, he gaped in amazement at the prone Ska'i. 'So that's why you shouted! But you didn't sound as if you were in any trouble.'

'So you took your time.' Halthris glared at him, wondering as so often before why she had taken Kettan as her first lover, seven years ago. He was so vain, with his golden jewelled quiver and scabbard, his intricately woven braids and over-handsome face: vain, and stupid. And one man's stupidity, out here on the steppe, apparently concealing any number of murderous Ska'i tribesmen in addition to its countless other hazards, could be fatal to all of them.

She silently gave thanks to Sarraliss, the Great Mother who watched over all women, for her deliverance from Kettan and from the tribesman, and turned to her brother. 'You speak some Ska'i, don't you? Ask him where the others are.'

Abreth grimaced. 'Even less than "some". You don't need any words to deal with them – either you kill them, or they kill you. Polite negotiation is a complete waste of time.'

'I don't think so – not in this case.' Halthris stared down at the Ska'i. He had not moved a muscle since having been felled by the cat: every fibre of his body was rigid with terror, his eyes distended, fixed on Fess's implacable, impassive face, while the blood, pumped by his frantic heart, soaked into the dry earth and grass beneath him.

'Hegeden's Wings!' said Kettan gleefully. 'Look at that – he's terrified of Fess!' He gave a whooping cry of triumph. 'What a marvel – the terrible Ska'i are afraid of cats!'

'This Ska'i may be – but what about the others?' Abreth pointed out. 'And don't make so much noise – we don't know where the rest of them are.'

'Which is precisely why I told you to ask him,' said Halthris in exasperation. 'A hundred of them could be lurking just the other side of the hill, for all we know.'

She clicked her tongue softly, and Fess gave a low, answering rumble deep in her throat. The tribesman, his face a white mask of absolute horror, pressed himself into the earth.

'See? He'll tell you. Either he thinks Fess is some kind of demon, or he's afraid she'll eat him alive as soon as I snap my fingers.'

With a resigned glance at his sister, Abreth stepped forward and leaned menacingly over the Ska'i. His freckled, open face usually radiated cheerful good nature, and his intimidating scowl was an incongruous distortion. But their captive, already half-dead from terror and loss of blood, seemed to find it convincing. To add weight to the threat, Halthris whistled the 'hold' signal, and Fess obediently put her other front paw on the tribesman's chest and thoughtfully flexed her claws a finger's breadth from his throat.

Abreth spoke three words of the harsh, guttural Ska'i tongue, his distaste plain in his tone. The man gulped, swallowed and whispered something too low and too hoarse to be heard. Fess stretched her claws again, and with a wild, desperate glance the Ska'i repeated the same phrase over and over, with the increasing shrillness of panic. Then abruptly his eyes rolled up, and his taut muscles relaxed.

'He's fainted,' Kettan said contemptuously. 'And I thought the Ska'i were afraid of nothing.'

'Well, obviously that one is,' Halthris pointed out. 'What did he say, Abreth?'

'I think – I *think* he said they were on the other side of the hill. Shall we go and look?'

'I will!' Kettan cried eagerly.

Halthris gave him one of her most withering stares. 'I can't think of a quicker way to bring the whole pack of wolves howling down on us. You stay here with Fess, and watch him – if there's any trouble, whistle, but I doubt there will be any. You know what's required, don't you, my lady?'

The spotted cat, briefly tickled under her bristly chin, began to purr. Kettan opened his mouth to protest, but Halthris grabbed her brother by the arm and pulled him away before their cousin could object. Moving with the swift, unerring deftness of hunting Tanathi, they vanished into the grass.

It was perhaps three bowshots, no more, to the top of the ridge. On the skyline, tumbled craggy rocks promised plenty of hiding places. But the Ska'i, like the Tanathi, were skilled steppe hunters, masters of concealment and cunning. Behind any one of those boulders a savage tribesman might be crouching, double axe in hand, eager to slaughter them and take their heads for trophies.

The soft undyed leather of their hunting tunics blended perfectly with the dull dun colouring of the autumn grass. They climbed upwards with increasing wariness, alert for every rustle, every movement that might betray a hostile presence. Once a young steppe hare, its fur already beginning to turn white for winter, bounced up almost from under Abreth's feet and sprang wildly away down the hill, and for a long while afterwards the brother and sister remained quite still, crouching beside a low, scrubby thorn-bush, listening intently. Only when they were sure that it was still safe did they move on.

At last, they reached the shelter of the rocks. The soft soles of their riding boots made quiet climbing easy. Halthris led the way, negotiating obstacles and crevices with ease and unthinking agility. Like her brother, she was tall for a Tanathi, and lightly built, but on the steppes their lean frames and wiry strength conferred a considerable advantage. With infinite care, she slid her face and upper body between two worn, lichened lumps of stone, and looked down at the broad rolling valley which lay on the other side of the ridge.

She remembered this place from previous occasions. Flat-bottomed and green, a small river ran through it after the infrequent but heavy spring and autumn rains, and it had often provided the Tanathi herds with good, lush grazing.

Not this year, however. This year, others had seized the opportunity before them. As far as her sharp eyes could discern, the floor of the valley was covered with vast numbers of animals, people, tents and wagons. Even at this distance, the sounds and smells of the huge camp soared clearly up to her in the still afternoon air: shouts, the neighing of horses, the sharp tang of smoke, the richer aroma of roasting meat.

This was not just a wolf-pack of Ska'i, an aberrant marauding band come north for a month of easy plunder before winter. This was the whole tribe, thousands upon thousands of them, the most ferocious warriors in all the known world, and each man trained and eager to kill without mercy . . .

The tent nearest to them was still a good way off, and half obscured by a group of hobbled, grazing horses, but she did not need to strain her eyes to know that the round objects suspended from a pole stuck in the earth outside it were the heads of Ska'i enemies, proudly displayed as evidence of prowess in war. And she wondered, with sickened revulsion, how many of those heads had long, braided hair, and had once spoken Tanathi.

A hand touched her, and she had the knife out of the scabbard before realizing that it was Abreth, unable to see past her and desperate to know what lay beyond the ridge. Her face white with shock, all the multitude of freckles stark on her skin, she put a finger to her lips and wriggled carefully backwards so that he could take her place.

He stayed there for a long time, and she knew that her feelings of amazement, hatred and fear must be similar to his. For centuries the terrible, bloodthirsty Ska'i, trained to war from infancy and devoted to Ayak the Devourer, wolf-god of Death, had inspired fear and horror in all who were unfortunate enough to cross their path. Even though the Tanathi lived far to the north of the Ska'i homelands, the two tribes had come into conflict perhaps four or five times during her twenty-four years of life. When her father had been a boy, there had been twelve individual clans of the Tanathi: now there were only ten, for Ska'i raiders had wiped out two entire bands, each numbering some five or six hundred men, women and children, all their songs and spells and stories lost and spilled scarlet into the parched earth.

That terrible fate would not, must not befall her and her brother and her friends.

After what seemed like a perilously long time, Abreth crawled backwards out of the cleft, and sat up beside her, his back against the sun-warmed boulder. Below them, on the western side of the ridge, the grassy slope, dotted with bushes, fell gently away into the shallow valley beyond, to rise again and again and again in the vast blue distance, until earth and sky, Sarraliss and Hegeden, became one. Within ear-shot, Kettan and Fess guarded their Ska'i captive: beyond, towards the bottom of the hill, the others, Channa and Sherren and Urdray, waited with the carcass of the stag. And much further away, far enough to be in no imminent danger from the Ska'i, the rest of their little group were camped with the horse herd, and eager for their supper.

Fifteen of them in all, twelve men, three women, all under thirty, all unmarried, charged with the annual duty of driving their surplus young horses to the great northern city of Zithirian for the autumn Gathering Fair. It was an important task, allotted only to the most skilled and competent of the clan's young hunters and riders, and a privilege eagerly sought. This was Abreth's sixth year, his sister's fourth, and she had always greatly looked forward to the weeks away from tribal restraint and discipline, the carefree laughter and sense of comradeship that always seemed to accompany them on the journey, the chance to marvel at the beautiful city and the strange, incomprehensible people who lived there, people who seemed to like staying in one place all their lives, with roofs over their heads, and who could not see that they inhabited a glorious cage . . .

There had been no awareness of danger, no word in the grass speaking of the horrible death lying in wait for them in the valley where they had planned to graze their horses the next day. She sweated to think of what might have happened if that hunted stag had not led them here, if she had not gone to find Fess, if the Ska'i had not attacked her on the hillside.

There were only fifteen of them, herding seventy young horses, prime Tanathi stock, sought all over the known world for their speed and endurance and spirit, and for their slender, deceptively fragile beauty. The price paid for their horses clothed the Tanathi in brilliant colours and fine city-woven wools, bejewelled weapons and garments in gold and silver, provided grain for winter fodder and spices and other luxuries for their food. If the Ska'i realized that such a prize lay almost within their grasp, and so inadequately guarded, they would descend on them like ravening wolves.

Abreth's expression of appalled and bewildered disbelief must mirror her own. He whispered hoarsely, 'There are *thousands* of them! Why? What are they doing here? And why haven't we heard anything?'

'Perhaps the Rerbresh are there as well,' Halthris said. Her hands were shaking, and sweat lay cold on her skin: she clasped her knees tightly, fiercely forcing herself to think. 'They are our enemies too, after all. If the Ska'i came northwards, the Rerbresh would join up with them. And we've spent all summer in the northern steppes, well out of reach of any word.'

'Didn't the Ska'i have a new chief last year?' said Abreth slowly, frowning. 'Perhaps this is his doing. But *why*? Why come so far north, with summer almost over? Unless – unless they plan to take our lands . . . or raid our winter valleys.'

Halthris felt sick. Each autumn, while the young men and women of each band brought their surplus stock to Zithirian for sale, the rest of the tribe, who had wandered in their separate clans all through the heat of summer, gathered in the sheltered land around Lake Raiyis, below the northern mountains, to weather the bitter storms of winter together. If the Ska'i were to discover that hidden refuge, the slaughter would be appalling: and anyone who managed to escape into the snow-covered steppes could stand no chance of survival. The whole of the Tanathi tribe, some six or seven thousand strong, would be exterminated.

She stared at her brother, willing herself to examine the situation calmly, to resist the rising panic that urged her to run down the hill and gallop away northwards to Lake Raiyis, to warn her family and her friends, her lover and all the people who gave her life meaning, so that they could take refuge in the merciless winter mountains, before a worse fate befell them.

'We can't be sure what they plan to do,' she said at last.

Abreth had always tended to jump flat-footed to conclusions. 'Of course that's what they're here for! What else can they want? Come on, Hal, let's go back, and wring the truth out of that demon-driven wolf-man before he dies on us.'

But the Ska'i warrior was still unconscious, his breathing shallow and his skin cold and clammy. Kettan, typically, had not attempted to staunch the bleeding. With angry impatience, Halthris fetched linen strips and ointment from the emergency kit she kept in her saddle-bag, and did it herself, while her cousin and erstwhile lover looked on in amazement. 'What are you doing that for? Why can't we just leave him to the kites, and go? He'll be dead in an hour or two, by the look of him.'

'Because the rest of the Ska'i will be sure to find him,' Halthris said, tearing cloth with her knife and wondering again why she had ever been so naïve as to take this vain idiot into her bed. 'If he dies, the kites will lead them to his body, so they'll know that enemies are about, and come after us. If he lives, he'll be able to tell them about us himself. On the other hand, if we take him with us, they'll never know what happened to him. He could have fallen into a gully, or met with a bear or even a leopard. And if I bind this wound, and the bleeding stops, we might just be able, with Fess's help, to persuade him to tell us why his tribe have invaded our territory.'

At her impatient, scornful tone, her cousin pushed out his lower lip like a sulky child and turned away with an injured shrug. He did not assist as Abreth and Halthris heaved the Ska'i man onto Kettan's horse, and trailed behind them down the hill, muttering darkly to himself.

Halthris had been worried that the signs they had left below the ridge – hoof-prints, blood, crushed grass – would betray something of what had happened to any curious Ska'i who ventured in search of the missing man. But as she and Abreth joined their three companions, thunder grumbled uneasily some way off, and a cold wind stirred her hair.

'Storm coming up from the west,' said Channa. He was the youngest of the party, a lanky boy of nineteen with unruly fair hair always spilling out of its braids. His tracking skills bordered on the supernatural, though, which accounted for his presence in this group of older, more experienced hunters. 'It'll rain soon – we'd best get moving, or we won't be back at the camp before dark. And by morning, the earth will be so wet and the grass so flattened that no one will be able to follow our trail.'

'I hope you're right,' Halthris said. 'May Hegeden hide us, and Sarraliss give us good fortune – we'll need all the luck we can manage, to escape from the Ska'i.'

By the time the six Tanathi eventually rode into their camp, it was indeed almost dark, and rain had been falling heavily for some time. The storm had forced them to lie flat on the open steppe until the worst of the lightning had passed, their well-trained horses prone beside them. Kettan had naturally grumbled at the delay, but as Halthris cogently reminded him, it was only prudent. Over the centuries, many foolhardy Tanathi had died in the flashing fires of a thunderbolt because they were too impatient to wait out a storm. So far, with Hegeden's help, they had escaped the Ska'i: except, it seemed, for Kettan, none of them had any desire to court death for a second time that day.

The four wagons had been drawn in a circle, in the lee of a low hill. Halthris was glad to see that someone had pitched one of their dome-shaped tents as well. Its smoke-hole was open, and trailing a reassuring white plume. At least there would be a fire over which they could roast the venison, and shelter while they ate. Beyond the camp, guarded by the two Tanathi on watch duty, the seventy precious horses stood hobbled, miserably resigned, their heads down and rumps turned in unison to the wind.

Urdray and Channa unloaded the haunches of deer, and carried them into the tent. The Tanathi who had been left behind in the camp crowded round, staring at the Ska'i man slung over Kettan's horse and urgently asking questions. What was he? Who was he? Why had they brought him back? Was he dead?

'If he isn't yet, he soon will be,' Halthris told them tersely, her cramped, numb fingers busy with the leather straps that tied their captive to the saddle. 'We'll put him in the tent – it's bound to be warm and snug in there.'

Abreth and Sherren carried the Ska'i inside the stuffy tent. An iron basket full of wood burned cheerfully in the centre, and the acrid smoke wreathed around the walls before finally finding its way out through the smoke-hole in the roof. The two Tanathi laid the tribesman down with scant ceremony, and Kettan glanced at the body dismissively. 'He's dead. I knew we should have left him for the kites.'

'You know very well why we didn't,' Halthris said with considerable annoyance. 'You're only sulking because you had to walk back here. If you can't say or do anything useful, get out.'

'Don't worry, little cousin, I'm going,' he said petulantly, and flounced out of the door.

On the soft, dry felt floor, the Ska'i moved, and muttered something. Halthris knelt beside him, and touched his forehead. It was ice-cold and clammy.

'Shock,' she said concisely to Abreth. 'I don't think he'll last the night – he's lost too much blood.'

She peeled back the stiff, soaked folds of the rough bandage around his shoulder and arm. The great raking wound that Fess had inflicted had ripped deep into the muscles, and the thick leathery skin had torn as if it were soft silk. The gashes were still sluggishly pulsing blood. If he had been another Tanathi, or a city-dweller, or even a Rerbresh, she might have pitied him, and done her best to save him: but for the savage Ska'i, she could feel no such compassion. He would have slain her and her friends with ruthless brutality, and she could not bring herself to offer him the mercy that he would have denied to her.

The man moved again feebly, as if struggling against invisible bonds, and cried out something. Abreth's head went up sharply. 'Quenait, he said, I'm sure of it – and I remember now, that's the name of their new chief. Apparently he's ferocious even for a Ska'i.'

Fierce enough to bring his entire tribe hundreds of miles north, to attack the peace-loving Tanathi at the onset of winter. Such a thing had never been known before, not for many lifetimes of men.

The captive muttered and twisted. Sherren looked at Abreth anxiously. 'Shouldn't we tie his hands? Then at least he won't be able to hurt any of us. They say a Ska'i can kill with just a touch of his finger.'

'So can almost anyone, if they know how,' Halthris said. 'But, yes, you're right – it would certainly be sensible. He may be badly hurt, but even in that state he could still be incredibly strong.'

'I'll stay with him all night,' Abreth said, as Sherren went in search of rope. 'I'm the only one of us who has any hope of understanding what he says – and I might learn something, even if he's raving.' He grinned at his sister. 'Lend me Fess? Just for the night, at any rate. If all else fails, she'll put the fear of Hegeden into him.'

'They don't worship Hegeden,' said Sherren, returning. He shivered suddenly, and made the guarding sign with the palm of his left hand outstretched, warding off evil. 'They worship Ayak. They sacrifice babies and children to him. I hope he dies.'

'So do I,' said Halthris. 'But not before he's told us why Quenait has come so far north.'

She and Sherren had their wish: the Ska'i warrior died just before dawn, when Iyal, the Morning Star, was still bright and high in the west. Save for those guarding the horses, Abreth was the only Tanathi awake. He closed the dead man's eyes and yawned and stretched, his tired mind trying to make sense of the little he had managed to glean from the prisoner's ravings. Then, stumbling from lack of sleep, he went to find his sister.

Halthris was in the wagon she shared with Inri and Chettay, the other two women. He unlaced the leather curtains and stuck his head inside. 'Hal? Hal, it's me, Abreth. Wake up.'

She was in her usual place, nearest the entrance, and sat up, instantly alert. 'What is it?'

'The Ska'i. He's just died.'

'Did he say anything?'

'A lot, but I couldn't understand most of it.' He paused, shivering in the night-sharp cold. 'Hal, we must talk, all of us – as soon as possible. Decide on a plan. If – if we do the wrong thing, go down the wrong path – it could mean death. Not just for us, but for all Tanathi. And there's no shaman with us, to guide us.'

The clan's shaman, Doresh, soothsayer and healer and weaver of spells, their link with the dangerous and capricious worlds of the spirits, the future and the dead, had of course stayed with the rest of the band, heading for the winter valleys. Without his prophetic trances and his skilled interpretations of all the omens, they were like children on the edge of an abyss, fumbling blindly in the dark with no light to help them.

Before sunrise, all fifteen Tanathi had gathered in the cook-tent. The dead Ska'i lay to the side, decently covered by an old rug, but the faded felt could not hide or disguise the sense of menace that seemed to flow out of the corpse like blood. More than one apparently down-to-earth hunter surreptitiously made the warding sign as they sat down.

Abreth looked round at the familiar faces of the young men and women he had known all his life: his sister, his cousin, his friends. He was the chief's son, and although the position was not in any way hereditary, he had his father's gift of command, effectively hiding any inward doubts, and the rest of the group had unquestioningly accepted him as their leader.

Halthris had that gift too, and her wits, and her temper and strength of will, were sharper. Abreth glanced at her rather warily, thinking that if his sister had been born a boy, she would undoubtedly have been chosen chief after their father. But since the Tanathi, although allowing their women enormous respect and freedom, had never yet elected a female leader, Halthris's many talents would be ignored. In a year or two, she would marry Vinnath, join his clan, bear his children and dedicate her life thereafter to the Hearth: all women, however skilled at hunting, came to it in the end. What a waste, thought Abreth, who admired his sister enormously, though he would have died rather than admit it to her.

'I've called us all together to decide what to do about . . . about that.' He jerked his head towards the shrouded body at the side of the tent. 'You already know what happened yesterday, and what we saw. The whole Ska'i tribe, and probably the Rerbresh as well, are camped less than half a day's ride to the east of us. I don't know for certain why they have come so far north at this time of year – but they're here, thousands and thousands of them. And they may be planning to attack our winter valleys.'

'Then someone must ride to Lake Raiyis to warn them,' Urdray said. 'Or perhaps we should all go—'

'What about the horses? If we take them with us, they'll slow us down,' Inri pointed out. 'And we can't just turn them loose to fend for themselves on the steppe, not with winter approaching.'

There was a brief, unhappy silence. Abreth went on. 'I watched over the Ska'i all last night, trying to learn something. I couldn't make head or tail of most of what he said, but he said "Tanathi" several times, and mentioned Lake Raiyis too. So I think we have to assume that our tribe is one of their targets, but not the only one – because he also kept saying "Zithirian", over and over again.'

'Are you sure?' demanded Kettan, with insulting disbelief.

'Of course I am – it's not a name that can easily be mistaken,' Abreth told him, wishing that Halthris had not raised their cousin's hackles yesterday: Kettan often spent weeks sulking. 'So perhaps they're going to attack Zithirian as well.'

'That's ridiculous – when have the Ska'i ever turned on a city?'

'When have they ever come north before?' Halthris mimicked Kettan with cruel accuracy. 'This new chief Quenait is obviously an unusually powerful and aggressive leader. Why shouldn't he attack Zithirian? It's the richest city in the world, apart from Toktel'yi. And the people are soft, and unused to war. I reckon it'd fall to him like a ripe peach.'

'Well, we must warn the Zithiriani too,' Abreth said.

'Why? They're not our responsibility—'

'Oh, do shut up, Kettan, before I knock your thick skull against the tent pole,' Halthris said furiously. 'Of course we owe them a warning. Where do all your precious gold and silver bracelets and brooches come from? Thin air? If Quenait captures Zithirian and plunders it and kills all the people, there'll be lean times for us all, even if he never attacks a single Tanathi.'

'She's right,' said Abreth. 'For our sake as much as theirs, we must warn them too. I suggest we split up. Two ride up to Lake Raiyis, and tell our people. Two more go ahead of us to Zithirian, and warn them that Quenait may move against them. The rest can follow with the horses – as Inri said, we can't leave them here, so we might as well take them to Zithirian as we always do. The city-dwellers could be in need of them, if they are attacked. And we're only two or three days' journey away, whereas it's nearly a week to Lake Raiyis. Well? What do you all think?'

The Tanathi were a peaceable tribe, but dearly loved an argument. In normal circumstances, Abreth's invitation would result in a prolonged and vigorous discussion, with opinions heatedly aired and denounced. But the presence of the Ska'i, singly in the tent and in vast numbers only a few hills away, had had a remarkably subduing effect. Urdray immediately slapped his hands, palm down, on his knees. 'Agreed.'

Halthris echoed him. 'Agreed.'

One by one the others followed eagerly, until only Kettan was left. With bad grace, he muttered his consent, so low that Inri, sitting next to him, could barely hear it. 'I suppose so.'

'Good.' Abreth looked round at his fourteen companions, his relief plain on his face. 'The only question now, is – who goes, and who stays? I think I should lead the main group with the herd.'

'My horse may not be the fastest, but he can go all day without tiring,' Channa said. 'I'll go back to Lake Raiyis, if you want.'

'In that case, I'll come with you,' said his older brother, Nayan. 'Someone has to look after you, and I suppose it ought to be me.'

Channa gave him an indignant stare. 'I'm perfectly capable of fending for myself. And your horse has the stamina of a butterfly.'

'Enough.' Abreth silenced them with a decisive gesture. 'Channa and Nayan go back to the lake. Take a spare horse each, and enough dried food for the journey, as much as you can cram into your saddlebags – you won't have time to hunt. Ride as quickly as you can, without risking your mounts of course. Channa, you know exactly where the Ska'i camp is – you can tell my father what has happened. If we discover any more news, we'll send someone after you.'

'The valley where they're camped – it runs from south to north, then turns eastwards,' said Inri, frowning. 'If they came up it from the south, if they have wagons—'

'They have.'

'Then doesn't that mean that they're planning to attack Zithirian rather than us?'

'It might do,' Abreth told her. 'But do you want to rely on it? Our people can shelter in the mountains and be safe all winter, though it won't be as easy or as pleasant as our usual camp. Better we hide, and survive with some hardship, than sit around in idleness and luxury, waiting to be slaughtered by the Ska'i.'

Kettan was fidgeting restlessly. 'I'll go to Zithirian,' Halthris said hastily, before he could volunteer. 'I've been there four times now, I know the city, and I can speak their language – not that it's very different from our own. And I know the way, too.'

Abreth looked at her dubiously. 'Are you sure? It'll be dangerous—'

'No more than riding with the herd. And I have Fess, remember. She's proved herself more than a match for any Ska'i.'

'I suppose so.' Abreth hesitated, unwilling to openly admit to his dependence on his younger sister. He had come to rely very heavily on her intelligence, her brisk common sense and her sharp sense of humour, that could make a joke out of the most desperate situation, and hearten everyone around her. 'You are the best person for the task.'

'I don't think so,' Kettan interrupted resentfully. 'We all know how the Zithiriani respect fine clothes and a lavish display of gold.' He clanked his bracelets pointedly. '*And* they despise women. I'll go.'

'No, you won't,' Abreth said decisively. Much though he wished that Halthris would stay behind, the thought of Kettan, brainless and conceited, blundering into the elaborate and formal court of the Zithirian King was at once laughable and appalling. Anything, even the temporary absence of his sister, was better than that. 'You've only been there once, Kettan – ten days camped outside the Sunset Gate, and you think you're an expert on city ways. Like it or not, you stay with me, even if I have to rope you to your horse like the Ska'i. Understood?'

Even the thick-skinned Kettan was beginning to realize how unpopular his continued opposition was making him. He flushed resentfully. 'Yes, cousin.'

'Good. Who'll go with Halthris?'

'I will,' said Urdray, forestalling Inri and Djekko by a whisker. 'I know the city well. Are you happy to have me along, Hal?'

She liked Urdray, who was large and cheerful and would not attempt to unbind her hair when they were alone together – unlike Kettan, who seemed to think he was irresistible to all women. Urdray was promised to a girl from the Emmesar clan, and due to marry that winter. She nodded, smiling. 'Of course I am.'

'So.' Abreth looked round his companions again. 'Are we agreed? Channa and Nayan to the lake – Halthris and Urdray to Zithirian. The rest of us will follow them, with the horses. If anyone has any valid reason for dissent – any *sensible* valid reason – then let them speak now, and not hereafter.'

It was the formal end to any meeting. Abreth waited out the traditional silence of thirty heartbeats, and then nodded. 'Good. Then we strike camp at once. Agreed?'

'Agreed!' they shouted all together, slapping hands on knees, and scrambled up with universal and eager relief.

Abreth watched them pour out of the tent. When the last had gone, he turned to Halthris, who stood beside him. 'Do you think I've done the right thing?'

In the dim light, her strong, freckled face was bleak. 'I think so. I just hope we can outwit the Ska'i. They're blocking our route to Zithirian – Urdray and I will have to make a long detour to get round them, and so will you. We don't know which direction they're going, or whether they have scouts or outriders.' She grinned suddenly, and slapped Abreth's back. 'You did well, big brother. You'll be Chief one day, I'll bet.'

All Tanathi were addicted to gambling, and would wager on anything. Abreth grinned back. 'I don't think so – you'll be married first. My black mare to your golden filly. Done?'

'Done. What are we going to do about the Ska'i? We can't just leave his body to the kites – the other wolves will be sure to find him, and follow our trail. The earth is soft further up the valley – I think it would be best to bury him there, as deeply as possible. You can take care of it – Urdray and I should go now, and so should the other two.'

'I know you must.' Abreth held out his hands to her, and she took them. 'Take care, little sister.'

'Don't worry – I will. And don't be afraid to keep Kettan in his place. Why I ever thought him so wonderful and handsome, I can't imagine. Surely I couldn't have been so silly, even at seventeen?'

'Of course you were.' Abreth grinned at her, hiding his emotion. 'Hal – if I don't speak to you again before you leave – goodbye, and good luck, and may Sarraliss walk beside you always.'

'And Hegeden go with you,' she said, and gave him a swift parting kiss. 'I'll see you in Zithirian – and keep well away from those wretched Ska'i!'

He watched her go, the smile frozen to his face, and then turned to begin dismantling the tent. She would be in no danger – she had Fess, and Urdray, and they could move much faster and more unobtrusively than the main group, who must guide the slow-moving herd.

Why then did he feel such a terrible fear for her safety?

CHAPTER
TWO

'They're dropping back!' Urdray's horse was galloping alongside hers. Halthris turned her head and saw his wide, gap-toothed grin, his blue eyes crinkled with incongruous amusement. 'Keep going, and we'll easily outrun them!'

A day after leaving the other Tanathi, they had trotted in happy ignorance round an outcrop of rocks and almost bumped into a party of half-a-dozen Ska'i, coming in the opposite direction. For a second, they had stared at each other in mutual astonishment: Halthris had even had time to note, with repulsion, the shaggy greased hair and moustaches, the stink of half-cured leather, and the wicked double axes at each tribesman's belt. And then the Ska'i leader had yipped a war-cry, and grabbed his bow.

Flight was their only chance. Halthris dropped the lead rein of the spare horse, whipped her grey round and urged him up the steep, rocky slope beside them, Fess bounding alongside. Behind her, Urdray kicked his mount in pursuit. An arrow flicked past her shoulder, and Ennim swerved and swept on, sure-footed amongst the grass and rocks and tussocks on the hillside. Another arrow, and another, as Urdray drew level with her, and then the top of the hill, and beyond it a gentler slope, flatter country, empty and featureless at first glance. Ennim plunged downwards, ears flat, foam flecking the bit. Halthris glanced back, saw a Ska'i halt on the ridge and bend his bow. She crouched low over the grey's neck, heard the whine of the arrow's flight, a thump, and a gasp from the man beside her. In a swift sideways glance, she saw him grinning again, but now in agony, his body taut with pain, and one of the long, barbed, deadly arrows jutting between his shoulder-blades.

The Ska'i, on their scrubby, inferior horses, were not following: they stayed on the skyline, yipping in triumph or threat, and waving their axes. Presumably, they were too pleased with the capture of the two spare mounts to bother with further pursuit.

Urdray was swaying in the saddle, clinging on to his chestnut's mane. Halthris reached out and grabbed the other horse's reins, slowing both animals to a canter. She said urgently, 'Wait – hang on – we can stop soon.'

'Keep – riding—' Urdray gasped. Blood had gathered at the corner of his mouth, and his face was chalk white. Halthris looked back. The Ska'i had disappeared, but she did not want to halt here in this level, exposed and pitilessly unsheltered terrain.

The sun was sinking before she found a suitable place, a gully seaming the eastern side of a low hill. By now, Urdray was slumped over his horse's neck: he had not spoken for a long time, and Halthris was afraid that he was dead. She slowed both animals to a walk, aware for the first time of the sweat of fear ice-cold on her skin, the ache in her arms from controlling two horses, the exhaustion threatening to overwhelm her.

There were some wind-twisted, stunted trees by a small pool of stagnant water at the bottom of the gully: poor shelter indeed, but much better than nothing. She halted Ennim, and slid stiffly down from the saddle. Fess stalked forwards, tasting the air: she glanced back at Halthris, and then slipped silently into the long grass below the rocks.

So at least the place was safe, for the moment. She touched Urdray's hand, and found it cold. Below the arrow, the back of his leather tunic was soaked with blood. With a gentleness that she feared might be wasted, she laid one arm across his back, braced herself to take his weight, and pulled him laboriously from the horse's back.

He was dead. His blue, sightless eyes stared back up at her. She closed them, not bothering to hide her tears. For the first time in ten years, she was utterly alone. There was no need now to be the stalwart Halthris that all her friends and family knew, who never wept, never despaired, never panicked.

But weeping would not bring Urdray back, or bury him, or light a fire. She sat beside his body for a while, thinking of him, his strength and good nature and willingness. Not the most intelligent of men, perhaps, but a good friend, and one whom she had loved and valued. And it was in such memories that the dead lived on, in the minds of those left behind them, when their souls had long since forgotten their earthbound existence and soared, wild and free as air, with Hegeden's eagles.

It was darkening fast when she rose, and took Urdray's gazelle-skin cloak, of which he had been so proud, to lay it over him. In the morning, she would cover him with rocks and boulders, and say the words that would give his soul to Hegeden. But for now, she must look after herself, make a fire, eat something, however little she wanted it, and sleep, for she would never reach Zithirian if she did not.

Fess came back as she was lighting a fire of dead branches and dry grass, bearing one of the miniature striped grass-deer in her jaws. Halthris took a plump haunch for herself and returned the rest to her feline partner, who carried it a little way off to dine while the meat roasted. When they had both eaten, woman and cat huddled together inside Halthris's warm, fur-lined deerskin cloak, staring into the heart of the fire.

She had not been so alone since her Ordeal, the rite of passage which all Tanathi must undergo before becoming adult. She had been fourteen, confident that she could survive for seven days on her own with only her horse, her bow and arrows and her knife. A leopard had nearly killed her, giving her scars on her arm which she would carry for the rest of her life, and only a lucky shot with her last arrow had hit a fleeing deer and thus ensured her successful survival. The experience had been a salutary lesson, and she had never forgotten how the steppe, home of the Tanathi, could also be their enemy.

But at fourteen, she had not had Fess. The cat pressed close to her, and Halthris stroked the thick, soft fur, tickled her under her chin to make her purr, and slept at last, warmed and comforted, while Urdray lay a few strides away, cold and stiff under his cloak, and the stars wheeled above them in their stately, never-ending dance, frozen sparks of brilliance in the unutterable blackness of the sky.

She buried Urdray the next morning, gathering rocks to lay on his corpse to keep the kites and other scavengers at bay, so that he could rest with dignity. The Tanathi raised earthen barrows above their dead, and the ridges above their winter valleys were bumpy with the mounds covering the ancestors of many lifetimes. But here, on her own, she could only give him what little shelter she could, and hope that it would be enough. And when the mound was finished, her hands rough and bleeding and her body aching with effort, she spoke the formal words that a shaman should properly utter at the interment of the dead.

'Farewell, Urdray, friend and companion and brother. Leave us now to seek Hegeden, to whom all souls fly at their ending: and may your hereafter be joyous and free, your hunting fruitful and your arrows unerring, your horse swift and effortless, your spirit unquenchable. And when our turn comes to join you, may we all ride together as we did in life, in happiness and laughter. Go now, in peace and freedom.'

She took two handfuls of dusty earth, and flung them up in the air above his grave. If his soul fled then, she did not see it, but there was a sighing rustle in the grass, perhaps the wind, perhaps not. She did not think that she had imagined it, though, for Fess turned her head towards the sound.

It was time to go. Halthris dusted off her hands, and fastened her pack to Ennim's saddle. Then, with a last look round at the gully, the pile of stones, the cold, scattered remnants of the fire, she turned, and mounted, and rode away eastwards towards Zithirian, with Urdray's chestnut led behind her, and Fess trotting easily by her side.

The silver city, men called it. Built of white stone quarried from beneath Mount Annako, sparkling where the light caught crystalline imperfections, it glistened in the sunshine, and the gold pennants that capped the pinnacle of each tall, slender, pointed tower flashed as the breeze turned them.

Halthris sat on her grey horse and looked down at Zithirian. This was the fifth time that she had visited the city, and she never tired of this view of it. Behind her, the steppe, endless, monotonous, receded in wave upon wave until it washed against the dark western forests, three weeks' ride away. But below where Ennim stood on the crest of the last hill, the grass surrendered at last to a neat stone wall, made of stacked rocks and boulders gleaned from the earth by the farmers of Zithirian.

Beyond that boundary wall, the land lay in orderly squares and rectangles, a tapestry of different colours: the yellow of unharvested grain or stubble; the rich brown of ploughed soil; vivid green fields grazed by plump sheep or cattle; the darker verdure of orchards of fruit or nut trees; the serried ranks of vines on sun-warmed slopes. This regimentation of nature, however fertile and successful, was utterly alien to the nomadic Tanathi: and yet, strangely, Halthris felt once more the subtle, insistent fascination of a land and a city said to be the most beautiful in all the known world.

To her family and friends, she was Hal, a practical woman who stood no nonsense from companions or lovers, who laughed and joked and seemed utterly careless of the darker, shadowy world that haunted many apparently more sensitive Tanathi. But it lurked in her soul too, to raise goose-flesh on her arms whenever the clan's shaman chanted his spells and incantations. And sometimes her dreams spoke to her ambiguously, to come true a week, a month, a year later, when she had all but forgotten them.

Zithirian spoke to her too, but the message was plain and unequivocal. Come to us, sang the slender towers and gleaming marble, the rich fields and the broad, shining River Kefirinn, with its burden of bright boats, swooping southwards with their brilliant, billowing sails. Come home, live here, and be happy.

It was another reason not to marry yet. If she did, she would be bound to Vinnath's Hearth, and she would never see Zithirian again. And something deep in her soul, unacknowledged to anyone save herself, needed that beauty, that music, to complement the endless days and nights on the steppe, the freedom that sometimes seemed illusory, the everpresent perils, the people who thought they knew her inside out, and in fact did not know her at all.

She tore her gaze away at last, and looked round. The folded hills, hazy, blue-shadowed, unchanging and apparently infinite, lay behind her. Somewhere there – below that ridge, or that one, nearly a day's ride away – lay Urdray, with a Ska'i arrowhead in his back, and all his cheerful eagerness finished for ever. She could see birds circling, minute black specks in the huge expanse of sky. If they were eagles, perhaps his soul had found its home. She raised her hand in salute, and turned back to face her next decision.

Fess sat beside her, waiting patiently. Last year, when the cat had been a yearling cub, she had caused a sensation amongst the Zithiriani, inspiring a mixture of terror and awed fascination in the city-dwellers. The Tanathi had been camped outside the walls, as they always did, and it had been easy for Fess to wander as she pleased along the river bank. She had been in no danger: the citizens were too much in awe of this savage, beautiful creature to dare any harm to her, and she had not hunted their sheep or cattle, though the fat farm animals must have been temptingly easy prey.

But this time, Halthris must go inside the city: and in the stone streets, amongst the stone houses, Fess would be frightened, bewildered, miserable. Best to leave her here, for she would be perfectly able to fend for herself. In a few days Abreth would arrive with the horses and the rest of their companions, and Halthris could call Fess back from the steppe and join them in their camp.

She closed her eyes, willing the cat to understand. The bond between them was close, and strange. Halthris had known only one other Tanathi, an elderly man from the Ustath clan, who had earned the allegiance of a hunting-cat, and he had not been able to explain it either. She knew, though, that Fess seemed in some peculiar way to be aware of her thoughts, for often she obeyed a signal before it had even been given. But Halthris had no idea whether the cat would be able to understand what was required of her, for this situation was completely new, and far more complicated than a simple hunting expedition.

She sorted her thoughts out into a logical progression of simple ideas, presenting them as pictures inside her head. Fess. Halthris going into the city. Fess staying behind, watching her. Fess hunting, eating, sleeping alone on the steppe. Halthris emerging from the city. Halthris putting the narrow, carved, silent bone whistle in her mouth, to summon the cat wherever she might be. And the last, happy image of Fess, leaping through the fields to meet her, and springing up in joyful welcome.

She opened her eyes. The cat was looking at her with that large, intently golden gaze, the oval irises dilated. Halthris felt the hairs rise on the back of her neck as a sensation of rather irritated and reluctant consent filled her mind.

'I'm sorry,' she said aloud. 'I know you don't like cities – noisy, smelly, restricting places! But I have to do this, Fess, I *have* to – and you'll be much happier out here for a few days than you would be if you were cooped up and gawped at in Zithirian. They might even want to put you in a cage.'

Fess growled, and the tip of her tail began to twitch very slightly. Halthris smiled at her, and slid down from Ennim's back to embrace her, and rub the tickly spot between the pointed, dark-furred ears. 'Don't worry. Stay here, and wait for me – I'll be gone a few days, at the most. I'll call you. And good hunting!'

Fess stood on the hilltop, looking down as Halthris rode through the last of the grass to the boundary wall. Then, she turned and slid sinuously back into the steppe.

There was a rough track leading between the fields, and Halthris urged her tired horse along it, Urdray's chestnut trailing wearily behind. She had intended to unpack her best tunic, with the leaping stags coloured red and yellow on chest, arms and back, and the glittering gold discs sewn at neck and hem: the Zithiriani admired brilliant colours and lavish displays of bullion, and the Tanathi always dressed in their finest clothes when bringing their horses to the Gathering Fair, so as not to seem at too much of a disadvantage when driving a hard bargain. Nevertheless, the city-dwellers undoubtedly considered them uncouth barbarians.

But it was too late now: if she stopped to change her clothes, she would not reach the city before sunset, when the gates were shut. And here, with four men hoeing cabbages only two fields away, was not the place to strip off her tunic.

They were staring at her, and one of them called something that she failed to catch. Doubtless they were wondering where the rest of her tribe were: the Tanathi never rode alone.

But Urdray was dead, and Fess left behind, and she had no choice. So she waved a greeting at the farm-workers, and went on, down into the wide rich valley of the River Kefirinn, and the silver city of Zithirian.

Inevitably, people began to follow her as she drew near to the walls. They laid down their tools, glad of the excuse, and left the fields to run after her, shouting questions. Their language was almost the same as hers, a different intonation, a more formal grammar, and after the first few moments of confusion, she found understanding flooding back.

'Tanathi woman!' a boy shouted, jumping up and down perilously close to the chestnut's heels. 'Where are the rest of you?'

'Where are your horses?'

'Is this one all you have?'

'Have you had sickness?'

She smiled and shook her head, pretending ignorant stupidity, and waved a vague arm back at the distant hills of the steppe. 'They follow. Soon.' If the Ska'i were indeed planning to descend like winter wolves upon this peaceful, lovely, gentle land, it would do no good at all to blurt it out now, and set everyone in a panic. She should first tell their Chief, or King, or whatever he called himself, and he could decide how best to defend his city and his people.

The great Sunset Gate lay open, flanked by its huge double towers, each from ground to pinnacle more than ten times the height of a tall man. The sun was dropping down to the tumbled horizon of the western hills, and flushed the white walls of Zithirian with a soft, glowing, rosy red. She could not halt Ennim, not with all these crowds around her, but the beauty of the silver city lay in front of her as she rode slowly up to the gate, and filled all her gaze.

There were several soldiers on guard at the Gate, with plain round helmets, bronze fishscale armour, and long, steel-tipped spears. They were huddled together, evidently conferring: then, as she drew near, two of them leapt in front of her, crossing the wooden spearhafts with a crash and blocking her passage. Despite his weariness, Ennim snorted and threw up his head. She tightened her hold on the reins and brought him to a sharp halt, so that he stood proudly in his blue harness, dappled and shaded like shadows on snow, a perfect and splendid example of Tanathi horse-flesh.

'Halt!' one of the soldiers cried, rather redundantly. 'State your business here, Tanathi woman, or leave Zithirian forthwith!'

The crowd around her had fallen silent, and waited in hushed expectation. Halthris regretted her red and yellow tunic, but it was too late now. She stared down at the soldiers with all the arrogance she could command, and said at last, 'I want to see your Chief. It's urgent, and very important.'

'Do you mean the King?' The young guard obviously took his duties very seriously. His square jaw was thrust belligerently forward, and his knuckles were white where they gripped the spearhaft too tightly. 'His High Mightiness, King Varathand of Zithirian, Fourth of his Name and Descendant of the Divine Ancestor Tayo, does not grant audience to such as you.'

If she made the effort, Halthris knew that she could match his high-flown language. But the Tanathi used words to ease communication, not to hinder it, and after the death of Urdray and her long hours alone, she was in no mood to be elaborate. 'I think you'll find that he will, when he discovers how important this matter is.'

The soldier laughed. 'Important? I assure you that none of your trivial barbarian affairs could possibly interest His High Mightness.'

She resisted the temptation to inform him that thousands of bloodthirsty Ska'i could shortly be hammering on this very gate, all eager to separate his thick head from his shoulders. 'You're wrong,' she said briefly. 'I have news for your King, news which might affect all the people of Zithirian. If you don't take me to him, you may live to regret it.'

'You dare to threaten me, you uncouth unwashed barbarian woman?'

There was a rustling of voice and movement around her. Halthris wished that she had kept Fess with her: the cat would surely have deflated this ridiculous boy's conceit with a single growl. She said with deceptive calm, 'No, I don't threaten you. But if your King finds that you have prevented me from giving this news to him, he won't be pleased.'

Another soldier pushed his way out of the congested gate, and joined his comrades. His helmet had a bright red plume in it, and he was considerably older than the two guards. 'What is it, Ranneko?'

'She says she must talk to His High Mightiness, Sir,' the aggressive soldier explained. 'She says that it is important, but she refuses to say why. And the sun will soon set – shall we drive her off, and shut the gates?'

'No,' said the officer. He looked up at Halthris assessingly. Like many wealthy Zithiriani, he was fair-skinned, with blond hair and blue eyes, and possessed an unquestionable air of authority. 'One Tanathi female hardly poses a grave threat to us, after all – and they have always been friendly, in the past. Is this true, woman? Have you news of importance for His High Mightiness?'

'Yes,' Halthris said, curbing the natural impatience that urged her to inform him that she would hardly waste time standing around talking about it, if she did not. 'And it's urgent – I must see him immediately.'

The officer glanced at the riderless horse beside her, and at the hundreds of eager, curious people pressed all around. 'You have come here alone?'

'My companion was killed. The rest of my friends are following more slowly, with the horses for the Gathering Fair. They sent me ahead with my news.' She stared intently at the officer, willing him, as she had willed Fess, to understand and to obey her wish. 'I don't want to talk about it here – at least let me in, let me see *someone* in authority—'

'Very well.' The man turned and waved the two soldiers aside. 'Tethan – Ranneko – let the woman pass. You may escort us to the Palace.'

A low buzz of surprised comment rose from the people around them.

'The Palace!'

'What news does she bring?'

'Must be important, then.'

And a lower voice, darkly cynical. 'Wants to see the King, does she? Bet she gets fobbed off.'

Ranneko seized Ennim's bridle, and the horse tossed his head free, butting the young soldier's face in the process. Halthris grinned unsympathetically. 'My horse is trained to resist any stranger who tries to handle him. He doesn't need your guidance, and neither do I. You can lead the chestnut, if you like.'

'Ranneko!' the officer said sharply, and the guard, nursing his bloody nose, took the reins of Urdray's horse with a look of acute resentment. With the red-plumed officer by her side, and the two spearmen following a respectful distance behind with the chestnut, trying to keep the crowds at bay, Halthris entered the city of Zithirian.

Last year, she and Abreth, escorted by a group of friendly and curious young citizens, had been given a quick tour of the sights, so she knew what to expect, but Ennim did not: his unshod hooves slipped and jarred on the stone paving, his eyes rolled as people jostled him, and only his rider's soft, unceasing encouragement, and his innate obedience to his training, kept him calm.

Zithirian held some thirty or forty thousand people – the equivalent of eight whole tribes of the Tanathi, who wandered over vast areas of empty steppe and moorland, penned up inside this walled-off bend of the River Kefirinn. She had often wondered what it would be like to live in a house, always to be in the same place, to have the same people as neighbours year in and year out, stone under her feet, stone all around her, and the only greenery the delightful but formal public gardens that were the city's most famous feature after its white walls and tall towers. Now, it seemed that she would at last be given a small taste of the life that had at once attracted and repelled her, ever since she first saw Zithirian.

The wide street that led from the Sunset Gate to the great Temple of Tayo in the heart of the city, was lined with trees growing in huge stone tubs. These were not the gnarled and wind-blown bushes of the steppe, but proud stately plants, freshly and vividly green, their shapes so neat and so similar that they must surely be trained and clipped by an army of gardeners. In their shade, people sat and gossiped and drank wine or fruit juice or aromatic, refreshing cups of kuldi, and stared with open amazement and curiosity at the barbarian woman riding past, with her escort of three solemn soldiers and several hundred noisy, excited Zithiriani.

Outside the main gate of the Temple, there was a little group of men and women in white robes, embroidered with golden birds. Halthris knew that the Priests of Tayo were a powerful force in Zithirian, feared, hated and respected. The young citizens who had befriended her and her brother, last year, had whispered that the Priests knew magic, and that their spirits could leave their bodies and fly anywhere, to spy unseen upon those who thought themselves safely alone.

She and Abreth had laughed at these wild notions, but now, seeing the implacable, ancient faces – why did all the Priests seem so *old*? – she began to wonder whether there might after all be some truth in the tales. A feeling of deep unease crept into her mind, a sudden sensation of acute self-doubt that was entirely foreign to her. Who was she to laugh at fanciful stories, when her own was more ridiculous by far, and even less likely to be believed? Surely the best, the only thing to do was to admit her error, turn her horse around and ride away from Zithirian. Such a proud, powerful and wealthy city could not possibly be at risk of attack from a wild rabble of nomadic tribesmen, however warlike and bloodthirsty.

A movement caught her eye, just before her hands twitched the reins to bring Ennim round. Two boys stood under the tree nearest to the Temple, one dark, the other so brilliantly fair that it must have been the flash of blond hair as he turned his head that had attracted her attention. She had a brief but indelible impression of a small, grubby yet perfect face, and a dark gaze that was disturbingly intent and unchildlike.

Then adults pushed in front of him, and the two children were lost to her view. She found her usual confidence abruptly restored. Her duty was plain: she must tell His High Mightiness of the pompous title, King Varathand, Fourth of His Name, about the menace lurking in the steppes, whether the Ska'i threatened Zithirian or not, whether her warning was heeded or not. And, stubborn and determined to the last, she would tell him to his face, however many obstacles, real or imaginary, blocked her path.

She had half expected the Priests to step out into the street and halt them, but they stayed by the Temple Gate, isolated in a circle of emptiness, fear and awe. Their eyes followed her, though, as she rode past, and she could sense once more that horrible unease, raising the hairs on the back of her neck.

The Temple occupied the centre of the city, and was circular, the outer perimeter studded with gold-capped towers. They had to ride right round this stone-built assertion of wealth and power, and then up the broad Ceremonial Way that led to the Royal Palace.

Here the wealthy lived, in sumptuous white stone houses that were very different in size and opulence, if not in basic design, from the crowded rubble-and-plaster homes in the poorer quarters of the city. Each dwelling in Zithirian, large or small, was built round a courtyard lush with greenery. All the rooms faced inwards, so the streets were lined with tile-capped walls, their blankness broken only by hefty, studded wooden doors, usually with a watch-grill set in them. This meant that, apart from the bright shops, taverns and eating-houses near the Sunset Gate, the city at first glance seemed an unwelcoming place. The effect was softened, though, by the profusion of plants, flowers, trees, growing in tubs, hanging from brackets, spilling over walls. Halthris had seen the arid steppe burst into glorious and transitory flower after the annual spring rains, but even hill after hill of scarlet poppies, bright blue windflowers, and the purple and cerise spikes called Hegedon's Wings, could not compare with this richness and variety of shape, colour and scent.

And everywhere there was water, running in conduits along the side of the street, pouring down artificial waterfalls, trickling into drinking-bowls, bursting from fountains. Ennim, who had not enjoyed a drink at all that day, could not resist the temptation. For the first time since his training, he took the bit in his teeth and turned aside, trampling across a verdant lawn of some low-growing, fragrant plant to stick his nose into the stone bowl beneath a public fountain, drenching himself, his rider and his escort in the process.

Halthris laughed, revelling in the spray of fine droplets, like warm rain on her dry, dusty skin and hair. She pulled off her cap and shook her head like a dog, while Ennim snorted and slobbered up the water and the sharp, tangy aroma of bruised herbs filled the air around them.

The three soldiers, soaked and discomfited, beat an undignified retreat, and the crowd laughed and pointed. She heard the word 'barbarian' repeated again and again, and grinned at them. These soft, extraordinary people might think her uncouth and savage, but their nice ways and fine clothes would be useless out on the wild steppes. She suspected that a group of pampered Zithiriani would not survive even a day's trek on horseback through the snows of winter: she herself had endured such conditions hundreds of times in her life.

Her sense of natural superiority restored, she managed to haul Ennim's nose out of the fountain, and guide him back to the Ceremonial Way, leaving a trail of hoof-prints across the battered thyme and camomile. Fortunately, he had shown no interest in any of the lovingly tended exotic plants in the garden, although the look of appalled horror on the officer's face indicated that his detour to the fountain was crime enough.

The Ceremonial Way climbed up the increasing slope of the rocky outcrop, jutting into the River Kefirinn, on which the Palace stood. Larger, and far more splendid even than the Temple of Tayo, it was similarly surrounded by glistening white stone walls, and garlanded with towers. Halthris looked up at the gold pennants capping each graceful sharp pinnacle, brilliant in the last of the sunlight against the deepening blue of the evening sky, and felt a sense of wonder. So much labour, to create something so beautiful, that was yet, to a Tanathi, as much of a prison as any dungeon.

She should surely be fearful of passing between those huge double towers, flanked by walls six men high, and guarded by enormous soldiers in gleaming bronze armour and luxuriantly plumed helmets, each wielding ceremonial lances twice as tall as they were. But she found no terror within her, no panic, only a strange, awed delight in this lovely edifice, mingled with an inquisitive and less exalted urge to see the inside of it.

It took some time to gain entrance, for the Zithiriani were addicted to elaborate ritual, and the Palace was protected from the vulgar common people by a dense and complicated wall of etiquette and formality. The crowds had dropped back as they approached the gateway to the Palace, and now watched from a respectful distance while the red-plumed officer requested safe passage for himself and Halthris, was refused it, requested it again in slightly different terms, was refused it once more, and finally demanded entrance in the name of His High Mightiness King Varathand, Fourth of His Name, in language so formal, convoluted and repetitive that small children were probably lulled to sleep with it. She was just beginning to think that they would be standing here until moonrise, when the soldiers whipped their lances upright, slapped their bronze-plated gauntlets against their shoulders with a startling, metallic clash, and chanted in unison. 'We hereby declare you friend, not foe, so you may pass within these walls, and your guest alongside you, by gracious permission and favour of His High Mightiness . . .'

The officer was beckoning to her. Ennim had gone to sleep, and woke with a start as she prodded him. The dark, cavernous mouth of the gate yawned at her: she sat proudly upright, her hands firmly gripping the reins, and urged her horse between the two ranked bulwarks of the Zithirian Royal Guard.

Inside the entrance, growing dim in the fast-fading light, there was a roofless tunnel of high walls, and more towers and another gateway ahead. A man in an embroidered tunic and trousers of fine blue wool was lighting the pierced bronze lamps hanging from brackets on the walls to either side of her. Above, Issir, the Sunset Star, had already begun to shine, and the chill invading the drowsy warmth of evening was an unwelcome reminder of the approach of winter. Here, so close to the Northern Mountains, the cold could be almost as harsh and intense as it was on the steppes.

More guards appeared, carrying iron-bound torches that flared dazzlingly and cast monstrous leaping shadows over the walls and across the stone-paved ground. Again the officer went through the ritual, tortuous questions, was denied, and at last received his ceremonial permission, while Halthris smothered a yawn and Ennim dozed again, his head dropping. She thought of Fess, out on the steppe, catching her supper and eating alone. Would the cat still be waiting for her, when she emerged at last from Zithirian? Or would she have vanished into the wilderness, forgetting the bonds forged by the past two years of love and companionship, to seek her own kind?

The officer was speaking to her, and she dragged her attention back to him, suddenly aware of how tired she was. He was asking her to dismount: her horses would be well cared for in His High Mightiness's own stables, there was a servant here to carry her pack, and the Court Chamberlain, who was responsible for all honoured guests at the Palace, to escort her within.

Ennim and the chestnut were led away, too exhausted to protest any more at these frighteningly alien surroundings, and Halthris turned to thank the red-plumed officer, for without his help she would undoubtedly still be sitting outside the Sunset Gate, pleading her cause in vain. But he had already gone, and she could hear the sound of tramping military feet, echoing back under the outer gate of the Palace.

She turned back to the Chamberlain. He wore the same blue embroidered tunic as the servant who had lit the lamps, but with a long, loose, fur-lined gown over the top. His middle-aged face was an impassive, expressionless mask. 'Madam, have you any weapons in your possession? You must lay them aside before you enter the Palace.'

Reluctantly, she drew her dagger, the one which she had thrown at the Ska'i, and afterwards rescued from the grass. It had a gold hilt and a steel blade, engraved with running cats. Her father had given it to her at the end of her Ordeal, to mark her entry into the adult life of the clan. To lose such a weapon, or surrender it to an enemy, was the deepest disgrace. She hesitated, then gave it to him.

'I thank you, Madam, and now do humbly beg and request you to walk with me.'

Trying not to outpace his rather mincing gait, she strode beside him into the innermost part of the Palace, while another blue-clad servant followed, carrying her old leather saddlebags as if they contained poisonous snakes.

She had never actually been inside a building before. Even on that tour of the city last year, they had eaten in the open air, in a tavern courtyard, and only peered through the gates of the Temple. It was so strange, so suffocatingly strange, to look up and see above her head, not the familiar open sky, but a ceiling painted an astonishing shade of blue, and gilded with stars that were, she realized suddenly, exactly the same as the constellations that hung at night above them all. The Gazelle, the Leopard, Hegeden's Crown and the Twin Foals of Sarraliss: all there, in their proper patterns, but in the wrong places, so that as she walked along the gently curving passage, she seemed to be turning first south, then east, then south again, then north . . .

All her attention fixed on the counterfeit stars, she failed to notice that the Chamberlain had stopped, and bumped into him. He waved her apology aside with sternly polite reproof. 'It behoves Madam to watch where she is going. I humbly do beg and request Madam to follow me now, and I will conduct Madam to the Lord Ansaryon.'

Halthris opened her mouth to ask who this was, and why she could not be taken straight to the King, and then thought better of it. She had asked to see someone in authority, and she seemed to remember, from what the young Zithiriani had told her last year, that the Lord Ansaryon was one of His High Mightiness's sons. He had three, as well as a daughter, and she and Abreth had learned quite a lot about them from their self-appointed guides.

So which one was Ansaryon? The drunken, bumbling heir to the throne of Zithirian, object of universal contempt? The effete, secretive, sinister Prince who was rumoured to dabble in all sorts of unsavoury pastimes? Or the sturdy young athlete of whom everyone had spoken with admiration and approval?

The Chamberlain led her down more curved corridors, the walls painted with astonishingly realistic scenes: landscapes, images of Zithirian, pictures of the mountains, ice festivals, gardens, courtiers, boats on the river, wild animals, all delineated with love, skill and accuracy. Beside them, the stylized birds and beasts of the Tanathi would seem crude and childish. But she had no time to stop and stare: the Chamberlain hurried on through this seemingly endless labyrinth, twisting and turning so that she lost all sense of direction. She saw no gorgeous lords or ladies, only servants hurrying about their business, all clad alike in that bright, uniform blue. Halthris tried to imagine what it would be like to have another human being at her beck and call, to fetch and carry for her, and failed. Tanathi men and women did their chores themselves, although certain notoriously lazy husbands were inclined to order their wives to do more than their fair share – yet another reason to avoid marriage.

She realized that this passage ended in a door, elaborately decorated round its edge with a pattern of fruit, flowers and autumn leaves. Two blue-clad servants stood impassively to either side of it, their hands clasped behind their backs. The Chamberlain halted, and raised his silver staff. 'This supplicant from the Tanathi Tribe wishes to beg audience with the Lord Ansaryon. May she be admitted?'

One servant stood as still as rock: the other touched his hand to his chest in acknowledgement, turned and slipped through the door. Halthris was beginning to feel like a parcel: a precious parcel, true, but just a piece of baggage nevertheless. Even a hunting dog might have inspired more warmth from the Chamberlain and the other servants than she had received. And she was accustomed to the directness and honesty of all Tanathi, even Kettan. This man had never met her eyes.

The servant returned. 'The Lord Ansaryon commands me to speak to you thus. His Gracious Highness is pleased to show your supplicant the light of his favour, for a brief while. If she has laid aside her weapons, and is of friendly intent, she may enter.'

The Chamberlain had already taken her knife. She spread her empty hands wearily. 'I have no weapons, and I am friendly.'

'Then she may enter,' said the servant, speaking to the Chamberlain, and opened the door. She walked past him, and into the room that lay beyond.

It was round, she saw with surprise: it must occupy the ground floor of one of the towers that bristled above the Palace. The curving walls were pierced by four long, narrow windows, shuttered against the cold night air. Around her, pictures even more lovely than those in the corridors swam before her tired eyes: she saw fantastic winged beasts in a frozen, exuberant dance, and birds with fire streaming from their plumage. There was a brazier, filled with glowing hot stones, in the exact centre of the room; several couches piled high with plump cushions; a carved wooden chest below each of the windows; and shelf upon shelf of ancient-looking leather covered objects. She stared at them stupidly, wondering what they were. Suddenly, the Ska'i seemed a very distant threat indeed: far more real was the very considerable danger that she would abandon etiquette, renounce ceremonial, succumb to temptation and fall asleep on that pile of soft tapestry cushions by the warmth of the fire . . .

A man stepped suddenly out from behind a lattice screen. Startled, she turned to face him, forcing her weary brain to concentrate. Like almost all Zithiriani of high birth, he was tall, his slight build to some extent disguised by the thick, furred robe which he wore over the usual tunic and trousers. Not so usually, all his garments were made of a deep yet glowing blue silk, the dark colour relieved only by a little exquisite embroidery around the neck. It was a far less showy ensemble than the Chamberlain's luxurious attire, but somehow the understatement was much more imposing.

She raised her eyes to his face. It was hard to tell his age – the city-dwellers had never been exposed to the cold winds and harsh sunlight of the steppes – but she thought that he was little older than she was, in his late twenties perhaps. His hair was cut in the Zithirian style, fringed at the front and shoulder-length at the back and sides, and so fair as to be almost ashen. His features were level and regular, his expression arrogant, and his eyes a strange, pale, iridescent silvery grey.

His gaze travelled over every detail of her hair, her face, her creased and dirty tunic, the empty scabbard at her belt and her worn leather riding-boots, and she stared stubbornly back, refusing to be intimidated.

'A Tanathi woman,' he said at last, his voice soft, cold, amused. 'How very interesting. I wonder what she wants.'

And the smile crawling across his delicate, beautiful face sent a chill to her heart.

CHAPTER
THREE

At least he was meeting her eyes, unlike every other Zithiriani she had yet encountered. Such directness was presumably a mark of rank. Halthris forced herself to remain still under his scrutiny, her hackles raised at the contemptuous tone of his voice, and the expression in those sinister, uncarthly eyes. Without turning, he snapped his fingers at one of the silent servants. 'Bring wine and food. Then leave us.'

Slowly, despite all her efforts at control, her heart began to increase its beat. This man was no drunken idiot: neither was he the hearty, athletic younger son. The Lord Ansaryon was rumoured to meddle in sorcery, to indulge in secret wild orgies that ended in ritual sacrifice, and even, so her informant had whispered, to summon the spirits of the dead.

Such things were unknown amongst the Tanathi. With much relish, and a certain amount of condescension, the young Zithiriani had explained exactly what such practices entailed. Abreth, trying unsuccessfully to conceal his horror behind a light-hearted façade, had commented that the King's second son sounded exactly like the Ska'i.

And now she was here, facing him, two strides away from his eyes and his hands, and the servants, on noiseless feet, were filing out, and she had no weapons to defend herself, no Fess to come leaping through the painted doors just in time to save her. But she was Tanathi, so her wits and reactions, not to mention her fighting skills, were surely far superior to this pampered royal pervert. At the very least, she could seriously damage that air of imperious arrogance, even if she did no actual harm to his person.

The food and wine was brought with astonishing speed, and set on a little table inlaid with some iridescent, silvery material, very similar to the colour of the Prince's eyes. There was a jug of wine, a bowl of water with a square linen cloth draped over the rim, bread, cheese, slices of cooked meat and pieces of chicken, a pot of some thick, creamy substance, and a silver dish heaped with different coloured sticks which she realised must be vegetables, cut in defiance of their original shape into the approximate length and

breadth of her little finger. It was very different from the typical
Tanathi supper of roast meat or broth, with flat bread to act as a
plate and to soak up the juices, but it looked delicious all the same,
and her stomach, which had known nothing but dried mutton for
nearly two days, growled hungrily.

The door had closed, and she was alone with him. He gestured
towards the table. 'Eat first. Then you may tell me what you want.'

Halthris suspected that once she sat down on that soft, blissful-
looking couch, she would be unable to rise again. She said stubbornly, 'I don't want anything. I have come to give you a warning –
or, rather, to give the King a warning, but they brought me to you.'

'A poor substitute,' said Ansaryon, with irony. 'Well, Tanathi
woman? What is this – warning? I'm dying to hear it.'

His tone sparked her quick temper into life. She said angrily,
'There are about eight or nine thousand Ska'i and Rerbresh
tribesmen camped three days' ride from Zithirian. They are planning to attack the city.'

Silence, save for the soft wind sighing outside the tower, and
the whisper of sound as the burnstones smouldered in the brazier.
The Lord Ansaryon was looking at her with disturbing intensity:
she found her head filled with pictures of the Ska'i, the vast camp,
the stinking, savage, ugly man who had so nearly killed her, and
she shivered. Such horrors seemed so far away from this cosy room
as to be purely a product of her imagination, and yet she knew the
menace the Ska'i posed was only too real.

'Tell me how you know this,' he said. 'And for Tayo's sake sit
and eat, woman – I'll learn nothing from you if you faint with
hunger and exhaustion.' He indicated the couch. 'Sit there, and
forget whatever stories you may have heard about me. Only half of
them are true.'

'Yes, but which half?' Halthris retorted.

For a moment, she thought her impertinence had angered him.
Then, disconcertingly, he laughed. 'The worst, of course. I repeat –
sit down and eat something, woman.'

'My name is Halthris,' she said. He must have noticed that she
had used no formal terms of address, but to call this unpleasant and
disturbing man 'Lord', as Zithiriani etiquette demanded, stuck in
her gullet.

'Then, Halthris – eat!'

She hated to obey him, even if it was pure common sense to do
so: he was right, she was desperately hungry, and if she did faint –
unlikely, she would probably fall asleep first – he was in a much
better position to take foul advantage of her. She was not some

prudish city-bred virgin, but the thought was revolting to a Tanathi woman who regarded her body as hers alone, to give or to withhold as she chose, and in her present state of utter exhaustion, the prospect seemed to loom absurdly large in her mind.

Deliberately, she waited a little longer, and then moved to the couch. Feeling him watching her, she began to eat with some care. She might be a barbarian, but she knew something of the behaviour expected at a Zithiriani meal. She washed her hands in the bowl of water, drying them on the towel provided. There was no knife, or spoon, laid out for her, so she used her fingers, as neatly as her hunger would allow.

As she demolished the bread and meat, she was aware that he had turned away, and was moving about the room: placing more burnstones on the brazier, checking the shutters, and finally sitting down at the table, his back to her. It did not make her much more easy in his company, but at least she was no longer conscious of his scrutiny. That had been uncomfortable, to put it mildly: she had felt as if his eyes could see right inside her head, as if skin and flesh and bone could melt before his power.

He had said that only half the stories were true. She remembered what she had been told, last year, and thought that even half was bad enough. But she had come here to give her warning, and she had given it, and her conscience was now clear. She hardly cared if he believed it or not: she only wanted to leave his unsettling presence, and sleep somewhere safe, and be out of this suffocating, starless, airless place, with its beauty and grandeur and wonderfully painted walls, before such a splendid prison drove her mad.

'Have you finished?'

Ansaryon was standing in front of her. She had been so busy eating that she had not noticed him getting up. Halthris looked at the empty plates and said with weary annoyance, 'No. As you can see, there is plenty left.'

'Why have you gone to so much trouble to warn us about the Ska'i, when you so plainly hate us?'

Startled, Halthris stared up at him. She said sharply, 'Dislike and hate are two very different things. And besides, where would we sell our horses, if Zithirian was destroyed?'

'Very true. So – the Ska'i have come north. Tell me everything you know, and how you know it.'

He was speaking almost as briefly and directly as a Tanathi. And as bluntly, she told him what she and Abreth had seen three days ago, about the delirious ramblings of the Ska'i prisoner, and about Urdray's death. He listened in silence, with no prompting, but she had the uneasy feeling that he knew what she would say, before she spoke.

The tale was soon finished, and she thought of Urdray, his spirit soaring free with Hegeden while his body rotted under the stones, and of how much she mourned his loss.

'Your dead companion. Were you close to him?'

Startled, she looked at Ansaryon. 'He was my friend,' she said, with simple sadness. 'Not my brother, or my lover, but my friend.'

'And your brother Abreth. He is coming to Zithirian, you say? So he will be able to confirm your story.'

'Then you don't believe me,' Halthris said flatly. 'I thought not.'

'I never said that. In fact, I do believe you. But if others at Court are to take your warning seriously, then your brother's evidence will add weight to your words.'

'Because I am a woman?'

'Because you are a woman, and there is only one of you as yet. Like it or not, Zithiriani – especially here at Court – still tend to think of the female sex in purely decorative and reproductive terms. I feel it is only fair to tell you that you will take them somewhat by surprise.'

For the first time, Halthris felt a touch of amusement. She fought it back, and said tartly, 'I had not expected anything else. And that being the case, it's surely better for you yourself to tell the King about the Ska'i. You're much more likely to be believed than I am.'

'Am I?' said the Lord Ansaryon, and a curious smile briefly crossed his face. 'I doubt that, somehow. I would probably be accused of spreading false and terrifying rumours for my own devious and despicable ends. If at least one live Tanathi can stand before the King and swear that every word of the warning is true, then there is a very faint chance that he will believe it.'

Halthris realized suddenly that this Prince of Zithirian seemed to be almost as much of an outsider at his own Court as she was. The insight did not make her warm to him, but she wondered, with a mixture of curiosity and repulsion, why he should be so alienated from the people around him, even his own family. She thought of her brother Abreth and her sister Tarli, their closeness and their support for each other, and, more distantly, the wisdom and love of their father. It was impossible to imagine any of his three children thinking or speaking of Charnak with the contemptuous tone of disrespect which Ansaryon had used to refer to his own sire. But from snippets she had picked up on her brief meetings with the people of Zithirian, it seemed that many thought, similarly, that His High Mightiness was neither high, nor mighty. Again, she could not envisage such a situation arising amongst the Tanathi, where each clan elected its chief by popular consent, and removed them from office in the same way. Charnak occupied his position because he was liked, respected and an intelligent leader. The King of Zithirian, by contrast, sat on the throne purely because he was his parents' eldest son, and not because he was peculiarly fit for the task. And if Abreth was right, and the Ska'i were planning to attack Zithirian, then to have a derided incompetent in charge was to invite disaster.

She began to hope that, when the Ska'i did appear, she and Abreth and all the other Tanathi would have long since fled to the comparative safety of the inhospitable Northern Mountains.

With some difficulty, she dragged her mind back to his last words. 'Then I hope that you and my brother and I between us can convince him, because if the Ska'i attack Zithirian when it is unprepared . . .'

'Then our heads will adorn their trophy-lances,' said Ansaryon, so exactly describing the horrible picture in her mind that the hairs rose on her arms. 'Don't worry – I have no intention of allowing that to happen. I believe you, and I will do all in my power to convince the King and his ministers of the urgency of immediate action – but I will need your help to do it.' He smiled suddenly, and she was almost persuaded that it was genuine. 'I shall skirt around the issue three times with abundant euphemisms and circumlocutions, in typical Zithiriani style. Then you and your brother can come in with the bludgeon of brutal truth and finish them off.'

By now, exhaustion was fogging her brain and dragging her eyelids down, and she knew that sleep was imperative. She got to her feet, stifling a yawn, and said firmly, 'Our plans will have to wait until tomorrow, when I have rested. Is there a room for me somewhere?'

'My servants have prepared one already, off my courtyard. Unless you would prefer to sleep in the open, under the stars?'

She might be a lowly and uncivilized barbarian, but she was not going to give him the satisfaction of seeing her prove it, however much she was perturbed by the thought of sleeping enclosed by four walls and a ceiling. 'That will not be necessary,' she said coldly.

'I didn't think it would be,' said the Lord Ansaryon, his voice dry. 'My thanks to you, Halthris of the Tanathi. I hope that you will sleep well, and I have high expectations of a further fruitful converse on the morrow.'

A servant had appeared, presumably in answer to a summons she had not noticed, and stood waiting for her by the open door. Too tired to indulge in further courtesies, she turned and followed him from the room.

And she was too weary even to notice that the ceiling above her soft, warm bed was a delicate, pale shade of blue, woven across with painted vines and flowers and birds, instead of the familiar flickering pattern of stars that had looked so kindly down on her in summer months, all her life long until this night.

'Madam?'

Her hearing and reactions sharpened by years of living on the steppe, Halthris came awake instantly and then wished she hadn't. Every muscle ached far worse, surely, than if she had spent the night on the cold hard ground. She sat up rather gingerly, and saw a young woman, clad in bright servants' blue, with a laden tray in her hands. The girl ducked her head with a gesture of polite subservience. 'Madam's humble servant, Kerrardi, trusts that Madam has slept well, and that her dreams were propitious?'

In fact, Halthris couldn't remember dreaming at all, but she nodded.

'I am joyed to hear of it,' said the maid. 'If Madam will permit this humble servant to present her with a simple repast which it is hoped will do something to assuage her hunger—'

'Oh, for Hegeden's sake, just put it down and go!' Halthris said, exasperated. 'Or we'll be here all day.'

In the next instant, she regretted giving vent to her feelings, sharpened by ravenous hunger at the sight of the food, for the little servant gasped and turned white. She put the tray down on the floor with a clatter and made a sign exactly like the warding gesture the Tanathi used to turn aside evil. Too late, Halthris remembered that in Zithirian, Hegeden and Sarraliss were heathen deities, and their worship strictly forbidden.

But she was not going to admit her error: only to Abreth and Tarli would she ever confess that she was in the wrong. She gave the girl a friendly smile, and said, as if nothing had happened, 'Thank you very much. That will be all.'

Her hands freed, the maid clasped them to her breast and bowed still more subserviently. 'As Madam wishes. Would Madam require the services of her humble servant Kerrardi in the preparation of a bath?'

'A what?' Startled, Halthris stared at her in bewilderment.

Then she remembered that the peculiar Zithiriani, their city admittedly awash with water, liked to immerse themselves in it at regular intervals, wallowing in their own dirt. Tanathi also bathed frequently, washing away grime in rivers and lakes far cleaner and fresher than the streams which flowed through the pipes and conduits so cunningly laid under the streets of the city.

Nevertheless, it would undoubtedly be more than pleasant to soak away the dirt and dust of her journey. She smiled again at Kerrardi. 'That would be nice. Thank you.'

'It is pleasing to Madam's humble servant to grant Madam's wish,' said the maid, with another bow. 'If Madam will allow her humble servant to enter the bathing room, she will draw the water for Madam. Would Madam desire her bath hot, or warm, or cool, or cold?'

'Warm, please,' said Halthris, and saw a look of surprise on Kerrardi's face. Was ordinary courtesy really so uncommon here in the Royal Palace?

Left in peace at last, she devoured soft, warm white bread, spread with some very savoury, salty black paste from a small pot, and washed down with the crushed scarlet juice of some fruit whose fragrance she vaguely recognized, but whose name she could not recall. Like her supper the previous evening, it was a meal at once simple, tasty and extremely satisfying.

The bath, too, proved wonderfully refreshing. She lay full length in an oblong marble tub, revelling in the warm silky water, surrounded by the aromatic odour of sweet herbs, and watching the dust of the steppe swirl around her in a gritty brown scum. She had dismissed the maid, finding her presence unsettling, and enjoyed now the luxury of being alone, with a full stomach, an alert mind and, at last, the opportunity to think in detail about what lay before her.

She knew from past experience that Abreth and the horses could not be expected until tomorrow at the very earliest – if, *if* they managed to avoid the band that had killed Urdray, or any other Ska'i that might be lurking across the route to Zithirian.

And the wheels of Palace protocol seemed to grind excruciatingly slowly. If they treated Abreth with the same ludicrously elaborate courtesy, she and her brother would not have the chance to give the King their warning in person for at least another two days, and more likely three, or even four. By which time, the Ska'i camp, even one so vast, could have packed its tents and its wagons, saddled up its horses, and be riding on inexorably towards its prey.

While she lay here wallowing in decadent and civilized luxury, the guest of a very dubious person indeed, even if he was a Prince, even if he did believe her story, Abreth could at this moment be lying dead in the long brown grass of autumn, or fighting for his life against Ska'i who knew nothing of kindness, or decency, or mercy, for whom her beloved brother was nothing more than a head to be severed from his neck, a battle trophy to advertise a warrior's prowess to the rest of his savage tribe . . .

Halthris ducked her head under the cooling water and emerged streaming and blinded by a curtain of soaked red-gold hair. She shook herself like a dog and stepped out onto the smooth, tiled floor. There was a pile of large fluffy cloths in which to wrap her wet body, and she pulled one round her, wondering at the feel of it: however did their weavers manage to achieve such softness? She rubbed herself briskly dry, and then pulled on her finest clothes, the garments she had wanted to wear yesterday for her entrance to the city: the blue silk tunic with the overlapping, chiming gold discs sewn at neck and cuffs and hem, and the stags in vivid scarlet and yellow leaping extravagantly across breast and back and arms. The green woollen trousers worn underneath, decorated with a single band of intricate gold braid down each outside seam, appeared almost plain by comparison. She buckled her best red leather belt round her waist, and dampened one of the smaller towels in the bath water, using it to rub the dust of her soft deerskin riding-boots. Then she attached two rows of looped golden chains to their upper edge.

The last and most important task was upon her: to reduce her wet, tangled mass of hair, the colour of hot new flame, to the six neat braids, plaited with gold and silver ribbons and thread, that were customary for all Tanathi to wear on ceremonial occasions. She took her silver and tortoise-shell comb from her pack, and began, with a certain nervousness fumbling her usually deft fingers. She did not want the maid Kerrardi, or any other servant, or, worst of all, the Lord Ansaryon himself, to walk in and discover her with her hair loose. It was a situation of such intimate privacy that to say 'They unbound their hair for each other' meant that two Tanathi had become lovers.

But no one entered, and she tied the last knot of gold ribbon on the last braid, with a little golden amulet, in the shape of a horse, hanging from the end. Now she was protected six times over, with a horse, for Sarraliss; an eagle, for Hegeden; a hunting-cat, for Sayni, the guardian spirit of her clan, and also for Fess; Emmesar, the swift-running hare; a deer to represent the faithful, loving Djarna; and a leopard, fierce and powerful, for Immith. It was an

unusual collection of talismans for a woman: but even amongst the
Tanathi, Halthris was not an ordinary woman.

Now she was dressed and confident in her finery, ready to face
the King of Zithirian in all his high mightiness. But no one came,
and her brusque manner seemed to have frightened the maid away
altogether. She put all her belongings neatly back in her pack,
checked her hair by running a hand down each braid, and added a
couple of blue lapis lazuli bracelets to the three of chased gold
already encircling her wrists. Then, bored, she got up and paced
about the room, examining the carved wooden intricacies of the
bed; the richly embroidered wall hangings, depicting, probably,
scenes from the Life of Tayo; the table, the chairs, the wooden
chest covered with painted birds in scarlet and orange and crimson,
and the ceiling pictures that she had been too tired even to notice
last night. Belatedly curious, she went next into the inner room,
where she had taken her bath. Where had the water come from?

Out of a spout set in the wall, seemed to be the answer, and
there was a handle beside it which, when pushed down with some
effort, yielded a gush of cold, clear water. There was a half-empty
cauldron, which had presumably supplied the hot, sitting on a
smouldering hearth in the corner. She delved under the scummy
surface of the bath, released the bung, and watched the cooling
remains pour out along a gutter running across the blue and white
tiled floor and under the wall into unknown territory. She wondered
where it would go. Presumably, since the Palace occupied the high
ground above the Kefirinn, her dirty water would end up polluting
the river.

Strange people, the Zithiriani. She grinned to herself, and went
back into the main room, her gold discs and amulets, chains and
bracelets, chiming together in soft harmony as she walked. She was
not going to skulk in this luxurious prison any longer, waiting like
some nervous supplicant to be brought into the Royal Presence as
though she were being done a vast favour. If they would not see
her, then she would go, and find Ennim, and ride out of the city to
wait for Abreth and the others, and for Fess.

She picked up her pack, strode out of the door, and stopped,
staring. Last night, led to her room so tired that she had barely
been able to put one foot in front of the other, she had not noticed
this courtyard, around which the rooms of Ansaryon's apartment,
like all Zithiriani houses, had been built. It was large, perhaps
thirty paces in either direction, not including the colonnaded
walkway on all four sides. As everywhere in the city, plants and
flowers grew in profusion, twining up the slender stone columns,

tangling together in a mass of colour over the tiled roof, and spilling over tubs and troughs.

In the exact centre was a stone fountain of astonishing and complicated artistry. Halthris, walking over to examine it, wondered how the water was induced to flow from the very top, in several streams that trickled down into shallow bowls and spouted again from each of them in a fine spray that sparkled in a myriad rainbow colours under the sun. There was no lever, no indication of how it worked. She peered fruitlessly up at the top, higher than a man, and then examined all the bowls, noting the little stone drinking birds carved on the rim of each one, and the fish etched under the surface of the water, so realistically depicted that she could recognize them all: the predatory but delicious pike, fat salmon, spotted trout, and crayfish with their long claws and waving feelers. Marvellous though they were, they offered no clues, so she knelt down on the wet stones and looked up at the undersides of the bowls.

'It comes from a cistern in the tower,' said a voice behind her. She leapt to her feet, nearly cracking her head on the curved stone above, and turned to see the Lord Ansaryon, standing watching her a few paces away.

He was wearing black today: the colour of crows and ravens, and of extreme ill omen, no Tanathi wore it unless gripped by inconsolable sorrow, and she shivered. Three servants stood behind him, all in that brilliant blue, and all studying her covertly.

But she had done nothing to make her feel guilty, and she met the Prince's chilly eyes without flinching. 'Does it? I wondered how it worked. And how does it manage to flow upwards, then? Sorcery?'

'Pressure of water,' said Ansaryon concisely. 'Now, Halthris of the Tanathi, I trust you slept well?'

'Very well indeed,' she told him, and saw the servants exchange glances, presumably noting her omission of his proper title. Well, she was a Chief's daughter, and surely his equal in rank, if they thought that such things mattered. And she would only give proper respect to those who had earned it. So far, the Lord Ansaryon had not.

'His High Mightiness King Varathand, Fourth of His Name, bids me inform his supplicant, Halthris of the Tanathi tribe, the privilege of a Royal Audience this afternoon, when the midday meal is ended.' The Prince's voice was formal and declamatory. 'In the meantime, Halthris of the Tanathi tribe is graciously permitted to enjoy the gift of His High Mightiness's benevolent hospitality.'

'This *afternoon*?' Halthris stared at him angrily. 'Why not now? I have rested, and bathed, and eaten, and I'm grateful for your kindness, but I am also heartily sick of kicking my heels here. I would rather go and tend my horse – or see the King *now*.'

The three servants, obviously shocked and affronted, gazed at her in horror. One of them even took a step towards her, as if to restrain her, but Ansaryon stopped him in his tracks with a swift gesture. 'If you were familiar with the practices and customs of our Court, Halthris of the Tanathi, you would know that His High Mightiness never, under any circumstances whatsoever, grants audience to anyone, not even the Emperor of Toktel'yi himself, before the midday meal has been eaten.'

'Why? Because he has to stuff his belly before his brain can work?'

As soon as the derisive words were out of her mouth, she knew that she had made a grievous mistake. The servants gasped, but Lord Ansaryon gave no obvious sign of disgust. Instead, he seemed to grow taller, and his silver eyes glittered. She forced herself to stand straight without flinching, unafraid to meet his gaze, although her heart had begun to pound erratically. Images of darkness and despair slid into her mind, and she repelled them desperately, determined to cling on to her pride and dignity, however little she deserved it.

'Tell me, Halthris of the Tanathi – do you normally make a practice of insulting your host? I would not describe the poorest peasant in such terms, if I had accepted his bread and his shelter.'

She would not apologize, not if he tried threats, or torture, or any of the unspeakable arts in which he was so hideously skilled. And she was beginning to suspect that those extraordinary eyes really could see inside her head – and put things there, too. She said firmly, 'No, I would not, either. But you forget the urgency of my warning. By the time I do see the King, almost a day will have passed since I arrived here – precious time wasted. And I don't like to think that all my efforts have been in vain, if the King fails to take me seriously. My friend Urdray did not die so that you could dither and delay while the Ska'i are preparing to attack you in overwhelming strength.'

The servants exchanged anxiously significant glances. 'Enough,' Ansaryon said sharply. 'I can see, Halthris of the Tanathi, that some instruction in Court ritual and etiquette is necessary if His High Mightiness is even to receive your supplication, let alone believe you. Accordingly, I suggest that you come with me now, to learn the proper rules of behaviour. Whether you follow them or not is your own affair, but His High Mightiness is not inclined to look favourably upon those he perceives as ignorant and boorish barbarians.'

It took a vast effort of self-control to hang on to her temper. Didn't he *care* about what was approaching, hidden in the rolling steppe lands where the Zithiriani seldom went? He had said last night that he believed her story. Why then this lack of urgency? Did he *want* the Ska'i to attack the city before it had a chance to defend itself?

Perhaps he did, for his own evil ends. She felt the goose-flesh rise on her arms, and shivered. If that were so, then the quicker she got out of this place, and free of Ansaryon's sinister clutches, the better. As soon as Abreth arrived, she would persuade him to leave the horses and ride back to the people of their tribe, who were honest, and straightforward, and could not ever imagine such a hideous betrayal of family and friends.

He had stepped aside, and gestured. The servants moved over to her, one on her left, two on her right. The implications were obvious, but she had no intention of abandoning her air of cool pride, and make an undignified scene. With all the things she wanted to say to His Gracious Highness the Lord Ansaryon simmering malevolently in her head, she walked forward to his side, her pack slung over her shoulder. 'Then if I am in such dire need of instruction, we had better start at once,' she said briskly. 'Will you lead the way?'

For an astonishing moment, she thought he was going to smile: the corners of his mouth tucked inwards, and his eyebrows rose. Then he inclined his head. 'Pray accompany me, Halthris of the Tanathi.'

She followed him out of the courtyard and along another painted corridor to a doorway she recognized. He opened it, stood aside to let her pass through, and shut it behind them. The servants waited outside, ready to burst in if she tried to knock him over the head with a stool or a wine pitcher in a fit of ignorant and boorish barbarian rage.

In daylight, the round room at the base of the tower looked somehow quite different, bright and pleasant rather than shadowy. The morning sun streamed in through the high, spear-shaped windows, and it was a moment before she realized that they were not in fact open to the breezes, but were filled with some marvellous material that let in light and not air. Around the edges, the small squares and rectangles were coloured, and the sun's rays flung lances of red and green, blue and gold and turquoise, glowing across the stone floor.

Halthris stood looking at it all: the couch, the cushions, the wall-hangings, the exquisite furniture, the air of soft and civilized luxury. It was certainly beautiful, she could appreciate that, but she could not relate these very pleasant and comfortable surroundings to the extremely nasty rumours she had heard. Hard to imagine foul rites taking place here, or in that lovely courtyard, although of course there must be three or four similar rooms above this one in the tower. Perhaps it was in one of them that the Lord Ansaryon practised sorcery, raised the dead, summoned demons, and indulged in revolting and bestial perversions.

She did not like him; she did not understand him; and beyond anything, she was afraid of him. But in him lay her only hope of convincing the King of Zithirian that the threat of the Ska'i was real. And so she must control her temper, cling to her proud dignity, and try to undo the damage that her hasty and thoughtless insult had done to the wary, fragile line of communication between them.

'The first thing to remember when in the Court of Zithirian, Halthris of the Tanathi,' he said just behind her, 'is to address those of rank always with their titles and honours. My servants are appalled that you do not speak to me with proper deference. Is that usual amongst the Tanathi, or do you give respect to your own leaders?'

'Only to those who have earned it,' Halthris said bluntly. 'And those who have not earned it, are not our leaders.'

The silence threatened to last for ever. He walked round to stand and face her, hands on hips. He studied her, and she gave him back stare for stare with unabashed and almost insolent boldness, making no secret of her dislike. He said at last, 'So, to be as blunt as you, I do not enjoy your respect?'

'No, you don't.'

Disconcertingly, Ansaryon laughed. 'And if I don't, I take it that my high and mighty father doesn't either?'

'I haven't even met him, so how can I respect him?' Halthris pointed out reasonably. 'And in any case, the fact that *you* obviously don't respect him hardly makes me more likely to do so. However you may pretend in public, you've made no secret to me of your contempt for him. And this time yesterday, you didn't even know I existed.'

'And now I do, with a vengeance,' said Ansaryon, and his laugh was almost rueful. 'Well, we've agreed that I don't like or respect my father, and that you don't like or respect me. I'll keep my feelings about you to myself, for the moment – beyond the suspicion that over the next few days, Halthris of the Tanathi, you will prove to be a considerable pain in my neck.'

'If that's the only way I can knock it into your thick head that the Ska'i are coming, before they chop it off your shoulders, then I'm glad I am.'

'Oh, I believe you. But my father is a different matter.' He gestured towards the couch. 'Sit down, and listen – and I'd be grateful if you would keep this conversation to yourself, while you are in Zithirian. It'll do neither of us any good to have my real opinion of my father, and of other members of my family, become public knowledge. But if your warning is to be heeded at all, then there are things you must know.' He paused, and sat down at the table, pushing his long, ashen fringe out of his eyes. 'First, and most important, the King. I presume, since you speak our language so well, and seem familiar with the city, that you have been to Zithirian before?'

Halthris sat on the couch, eyeing him warily. She was far from ready to relax in his company yet. 'Yes, I have,' she said. 'This is my fifth visit.'

'So you must have heard stories about my family, as well as the rumours about me?'

'Yes,' said Halthris.

'Then you will have heard, no doubt, that the King my father is a dull-witted senile incompetent who never stepped out of his mother's shadow, and leaves the government of the city to his corrupt and venal ministers?'

'Not to mince words – yes.'

'Well, in this case rumour hasn't lied,' Ansaryon said quietly. 'My father is sixty-eight years old, and his long life has given him neither wisdom nor intelligence. Now he is all but a dotard. The Queen, my mother, was very different, but she died twelve years ago. My elder brother Cathallon is a pathetic figure – he took to drink a long time ago, and now only lives for the next bottle of wine or ral.'

'Ral?'

'It's a very strong spirit, and rots a man's gut if he drinks it for long enough. No one takes much notice of Cathallon any more – or rather, they pretend not to see him.' His mouth twisted bitterly. 'Court life is conducted on two levels. On the surface, everyone observes the rituals and behaves with absolute correctness. And underneath it all lies a seething mass of intrigue, rivalry, corruption and immorality. People will see you as my creature, my protégée, even my lover. They will think that I am using you for my own hidden purposes, and they will try to use you for theirs. Trust no one, believe no one, reveal nothing to anyone – except, of course, the message which you have come here to deliver. And that way, if you are lucky, if the Ska'i allow it, you may escape from Zithirian with your barbarian pride intact.' He studied her speculatively, and then added, 'So – what are you thinking, Halthris of the Tanathi?'

'I'm wishing I'd never offered to come here,' she said.

'Are you always so blunt?'

'Yes – and you'll find most of my people are the same. We dislike pretension and hypocrisy.' She stumbled over the difficult syllables, and added, 'The words for them don't even exist in our language.'

'Then you'll find a great deal to dislike in Zithiriani. Is your brother more diplomatic than you, or does he call a spade a shovel too?'

Despite herself, Halthris smiled. 'He's better at persuading people, I think. I want to shake them into seeing things my way. But I shall do my best not to shake some sense into the King, I promise you.'

'I doubt you could. My grandmother never managed it, and she was one of the most formidable rulers in all Zithirian's history. Yes, don't look so surprised – the city has had two reigning Queens, and my grandmother Tesi was the second of them. She did much, once she came to the throne, to improve the status and position of women here. The fact that you will be allowed an Audience at all is due to her reforms. Up until her time, women could attend Court, but not any formal ceremony or reception or discussion.'

Halthris thought of Tanathi clan and tribal Councils, where anyone who had successfully endured their Ordeal had an equal voice, man or woman, Hearth or Hunter. She tried to imagine living in a world where her opinions did not count, could not even be heard, and failed.

'But despite Queen Tesi's reforms, you'll find that such attitudes to women are still common, especially amongst the older and more powerful courtiers and councillors. They think that females are weak, stupid, easily led and not to be trusted.'

'And do you think that?'

'After meeting you, Halthris of the Tanathi, I suspect that my views on the frailer sex, as women are called here by those who should know better, will undergo radical alteration. But what really matters is that you enter the King's presence, as is customary, with due humility, reverence and respect: that you address him every time you speak as "Your High Mightiness": and that you tell your story clearly and convincingly.'

'And if I don't?'

'Then my father has the perfect excuse to do nothing – not that he has ever needed any excuse, even with nearly ten thousand Ska'i at the gates. At best, he will call up the reserve soldiers from the city and the farms, strengthen the defences, and bring in the winter supplies early.' He looked up, frowning suddenly. 'Why? Why have the Ska'i chosen to move now, when in a month's time the snows may arrive, and everything will be frozen?'

'Including the river,' Halthris said, on a flash of inspiration. 'When the river freezes . . .'

She paused, and Ansaryon finished for her. 'When the Kefirinn freezes over, two sides of Zithirian are virtually defenceless. Oh, whoever planned this is no fool. Do you know anything about the Ska'i, beyond your own encounter with them?'

'We hear a little, now and then. The tribe whose lands separate us, the Rerbresh, are not so hostile – they buy our horses, when they're not trying to encroach on our summer grazing. So we know from them that the Ska'i have a new chief. His name is Quenait, and he's supposed to be ferocious, even for a Ska'i. Certainly he seems to have united the whole tribe, and probably the Rerbresh as well. Apart from that, we only know what everyone knows about them.'

'So this new chief Quenait may have ambitions to capture a city. It's a strange ambition for a savage nomad.' He glanced at her. 'Or of course your brother may have misunderstood – they may only be seeking to expand their territory. In which case, the Tanathi are probably in more danger than Zithirian.'

'We've sent warning to our winter valleys,' Halthris told him. 'But Abreth was certain. The Ska'i kept on talking about Zithirian, over and over again. Why would he do that unless they were planning to attack you?'

'I'm sure my father will think of a good reason.' Ansaryon smiled grimly. 'Best to abandon your honesty, I think, and lie a little for the good of your cause. Don't look so aghast, Halthris of the Tanathi – you can't tell me that lying is unknown in your tribe?'

'No, it isn't,' she admitted. 'But I'm afraid that it isn't something that comes naturally to us.'

'Then you'd better learn fast – just as you must also learn hypocrisy and subservience. You've come into contact with civilization now, Halthris of the Tanathi – and like it or not, you've already been corrupted from your pure barbarian ways. Being willing and able to sleep under a roof is a sure sign of it.'

'We have tents,' Halthris pointed out. 'We don't spend every night under the stars – and certainly not in winter.'

'Do you not? I shall have to find out more about your interesting customs – but we shall discuss that later. First, I must instruct you in what you must do this afternoon. If I don't, I'm certain that my father will refuse to listen to you.'

And much as she disliked the prospect, Halthris knew that he was right.

CHAPTER
FOUR

'Welcome His High Mightiness King Varathand of Zithirian, Fourth of His Name, Descendant in the First Line of the Divine Ancestor Tayo, Wearer of the Silver Crown, Ruler of the Silver City, Wielder of the Silver Spear – all those here present, kneel before him!'

With a smooth, practised rustle of silk and satin, the Court of Zithirian made obeisance to its master: and with rather less practice, and markedly less enthusiasm, Halthris of the Tanathi did likewise, her gold ornaments singing gently.

The Throne Room occupied the first floor of the great central tower of the Palace. Below were the clerks' quarters, where the administrative business of running city and state was carried on: directly above lay the Council Chamber, and on the third and fourth floors, other rooms. Ansaryon had described for her the magnificent solid silver throne, in the form of a divine firebird with wings outstretched to protect the monarch, and the fabulous murals, painted by a famous and long-dead master of the art whose work had even decorated the Imperial Palace in Toktel'yi. Even so, the first impact of this huge circular room, glittering with astonishing beauty and splendour, had taken her breath away.

She had waited for a long time, standing quietly with the other supplicants, the object of much covert attention. Zithiriani courtiers seemed reluctant to display their curiosity openly, so no one approached her, but she could feel eyes feeding avidly off her from all sides.

Ansaryon had warned her that she would be one amongst many, people who wanted mundane favours, a grant of land, pardons for themselves or for a relative, righting of petty injustices. 'The Chief Minister has a list of petitioners, and decides who will speak first. I have ensured that your name is at the top.' He had given her that chilly, almost hostile smile. 'Well, Halthris of the Tanathi – I have done what I can for you. You have received your instructions, you know what you must do, and you are wearing enough gold to make the Court sit up and take notice – although I suspect you'd be an object of acute interest even dressed as a peasant. Once you enter the Throne Room, it's up to you. I'll be there, as will my brothers and my sister, and all the most important ministers and officials of the Court – but I will be able to give you no more help, nor reveal that I have even spoken to you, though of course by now everyone in the Palace will know that you were brought first to me, and are lodged in my apartments.' He smiled again, and this time, she was sure, his eyes were nearly friendly. 'It's up to you now. If the Ska'i are coming, then the fate of Zithirian and all its people may well depend upon your conduct this afternoon.'

'Don't worry,' she had told him, feeling herself almost liking him. 'I won't let them down.'

But now, kneeling encased in scarlet and blue and gold, her bright hair braided, a figure of barbaric colour and splendour even amongst the magnificence of the Zithirian Court, she was by no means so certain of success.

He had told her to keep her eyes downcast. It was considered very bad manners to look at anyone directly, and most of all the King, but she could not resist a discreet glance as, with a slow, measured step, Varathand, Fourth of His Name, entered the Throne Room, his children beside him.

What she saw did not encourage any optimism. The man was clad in an extreme version of the grotesquely fantastic Court dress, a huge garment of rigid heavy silk, falling outwards from the shoulders straight to the ground. It was so thickly embroidered, with a great silver and white firebird in full display from chest to hem, that Halthris could not make out its background colour. Above all this magnificence, the King's shrivelled head and neck poked out from the top of his gown exactly like a tortoise peering from its shell. Indeed, so strong was the resemblance – Varathand was balding, with a beaky nose, sunken eyes and no discernible chin – that Halthris found herself urgently smothering a strong desire to laugh.

Fortunately, the King's features had not been transmitted to his offspring. On his right, the place of honour, stood a tall, stooping man who must, she supposed, be the Heir, Cathallon, the notorious drunkard. At first glance, he did not appear to be such a hopeless degenerate, but she noticed the coarsened, reddened skin, the bloodshot eyes, lank blond hair and general air of mental weakness, and knew that Ansaryon had spoken the truth. Like his father, no splendid garment could disguise this man's feeble and ineffectual character.

Ansaryon was there too, as he had promised, a pace or so behind King and Heir. He bore a certain resemblance to his older brother – the height, the slender build, the lint-pale hair and almost colourless grey eyes – but there was intelligence, strength, even humour in his face, instead of Cathallon's dull vacuity. Beside him stood a young woman in azure and gold, her silver-gilt hair flowing down her back and breast in profusion, who must be his sister, the Lady Zathti. Her features were beautiful and delicate, but her eyes darted round the room like those of a cornered rabbit, and her soft mouth was trembling as if this gathering terrified her, although she must surely attend it nearly every day. A poor creature, Halthris thought with brief pity: no wonder she had no husband, although she must be well past the age for marriage.

The King and his three eldest offspring, all apparently either vicious or feeble-minded, or both, seemed notably unworthy of the grovelling respect given to them by their Court. But on Varathand's left side stood a man who was surely Tsenit, the youngest son, and he was in all respects utterly different. Shorter and stockier than his brothers and sister, the stiff absurdity of the Court dress could not disguise his athletic, muscular body. Halthris glanced at him again, covertly, with a skill just learned from the men and women kneeling around her. She could imagine this young Prince, with his dark curling hair and strong, regular, open face, urging soldiers into battle, or riding through winter snow, or leading the hunt. He exuded an air of capable energy that the rest of the family entirely lacked.

And by the peculiar, ridiculous laws of Zithirian, he was the one son of Varathand who seemed most worthy of the throne, and the one least likely to inherit it. She could not believe that the people in this room, or any of the other citizens, would willingly accept the dismal Cathallon as his father's heir, rather than the vigorous, capable and popular Tsenit.

It would never happen that way amongst the Tanathi, Halthris thought, notching up yet another weight in the balance against this supposedly superior civilization.

The Chief Minister had begun to speak, and suddenly, start-lingly, she heard her name pronounced in the stiff, formal accents of Zithirian. 'Halthris of the Tanathi – rise, and step forward to state your case and receive the wisdom and justice of His High Mightiness King Varathand, Fourth of His Name—'

The endless, pompous titles washed over her. She rose in one fluid movement, keeping her eyes downcast, and began the slow ritual that Ansaryon had taught her. One pace: stop and bow the head. Two paces further: bow from the waist. Three paces more, and kneel again, hands clasped to the breast in supplication, and wait for the King to speak. 'And don't, whatever you do, make your paces too long, or you'll finish too close to him – and no one, save for those favoured few intimates, is allowed to come within touching distance of the King, on pain of losing a hand.'

She had not made her paces too long. She knelt, and heard a thin, reedy, querulous voice. 'Rise, Halthris of the Tanathi – rise, and state your case.'

It seemed so unnatural not to be able to look him in the eye. She concentrated her gaze upon the head of the silver firebird, embroidered on his chest. The silk beneath it was of a rich turquoise colour, she noted with one part of her mind. She took a deep breath, and began the speech she had rehearsed with Ansaryon that morning.

'This supplicant humbly begs for the benevolent attention of His High Mightiness to the message which this humble ambassador of the Tanathi tribe brings to His High Mightiness from her people.'

She glanced swiftly at his face. Like a mask, it displayed no expression whatsoever. For a moment, a wild surge of impatience washed over her, and she longed to scream, 'The Ska'i are coming, you stupid old man – do something, or they'll kill you all!'

But if she did, they would think her mad – they would fling her out at best, imprison her at worst, and her warning would be ignored. So she paused, summoning all her self-control, all her calm, all her intelligence, and then spoke again.

'This humble ambassador brings to His High Mightiness news of the utmost importance. The savage tribe who call themselves the Ska'i have chosen a new chief, named Quenait. He surpasses all his people in cunning, in evil, in ferocity and in ambition. He and every one of his warriors have left their lands in the south. They have joined with the Rerbresh tribe, and together they number eight, perhaps even ten thousand. I myself saw their camp, three days' ride to the west of this city. Quenait is planning to attack Zithirian, Your High Mightiness, and you are all in desperate danger.'

As she finished, she heard the murmuring rise all around her, mingled with sharp gasps of shock or disbelief. Well, Halthris thought grimly, at least my news has had some effect. She risked another glance at Varathand, and saw with dismay that no reaction showed on his face: no alarm, no fear, no determination, no belligerence, nothing. However, the Heir, Cathallon, was staring at her slack-jawed with bewilderment, and the Lady Zathti, her hands clasped shaking together, was obviously in some state of agitation.

The King spoke, his voice even more tremulous than before.

'Halthris of the Tanathi states that she has seen the camp of the Ska'i. How then was she able to escape, when their ferocity and lust for blood are legendary throughout the known world?'

Trying, without much success, to speak in the same convoluted way, Halthris described how she had nearly been killed by the Ska'i warrior, and of the events that had followed. The whispers had died away, and there was absolute quiet in the Throne Room: the only sound, apart from her own voice, was its echo in the high, vaulted air above her.

When she ended, on the tale of Urdray's death, a mouse's footsteps could have been heard crossing the floor. 'And so Halthris of the Tanathi brings this urgent news to His High Mightiness, out of the love she and her tribe bears for His High Mightiness and his people, and fearing that the Ska'i mean to attack Zithirian.'

Her words hung ominously in the void. The silence continued. She did not dare to look up: already, she had been far more blunt than Ansaryon had advised. Above anything, she wished for Abreth, who was no more steady and courageous than she was, but whose presence would lend her some much-needed support. Tanathi were not accustomed to being alone, surrounded by strangers.

The King's thready voice interrupted her thoughts. 'What credence shall we place in the word of one Barbarian woman? It seems to us that she may have exaggerated the situation out of all proportion. Such people as the Tanathi are not civilized: they cannot read, or write. It appears likely to us that they cannot count, either. Surely Halthris of the Tanathi has seen a camp of, at most, a hundred men, and with the eye of fear has enlarged their numbers in her mind.'

'Your High Mightiness – I know what I saw.' Halthris gripped her hands together and stared down at them, using all her strength to contain her anger. Of course she could count – all Tanathi were used to assessing the numbers of their stock herds, quickly and accurately. 'My brother Abreth saw them too. He will arrive here tomorrow, or the next day, to confirm what I have told you. I repeat – the Ska'i are coming, and they mean to attack Zithirian. They are merciless head-takers, and they will spare no one – not even women, or children, or babies – save to take them as slaves, to sacrifice later to Ayak, their wolf-god of death. If you do not defend yourselves, they will slaughter all of you, and plunder and destroy your city.'

She thought she had gone too far. Behind her, there were several gasps – probably at her blunt manner rather than at her words. Then a new voice, young, brisk and confident, broke in.

'Has Halthris of the Tanathi any other proof that Zithirian will be their target?'

It must be Tsenit. She was sweating with the effort of keeping calm, of maintaining her subservient pose, eyes down, unable to see anyone's expression. She said slowly, 'The testimony of the prisoner we took is our only direct evidence. But the camp that we saw was in a valley that my people know well. It runs from south to north, then turns eastward, towards Zithirian. Even in such vast numbers, they could be here tomorrow. And although the city walls are high, the farms and settlements in the countryside are completely defenceless. If their inhabitants are not warned, and given the chance to take refuge in Zithirian, the Ska'i will kill them all.'

'Another question has not been asked, or answered. Why would a savage nomad such as this Quenait wish to attack Zithirian? He can know even less of cities than the Tanathi. Surely, raiding the borders of the Empire, or other steppe tribes, is more to his taste?'

She said carefully, 'His High Mightiness's city is fabled throughout the known world for its wealth. As His High Mightiness can plainly see in the person of this humble ambassador, all barbarians worship the glitter of gold and silver. Quenait may well be driven on by a thirst for plunder. And he may feel that Zithirian is more easy and more rewarding to capture, than to raid the barren border towns of the Toktel'yan Empire.'

'May – might – it seems to us that there is no certainty in any of this.' The King's voice was bored and tetchy. 'Halthris of the Tanathi has stated her case with typically barbarian passion, but she has not yet convinced us that there is any true threat to us from these Ska'i. When her brother arrives, we shall consider hearing what he has to say. Until that hour, Halthris of the Tanathi may live at peace and in comfort under our roof, and enjoy our hospitality. We hope that her barbarian customs and ways will not make her unwelcome. We dismiss her with honour, and our thanks.'

A hand was under her elbow, guiding her backwards. Through a fog of incredulous rage, Halthris forced herself to make the ritual obeisances. I hope Quenait slices off your stupid head in person, you silly old goat, she thought furiously. It's no more than you deserve. The real tragedy is that all your innocent people might have to pay the price for your incompetence as well.

She looked up at last as the impassive officials escorted her from the chamber. The King, resplendent on his wonderful silver throne, was already listening to the next supplicant, his three very different sons standing attentively beside him.

It was a great pity that they hadn't taken her to Tsenit first, instead of to Ansaryon. He certainly looked as though he could persuade the King to defend the city – and he was supposed to be Varathand's favourite child. Curiously, Ansaryon, in his description of his family, hadn't mentioned either Zathti or Tsenit. She was rapidly coming to the conclusion that the murky undercurrents beneath the Court's rigid façade were far deeper and more unpleasant than Ansaryon had hinted. And she, Halthris of the Tanathi, honest and outspoken and impatient, was cast adrift here, without paddle or star to guide her, and aided only by her wits and her courage.

Well, she thought, as the door to the Throne Room shut firmly behind her, and she was given into the charge of another servant, bravery and intelligence have not failed me yet. She vowed that somehow, by any means possible, she would extract herself from this lunatic place, and take refuge with Abreth and her friends and the rest of the tribe in the sane safety of the mountains, far from a city where blind stupidity, viciousness and jealousy could reign unchecked over thousands of innocent people.

The servant led her down the spiralling stairs of the tower, past other menials in their brilliant blue, and men in the dark yellow robes of officialdom. At the foot of the stairs, another servant stepped forward. 'It is humbly requested that Halthris of the Tanathi accompany me now.'

The surprised expression of her original escort told her that he had not expected this, and the young, plump face of the second man was not one she recognized. She said, 'Where do you wish to take me?'

'It is humbly requested that Halthris of the Tanathi accompanies this humble servant,' the young man repeated firmly.

The other made a swift bow and scuttled away, and Halthris found her arm gently taken. 'That's not necessary,' she said, shaking him off. 'I will do as you wish, and I am not your prisoner.'

Some of her anger had infiltrated her voice, and the plump servant snatched his hand back as if stung. He turned and walked off down the twisting corridor, and she followed him, curious but not apprehensive. Who wished to see her? Was she to be granted a private word with the King, or with one of his ministers?

The passage in the heart of the tower unwound before her, illuminated by lanterns whose flickering light made the painted walls seem almost alive. She was beginning to get her bearings, and recognized some of the pictures as they passed. Then the servant led her down a turning to the right, and right again, and she found herself suddenly in a courtyard like the one in Ansaryon's apartments.

Alike, but not the same. Instead of a fountain, the centre was occupied by a wide pool, with a low wall around it, and steps leading up and into the water. There were no flowers, but a rich green vine twisted up the stone columns supporting the roof above rooms and walkway. Around the edge of the courtyard stood several stone statues, nearly life-size and carved with that astonishing realism which seemed to be characteristic of Zithirian art. They all depicted young men in athletic or war-like poses: one was throwing a spear, another making ready to run, the third and fourth engaged in a wrestling match. The whole effect was of a vigorous and masculine austerity, very different from the luxurious comfort of Ansaryon's quarters.

'I hope you were not alarmed by your abduction?'

It was a familiar voice. She turned to see Tsenit, still in his formal robes, walk forward from under the shadow of the colonnade. His vigorous, purposeful stride was very different from the rather languid, mincing walk of most Zithiriani. He gave her a cheerful, friendly smile, revealing very white teeth. 'Welcome to my apartments, Halthris of the Tanathi.'

'Thank you,' she said. She already liked this young man far better than the rest of his family, but she was not yet prepared to give him his proper title. 'I wasn't in any way anxious – just curious.'

'And so am I.' Tsenit stopped a few feet away, and surveyed her with frank appraisal. His eyes were a bright and sunny blue, contrasting attractively with the wavy dark brown hair framing his face. 'I want to know why a Tanathi Chief's daughter would risk her life to come here to give us a warning that may well be ignored – and why she brought her news first to Ansaryon, of all people.'

'I didn't have any choice in the matter – I was taken straight to him,' Halthris said. 'I did ask to see the King, but no one took any notice.'

'My father is old, and not in the best of health – as you may have seen,' Tsenit said. 'He finds even these brief afternoons dispensing justice a considerable strain, and he has now devolved much of his work onto other shoulders. My brothers and I bear the burden as best we can.'

'You don't seem to find it very irksome,' said Halthris drily.

Tsenit laughed. 'Oh, I do, I do – I would much rather be out in the countryside, riding or hunting, than cooped up in that stuffy tower and slowly disappearing under a mountain of paperwork.' He grinned, and she could not help grinning back. 'As I'm sure you understand, Halthris of the Tanathi.'

'I think I do,' she agreed, liking this cheerful and friendly young Prince far better than his strange and rather sinister brother. 'But I would like to know why I have been brought here.'

'All in good time.' He turned and snapped his fingers. Two servants came forward, and with swift hands unbuttoned the preposterous silk gown and removed it from his broad shoulders. Underneath, he wore a simple belted tunic in cream linen, and dark blue trousers tucked into soft leather boots very like hers. He stood hardly taller than she did, but she had not imagined his powerful build. Unlike Ansaryon, Tsenit obviously spent his free time in energetic and healthy exercise.

'That's better,' he said with relief. 'Those robes are so heavy, they stand up on their own. The courtiers vie with one another to see how much floor space they take up. The Chief Minister's wife has a new gown which won't fit through the Throne Room door – she has to squeeze through sideways. Come with me, Halthris of the Tanathi – I want to show you something.'

Bemused, she followed him out of the courtyard, along a brief passage and through a plain wooden door. Beyond it, a flight of stone steps wound upwards into gloom, illuminated by more hanging brass lanterns.

'I trust you're fit, Halthris of the Tanathi,' he said with a cheerful smile, and began to trot up the stairs. She stared at his retreating back for a moment and then, rising to the challenge, ran in pursuit.

Stairs were almost outside her experience, and much harder work to climb than she had assumed. On and on they turned, in that dangerously dim light, seemingly endless. Sweating, Halthris tried not to gasp for breath, aware of aching legs and dry throat. She passed doors at regular intervals, but there were no windows, no way of telling how high she had ascended. She remembered the clan's Storyteller, sitting by a summer fire with a ring of children around him, all enthralled by the tale of Foolish Gan, a favourite character in Tanathi legend, who thought he could reach the moon by climbing Annako, the highest of the Northern Mountains, and was frozen solid in the snow until an ice-bear licked him back to life.

Suddenly, she reached light, air, space. The surprise of it stopped her in her tracks: she hung in the doorway, gasping, while the wind whipped her braids across her face and the sun blinded her.

'Well done,' said Tsenit, in slightly condescending tones that reminded her instantly and incongruously of Kettan. 'You're the only person to have run all the way up here without pausing for breath – apart from me, of course.' He smiled, and Halthris began to revise her opinion of him. Where physical fitness was concerned, Tsenit seemed to consider himself supreme.

Of course, given the lazy and pampered lifestyle of the Royal Family, his conceit was probably quite justified, but she was still irritated by his arrogance. She calmed her breathing, achieved control over her sweaty, shaking limbs, and walked out onto the roof of the tower.

The centre was occupied by a steeply sloping spire, spearing towards the sky. On its peak, the likeness of a fearsome winged beast, made of beaten gold, glittered in the sun as it roared soundlessly westward, into the wind. She found the racing clouds above it made her feel dizzy, and hastily diverted her gaze.

'Here.' Tsenit was beckoning to her. 'Come and look at this, Halthris of the Tanathi.'

She walked the few steps across to where he stood by the rampart. Keep calm, Halthris: think slowly, act carefully, don't panic. The thought that only a pile of precariously balanced stones kept her at this unnatural height was at once absurd and terrifying. A white snowbringer floated past on pointed wings, its beady dark eye glancing at her curiously, and her sense of deep disturbance increased. If Hegeden had meant us to invade his realm, she thought, the sweat breaking out afresh on face and back, he'd have given us wings as well.

'You're not afraid of heights, are you?' said Tsenit, hitching himself casually on the rampart with a nonchalance that astounded her. 'I thought you Tanathi feared nothing and nobody.'

'Everyone has one weakness, at least,' Halthris said. She did not like the thought that he had discerned her terror so easily, but there was no point in denying it if it was that obvious. Keep calm, her sensible inner voice kept urging her. Orientate yourself. You are facing north-east, for the afternoon sun is on your back. Don't lean over the edge: concentrate on what lies in the distance first.

She looked, and then gazed again in wonder. The three greatest peaks of the Northern Mountains, Sargenn, Annako and Estray, floated in all their marvellous glory, cloud-free in the sunlit air, like some fabulous dream made real. She felt as if it would be possible to reach over the parapet and touch them, so close and clear they seemed.

'Magnificent view, isn't it?' said Tsenit. 'Estray is the nearest, to the left. It's almost fifty Toktel'yan miles away. Annako is the peak behind it, and Sargenn is away to the right. Usually they're hidden by cloud, this late in the year.'

'Not so late,' Halthris said. 'The snows are at least a month away, surely.'

The wind gusted round her, icy chill despite the sun. A snowbringer glided past again, and she realized that there were several of the small, graceful white birds, harbingers of winter, drifting round the tower. During the summer, they roamed far to the north beyond the mountains, in lands where no Tanathi had ever trod, but which were believed to be bleak and featureless plains, inhabited only by hairy beasts and terrible howling demons. As the cold poured down from this unknown territory, it swept the snowbringers ahead of it, and their arrival was a certain sign of imminent winter.

'I think they will come early, this year,' Tsenit said. 'And with the snows, the dark, the cold, the wolves – and the Ska'i.'

'Then you do believe me?'

'I think so, yes – you would not have come here alone if your story had not been true. Unlike my brother Ansaryon, I have the trust and confidence of His High Mightiness – it was a great pity you weren't brought to me first. But although his reaction did seem very unpromising, I shouldn't be too disheartened. My father always needs a great deal of persuasion to convince him that action is needed – whether it's changing the rate of the Land Tax or answering the threat of invasion. But he does not have a completely closed mind, I assure you. Give me a few days to work on him, and you'll see some result.'

'Thank you,' Halthris said, since his expectant pause seemed to demand her gratitude. And she was grateful – certainly, Tsenit appeared to be a much more useful ally than Ansaryon. But a few days might be too long. In a few days, the Ska'i might be advancing over the fertile green and gold fields along the Kefirinn, slaughtering unsuspecting farmers and families who had had no warning of their approach because of Varathand's dithering. She added, 'If they moved fast, the Ska'i could be here in a day or two.'

'Then I shall have to work hard,' said Tsenit. 'Don't worry, Halthris of the Tanathi. I have it all in hand. You can enjoy a little civilized luxury, and soon your brother will be here, and his story will add credence to yours. Anyway, I didn't bring you all the way up here to discuss the Ska'i. I wanted to show you the city. Don't be alarmed, the parapet is quite safe – you can't possibly fall.'

Once more, his condescending tone raised her hackles. But she hid her irritation, and her fear, and stepped up to the sun-warmed, silvery stone, quarried from the glittering white cliffs of Annako and brought to this place nearly three hundred years ago by the renegade Tanathi Tayo, to enhance and glorify the mean huddle of riverside huts he had taken over, and preposterously dignified with the title of city.

'There you are,' said Tsenit, taking her arm in friendly fashion. 'Halthris of the Tanathi – behold Zithirian!'

She would have appreciated the sight much more if it had not unleashed a wave of dizziness. The Palace stood on a rocky eminence, around which bent the swift-running waters of the Kefirinn. Immediately below her, the jumble of buildings around the central tower finished abruptly, to be replaced by the inevitable garden, brilliant with flowers, spurting with fountains, mirrored with ponds and pools. A lower wall, with squat round towers set into it at intervals, stopped the lush greenery from falling over the cliff into the river. Distantly, she saw another, smaller stream tumbling into the Kefirinn from the north, and just above this confluence, foaming white water and the dark jagged teeth of rocks.

'That's the River D'yenn, which rises between Sargenn and Annako,' said Tsenit, pointing. 'And those are the first rapids on the Kefirinn. Ships can sail all the way up from Toktel'yi to Zithirian, but no further. There are ten rapids between here and Lake Raiyis, the source of the river, but it is possible to take a boat up there, if it is small enough to carry around the rough water.' He turned her to face southwards, into the sun. 'There are the docks. The Divine Ancestor had them dug out of the marshes below the Palace Rock. Fifty ships can tie up there at once, in the height of the season, but now of course there are only a few left. The Last Ship is due any day – and when it arrives, the Gathering Fair will be held. But of course you've been to the fair in past years – you know all this.'

'Not all of it,' said Halthris, wondering how he had found out that this was not her first visit to Zithirian. But of course he must have guessed it, from her command of the language if nothing else. She obediently listened to his description of the docks, the warehouses stuffed with the produce of Zithirian – gold, silver, embroidered textiles, furs, wine, grain – to be exchanged for the spices, silks, cottons, oils, exotic fruits and animals, scented woods and precious stones, that were sent north from Toktel'yi and the distant, fabled islands of the Archipelago. And under the spell of his enthusiasm, Halthris began to yearn for a glimpse of those strange and wonderful places, where the people had skins of brown or rich black, where the heat all the year round was greater than the hottest summer afternoon on the steppe, where strange gods were worshipped and mountains spat fire and smoke, and the islands crowded so thickly that no man or woman had ever listed or even counted them.

'I've been to Toktel'yi, you know,' said Tsenit, with an air of pride that made him seem suddenly very young. 'It's almost a disappointment – huge, of course, the largest city in all the known world, but nowhere near as beautiful as Zithirian. Most of the buildings are made of mud brick or wood, except for the Imperial Palace – and that's built of Annako stone, just like this tower!' He stroked the sparkling parapet as if it were a living thing. 'Zithirian is the best, the richest and the most lovely place in all the world – even a barbarian can see that, even the Toktel'yans admit it.' He smiled at her, and the effect was dazzling. 'Now come and see the other side – the view's even more spectacular, if that's possible.'

Halthris was drawn by his warm, insistent hand around the central spire, through the sudden chill of its shadow, and out again into the windy sunshine beyond. She was becoming more used to this, but still did not like to approach the parapet too quickly. As before, she fixed her eyes first on the further horizon. In contrast to the sharp, crystalline clarity of the Northern Mountains, marching away into the distance on her right, the endless blurred dun grass of the steppe lay in front of her, featureless and hazy, receding to a smudged horizon far to the west. She said in surprise, 'It seems quite flat from up here – but it's all valleys and hills and moorland.'

'The effect of height and distance,' said Tsenit. He took her arm again, and drew her close to the edge. 'Look down there – look at the city, Halthris of the Tanathi. Isn't that a sight just as marvellous as the mountains?'

Below her, beyond the towers and walls of the Palace, lay Zithirian, and she gazed down on it as if she were a snowbringer, soaring in the crisp air. She could see the countless little courtyards, the maze of narrow streets, the fat, gilded white towers around the great central Temple of Tayo, the outer walls of the city, and beyond them, the rich fields up and down the valley of the Kefirinn, which fed the thousands of citizens crowded into the houses below.

'Look!' cried Tsenit suddenly, and turned her abruptly to face south, his hand on her back. 'The Last Ship – I can see it coming, the Last Ship!'

Far, far away down the Kefirinn, so small that even Halthris's keen eyes could hardly discern more than a flash of light and colour, there was, perhaps, a tiny moving sail. Forgetting her earlier fears, she leaned over the parapet, shading her eyes against the sun. 'How can you tell?'

'He's guessing, I expect.'

It was Ansaryon's voice. Tsenit sprang away from her as if stung, his dark brows pulled together in a grimace of anger. 'What are you doing here, brother?'

'I came to find a certain barbarian woman,' said Ansaryon. 'Your servants told me you were both up here.'

Halthris turned away from the rim of the tower with some relief: she hadn't realized how dangerously far she had leaned over it, in response to Tsenit's infectious enthusiasm. The Lord Ansaryon, once more in his sombre black, stood a few paces behind them, the wind blowing his pale silky hair into rats' tails around his lean, overbred face. He added, a sneer in his voice, 'My young brother loves more than anything else to look down on things – and on people.'

Tsenit flushed. He said, 'You've no business here. Go away. Halthris of the Tanathi is my guest for the afternoon, and she wishes to stay and admire the view.'

Ansaryon's eyes hooked her gaze before she could avoid it. 'Do you wish to stay with my brother? Or have you had enough of heights for the moment?'

She opened her mouth to announce her preference for Tsenit's company, even in this unnatural place, and found to her horror that she was saying something quite different. 'I think I have. If you will permit me, Lord Tsenit, I will return now with the Lord Ansaryon to his apartments.'

'But—' Tsenit began, his face an almost comical mixture of rage and indignant bewilderment.

'You heard her. She wishes to leave with me.' Ansaryon stretched out a long, pale hand, adorned with a single dark-stoned ring on the middle finger. 'Allow me to escort you down, Halthris of the Tanathi. Goodbye, brother.'

She descended the endless stairs in an appalled silence, struggling to control her fear and anger at the man who followed a few steps behind her. She did not want to come with him – she did *not*. There were certain aspects to Tsenit's character which did not appeal, but a little conceited arrogance was surely a common trait in princes, and he was certainly nicer, more friendly and approachable than his strange elder brother.

She had intended to say that she would stay on the tower, and had instead uttered words quite different. And she was sure that Ansaryon had made her say them.

The implications were terrifying. She had already suspected that he might be putting pictures into her head, much as she communicated with Fess. But she had never tried to force the cat to do something she did not want, or which was against her nature. It seemed, though, that Ansaryon had just done that to her.

She had always been in control of herself and her destiny. No one in her tribe, not her father, nor her long-dead mother, nor her brother and sister, had ever been able to mould her: she had always followed her own path, regardless. And now all that confidence and certainty had been stripped away from her, and she teetered on the brink of an abyss just as dreadful as if the stones of the parapet had vanished as she leaned against them.

For if Ansaryon could frame her thoughts and dictate her words, presumably by means of his evil sorcery, then she was lost. She would be his creature, forced to obey his every desire, and to be his slave for ever more.

CHAPTER
FIVE

'I won't do that again – I swear it.'

They stood in Ansaryon's tower room. A tray of food and wine had been placed temptingly on the table, but Halthris was not hungry – in fact, she could not imagine ever being hungry again. Sick with fear and loathing, she stared at the man who had reached inside her head to manipulate her thoughts, her words and her actions, and wondered with remote despair what he meant.

'Listen, Halthris of the Tanathi – *listen* to me!'

He came up close to her, within touching distance, and she couldn't stop herself backing away from him. She bumped into something sharp and solid, perhaps the edge of the big table, and began to shake.

'Listen,' Ansaryon repeated. His voice was low, intense and urgent. 'I know what you're feeling – believe me, I *know*. I too have had my mind invaded, and suffered the terror and the humiliation of being under someone else's control. And I won't do it to you again.'

She stared at him. 'I don't believe you. You've been putting things into my head since I first came to you, haven't you? And reading my thoughts, too. I'm not stupid – I've heard of such things. The Ska'i shamans do it. One of them made a hundred men walk off a cliff, once, just to demonstrate how powerful he was.' She could not stop her trembling, but she could at least keep some dignity. 'I can't stop you, can I? But I can tell you that I'd rather die than submit to – to whatever you want to do with me.'

'I don't want to do anything to you,' Ansaryon said, his voice suddenly harsh. 'Halthris, I had a reason, a very good reason, for making you leave the top of Tsenit's tower. I can't tell you why, for another very good reason, but I hope that one day I'll be able to explain it to you. In the mean time, you have my promise that from now onwards I will make no attempt to reach your mind without your consent, or to influence your thoughts, or to control you in any way whatsoever.'

'Your promise? I wouldn't trust you further than a flea's jump.'

Ansaryon stared at her for a moment. The pupils of his eyes

were darkly dilated, the iris reduced to a silver circle around desolation. He said softly, 'I swear to you, by the powers of Tayo, that I will keep my word. And if I do not, may Ayak and all his wolves devour me, and cast my soul into oblivion.'

Silence. Halthris shivered, as if the death-god's shadow had swept over her. She whispered, 'That oath can never be broken.'

'And I will never break it.'

For a long, long time their eyes met, and she felt no more invasions of her thoughts or her self. Instead, curiously, she was tempted to let her mind reach out to his. It was an impulse she immediately suppressed, but she could not deny that it had existed.

And now she did not know what to think. She had been so sure that he meant her harm, that he intended to turn her into something resembling the gibbering, soul-bereft mind-slaves that were rumoured to serve the shamans of the Ska'i. But instead he had apologized, and he had sworn, with an oath that could only be abjured on pain of the most hideous torment, that he would not invade her mind again.

Could she trust him? Or was his soul already so far beyond redemption that to take Ayak's dreadful name in vain meant nothing to him?

'You still don't believe me, do you?' he said at last. 'And I can't say I blame you, Halthris of the Tanathi. After all, I myself told you not to trust anyone here – anyone at all.'

'Not even Tsenit?'

'Especially not Tsenit,' said Ansaryon, and there was a note of such savagery in his voice that she almost flinched. 'Are all the Tanathi really such shining examples of truth and honesty that you haven't yet learned the dangers of judging only by appearances?'

'No,' said Halthris, defensively annoyed. 'But I can recognize jealousy when I see it.'

'*Jealousy?*' Ansaryon stared at her in genuine bewilderment, and then began to laugh. 'Oh, no, not jealousy, Halthris of the Tanathi. Why should I be jealous of Tsenit? Because he is handsome, athletic, outgoing, extremely popular, and my father's favourite? Believe me, I am not jealous of anyone, least of all Tsenit. I have no interest in sports or warfare, I don't care what people think of me, and above all I have no desire to be doted on by that slobbering senile old idiot who calls himself my father. You're right, I have no love for my younger brother, but jealousy isn't the reason.'

'What is it, then?'

'There are several, and I have no intention of sharing them with anyone, including you. It should be enough to say that I don't trust him – and neither should you. Don't trust anyone in the Palace – not even me.'

'Not *even*? Shouldn't that be "especially"?'

Again he laughed, more warmly, and she was surprised to see something that might, incredibly, be admiration in his face. 'Very well, if you insist – especially not me. As I said, I don't care what people think of me – but even so, few people have ever answered me back as sharply as you do, Halthris of the Tanathi.'

'A pity they haven't more often,' she observed waspishly. 'My people make a point of bringing down those who get above themselves.' She grinned suddenly. 'I have a particularly infuriating cousin to practise on.'

In the space of a few moments, the atmosphere between them had drastically altered, from fear and hatred to a certain warmth, almost friendship. No, she did not trust him, and she would remain on her guard. But, almost unwillingly, she was beginning to like him a little.

He was smiling, and there was no hostility left in his eyes. 'Amongst all the other things said about me, you must have heard that I am something of a scholar – a person who pursues knowledge. Does that mean anything to you?'

'Not much,' said Halthris, a little puzzled by the conversation's sudden change in direction. 'Knowledge is all around us, surely – you don't have to chase it.'

'For you, it is indeed all around you – in the steppe, in your stories, in the world you inhabit – you eat it and breathe it and dream it, and most of it must be vital to your survival. But in Zithirian, life is not so simple. There are so many people, so many skills, so many stories that one man, or woman, could not learn them all in a hundred lifetimes. Instead, we have written everything down – in books.' He turned and swept a hand towards the shelves of leather-covered boxes that covered all the space between two windows. 'Those are books, if you hadn't realized what they were. Had you? Have you heard of writing, or books?'

'Of course I have,' Halthris said. 'Even a barbarian woman is not completely ignorant.'

'But of course you have no need of such things yourself,' said Ansaryon, ignoring her sarcasm. 'All the knowledge a Tanathi requires for life can be contained in the head.' He turned and selected a volume. 'Here – look at this.'

She had never seen a book at close quarters before, let alone handled one. It felt astonishingly heavy for its size. She tried to turn it over, and found that the outer casing could be peeled back, to reveal scores of small, thin sheets of what must be paper, bound together somehow and fastened to the thick leather-clad wood.

Curious, she laid the book down on the table and leafed through it. Many pages were covered in tiny black marks, like a host of strangely-shaped insects. But to her wonder and delight, she found pictures everywhere of animals and birds, beautifully drawn and brilliantly coloured. She recognized the white snowbringer, with its dark eye and pointed wings: a silver-headed eagle, Hegeden's own companion, fiercely magnificent even in miniature; and, most lovely of all, the mountain tiger, so rare she had only ever seen one once in her life, with its clouded black and grey stripes, its bushy tail and keen yellow eyes.

'Beautiful, isn't it?'

Ansaryon's voice broke the enchantment at last. She looked up, a forgotten smile on her face. 'How – how did he *know*? How could he put it all down so exactly? I can almost see it move. Is – was it some kind of sorcery?'

'Rather more mundane, I'm afraid. The book was made in the time of my great-great-grandfather, Tsenit II, who died nearly a hundred years ago. He kept a menagerie in the Palace gardens, and employed many artists to paint them. There are many copies of this book, but the pictures in this one are the finest anywhere.'

'You mean – there was a *live* mountain tiger? Here in the Palace?'

'Yes, kept in a cage. Mountain tigers, mountain goats, steppe deer, rock rabbits, spotted cats, eagles and other birds – King Tsenit paid hunters to go into the steppe or the mountains to capture animals alive and bring them back so that this book could be made – an accurate description of all the animals and birds to be found within the borders of Zithirian, from eagles to sparrows, from mice to tigers.'

'But *why*?' asked Halthris in bewilderment.

'Because if he didn't, he wouldn't *know*. You do – you probably recognize all the animals in the book. There isn't one whose name you don't know, and its habits, its size, its appearance, whether it's dangerous, or good to eat. But you're a Tanathi – you absorb all that knowledge in childhood, because it's vital for your survival to remember that mountain tigers often live in caves, or that grass deer are solitary but nooka antelope are not. Well, it wasn't necessary for my great-great-grandfather to be aware of such things – he didn't hunt on the steppe, his food arrived well-cooked on plates and bore little resemblance to the animal it once was. But he wanted to know – he wanted to find out. And so, like me, he was called a scholar.' He grinned suddenly. 'Some people would say that a scholar is one who uselessly pursues useless facts. There's an element of truth in that.'

'But this isn't useless.' Halthris looked down at the book. 'This is beautiful.'

'You have no need of it, though – you know it all already. Nor have I – I'm hardly likely to encounter a mountain tiger in the streets of Zithirian. But some people, myself included, find such information fascinating, even if they're never going to make use of it. Isn't there anything that you would like to know more about, even though you have no real need?'

She said slowly, 'Yes. Yes, there is. I've heard a few stories about the lands to the south – the Toktel'yan Empire, the Archipelago – I'll never go to those places, but I would very much like to know more about them.'

'And I shall never live with your tribe – but I would like to know more about the Tanathi, and their customs.' He glanced at her. 'Telling me about your people can't do any harm – and it might occupy the time until your brother arrives. My great-grandmother, after all, was a Tanathi woman.'

'Yes, I know. Her name was Djerrin, and she was of Sayni's Clan, which is mine. Is that why you are curious about us?'

'Partly, yes. And, of course, I would like to learn more about your people, purely for the pleasure of adding to my useless store of knowledge.'

'I'll try to tell you what you want to know,' Halthris said. 'As you say, it will pass the time until Abreth comes.' *If* he comes, said the voice of dread in her mind. 'Only the lore of a shaman is forbidden to be revealed to outsiders. And since I'm not a shaman, I couldn't tell you much about them anyway.'

'The practices of the shamans are not what I had in mind.'

'Why not? Because you know and employ them already?'

'One of these days, Halthris of the Tanathi, your sharp answers will get you into considerable trouble. They don't worry me – indeed, as you've probably realized, I rather enjoy them. It's a refreshing change from obsequious courtiers. But it might be wise to curb your tongue outside this room.' He crossed to the table, sat down, and pulled a pile of paper towards him. 'Well, we have the rest of the afternoon at our disposal, Halthris of the Tanathi, and the evening too. Where shall we begin?'

*

At first, Halthris's life in the Palace was extraordinarily uncomfort-able. Despite the luxury of her surroundings, the soft bed, the warmth, the daily baths, the excellent food and efficient servants eager to supply her every need, she longed acutely for the freedom of the steppe, for Fess's warm companionship, and to be able to see to the far horizon instead of only to the next wall. She was, however, profoundly grateful that Ansaryon did not suggest taking her up to the top of his tower. She had had several nightmares about falling off Tsenit's.

The younger Prince had not attempted to contact her again, which was strange, given his earlier and effusive overtures of friendship. After some thought, she sent him a brief message, dictated to one of the ubiquitous servants. There was no reply, which worried her. With every day that passed, the urgency grew greater. If he was using his influence as Varathand's favourite son to persuade the King to prepare for the coming of the Ska'i, then she had no knowledge of it.

And she had no way of discovering what was happening, even elsewhere in the Palace. The two servants assigned to her, the girl Kerrardi and a young boy, only smiled and shook their heads when asked about the King, about Tsenit, about events in the city. And several times she tried to leave Ansaryon's apartments, only to be gently but firmly returned to the courtyard. She was not really being treated like a prisoner, save in one vital respect: her freedom was denied to her.

Being Halthris, she asked Ansaryon bluntly why she was being held captive, and received a less than blunt answer. 'You are not a prisoner. I just thought it was best to keep you in my quarters for your own safety, that's all.'

'Yes, but *why*?'

And he smiled at her infuriatingly. 'Why? Best for you not to know that at present, I think, Halthris of the Tanathi.'

So she still did not trust him. She wondered if, for terrible reasons of his own, he wished to overthrow Zithirian with Quenait's help. In which case, to keep her here, impotent and ignorant, until the city was attacked would suit his purpose very well.

But although she knew that this was, horribly, a likely expla-nation for her situation, she did not now think that it was true. For the more time she spent in Ansaryon's company, describing the life, customs and lore of her tribe while he scratched incomprehen-sibly on his paper with ink and reed pen, the more she was coming to see him as a friend, despite all her misgivings. Yes, he was insufferably arrogant and secretive; yes, he had moods of deep black anger and bitterness which he could not quite hide from her; yes, he seemed to hold an alarmingly large number of people, especially the other members of his family, in considerable contempt. But he was quick, intelligent and perceptive: his genuine interest in the Tanathi was very flattering, if bewildering; and his manner was markedly more open and friendly than at their first encounter. She found it increasingly difficult to believe all those terrible stories. Surely, if he sacrificed babies, or violated virgins, or called up demons and the dead in those upper tower rooms she had never seen, then she would *know*?

She asked him several times whether his father had made any attempt to warn his people about the Ska'i, or to strengthen the city's defences, and always received a less than informative reply. 'Let's just say that I'm doing my best, shall we? When your brother comes, it'll be different.'

Halthris wished she shared his certainty. In her mind, 'when' had long since given way to 'if'. She had made the same journey across the steppe in two days: surely, the fact that Abreth had failed to arrive after five, even though the herd of seventy young horses would have slowed him down considerably, meant that disaster had overtaken him and his companions.

And then, late in the afternoon of her sixth day in Zithirian, in cold and rainy weather, a servant knocked at the door of the tower room, and delivered his message in the usual convoluted style that still irritated Halthris intensely. But all her annoyance was forgotten at the words which told her what she had been hoping and waiting for all this time to hear.

A party of Tanathi tribesmen were outside the Sunset Gate, with a herd of horses, and wished for news of their two companions, believed to have already reached the city.

'I'll go to them now, and tell them that the Lady Halthris is here in the Palace,' Ansaryon said, rising to his feet. As she stared at him in angry bewilderment, he dismissed the messenger and gestured to his personal servant. 'Mearko – bring me my blue gown, and then order an escort for me.'

When the man had gone, he forestalled her furious questions. 'Listen – I know what you want. You want to rush down to the Sunset Gate to greet your brother and your friends.'

'Hegeden's wings, of course I do,' Halthris snarled. 'What possible right have you got to keep me here? Why can't I see him – *why*? Let me out of here, or I swear I'll break the neck of anyone who tries to stop me.'

'*Listen*, will you?' Ansaryon's eye glittered, and his voice, reduced to a hissing whisper, had a compelling quality that at last won her silence, if not her assent. 'If I escort Abreth straight to the King in public, then he can tell him about the Ska'i without any suspicion of collusion with you – or with me. No one will be able to accuse you of concocting a story together – or say that I have influenced him, for that matter. When Abreth has spoken to the King, *then* I will bring him here to you. Do you understand?'

She did, but her anger was still sharp. 'Who in Hegeden's name will accuse us of lying? Why should we lie? How would it benefit us to make up such a story if it wasn't true?'

'I don't know off-hand, but I'm sure certain people could persuade the King my father that day was night if they tried hard enough. If Abreth goes straight to him now, it strengthens your case enormously. You do see that?'

Unwillingly, Halthris nodded. 'Yes. Yes, I suppose I do.' She paused, feeling suddenly that the words she was about to say almost constituted a betrayal. 'When my brother has spoken to the King . . . I wish to leave the city with him, and join our companions.'

There was a small, strange silence. Then Ansaryon said, 'Of course you may. You were never a prisoner here. I shall miss our conversations, though – I have much enjoyed learning about the ways of your people. And your hunting-cat must be pining for you, after so long apart.'

'Fess? She never pines for anyone,' said Halthris. 'She is utterly self-reliant. But I think, even so, that she'll be glad to see me.' She paused, and added, with Zithiriani formality, 'If I do not have the chance to do so later – I thank you, Lord Ansaryon, for all the favour and honour which you have shown to me, and the help which you have given to me.'

His smile was sudden, and warmed her into a similar response. 'That's the first time you've addressed me as "Lord" – have I earned your respect at last?'

'I think you have,' she told him, feeling oddly embarrassed. 'I don't deny that once I thought otherwise – but now I truly believe that you are my friend.'

'I was never anything else, if you had but known it,' he said softly.

The servant returned then, bringing the midnight-blue over-gown that he had been wearing when they first met. Although he lacked Tsenit's solid, muscular build, she thought that Ansaryon, when he wanted, could make his lean height regally imposing. She hoped that Abreth would be suitably impressed: and she returned to her room, humming happily, to make herself ready to greet her beloved brother, with a sense of joyous freedom that she had not truly felt since entering the gates of Zithirian.

She had soon packed her belongings, and then she had a long, long time at the mercy of her thoughts. It was, after all, perfectly possible that Abreth was not with the rest of the Tanathi, that he had indeed been killed by the Ska'i: the messenger had spoken only of a group of tribesmen, which could indicate any number from two or three upwards. Outside, as the day wore tediously on, the rain dwindled to nothing, and the sun emerged hesitantly from behind thinning clouds. Bored and apprehensive, she went out to sit on a stone bench by the fountain, ignoring its damp surface, and watched the wet stones of the courtyard gently steaming in the warmth of the sunlight. In the rooms around her, the subdued bustle of Palace life continued, but Halthris occupied her own small bubble of isolation, and let her thoughts drift away to memories of the steppe, so different from this.

And yet, and yet, she knew already that she would be curiously sorry to leave Zithirian.

A soft footstep intruded on her daydream, and she looked up, and saw Abreth standing a few paces away in the shadows under the colonnade, staring at her.

Wild with sudden joy, she called his name, leapt up and ran into his embrace. For a long while they hugged each other wordlessly, delighting in the relief and comfort of reunion: then, Halthris drew away from him, hoping that he would not notice the tears in her eyes. She said scoldingly, 'Whatever took you so long? You must have been to Gulkesh and back!'

'Kettan, who else, blundered into a band of Ska'i,' he told her, trying not to sound too defensive. 'We had to run south for two days to give them the slip. But don't worry, we're all safe – even Kettan, unfortunately. Djekko and Iriyan have got a scratch or two, though nothing serious, and we lost a dozen horses when I cut them loose to delay the pursuit. I thought it was better the Ska'i had some of our stock, rather than kill us all.' Knowing already what the answer must be, he added, 'Where's Urdray?'

'He's dead,' Halthris said sadly, and told him what had happened. They embraced again for a while, in silent and mutual sorrow, before she went on. 'Well? Have you seen the King?'

'Yes, and a very unimpressive sight it was too,' Abreth told her grimly. 'The thought of that pathetic old fool providing Zithirian with effective leadership beggars belief.'

'I know – but did he *listen*?'

'Well, he *seemed* to – but he certainly implied that he was more ready to trust me because I was a man, and therefore not prone to "feminine fears and exaggerations",' Abreth said. 'And don't look at me like that, Hal – I'm only repeating him, word for word. He then told me that it was more likely that the Ska'i would attack the Tanathi and we should all go to Lake Raiyis as soon as possible, said that Zithirian was perfectly capable of defending itself against a few barbarians thank you very much, and goodbye.'

'And that was it?'

'That was it. Escorted out of the Throne Room, along so many passages I thought I was in a rock rabbit's warren, and here I am. And very glad to see you, Hal – I was beginning to think they were holding you prisoner.'

'Not so long ago, I thought the same.' She glanced round at the empty courtyard, and then said very quietly, 'I've been the Lord Ansaryon's guest, and treated very well, but when I asked to leave the Palace, even leave his apartments, I found I couldn't. He said it was for my own safety.'

'Well, you remember what they were all saying about him last year – no one in Zithirian likes or trusts him. One of those people who gave us supper in that tavern told me that Ansaryon is planning to seize the throne, when the King dies – which won't be very long, by the look of him.' He stared at his sister in bewilderment. 'Hal, what *is* going on here?'

'I don't know – I wish I did. I feel like a counter in a very complicated game of tek. All I know is that the whole of the Royal Family seem to be intriguing against each other – and that they're all so busy plotting that they haven't time to do the really important things – like saving Zithirian from the Ska'i.' Her voice grew rich with scorn. 'I've been used by one faction against another – Ansaryon's enemies don't believe me because I'm under his protection, his younger brother, the one everyone likes, swore he'd do his best to influence the King and then doesn't seem to have done anything at all – and what with one thing and another, sometimes I wish the Ska'i would come and knock some sense into their stupid heads!'

'Do you mean that?'

Ansaryon had entered the courtyard behind them, noiseless as usual. Abreth whirled round, his hand going to his dagger before he remembered that it had been courteously but firmly removed at the outer gate of the Palace. He stared at the Prince in angry disbelief. 'I didn't know you spoke our language.'

'It isn't so very different from ours,' Ansaryon pointed out. 'Indeed, in Tayo's time it *was* the same. A few different words and meanings, a more complicated and elaborate grammar, that's all that has changed here in nearly 300 years. Well, Halthris of the Tanathi? I take it that since you are now reunited with your brother, you wish to return with him to your companions?'

'You know I do,' Halthris said. She glanced at Abreth's hostile face: evidently, his experience of Ansaryon so far had only confirmed the alarming stories they had been told about him. She added, smiling, 'If you had not interrupted us, I would have had the chance to tell my brother that despite the fact that I know next to nothing about what you call the "politics" here, and like what I know even less, I have come to regard the Lord Ansaryon as my friend. And if he is my friend, he is yours as well – so unravel that horrible scowl, Abreth son of Charnak, and show the man some courtesy.'

'Courtesy?' Ansaryon said, and grinned. 'That advice from you, Halthris of the Tanathi, is akin to the Emperor of Toktel'yi advocating a life of simple austerity. Let me tell you, Abreth, that I have never met anyone ruder or more forthright than your sister. I had to keep her here for her own safety.'

'So you said,' Halthris reminded him quietly. 'But not for the reason you've just given, I think.'

Her eyes met his, with significance. After a while he smiled rather grimly, and shrugged. 'Believe me, you are both better off in ignorance. My advice to you both is to return now to your friends, sell your horses as quickly as you can, and then ride back to your people as if Ayak's wolves were at your heels. And leave us to ourselves, or to the Ska'i – sometimes, you know, I'm not sure which is which.'

'I am,' said Abreth grimly. 'You've never even seen a Ska'i warrior, have you? Well, we both have. They're ugly, squat, powerful little men – they ride shaggy ewe-necked ponies that can trot all day, and all night too, without getting tired – and they're dedicated from birth to Ayak the Devourer. And because they're all Ayak's, they think it's blasphemous to attack and kill each other, so they curry his favour by killing everyone else they come across, instead. The words for mercy, love, or peace don't exist in their language, but they have twenty-seven expressions meaning "death". And they collect heads, Lord Ansaryon – they dry them in the sun and hang them by the hair from their trophy lances, men's heads, and women's and children's too. The more heads a Ska'i warrior can gather the more likely Ayak is to grant him long life. They believe that the wolf won't want to devour them as long as they can give him lots of other lives in their place. How many heads does

Quenait have outside his tent? Hundreds, I'll bet. And he may not be able to get inside Zithirian – he's only a barbarian savage, after all – but he'll kill every living person outside the walls, if he can catch them. If you tell your father that, I don't think he'll still be so certain he's safe.'

'I have told him,' Ansaryon said. 'Several times. Unfortunately, I'm not the only one giving him advice – and there are many whom he favours more than me.'

Abreth stared at him. He said finally, in tones of angry resignation. 'Well, it's up to you now. We've done our best to warn you, to help you – if you won't take any notice, it's not our fault. Hal? Shall we go?'

'Yes,' she said. 'My pack's all ready – I'll go and get it.' She turned and went back to her room.

Ansaryon was looking at Abreth with something almost like amusement in his face. He said, 'Your sister told me that you were not as blunt as she is. For once in her life, she appears to have been wrong. But, refreshing as your honesty may be to one who has lived in this festering pot of intrigue and deception all his life, it is also dangerous. So are politics, in Zithirian. Do you have that word in your language?'

'Politics?' Abreth pronounced the unfamiliar syllables with care. 'No. What does it mean?'

'Affairs of state – the business of government – and also, all the plots and behind-the-door dealings and playing off of one person or faction against another. It's all to do, basically, with power. An alien concept, amongst the Tanathi?'

'No,' said Abreth, with a reluctant grin. 'Not at all, especially in the winter months.'

'That's when you choose your Chiefs, isn't it? Yes, Halthris has told me a lot about your customs. She also, in her own inimitable fashion, made it quite clear that she considers them far superior to those of Zithirian.'

'She's right,' Abreth said. His initial antipathy to this peculiar and somewhat alarming man was beginning, rather against his better judgement, to give way to a reluctant liking. He could still quite easily imagine him indulging in the hideous rites those young Zithiriani had described in eager whispers last year, over cups of sweetened wine in the tavern courtyard. But Halthris had come to no harm here, under his protection: indeed she had even referred to him as her friend. And Abreth, although two years older than his sister, had always tended to defer to what he considered to be her superior judgement. Hal seemed to act instinctively, without thinking, and yet she was rarely wrong, and never made a fool of herself. In contrast, he needed time to come to a decision, and usually worried about it afterwards. Both his sisters, Halthris the younger and Tarli the elder, had always teased him about his active conscience.

'She's right in my opinion too,' Ansaryon said, and glanced round as Halthris came out into the courtyard, her pack slung over her shoulder and her flame-coloured hair bright even in the shadows. 'Your horses are waiting for you in the Outward Court. And if I were you, I'd sell your herd tomorrow, for whatever price you can get, and return to Lake Raiyis. If the Ska'i go there, your people will need you – and if they do not, well, the defence of Zithirian is our own business. We are not worth the useless expenditure of Tanathi lives. You have risked a great deal to bring us your warning, and if we choose to ignore it, that is our tragedy, not yours. We do not expect you to die for us, as well.'

His voice was quiet, and desperately bleak. To Abreth's astonishment, Halthris seemed to be almost distressed. Then she gave herself a little mental shake – he could see it in the way her shoulders straightened, and her eyes narrowed – and smiled, the old, brave, resolute smile with which she always faced difficulties and danger. 'Next year, my Lord Ansaryon, I shall remind you of your wild imagination over a cup or two of Hailyan wine, at the Wild Goose Tavern.'

'I shall have to come in disguise,' Ansaryon said, smiling suddenly in return. 'Princes of Tayo's Divine Blood are not supposed to demean themselves by drinking in taverns – even one as respectable as the Wild Goose. But, yes – I shall hope very much to see you both there, Halthris and Abreth of the Tanathi.'

He held out his two hands, in the gesture of friendship common to all the known world, and Halthris took them after a brief hesitation. 'Goodbye, my Lord Ansaryon,' she said formally. 'May your journeys be light, may your days be bright, and the darkness of night never hide you from sight.'

It was the traditional Zithiriani farewell, spoken by those who did not expect to see their friends again for a very long time, if ever: words very similar were part of funeral ritual. Abreth noticed that the Prince did not offer the hands of friendship to him, although he smiled and wished them both a safe journey in return.

Then the blue-clad servants arrived almost instantly, to escort them back to their own people, their own world, loved, familiar and above all, despite its many uncertainties and dangers, secure, compared to the deep, dark and perilous waters of the Zithiriani Court.

It was almost dark when they finally arrived at the camp, and the air had turned much colder, with a sharp northerly tang to it. All along the winding corridors of the Palace, through the outer courtyards, and during their passage out of the city, Halthris had said very little, and her face was as unyielding and formidable as the slopes of Mount Annako. Abreth tried to distract her with tales of Kettan's appalling behaviour over the past few days. He had disobeyed orders, kept up an unceasing mutter of complaint about everything and everyone, and finally made such a nuisance of himself with Inri that Sherren, normally the mildest and most conventional of men, had been goaded past bearing and had punched Kettan in the eye at supper in front of everyone, a breach of good manners that had afterwards deeply shamed him, although everyone blamed Kettan.

But even this sorry story did not lighten her mood, and for the rest of the way they proceeded in silence. Abreth longed to ask what had happened to her in the Palace: not only was he desperate to satisfy his overwhelming curiosity, but he hated to feel that there was anything which his sister did not wish to share with him.

But even if she had wanted to confide in him, all chance of it was gone the moment they entered the camp, in its sheltered hollow down by the river. Even Kettan joined in the welcome, undeterred by her scathing reference to his truly splendid black eye. Not even the news of Urdray's death could shadow this reunion: laughing and smiling at last, Halthris was drawn into the bright crowd of faces around the fire in the centre of the ring of tents. There was hot roast meat (Inri, ever practical, had organized the purchase of a spring lamb from a farmer who had brought his flock to sell it at the Gathering Fair), jugs of wine and spiced gellin, the Zithiriani peasant drink made from fermented honey, very thick and warming, and fresh scented risen bread, a luxury that the Tanathi, who did not use ovens, never tasted except at Zithirian. The gathering was loud and convivial, and ended in song, led by Halthris, who had a strong, clear, tuneful voice, and a gift for improvised parody.

Abreth, watching her unhappily, was confused by the strength of his feelings. As children, they had been so close. He would have done anything for either of his sisters – even died for them. So why, oh why, did she shut him out at the very moment when, surely, she must need his brotherly support and friendship the most?

Something had happened during her days in the Palace, to

change her. Surely Hal, so energetic, forthright, honest, so positive in her judgement of right and wrong, would never claim true friendship with an effete Zithiriani Prince with a sinister reputation for sorcery and other, even more repellent practices? Had she fallen victim to some terrible spell?

He worried about it all evening, a state of mind not helped by the wine and the gellin, and at last, his head spinning and his throat dry and aching with too much smoke and song, stumbled into his fur-heaped bed in the tent he shared with Djekko, Iriyan and Sherren. Sometime during a long, dark and restless night, he afterwards remembered feeling cold, and pulling more furs and felt blankets up over his shivering body.

And in the morning he woke, still cold, puzzled by the blinding brilliance of the light flooding into the tent as Djekko opened the door-flap. He sat up, staring. Sherren was kneeling by the entrance: he made the warding sign, and said softly, 'Hegeden help us all!'

Outside, the ground was covered with a thick, deep, soft layer of snow.

CHAPTER
SIX

'It's impossible!' Once more it was Kettan, denying the obvious. 'There are *three more months* to midwinter!'

'Can't you believe the evidence of your own eyes again?' said Halthris. She bent, picked up a handful of snow and threw it at him in a gesture that might have been playful, but was not.

'Ow!' cried her cousin, wiping the mess from his arm. 'That hurt!'

'I doubt it,' Halthris said unsympathetically. 'It's definitely snow, wouldn't you agree? Real, genuine, cold, wet, snow – at least a month early, but snow all the same. Abreth? Shall we call a meeting?'

Chettay came wading back: it reached almost to the tops of her boots. 'The horses are all right, but pretty miserable. Like us, they weren't expecting it, and they've all still got their summer coats.' Her breath blew great puffs of smoke into the clear, frosty air, and she waved a hand at the grey clouds bunched menacingly over the Northern Mountains, far away across the river. 'And there's more to come, by the look of it.'

Sherren was gingerly touching the snow as if he had never seen it before. He raised a handful to his lips and tasted it. 'Looks like sorcery to me.'

'Looks like more snow, too – Chettay's right,' Abreth said irritably. He had a headache – surely due more to the terrible blazing intensity of the sunlight than to the few small cups of gellin he had drunk the night before – and it was difficult to think clearly. But this needed urgent discussion. Sorcery or not, the snow was only too real, and their plans would have to be altered.

A little later, the twelve remaining members of the Sayni clan's horse traders sat round the brazier in the hearth tent. Although smoky and stuffy, at least it was warm in here, and Djekko, who could always be relied upon to think of food, had laid a stack of flat griddle cakes on the bars above the brazier, to singe over the heat.

They were charred, but delicious. Abreth found the thick, chewy unleavened bread enormously satisfying, and a cup of melted snow, pure and clear and bitterly cold, washed it down very refreshingly. His headache had receded to a dull throb, almost possible to ignore, and he had had time to think. So, by the looks on their faces, had his companions.

'Whether Sherren's right or wrong, whether there is sorcery at work, I don't know,' Abreth said soberly, staring round at the others. 'But the fact remains that snow has fallen very early, and for the first time in my memory, at least, winter has come while we're still in Zithirian. We can either stay here and wait for a change in the weather—'

'Unlikely, to say the least – once the snows come, they usually stay until the spring,' Inri pointed out.

'I agree – unlikely. Or we can sell our horses cheaply, and go back to Lake Raiyis as soon as possible. If we follow the river valley, there are plenty of farms and settlements where we can shelter if there are blizzards. I know it's more direct to go straight across the steppe, but conditions up there would probably be much worse.' He glanced at his sister, but Halthris was gazing into her untouched cup, as if the water reflected something quite different from her intent, freckled face.

Feeling more than usually adrift, Abreth continued. 'And then there are the Ska'i. Where are they? Are they going to attack Zithirian, or the Tanathi? Is this unseasonable weather something to do with them?'

'Their shamans can do almost anything if they give Ayak enough blood,' Sherren said. 'It *must* be their doing – it *must*. It's too much of a coincidence.'

A muttering around the brazier indicated that several Tanathi agreed with him. Abreth held up his hand for silence. 'All right. Assume the snow *is* caused by sorcery, and not just an unlucky change in the weather. Assume that it's the work of the Ska'i shamans – although I must say I've never heard of them being able to affect the weather so drastically before. That indicates that they might attack Zithirian at any moment.'

'Why?' Kettan demanded. 'Why should they want winter to come before they attack? It doesn't make sense.'

'Because the rivers will freeze,' Halthris said. She raised her head, and looked round at the others. Abreth saw that her face was white under the liberal scattering of freckles, and there were deep shadows under her blue eyes, as if she had not slept. 'In a day or two, the Kefirinn will be frozen over. There's already a crust of ice several paces out from the bank. And when it's covered the river, Zithirian will be defenceless on two sides.'

'No, it won't – what about the cliffs under the Palace rock?'
Kettan objected.

'Easy to climb. And you can just walk up the steps at the ferry
crossings and enter the city through gates that are only guarded by
a few soldiers. There are no proper defensive walls anywhere along
the river, except by the Palace – only gardens going down to the
water.'

'Haven't you warned them about it?' asked Chettay.

'Yes, we have – but they won't take any notice,' Halthris told
her. 'Zithirian imagines that its size and splendour make it invulner-
able. Everyone seems to think that a pack of barbarians wouldn't
even dare to ride within a day's march, let alone attack them. The
Toktel'yans took the city, true, but that was many lifetimes ago,
and they broke in through the Sunset Gate, before it was enlarged
and strengthened. No one, ever, has attacked across the frozen
river, and so the Zithiriani believe that no one ever will. Yes, I
know it's ridiculous, but they've been living soft and pampered lives
for so long that they've forgotten what real warfare is like. They
think the Ska'i will ride down from the steppe, raid a few farms,
drive off the cattle and go away again. I've tried to tell them that
this time it's different – believe me, I've tried. And of course,
there's always the chance that they may be right – that the Ska'i
will attack the Tanathi, and leave Zithirian alone. But whatever is
going to happen to the city, I think we should go, and go quickly.'

People were nodding. Abreth said quietly, 'The King told me
to leave before it was too late. So did the Lord Ansaryon. Are you
sure that you're not just acting as their mouthpiece?'

Halthris jerked round to face him, her long amber-gold braids
swinging. She said angrily, 'No, I'm not. *You* think we should go
too – you've already said as much. But the fact remains that if the
Ska'i attack Zithirian, twelve Tanathi to help defend it won't make
any difference. But if the Ska'i are heading for Lake Raiyis, then
we'll be needed there urgently. We can't help Zithirian, but we can
help our own people. And that, surely, is where our hearts and our
duty lie.'

He had never heard Halthris, his practical and unsentimental
sister, talk like that before. She caught his eye and smiled.
'Wouldn't you agree, brother?'

'Who's leading this band, that's what I'd like to know,' muttered
Kettan darkly.

'Agreed,' Abreth said, ignoring him. 'I think that we should sell
the horses – always assuming there are any buyers for them in this
weather – and leave as soon as we can. Tomorrow for preference,

or the day after. Even travelling as fast as we can, it will take us ten or twelve days in this snow to reach the winter valleys. Are you all agreed?'

Two by two, the hands slapped on knees in assent. Halthris and Sherren were the first, Kettan once more, grudgingly, the last.

'And let's hope it is Zithirian that they attack,' Inri whispered to Halthris out of the side of her mouth. 'Or our journey back to Lake Raiyis might prove rather eventful, to say the least.'

To the surprise of everyone in the Tanathi camp, the early snow did not seem to have alarmed the people of Zithirian: indeed, rather the opposite. Stalls for the Gathering Fair had already been set up on the broad green field outside the walls of the city where it was traditionally held, and now hordes of citizens crowded round them, indulging in an orgy of spending. They bought luxuries and trinkets, oils for cooking and lighting, horse harnesses, cloth, potions, perfumes, exotic animals, meat on the hoof, gloriously embroidered garments – and horses.

By midday, all the best of the Tanathi stock had been sold, and many of the more indifferent ones, and the secret box built into one of the wagons was full of silver bars, gold Toktel'yan coins, jewellery, precious stones and other valuable items taken in payment. Normally, much of this wealth would have been used to purchase the bulkier goods which the tribe would need for the coming months of hardship: honey, grain, dried kuldi leaves, cloth, metal, dried fruits, barrels of wine and wooden casks of gellin. But as Inri pointed out, if they wanted to reach the winter valleys as quickly as possible, burdening themselves with two or three extra wagon-loads would slow them down and make travelling through the deep snow still more difficult. Such items were necessary, certainly, but their absence need not mean disaster. The Tanathi were a tough and hardy people, used to privation and discomfort. In these unprecedented circumstances, they could manage without for this winter.

By mid-afternoon, snow had begun to fall again, lightly and delicately: but the grim leaden sky in the north spoke of blizzards to come, and the air was even colder than before. The stall-holders in the fair were beginning to pile their remaining wares onto hand barrows or carts or donkeys, to be taken back to the safety and shelter of their farms, or their houses in the city. But there were still plenty of people thronging the alleys between the booths, driving last-minute bargains with eager, calculating eyes. Children shrieked and ran and fell and rolled and threw snowballs, a group of hardy archers competed with numbed fingers for a bag of silver, and over on a platform near the Sunset Gate, two wrestlers, naked save for shortened trousers and blue with cold, grappled shivering for a successful throw.

Halthris, sitting on Ennim at the edge of the crowds, the object of friendly smiles and more covert, assessing glances, could not rid herself of a most unpleasant feeling of impotent despair. Once, as a child, she had watched a family of appealing, sandy-coloured, large-eared rock rabbits playing on the hillside below her. And then she had seen a steppe fox slinking through the long grass above them. The baby rabbits, too young to be aware of the danger, had played on oblivious, until the fox sprang down amongst them, dealing instant death with every bite. Not one had survived.

Just so, it seemed to her now, the people of Zithirian, breathless and happy, their faces glowing with cold and exertion, passed her by in ignorance of their fate, carrying the goods they would never live to enjoy, to homes that would soon be wrecked and plundered by the Ska'i.

Unable to watch any more, she left the crowds and rode away towards the steppe. Ahead of her, the slopes above the valley of the Kefirinn were girded, half way up, by the low stone wall that separated cultivation from wilderness, and civilization from the barbarian hordes. Here she stopped, looking up at the humped, snow-covered grass, while Ennim blew clouds and stamped his feet impatiently. In Tanathi fashion, his hooves were now encased in leather boots, neatly tied below the fetlock, to prevent snow balling up inside his feet and laming him. He pawed at the ground and soon exposed a few tussocks of wet grass, which he began to eat with relish. Tanathi horses might appear slender and delicate, but in reality they were as tough as their riders. They had to be, to survive winter on the steppe.

Halthris stared up at the hillside, and emptied her mind slowly and deliberately. With equal care, she constructed a mental image of Fess, running through the snow with her peculiarly graceful, bounding stride. Her eyes closed, she concentrated on that vision, sending out her love and her call to the hunting-cat, wherever she might be.

She had already tried three times to summon Fess from down in the camp, and failed. Out here in the silence, however, it was easy to collect her thoughts. Around her, everything was hushed, waiting – for what? For the blizzards that had obliterated the view of the Northern Mountains, and would soon sweep across the lush, snow-covered valley behind her? Or for the Ska'i?

She opened her eyes. A shape, tiny against the vast domed horizon of the hill, appeared suddenly on the sharp white rim of her view. Holding her breath, Halthris watched intently, and then sighed in relief. The graceful exuberance was unmistakable. Fess had heard her at last, and was coming back to her.

In an astonishingly brief time, the spotted cat had descended the hill, bounding through the soft, thick snow and leaping over the waist-high wall as if it were a grass-tussock. Halthris dismounted and ran to greet her, and Fess sprang up to place her paws on her shoulders, knocking her flat on her back in the snow.

It was cold and wet, but Halthris did not mind. Fess's warm weight was on her chest, she was rubbing the ticklish spot under the cat's bristly chin, and listening to her purring, a loud and rhythmic rumbling of happiness.

'Sorry, Fess,' Halthris apologized silently in her mind. 'Sorry I was so long coming back – I couldn't help it. Have you been all right?'

The harsh fur under her hand still covered plenty of flesh, but a feeling of reproach crept into her mind. 'You said you would only be gone a few days. Instead, it was many. And now there's this snow come early. AND the horsemen.'

The image filled the spaces in her head with slow, horrible clarity. Three or four Ska'i, fur-clad and shapeless on their shaggy ponies. One called soundlessly, and raised his bow, and shot.

The picture broke up in sudden pain. Halthris sat up, her heart pounding, her hands feeling urgently along the cat's haunch. There it was: a long, raking gash that had scored fur and skin, but seemed to have done no worse damage. She forced her mind into logical thought. The Ska'i. Fess had encountered the Ska'i. She would not have strayed far from Zithirian: from past experience, not out of reach of mind call. And that could be heard no further than an hour's ride, or less.

Which meant that the Ska'i were now quite probably just over that ridge, lurking in the valley beyond, gathering their strength for an assault on the silver city, lying unsuspecting behind her, three Toktel'yan miles away . . .

Keep calm. Don't panic. She bent her head, closing her eyes against Fess's intent yellow gaze. Contact her again – find out more.

She asked the silent questions. 'When was this?'

'Yesterday,' said Fess, although her way of communicating the information was far more long-winded, involving images of dawn, night, sunset, and finally the deceptive warmth of afternoon sunshine in autumn.

'*Before the snow?*'

'*Of course before the snow.*'

'*How far?*'

Through the cat's eyes, she saw the boundary wall, the crest of the ridge behind it, and the long slope down beyond, another, shallower hill, and then . . .

Ska'i. The whole camp, thousands of them, horses, wagons, tents, teeming with squat slit-eyed Ska'i and a few of the taller, hawk-faced Rebresh, with horse-tail plumes in their dark hair. Not only did she watch with Fess's eyes, she had the use of her sense of smell too: the stink of dust, rotting meat, faeces, unwashed bodies, filled her quailing nostrils. Above the camp, kites hovered, eagerly seeking something to scavenge, and scrawny hunting-dogs fought over a reeking bone.

Gasping, Halthris opened her eyes. There was no dust, no camp, only the bleak pure clarity of the empty, snow-covered fields. Sensations of wet chill assailed her suddenly: shivering, she scrambled to her feet and called Ennim. The grey came ambling over, his pink nose dusted with melting snow crystals. She sprang onto his back, gathered up the reins and turned to call Fess.

The cat was standing quite still, staring up at the steppe. Her hackles were raised in a stiff crest all along her back, and her tail had bristled out to twice its normal diameter. As Halthris stared at her, she growled menacingly, low in her throat, and the tip of her tail began to twitch.

Ennim had also sensed something: he was gazing fixedly in the same direction, his ears pricked. Halthris shaded her eyes against the flat brilliance of the snow, blinking.

There was movement on the hard edge where white hill met lowering grey sky. And then a horseman appeared, and another, and another: her blurred, snow-blinded eyes refused to count them. She knew what they were, though. Small, furry ponies, surprisingly swift, carrying fur-wrapped riders who wielded stout, accurate bows and the deadly double-headed axes that could sever her neck in one sweep.

Halthris yelled to Fess, turned the horse, and kicked him unceremoniously into a gallop, back across the fields to Zithirian.

She glanced round once or twice, and each time there were more and more riders on the ridge, until they ceased to become individuals and merged into one long, vast, black line. None pursued her: their strength was so overwhelming that they probably thought they could afford to let her go.

A man was herding a flock of sheep from field to farmyard: she shouted at him as she swept by, saw his amazed face and heard his cries, and hoped that he had understood enough to take action and see his family safe.

The snow on the fair-ground was chopped, filthy and piled into huge grubby heaps, and the green grass revealed by the sweeping seemed shockingly vivid. There were still many people here, packing up stalls, even some buying and selling, although sunset could not be far off. They stared at her in astonishment, scattering in front of Ennim as he galloped for the Sunset Gate, screaming at Fess leaping beside her, their faces white with sudden fear, and she cried her warning until her voice grew hoarse and cracked. 'The Ska'i! The Ska'i are here! Run to the city!'

There were soldiers on guard at the Gate, and several of them, seeing the commotion, ran forward with their spears raised, to block her way. She halted Ennim, and he stood trembling, his dappled hide slick and dark with sweat, his hot breath blowing great holes in the snow beneath his lowered head.

'The Ska'i are coming!' Halthris shouted, as loudly as her shattered voice would allow her. 'Look – look up on the steppe.'

Beyond the tents and stalls, the road and the fields and the low roofs and trees of distant farmsteads, the hills rose in gentle curves. She had wondered if the Ska'i would still be there. Perhaps she and Fess had imagined them: perhaps this panic had been for nothing.

They were still there. The people clamouring round her stared, and their voices fell suddenly silent. The youngest soldier, who could not have been more than eighteen, turned very pale, and swallowed. The man beside him made the warding sign with sudden savagery: a woman in the crowd sobbed with fear, and someone, his voice low and vicious, was cursing all barbarians, all savages, with endless torment.

An officer appeared, with a red plume in his helmet. With relief, Halthris recognized him as the man who had escorted her to the Palace when she had first come to Zithirian. Everyone began to speak at once: he silenced them with a shout and turned to view the distant menace on the horizon.

Judging from the way the line had stretched out along the ridge, there were now thousands of them: a horde of terror beyond all imagining, a threat which Zithirian's King could not now possibly ignore. The officer's face was blank of all expression as he surveyed the extent of the Ska'i forces. The sinking sun had emerged fitfully

amid racing clouds, and as a shaft of light swept along the distant
hills, it sparkled again and again on weapons and armour. Even
from three miles away, there was no mistaking the doom which
awaited them all.

'Into the city, all of you – *now*!' The officer took decisive
charge, his voice sharp with urgency. 'No, don't go back for your
goods – go *now*! Tethan, Unya, round up all the stragglers and get
them inside the Gate.' He gestured at the other soldiers. 'You four,
get back to your posts, and let everyone in – *everyone*, do you
understand? Unless they're Ska'i, of course.'

'How – how can you tell?' asked the boy soldier, his teeth
chattering.

'Because they'll be wanting your head off your shoulders, you
fool,' said one of his comrades, not unkindly. 'Come on, lad – *run*!'

The officer glanced up at Halthris, and smiled grimly. 'So you
were right after all, Tanathi woman. Satisfied?'

'No,' Halthris said. 'I wish – I wish they'd believed me when I
first told them.' She found herself shivering, and it was not from
the cold. 'My people – there are only twelve of us – can we come in
too?'

The officer's eyes dropped to the knife at her belt, the bow-case
and arrows slung from Ennim's saddle. Halthris said quickly, 'Don't
worry – we will fight. For you, not against you. And my brother
knows a few words of the Ska'i language, which might be useful.'

'Of course you and your companions may enter,' the officer
said. 'And bring your horses as well – though I doubt there'll be
any room for wagons or tents.'

'If all the country people take refuge in the city, I don't suppose
there will.' Halthris glanced back at the faraway hills. The Ska'i had
not moved: perhaps they knew what terror their mere appearance
had inspired. Screaming people were running past towards the
Gate, clutching bundles, dragging bewildered children by the hand.
One abandoned toddler, so bundled up in his winter tunic and hat
and leggings that he could barely move, stood howling in the middle
of the tumult: then a woman rushed up, swept him into her arms
with a shrill scolding cry, and carried him into Zithirian.

'Thank you, Tanathi woman,' the officer said suddenly.
Startled, Halthris turned and met his blue gaze. 'My name is Invan,'
he added. 'Please, count me as a friend.'

'Of course,' she said. She had seen that look in a man's eyes
before, although here, now, in this perilous situation, such obvious
admiration seemed utterly out of place. But she leaned from the
saddle to give him the two hands of friendship. 'My name is

Halthris, of Sayni's clan – and this is my hunting-cat, Fess. She is quite safe with my friends, but she has one Ska'i to her credit already, and the mere sight of her seems to scare them out of their wits.'

'A pity you don't have more than one of her, then,' said Invan. 'I must go – Tayo be with you, Halthris of the Tanathi!'

At their camp, her companions were already aware that something was happening: the commotion around the Sunset Gate and in the fair-ground could plainly be heard. As Halthris rode up, Chettay was calling down from one of the willow trees by the river bank. 'It's the Ska'i all right – they're all along the ridge over there!'

'You're right,' Halthris said. She kicked her feet clear of the stirrups and dropped down to the ground. 'They're just sitting there taking a good look at us for the moment. If they could see that far, I'm sure they'd enjoy the effect they're having. Everyone's in a state of absolute terror.'

'Well, at least the Zithiriani will have to believe us now,' said Inri. 'Let's hope they've got the intelligence to make *some* preparations.'

'But what about us?' demanded Kettan. 'What do we do? We can't just sit here and wait for the Ska'i to cut all our heads off. I vote we strike camp now and ride up the river to Lake Raiyis.'

'We can't,' Abreth pointed out. 'The Ska'i would fall on us as soon as we moved, and we wouldn't stand a chance.'

'The only chance we have is to take refuge in Zithirian,' said Halthris. She looked round at them all, seeing varying degrees of shock, resignation, fear. 'We shall have to abandon the tents and the wagons – there isn't time to dismantle them. But we can bring in all our weapons, the horses, and the gold and silver. There's no point in leaving that behind as a free gift for the Ska'i. And for Hegeden's sake let's hurry – we may not have very long.'

In a surprisingly short time, the Tanathi were ready. Twelve people, nine men and three women, with their weapons, their bundles of personal possessions, and, shared between Abreth, Sherren, Vondrak and Djekko, the wealth their horses had earned them. Twenty-six riding horses, with their tack and trappings, and a further seventeen young animals, those which had not so far been sold, and which were mostly the bad-tempered, the strangely coloured, or those in some way defective of conformation. Halthris was tempted to suggest that these be turned loose to fend for themselves: unbroken and of mediocre quality, they would be of little use either to the Ska'i or to the Zithiriani. But then she thought of the winter to come, with perhaps four or five months of snow, and the possibility that the Ska'i would prefer to sit down around the city and starve it into submission, rather than attack at once. In which case, they might all be glad of some horse-flesh, before spring came.

Through all the bustle of packing and making ready, their eyes kept rising to the distant skyline. It was still rimmed with those tiny black dots, so small and far that they might have been taken for deer, or cattle, or wild horses, if the Tanathi had not known for certain what they were.

'I wish they'd *do* something,' Kettan grumbled resentfully as he piled his precious clothes and surplus jewellery into the middle of the leopardskin cloak of which was particularly proud, although it had been his father's kill and not his. 'Attack, or disappear – anything rather than just sitting there like a row of ravens waiting for the feast.'

'Don't wish too hard,' said Sandresh warningly. He was the only Tanathi placid and long-suffering enough to be willing to share Kettan's tent, but even his supply of patience had limits on occasions such as this. 'What you least want might be granted.'

By common consent, what they could not carry would be burned so that the Ska'i should not have it, and so Abreth and Iriyan went round to each tent and wagon before they left, placing glowing burnstones from the brazier inside. And as they turned towards Zithirian, a pall of dark smoke rose from the camp behind them, an ominous portent of what might come.

At last, some sense of urgency seemed to have penetrated the rulers of the city. As the twelve Tanathi rode up to the Sunset Gate, a score or more horsemen galloped out, all heavily armed. Some turned south, and vanished along the meandering road that followed the course of the Kefirinn and led eventually to the city-state of Minassa, then Tamat, on the borders of the Empire, and finally, a thousand miles away, the great city of Toktel'yi itself, heart of a land so warm that no water ever froze, and where snow was unknown. The rest rode away north, along the rich valley, with fields and orchards, farms and vineyards lining the banks of the river until the channel narrowed and the impassable mountains touched rocky feet into the ice-cold, turquoise waters of Lake Raiyis.

'Where are they going?' Djekko wondered aloud.

'Warning the countryside, I hope,' Halthris said. She wondered what the farmers could do to defend themselves, once the Ska'i had descended from the steppes. Those living nearest to Zithirian would be able to take refuge in the city, but people in outlying areas would not have the time. Perhaps they would have the sense to take their wives and children and animals and flee across the Kefirinn and into the foothills of the mountains. But in this bitter cold, where would they find shelter? The snow would kill them, if the Ska'i did not: and the frozen river would not protect them.

She had a sudden dreadful vision of people running, screaming, across an open expanse of ice: men, women and children, slipping, dodging, mad with terror, while the laughing Ska'i rode amongst them like hunters amidst a herd of deer, hacking them down one by one until the snow was scarlet with blood and none, not even the smallest and most defenceless child, remained alive to plead for the mercy that a Ska'i would not understand . . .

Feeling sick, she rode with Abreth up to the Gate. The soldiers on guard stood aside to let them pass, and an officer, not Invan, came up. 'Tanathi friends, I am instructed to direct you to your allotted quarters. His High Mightiness King Varathand—'

'Fourth of His Name,' Halthris muttered to her brother.

'Fourth of His Name, has most graciously decreed, in acknowledgement of the signal service which you have performed by giving warning of this attack, that you all be allowed space within the Royal Palace itself. Your mounts will be housed in the Royal Stables, and you will enjoy all the privileges and hospitality of the Royal Guard in the barracks.'

'And in return, he expects us to fight for him, I suppose,' said Kettan mutinously.

'Of course. What did you think we were going to do? Sit on our backsides and play tek all winter?' Abreth hissed back at him. 'Unless you want to go back to Lake Raiyis now, of course. I for one won't stand in your way.'

As he expected, this effectively silenced his cousin, although if looks could kill, both he and Halthris would have been shrivelled in the saddle, then and there. The little cavalcade of Tanathi, each with two led horses, passed beneath the great double towers of the Sunset Gate, collecting a small escort of three or four soldiers and the officer, and began their slow progress through the confused, noisy, crowded streets of Zithirian up to the Royal Palace on its outcrop of rock above the Kefirinn.

They were jostled by weeping women, men pulling on their armour as they ran towards the walls, other men brandishing makeshift weapons, lost wailing children, country people with all their possessions piled on backs or horses or handcarts, several of the small, fine-boned golden Zithirian cows, each with collar, lead and bell like hunting-dogs and all mooing and skittish with fright, a flock of sheep, and finally, in the tree-lined Ceremonial Way just beyond the Temple of Tayo, two massive six-ox wagons, locked wheel-hub to wheel-hub and blocking all further progress.

The trees, in their huge tubs, had been blasted by the cold, and beneath the bare, snow-frosted branches withered leaves lay in heaps, mixed with piles of filthy snow swept from the paved street. All the flowers were dead, hanging sad and blackened from the walls of house or tavern. Everywhere there was panic, confusion and despair.

'They're running about like headless chickens,' said Chettay, in some contempt, as the drivers of the entangled wagons came to blows in front of their bemused oxen. 'Isn't there anyone to lead them? They haven't got a chance against the Ska'i unless someone takes charge. What's the King doing, for Hegeden's sake?'

She was speaking Tanathi, swift and idiomatic, and in this chaos Abreth doubted that anyone in the crowds pushing frantically past them had the leisure to stop and listen, let alone understand. All the same, he glanced hastily round and then shook his head. 'Hal says he couldn't fight his way out of a grass basket, and from the little I've seen of him, she's right. Gods, what a mess!'

'Well, whatever Kettan may be thinking, it's hardly your fault,' said Chettay. She was a handsome girl, with curly light-brown hair in four braids, and a neat round face that was almost wistful in repose. Abreth, who had recently been thinking that it was time to choose a wife and live with her in his own tent instead of with his bachelor friends, grinned at her wearily. 'I'm glad you think so. Sometimes I'm not so sure.'

'But it isn't,' said Chettay earnestly. 'You did the right thing. If we hadn't met the Ska'i, we'd have come here anyway, completely unprepared.' She smiled, and reached over to touch his hand. 'Don't worry, Abreth. We're safer here than anywhere else, and I don't mind sleeping inside stone walls for a while.'

Even he could see that her reasoning was a little faulty, but her unconditional support and admiration were very welcome after Kettan's simmering resentment and Hal's abrasive, sisterly honesty.

A shout went up, and then a sudden brazen fanfare sounded. People stopped and turned, their faces suddenly alive with eager hope, and the cry began. 'Tsenit! Lord Tsenit! Long life to Lord Tsenit!'

The Tanathi, stuck behind the wagons, stared at the procession coming the other way, down from the Palace. The two brawling wagon-drivers, rolling in the snow and punching each other with dreary malice, struggled suddenly apart and stood, heads hanging in shame, beside their teams. The citizens pushed past and held their children up to see, and their cheers swelled in crescendo. 'Lord Tsenit! Save us, Lord Tsenit!'

The young man whom Halthris had last seen standing on top of his tower, gazing with baffled rage at his brother Ansaryon, was, in defiance of Zithiriani custom, sitting on a horse rather than being carried in a richly decorated chair. The animal was white, and obviously of Tanathi breeding: it looked magnificent, and so did Tsenit. His dark head was bare, but he was dressed in an armoured tunic of gleaming bronze. A long sword in a jewelled scabbard hung at his side, and he carried a steel helmet, lavishly adorned with white plumes, in his left hand. He sat quietly, smiling slightly as the roars of adulation and entreaty rose to a peak around him, and then raised his hand.

The noise drained swiftly away. Tsenit scanned the crowd, still smiling. He snapped his fingers, and soldiers ran forward. In a few moments, the wagons had been freed, and the two drivers were bowing their heads and crying their thanks and apologies.

'Enough!' The Prince's voice was not loud, but it was very clear, and carried all round the street and up to the gilded portals and towers of the Temple. 'This is a time of great peril for us all, but with the help of the Divine Ancestor Tayo, for whose assistance I have come here to pray, the people of Zithirian – the *great* people of Zithirian – can turn on these vicious and heathen savages, and drive them back to their own lands. If you fight as I know you can fight, not one in ten of the Ska'i will ever return to their homes. Will you fight them?'

The answer came roaring back ten thousand fold. 'Yes, yes, *yes!*'

'Will you drive the enemy from our country, and kill the barbarians?'

'Yes!'

'Will you obey your leaders, and the orders they give you, so that we may win a glorious victory?'

'Yes, oh yes!'

'Will you join together, all the people of Zithirian, to meet and defeat this menace, utterly and for ever?'

'Yes!'

'Knows how to inspire a crowd, doesn't he,' Abreth commented softly, watching the performance with admiration.

'Most of Zithirian thinks he should be the next king – and on this showing,' Halthris said, 'I'm inclined to agree with them.'

'Go now to your homes, all those of you who have no duties

assigned to you yet,' Tsenit went on. 'Your Quarter officials will come to each household in turn. All households will be required to take in refugees. All households must make a true and complete list of all their stocks of food, oil, burnstones, medicines and weapons. All able-bodied men between the ages of sixteen and sixty must prepare to serve in the defence of our glorious city. To make our task easier, and for your own protection, there will be a curfew imposed from midnight tonight. Save for a period of two hours around midday, all women and children must stay in their homes, lock and bar their doors, and shutter their windows. So must all those not on official duty. Only those defending the city can move freely during the curfew. When it begins, two blasts of the Sacred Horn will sound from the Temple, and one blast will announce its end. The Quarter officials will ensure that all this is understood in due course. Now, go to your homes or to your posts – and remember that the Divine Ancestor is our guardian. With his help and protection, Zithirian is great – Zithirian is mighty – Zithirian is powerful!'

A great roar of approval and acclaim burst from the crowds. A few doves, gently multi-coloured in pink and grey and white, who had been huddling disconsolately in the bare trees, flew upwards in alarm, their wings clapping. Ennim snorted, and several of the young unbroken horses reared and squealed in fright. By the time they had been calmed, Tsenit had ridden past, with a smiling acknowledgement in Halthris's direction, and on to the Temple.

Already, amazingly, the citizens were dispersing. The faces moving by were often tear-stained, but calm and determined, filled with new hope. Whatever Halthris's private thoughts about Tsenit – and they were almost as confused as her views on his brother Ansaryon – the King's youngest son was certainly a gifted and inspiring orator.

But it would take more than good leadership alone to transform these pampered, peaceful, luxury-loving people into a force capable of withstanding the ferocious hordes of Quenait's Ska'i. And as she and the rest of the Tanathi plodded up the steep Ceremonial Way to the Royal Palace, Halthris wondered if their decision to join the defence of Zithirian would bring all of them to their deaths.

CHAPTER
SEVEN

'But why are they just sitting there waiting? Why don't they *attack*?'

The Ska'i had come down from the ridge overnight, and the city had woken from a fitful and uneasy sleep to find the distant skyline no longer prickled with horsemen. For a few joyful heartbeats, the watchers on the towers and along the ramparts had believed that the menace had gone altogether. Then they saw movement amongst the trees, a mile or more away, and soon the word was passing up and down the lines of men. The enemy had advanced, and was encamped, in apparently overwhelming strength, within sight of the Sunset Gate.

And there they stayed, dark and hideous against the snow like some vast predatory monster, around a newly-abandoned farm-stead. Everyone could see them, and see too the horsemen, the wagons and spare mounts and pack animals, streaming down from the hills to join them. It was obvious, even to the most optimistic Zithiriani, that they numbered many thousands.

The only member of the Royal Family to appear that dreadful morning was Tsenit. Halthris, posted with the rest of the Tanathi on the walls just to the right of the Sunset Gate, noted that he seemed to be everywhere: rallying men on the ramparts, making inspirational speeches from the steps of the Temple, and organizing the defence. On his orders, scouts were sent out, to discover how many Ska'i threatened them, and whether there was any likelihood of imminent attack.

They all watched the men ride out, on fast Tanathi horses. The morning crept by, and none returned. At midday, one booming blast from Tayo's sacred horn announced the temporary lifting of the curfew. Women and children scurried into the streets to exchange news and rumours, draw water from the public fountains, or to take food to their menfolk on the ramparts. Still the Ska'i did not move, and amongst the watching defenders, nerves and tempers audibly began to fray.

'Why don't they *attack*?' cried Kettan, next to Halthris, and she nudged him sharply. 'Don't shout so loud. Everyone will think you want them to.'

'I do,' said her cousin sullenly. 'Anything's better than this.'

'Look!' Abreth, on her other side, was pointing over the ramparts. 'I can see something moving – someone's coming! Is it the scouts?'

All along the walls, men craned to see. Carefully, Halthris peered over the edge: bitter experience had taught her a healthy respect for Ska'i archery.

These were indeed horsemen, but not the returning scouts, for they were mounted on scrubby little ponies. Behind each warrior, something dragged in the snow. With an awful feeling of apprehension sprouting in her mind, Halthris shaded her eyes for a better look. Then, she bent and carefully nocked an arrow to her bow. Like all Tanathi Hunters, she was an excellent shot, supremely accurate to about a hundred paces, and with a good chance of hitting her taget up to about twice that distance.

The Ska'i, about a score of them, evidently thought little of Zithiriani archery skills. They rode out into the broad open space where the fair had been held only yesterday, the heaps of dirty snow all covered by the new pristine fall from last night's blizzard. Halthris glanced to either side, and saw all eleven of her companions similarly positioned, their arrows nocked and ready. A hundred paces more, and the Ska'i would be in range.

Fifty paces. Abreth said softly, 'Wait until they get really close. Shoot when you're ready, and keep shooting until they run.'

'Those are *bodies* they're dragging behind them,' Chettay said, with horror. 'Are they the scouts?'

A low wail from Zithiriani further along the ramparts indicated that others thought the same. The Ska'i yipped in insolent triumph, and wheeled their mounts so that they ran parallel to the walls, about a hundred paces away.

'*Now!*' Abreth cried, and with the speed and skill honed by constant practice since early childhood, the Tanathi loosed their arrows.

The yips changed abruptly to yells of pain or anger, or were cut off altogether. Suddenly, there were bodies on the ground, empty saddles, milling horses. Halthris nocked another arrow, aimed carefully for a Ska'i in a bronze-plated tunic, who appeared to be their leader, and shot. With vindictive satisfaction, she saw him clutch at his throat, the vulnerable gap between helmet and body armour, and topple sideways into the snow. At last, Urdray had been avenged.

There were only two warriors left upright, and they turned their mounts away from the city and that swift, lethal rain of arrows, and whipped them into a frenzied gallop back towards the safety of the Ska'i camp, followed by the derisive and victorious cheers of the defenders. Despite the grim fate of the unfortunate scouts, Zithirian had definitely won the initial encounter.

A party of the most daring soldiers ran out from the Gate to retrieve the corpses of their comrades, each lacking its head. Snow began to fill the air, in tiny drifting flakes, and it was bitterly cold: the ice along the Kefirinn had widened so that only a narrow channel was left free in the middle of the river. Halthris, like her companions, was wearing all her tunics, her fur-lined boots and gauntlets and her deerskin cloak, and still felt frozen. Beside her, Fess sneezed as a snowflake tickled her nose, and sidled along the walkway until she was snuggled inside Halthris's cloak. The shared warmth was very pleasant for both of them: Fess, like all cats, hated to be cold and wet.

The bodies of the scouts – not one had escaped – were brought back in to howls of rage and grief, but the dead Ska'i remained sprawled in the snow, a most welcome reminder of the defenders' first small victory. With a hundred of us, instead of just twelve, Halthris thought, we could keep the Ska'i at bay for a long time.

If only winter had not arrived so early, rendering Zithirian appallingly vulnerable. Otherwise, it was hard to understand why Quenait had brought all the warriors of his tribe so far north, to throw them at the high walls and sophisticated defences of a city. Houses, farms, villages and other small and defenceless settlements were their usual prey. Why should the Ska'i risk failure, and terrible loss, by besieging the mighty Zithirian?

It did not make sense, unless they knew that they were certain to succeed. The thought chilled her. Once more, she thought of Ansaryon. Was he planning to betray his family, his city, his people, to this pack of cruel and merciless savages?

She could not reconcile that possibility with the man who had sat at his desk and written down her descriptions about life amongst the Tanathi. Whatever the sinister skills he possessed, those days had taught her that he was also a man with a deep and genuine curiosity about her tribe: men, women, children, their weapons and their clothes, their customs and rituals and language, and the animals, plants and landscape of the lands in which they lived. He had talked to her with warmth and intelligence: he had wanted to *know*. And this hunger for knowledge must surely indicate a hidden delight in all the marvels and splendours of the world, from the peaks of Annako and Estray to the burrows of the grass-mouse or the clouds of blue-lace butterflies that drifted across the steppe in high summer.

And there was the evidence of his apartments. She knew, from what he had told her in the course of casual conversation, that the decorations and furnishings had been his choice. He had appointed artists and craftsmen, he had discussed with them what he wanted, and had supervised their work. And a man who loved such beautiful surroundings, who filled his courtyard with flowers, who had designed that wonderful fountain, could not, could *not* be plotting to destroy everything he had helped to create.

Men who had dedicated themselves to the worship of Ayak the Devourer did not celebrate life. And without any proof save her own intuition, she was certain that Ansaryon was not in league with the Ska'i.

An inconvenient voice inside her head reminded her that she had been wrong about Kettan. For six months she had thought that he was the gift of Sarraliss, until at last his behaviour had opened her eyes to the truth about him. But she had been only seventeen, and he was her first lover. We all make mistakes, Halthris told herself, with a wry smile. And I've been paying for that little error ever since.

She looked up, and straight into the silver-grey eyes of the Lord Ansaryon.

It took all her self-control not to reveal her shock: it was as if her thoughts had summoned him. He stood on the walkway, dressed today in blazing red, heavily embroidered with gold thread and precious stones, with a fur-trimmed gown over the top. His only concession to military necessity was a steel, blue-plumed helmet tucked in the crook of his arm, and a very ornate sword hanging from his belt.

'You startled me,' Halthris said. She could see all the Tanathi staring, and the men of Zithirian kneeling in obeisance. 'I wouldn't advise you to stand upright just here, my Lord,' she added, eyeing his clothes. 'That colour can be seen for miles, and there must be any number of Ska'i bowmen who'd be tempted to try their luck.'

'At this range? Unlikely, surely,' Ansaryon said, but he dropped down to a squatting position, so that his distinctive ash-blond head was below the level of the wall. 'Halthris of the Tanathi, I bring you a message from His High Mightiness – is that your cat?'

Fess had been hidden beneath her cloak, but the near approach to the stranger had brought all her protective instincts to life. She pushed her head out from the concealing deerskin, and growled warningly.

'Yes, this is indeed my hunting-cat Fess.'

'Is she likely to go for my throat, or is all that fearsome posturing just a pretence?'

'Not at all,' Halthris told him. 'If I snap my fingers, she'll attack. If you remember, she killed that Ska'i tribesman, the one who told us that Zithirian was in danger. He was terrified of her.'

'I'm not surprised.' Ansaryon knelt in the ice-crusted snow, his bare head frosted with new flakes. 'Are you going to attack me, Fess?'

Golden eyes stared into silver. For the space of several heartbeats there was no sound or movement from either of them. And then Fess made a curious noise, almost a whimper, in her throat, and crept forward to push her head under Ansaryon's outstretched hand.

Behind her, Abreth drew in his breath sharply with amazement. Halthris, who suspected how the Prince had done it, smiled thinly as the big spotted cat began to purr happily beneath Ansaryon's gently caressing fingers. 'You are honoured,' she said drily. 'Fess does not give her love to passing strangers.'

'I hope I am not just a passing stranger,' Ansaryon said. He stood up, and Fess, with one last eloquent look, moved back into the shelter of the cloak. 'As I was saying – His High Mightiness King Varathand of Zithirian, Fourth of His Name, has been informed of the splendid display you and your comrades have today given of Tanathi prowess in warfare, and in recognition of your services, commands you to leave your positions on the walls, and return to the Royal Palace to continue your duties there. His High Mightiness wishes to enjoy the additional security that their presence amongst his personal bodyguard will confer upon him.'

In other words, thought Halthris angrily, he's so scared that he's prepared to endanger the whole city in order to safeguard his own life. True, there were only twelve of them, but their skill with a bow must far exceed even the Zithiriani soldiers', and their shooting had already given the citizens an enormous boost to morale. If the Tanathi were called back to the Palace, it would cause considerable damage to the mood of cautious and determined optimism amongst the defenders.

She said carefully, trying to conceal her fury, 'I do not think that our talents would be useful within the confines of the Palace. We are not an aggressive people, so we have no practice of close-quarter fighting. Our skill is purely with the bow. And surely out here on the walls we can be most valuable to the defence of the city.'

'Perhaps,' Ansaryon said. 'But it is a great and almost unprecedented honour for strangers to the city to be invited to join the Royal Guard – and it will be taken as a very offensive insult, if you refuse the King's command. His rage and disappointment might even be so great that he would order that you and your companions be ejected from Zithirian, to take your chance with the Ska'i.'

'Did *you* suggest this to the King?' she hissed. Honour it might be, but she herself had no desire to waste her time and her skills defending the doddering old idiot whose incompetence and procrastination had put his city and his people in deadly danger.

'No, I did not,' Ansaryon said softly. 'I am afraid that the King commands you, Halthris of the Tanathi – and you cannot refuse.'

She glared at him, challenging him to invade her mind again. He merely smiled, and stood aside so that she and the others could pass him on the narrow walkway. 'Pray accompany me now, Abreth and Halthris and your companions.'

Although he had come up onto the ramparts alone, she saw soldiers at the foot of the next flight of steps. So they truly had no choice. She glanced round, seeing Abreth's angry, bewildered face, and Kettan's indignation, for once entirely appropriate, reflected in the expressions of the other nine.

'Very well, we will come,' she said at last, without any show of enthusiasm.

The men of Zithirian, with their puny bows and blunt spears and ancient swords, crouched on the walkway and watched the Tanathi go. Halthris heard the mutterings of fear and rage rise behind her, and felt sick. Despite their small numbers, they had already proved that they would be vital if the Ska'i attacked. And now the defenders must watch as they were ordered away to protect their despised King, abandoning the citizens, so it must seem, to their fate. The effect on their morale would be devastating.

She wondered where Tsenit was: perhaps she could appeal to him, and ask him to use his influence with his father. But she could hardly talk of this to Ansaryon, whose hatred of his younger brother seemed so unreasonably extreme.

And Tsenit, who had been very much in evidence earlier in the day, was now nowhere to be seen.

The curfew horn blared out again as they passed the Temple of Tayo, and the streets began to empty. It was a sensible precaution – in the event of a Ska'i attack, the women and children would be far safer locked inside their courtyard houses than milling about in the streets. But it still seemed harsh and unnatural. She pitied those who must wait in terror, starved of news, unable to defend themselves, and dreading the barbarian onslaught. At least, she and her companions were not helpless spectators. Whatever happened, whether they lived or died, they would have the chance to fight for their own lives, and for Zithirian.

The King was in the Throne Room, his ministers all around him. He had seemed ancient and decrepit before: now, in the face of possible disaster, the little royal dignity he still possessed had completely deserted him. Halthris stared with contemptuous pity at the pathetic, shrunken old man, weeping in terror, huddled in a corner of the huge silver throne.

And beside him, his face almost alight with purpose and determination, was his youngest son, Tsenit.

All at once, she knew who had told the King about the Tanathi success against the Ska'i. And she wondered rather bitterly why he had done it. Tsenit seemed to be a competent commander, and he must know the effect that the order to withdraw the Tanathi to the Palace would have on the other defenders. He must know, too, that their archery skills would be wasted in close-quarter fighting. So why? Was it to placate and encourage the King?

Certainly, Varathand seemed to gain some strength from their arrival. He sat upright, wiped his face with an exquisitely embroidered square of linen, and thanked them in a faint and quavering voice for obeying his orders so promptly. All around the great room, the Zithiriani aristocracy stood like statues, armoured in their rigid and preposterous court robes as if the only disaster that threatened them was the loss of that inhumanly formal control. There was no sign of the Heir, Cathallon – presumably drowning his fear in his apartments – but the Lady Zathti, Ansaryon's sister, stood trembling amidst a little crowd of women, her hands constantly plucking at the embroidery on her green satin gown.

Beside Halthris, Tanathi faces expressed unease, or disbelief, or, in Kettan's case, outright contempt for this deeply unimpressive court, all show and no substance.

Except for Tsenit. Except, perhaps, for Ansaryon. And she and Abreth, through a mixture of misplaced loyalty, courage, and the desire to help Zithirian, had plunged themselves and their friends into this nightmare. With the fearful clarity of hindsight, Halthris knew that when their captive Ska'i died, they should have taken their horses and their hopes of gold, and turned back to Lake Raiyis and the rest of their tribe. Then at least they would not have been

trapped here, forced to defend the indefensible, and possibly facing
a horrible death under a Ska'i axe.

Quenait's men would surely soon attack: they were not here to
admire the view. But the afternoon wore on towards dusk, and
nothing happened. No further movement from the Ska'i was
reported by the stream of messengers from the city walls. The snow
stopped again, and the sun came out, shining brilliantly through the
richly-coloured glass windows of the Throne Room. Those who
waited within could hear the steady dripping outside, as the snow
and ice began to melt. It seemed like an omen of hope.

But the cold returned at sunset, and invaded every part of the
Palace, despite the profusion of braziers pouring out heat. Outside
the sky, scarlet and crimson and purple over the western steppe,
was a breathtakingly beautiful reminder of the colour of blood. The
men guarding the walls, cold, stiff, sick of waiting, sick with terror
for themselves and their families, made the warding sign and
whispered prayers to the forbidden deities, Hegeden and Sarraliss,
whose place in the hearts of the people of Zithirian had never been
usurped by the alien and allegedly divine Tayo.

The moon rose, full and clear and cold, to cast its merciless
light upon the snow-covered city. It was almost as bright as
morning, and the defenders, trying to encourage themselves and
each other, whispered that the Ska'i would try nothing tonight, for
any movement would be instantly spotted from the walls.

Soon the word went round. By order of Tsenit, eight men in
every ten were to return to the barracks, or to their homes, for rest
and food. Those who remained would be relieved in due course.
The lucky ones bade their comrades good night and hurried off to
bed: the others huddled beneath their cloaks and tried not to fall
asleep. Apart from the necessity of keeping watch, such fierce cold
had a way of stealing the life from a man, if he did not stay awake.

In the Palace, the King, his family and his courtiers had retired
to their separate apartments. Some five hundred members of the
Royal Guard had been distributed round the Palace walls, and the
gate was locked, barred and guarded. The off-duty soldiers slept in
their barracks. The tension of waiting, the atmosphere of fear and
helplessness, seemed to have disappeared. Whatever the morning
might bring, tonight Zithirian was safe.

At midnight, the citizens still on duty on the ramparts were
prodded into wakefulness, and told to go home. Their place was
taken by soldiers of the Guard, looking reassuringly military.
Knowing that the defence of the city was in good hands, the men
stumbled through the empty streets, shivering and yawning, and

hammered on their doors, shouting for their wives or mothers, sisters or daughters to let them in.

They did not notice the clouds rushing silently up from the north, obliterating the distant silvery mountains, banishing the moonlight, and then emptying a deluge of swift whirling snowflakes onto the city below, and on all the lands and fields around it.

The shouting and screaming woke Halthris. She sat up with a jerk, heart pounding, wondering for a moment where she was. Above her, the stars marched in strange patterns, and the flickering yellow light was surely not the moon . . .

She was sitting on a wool-stuffed mattress in a small guard-chamber, just outside the entrance to the King's apartments. With the periodic obstinacy of the weak, he had insisted that six Tanathi protect his own quarters, and the rest be placed outside the Lady Zathti's rooms nearby. Abreth had volunteered for that task, and had taken Chettay, Kettan, Iriyan, Karbra and Sandresh with him.

'What is it?' Inri's voice was startlingly close. 'Is it an attack?'

'Must be.' Halthris scrambled to her feet. Beside her, Fess was crouching, every hackle bristling. She bent, pulled the dagger from under her pallet, and thrust it into the scabbard at her belt. All around her, the others were doing the same. Inri, Sherren, Djekko, Grinya and Vondrak: her friends, her comrades, who had lived together in Sanyi's clan all their lives. And who perhaps were doomed to die together, too.

'So, what do we do now?' asked Djekko. He was the only one of them who carried a sword, and the lamplight gleamed dully on its broad, polished blade. 'Is this the only way into the King's apartments?' He used the Tanathi word meaning 'a group of tents'.

'I don't know.' Halthris stood at the doorway, looking out into the corridor beyond. They had been given no orders, for despite the King's terror, no one had anticipated a night attack. And the screaming, the noise was so close that it must surely come from inside the Palace.

'The King! The King!' A man in blue livery came running down the corridor, carrying a lantern. His shadow swung wildly to and fro across wall and floor and ceiling, and he was panting for breath. 'Attack – treachery – save the King!'

Halthris stepped out into his path, knife in hand, blocking the entrance to the King's room. 'What's happened?'

It was the same pompous Chamberlain who had originally escorted her to Ansaryon. Consumed with terror, he stared at her, his breath coming in huge shuddering gasps. 'Are you – are you part of the plot?'

'What plot?' Inri demanded. 'Our duty is to guard the King. Tell us – have the Ska'i attacked?'

The Chamberlain obviously thought the two barbarian women were going to kill him: his mouth opened and closed in panic. Halthris pushed her knife into its scabbard, and nudged Inri. The other girl did the same.

'We're here to guard the King and keep him safe,' Halthris said, keeping her voice calm and reassuring. 'Please, tell us what has happened – then we can carry out our duty.'

'The Ska'i,' said the Chamberlain, and made the warding sign. 'The snow fell – falling still – blizzards – there's surely sorcery at work! Before we knew it, they were in the city – and now they've got inside the Palace, I don't know how – it must be treason, it must be! How could they get in? The gates were barred!'

Halthris felt cold with fear. She had been right, her instincts had been right – someone had betrayed Zithirian to the Ska'i. But who? And why?

It must be Ansaryon. He was a sorcerer, and he was said to covet the throne. And although her own experience of him had spoken otherwise, the stories and rumours about him certainly indicated that he was a man ruthless enough to enlist the terrible Ska'i as his allies, in order to wipe out the rest of his family and make him King.

With grief and rage burning her heart, she vowed silently to Hegeden, dispenser of justice, that if she had the chance, she would kill Ansaryon.

The shouting was getting nearer. Suddenly, horribly loud and clear, she heard the high-pitched yipping war-cry of the Ska'i. The Chamberlain's face crumpled with terror, and he thrust his way between the two women and flung himself at the door to the King's apartments, pummelling it with his fists and sobbing incoherently.

Frantically, Halthris tried to think. If the Ska'i were coming, if treachery were involved, then it was no use trying to fight. The only way to protect the King was to take him away from Zithirian, now, before he could be caught and killed. And if it *was* treachery, the rest of the Royal Family were also in mortal danger – except for one.

She tried to visualize the layout of the Palace, glimpsed so briefly from the top of Tsenit's tower. If they could get the King into that garden around the edge of the rocky outcrop, through the wall somehow – there must be a gate – and over the frozen Kefirinn . . .

She turned, swiftly decisive. 'Inri – go and find Abreth. Tell him what's happening, if he hasn't already guessed. Tell him we've got to get the King and the rest of his family away, and all the courtiers, or they'll be killed. Tell him to find Tsenit – persuade one of the servants to help. We must get everyone out of here and into the Palace gardens and over the river, as soon as we can.'

Inri nodded, and ran off down the corridor, towards the heart of the Palace. Halthris turned, pulled the wailing Chamberlain aside, and thrust her shoulder at the door.

It had obviously been barred from the inside, presumably by the King's panic-stricken attendants, and only gave way when Sherren and Vondrak, the heaviest of her male companions, came to help. The passage beyond was filled with servants brandishing makeshift weapons – cooking pots, pieces of broken furniture, tongs from a brazier. They fell back screaming before Djekko's sword. Halthris shouted at them that the Tanathi were friendly, but they were too terrified to listen, and fled.

She ran up the corridor behind them, opening doors, looking for the King. Then she remembered that each suite of apartments had its own tower. Surely, Varathand would be there.

He was. He lay crumpled on the floor between two chairs, his hands over his face. In front of him stood a short, sturdy, middle-aged man who bore a considerable resemblance to Tsenit, though his dark curly hair was sprinkled with grey. He held a sword in one hand and a spear in the other, and raised them both menacingly. 'Come any nearer, Tanathi traitors, and I'll kill you!'

'We're your friends!' Halthris cried, halting in the doorway. She had seen him at her first audience in the Throne Room: he was the King's much younger brother, Lord Tayma, and evidently a man to be reckoned with. 'The Ska'i are in the Palace – if we can reach the gardens, we've a chance of escaping across the river – please, Lord Tayma, help us get the King away, or he'll be killed!'

Varathand's brother stared at her suspiciously. He said, 'Where are the servants?'

'Gone – I think they've gone into the courtyard. They're too frightened even to listen to me, let alone help.' Halthris glanced at the quivering, pathetic figure on the floor. 'He asked us to guard him, my Lord – please let us do our duty – we must save him, and you, if we can.'

Lord Tayma turned suddenly and knelt down by the King. He

gathered the sobbing old man into his arms, and struggled upright. 'If he's worth saving,' he said, and his mouth twisted with grief and anger. 'I'll carry him, Tanathi woman. Follow me. There's a door to the garden behind that screen.'

'Horses,' Grinya said behind her. 'We'll need horses, or we won't get far. Is it possible to bring them down to the river?'

'Yes,' Tayma said. 'Go along the outer wall, as far as you can, next to the servants' quarters by Tsenit's tower – there's a gate in the wall, and a ramp down to the river. It'll be locked, though – hasn't been opened in years.'

'We'll get through it somehow,' Halthris said.

Hard on her words came the yip of Ska'i warriors, appallingly loud, and the screaming soared suddenly to new and terrible heights. Djekko ran past Tayma, pushed over the light painted screen, and flung open the door behind it.

Icy air blasted in, mixed with flurries of flying snow. No one had realized the change in the weather. Too late, Halthris thought of her deerskin cloak, left behind in the guardroom.

At her side, Fess sniffed and then trotted forward. She paused on the threshold, her golden eyes looking back at Halthris, and then bounded out into the night.

Running feet behind them, and more yipping. Tayma said urgently, 'Get the horses – the barracks are on your left as you go into the garden – there's a door in the wall, and the stables are just beyond them. I'll carry the King down to the gate and wait for you.'

He gave them a swift smile, and followed Fess. Halthris said quickly to the four Tanathi still with her, 'Go and get as many horses as you can. Ours, or not, it doesn't matter – just hurry! I'll try and find Abreth and tell him about the gate.'

When they had run out into the snow, she set the screen back upright in front of the door. With luck, the Ska'i might not notice what lay behind it: she hoped that they would be too filled with battle frenzy to look too carefully. From the dreadful sounds now coming from the King's courtyard, Quenait's warriors were bent on butchering anyone they could find.

She shut the door behind her, cutting off that terrible noise. In front of her lay the darkness of the blizzard, but even as she stared into the snow, trying to make sense of where she was, the flakes began to diminish, and it seemed a little lighter. She glanced up and saw, faint and ragged through racing clouds, the silver disc of the moon, sacred to Sarraliss and also to Tayo, aloof above the towers of Zithirian, oblivious to the hideous slaughter taking place in the corridors and courtyards and chambers of the Palace.

To her left, the wall of the barracks, and then one of the squat outer towers, black against the lesser gloom of the sky. To her right, the humps and bumps, the snow-disguised ornaments and frozen ponds and dangerously shrouded obstacles of a typically elaborate Zithiriani garden.

Cursing all gardeners under her breath, Halthris ran in search of her brother.

EIGHT

The Ska'i attack had had an extraordinary effect upon the Lady Zathti. Everyone knew that the poor creature was weak-minded and terrified of her own shadow, and so Abreth had expected to find her fainting with fear. Instead, she was as still and pale and immobile as a statue, save only for the words issuing from her bloodless lips. 'If the barbarians have taken Zithirian, then I will not leave my father or my brothers!'

'But my lady, my lady—' The protests of the half-dozen women clamouring round her rose to a frenzy. In their still centre, Zathti shook her head. Robed in a plain linen shift, her silver-gilt hair pouring loose down her back, she was breathtakingly beautiful. 'No. I will *not* go. Save yourselves.'

'They're right, Lady,' Abreth said urgently. 'My comrades will save your father – we can save you all if you'll only come with us now – *please*—'

'No!' Zathti screamed suddenly. Her face was distorted, her pale blue eyes glistening with fervour. She's mad, Abreth realized with horror. She's mad, she *wants* to die.

The sounds of terror and slaughter were getting closer. Kettan pushed his way through the cluster of women, ignoring Abreth's shout. He grabbed the Princess of Zithirian by the shoulders, and shook her violently. '*You* may want your head lopped off, you stupid bitch, but we don't. Now come *on*!'

Quick as a snake, Zathti whipped something from the sleeve of her robe and struck. Kettan cried out and staggered back, his beauty entirely spoilt by a vicious gash slicing across his face and pouring blood.

'I said – *leave me*!' Zathti hissed, and the long slender knife in her hand glittered evilly. 'Go, all of you – *go*!'

And there was suddenly the sound of many running feet, high exultant yipping, and the vanguard of the Ska'i poured down the corridor and burst into Zathti's tower chamber.

Chettay flung her spear. The first man through the door stopped dead with a gasp, his hands clutching at the shaft protruding from his chest. The object which he had been carrying fell to the floor with a soggy thud, and rolled in a track of blood almost to the middle of the floor. As the Ska'i warrior toppled backward, one of the ladies cried, 'His head! It's Lord Cathallon's head!'

Halthris, flinging open the door from the garden as the women screamed, recognized with horror the coarsened, drink-blurred features of the Heir. Then she saw his sister Zathti push past Abreth and Kettan, the knife high in her hand. With a look of insane joy on her face, she ran straight at the Ska'i.

Halthris did not wait to see the inevitable. She ran to the nearest woman, grabbed her by the arm, and thrust her through the door into the garden. The others, screaming, followed her into the cold and the snow. At least they might have a chance of escaping the Ska'i, even if they risked freezing to death in their flimsy robes. She turned to yell at her brother, and saw Sandresh go down with a thrown knife in his neck. Zathti was dead too, hacked down in a great pool of blood. Kettan stood staring stupidly at Abreth, Karbra and Inri, who were slashing at the Ska'i with their spears.

'Get back!' Halthris cried, knowing that they had no chance. Iriyan ran forward to join them, Sandresh's sword in his hand. She shouted again, grabbed Chettay, pushed her outside. Then Kettan, still bewildered and mopping his gashed cheek. 'Get out – save yourselves – we've no chance otherwise – *please* – ,' she shouted, almost sobbing, certain Abreth would be killed. '*Go!*'

As she spoke, both Karbra and Iriyan fell beneath a forest of slashing axes. More Ska'i ran up the corridor, yipping, eager to kill. The two other Tanathi turned and ran towards the garden door. A warrior flung something, and Inri stumbled forward, a thrown axe jutting from her back. Behind her, Abreth pulled it out: she gasped, and he gripped her under the arms and dragged her outside.

Halthris retrieved two spears from the floor and stood guard in the doorway, staring in horror at the Ska'i, mortal enemies of all other humans. Her friends lay a few paces away, dead or dying: a tribesman bent, and hacked, and with a shriek of glee sprang upright with Karbra's head, still pouring blood, hanging by its braids from his fingers. With savage accuracy, she flung one of the spears at the man and saw him fall, Karbra's head dropping from his lifeless fingers. Then she hurled the other weapon into the pack of howling fiends, shut the door on them, and ran for her life.

The snow had stopped, and the moon was almost clear of clouds. It meant that they could see, but also be seen. Ahead of her, two figures hurried, supporting a third between them, with another alongside. She shouted her brother's name, and saw him turn. 'There's a gate in the outer wall – at the far end of the garden

– the King's brother told us about it – Djekko and the others have gone for the horses.'

'The others?' said Chettay. Her round face was streaked with tears, shining in the moonlight. She had always been the most gentle, the most sensitive and soft-hearted of their group. 'Then they aren't dead?'

'Not as far as I know – not yet, anyway.' Halthris glanced behind her. 'Here come the Ska'i – *run!*'

The tower door was open, yipping warriors plunging through it into the garden. Abreth and Kettan, carrying Inri awkwardly between them, lumbered into a trot. Halthris glanced back, and saw men and horses burst from a gate in the wall of the barracks, some fifty paces behind them.

'It's them!' Chettay cried, her voice shaking with relief. 'I can see Sherren, and Grinya—'

Horses, a score or more, some mounted, some riderless, and soldiers too, the plumes and shining steel helmets of the Zithiriani Royal Guard unmistakable in the bitter clarity of the moonlight. With a yell, they fell on the Ska'i, while the animals, ridden or guided by the four Tanathi, plunged towards Halthris over the lumpy snow. It was a scene of apparently wild confusion, but Sherren, their best handler of horses, was yelling directions and whistling the herding signals that all Tanathi mounts learned as foals. Halthris ran forward and grabbed the animal passing nearest to her. It was Sandresh's black, a good reliable sort, not too tall and with a smooth steady action. He wouldn't be needing it now, but Inri would.

Behind them, the fighting was rising to a peak of ferocity. Abreth and Kettan pushed Inri into the black's saddle. In the moonlight, the patch of blood on her back was as dark as the horse's hide, but she sat upright, gathered the reins, and urged her mount towards the gate. The rest of the Tanathi followed her, dodging through the snow-covered garden.

Halthris, ducking under ornamental trees of peculiar shape, limping from a heavy fall on an ice-covered pond, her left hand shredded in an unfortunate encounter with a thorn bush, knew that the courage of the soldiers had given them the precious few moments necessary for escape. If they could open the gate before the Ska'i overwhelmed the Guards, they stood an excellent chance, for the tribesmen would be too intent on the easy slaughter, plunder and collection of heads to waste valuable time and effort chasing a few well-armed fugitives. If they could get across the Kefirinn, they could take the King . . .

Where? She had no idea. Lord Tayma seemed a capable man, he would surely know of some safe refuge and guide them there. She agreed with him, Varathand hardly seemed worth saving, but he had ordered the Tanathi to protect him, and so they must do their utmost to obey. It was unthinkable to abandon him to the awful fate that had already befallen his eldest son and his daughter.

The garden narrowed at its far end, finishing where the outer wall joined a wing of the Palace. She had never been here before, but she had looked down briefly from Tsenit's tower, which stood where the wing met the central building. It was that tower which cast the long shadow plunging the furthest corner of the garden into darkness. There were people there, she saw as she ran up: the black, with Inri drooping over its neck; several other horses, Djekko clinging to their reins as they snorted and shuffled nervously; and, with his shoulder to the door leading to safety, the short, sturdy figure of Lord Tayma.

'It's locked,' the King's brother gasped, as she and Abreth arrived, with Kettan and Chettay just behind. 'I can't budge it!' He hurled himself again at the wood, grunting with effort.

'An axe,' Halthris said. 'Anyone here got an axe?'

'I have.' Her brother pushed forward with the weapon in his hand. With a shiver of revulsion, she recognized it as the axe which he had pulled from Inri's back: one of the wickedly sharp curved edges was still smeared with her blood. But this was no time to be squeamish, and the screams and yells behind them, followed by a shrill yip of triumph, told them that they did not have long.

Abreth swung the axe at the door. Chettay, kneeling in the snow beside Inri's horse, was stringing her bow, which she still carried. Halthris had left hers behind in the Palace, but she saw that both Sherren and Vondrak, sitting their restless horses, had arrows nocked at the ready.

'Here they come,' said Grinya. He was standing on his mount, keeping balance with effortless skill: Tanathi learned such tricks in early childhood. 'A few Zithiriani soldiers left, running this way – and all the Ska'i after them like a wolf-pack. Give me your bow, Chettay – quick!'

She passed it up to him. Abreth's blows with the axe were getting wilder, and seemed useless. Halthris realized that they were going to die here, trapped like rats in the corner of the garden, and the King and Lord Tayma too.

Where was the King? She looked round and saw him huddled on the back of one of the horses, whimpering with terror. Grinya aimed, and shot, and a shriek went up from the running Ska'i. Oh, hurry, Abreth, hurry, Hegeden lend you strength and Sarraliss guide your strokes—

Chettay had Vondrak's sword, and stood between the horses, ready to face the enemy. Beside her, Lord Tayma had also drawn his sword, his face grim. Halthris joined them, feeling singularly vulnerable with only her knife in her hand. If they could hold off the Ska'i for just a little longer, some of them might have a chance of escape.

Kettan pushed in next to her, grasping a spear. At this moment, petty quarrels seemed irrelevant. She grinned at him, and saw his look of surprise. Then he said, 'That soldier – it's the Prince!'

For a heartbeat, she thought he meant Tsenit. Then she saw the unearthly light shining on pale hair, the familiar slender build, the elaborate sword in his hand, and recognized Ansaryon. Behind him and beside him ran perhaps a dozen soldiers of the Royal Guard, several obviously wounded. And hot in pursuit, yelling in triumph, about a score of Ska'i.

The sweat was pouring off Abreth, despite the bitter cold, and his breath steamed in the air like a dragon's. He glanced round, took in the desperate danger facing them all, and swung the axe again at the stout wooden planks. The blades were blunted now, but there was a hole on three sides of the iron-bound lock, and only a few more blows should free it. If, *if* Hegeden granted him the time. With the strength of utter despair, he put all his weight behind the next stroke.

And the door shuddered beneath the force of it. Abreth saw, with sudden wild hope, that the lock was now only hanging by a few splinters. He wrenched it away from the ragged wood and cried, 'It's open! Hurry – *hurry*!'

Halthris saw Ansaryon running, leaping over snowdrifts, and wished she had a bow, like Grinya and Vondrak and Sherren, so that she would be able to kill him. Behind him and the soldiers and the Ska'i, flames leapt suddenly from the lower windows of the Palace, and she heard screaming even above the screeches of the pursuing tribesmen.

And then the Prince and his soldiers had reached them, and were turning, weapons raised, to face Quenait's savages. The Ska'i halted, some ten paces away, and she saw them brandishing their spears and axes, and an archer take aim and shoot. Behind her, a thud and a gasp: she turned, fearing Abreth had been hit, and saw King Varathand bent backwards, his hands plucking frantically at the air, an arrow in his chest. Then, he toppled like an old sack of grain to the ground.

So their obligation was ended. Sick with fear, sick of fighting, she faced the advancing Ska'i once more. Another arrow, another and another – several swished harmlessly past, but Lord Tayma gave a sudden cry and fell, and two of the soldiers were down. In reply, the three Tanathi bowmen were shooting steadily and accurately, apparently unscathed, and there were several Ska'i lying in the snow.

'The door's open!' Abreth screamed, above the noise of battle and the rising roar of the flames. He gestured wildly at the gateway to freedom, to safety, but no one seemed to have noticed. With a sob of despair, he ran forward and grabbed the reins of one of the frightened riderless horses blocking his way. 'Hal! Chettay! Mount up and *go*!'

Chettay heard him, and gave him a frantic look of hope mixed with despair. More arrows, and suddenly Vondrak was gone, his bow dropping into the snow beside his body. Abreth pushed the reins into Chettay's hands and shouted again to his sister. 'Hal! HAL! Take a horse – *run*, while we've still got the chance!'

A dark, mottled shape slid out of the shadows behind them and rushed forward, snarling. 'Fess!' Halthris cried sharply, and the cat crouched down a few paces in front of her, tail lashing, hackles up, teeth bared. The Ska'i fell eerily silent: they stared at the cat in horror, and slowly lowered their weapons.

Mercifully, Sherren had understood, and he and Grinya were guiding their horses round and edging back to the doorway. Did the Ska'i know that they could escape? From the looks of glee on their faces, before Fess's appearance, they had thought their quarry trapped and ripe for slaughter.

Halthris looked round. Inri gone, Chettay, several horses. The few defenders left standing – Kettan, Ansaryon, four soldiers – stepped back into the shadow of the tower, glancing behind them, while Fess kept the terrified Ska'i at bay. She waited the longest, standing straight and proud and foolishly alone, while the others melted back towards safety. Then she heard her brother shout, yelled to the cat, and ran.

A horse reared in front of her. She grabbed its reins and hauled herself into the saddle. Fess snarled and sprang, and a Ska'i went down under her raking claws, screaming. As the sound ended in a gurgling moan, she saw Ansaryon struggling to his feet, slashing wildly at another tribesman with his sword. A riderless horse, Vondrak's, jumped sideways away from the clashing weapons, and cannoned into hers. She leaned over, clutching at its bridle, and managed to get a hold as the frantic animal stumbled. 'Ansaryon – Lord Ansaryon! Here!'

He heard her. She saw his pale face, his hand outstretched, and then a Ska'i lunged at him with an axe. One of the Royal Guard thrust his sword into the man's back, and then Ansaryon was scrambling onto the horse in an undignified flurry of limbs and clothing.

'Through the gate!' Halthris yelled at him, and urged her mount at the dim opening, with no idea of what lay beyond it. She ducked her head as the horse plunged through and onto a steep ramp, cut out of the rock. Just as Tayma had described, it led directly down to the frozen river.

She saw a string of horses, some riderless, clattering ahead of her. The moon shone brightly over the wall, and she could see quite clearly the broad white expanse of the Kefirinn, the further rocky bank, and freedom.

It did not seem possible, even now, that they might escape. Her horse's hooves slithered in the thick snow: two of those in front of her had already fallen. She glanced back. Ansaryon followed her on Vondrak's chestnut, riding as if he had never sat on a saddle in his life, and behind him came Kettan, more loose horses, and three or four soldiers, running for their lives. Fess was loping just beside Ansaryon, her hackles still bristling and her ears flat.

The leading rider had paused at the foot of the ramp, where it ran under the snow-covered ice. He leaned forward to give his mount an encouraging pat, and Halthris knew that it was Abreth. Then, he urged the animal forward, onto the river.

It did not give way. She saw his white face, his waving hand, and heard his shout. 'It's all right – come on!'

Next came Inri, recognizable from her awkward posture as she huddled over the horse's withers. Sherren, Grinya, Djekko, Chettay, all persuading their mounts onto the frozen Kefirinn. Was it thick enough to hold them? Would that smooth, innocent, pristine whiteness break above the ice-cold, deadly waters in the middle of the river, where the current would be stronger and the ice at its thinnest? She did not know, but crossing it gave them their only hope of escape.

As she reached the foot of the ramp, she heard the yipping Ska'i warcry again, and looked back. They were pouring out of the gate, far more of them now than the score or so who had faced them in the garden. One of the Royal Guard turned, sword in hand: they cut him down and streamed, screeching, over his body. Several knelt to shoot. Halthris jabbed her heels into her mount's flanks, and slapped his rump with a yell. The horse sprang out onto the ice. She glanced back again. Ansaryon was still following, then

Kettan, and two or three soldiers who had managed to clamber onto riderless horses. I was going to kill him, she remembered, urging the chestnut across the frozen river. But she had realized, as he fought beside her in the garden, that he could not be the traitor, not if the Ska'i were trying to murder him. It didn't make sense.

Ahead of her, Abreth's mount was scrambling up the further bank. The ice had held. Still doubtful, she steered her horse exactly along the tracks left by the others. An arrow slashed through the air beside her, and fell into the snow. A riderless horse veered away from them, shrieking, and crashed through the ice not fifty paces away. As it disappeared into the water, she heard the frozen crust hiding the Kefirinn creak and sigh. Her bay gelding stumbled, and for a dreadful instant she thought that they would go through the ice too, but the animal struggled on, ears back, slipping with every other stride on the treacherous surface.

The bank loomed up in front of her and above it Abreth's face, mouth wide, yelling encouragement. Fess sprang up in two easy bounds. Her horse leapt off the ice, scrabbled and heaved itself up and over. She brought it to a shuddering halt, and turned in the saddle. Here was Ansaryon, kicking his mount up from the river, and the soldiers behind him. And beyond, out of effective range now, the Ska'i yelled and flourished their weapons on the other bank. Above them, sharp in the moonlight, she could see the thin diagonal line of the ramp, vanishing into the rocky shadows beneath the outer wall of the Palace.

And behind it rose the towers, lit by an eerie mixture of steady, relentless moonshine and the red, evil, flickering glare of many fires. Clouds of black and scarlet smoke boiled up into the icy air, and hung in a pall above the city.

She turned abruptly away from the sight, afraid and ashamed of the grief wrenching at her heart. She was Tanathi: what was the fate of Zithirian to such as her? And despite the terrible deaths of her friends, she was alive, and unhurt: so was her beloved brother, and Kettan, Djekko, Sherren, Grinya and Chettay. And Inri might survive, though it did not seem likely. Eight Tanathi out of twelve; Fess; three of the Royal Guard; and the Lord Ansaryon, last of all his family, and the fleeing King of a fallen city and a slaughtered people.

'What shall we do? Where shall we go?' Chettay cried, suppressing a sob without much success.

Ansaryon rode forward. In the pure black and white clarity of the moon's rays, he looked like a creature from another world, his fine-boned features reduced to flat planes of light and shadow, his

ashen hair hanging over his eyes. Halthris wondered what he was
thinking, feeling, knowing that his world, the safe cosy city where
he had lived all his life in pampered and decadent luxury, had been
so suddenly and terribly destroyed.

Nothing showed in his face, however. He said clearly, 'I know
where we will be quite safe from any Ska'i. But it's a long ride, and
a very hard one in winter.' He surveyed them all, the eight Tanathi
and the three soldiers. 'Two days at least, perhaps three if the
blizzards return. Are you willing?'

'Yes,' said Inri, her voice taut with pain, and the rest echoed
her.

'Then come with me,' said Ansaryon, First of His Name, King
of Zithirian: and rode away from his shattered, burning city without
a backward glance.

'The Ska'i! The Ska'i are following us!' The soldier who had been
on watch came scrambling down from the high pinnacle of rock
above their camp. 'They must have been riding all night – they're
only a mile or so behind us!'

Halthris, kneeling beside Inri and trying to force some melted
snow between her friend's chattering lips, felt despair rush back
over her like flood water, surging into every part of her body and
soul. She put down the cup and stood up wearily.

They had ridden all through the first night, and for most of the
following day too before Ansaryon had called a halt and ordered a
camp in this comparatively sheltered place, a wide cleft between
rocks. Above, to their left, reared the vast cloud-veiled bulk of
Mount Estray, and the usually swift torrent of the River D'yenn
separated them from the mountain. The ice covering its falls and
rapids was frozen into spikes and shards by the speed of winter's
sudden descent.

She had no idea where they were going, save that they were
heading northwards, into the impassable, inhospitable mountains.
All her attention had been given to Inri, who had collapsed in a
fever half way through the previous day. Halthris had taken her up
on her horse, to keep her warm, and the two of them had huddled
together with Fess last night, in the inadequate shelter of Inri's
cloak. Fortunately, Sherren had thought to bring his pack and
Djekko's with them, so at least they had had something to eat,
albeit the hard bread and dried meat that comprised Tanathi
emergency rations. They had even lit a small fire, enough to heat
the melted snow, and Chettay had sprinkled a generous handful of

dried leaves into the bubbling pot, to make the refreshing and heartening drink that Tanathi and Zithiriani alike called kuldi.

Inri had been too ill to eat anything. Halthris had washed and dressed the hideous wound in her back with makeshift bandages from her cleanest tunic, but feared that the sharp blade of the Ska'i axe had penetrated a lung, for it obviously hurt Inri to breathe, and pink-tinged froth was gathering at the corners of her mouth. But she had somehow survived the night, and might live long enough to reach their destination, wherever it was. Ansaryon had told them that it was two or three days' ride from Zithirian, so Halthris had hoped that surely they would soon be safe.

The Prince, or King, had led them in silence, unnaturally stiff and upright on poor Vondrak's big, raking chestnut. The soldiers rode behind him, in numb misery. The Tanathi, shocked by the terrible violence of the Ska'i attack and by the narrowness of their escape, and grieving for their four dead comrades as well, were too immersed in their own sadness to make any attempt to breach the invisible wall that surrounded Ansaryon. And Halthris, the only one who had communicated with him on close and human terms, was entirely occupied with helping and tending Inri.

It could have been worse, she kept telling herself, when the snow was falling again, and her arm ached from holding her friend upright on the horse, and it was beginning to seem as if they would ride into the mountains for ever, or until they froze to death in the blinding blizzards that threatened to engulf them . . .

Or until the Ska'i caught them. The Ska'i, doubtless well fed, warmly clad, bristling with weapons and eager to hunt down their cold, exhausted prey. She glanced down at Inri, seeing the other girl's gaunt, pain-filled face, and knew that she herself would kill her in the final attack, rather than give any Ska'i the opportunity.

'Stay still,' Ansaryon said sharply. He was standing by the rough trail they had followed, looking back towards where Zithirian lay, many miles behind them and out of sight behind the intervening peaks, its position indicated by a dull smudge of smoke, pale against the snow-laden sky. 'Nobody move – or speak.'

Above them, the snowy mountainside soared up into the clouds. Halthris saw Ansaryon stretch out his hands towards the rocks above the place where the Ska'i must be. There was a grove of pine trees, bowed under their frozen burden, a cliff, and then a precipitous white slope vanishing up into the mist. As she stared, the King of Zithirian flung back his head and let out a piercing, eerie shriek that raised the hairs on her neck and startled all the horses.

The sound bounced and echoed off the stone walls and ramparts of the mountains around them, and hung frozen in the icy air. For a long, long moment nothing happened. And then Halthris heard a low, distant, muttering sound, like thunder a very long way off. As she wondered what it could be, Abreth cried out, and pointed, and Fess, every hair bristling with fear and her ears flattened, crouched down next to Inri.

The whole mountainside seemed to be moving. She stared in astonishment. No mistake: the sheet of snow hanging above the narrow pass was sliding downwards, so slowly that she had not noticed it at first. As they watched, though, it began to pick up speed, and the sinister rumbling noise increased. The avalanche sprang suddenly off the cliff in a vast white cloud and smashed through the pine trees below, brushing them aside as if they were twigs. Then the vast mass of falling snow swept over the last rocks, gathering stones and boulders as it passed, and roared over the trail and the frozen river D'yenn, to crash against the sheer wall of rock that plunged down from Mount Estray.

And then there was silence, utter, profound, chilling.

Ansaryon turned, and dropped to his knees in the snow, his head hanging. The Tanathi stared at him with a mixture of amazement and terror: Sherren, white and shaking, made the warding sign. The soldier who had given warning of the Ska'i began to clamber back up to the lookout point. His voice, calling down, was loud with triumph and relief. 'They've gone – all gone – swept away – there isn't a sign of them!'

Halthris walked over to Ansaryon. She looked down at him, and cleared her throat softly. 'Are you all right?'

The King of Zithirian glanced up, and then sat back on his heels, pushing the lank damp hair away from his eyes. Like all of them, he was still dressed in the clothes he had worn during the attack, and indeed the day before: that startling scarlet tunic and trousers, now dark with damp and dirt, and still covered by the long, sleeveless furred gown, likewise suffering from the effects of the weather and the journey. His face was absolutely colourless, his lips pale, and his silvery eyes glittered from under shadowed lids. He smiled at her, with difficulty. 'You see? Sorcery does have its uses, after all.'

'I was thinking exactly the same thing myself,' Halthris told him. 'At least we are safe now – unless they send another lot in pursuit.'

'It couldn't catch up with us in time. We should reach Sar D'yenyi by dusk.' Ansaryon got clumsily to his feet: the effort of rousing the avalanche seemed to have exhausted all his energy. He stood gasping, his breath pluming in the air between them. 'Your friend – will she last that long?'

'I don't know.' Halthris stared at him with sudden and considerable concern. 'Will *you*? Does anyone else know the way to this place – this Sar D – D'yenyi?'

'No. No one else. This pass doesn't lead straight to it – you have to turn off – the river goes between high cliffs and then out again.' He looked at her and smiled. 'Don't worry, Halthris of the Tanathi. I won't drop dead and leave you stranded in the mountains. Nor will Inri die on the journey, if you give her this.'

She gazed suspiciously at the small lump of sticky, amber-coloured substance which he held out to her. 'What is it?'

'Kuldi. Most people just use the dried leaves, but this is compressed sap, much stronger and more effective. It's a medicine, rather than a drink. If you melt it into a cup of boiling water, it'll put new heart and strength into her. Go on – take it. You should have time to brew it before we go.'

Halthris did as instructed. The pungent aroma rising from the thick, viscous liquid made her eyes water, and she coughed as it caught her throat. She did not think that Inri would be able to drink it, but the other girl, supported by Sherren, sipped from the steaming wooden cup that Halthris held to her lips, and managed to finish it right down to the dregs, though she had to stop several times to catch her breath. Afterwards, Halthris was relieved, and secretly rather surprised, to see that there was now a little colour in Inri's drawn face, and her breathing seemed easier.

Abreth, Grinya and two of the soldiers had gone back down the trail to the site of the avalanche, and reported that no living thing could be seen, although they had found several dead horses, and the broken dead bodies of half a dozen Ska'i. They had brought back some saddle packs containing clothing and food, and this was distributed, delaying their departure still further. It must have been almost midday, although the sun was hidden behind the thick dark-grey clouds, by the time they left their camp site and continued along the narrow pass.

As if the mountains had been malevolently waiting for this moment of hope, the blizzards overwhelmed them before they had gone more than a mile.

Fortunately, one of the salvaged Ska'i packs had contained a bundle of rope. It was not long enough to tie all twelve remaining horses together, but Sherren, Abreth and Djekko managed to link seven of them, working in a blinding hail of snow with hands numb with cold even inside their thick leather gauntlets. The Tanathi, tough and inured to discomfort, were coping well in these desperately dangerous conditions. Even Inri, so seriously hurt, seemed happier huddled in her cloak on Grinya's horse than the three soldiers of the Royal Guard, who had only their bronze armour and helmets to protect them from the weather, and whose horses, by tacit consent, were amongst those roped together.

Ansaryon led the procession, his sure-footed Tanathi-trained horse picking its way over rocks, past crevasses and round boulders as if it had been bred in the mountains. He seemed to have retreated once more into that remote and impervious shell, speaking to no one and apparently oblivious to the cold. Behind him came the loose Tanathi, Halthris with Fess beside her, Djekko leading Inri's mount, and Abreth holding the reins of the first of the roped horses, which was Kettan's. Looking back, Halthris could barely discern her brother through the blurring snow, and could not see those behind him at all.

They made painfully slow progress along that narrow divide between the two mountains, Estray on the left, and part of a lower range called Mondir on their right. Each rider's head was bowed under the weight of snow settling on hood and back, so that they seemed like a group of shrunken frost giants, white and hoary. The horses were all Tanathi, and used to such conditions, even of this severity: they plodded on, snow-mantled and tireless, heads lowered against the ferocious north wind. Fess was also accustomed to hardship, but heartily disliked being cold and wet. She looked so miserable that Halthris, not without misgivings, let her jump up onto her saddle-bow. Her own horse, Ennim, had been trained to tolerate the outlandish extra weight, but he, alas, had not been amongst the mounts freed from the Palace stables. She had poor Karbra's bay gelding instead, and she had wondered if he would allow the cat on his back.

He certainly did not seem to like it very much, and snorted and side-stepped as Fess snuggled against her chest, under the stinking, badly-cured Ska'i cloak that had been doled out to her. But the bay soon settled down, with some rolling of eyes and flattening of ears, and resumed his patient trudge through the blizzard. Obviously, he did not relish the extra burden, but was too cold and exhausted to feel like doing anything to dislodge it.

As Ansaryon had said, the D'yenn flowed through a precipitous gorge, and at its entrance the trail left the river bank. By this time, it was almost dusk, and the light was diminishing fast. As they halted, however, the steady fall of snow thinned a little, and it became possible, just, to see more than a few paces ahead of them.

Halthris urged her horse up to Ansaryon, who had halted, staring up at the jagged jumble of rocks in front of them. 'Is this the place where we have to turn aside? Where do we go?'

He was silent for so long that she wondered if he had heard her. But just as she was about to repeat her questions, he turned his head and stared at her, as if returning from a very great distance. He also wore a Ska'i cloak, made from a huge and shaggy brown bear skin. The head was still attached, forming a grotesque hood: even under a blanket of snow, she could see the black nose and snarling teeth. Beneath it, his face looked worse than Inri's: bloodless, hollowed, desperate. Sorcery surely doesn't drain so much out of you, Halthris thought. He's sick, or hurt.

'Up there,' Ansaryon said, pointing. His voice was no longer clear and pleasant, but had degenerated to a harsh whisper. 'Up there to the right, over the shoulder of the hill, down, and onwards. It rejoins the river not far away. Just follow it, and you'll come to Sar D'yenyi.'

'You're coming too?' Halthris said sharply.

'I hope so. I'm just telling you – in case – it's not easy, that climb. Especially in conditions like these.'

'The snow seems to be easing off slightly.' Halthris glanced up at where the mountains should be. 'We must try to get over before darkness comes.'

'Exactly.' Ansaryon bent his head under the hideous bear's teeth, and she had a sudden and extraordinary sense of the strength and tension of the sorcery hidden within him. It felt like the heat from a fire, or from the sun: she would not have been surprised to see the snow turn to rain around them, so intense were the waves of power radiating from him. She stared in awe and wonder as the wind dropped and the snow died away to a scattering of tiny flakes. Over there, on Estray, the blizzard still raged, blotting out the mountain: but their little group of horses and riders stood in the sudden clear heart of the storm, and in front of them their route lay plainly visible, winding over the ridge beside the gorge.

'We don't have much time,' Ansaryon said, raising his head suddenly. He glanced round at the others, and gestured urgently. 'Come on – on, before darkness falls!'

Wearily the horses struggled up the steep incline in his wake. Halthris, feeling the hum of sorcery tingling all around her like some vast invisible creature, wondered if anyone else had noticed. Certainly even Sherren, notoriously superstitious, seemed to be taking this extraordinary situation for granted, as if it were perfectly natural for twelve riders to be isolated in their own bubble of clear weather while moving through a raging blizzard. Perhaps he was so tired he hadn't noticed.

They reached the top as the light began to fail in earnest, and made their way slowly down the other side, following Ansaryon. As they reached the bottom, the snow began to fall fast around them, and within a few heartbeats it was as thick as before, and darkness was upon them.

Abreth shouted, and the procession came to a slow, ragged halt. One of the soldiers had succumbed to cold and exhaustion, and fallen from his horse. He was numbly apologetic as he struggled to his feet with Djekko's help, and managed to clamber back into the saddle, but it was plain that he could not endure much more.

Halthris rode her horse up to Ansaryon. 'How much further?'

Again, he took some time to reply. 'There's a place where we can rest, a cave just off the trail – not far – we can get some sleep and move on in the morning.' She could only dimly make out his face now, but for an instant she saw the glimmer of his eyes. 'We've got to find shelter, or we'll all die – even you Tanathi.'

'We're nowhere near dying,' Halthris said firmly, although she thought with fear of Inri, still wrapped in Grinya's arms and Grinya's cloak, who might be dead already. 'But you're right – we must have some rest. Lead us to the cave, then.'

To her surprise, it was huge, with a narrow entrance widening to a broad high chamber beyond. Even more amazingly, it was equipped as a refuge. Wooden boxes at the back proved to contain skins and blankets, kindling and wood and the stone and steel necessary to make a fire, and rush-lights dipped in tar. There were also bales and bundles of hay and straw, burnstones, and even a tripod and a couple of large cooking pots, together with a collection of wooden cups and plates.

'There are several of these places along the pass,' Ansaryon said. 'It's a long hard journey to Sar D'yenyi, and they have saved many lives.'

The Tanathi fell upon the boxes with cries of astonished delight. It was not long before the cave seemed almost cosy. The twelve horses were picketed just inside the entrance, sampling the hay, which was rather musty but certainly much better than nothing. Behind them, Sherren and Chettay had lit a fire, which blazed obediently, and there was already a pot of snow hung over the flames. Djekko had jammed several rush-lights into convenient cracks in the cave's rocky walls, and Halthris collected most of their remaining food to make a kind of stew which, though not particularly palatable, would at least fill empty bellies and put heat and heart into frozen souls.

At last, utterly worn out, one by one the twelve fugitives snuggled down on their straw beds, feeling warmer and more comfortable than at any time since leaving Zithirian. They were surely now safe from pursuit: they had the promise of a blissfully restful night before them: and tomorrow, they would reach their destination at last. Even Inri, who had drifted in and out of consciousness all day, appeared to be better, and had eaten a little of the stew. It seemed suddenly quite probable that they would survive, and with that thought, sleep was easy.

Halthris woke before dawn, and found several Tanathi gathered round the fire, boiling water for kuldi. Once more the refreshing aroma wafted through the cave, rousing those still asleep. Inri was sitting up, smiling, some of the shadows gone from her eyes, and the soldier who had fallen from his horse the previous day was obviously almost restored to normal.

They breakfasted on burnt bread, then extinguished the fire and returned the cave to its former state, so far as was possible. Outside, the clear brilliant light indicated sunshine. When Halthris peered through the narrow opening, the brightness almost blinded her, but she could see Estray in all its majesty, the perfect symmetrical peak where the Divine Tayo had supposedly been translated to Paradise, towering up into the sky, each rock, each precipice, each slope sharply delineated by the rising sun until the final, distant pinnacle piercing the blue.

With eagerness, they packed, saddled the horses, and rode out into that dazzling glare, towards Sar D'yenyi.

The sun was still a little below its zenith when Ansaryon urged his horse to the top of a low hill, round which the river curved in a torrent of snow-covered ice. He halted, and shaded his eyes: then, he turned and beckoned them onwards.

Halthris reached him first. She reined in her chestnut, and stared in wonder.

In front of them, unutterably, achingly, blindingly white, stretched a frozen lake, cradled at the feet of the mountains: Annako, Estray, Sargenn, Mondir. Their distant foothills plunged down into the ice, sheer and straight, but the nearer shore was gentler, though strewn with rocks.

And not far out into the lake, another, much larger rock reared up out of the solid water, crowned with towers, spires, pinnacles, a Zithirian in perfect miniature, casting spears of indigo shadow across the snow.

Ansaryon was speaking softly, rhythmically under his breath. He looked as a dying man might, seeing water in the desert, or shelter after storm. He glanced at her, and smiled. 'There it is – Sar D'yenyi, the High Citadel, the secret stronghold of Zithirian.' And as she gazed, enchanted, he began to recite the words of a poem, or a song.

> Though skies may fall, and put an end to dawning:
> Though seas run dry, and fiery mountains roar:
> I once saw Sar D'yenyi in the morning,
> And my heart is filled with joy for ever more.

'It's so beautiful,' Halthris said in wonder. 'Who built it?'

'A friend of Tayo – his right-hand man, Rendeth. It was intended as a refuge in times of trouble, and also to guard the quarries and the gold and silver mines in the mountains. Only the King and certain favoured members of his family and Court were ever allowed even to know of its existence, let alone come here. And as I'm sure you now appreciate, it's not easy to find by chance.' He gestured at the mountains. 'That tallest one is Annako, where all the stone that built Zithirian, and Sar D'yenyi too, was dug, and floated across the lake and down the valley of the D'yenn on rafts and rollers. And the other peak, the one with the sheer face and the slanting summit, that's Sargenn. The gold and silver you are wearing come from its heart. There are several settlements there across the lake, of miners and their families, governed by the Lord of Sar D'yenyi.' He paused, and then said bleakly, 'Who until two days ago was the King's brother, Lord Tayma.'

Halthris thought of that man, and the manner of his death and his brother's, and an unpleasant thought occurred to her. She said quietly, 'Those Ska'i – in the Palace gardens – they *meant* to kill the King, and Lord Tayma, and you, didn't they? They singled you out. The Chamberlain was shouting something about treachery – someone must have opened the city gates for them, someone let them into the Palace, someone told them to kill all the Royal Family. Who was it, Ansaryon? Do you know?'

His face was still turned towards the glory of Sar D'yenyi, his straight, uncommunicative profile as still and pale as if carved from Annako stone. She waited, hearing the voices behind and beside her, the cries of wonder and gasps of delight as their companions reached the summit of the ridge and saw what lay before them. And when he spoke at last, so softly that only she could hear him, she already knew the answer.

'It was my brother Tsenit,' said Ansaryon, King of Zithirian.

PART
TWO

CHAPTER
NINE

The icy surface of the lake was rough and ridged under the wind-blown snow, and drifts had piled up against the shore, sculpted into fantastic curves and ripples and cliffs. The horses struggled belly-deep through them before suddenly pushing free out onto the frozen water. Ansaryon led them, as he had done all the way from Zithirian, and his face was once more empty of feeling, as if he had never gazed at the glorious prospect of Sar D'yenyi and revealed, as he spoke that brief fragment of poetry, a depth and intensity of emotion that Halthris had never suspected.

What did lie behind that impassive, colourless mask, schooled too well by the empty rituals of the Zithirian Court? Did he feel sorrow for his dead father and brother and sister, and bitterness or rage towards Tsenit? His expression now gave absolutely nothing away. And yet she had not imagined the joy and the grief, tangled together in his voice.

She wanted to ask so many questions. If this had been Lord Tayma's stronghold, who occupied it now? His wife and family, perhaps? Who would greet them, and give them shelter? And she thought too of Tsenit. Was he still alive? How long had Ansaryon suspected his treachery? And how, how could a young man so popular, apparently so likeable, have delivered his home, his family, his city and his people into the ravening and bloodthirsty arms of Quenait and his tribe of wolves?

Only Ansaryon could tell her, and Ansaryon ignored her and all the others, riding at the head of the fugitives with that unnaturally stiff and rigid posture, his gloved hands clenched on the reins, never taking his eyes off the walls and towers crowning the rocky island ahead.

She had wondered how they would climb up to the citadel, but as they came closer, she saw that there was a low platform of dressed stone jutting out of the ice, and a large collection of boats tied up to it and gripped fast by the frozen water. From the quay, a ramp cut into the rock zig-zagged up the steep side of the island, until it reached a gate, flanked by two towers, set in the south-facing wall of Sar D'yenyi.

The gate was shut. The sun shone with the blazing, adamantine brilliance of a diamond, on the snow, the rocks, the silver walls and soaring spires. Ansaryon reached the quay, and looked up. Halthris saw movement on the ramparts above the gate. She realized suddenly that he was still wearing the Ska'i cloak, and that he was easily within range of any competent archer within the citadel.

As the thought struck her, he pushed the gruesome hood back and shook his head and his hair free. For a few heartbeats, there was utter silence in the clear, still, ice-cold air. Then he shouted, his voice carrying and echoing and bouncing amongst the rocks as if he thought to start another avalanche. 'To the Lady of Sar D'yeni – the Lord Ansaryon and his party beg entrance and shelter.'

Another silence. More movement on the walls. And then suddenly, the great gate began to open, and Ansaryon spurred his horse up onto the quay, and then to the ramp.

They followed him, weary but buoyed up with relief and gratitude for their escape. Later would come the grief, the guilt, the endless discussions about what had gone wrong, and how disaster might have been averted. But for now, it was enough to know that they were safe, and that by a miracle, and Ansaryon's leadership, they had survived.

The King reached the gate, passed under it, and into the courtyard beyond. It had been swept clean of snow, revealing subtly coloured blocks of stone laid in a swirling spiral pattern of blue and grey and green. The space was thronged with people, staring suspiciously at them. Some were armed with swords, spears or bows. And in the exact centre of the spiral a girl stood, wrapped in a warm fur cloak, dark-haired, very small, very young. Her eyes were wide with astonishment as the tattered and disreputable band of fugitives filed into the courtyard, but she displayed the cool self-possession that seemed to be typical of all aristocratic Zithiriani.

'Greetings from the Lord Ansaryon to his beloved cousin the Lady Kefiri.' His voice was still clear, but rapidly losing its power. 'Lady, I very much regret that I bring you news of great grief and disaster, and you must prepare yourself for the worst.' He paused, and the girl's face paled, while the people around them fell silent, their expressions suddenly full of apprehension.

'The city of Zithirian has fallen to the Ska'i. The King is dead, and the Lord Tayma, and the Heir, and the Lady Zathti, and all the Court. We have barely escaped with our lives – we crave shelter, and rest, and care for the wounded. These are my friends of the Tanathi tribe, Abreth son of Charnak and his sister Halthris and their comrades. They fought like lions in defence of the King, and four of them died.' He was almost whispering now, and Halthris, urging her mount unobtrusively closer, saw that he was only holding himself upright by sheer strength of will. 'I am sorry, Kef,' he added, his voice suddenly twisted with grief. 'So sorry, to bring you such news – your father is dead, he died fighting bravely—'

'And Tsenit?' said the girl. She was almost as white as the walls of the central tower behind her, but still held to that desperate self-control. 'You – you didn't mention Tsenit.'

As the people began to murmur, Ansaryon said clearly, 'Tsenit is the traitor. Tsenit's orders let the Ska'i into the city and the Palace. Tsenit commanded that all the rest of his family should be slaughtered. Thanks to the Tanathi, the King and your father were almost saved. And in the name of Tayo, our Divine Ancestor, I ask you, Kefiri, daughter of Tayma, son of Tesi, to avenge our deaths and expel the Ska'i from Zithirian!'

All around them rose cries and moans of grief, of horror and amazement. And as the Lady Kefiri stared at him, Ansaryon slumped suddenly forward in the saddle, and slid slowly down to lie in an untidy heap on the stones.

Halthris reached him first, and saw what the cloak and the scarlet gown and tunic had disguised for too long: blood, soaking the cloth, staining the saddle, and tinging the wet ground where he lay with red. She turned him over, saw the empty face, the sickening pallor, and laid a hand to the side of his throat. There was still a pulse, but it was not strong.

'Ansary!' The Lady Kefiri flung herself down beside him on the bloodstained cobbles. Her curling black hair flowed loose, in Court fashion, and she dragged it out of the way with a small, impatient hand and stuffed it under the neck of her cloak. Halthris had thought her a child, but realized now that she was obviously older than she appeared. She said, gasping, 'Is he dead?'

'No, but he soon will be if we don't stop the bleeding,' Halthris told her. I should have known, she thought, turning to gesture to Abreth and Sherren, who were still sitting on their horses, gaping stupidly. I suspected something was wrong – I should have done something—

And the desperation of her sudden fear for him astonished her. At last her initial dislike, mistrust and suspicion had vanished, and she had come to respect him, both for his powers of endurance, and, more reluctantly, for the skills of sorcery that twice had saved them all. But she had not realized until now that she cared so much whether he lived or died.

The Lady Kefiri was calling for help, and Halthris found herself elbowed aside by a dozen eager volunteers. Feeling suddenly superfluous and unwanted, she moved aside out of their way, and watched as the frighteningly lifeless body of the King of Zithirian was lifted gently onto a stretcher and carried away. And she shivered, but not from the cold: for she had seen the grey marks of Ayak in his face.

'Hal-thris?'

The Lady Kefiri came up to her. She was tiny, hardly reaching to Halthris's shoulder, and the mass of curling brown hair, the roundness of her face and the wide, blue, tear-filled eyes made her seem very young, but her air of self-possessed determination was distinctly unchildlike. She said, 'Your name is Hal-thris? Of the Tanathi? We – it seems that we have much to thank you for.'

'We did not do enough,' Halthris said sadly, knowing it was true, and yet unable to see how it could have been otherwise. 'The King is dead, Zithirian destroyed—'

'You did your best,' said Kefiri. 'If Tsenit – if Tsenit is a traitor, then not all the armies of Toktel'yi would make a difference, in the face of such a vile betrayal.' She drew a deep, shuddering breath. 'Come inside – you and your people. There is hot food for you, and warm beds – and I see that one of you at least is hurt. We have a Healer here who is very knowledgeable and skilled, and he will tend you.'

'And Ansaryon?'

Kefiri gave her a long, assessing look. 'Were – are you his friend – his true friend?'

'Yes,' Halthris told her, and spoke the unadorned truth.

Kefiri gazed at her, with eyes that were as deeply blue as snow shadows. Then she shook her head. 'I – I fear he may be beyond helping. Not the wound – something else. Perhaps we can talk later, in private. There are things you do not know, which you should – but only after you have eaten, and rested. The horses will be well tended.' She glanced at Fess, waiting with patient misery by Halthris's side. 'Your cat is welcome too. Will she be happy, within walls?'

'As long as there is a space by a fire, and food for her, and my company, she will be happy,' Halthris said: and Fess followed her into the great central tower of the fortress with an aura of relief and hungry anticipation almost visible around her.

The inhabitants of Sar D'yenyi were friendly, sympathetic and eager to make a fuss of the fugitives. They were ushered into a huge circular chamber that was obviously the heart of the citadel.

A dozen braziers full of glowing burnstones stood round the walls, and more were brought, making the room almost hot. Tables had been set up, and food arrived: thick steaming broths, warm spiced wine, fresh risen loaves of bread, soft and fragrant, hunks of roast meat and hard yellow cheese, jars of summer fruit preserved in honey. The Tanathi and the soldiers fell like wolves on the loaded plates, so hungry that some did not even bother to remove their soaked outer garments.

When they were at last replete, a man who was obviously the Chamberlain of Sar D'yenyi came to escort them to their quarters. There, he said, smiling, fresh clothes and warm comfortable beds awaited them, the Healer was on hand to tend any hurts they might have, and everyone in the citadel was at their beck and call. If they needed anything at all, they had only to ask, and it would be given.

The food had wrought a dramatic improvement in Inri, but Halthris ignored her protests and requested the services of the Healer. He was a tall, thin, elderly man, with kind eyes and deft, sensitive hands, and his bag contained an impressive array of pots and potions, as well as a selection of clean and gleaming instruments. He examined Inri's back with great gentleness, gave her a spoonful of a thick amber syrup that made her drowsy almost at once, and then carefully bathed the deep, hideous wound before stitching the ragged edges together with a needle and thread, exactly as if he were sewing a leather garment together, but so swiftly and skilfully that Inri, her eyes closed, never moved.

'She'll do well enough now,' he said, rising to his feet. 'She's lost a lot of blood, of course, and the right lung is damaged. It will take a month or so of good care, but she will recover, I assure you. The wound is clean, and has not festered.' His eyes crinkled in a sudden smile. 'You Tanathi are a tough tribe indeed. An injury like that would have finished most men off.'

'Thank you,' said Sherren, his face glowing with relief. 'I thought she was going to die—'

'Takes more than a Ska'i axe to kill me,' Inri muttered on the edge of sleep, and Sherren, tears in his eyes, knelt by her bed and took her hand in his.

The other Tanathi, who had watched the Healer with interest – his methods were very different to the mixture of potions, chants and ritual employed by their own shamans – quietly slipped out of the room, and left the two alone. Halthris noted that even Kettan, who had obviously fancied his chances with Inri, now seemed to accept Sherren's superior claim. But since the attack on Zithirian, he had been unusually subdued: almost tolerable, in fact. Perhaps the narrowness of their escape, and the violent and brutal deaths of four of their friends and companions, had permanently changed him for the better.

Knowing her cousin too well, she rather doubted it.

Now that Inri was at last safe, she had time to think of Ansaryon. As her companions drifted off to the other rooms allotted to them, presumably to rest or talk, she approached the Healer. Like all the people she had met today in Sar D'yenyi, he was warmer and more friendly by far than anyone had been in Zithirian, and she had no fear of being rebuffed.

'You do not need to worry about your friend, Tanathi woman,' he said with a smile. 'Barring some unforeseen disaster, she will make a full recovery – though it will probably take all winter to restore her to health. No more journeys through the snow for a while, eh?'

'I certainly hope not,' Halthris said. At this moment, the thought of staying in this lovely, remote and welcoming refuge for nearly half a year was extraordinarily attractive. Although someone, soon, must somehow brave the weather and find the rest of their tribe, to tell them what had happened . . .

Her exhausted mind was beginning to wander. She dragged her thoughts firmly back to their original track. 'And the Lord Ansaryon? How is he?'

The Healer's face became suddenly serious, and he shook his head. 'Unfortunately, I cannot be so optimistic. I have done my best for him, but it may not be enough. This is an evil day, Tanathi woman – an evil day for Zithirian, and for Sar D'yenyi, and for all Tayo's children. Let us pray to the Divine Ancestor that the Lord Ansaryon lives to avenge the murder of his family, and to slay his evil, treacherous brother.'

But Halthris realized suddenly that Ansaryon had not expected to live, for he had charged his cousin Kefiri with the sacred duty of vengeance. Through sorcery, or through a more ordinary human obstinacy, he had held death at bay all through that terrible journey, to bring them safe to the refuge that he alone had known how to find. And now, his task ended, the strength of will that had kept him alive had ended too.

She said softly, 'We all owe him our lives. May I see him, do you think?'

'I was coming to find you, to ask if you wanted to,' said Kefiri.

She was dressed all in white, a plain loose long-sleeved gown, with no embroidery, no bodice, no jewels, and her hair loose down her back. Halthris knew enough about the customs of Zithirian to recognize the colour of mourning: and although she realized that Kefiri must be wearing it out of grief for her father, Lord Tayma, a chill invaded her heart, foreshadowing another death. She said, 'Is he dying?'

'We don't speak of dying until death has actually occurred,' the Healer told her gently. 'If there is still breath in the body, then there is hope of life. And if you have any skills that might save him, Tanathi woman, then you may use them with my blessing.'

Sadly, Halthris shook her head. 'No, I have not – I am no Healer.'

Kefiri gave her a small, wan smile. 'Come with me, Halthris, if you wish.'

She was led down a long, curving stone passage, unpainted but otherwise eerily similar to those in the Palace in Zithirian, and up a flight of stairs that seemed to meander through the walls of the great central tower in a gracefully haphazard fashion. Tall narrow windows, filled with that strange transparent material, let in sparse, pure light to illuminate or adumbrate the texture of the stones, steps and walls as if that were their only purpose, and their ordinary function unnecessary. But with each ascent Halthris could glimpse the lesser towers of Sar D'yenyi, diminishing below them.

The topmost room had much wider windows, and only the mountains were visible now. She thought of Tsenit's tower, and the fear that had gripped her, founded on the unnaturalness of being so far above the earth without wings on her shoulders or earth beneath her feet. Here, surely, she stood higher, far higher, and yet she had no sense of danger, and no terror.

But there was a different kind of fear in her now. The room was dominated by a huge high bed, in which three or four people could comfortably have slept. But there was only one man in it, and his body scarcely disturbed the quilts and furs and blankets heaped above it. Halthris walked forward, and looked down at Ansaryon, King of Zithirian, and felt like weeping.

Three were women in the room, busy with bowls of water, medicines, bandages. At Kefiri's nod, they left, without any of the obsequious gestures that had demeaned the servants in Zithirian. When the door had shut behind them, she reached forward and gently unpeeled the bedclothes.

Ansaryon did not stir, although Halthris heard the faint whisper of his breath. From neck to hip, his body was wrapped in bandages, some already stained with blood.

'He has been hurt in three places,' Kefiri said. Her voice trembled, but she went on bravely. 'In the shoulder – that was probably an axe. Several of his ribs are broken, and he may be bleeding inside. And something has gashed him across from side to hip – a glancing blow, the Healer said, if it had been harder it would almost have cut him in half – ' She gave a gasping sob, and a tear slid suddenly down the side of her nose. 'He rode all the way from Zithirian in a blizzard, hurt like that – didn't anyone *notice*?'

'I suspected that he might be wounded,' Halthris told her. Since Kefiri seemed to be on the verge of breaking down altogether, she reached past her and drew the covers up again, over the unresponsive body. 'I know now that I should have done something – but I thought it might have been because of the sorcery.'

'He used *sorcery*? On the journey?'

Halthris glanced round, surprised at the sharpness in the girl's voice. 'Yes, twice. He raised an avalanche, which killed the Ska'i who were following us. And then he kept the blizzard away from us, when darkness was falling, just before we reached the refuge cave where we spent last night.'

'I know the place,' Kefiri said. She had regained her composure, and looked very pale, but thoughtful. 'No wonder – no wonder he collapsed. Father always used to say that he was the most stubborn of all of us – he would *not* give in, ever – everyone thought he was weak and degenerate, because he wouldn't take part in the Bridal Race – do you know what that is? Every year in the spring, the young men compete in it, and it's a matter of honour and pride to complete it at least once. They run round the city walls, from the North Dock to the South, and then swim across the Kefirinn and back. It's quite dangerous – often, someone drowns, the river is very cold and swift after the thaw. No girl will look at a man unless he's run in the Bridal Race. Cathallon – the Heir – had to be rescued by a boat when he tried it. Tsenit . . .' Her mouth twisted with savage bitterness. 'Tsenit ran the race every year, he made a virtue of it, showing off how tough and strong he was. And Ansary refused to leave his books to take part, even though almost everyone despised him for it. He said he couldn't see the point, since he had no plans to marry anyway. And in reality he was stronger than any of them – I just wish he hadn't chosen this way of showing it!'

'He did it to guide us here to safety,' Halthris reminded her. 'No one else knew where Sar D'yenyi was – we would have died, but for him.'

'I know that,' Kefiri said. She stared down at her cousin's empty face. 'But I'm sure that he wanted to prove something as well, even if it was only to himself. And now he will die of it.'

Halthris, her heart sick, said quietly, 'You told me in the courtyard that it isn't just his wounds – that there is something else wrong. What is it? Is it to do with sorcery?'

There was a long, long silence. She heard the soft whine of the wind round the tower, distant voices, the faint, difficult, irregular sound of Ansaryon's breathing. Then Kefiri looked round, her eyes haunted. 'Yes. Yes, it is. If I tell you, will you swear to tell no one else? *No one*, not even your brother, or your companions. Only I know, and the Healer – and if you are his true friend you should know too – do you swear?'

'I swear it,' Halthris whispered. 'On the heart of Sarraliss.'

Abruptly, Kefiri left the bedside and went over to the brazier. She held out her hands to the warmth: they were shaking, and the nails were bitten down to the quick. She said, 'My cousin is a sorcerer. You knew that – even if you had not seen him use his powers, you must have heard the rumours.'

Halthris nodded.

'But do you know what gives him those powers? Sorcerers are not born, they are *made*. In Zithirian, only the priests of Tayo are permitted to use magic. For anyone else to be a sorcerer is a crime punishable by death. But there's a secret society called the Mazath. Ansary has been a member of it for ten years – since he was about sixteen or seventeen. Everyone in our family knows it. And of course there are rumours in the city, but no one has ever dared to prove it. As he is a Prince of the Blood of Tayo, only the High Priestess of Tayo would have the authority to denounce him, and she never has.'

'So what is it that makes him a sorcerer?'

Kefiri rubbed her hands above the burnstones. 'There is a drug which gives the powers of sorcery to anyone who takes it. It's called Annatal, which is the name of the island in the Archipelago, south of Toktel'yi, where it comes from, and it's very rare, and expensive. You have to take it regularly, and for as long as you do, you can work magic. Of course, there is a lot of training involved – that's why the Mazath was formed, to teach initiates how to use their powers. And even with the drug, they can't do very much. Influence the weather, create illusions, leave their bodies and move about in spirit – the Priests use it to spy on people. All very petty, really. But there's always the chance that someone taking the drug will discover how to gain *real* power. And I suppose that's why they take Annatal, because there are too many dangers involved otherwise.'

'What dangers? Of being found out?'

'Partly, yes. But Annatal itself is dangerous. If you take it over a long period of time, it ages you. Have you noticed how old all the Priests of Tayo look? It's because they're addicted to Annatal. Once you've been taking it for fifteen years or more, you begin to age faster and faster. The High Priestess is only just over fifty, but she looks thirty years older than she really is – and she'll probably live to be a hundred and twenty, because despite ageing you, Annatal also prolongs your life. The process hasn't begun in Ansaryon yet – I don't think he's been taking it for long enough. But that isn't the worst. Annatal is highly addictive. Those who start to take it have to keep on taking it for the rest of their lives. They have to, or they die.'

'And that is what is wrong with Ansaryon?'

Kefiri nodded. 'Yes. There is no Annatal here in Sar D'yenyi – my father loathed such things, he would never allow it, despite the fact that many of the young men at Court indulged in it. And Ansaryon did not bring any with him. I searched his clothes, and his pack – there was nothing. I don't think he can have had any since he left Zithirian, nearly three days ago. And it usually takes only five days without the drug, to die.'

Halthris stared at the unconscious man in the bed. She said numbly, 'What will happen?'

'The Healer told me. He has never seen it himself, but his teacher was once ordered to tend a man accused of sorcery, who was in prison in Zithirian. Of course, there was no need to execute him – they just withdrew his Annatal and waited for him to die. It was proof of sorcery, and his punishment, at the same time. There will be fever, delirium, sweats and convulsions. Then, if these do not kill him, he will lapse into a coma, and die.' She turned to Halthris, her face raw with grief and despair. 'I don't want to sit and watch that happen to him – I *don't*! And yet he is my cousin, the last of my family left except for that viper Tsenit – I have no choice.' Her voice sank to a whisper. 'You are his friend, too. Will you stay with me, and share the burden? I don't – I don't think I can bear it very well on my own.'

'He saved our lives,' Halthris said. 'For that, and for our friendship, of course I will help you.'

And then Kefiri broke at last into a storm of weeping, and Halthris took the Lady of Sar D'yenyi into her arms like a child, and tried to give her comfort, when no comfort could possibly alleviate the agony of such loss. And she grieved too, on her own account, for the man she had only just begun to know and respect, and who would be snatched away from her untimely, before the full flowering of their friendship.

The Healer had not lied. Before nightfall, Ansaryon's deep unconsciousness had given way to a restless sleep, and thence to a violent and hideous delirium that no sedative could allay. All night he struggled in the grip of unspeakable dreams and hallucinations, tossing, thrashing, shouting in languages that Halthris did not know, or in the rich, empty cadences of Zithiriani. He saw demons, creatures of ghastly evil, the monsters whom he had supposedly summoned from the Underworld where they lurked. And he saw too the dead: his father, the mother who had died many years ago, his brother Cathallon, and above all, frail, beautiful, insane, his sister Zathti, his twin. Over and over again he spoke her name, and begged her forgiveness. What he had done to her, he did not say, and no one knew, but bitter anguish and remorse filled his voice.

Halthris could hardly bear to listen to his ravings. This frenzied, tormented madman was so appallingly different from the controlled, unemotional and civilized Prince of Zithirian that they did not seem to be the same person. But she had promised Kefiri that she would shoulder some of the burden, and so she stayed by the bed, helping to hold him down during the worst convulsions, sponging his burning body in brief intervals of calm, and listening all the while to that once pleasant voice rambling, shouting in rage or terror, whispering in grief and despair, laying bare all the tortuous and intimate landscape of his soul.

Only the Healer, Mellok, was with them, and Halthris was glad of it. She did not know what her companions thought of her absence, and did not really care. But Abreth brought Fess up to the tower chamber, and the cat curled up close to the warmth of the brazier. Her ears flicked at every sound Ansaryon made, but she was obviously content to be in Halthris's presence, even in these circumstances.

As dusk approached, the day after their arrival at Sar D'yenyi, Ansaryon's fever rose suddenly to its height. Kefiri, her face pale and pinched with despair and lack of sleep, tried to hold onto one flailing arm, and was hurled to the floor. As Halthris bent to help her up, Mellok cried out suddenly, and stumbled back from the bed. Ansaryon struggled to a sitting position, his eyes wild, glittering, unseeing. He stared past them to the curved wall beyond, and his head moved in a savage gesture of denial. Then, he flung out his hands.

Lightning, blue, forked, crackling, leapt from his fingers and arced across the room. Kefiri screamed, and Mellok dropped to his knees. The air was suddenly sizzling, full of power. Halthris felt the hair rise on her head, and sorcery prickled her skin. Ansaryon seemed to pulsate with an eerie, lambent glow: then, his voice hissing and unrecognizable, he spoke the terrible words of the Curse of Ayak.

'May Hegeden forsake you, may Sarraliss forswear you, may Tayo forget you – may the wolves tear out your tongue, slaughter your heart, devour your soul: you have lived in evil, may you die in evil, in fear, in agony, in everlasting torment – you are Ayak's, D'thliss, and to him may you return!'

Light flared up, a great sheet of cold fire so blindingly brilliant that Halthris covered her eyes. Then all the tension left the air, and there was silence: utter, deathly silence.

'Halthris?' Kefiri touched her hand. 'Halthris, are you all right?'

She was shaking. Mellok was muttering a prayer. After that curse, Halthris thought grimly, it had better be an effective one. She realized that she was crouched on the floor. Slowly, stiffly, she removed her hands from her eyes and sat up.

The room was peaceful, as if that terrifying exhibition of raw sorcery had never taken place. But Fess, every hair stark on her back, her tail bristled and her eyes huge, cowered behind the brazier, gazing at the bed as if its occupant were about to transfix her with a lightning bolt.

Halthris rose to her feet. Her knees felt wobbly, and she was trembling. Hesitantly, dreading what she would find, she stumbled the few steps to the bed.

Ansaryon lay sprawled on his side across it, his head buried in the twisted blankets. She turned him onto his back. His face looked very young and vulnerable beneath the rats-tails of his sweat-soaked hair. It did not seem possible that he had unleashed such power, and yet she had not imagined it, nor the terrible hatred with which he had laid Ayak's dreadful curse on someone named D'thliss.

Unbelievably, he was not dead. There was still a faint, staggering pulse, and he was breathing, just. Mellok finished his prayer, his face a ghastly grey, and examined his patient with shaking hands. 'Yes, he is still alive – but not for much longer, I fear. This is the last stage. Soon he will slip peacefully away. The best we can do for him now is to watch over him as he leaves us.'

Quietly, nervously, avoiding each other's eyes, they made him comfortable, renewing bandages, wiping the sweat from his face, laying him back gently on the pillows. It was now dark outside, and snowing hard, the flakes whirling against the windows. Kefiri summoned servants, who came with tapers and lit the wall lamps all round the room until it was almost as bright as day, though not with the brilliance of sorcery. Food arrived, but none of the three watchers could eat more than a few mouthfuls. The cups of hot kuldi, though, were very welcome: with every sip, Halthris felt a little strength returning to her numbed and exhausted mind.

Kefiri had fallen asleep in her chair, looking utterly drained. She was only seventeen: by comparison, Halthris felt immeasurably ancient. Mellok, too, seemed to have been aged ten years by what he had seen: his face was hollowed with fatigue, and his hands still trembled as he gulped down the kuldi. Halthris sat amongst cushions on the floor, her arms round Fess, who pressed close against her, both offering and receiving comfort.

'*Don't worry*,' she said in her mind to the cat. '*It is nearly over. Soon he will be dead, and I had rather he died than face such torment again. No one should have to endure such things, no matter how evil they are – and I know that he is not evil, whatever has happened in the past, whatever he has done.*'

And Fess, in her own way, let her know that she understood, and somehow shared her grief.

Halthris slept at last, and woke to darkness, thick, cold, impenetrable. All the lamps must have gone out. She felt harsh warm fur beneath her cheek, and knew what had roused her. She sent her greeting to Fess's mind in return, and found that the cat was fast asleep.

But something, someone, had summoned her.

It came again, the merest whisper inside her head. '*Halthris, are you there?*'

'*I am here*,' she said soundlessly. Her heart was beginning to pound, the rhythm of hope, or of fear, she did not know which. It was so faint, this tenuous communication of the spirit, that she could hardly discern it, and yet she knew with utter certainty who spoke to her.

'*I promised*,' he said. '*I know I promised not to invade you. I'm sorry – I have no other choice.*' There was a pause, as if he were gathering strength, and then he went on. '*Come to me – I need you – Halthris, will you come?*'

'*I will*,' she said, and rose to her feet. Fess stirred, but made no sound: perhaps, in some strange way, she knew what was happening. It was only a few steps to the bed, but she misjudged the distance, and banged her knee painfully on the wooden frame. By now, her eyes were becoming accustomed to the dark, and she could make out, very faintly, the shape of his head on the pillow. She could not tell if he was looking at her, but she groped for his hand, and found it, and held on.

'*Thank you,*' said Ansaryon inside her head. She felt a slight movement of his fingers against hers: they were very cold.

Halthris said, wordlessly, '*I thought you were dying.*'

'*So did I.*' His tone was faintly, drily ironic. '*But it seems that I am not – not yet. I think I need your help, though, Halthris of the Tanathi. Keep my mind here – keep me with you – can you do that?*'

'*I don't know. I can try. What do you want me to do?*'

His answer was completely unexpected. '*Can you sing?*'

Halfway between a sob and a laugh, she spoke aloud. 'Yes – yes, I can sing.'

'*In your mind,*' said Ansaryon, with a touch of exasperation. Already, his thought-voice seemed a little stronger. '*Anything – one of those interminable Tanathi lampoons if you like, I don't mind – rhymes, poetry, ballads, nonsense – anything.*'

'*Why?*' she asked, bewildered. '*How will it help?*'

'*I don't know – I just feel that it will.*' His hand gripped hers in a sudden spasm. '*Oh, for Tayo's sake, Halthris – sing!*'

She had a good voice. Once, as a child before her Ordeal, and the realization that she desired only to be a Hunter, she had wanted to become apprenticed to the clan's Singer, Umay. For over a year she had sat at his feet, learned his songs, remembered the tunes, and made up words of her own in emulation or parody. The Tanathi used music to celebrate deeds of courage, to deflate pretension, and to record and comment upon the life of the tribe and its members, so hers had not been a trivial ambition, and she knew that if her feet had followed that road, she would have made a good Singer. On hunting trips away from the clan, she still entertained her companions with songs, both her own and other people's.

But this was utterly different. How could she sing without sound? For a few heartbeats, she was stabbed by cold spears of panic. Then, from nowhere, a fragment of rhyme entered her mind.

> '*Cold the wind and grey the weather,*
> *Hunters riding close together,*
> *On each head an eagle's feather,*
> *Hegeden guards them all.*'

'*It doesn't make much sense,*' she said apologetically. '*It's just a children's song – it's all I could think of.*'

'*I told you. It doesn't matter. Anything.*'

Mention of Hegeden had cleared her mind. She gave him the

full chant, learned from Umay, of the Eagle's lament for his mate Kin'gir, lost among the winter mountains. Then, to redress the balance, the story of Sarraliss, mother of all humans, and the creation of the First Horse, born of earth and wind and joy: and, descending from the sublime to the ridiculous, the song of Foolish Gan and the Bull-shaped Rock.

She felt his amusement as she finished, and it was a completely new sensation: Fess, being a cat and permanently on her dignity, had no sense of humour whatsoever.

'*We share the same stories, you and I,*' he said. '*My nurse told me that one. Come on, Halthris of the Tanathi – surely you know more songs than those?*'

So she sat there in the dark, holding the hand of a man whose body seemed to be lifeless, but whose mind, despite the suffering he had endured, was still, astonishingly, capable of this strange and soundless communication of thoughts and emotions. She sang the tale of Djarna, the deer, and her faithful devotion to her beloved S'yar, the stag; a selection of children's lullabies and scraps of song; the ballad called the Tragic Hunter, in which a Tanathi widow mourned her husband, slain by a leopard; and How Hegeden Made the World, which told of the Creation, and in its full form took five nights to relate.

Even ruthlessly pruned, she found it exhaustingly long. Towards the end, describing how Hegeden found two twigs for his nest, accidentally dropped them into a river and transformed them into the First Man and the First Woman, she realized that she was chanting aloud, and hastily switched back to thought-speech.

'*You're very tired,*' he said, when she had finished. '*I'm sorry – but if you can stay awake till dawn – keep me here – don't let me go—*'

'*I won't,*' she promised him, frightened by the sudden desperation in his silent voice.

'*Your mind is full of questions, Halthris of the Tanathi. I can't answer all of them – not yet – but some of them I will. Tomorrow, perhaps?*'

'*If—*' she began, and he finished for her. '*If I survive this. You are my anchor, Halthris of the Tanathi – you are holding me here. If the sun shines on my living face, I feel – I know I will not die.*' She sensed his dry irony again. '*Not yet, anyway.*'

'*Have you any songs?*' she asked him. '*Are you strong enough to sing me some?*'

'*I don't know. All I can do is breathe, just, and speak to you silently, and listen. Not unpleasant, save for the darkness lurking. Almost like floating on an invisible sea, warm, comfortable – and dangerous.'*

'When we first saw Sar D'yenyi – what did you recite then? It was beautiful.'

'That's just a fragment of song – part of a very long poem written by a man called Sethearna, who lived a hundred and fifty years ago, in the time of Queen Zathti, when Zithirian was invaded by the Toktel'yans, and the Royal Family and the Court took refuge here in Sar D'yenyi. When the Toktel'yans had been driven out, he wrote a poem in celebration called "The Defeat of the Emperor". It's partly narrative, partly praise of the Queen, partly songs that can be sung separately, in their own right. That one is called "Sar D'yenyi in the Morning".'

'Can you recite it now?'

There was a pause, and she felt again the movement of his fingers in hers, and the smile he was too weak to make in reality. 'I can't remember all of it.'

'Try.'

Softly, the words stole into her head, and she saw again in her mind the sharp, agonizing beauty of the towers soaring up out of the ice, the lances of blue shadow, the glittering walls.

> 'Though skies may fall, and put an end to dawning:
> Though seas run dry, and fiery mountains roar:
> I once saw Sar D'yenyi in the morning,
> And my heart is filled with joy for ever more.
>
> My love has fled me, gone and left no warning,
> My grief will walk beside me all my days:
> But I saw Sar D'yenyi in the morning,
> And the glory set my spirit all ablaze.'

It was growing light. She turned her head and saw his face on the pillow, whiter than the linen. His eyes were closed: he seemed asleep, or dead.

'Don't worry, I'm not,' he said. 'I've thought of another song. Listen, do you recognize this?'

It took her three lines to realize that this apparently commonplace children's counting rhyme masked a very simplified version of 'How Hegeden Made the Animals'.

> Eagle on his eyrie sat
> One by one the mountain cat.
> Eagle winging high above
> Two by two the gentle dove.
> Eagle flying far and near

Three by three the faithful deer.
Eagle floating out of sight
Four by four the greedy kite.
Eagle filled with all our hope
Five by five the antelope.
Eagle hanging in the air
Six by six the running hare.
Eagle flies and does not sleep
Seven by seven the leopards creep.
Eagle never will forsake
Eight by eight the silent snake.
Eagle flies out of the sun
Nine by nine the wolf packs run.
Eagle always soaring free
Lord of men will ever be.

'I thought that the worship of Hegeden and Sarraliss was forbidden in Zithirian,' said Halthris, when he had finished.

'So it is – but they sing the songs, just the same. My nurse taught them to me. It was only later that I realized their significance. There are many songs which would displease the Priests of Tayo. This one, for instance.'

'Beware the horses of the night
Lest they thy sleeping soul affright
The Harper keep you safe till light,
And guard you from all harm.'

'The Harper of the West,' Halthris said. 'The rain-bringer, the song-singer. Is he known in Zithirian too?'

'All the children love him. The best, the most meaningful, the most beautiful songs are the children's. And no one, not even the Priests of Tayo, can take them away.'

'I don't think I like the Priests of Tayo very much.'

'I don't blame you. Very few people in Zithirian do. Is it light yet?'

'Yes, though I don't think the sun has risen. Kefiri and Mellok are still asleep.'

'And Fess?'

'She's looking at us. Can you reach her mind, too?'

The cat was staring at Ansaryon, her yellow eyes shining. Suddenly, without a sound, she rose to her feet and leapt lightly onto the bed. Her blunt, whiskery muzzle sought and found Ansaryon's other hand, and began to wash it.

'Yes. She despises most humans, but she's prepared to make an exception for me. And for you, of course. Halthris?'

'Yes?'

'Kef and the Healer will wake soon. I think it's best if he doesn't know what has happened. Kef will understand – you can tell her later. For now, just say – just tell them that I am not dead. Once the sun comes, I shall be safe.'

'How can you possibly know that?'

A pause. 'I don't,' said Ansaryon. 'I'm just guessing. But I do know that Ayak – Ayak doesn't like to take his favourite victims in daylight.'

'His favourite?'

'Undoubtedly.' His wry smile was clear in her mind, even if his face did not alter. 'Ayak would love to get his fangs in me. I have used his name, but I am none of his, I promise you.'

'I know you are not. I knew a long time ago.'

'Did you? You surprise me.' Once more, she felt the pressure of his fingers. 'Is the sun risen yet?'

There was a fanfare of scarlet and gold beyond the eastern window. Halthris stared at the glory of it, and let him see through her eyes. As they waited, she said, 'What about the night to come?'

'I shall be stronger then. This weakness will not last for ever. And in any case, I have my anchor, my Harper of the West, to guard me from all harm.'

She knew that he meant her, and despite her weariness felt a surge of joy. Then her down-to-earth nature reasserted itself. 'What's an anchor?'

Again, the sensation of amusement. 'I'd forgotten that you might not know. It's a device – a very heavy stone, or a piece of metal – on the end of a long rope. You throw it overboard from a boat, and it stops it moving.'

With his mind's eye, she saw one of the graceful Kefirinn ships, sleek, shallow, fast, floating on the wide sunlit stream of the river, its bright sky-blue and turquoise sail echoed in the still water beneath. A man stood in the bows, bare-legged, wearing the brief tunic of a Toktel'yan labourer. He picked up a strangely-shaped object, made of several pieces of iron with a rope attached to one end, and pushed it over the side. It sank with a splash, and the ship, which had been drifting dreamily with the current on a day almost windless, turned slowly round and stopped, tugging gently on the rope disappearing into the water.

'You see? An anchor in use. That ship is the Golden Harvest – I *sailed in her once, down to Toktel'yi. Have you ever been in a boat, Halthris of the Tanathi?'*

'Of course not. Tanathi prefer dry land, earth – we mistrust boats, and towers.'

She looked up, smiling, and saw that the sun, unseen behind the sharp spike of Mount Sargenn, had touched the distant peaks with amber and gold.

'*Sunrise.*' His voice in her mind was suddenly faint with relief and delight. Abruptly she realized the enormity of mental effort that had kept him conscious all through their silent conversation, although the effects of withdrawal from the drug had left him too weak even to open his eyes.

'*Thank you,*' he added. '*I owe you my life, Halthris of the Tanathi, worthless though it may be. You can let me go now – don't worry, it will only be sleep, I promise you.*'

'*How can you know?*' she cried, feeling him slipping away from her into emptiness.

'*I know. Trust me. I will speak to you soon . . .*'

He was gone. An irrational sense of loss, acute, agonizing, flooded her mind. She buried her head in her hands, and tried not to weep.

'Halthris?'

Her name, spoken aloud, was almost unrecognizable. She looked up and saw Kefiri staring at her in alarm. 'Halthris – what is it? Is – is he dead?'

'*It will only be sleep. I promise you.*' She turned and gazed down at Ansaryon. He had not apparently moved at all, but there was a subtle difference in his face, and the grey marks of Ayak's fangs were gone. She put a finger on the pulse-point just below the sharp line of his jaw, and felt the beat of his heart, slow, strong, reassuringly steady.

'No,' she said, letting joy displace grief at last. 'No, he is not dead.'

CHAPTER
TEN

Not dead, but hardly alive either. Mellok the Healer refused to believe it at first: then, when his own examination of the patient confirmed that, against all the odds, all the teachings, Ansaryon had survived, he became convinced that Halthris must be responsible. To his flood of eager questions, she had only one answer. 'I didn't do anything, and I didn't give him anything. I just sat beside him, and held his hand.'

But it was obvious from his awed, wondering expression that Mellok thought that she had used some kind of unknown and powerful Tanathi magic. She wanted to tell him the truth, but Ansaryon had asked her not to, and she would respect his wishes.

When it became clear that she was not needed for the moment, she called Fess, who was still lying on the bed – enjoying its comfort, she suspected, rather than from any sense of loyalty or devotion to its human occupant – and told Kefiri that she was returning to her room for a while.

Kefiri's face revealed that she, too, believed that Halthris had saved Ansaryon with hidden powers. 'Shouldn't you stay?'

Halthris shook her head. 'There's no need. He's asleep, and quite safe for the moment. You should get some sleep, too. That's what I'm going to do.'

Kefiri studied her, a frown between her strongly-marked brows. She said softly, 'You *did* do something, didn't you?'

Mellok was discussing medicines with one of the women. Halthris dropped her voice to a murmur. 'Yes. He asked me to keep him here, and I did.'

'But I didn't hear you—' Kefiri stopped suddenly, and she stared at the Tanathi woman with sudden realization. 'So *that* was it! But you don't take Annatal, do you?'

'No. I wouldn't know what it was if it appeared on my supper plate.'

'Then you must have some natural power of your own.' Kefiri chewed thoughtfully at a ragged nail. 'That's supposed to be impossible. But whatever the reason, I think you saved his life last night, and so I thank you for it, from my heart.'

'I was his anchor,' Halthris said, remembering. 'That was all.' She paused, and then added, 'He may wake, and ask for me – if he does, can you send someone to find me? Especially if it is near sunset.'

'Of course I will,' said Kefiri, and to the other girl's surprise, reached up on tiptoe and kissed her cheek. 'You are his friend, and now you are mine too. Sleep well, Halthris of the Tanathi.'

But her mind was too restless, too active to sleep. What she really needed was time alone, to think about what had happened, and ponder the implications. She wandered down the stairs of the central tower, Fess at her heels, and nearly bumped into a small boy standing at the bottom, gazing upwards. He wore the ubiquitous tunic and trousers of all Zithiriani, but they were unusually ragged and dirty. Under the veneer of grime, his lank unwashed hair was startlingly pale. He stared at Halthris in obvious bewilderment, and she smiled. 'Are you lost? That's all too easy, here. I'm going to the Tanathi quarters – what are you looking for?'

The child shook his head. His eyes, under the thick uneven fringe of hair, were surprisingly dark for such a fair colouring. She had a sudden sense of unease, as though something quite alien and unchildlike had looked out at her. He said in a whisper, 'I don't know. What's up there?'

'Lots of rooms, one above the other, in the tower. I shouldn't go up there, if I were you – the Lord Ansaryon is still sick, and mustn't be disturbed.'

A low growl interrupted her. She looked round in surprise and saw Fess staring at the child. Every hackle was raised, her tail had grown to twice its normal size, and her teeth were bared. Halthris said sharply, 'Fess! Don't be silly – he can't hurt you!'

Reluctantly, the cat slunk past the boy, still bristling, and sat down beside her partner. Halthris rubbed the top of her head reassuringly, feeling the animal's fear and hatred still seething around them both. When she looked up, the child had gone.

Abruptly, Fess's ears went up, and she glanced round at Halthris.

'It's all right, he was just a lost little boy, that's all – not some demon or sorcerer,' she said firmly. 'Come on, let's find our quarters.'

She had wanted privacy, but her suspicions proved correct. As soon as she walked through the door of the room which had been allotted to her and the other two Tanathi women, Sherren leapt up from the side of Inri's bed with a cry of delight. 'Hal! There you are at last! Inri's been wanting you—'

'Didn't Abreth say where I was?' She glanced longingly at the empty and inviting comfort of her bed in the far corner, and then turned her attention to Inri. She was sitting up, there was healthy colour in her face, and a well-cleaned plate and bowl lay on the floor beside her bed. 'I was with Ansaryon. The Lady Kefiri wanted my help, I can't think why. Anyway, it seems he's not going to die just yet, so I thought I'd come back and see how Inri is.'

'Much better, as you can see.' Sherren's young, fresh face was smiling in welcome. She wondered what he would think if he knew just what she had seen, and done, over the past day and night. 'You do look tired, though, Hal. Haven't you had much sleep?'

'Not much, no.' She grinned at Inri. 'I can see they've been feeding you properly.'

'More than I can eat, usually.' The injured girl leaned back gingerly against the heaped pillows, her green eyes shining. 'Thank you, Hal – thank you for helping to save me from the Ska'i.'

'You're my friend – of course I'd help you.' Halthris felt embarrassed, remembering, too, Kefiri's gratitude. She had only done what was asked and expected of her: there was no need, surely, for such praise. 'Anyway, Grinya did all the hard work.'

'I know – he's been telling me not to eat too much, or his poor horse won't be able to carry both of us next time.'

The door opened to admit Abreth. 'I thought I heard your voice – hello, little sister!' He embraced her heartily. 'How is Ansaryon?'

'Sleeping. It looks – it seems as though he might recover eventually – if Hegeden wills it.'

'Well, anyone hurt as badly as he was will take some time to get over it,' Abreth pointed out. 'I must say, my opinion of him has soared. I thought he was just another fragile city-dweller, certain to shrivel up and die at the first touch of hardship.'

'I thought so too,' his sister said. 'And I'm very glad we were wrong, because he certainly saved our lives on that journey.'

And last night she had saved his, so now they were equal.

'Have you eaten yet?' Abreth went on. 'Because there's plenty of our breakfast left – they're very generous with their food here – and Djekko has challenged Kettan to a game of tek. Just the two of them, no other players. Grinya's keeping the bets, and so far almost everyone has put something on Djekko.'

'And I will too – he's a master at tek.' She thought of something. 'How will they play without a carpet?'

'Chettay is drawing it out now – we asked for a big piece of that paper stuff, and some charcoal. It's not perfect, but it'll do.' Abreth's face was exuberant at the prospect. All Tanathi loved to play tek, which was a complicated game of skill and strategy, involving up to six players moving counters on a specially woven carpet of intricate design. A good contest between evenly-matched players might last several days, and there was always feverish betting on the outcome, on the final score, and even on the length of the game.

Grinya put his head round the door. 'We're ready. Hello, Hal – want to bet?'

'I'll wager a couple of bracelets on Djekko, but no more. I don't trust Kettan not to improve his game.'

'He'll need to raise it a long way to beat Djekko. Well, Inri? Can you muster the strength to come and watch?'

Soon, all eight surviving Tanathi were crammed into the small room occupied by Djekko and Grinya. The two wooden-framed beds had been pushed to one side, leaving the floor clear, and in the space lay a large rectangular piece of paper, rather longer and wider than a prone man. Chettay, working from top to bottom with her stick of charcoal, had drawn a squared and segmented spiral pattern moving inwards to the centre, which was marked by a circle. At irregular intervals the firm lines of the spiral were broken, marking the places where a contestant could cross one of his counters over to block his opponent's path. As befitted a top player, Djekko had his own hexagonal dice, a handsome object made of polished bone with inset gold dots on each face. He also had his three counters, in the form of silver cats. In contrast, Kettan had taken three of the gold talismans from his braided hair, a hawk, a snake and a bear, and laid them down on the figure of Sarraliss and her mare Chy, which always marked the start of the game, at the bottom left-hand corner.

'Please try not to smudge it,' Chettay was saying anxiously, her eyes on her handiwork. 'It's taken me since yesterday evening – oh, be *careful*, Kettan!'

'I'm being careful.' It was noticeable that Kettan was wearing hardly any jewellery: only his talismans, a couple of bracelets of almost plain gold, and a silver and amber neck-ring. He settled himself cross-legged on the floor beside the paper, and studied the pattern critically. 'It's not straight.'

'Doubt you could have done any better,' Djekko said. 'Right – who'll take the dice?'

The actual throwing was a matter much too important to be left to the players themselves, and was generally allotted to a mutually-agreed onlooker.

'Hal,' said Abreth at once.

Hastily, she declined. 'No. I'm going to get some sleep in a moment – I've been awake for most of the night.'

In the end, Chettay was chosen – Kettan having rejected Sherren because he suspected that their personal animosity might affect his judgement, and Grinya because, as the keeper of bets, he had a pecuniary interest in the result. The dice was thrown to determine the starting order, and in a hushed, absorbed silence, the game began.

By the time the players had moved their counters half way up the first arm of the spiral, it was obvious that this time luck was on Kettan's side, and that the contest would be a long one. Halthris got to her feet and slipped quietly out of the room. She would be able to snatch some privacy, even some sleep, and there looked to be no prospect of the game ending much before sunset.

Fess was lying curled on her bed, her black nose hidden beneath the fat, furry end of her long tail. She opened one baleful eye as her partner entered, and then closed it again dismissively.

'Don't worry,' Halthris said, grinning. 'I wouldn't dream of disturbing you.' She pulled off her soft leather boots and flopped down on Chettay's bed, which was the one most likely to remain unwanted for some time.

At last she was alone, safe from curious eyes and inquisitive probings. But her own mind was full of questions, and as soon as she lay down, Chettay's warm fox-fur cloak pulled over her, they rose up clamouring. How could Ansaryon speak to her, and she to him? Was it the same method which she used to communicate with Fess? What linked their minds, if not the mysterious, deadly drug whose absence had nearly killed him? *Did* she have concealed powers, as Kefiri had suggested? If so, how had he known about them? Why had he used her for his anchor, rather than his cousin Kefiri, who obviously knew him far better? What was the significance of the wolf-god of death, Ayak the Devourer, beloved of the Ska'i? And who, or what, was D'thliss, whom he had cursed in Ayak's name?

There were no answers yet, but he had promised to give her some later. For now, her eyes were closing, and sleep, blissfully welcome, was creeping up on her. She allowed herself to drift into slumber.

Fess growled. Halthris came awake with a start and sat up, the fox-fur cloak slithering like a live animal to the floor. The cat was crouched on the end of the other bed, hackles erect, glowering at a small, ashen-haired figure standing in the centre of the room.

It was the child again. He still wore that strange, bewildered look on his grubby face, and she smiled at him, despite the abruptness of her waking. All Tanathi loved children, and thoroughly indulged and cherished the young of their tribe. 'Hello,' she said gently. 'Are you still lost?'

The boy started, and looked round at her. He was perhaps seven or eight years old, and would be very attractive if it were not for the dirt on his face and clothes, and his general air of hunger and poverty. He shook his head mutely.

'Well, this is my room – I share it with Inri and Chettay. I'm Halthris, of the Tanathi tribe. All the others are next door, there's a game of tek in progress.'

The child was looking at her as if he had no idea what she was saying, although she had spoken clearly in good Zithiriani. Fess had stopped growling, but her tail twitched rhythmically, and her eyes glittered a savage yellow.

'Why don't you go and watch the game?' she suggested gently. 'I'm trying to get some sleep here, and I'd be very grateful for some peace and quiet.'

For a moment more, his deep eyes stared at her, and she was struck again with that profound sense of unease, even of despair, so that she wondered what she was doing here, why she had ever fought for Zithirian, ever tried to anchor a flawed and fading mind to light and life . . .

He nodded suddenly, and smiled. It lit up the whole of his face: his eyes danced, his cheeks dimpled, he was a little boy again. He sketched the Zithiriani salute of child to adult, knuckled hand on bowed forehead, and then turned and ran out.

'What's your name?' she said, but he had already gone.

Puzzling over it, but not for long, she reached down and pulled the fox-fur back over herself. As she snuggled into its silky warmth, Fess left the other bed and insinuated herself underneath the cloak, purring. She gave her human partner a roughly affectionate lick on her chin, and tucked herself against her side. Within a few heartbeats, they were both fast asleep.

Five times in two days, the trumpets sounded: and five times, fugitives from the captured city of Zithirian had straggled wearily across the ice and into the haven of Sar D'yenyi.

First had been Ansaryon and his strangely assorted band of Tanathi and soldiers. The other refugees were all members of the Court, or the Royal Guard; no women, no children, no ordinary citizens, for they would not know where the High Citadel was, and would be unlikely to survive the journey if they did. The fact that Ansaryon had endured it, hideously wounded and suffering from Annatal withdrawal, was a miracle in itself. His continued refusal to die aroused in his young cousin Kefiri a mixture of admiration, pride and relief. She had lost so much in this terrible disaster: Ansary's tenacious hold on life was the symbol of hope to which she clung.

There was a great deal to do, and she threw herself into organizing it all with a frantic urgency that betrayed her desperate need to keep grief at bay. There were people to feed, to tend, to find accommodation for. Messages had to be sent to the mining and quarrying settlements, far into the mountains, and also to the remoter farms in the Kefirinn valley, on the other side of Estray. Winter had come a month early, but at least they were well prepared for it: Sar D'yenyi always was. The rocky island on which the citadel stood was holed like a sea sponge with tunnels and underground storage chambers, packed with dried meat and fish, grains, honey, hay, preserved fruits and vegetables, oil, burnstones, bales of furs and cloth, spices, medicines . . . if necessary, the inhabitants could be fed, clothed and warmed for a year without running short. And being surrounded by a mountain lake, fresh pure water had always been abundant.

Still, she checked the inventories and the stores with her Chamberlain, just to make sure. After all, Tsenit knew about Sar D'yenyi, and must have guessed that many fugitives would make their way here. But did he know that Ansaryon was still alive?

If he did, then, sooner or later, the Ska'i would appear at her gate, too.

Against that day, she ordered the defences to be checked and strengthened where necessary. Up on Estray, a cave above the tree line gave a perfect view, when clouds and mist did not obscure it, of much of the trail leading to Sar D'yenyi. In past times of danger, it had been used as a look-out post, with a signalling system to warn of approaching enemies. She discussed it with Ramath, the Captain of the Guard, and ten men and their supplies were sent up there, with orders to have someone on watch like a hawk at all hours of the day, and night. But the frozen lake presented the most serious problem for the defenders: while winter remained, it would be a permanent bridge over which attackers could reach the island. She must ask Ansary what to do, when he got better.

When. That first day, after the terrors of his fever and the sorcery which had flung lightning all round his chamber, she had hardly dared believe that he lived, let alone that he might recover.

The deep sleep into which he had sunk, after Halthris's mysterious intervention, was so terrifyingly similar to the final coma which Mellok had described. But the Healer assured her that it was true slumber, and that the strength of her cousin's heart and breathing increased by the hour.

It was all the Tanathi woman's doing, Kefiri was sure. She did not quite understand how, but it was connected with the thought-link all Mazath used. She had not realized that anyone who wasn't Mazath trained and using Annatal would have the power: but Halthris evidently possessed it, although she had seemed almost as bewildered by what had happened as Kefiri was.

She liked the Tanathi woman. She would have liked her anyway, for Ansary's sake: she was ten years younger than her cousin, and had always idolized him – almost as much as she had idolized Tsenit.

She shied away from that path of thought, just as she steered her mind past images of her father, her other cousins, her uncle the King, the men and women who had peopled her childhood, all dead, horribly murdered and mutilated by savage and bloodthirsty warriors, amidst the flaming wreckage of the most beautiful city in all the known world.

So she inspected the stores, and welcomed the fugitives, and listened calmly to their harrowing stories of death and destruction and hardship. And whenever she could, she climbed the stairs to the high tower room where Ansaryon lay.

On that first day, he slept almost until dusk: the sun had already disappeared behind Estray, and there were clouds gathering ominously round Annako, in the north. It was probably snowing now, at the other end of the lake. Despite the braziers, the room felt chilly, and Kefiri tucked her hands into the loose-fitting sleeves of her mourning gown. She had three woollen shifts on underneath, and still the cold struck through. She could not remember a winter so bitter, so early, in all her seventeen years.

'Lady Kefiri!'

The voice of one of the attendants pierced her thoughts. She turned away from the window. 'What is it, Serrenni?'

'Lady – come, quick!'

She flew to the bedside. Ansaryon lay there, still flat and unmoving under the heaped covers, but his eyes were open, and he was smiling at her. She bent and kissed him, something that she would never have dared to do when he was well. Despite her adoration of him, she had always been a little frightened of her cousin.

'You have me at your mercy,' he said, barely above a whisper. 'But please don't fuss over me too much, Kef. I'm not worth it.'

'Let me be the judge of that,' she said briskly, to hide her emotions. 'How are you feeling?'

'Weak.' The smile spread slightly. 'And before you ask the inevitable question – yes, I think perhaps I could toy with a little broth.'

The women, who had licence to fuss, helped him to sit up, exclaiming in sympathy as he winced in pain. The effort left him gasping, his forehead soaked in sweat. Serrenni, giving an excellent imitation of a motherly hen, clucked and leaned over to wipe his brow. He frowned and said, without opening his eyes, 'Send them away, Kef – for the love of Tayo, send them all away!'

She stared down at his mutinous face for a moment, then sighed, shrugged and gestured. One by one, Serrenni and her assistants put down their bowls and cloths and bandages, and with aggrieved expressions filed out.

'Wonderful,' Ansaryon said. 'Now call one of them back and ask her to fetch Halthris.'

Exasperated, but also pleased because this contrariness was a good sign, she marched to the door, opened it, and recalled Serrenni.

Halthris had slept for most of the day, deeply and dreamlessly, and woke to find the game of tek still in progress, with several turns of the spiral yet to go, and Kettan, astonishingly, still in the lead.

'There's a bridge two or three throws ahead,' said Grinya as she peered down at the paper, which by now was so smudged as to be almost indecipherable. 'If Djekko gets the right number for any of his counters, he can leap across and block Kettan's leader in its tracks.'

'Unless Kettan beats him to it – he only needs a couple of lucky throws.' Halthris glanced at the bet-taker. 'I don't suppose you'd take a bracelet on my beloved cousin? Just for luck, you understand.'

'All right, but just the one – it's much too late in the game, really,' Grinya told her cheerfully. 'I should pray for Sarraliss's hand on the dice. That's strange – where's he gone?'

'Where's who gone?' She looked round the room, but all the Tanathi seemed to be present, absorbed in the game.

'The boy – fair-haired, rather dirty, eight or so. Funny, I didn't see him go, but he's been hanging round for most of the afternoon.'

'I've seen him a couple of times today. He never says anything – I think he's quite shy. But he's got a lovely smile.'

'Bit young for you, isn't he?' said Grinya teasingly.

'Don't be a fool. I don't know where he comes from. Perhaps he's another refugee – several arrived today, apparently. Certainly he stands out like a sore thumb. And he always seems lost.'

'Poor little lad,' said Grinya carelessly. 'Still, he certainly enjoyed the game. Chettay was explaining the rules to him. Does that woman want you?'

One of Ansaryon's attendants was peering round the door. As soon as she caught Halthris's eyes, she nodded and beckoned.

'I'd better go,' Halthris said. She took off an amber bracelet, one of her cheapest, and dropped it into Grinya's expectant hands. 'I always did like to hedge my bets.'

As she left the room, Djekko's crow of delight signalled that he had indeed managed to block Kettan's counter. Since overtaking an opponent was forbidden, her cousin would have to retrace his moves and find another bridge. The game looked like going on all night, and she was glad. If it took up everyone's attention, she would be free from awkward questions. They would be unlikely to understand the new bond between her and Ansaryon, so strong and secret and extraordinary, and they would undoubtedly think that she ought to be with her own people, rather than with the Prince of Zithirian, no matter how great the debt they owed him.

Ansaryon was sitting up in bed, and Kefiri was spoon-feeding him from a small blue-and-white pottery bowl, decorated with graceful flowers in the exquisite Minassan style. The sight gave her sudden and joyful hope. He had assured her that he would not die, but until she saw the smile on his face, the faint but unmistakably healthy flush of colour across his cheekbones, and the glitter of those unearthly silver eyes, she had not really believed him.

There was no one else in the room, and the woman who had escorted her was already half-way down the stairs. She caught an echo of his silent welcome, and with it an astonishingly strong sense of pleasure and delight at her appearance. 'Hello,' he said aloud. 'Have you slept?'

'Long and soundly.' She stopped by the bed, Fess at her side. 'And have you?'

'I certainly have.' He paused to swallow another mouthful of what appeared to be thin soup, although a remarkably aromatic and heartening smell was wafting with the steam from the bowl. 'And for Kefiri's sake, I think we will refrain from using thought-link.'

'I'm not a Mazath, nor do I possess any powers of my own,'

said his cousin, rather shyly, and scraped round the bowl to fill a last spoonful.

Ansaryon opened his mouth like a comically obedient fish, making Halthris smile and the younger girl giggle. When the soup was finished, he said thoughtfully, 'But you have, Halthris of the Tanathi. You must have – because you talk to Fess in thought-speech, don't you?'

'I've never thought about it until now – it just seemed to be the natural thing to do. And it isn't really *speech* – I put pictures into my head, sometimes deliberately, and at other times she knows what I want her to do almost before I've realized it myself, when we're hunting and everything happens very fast. But when – when we talked last night, that was different. The same method, but different.'

'Like using a pen to write words, instead of drawing pictures,' Ansaryon observed. His voice, though weak, was his own again, subtle, pleasant, and drily ironic. 'How many Tanathi have hunting-cats?'

'At present, I think only I have. But I've heard of others in the past. I once spoke to an old man who'd had a cat in his youth, and found that he'd used much the same way of communicating with it as I do with Fess. Whether all Tanathi have such abilities I don't know – but I don't think we can, or we'd surely use it to control our dogs and horses as well.'

'Oh, dogs and horses don't have the right minds for it,' said Ansaryon, and stretched out his hand to Fess. 'Whereas cats, being altogether superior beings, are naturally adept at thought-link.'

'Shameless flatterer,' Halthris said, smiling at the cat's look of blissful contentment as he scratched under her chin.

'The art of being a successful courtier is founded on the mastery of flattery. Which is one reason why you will never do well at the Court of Zithirian, Halthris of the Tanathi.'

'There is no Court of Zithirian,' said Kefiri, in a small bleak voice. 'There is nothing left.'

'Oh, I think you will find that there is,' Ansaryon told her grimly. 'If he is still alive – and I am certain that he is – Tsenit will have made sure that there is something left for him to rule over.'

Tsenit. The name, with all its unpleasant associations, hung in the air like a curse. Halthris glanced at Kefiri, and saw that her eyes were filling with tears. The younger girl briskly wiped her face, and said sadly, 'I know that we must talk about Tsenit. But you should be aware, Halthris, that until – until three days ago, I thought I was going to marry him.' She swallowed, and went on in a low, determined voice. 'And I also thought that I was in love with him.'

Suddenly, Halthris was filled with pity for Kefiri, whose world and illusions had been brutally shattered in a way that made her own troubles seem distant and trivial.

'You needn't feel sorry for me,' said the Lady of Sar D'yenyi, rather bitterly. 'It was my own fault. Ansary told me I'd be a fool to marry him, and I didn't listen.'

'But he deceived everyone else – certainly, I was completely taken in, I thought he was the best of a rather rotten bunch, Hegeden help me.' Halthris stared at Ansaryon, frowning thoughtfully. 'He was the most popular person in Zithirian, right up until the attack. The citizens were eating out of his hand – what will they do when they find out he betrayed them?'

'At a guess, he'll have put the blame on me,' Ansaryon told her. 'If you dug deep enough, I think you'd find all those ugly rumours about me were started, and spread, by Tsenit and his faction. I think, too, that he and his chief accomplice have been planning this for a very long time – at least two years, if not more.'

'His accomplice?' Kefiri said, her eyes wide. 'Who is that?'

'A powerful, ambitious and totally ruthless woman who goes by the name of D'thliss – and who is also the High Priestess of the Temple of Tayo.'

And whom he had cursed with Ayak's name, in his delirium. Halthris shivered, remembering those sinister, shrivelled figures in their white and gold robes who had stood outside the Temple as she rode past to deliver her warning to the King – warning of an attack which perhaps they had known about already. Had one of them been D'thliss?

'She is evil, that woman,' Kefiri said with a shudder. 'I was a pupil at the Temple School for five years – I persuaded Father to let me come home two years ago – and I hated her. Most of us did. She seemed to be able to fill you with misery and despair just by looking at you. We couldn't understand why the other priests and priestesses elected her when Maltair died – but even the nice ones seemed to be under her spell.'

'She manipulates minds,' Ansaryon said quietly. 'She manipulated mine for nearly two years, until I managed to break free of her. Then she drew Tsenit into her web, and sucked all the goodness and decency out of him. He is not a Mazath – that makes him less susceptible to her more unpleasant methods of control, but it also means that in other ways he is more vulnerable. She is very clever, she can discover your most secret weaknesses and cravings, and make use of them. He is extremely ambitious, and I think he has always wanted to be King. So she encouraged him to the point where he was willing to have his whole family slaughtered, and Zithirian sacked by barbarians, to achieve his heart's desire.'

'But if you knew the truth about him, why didn't you *say*?' Kefiri cried.

'I did say. I told you not to marry him, didn't I?' There was a touch of bitterness now in Ansaryon's quiet voice. 'But unlike D'thliss, I have no powers of prophecy or foresight. I knew he was vain, conceited, ambitious and unscrupulous, he was much too friendly with D'thliss and I didn't trust his influence over the King. But I had no idea how low he would sink. Believe me, Kef, until the Ska'i appeared on our doorstep, I thought he only wanted Sar D'yenyi, and that was why he had suggested marrying you.'

'I didn't think that . . . I really believed that he loved me.' Kefiri looked down at her bitten nails, her face flushed with shame. 'What a fool I was! I believed every word he said, I swallowed it all whole—'

'I did too, remember?' Halthris told her. 'I thought it was a great pity that he was the youngest son and not the eldest – I thought he would make a far better King than either of his brothers, or his father. When Ansaryon warned me against him, I thought he was just jealous of his popularity.'

'You're right – at first I was, when my father thought he could do no wrong, and I could do no right. Then I began to realize that Tsenit has no moral restraint – no concern at all for anything save his own sweet self. He and D'thliss make a good pair.' He glanced at Halthris. 'Do you remember when he took you up to the top of his tower at the Palace?'

'I don't imagine I'll ever forget it. I was convinced I'd fall off.'

'If I hadn't come up, and *made* you leave with me, I'm pretty sure you would have done. With a little helping push from Tsenit, of course.'

His voice was utterly serious. She stared at him in astonishment. 'You mean – Tsenit was going to *kill* me? But *why* – why would he want to do that?'

'Because of your warning about the Ska'i. I think that he and D'thliss had invited Quenait to attack Zithirian some time ago – D'thliss because she, like the Ska'i, is a devotee of Ayak, and Tsenit because he thought it would be a good way to eliminate the rest of his family without any of the blame attaching to him. Indeed, he could present himself as the brave and loyal saviour of the city, once it was all over, and announce that I was the traitor. When you arrived with your inconvenient news, he must have been very worried. True, he was the King's favourite, and he was doing his best to convince him in private that you were some ignorant barbarian woman who was making a fuss about nothing – but there was always the danger that others would take you more seriously. So he decided to push you off his tower – a sad accident, how tragic, the poor woman was not accustomed to heights and leaned over too far. And by the time your brother arrived, it would be too late.'

'Oh.' Halthris shivered, remembering her fear, her dizziness, and Tsenit's guiding hand pressing the small of her back. So her instincts had been right. She added slowly, 'But if you didn't know what your brother was planning – why did you come up to the tower?'

'I didn't *know* – but I didn't trust him, and I suspected that he might have something to do with the approach of the Ska'i – although at that stage I still had no idea of the full scope of his treachery. I thought something was odd, some instinct told me you might be in danger, so I followed you up. But I could hardly spring dramatically across the roof crying murder, not without informing Tsenit that I was suspicious of him. So I took you away from the danger in the only way I could, in the circumstances. If I was wrong, no harm was done – and if I was right, I had saved you. And as soon as I saw the fury on his face, I knew he'd planned to kill you.'

'I'm sorry,' Halthris said. 'I was furious too – I thought you were going to make me a mind-slave.'

'The Ska'i do that, apparently. I understand why you were so angry, then. I did apologize, if I remember, and promised not to invade your thoughts again, without your permission. But I couldn't tell you why I'd done it, in case your mind was "overheard". The less you knew, the better.'

'Who would "overhear" me? Tsenit?'

'No – he has no latent powers or talents in that directions, I'm certain. As a rule, only Annatal gives you such abilities – and Tsenit is much too vain of his looks and his body to damage them by taking it, whatever advantages it might confer. It also means that it is quite difficult to enter his mind. Effective thought-speech requires training in listening as well as in speaking. Those who have never practised it usually have strong natural barriers. I can pick up someone's general emotions and feelings, but I can't actually overhear thoughts, unless the other person is similarly trained, and wants me to listen. In addition, most Mazath, and priests, learn to defend themselves against coercion and manipulation. Some of them are better at it than others.'

Halthris said thoughtfully, 'Then – if you can only command people who are already thought-speakers, why did you do it to me? You couldn't have known—'

'Not for certain, no. But when you described the Ska'i to me, I found I could see them with your eyes. I suspected then that you might have latent power, although it's something that orthodox Mazaths think cannot exist – possibly because they don't like the idea that some people don't need Annatal to become thought-speakers or sorcerers. And there was Fess, too. The bond between you, as you described it, seemed to owe much to thought-linking. So in desperation I tried to command you, and it worked.'

'I'm very glad it did.' Halthris grinned at him. 'Or I'd probably now be dead. Two to one.'

Kefiri was looking at her, puzzled. She explained. 'Ansaryon has saved my life twice now. Once on the tower, and once on the journey here.'

'Twice on the journey,' he reminded her, and laughed. 'Whereas you, I fear, have only saved me once. I'll have to keep you at my side when we retake Zithirian, Halthris of the Tanathi, so that you can discharge your debt.'

When. With sudden alarm, Halthris realized that it was almost dark. But as the fear entered her mind, Ansaryon's fingers touched hers, and he smiled, and shook his head very slightly. *'Don't be afraid,'* said his voice within her mind. *'Ayak has no further dominion over me. I am no longer weak enough to be in danger from him, and the darkness holds no more peril.'*

'I don't understand Tsenit,' Kefiri was saying, in distress. 'Why couldn't he have been content with me, and Sar D'yenyi? Why did he and D'thliss have to bring in the Ska'i, and destroy so much?'

'I'm sure D'thliss suggested it. Even Tsenit's ruthlessness, on its own, couldn't have stretched that far. But she wants to rule Zithirian. My father was old and senile, and according to his Healers had only a few months left to live. Cathallon was a slobbering wreck, likely to drink himself to death within a couple of years. D'thliss takes Annatal, of course, so she can expect to live until she's at least a hundred – and she's only fifty now. She wants power for life. She tried to use me, and in the end she failed – because I was a Mazath, and could resist her, not because I was stronger than my brother, or morally superior. So she turned to Tsenit, and corrupted him instead, feeding his ambition. He is under her control and her spell. She will install him as the figurehead of her rule, and do as she likes through him. So far, almost everything has gone according to her plan, I suspect. If we have any more news from Zithirian, I think you'll find that Tsenit has been proclaimed King amid popular relief and rejoicing, the Ska'i have obligingly gone back to their homeland, and most of the city is surprisingly undamaged and rapidly returning to normal. All as she wished, save for one thing – I am still alive.'

The silence was long and deep. The limited light from the two wall-hung lamps made a small, brave defiance against the darkness outside the windows, where it was snowing once more.

'But if they realize you're here . . .' Kefiri said at last.

'Yes, it hardly seems logical that I would try to seize the throne and then run away, does it? But D'thliss is quite capable of concocting some story to explain my unexpected survival. And also quite capable of sending an army up here to finish me off – and all the other fugitives as well.'

'Sar D'yenyi has never been taken,' Kefiri said proudly. 'Nor will it be, if I have anything to do with it.'

'But D'thliss is a sorcerer—' Halthris broke off, and added, 'And you are too, of course.'

Another silence, taut with significance. Then Ansaryon said softly, grimly, 'Only when I was taking Annatal. Now, I think you'll find I have no powers left.'

Kefiri stared at him in surprise. 'But you can still thought-link with Halthris, can't you?'

'Yes. And we've already established that it's an ability which doesn't necessarily depend on Annatal. If D'thliss discovers I am here, she will also know that my powers have gone. And with the ice making it easy to reach the citadel, and lacking my sorcery to defend you, Sar D'yenyi stands in mortal danger.'

Halthris felt fear clench her stomach. Kefiri put her hands to her mouth, her expression suddenly full of despair. And Ansaryon's face, in the shadowy light, was a bleak, immobile mask.

CHAPTER
ELEVEN

Most of the Royal Palace of Zithirian was a blackened, smoking ruin, restored to a peculiarly melancholy and deceptive beauty by the snow heaped upon charred stone and broken beams. No one approached it, although it would have been quite possible to evade the few guards, and pick over the debris for anything worth looting: jewellery, weapons, anything of value that the fire or the Ska'i, expert plunderers, might have missed. But the surviving citizens were too terrified and shocked to do anything but skulk in their homes. The streets were deserted, even during the hour at midday when the curfew was lifted, and the few who dared to emerge did so only because they were desperate for food or water.

The first and overwhelming emotion for everyone, after the hideous night of the Ska'i attack, had been relief, that the bulk of the city seemed, miraculously, to have escaped the destruction and slaughter that had taken place at the Palace. Men counted themselves fortunate that they had been spared duty on the walls that night, without pausing to wonder why that had been so, and huddled in their houses, polishing makeshift weapons, barricading doors and windows, keeping warm with their wives and children and waiting in terror for the Ska'i to break in past their pathetic defences and massacre them all.

All that first day they waited. In the Embroiderers' Quarter, in the north-western segment of the city, Kaydi Gandar's Widow wished, for the first time in two years since her late and unlamented spouse had died, that she could have him back, for two teenage sons and one lame servant would be useless against any attack. She suspected that any man short of a full-powered sorcerer would be useless, but it would certainly make her feel better to have pompous, arrogant Gandar bear the brunt of the barbarian axes, while she and the boys and Shilda hid down the well.

But the Ska'i did not come. All day it snowed heavily, and the smoke from the burning Palace hung over the city, the nauseating stink of charred corpses infiltrating every cranny of her fresh, spotless house. In the afternoon her younger son, Herris, who was thirteen and recklessly irresponsible, climbed up onto the roof when she wasn't looking, and returned to report that the shouting and screaming had more or less stopped, that the whole Palace seemed to be still ablaze, but that, amazingly, the city itself was apparently undamaged. Nor were there any Ska'i to be seen.

She cuffed him furiously but he dodged all but the first blow, grinning at his own successful daring until she had to grin back. Herris was such a problem, and yet so likeable that she could never be angry with him for long. Her elder boy, Thobin, was a different matter: quiet, diligent, hardworking, he had her talent for embroidery, and she would pass the business on to him. She was not sure what lay in the future for Herris, out at all hours, untidy, wicked, uncontrollable. He would probably end up as a pickpocket.

Then the hammering and shouting had begun at the door. In a panic that she laughed now to recall, she and Thobin were half-way down the well before Shilda managed to convince them that it was only old Djembeth from across the way. As the Snowbringer Street representative at the Quarter Hall, the administrative centre for their part of the city, he had the duty of passing on news.

And astonishingly, the news was good – good for ordinary citizens, anyway. Their lives and property were to be spared, but they must stay in their houses on pain of death, unless during the hour when curfew was lifted, at midday. Contrary to popular belief, the Ska'i were not a pack of bloodthirsty savages, but would show mercy to anyone not connected with the Court or the Royal Family.

'And what has happened to them?' Kaydi asked, with curiosity but not much regret: the King of Zithirian and his family, with one exception, were not universally beloved.

'They're all dead except the Lord Tsenit, Tayo preserve him!' said Djembeth. He cackled gleefully. 'Tsenit will soon sort those Ska'i out and send them packing, you'll see, Gandar's Widow. I'll shed no tears for the rest. Reckon it all turned out well after all, eh? We're shot of that useless Varathand and his drunkard heir and the evil sorcerer and the half-wit girl – and got the only good one of the bunch for our King. If that Ska'i chief happens along this street, I'll kiss his boots for him!'

'I'll hold you to that, Djembeth,' said Kaydi. She had never cared much for the old windbag – any friend of Gandar's was no friend of hers. 'But what's happening? Are the Ska'i going or staying?'

'Don't know,' Djembeth said dismissively, as if it were a matter of small importance. 'Tsenit will be King, and that's all that matters. A strong ruler for Zithirian at last!'

'It's all worked out very conveniently for him, hasn't it,' Kaydi said waspishly. 'How kind of the Ska'i, to save him the job of wiping out all his family. How much d'you reckon he paid them? A licence to plunder the Royal Palace for three days?'

A look of shocked horror quivered over Djembeth's seamed, plump face. 'Gandar's widow! That is a disgraceful slander! You shouldn't even think such things, let alone say them – even to an old friend.'

She was wet and slimy from the well, she had scraped some skin off her right thumb and probably wouldn't be able to sew anything for days, and her patience with him, with the Ska'i, and above all with any of the Children of Tayo, dead or alive, had finally expired. 'Oh, bugger off, you fawning old fool,' said Kaydi Gandar's Widow, and shut the door in his face.

Later, of course, she acknowledged that she might have made a mistake. In the petty world of Quarter politics, Djembeth wielded real influence, fawning old fool or not. If the miracle happened and Zithirian returned, somehow, to something resembling normality, he could make life very difficult for her out of pure spite. Road repairs could be sited to block her door and discourage her customers, her market licence would probably be in danger, and it might prove impossible to find anyone to take Herris on as an apprentice.

Of course, it might prove impossible anyway. Her younger son already possessed a small but growing notoriety, and it would be a brave craftsman, or woman, who let him into their workshop and undertook his training.

But at least Djembeth had told them that they were safe – for the moment, at least. And despite her cynical words to the old man, she too could see that this terrible invasion might indeed be a blessing in disguise, if it had swept away all the rotten, decadent members of the Royal Family and left only Tsenit, young, able, and popular. He would get rid of the Ska'i, rebuild the Palace, and found a new and stronger dynasty.

Not unnaturally, Djembeth thereafter avoided Kaydi's door, and so Herris, with glee, became their source of news. Their house, although self-contained around its courtyard and well, was one of a small block of seven, and it was not difficult for a young and agile boy to climb onto the roof, negotiate the steep snow-covered tiles, and speak to those in the other houses, without breaking the curfew. At first, Kaydi worried for him: scampering across the ridges and gutters, she feared he would fall or, worse, present an excellent target for some Ska'i archer. But as the days crept by, and

Herris's snippets of gossip became more and more interesting and valuable, she relaxed.

From him she learned that the Ska'i had withdrawn from the city, and were now camped outside the walls. Tsenit was apparently negotiating for their departure, and this was not the sign of weakness that it might appear, for the tribesmen's numbers seemed so overwhelming that, surely, they could have taken the whole city and slaughtered its inhabitants with little trouble and fewer qualms.

So for five days they existed snugly in their warm, cosy little house: a workroom, a kitchen with hearth and oven, where they all tended to congregate in idle moments, a storeroom off the kitchen, and three small bedrooms along two sides of the tiny courtyard, where she, her two sons and Shilda slept. A prudent and thrifty housewife, Kaydi had already stocked up for the winter, so its unprecedentedly early arrival had not caught her with bare shelves and empty jars and barrels, unlike many others. They had the well, a heap of black burnstones in a lidded stone locker in the courtyard, and flour, dried meat, honey, grains and wine and gellin, in sufficient quantity to last until spring. She had no intention of venturing out, even in the hour between curfews, until she was sure it was safe.

And then, shattering all their tentative hopes, the Ska'i came.

Six of them, to be precise, with a young and plainly terrified soldier of the Royal Guard to gain admittance. If it had not been for the reassuring sight of his familiar fishscale armour and steel helmet, she would never have opened the door. And once the bolt had been drawn back and the bars lifted, the tribesmen pushed past her and into the narrow passage that led to the courtyard. They were small, squat and stank of rancid fat and ferocity. Kaydi, who had been toughened by her difficult marriage and was not the sort to scare easily, found herself sick and dizzy with revulsion and fear.

'They want food,' said the young soldier hastily. 'You'd better give them what they're after. Then they'll go.'

'And come back tomorrow, and the next day, and the next, until we all starve?'

'No – not at all – it's all been agreed with the King,' the boy gabbled. 'Snowbringer Street contributes today, Vine Row tomorrow – everyone will take their turn. It's all been arranged fairly, so the burden is shared.'

'So when are they going?' demanded Kaydi, anger defeating fright. 'This year? Next year? Sometime? Never, I bct.'

'Please – *please*, Gandar's Widow, don't make it worse for

yourself,' the young soldier hissed urgently. 'Don't give them any excuse to – to—'

'It's all right, I won't,' said Kaydi, who had observed the wickedly sharp double axes at each Ska'i belt. 'I just hope they won't be too greedy, that's all.'

She marched through into the kitchen. The Ska'i followed her, their eyes darting eagerly about, as if noting her possessions for future reference. Hers was not a rich household, but it was comfortable. She had a good set of copper plates and bowls displayed on a shelf, some very old and beautiful pieces of Minassan pottery which she loved, and which were surely no possible use to the Ska'i, and a few pieces of jewellery which had belonged to her own mother, or to Gandar's. The money, the gold and silver bars and rods and coins of Zithirian currency, was buried under a loose stone in the corner of her bedroom, and only she knew where it was. She resolved to put the jewellery there too, as soon as the Ska'i had gone.

She flung open the storeroom door with sarcastic ceremony, and the tribesmen thrust past her in a reek of unwashed bodies and badly-cured leather. They certainly knew what they wanted: she watched angrily as a tall jar of best Hailyan wine, a barrel of dried meat and a dozen pots of honey were carried past her, through the kitchen and out into the street. Thobin, his face pale, stood by the hearth, with Shilda beside him. Herris was nowhere to be seen, and she hoped that if he was up to no good, he would have the sense not to let the Ska'i catch him doing it.

He was on the roof. As soon as the men had gone, he dropped down into the courtyard, his sleeveless leather over-tunic damp with melted snow. 'They've got a *huge* cart and it's full of things already, and they're going to every house in the street.'

'Well, they have to feed their army somehow, I suppose,' Kaydi said. 'At least they didn't take very much from us.'

'Not this time,' said Thobin anxiously. 'But they're bound to come back. There are thousands of them – they can't live on snow and plunder.'

And there were still three turns of the moon till Sundim, the dark of the year, and two turns beyond it at least, until the start of any thaw. Kaydi forced her thoughts away from the paths of doom, and spoke briskly. 'Well, there's broth in the pot and herb bread warming in the ashes. Shall we all go and eat?'

It was a subdued meal. Even Herris did not seem inclined to indulge in his normal chatter, and Thobin, still pale with fear, barely touched his food. At the best of times, Shilda was a taciturn, brooding man, and today had completely given up any attempt at communication. Looking at his surly, unshaven face, Kaydi wondered why she had ever agreed to take him on. But he was a good worker, within his limits, he was her distant cousin, and she felt sorry for him. It was not his fault that a childhood fall had left him lame and unfit for any work heavier than light household duties.

'Ma,' said Herris, interrupting her thoughts. 'Ma, when the soldier was knocking on our door, he said, "By order of King Tsenit, Third of His Name". *Is* he King, then?'

'Well, if all the rest of his family are dead, I suppose he must be – although he hasn't been Chosen or Crowned yet, has he?'

'I think I'd have heard about it if he had been,' Herris pointed out with a grin. 'So, if he's King, why is he helping the Ska'i? Why doesn't he tell them to bugger off?'

'Herris! Watch your language, or you'll feel my hand!'

'But you said it to Djembeth,' her son reminded her slyly. 'Anyway, I'm almost grown, I can say what I like. Why doesn't he get rid of them?'

'Perhaps he can't. There are rather a lot of them, after all. And I don't suppose there are many soldiers left.'

'Yes, there are. Kenmet Rigan's Son has been out to get water, and he told me there are still soldiers everywhere. On the ramparts, at the gates, guarding the Temple, guarding the Palace, what's left of it, patrolling the streets – everywhere. And the Ska'i are all camped in the fair field. Kenmet said you can smell them from the walls.'

'Kenmet? Not you?'

'Ma! I haven't been in the streets at all – I've stayed on the roofs.' His rather thin, large-eyed face assumed its most innocent expression. 'Honest I have, Ma. But even if I *did* go out during the curfew, the chances are I wouldn't get caught – I can run much faster than any soldier.'

'I don't care – you don't go outside without my say-so, whether the curfew's been lifted or not. Understand, Herris?'

'Yes, Ma,' said her younger son, looking down at his bowl, the perfect picture of docile obedience.

It was just as well that Kaydi didn't see him a few hours later. Night had come with the swiftness of winter, and it was snowing heavily. She had made the mistake of assuming that he was in the room he shared with Thobin, playing some quiet game with his brother, and welcomed some privacy in which to hide her jewellery, and some of the more precious silks, trimmings and fabrics from the workroom: cloth of silver, amber and turquoise beads, gold thread.

Herris, with a delicious sense of adventure, shinned up the trumpet vine that grew along the side of the courtyard, scrambled over the roof, and after a cautious inspection, dropped unseen into the empty street. Most householders were too frightened to light the lamps outside their doors, and in this snowstorm, with darkness all around, he felt quite safe. And even if patrolling soldiers did see him, he knew every alleyway, every passage, every twist and turn of the labyrinthine Embroiderers' Quarter. They would never catch him.

As arranged earlier in the day, he met up with Kenmet, a small, pale, red-haired boy with even more daring than Herris, although his wits were not as sharp. They grinned at each other through the whirling snow-flakes, and then slipped like disreputable ghosts through the deserted lanes of Zithirian, looking for excitement.

In her secret chamber under the great central Worship Hall of the Temple of Tayo, the High Priestess, D'thliss, was attempting to calm the fears of her protégé, the new but as yet unCrowned King of Zithirian.

Tsenit hated this place. He was a man who appreciated fresh air, exercise, open spaces. Every time he entered this foetid, stinking lair, full of reeking and nameless objects and presided over by a wolf's head reverently set about with tallow candles, made from the fat of he dared not guess what creature, the bile rose in his throat. But there was nowhere else they could meet in secret, and he owed D'thliss everything. So he swallowed his revulsion, and sat gingerly in the dilapidated chair with his legs carelessly crossed, attempting to give an impression of casual nonchalance.

D'thliss, who was, like all Tayan priests, a skilled sorcerer and addicted to Annatal, was well aware of Tsenit's feelings, and revelled in them. So she frightened the fool, did she? So much the better. He had been eating out of her hand for years, he had eagerly swallowed the poisonous lies she had whispered in his ear, and to achieve his ambitions he had agreed to the wholesale slaughter of his own father, uncle, brothers and sister, not to mention the entire Court: Ministers, officials, aristocrats, servants, the lot. Now, with their ultimate prize almost secure within their grasp, was not the time to have doubts.

'I don't like the thought of it,' said Tsenit, frowning petulantly.

'They ought to be given a decent burial. Can't Quenait send the heads back?'

'You forget. They are battle trophies, sacred to Ayak. It would be a grave insult to take them away from the warriors who have earned them.' D'thliss smiled at him, knowing full well the effect the sheer evil of her expression would have. 'If you bury your father and your brother and sister in wooden coffins, as is the custom, no one's going to notice if they've got heads or not.'

'I still don't like the idea of my father's head on a Ska'i lance—'

'You weren't so fussy six days ago,' D'thliss observed maliciously. 'You said you couldn't wait to see him grinning from a spike.'

Tsenit shifted uncomfortably on his chair. 'And another thing. Ansaryon's body hasn't been found yet, has it?'

'Ah.' D'thliss glanced at him assessingly. 'I was wondering when you'd realize that.'

Her protégé leapt up and glared at her. 'You mean you *knew*?'

'Of course I knew. I make it my business to know everything.'

'But why didn't you *tell* me?' Tsenit's voice cracked with anger.

'I didn't think it necessary. Now sit down and listen.'

Reluctantly, the King-Apparent of Zithirian fumbled for his seat and obeyed, never taking his eyes off her. 'Is – is he still alive?'

'He may be.'

'I thought you said you knew everything.'

'*Almost* everything. Certainly he was alive last night.'

'Last *night*? Then – then he didn't die in the attack!'

'How astute of you,' D'thliss said, with unpleasant sarcasm. 'No – unfortunately, he survived it. Not because of Ska'i incompetence, I can assure you. As ordered, they killed Varathand, Cathallon, Zathti and Tayma, but your dear brother managed to escape with the help of those thrice-cursed Tanathi – may Ayak devour their souls!'

The candles around the wolf's head shivered suddenly. Tsenit, the goose-flesh stark on his skin, surreptitiously made the warding sign. He said angrily, 'Where is he, for Tayo's sake?'

'Where do you think? Sar D'yenyi, of course.'

'Then I'll send the Ska'i after them. The lake will be frozen – that place isn't impregnable, you know, whatever the stories.'

'Quenait refuses.'

Tsenit stared at her in disbelief. 'You mean – you've already discussed it with him? Before you even *told* me that my brother's still alive? How dare you! Who's King here, eh? Me, me, *me* – not some dried-up witch of a priestess with a mangy wolf-head in her lair!'

He would have said more, but D'thliss had risen to her feet. The accelerated ageing process inflicted by Annatal had shrunk her bones and shrivelled her skin, but in the light of Ayak's candles she was still a menacing figure. Her many shadows flickered behind her, looming vast and evil over the crowded walls. Tsenit, rigid with sudden horror, stared up at her, the words drying in his throat.

'If you insult Ayak again, you will die for it,' D'thliss whispered. 'Slowly, horribly, painfully. Understand me, *boy*? You are nothing, *nothing* without me. Where would you be if I hadn't taken an interest in you? You'd never have set your sights beyond Sar D'yenyi and that immature little virgin you'd have to marry to get it. You owe me *everything*, and don't you forget it. I've made you King, and believe me, I'll bring you down to dust with a snap of my fingers if you so much as step out of line. Understand?'

Too terrified to speak, he nodded frantically.

'Good. I'm glad you see sense. Now, we have a good deal still to discuss.' D'thliss sat down again, smiling maliciously. 'What, for instance, we do about Ansaryon.'

'He has to be killed,' Tsenit said, his voice a thin and feeble travesty of his normally hearty tones. 'By the law of Zithirian, he is now King, not me.'

'True. But laws can be changed, after all. The succession can be altered in your favour – especially if the citizens believe that it was Ansaryon who betrayed them to the Ska'i.'

Tsenit's mind, never extraordinarily quick, was beginning to work again. 'But that doesn't make sense. He wouldn't arrange the attack and have his whole family killed to become King, and then run off to Sar D'yenyi leaving it all to me.'

A smile stretched D'thliss's face, pleating the deep folds of dry skin around her thin mouth. 'Oh, I think you'll find they will believe it. They love you, after all, and they hate and fear Ansaryon. You can tell the story yourself – how you caught him in the act of slaughtering your father and your uncle, with the help of those treacherous Tanathi, and managed to chase them out of the city. It'll make a fine heroic tale for the bards – if there are any left, of course. I told Quenait to kill every man and woman in the Palace, and he's very thorough. His warriors have eight hundred and forty-three fresh heads on their lances. You have the luxury of constructing your government and your Court, as well as your Palace, from scratch. Don't look so squeamish, boy. I can't abide futile regrets. What's done is done, and no going back. You're committed now.

The throne is yours – your brother poses no threat to you. Forget about him, and take it!'

'Tsenit stared at her unhappily. 'He's no fool – and he's not a coward, either, despite all the rumours we've been spreading. I can't see him sitting meekly in Sar D'yenyi for the rest of his life, content to let me have what should be his. And anyway, I can't afford to let him. Sar D'yenyi controls the mines in the mountains. Without gold and silver, Zithirian's worth *nothing*.'

'So, you wait. Quenait only refused to attack the citadel *now*. His warriors are weary, and in any case they've got enough food and plunder to keep them happy till Sundim. In these blizzards, they won't move.'

'Can't you control the weather?'

'I brought winter early, true, but it's out of my hands now. The sun is still quite high. If I stop the snowfall, it will melt what's already fallen – and the ice as well. No chance of taking the citadel then, for a couple of months probably. It's a shame that Quenait isn't as amenable as I'd hoped. However, you can be sure that sooner or later he'll be happy to attack Sar D'yenyi, as soon as it's practicable. After all, he'll have every incentive. I've promised him a share of the gold.'

'You *what*? You had no right—'

'I have every right. You are King of Zithirian, Tsenit, by my agency and my permission. I thought I'd already made that clear. Do as I say, and you'll have a long and happy reign, and you and the city – and the Temple – will flourish. With luck, you'll marry some pretty and insipid Princess who'll give you an heir, to be trained under my close supervision.' She smiled as she contemplated this glowing view of the future. 'But I'm afraid you will never be rid of me, young man – never. We are bound together, like it or not – we will rise together, and if you turn against me, I'll make sure we fall together. Understand?'

'Yes, High Priestess,' Tsenit muttered, like a naughty school-boy, and in his blue eyes and open, likeable face, there was the final acknowledgement of defeat.

She smiled again, almost with warmth. 'Good boy. You may go now. Have it announced throughout the city that the coronation will take place in three days' time. The curfew can be lifted after that, too.'

'Very well.' Tsenit, his expression already full of the relief he could not hide, was edging towards the door. He paused, his fingers on the handle, and said slowly, '*How* do you know that Ansaryon is still alive?'

'I know.' D'thliss gestured imperiously at him. 'But my methods are not for you to learn. Go – you must be dying to breathe fresh air.'

She cackled as the discomfited young man hurried from the room. Stupid boy! But so very fit for her purpose. Her only regret was that she had wasted so much valuable time trying to corrupt Ansaryon first. She had been so sure that he would readily fall into her web, that the restive, rebellious mind that had led him to become a Mazath would also persuade him to betray his family. Too late, she had discovered that he still retained some unsuspected moral sense: and his Mazath training had helped him to break free of her domination. She wished now that she had had him killed years ago, but his death might have thrown suspicion on her, however carefully she planned it. In any case, what he had done while still under her influence had been so despicable that he would never dare to denounce her, for fear that she might reveal the dreadful crimes that he had committed.

Like Tsenit, he was still bound to her: his guilt ensured his silence. But even so, he was dangerous. Tsenit for once was right: his brother could not be allowed to sit unmolested at Sar D'yenyi, a focus for discontent, opposition and rebellion, and, worse, diverting the rich fruits of the mines away from Zithirian.

When the time was ripe, Quenait would deal with him. And meanwhile, she could watch almost every move he made, from a distance of a hundred miles, and without leaving the Temple.

She smiled again, and sent her mind in search of the one she wanted.

After the closed, claustrophobic lanes and streets, Zithirian's docks seemed alarmingly exposed. The wind, blowing from the north, swept along the quaysides and between the low, squat warehouse buildings, piling drifts against walls and doors. Some of these were hanging off their hinges, and Herris knew that behind them the cavernous spaces would be looted and empty. Over there, on the other side of the dock, one row had been burned out completely.

'Let's go in there,' Kenmet whispered, pointing at the nearest gaping entrance. 'See what we can find.'

There were times when his friend's rashness made even Herris uneasy. He shivered inside his layers of wool, fleece and leather. 'Not likely! There might be bodies, or soldiers lying in wait, or – or *anything*!'

'Coward!' Kenmet jeered derisively. 'Coward, coward! *I'm* going in, even if you haven't got the guts.'

As he had intended, this taunt had the desired effect. Herris drew himself up indignantly. 'Course I'm not scared. But it'll be much darker in there than it is out here. How will we see?'

'I've brought a candle.' Proudly, Kenmet unbuttoned his tunic and pulled out a rather soft-looking stub of tallow. He straightened the wick and grinned at Herris. 'See? I always come prepared.'

Together, they slunk along the quay, keeping close to the buildings. There were four warehouses in this row, facing onto the arm of the dock, and all seemed still sealed and intact except the one at the end.

'Pity we can't break into them,' Kenmet whispered, nodding at the barred doors. 'Think of the riches inside!'

'Gold and diamonds!'

'Jewels and silver!'

'Spices and potions from distant lands!' Herris declaimed poetically. 'Silk from Kerenth, land of beautiful women—'

' – furs and figs and raisins—'

' – wine, grain, honey—'

' – sugar loaves and kuldi—'

'And fabulous finery from fantastic far-flung fields!'

Giggling and hushing each other, they came to the yawning door. Some belated sense of caution overcame them as they peered into the looted warehouse.

Nothing moved, nothing was visible: they hovered on the edge of a vast chasm of darkness that might hold any horror. Herris could hardly see Kenmet's face, but he sensed his friend's fear. Perhaps they wouldn't go in after all.

Just as relief began to creep up on him, the other boy grabbed his sleeve, and pulled him through the doorway.

Kenmet immediately knelt down just inside, out of the wind, and began to struggle with flint and firestick. Light flared suddenly, dazzling Herris despite the smallness of the flame. Blinking, he watched as his friend carefully lit the candle, his fingers wrapped in cloth to stop the hot melted fat burning his skin. Then Kenmet rose to his feet and lifted up his hand.

Such a limited light was almost worse than none at all. They could see for a little way around them, but the rest of the huge space was plunged into absolute gloom. Herris looked down, and saw a length of torn and spoilt cloth a few feet away. Beyond it, broken boxes, scattered shards of pottery, and a dark sticky puddle that could have been wine, or blood, gave mute but eloquent testimony to the violence of the looters, whether Ska'i or Zithiriani.

'Come on!' Kenmet was tugging at his sleeve again. Reluctantly, but with a certain delicious and fascinating sense of danger, Herris followed him towards the centre of the warehouse.

Every so often, they paused to examine the debris, and found several items overlooked by the looters. There were some lovely beads like flowers imprisoned in glass, in shades of turquoise and sky blue, amethyst and purple; an ivory carving of Toktel'yan workmanship, representing a peculiar beast with a humped back, a long neck and a very disagreeable expression; a crushed and dirty bag full of peppercorns, worth several silver bars; a delicate filigree gold brooch, stamped on and twisted out of shape; a bundle of exotic coloured feathers, some still intact; and several fragments of beautifully embroidered cloth, intended for export to Minassa or Toktel'yi or the far-off, fabled islands of the Archipelago.

But there were no bodies: not visible ones, anyway. Now convinced that nothing unpleasant lurked in the looted warehouse, even Herris grew more confident, and picked over the remains of what had once been some unfortunate merchant's wealth with a bold and increasingly discriminating hand. No to the trampled furs, muddy and ruined, that would have been worth a fortune in pristine condition; no to the chipped or broken pieces of Minassan pottery. Strangely enough, the beads were the only things he really wanted: his mother would love them. The rest he kept because Kenmet was also busy scavenging, and would have them if he didn't.

They were so engrossed, despite the dark, and the eeriness of this abandoned place, and the bitter, bitter cold, that they did not hear anything until a brighter light flared suddenly, and a voice yelled echoingly across the length of the building. 'Stop! You there, stop, or be shot!'

Soldiers. They were gathered in the entrance, blocking their escape. In one terrified glance, Herris saw their crowded shapes, the plumes of the officer, the brilliance of the lantern lifted up on a pole, and knew that they were doomed.

There had been ral in the warehouse: the acrid scent of the spirit had lingered in his nostrils for some time. The heap of ruined silks just beside them was soaked in it. Herris snatched the candle from Kenmet's hand and dropped it onto the pile. Flames leapt up violently. One of the soldiers yelled, and the two boys ran.

There was a window at the back of the building, small and high. 'They won't see us yet, not with that fire between us and them,' Herris gasped. 'Come on, Kenmet – this is our only chance!'

The glass and shuttering were broken: presumably the looters had got in this way. The sill was just in reach of his fingertips. He jumped, clung, and dropped back, cursing. Kenmet yelled something: the burning silk would not hide them much longer. Herris gritted his teeth and leapt again. This time, he managed a better hold, and could grab part of the frame to pull himself up. Once on the sill, he turned and stretched a hand down for Kenmet.

His friend was much smaller and lighter, though there was only a month's difference between them. It was quite easy to haul him up, but as Kenmet scrambled onto the narrow sill, Herris overbalanced. With a cry of dismay, he fell backwards into the night, the other boy on top of him.

If it had not been for the snow, they would certainly both have been hurt: the window was a man's height above stone paving. But there was a thick soft drift below to break their fall, and all Herris suffered was the pain and indignity of Kenmet's elbow in his eye. But there was no time to linger: already, shouts indicated that the soldiers had realized their escape. Muffled in frozen snow like frost giants, the two boys struggled out of the drift and ran for their lives.

Herris had no idea where they were going. He knew only that there was a stitch in his side, that the soldiers, being bigger and stronger, were gaining on them, and that he wanted desperately to be home, safe and warm and secure with his mother and brother. They dodged down an alleyway between two large merchants' houses, crossed a broad avenue that must be the Ceremonial Way leading up to the burnt-out Palace, and plunged into the wide and salubrious streets of the Goldsmiths' Quarter.

Behind him, Kenmet was gasping. Herris risked a glance back and saw his friend stumbling erratically through the snow, mouth open, arms flailing. And at the end of the street, a couple of soldiers suddenly appeared. One shouted: the other nocked arrow to bowstring.

There was an alleyway, a tiny narrow passage between two high walls. Something made him grab Kenmet's hand and pull him down it, ignorant of where it might lead, knowing only that it offered some chance of safety.

'Here! In here!'

Hands clutched at him: he tried to fight them off, and a boy's voice hissed furiously, 'Leave it, you idiot, we're trying to *help* you!'

He was pulled along an even narrower lane, the walls on either side so close he could have touched them both. Kenmet was running behind, wheezing: too late, Herris remembered that the other boy had some disease of the lungs that afflicted him whenever he did anything too strenuous or stressful.

'Here – down under here, and keep quiet!'

It was a bush, snow-laden. Too frightened and bewildered to argue, he dived beneath the branches. Kenmet almost fell in beside him, and crouched down like a hunted animal, struggling to control his gasping breaths. Footprints, Herris thought, in sudden panic. It's almost stopped snowing, we must have left a trail that a blind man could follow – they'll be here right away, they'll find us, they'll kill us—

He peered frantically through the burdened branches, and saw only pristine, untouched snow.

'They've gone past,' said the boy who had rescued him.

In the sudden pause, he heard Kenmet's ragged breathing and, more distantly, the shouts and running feet of the pursuing soldiers, dwindling away into nothing.

Herris drew a deep, shaky breath. 'Thanks,' he said. 'I'm sorry I fought you – I didn't think—'

'That's all right.' The other boy was almost invisible in the darkness, but Herris thought he saw him smile. 'I'm Lelya, and this is Bron.'

Until now, he hadn't realized that there were two of them. He could see nothing of the other child except the glimmer of pale hair. 'I'm Herris,' he said. 'And my friend Kenmet. We're from Snowbringer Street, in the Embroiderers' Quarter. Where do you live?'

'The Temple,' said Lelya.

The Temple. Home of priests, of sorcery, and of a deeply unpopular religion. Herris swallowed. 'Then – I think perhaps we'll be going.'

'Don't be stupid,' Lelya said sharply. 'We may live there, but we're not part of it. We wouldn't be out here during curfew if we were. We hate the Ska'i as much as you do.'

'But – if you live there – are you at school there?' Only the wealthy sent their sons and daughters to be educated by Tayo's Priests, and Lelya's speech, full of quick idiom and slang, was not that of some pampered rich child.

'Not likely. My grandmother's one of the Priests. But she lets us do more or less what we like – most of the time, she doesn't care what we get up to. Bron's my foster-brother. We often come out at night – especially now.'

'We were in one of the warehouses,' Herris told him. 'We found some oddments – beads, carvings, that sort of thing.'

'I don't think the looters have left very much behind,' Lelya said.

Kenmet coughed suddenly, and Herris put his hand over his friend's mouth. 'Shush, or they'll hear us!'

'No, they won't.' The other boy, Bron, spoke for the first time. From the sound of his voice, he was much younger than Lelya. 'They're a long way off – nearly as far as the riverside.'

Herris felt the back of his neck prickle. 'How do you know?'

'I know,' said Bron, with utter and simple certainty.

This cold, cramped position was distinctly uncomfortable, and Kenmet was obviously in some distress: besides, Herris was suddenly becoming very uneasy. How *did* the boy called Bron know where the soldiers were? And why had they all left no betraying footprints?

He looked out again. The smooth white snow, glimmering in the darkness, showed no sign that anyone had ever run across it to the bush.

And yet all four of them had.

The Temple. Lelya and Bron lived in the Temple, festering with sorcery, the only place in Zithirian where it was allowed. The very thought made Herris want to run away. He touched Kenmet's shoulder reassuringly. 'I ought to take him home – he isn't well. But I don't know where we are.'

'We're in one of the public gardens,' Lelya told him. 'The one on Antelope Street – do you know it? Take first left, second left, first right, and you come to Sargenn Avenue. Know where to go after that?'

'Of course I do,' Herris said impatiently. He was now desperate to leave the disturbing company of two children who might or might not be apprentice sorcerers, and who at any moment could change him and Kenmet into something unpleasant. He ducked his head and crawled out from under the bush, shaking a lot of icy snow down the back of his neck in the process. 'Come on, Kenmet, let's go!'

The bush heaved again, losing most of its load, and the three other boys emerged. Herris glanced covertly at Lelya. About his own age and height, thin, dark: no more detail was visible, and he didn't even know if he would recognize him again. In contrast, Bron had hair of ashen pallor, and was probably seven or eight. Apart, the two Temple boys would be safely anonymous: together, they were distinctive.

And definitely to be avoided. Herris took Kenmet's hand: he

was shivering and trying not to cough, all his earlier bravado gone. 'Goodbye,' he said. 'And thank you.'

'There's no need to be frightened of us, you know,' Bron said unexpectedly. 'We *are* your friends, really we are.' He grinned suddenly, and Herris felt all his unease vanish in the warmth of the younger boy's smile. 'Goodbye – and good luck! We'll see each other again soon, I expect.'

They walked away from the white, shrouded garden, and Herris looked back as they turned the corner. The two Temple boys had disappeared, but behind him and Kenmet, reassuringly dark and familiar, was a firm trail of footprints in the deep snow.

CHAPTER

TWELVE

Sundim, amongst the people of Zithirian, was a time of celebration: an act of defiance against the cold and the dark, and an affirmation of hope, for now the days would lengthen, the thaw would soon begin, and spring at last would touch the frozen lands below the Northern Mountains with warm green fingers.

Feasting, drinking, singing and dancing were the traditional activities of the festival. Usually in country homes a cow or sheep was killed and roasted, an act of extravagance that was very heartening in such dead, dreary days. If the weather permitted – which happened surprisingly often – there would be games outside in the snow or on the ice of ponds, rivers or lakes. Despite the bitter cold and the hardships of winter, everyone looked forward, in the gloomy days of autumn, to the turning of the year.

The inhabitants of Sar D'yenyi were no exception, and the Lady Kefiri had spent much time and energy planning a Sundim celebration that would raise the morale of her people and help them to forget, for a few days, the terrible things that had happened to Zithirian.

Over the past three months, a steady flow of refugees had found their way to Sar D'yenyi. Some had come direct, in varying states of distress, to hammer on the doors of the fortress: these were the people who for one reason or another knew where it was, and had managed to negotiate the inhospitable, snow-bound passes. Others had been discovered wandering in the mountains or sheltering in caves, starving, dying, desperate. Now Ramath, the Captain of the Guard, sent out regular patrols to pick up such fugitives, and they were still being brought in at the rate of perhaps a score a week. Some died, but the effects of rest, warmth and food on the others were heartening.

These extra mouths almost doubled the existing garrison. Kefiri, checking stores and rations, was very glad that the citadel was so well stocked with food and fuel. Space, however, was not so abundant, and the numerous small rooms in the outer walls and towers were packed with people. Mattresses filled even the corridors, and food was doled out twice daily on a shift system, for there were not enough plates, bowls and cups to go round.

Once they were fit to be interviewed, the new arrivals were gently questioned by Kefiri and her chief officers. A surprising number proved not to have come from Zithirian at all, but from the outlying farms, settlements and villages scattered up and down the Kefirinn valley, now apparently being plundered by marauding bands of Ska'i. Sometimes whole families had fled together, and miraculously survived cold and hunger until located by the patrols. More often, however, those who reached Sar D'yenyi had terrible, harrowing tales to tell of friends and relatives less fortunate who had succumbed to the Ska'i, or to the savagery of a mountain winter: mostly the old, the very young and the sick. By Sundim, five hundred and twenty-seven fugitives had arrived at the citadel, not one over sixty years of age, and perhaps only thirty or forty babies and children amongst them. Come spring, the melting snow would expose many small corpses to the greedy gaze of the kites.

Those from the countryside had little to tell of the situation in Zithirian. All too often, the first they had known of the invasion of their country was when a band of Ska'i swept down to plunder farms and settlements of food, before setting light to the buildings and chasing the terrified survivors into the mountains. But in the city, apparently, it was quite different. Again and again, refugees – usually soldiers, or members of the aristocracy – told the same story. Most of Zithirian had been left largely intact, apart from the Palace, which had been wrecked, looted and burned so thoroughly that all but the central tower and a few other buildings was hardly more than a heap of stones. Everything else – the houses, the Temple, even many of the warehouses by the docks – had somehow escaped the murderous and destructive attentions of the Ska'i.

The most detailed and damning account came from an officer in the Royal Guard, a tall, authoritative, fair-haired man called Invan. He arrived at the head of a group of young soldiers, almost a month after the city's fall, and was painfully honest about his own part in the initial attack.

'The Ska'i were camped outside the gates, about a mile away. Tsenit took charge of the defence of the city: he's been trained as a soldier, after all, and he's very competent. Up until midnight, we were at the barracks, waiting for the call. Then we were told to replace the men on duty on the walls. They were ordinary citizens, mostly.'

'And you didn't suspect anything?'

'Not a thing. We all trusted Tsenit. Most of them still do – they can't see what's staring them in the face. Don't want to see it, I suppose. He seemed . . .' Invan stopped, and shook his head in bewilderment. 'So open, so pleasant – everyone liked him. Most people used to say what a shame it was, that he was the youngest son, and not the eldest.'

Kefiri sat and listened in perfect calm, her dark hair streaming down. The feeble sunlight of a winter morning fingered its way into the Council Chamber, striking pale metallic glints from the gold, netted cap pinned to the back of her head. Somehow, the look of earnest determination on her face made her seem even younger than she was. No one could have guessed at the rage, hatred and self-disgust churning behind her still, blue gaze.

Tsenit, so different from almost all the others of his family. Tsenit, who, with his dark hair and athletic build, very much resembled his uncle, her father. Was that why she had so readily assumed that he was as honest and loyal as Tayma had been?

Tsenit, who had murdered father, brother, sister, uncle, as surely as if his own hand had wielded the axe. And she, silly fool, had believed that she loved him, and that he loved her. It didn't matter that almost everyone else had been deceived too: the guilt, the grief, the wound to her self-esteem, were all too vast to be blown away with a few soothing words.

She turned her mind back to what Invan was saying. He and his men had taken up their positions on the walls: then Seardrith, Commander of the Royal Guard, had come in person to give his orders. They were to stay in position. Whatever happened, they must not move. Any soldier who came down from the ramparts would be killed. He had repeated it, several times, and then had added, his voice intense, 'It's for the best. Remember that, Invan. Whatever you see and hear – remember, this is for the good of Zithirian.'

So when someone opened the gates in the middle of the blizzard, and the Ska'i came pouring into the city, Invan and his men stayed where they were. Others, disbelieving, ran down to confront the invaders and were slaughtered to a man, their fate glimpsed and heard by those still on the ramparts. Frozen, snow-covered, horrified by the betrayal, shamed by their cowardice, they had obeyed Seardrith's orders and crouched there, listening to the distant screams and shouts as the Palace was sacked. Later, as the snow died down, they watched it burn.

They stayed there all night, not daring to move, staring at the greedy flames, the black towers stark against that hideous crimson and orange glare. And at dawn, Tsenit came, with Seardrith, and an escort of the Royal Guard.

There had been a plot, though it was not then explained who had been involved. The gates had been opened to the Ska'i, and they had attacked the Royal Palace, killing almost everyone inside it, including the King, the Heir, the Lord Tayma, the Lord Ansaryon and the Lady Zathti. Seardrith, who had been involved in the plot, had seen the error of his ways at the last minute, and had warned Tsenit just in time for him to escape death. The Ska'i were still occupying the Palace, but could be persuaded to leave the city by a show of strength. Accordingly, all the soldiers were now ordered to eject them.

'And at first I swallowed every word of it,' Invan said now, grimly. 'But then I started thinking – especially when thousands of Ska'i came trooping out of the Palace, all hung about with heads and plunder, as meek as children. As if they had been *told* to surrender. And the only person who could have given them such orders was Tsenit. Then the word was put about that Ansaryon was the traitor, Ansaryon had let them in. But I didn't believe that either. Why should the Ska'i kill him, if that were so? And there were all kinds of rumours. Certainly, no one had found his body. But where was he? Many people, I'm sorry to say, still think that he was the villain of the piece, in defiance of logic and common sense. Tsenit is their hero. But the more I watched him, the more I was sure. He planned everything – he murdered his own family. Now he's the Crowned and Chosen King, and he's holding court in what's left of the Palace – the Central Tower is still intact – and behaving as if everything is back to normal. But the Ska'i are camped on the Fair Field, and taking what they like from the citizens. Oh, it all started fairly enough, a rota worked out, but now they just come in and rob people at random, and anyone who resists ends up as a head on a trophy lance. I've tried to stop it, and got this for my pains.' He held up his left hand, to show a scabbed, angry gash across the knuckles. 'Tsenit claims he has them under control, but he's as terrified of them as everyone else is, I think. Their chief, Quenait – I've seen him once or twice, and he has a look fit to freeze your soul. And he has a shaman who goes everywhere with him – Tayo's blood, I've never set eyes on a more evil-looking wizard. If Tsenit thought he could get that pair to dance to his tune, it's probably the biggest mistake of his life.'

'So what finally made you decide to leave?' asked Ramath, the

Captain of the Guard, in tones that did not quite disguise his contempt.

Invan was no fool: he glanced up at the tiny, slender girl sitting opposite him in a shaft of sunshine. 'I'm not proud of myself,' he said shortly. 'But if I had done the decent, honourable thing, I wouldn't be here now – my head would be hanging by the hair from a Ska'i lance. And that wouldn't have done anyone any good.'

'I understand,' said Lord Tayma's daughter. 'And I'm glad you escaped, Invan. The more people we can gather here now, the better our chances of overthrowing Tsenit.'

'I don't trust him,' Ramath said. He was notoriously as stubborn as a mule. 'He could easily be a spy.'

Invan flushed indignantly. 'No, of course I'm not! I hate and despise Tsenit and what he's done to Zithirian, I loathe those bloodthirsty barbarians, and I don't much like the Temple either – it wouldn't surprise me if the Priests didn't have something to do with all this, the Ska'i haven't laid a finger on them.' He turned in appeal to Kefiri. 'Lady, believe me, I'm no spy – I'll swear any oath of loyalty you like—'

'Once a coward, always a coward,' Ramath muttered.

'I don't think so,' Kefiri said softly. 'I think he wants to make amends. My father mentioned you several times, Invan, and always spoke of you very warmly. I revere his memory and his judgement, and so I will gladly welcome your offer of service.'

Invan swore the oath of loyalty then and there, kneeling before her, his hands on his breast, while Ramath looked on with an expression of barely concealed disgust. Then Kefiri smiled, and spoke the traditional words of acceptance. 'Invan son of Marnaya, I take your heart, your head, your hands, your body. As you serve me and mine, so will I serve you and yours. In the name of Tayo the Divine Ancestor, be steadfast, loyal, brave and true.'

And the sunlight, falling on his yellow curling hair, turned it to gold, the colour of faith and strength.

Into the hush, Kefiri spoke again. 'I thank you, Invan, from my heart. You haven't even had time to eat yet, have you? My Chamberlain is outside – he will show you where to go.'

Invan had risen to his full and considerable height, but still hesitated. He said slowly, 'Thank you, Lady. But first I must ask you something. I left Zithirian because of the rumours I heard in the Palace. It was being said that Ansaryon was not killed in the fighting – and certainly, his body was not buried, nor was his head seen being carried by the Ska'i, although all the rest of his family's were recognized. Of course, Tsenit has announced his death, but I wouldn't believe him now if he said snow was white. Is it true? Is Ansaryon alive?'

Kefiri glanced at Ramath, and then smiled. 'Yes. Yes, he is, and he is here in Sar D'yenyi. He was sorely wounded in the fighting, and for a while we thought he would die, but he is now slowly recovering. You may see him later, if you like, although I should warn you that he keeps to his room, and still tires very easily.'

Invan's face was filled with sudden glee. 'But – if Ansaryon is still alive, then Tsenit cannot be the true King!'

'Agreed,' said Ramath. 'But he has been formally Chosen by the people, and Crowned in the ancient ritual. And he's in possession of the city. It's going to take rather more than the efforts of a few refugees in Sar D'yenyi to shift him.'

'We'll ask for help,' Kefiri told him. 'Minassa, Lelyent, even Toktel'yi – it's in all their interests to have the Ska'i and Tsenit defeated.'

'They may well refuse. Certainly Toktel'yi will,' said Ramath gloomily. 'The Emperor's spies must already have told him what's happening. Come summer, the known world will be fighting over Zithirian's gold like dogs over a bone.'

Kefiri looked at him. Ramath was older than her father had been, nearly sixty, and his vast experience had left him cynical, pessimistic, always inclined to do nothing rather than risk men and money in anything that he perceived to be a lost cause. In minor matters – running the garrison, organizing patrols, training soldiers, all the day-to-day duties of his position – he was unsurpassed, but she knew now why her father had once said that he would leave Ramath in Sar D'yenyi rather than take him into battle.

She said carefully, 'I think that's a matter more fit for discussion at another time. Ansaryon, of course, will lead us – he is our rightful King. I suggest that we wait until he is fit enough, before deciding our strategy. And there are other voices to be heard, too. Don't forget the Tanathi – they are our allies, we must include them in any decisions.'

'Tanathi?' Invan looked up keenly. 'I thought they had all died when the Palace was overrun.'

'Some did, but eight of them survived, and Ansaryon brought them here. Two of them have gone back to the rest of the tribe, to warn them about the Ska'i, but the others are still here. Abreth is their leader.'

'Abreth – I remember him. Is his sister also here?'

Ramath shot Invan a sharp glance, but Kefiri, young and innocent, hadn't noticed the sudden raw hope in the soldier's voice. She said, 'Halthris? Yes, she is.'

'I am glad – very glad.' Invan smiled with relief. 'I was convinced they were all dead. If King Varathand had heeded their warning, many lives would have been saved, and Tsenit's evil plan would not have succeeded. We owe them a great debt.'

'We do indeed,' said Kefiri, and saw the look of irritation on Ramath's face. The Captain mistrusted the undisciplined, free and informal Tanathi, and refused to believe that a pack of barbarians could have anything worthwhile to contribute in the retaking of Zithirian.

More than ever, Kefiri wished for Ansaryon's help. He was a man, older, experienced, and moreover their leader and King by right, however unassailable Tsenit's position seemed. Ramath had known her since she was born, and despite her superior rank, quite obviously still thought of her as a little girl.

But Ansaryon had stayed in his room for months. At first, of course, he had been too weak and ill to do anything else, and the process of recovery had been painfully slow. One of his wounds had become infected, and once more his life had been in danger. Mellok's skills had eventually turned the tide of death, and since then her cousin's strength had gradually come back. He could now walk without difficulty, and although he still tired very easily, she had felt for some time that he was, in fact, capable of doing far more than he allowed to appear.

But instead he kept to his room, reading or sleeping or just sitting staring into space, and she had no idea how to penetrate that obstructively indifferent façade. Even Halthris, whose mind had once spoken to his, and saved him from death, seemed baffled and angered by his apparent rejection of her companionship. Her own friendship with Halthris was rapidly growing, and Kefiri found herself increasingly annoyed with her cousin, for the Tanathi woman's sake as well as her own.

Invan left, escorted by the Chamberlain, to find food and a bed somewhere in the crowded towers. Ramath also went out, to check over some military matter. Alone for a brief and blessed while in this seething place, Kefiri walked to the northern window and stared out.

Below the tall central tower, the walls and cramped open spaces and jumbled buildings of Sar D'yenyi clustered precariously on the citadel's fragment of rock, the snow thick and untouched on roofs and ramparts, and trampled and dirty on the ground. Beyond, the dazzling white expanse of the lake stretched nearly thirty miles away from her, frozen and lifeless. And in the distance lay the mountains, pregnant with the gold and silver and glittering stone that had made Zithirian so wealthy, and also ensured that it would forever be a target for greedy plunderers like the Ska'i . . . or the Toktel'yan Empire.

The mountains were so beautiful, so far away, so deceptively fragile, silver spikes glittering against the pale blue winter sky. For aeons they had stood impassively as empires rose and fell, cities were founded, flourished and died, and the lives of men and women seemed puny and pointless when set against the everlasting might of those distant, unchanging peaks. Sargenn, Estray, Annako, Mondir . . . they would still be there, remote and stern, when she and her fortress and all that she loved had withered into the dust of history, their names lost and their battles, passions and hatreds forgotten.

She turned, and saw to her surprise that she was not alone in the Council Chamber after all. A child stood just by the door, small, dirty, unkempt, with the unmistakable aura of poverty, neglect and hunger clinging to him. Startled, Kefiri said sharply, 'What are you doing in here?'

The boy said nothing, but his dark eyes, almost hidden behind a lank curtain of filthy, ash-blond hair, seemed suddenly to bore into her soul. A despairing sense of the sheer hopelessness of the struggle washed over her. What was the point of resistance? In a hundred years' time, they would all be dead.

Someone knocked, the door swung open, and Halthris stood on the threshold. At her entry, the child jumped, and turned as if to run away, but the Tanathi woman blocked his path. 'Hello,' she said. 'I haven't seen you around for a while. Where have you been hiding yourself?'

'Do you know him?' Kefiri asked, puzzled. She was not sure if she had seen the boy before: there were so many refugees that she had lost track and count of all but a few. But there weren't many children amongst them.

'Oh, I've seen him several times, but not for a month or more. My name is Halthris.' She smiled at the boy. 'What's yours?'

The child glanced back at Kefiri. This time, his eyes only revealed fear. At last he said, in a voice so quiet that it could barely be heard, 'Bron.'

It was not a familiar name. People in Zithirian, and amongst the Tanathi, were usually called after birds, animals, flowers, rivers or other natural things. Kefiri meant frost or ice, and was taken from the same root as the great river by which Zithirian stood. Halthris was water-child in Tanathi, and Ansaryon's name was linked to the word for the moon's crescent, Ansar.

But Bron meant nothing, in any of the tongues Kefiri knew: Zithiriani, Tanathi, Toktel'yan, or the liquid, beautiful language spoken in Kerenth, land of women.

'Well, Bron, are your mother and father here too?' Halthris was speaking with quiet reassurance.

The boy shook his head, and whispered, 'They're dead.'

'Then who looks after you?'

Bron swallowed. If it had not been for the dirt, and the blue, pinched look of hunger and tiredness, he would have been a beautiful child: the combination of that hair, almost white, and the deep dark eyes was very arresting. He said hesitantly, 'My – my grandmother. And my foster-brother.'

'Then hadn't you better get back to them? They'll be wondering where you are.'

The boy nodded. Kefiri said quickly, 'Are you hungry? Do you get enough to eat?'

He shook his head again. 'Sometimes I don't.'

'Well, there's plenty of food for everyone here – no need to starve,' said Kefiri kindly. 'Go and ask Nayarmi in the kitchens for one of her special cakes – that'll soon fill you up. And say the Lady Kefiri sent you. Go on – off you go, quickly, before the dinner-time rush!'

'Thank you, Lady,' the boy whispered. He smiled suddenly, made the child's salute, and ran outside.

Halthris came in and shut the door. She said slowly, 'There's something odd about that child. He makes me very uneasy. And Fess loathes him – every time she sees him, she bristles up as if he's a mortal enemy.'

'How strange. She can't possibly see a little boy as a threat, can she?'

'I don't know. But her fear of him is very strong – I can feel it.' Halthris paused, and then added, 'She reacts in the same way to sorcery.'

'That poor half-starved child can't be a sorcerer!'

'I know he can't. But there is something peculiar about him, even so. He doesn't seem to belong anywhere – he's always on his own, always dirty, always hungry, though everyone else here is clean and well-fed. I haven't seen a sign of this grandmother and foster brother. And his name – Bron. It isn't Zithiriani, is it?'

Reluctantly, Kefiri shook her head.

'I don't think he's a sorcerer himself,' Halthris went on thoughtfully. 'He's a child, a real child – did you see that smile? But the feel of power clings to him – I can almost smell the scent of magic.' She smacked her hands together in sudden frustration. 'I *wish* I could talk to Ansaryon!'

'So do I,' said Kefiri emphatically. 'Ramath thinks I'm still a babe in arms – Invan obviously feels the same—'

'Invan? An officer in the Royal Guard?'

'Yes – he arrived here from Zithirian this morning with some of his men, and he had a lot of news.' Kefiri frowned at her friend. 'Do you know him, then? He asked if you were here, he seemed very glad to hear you were alive.'

'Did he? I've only met him two or three times, but he was very helpful – he brought me to the Palace when I first came to warn the King.' Halthris thought of the tall, handsome soldier, his frank smile, the warm appraisal in his face. Vinnath, the man whom she had agreed to marry last winter, seemed now to be part of another world, a different life that knew nothing of walls, or sorcery, or the murderous treachery of Tsenit and the hideous brutality of the Ska'i. The past few months had changed her, and she suspected that if she met Vinnath now, she would not remember his face, and he would not recognize her.

But if she no longer wanted Vinnath, she was not at all sure that she wanted Invan instead. She had no idea what she did want, save that she was beginning to wish that she had volunteered to go with Grinya and Djekko and make the long, dangerous journey to Lake Raiyis in search of their tribe. Suddenly, she longed to ride, and feel the wind again, to see sky above and earth below and the endless grass and hills of the steppe behind and before her. It was a land hostile and unforgiving, but still, even now, her home and the symbol of freedom.

'Ramath is sure he's a spy,' Kefiri said.

For a few heartbeats, Halthris could not think what she was talking about. Then she remembered. 'Invan? A spy? I shouldn't think that's very likely. For a start, if he were spying for Tsenit, how would he get any information back to Zithirian? Hundreds of people must have died in the mountains, and it can't be an easy journey, even in summer.'

'We use pigeons to carry messages between Sar D'yenyi and the mining towns on the other side of the lake,' Kefiri told her. 'But that was my father's idea, and although he'd thought of doing the same between here and Zithirian, he never got around to it. No, you're right – of course Invan isn't a spy. Ramath thinks the worst of everything and everyone, that's all.' She sighed, and sent a look of earnest appeal to Halthris. 'Please – will you talk to Ansaryon for me? I know he's been very unapproachable lately, but I think you have more chance of success than I have. You seem to be able to reach him in ways that I can't.'

'Not recently,' Halthris pointed out. She was not Kettan, to take offence at the most trivial matter, but it was undeniably very difficult, after the extraordinary closeness of thought-link, not to feel annoyed when Ansaryon behaved as if she were invisible.

'I know,' Kefiri said unhappily. 'When I think of what he has suffered, what has happened to him, I can understand why he sits and broods up there. But there's so much to be done before we can get rid of Tsenit, and I can't possibly manage it all on my own. He's the rightful ruler of Zithirian, not me, he should be leading us and planning our campaign – and he doesn't seem to care, or even to *notice*. I can't face his indifference again, not yet – will you go, please, Halthris?'

The thought of trying in vain to penetrate Ansaryon's apparently impregnable defences yet again was a deeply disheartening one, but Halthris liked Kefiri very much, and admired the astonishing competence and energy with which this untried seventeen-year-old kept charge of a fortress containing over a thousand men, women and children. She nodded, trying to conceal her lack of enthusiasm. 'I'll try – but I don't hold out much hope of success.'

'You're almost as bad as Ramath,' Kefiri said, smiling with relief. 'But thank you, Halthris. And good luck!'

It was the day before Sundim, the shortest, bleakest, darkest day of the year. Halthris, climbing the stairs that wandered around the central tower within the thickness of its outer walls, glanced out of the narrow windows as she passed them. Children were playing on the lake to the south of the island, and she could hear their far-off shrieks of laughter. Tomorrow, Kefiri had told her, there would be races for wearers of the polished bone ice-sliders, matches of a game called Pella which was apparently very popular, horse-sledge races, archery contests, an ox roasted on the ice, dancing, music . . .

'Unless it snows, of course,' the Lady of Sar D'yenyi had said dismissively, as if the weather would not be so unkind as to cheat them of their Sundim celebrations. 'In that case we'll have to fit it all indoors, somehow.'

It was almost midday, so there was still some while to sunset. Zithiriani measured time in years, months, days and hours, and counted its passage with calendars and marked candles, a practice which Halthris had always found strange and incomprehensible. There was surely no point at all in calculating the progress of darkness, and in daylight the sun was a perfectly adequate indicator. She glanced up at it when she next passed a south-facing window. Yes, at its zenith. Time for a ride, if she wanted.

And she did want it. For three months, she and her companions had lived packed cheek by jowl in their small rooms, arguing, gambling, singing, playing endless games of tek, and going out when the weather permitted to practise their shooting. It was what all Tanathi did during the winter months, save that here there was no need to hunt, and the walls were made of stone, not leather or felt.

Perhaps a hunting expedition might be a good idea. There must be game in the forests around the lake. Goats, possibly, or deer, or even the rare and solitary mountain tiger. She was beginning to plan it, and hoping that Sherren would not murder Kettan before a good day's hunt could lift morale and defuse short tempers, when she arrived at the door of Ansaryon's chamber.

She knocked, and received no reply. Feeling rather foolish, she knocked again, and waited. At last footsteps came up to the other side of the door, and it opened to reveal one of the serving women, broom in hand and her hair tied up in a scarf. 'I'm sorry – Lord Ansaryon isn't here.'

'Not here?' said Halthris, in astonishment. 'Do you know where he's gone?' To her certain knowledge, he had not left this room since being carried into it half-dead, three months ago.

'I'm afraid I don't,' said the woman apologetically. 'But he was dressed for outdoors.'

Well, perhaps this was a good way of killing two deer with one arrow. Halthris thanked her, and ran back down with feet that seemed to fly. In the Tanathi quarters there was another game of tek in progress, involving Kettan, Inri, Sherren and Abreth, with Chettay keeping the bets, and a very lively affair indeed, to judge by the noise coming through the door. She went into her own room, pulled her sheepskin tunic out from amidst her bedding – it was bitterly cold at night, even with a brazier lit – and put it on. Thick riding gloves, Inri's fur-lined cloak and her outdoor fleece-filled boots completed her attire. She did not consider stopping to tell any of the other Tanathi where she was going: somehow, she did not care for the thought of any company save Fess.

Despite its situation on an island, Sar D'yenyi had stables for about fifty horses, and she made her way there with some difficulty. Everyone seemed to be busy with the preparations for Sundim, and the great courtyard inside the gate was thronged with people bustling to and fro on vital errands. Once in the stables, she located the horse she had ridden from Zithirian, Karbra's stout bay, now considerably fatter from good hay and little exercise. She refused the groom's offer of help, and saddled and bridled him herself, remembering also to tie the leather snow-shoes over his hooves. With her bow, quiver and knife, at last she was beginning to feel like a true Tanathi again.

'Lord Ansaryon,' she said casually to the groom. 'Has he come back yet?'

'No – he went out hours ago. Took one of your people's horses, too – the big iron grey. You the search-party, eh, Halthris?'

He was a large, cheerful man with the far-seeing cycs and prematurely lined face of the mountain or steppe dweller. Over the past three months, they had become quite friendly, exchanging training methods, horse medicines and knowledgeable banter. She grinned at him. 'Possibly. Any idea where he went, Greeyak?'

'None, but he rode off towards the Estray bank. You'll be able to follow his trail. There shouldn't be any more snow till nightfall.'

He was right: the line of hoofprints led away direct towards the western edge of the lake. The noise of the laughing, scampering children diminished behind her as she kept her mount to a brisk trot, Fess loping easily beside her, snuffling the air. The ice-covered lake seemed as solid as earth, only the ridges and ripples of wind-blown, frozen water betraying what really lay beneath the bay's muffled feet. It was quite still, and the vast blue sky vaulted above her, cloudless and unfathomable. Ahead, beyond her pluming breath and the two curved, furry russet ears, she could see the distant shore of the lake. Trees, snow-mantled pines, crowded down to the edge, and above them the foothills of Estray piled up, ridge upon ridge, until they merged with the sheer cliffs and snowy, perfectly symmetrical peak of the mountain which Tayo had chosen as his gateway to Paradise. There was no sign of Ansaryon.

After the sunlit brilliance of the lake, it was startlingly dark under the trees. Nothing moved, no birds called. Halthris strung her bow, and studied the ground. Even in this sparse snow, there was no excuse for missing tracks and signs. The hoofprints of Ansaryon's mount led purposefully off up the slope, and the tiny slotted marks of a forest deer, small, swift and shy, meandered across it. A hare and several birds had also wandered here. She called to Fess, who was looking round her with interest, and urged the bay horse upwards through the trees, wondering what she would find on the other side.

It was a long climb. She saw two deer browsing on the pines, but failed even to nock an arrow before they scented her and Fess, barked an alarm, and plunged away, deeper into the woods. The silence was thick and oppressive: she could imagine demons or other evil creatures lurking in the undergrowth. It was said that the great western forest on the other side of the steppe contained trees which moved, with branches that reached down to strangle unwary travellers. But Fess was eager and unruffled, so no such perils could be hiding here.

The cat caught an unwary hare, and brought it back to her. Halthris praised her, promising her a feast later, and hung it from her saddle. Now, she had something to show for her folly in riding out alone, and a ready excuse should she meet Ansaryon.

If she found him. The trail went on and on, zig-zagging up through the ranked pines. Above her, winds began to stir in the branches, and every so often clumps of snow cascaded downwards, once hitting her on the shoulder. She shook it off, calmed her sweating, nervous horse, who obviously hated the forest, and persuaded him onwards.

It was becoming lighter ahead, and then, surprisingly abruptly, the trees ended and they emerged into the open. She halted her mount and looked around, blinking in the sudden sunlight.

On either side of her, the forest finished in straggling clumps of snow-bowed pines. Ahead lay a smooth, even slope rising up to a bumpy ridge. Beyond that, she could see the summit of Estray, high and magnificent, with an encroaching veil of cloud beginning to blur its peak. Frowning, she studied the sky. No doubt of it, snow was gathering over the farther mountains in the north. An icy wind brushed her face, and she pulled up the hood of Inri's cloak. Greeyak had been wrong: there would definitely be blizzards before sunset.

And still Ansaryon's trail led on, up the mountainside and out of her sight. Halthris shivered suddenly, feeling a chill presentiment of disaster. Alone, he had ridden into this wilderness, as purpose-fully as if going to meet someone – or something. And she was beginning to wonder if he intended to come back.

Kefiri needed him: so did Sar D'yenyi and all its people. Without him, they had no hope of recapturing Zithirian. And Halthris could not bear the thought of Tsenit enjoying the fruits of treachery and murder unmolested. The Tanathi were not a warlike tribe, but they had a fervent belief in justice, and in vengeance.

She reached the top of the hill, and stared keenly at the wide, shallow valley on the other side, the higher, rockier slope beyond it. Up here, the winds of winter had blown the snow from the ridge, exposing a few tufts of frozen grass: poor fare, but tempting, even so, to her tough Tanathi horse, who pawed the ground and then began to graze, with a chinking of bit against teeth.

In all the vast expanse of the mountains, nothing moved, nothing stirred. She twisted in the saddle and looked back. Sar D'yenyi lay like a jewel in its frozen setting, outlined by its own shadow. She saw the flash of a pennant flying from the central tower, and the tiny dots of the children, playing on the ice. The sun was still shining on the lake, but as she watched the clouds crept nearer, plunging her and the ridge into shadow. The summit of Estray was no longer visible, nor were the mountains at the far end of the lake. The wind blew stronger, whipping the black hairs of the bay's mane, flapping her cloak. She was well protected within her layers of wool and leather and fleece, but her face felt the suddenly stinging cold.

She turned back towards the mountainside, and as she did so a distant movement caught the edge of her sight. She sharpened her gaze, shading her eyes with her hand, for even out of the full glare of sunshine, this great almost featureless swathe of snow was brilliant enough to dazzle.

Yes, there it was again, perhaps half a mile away as the eagle flew, at the foot of the rocks. Too large for a deer or a goat, much too small for a frost giant – if she believed in such things. Her eyes narrowed and straining, she realized that it was a horse – a dark grey horse, riderless, standing amidst the boulders.

Halthris jabbed her heels into the bay's flanks. The animal flung his head up in surprise, and she urged him down the hill with a yell. The snow became deeper, filling the natural hollows with a smooth white blanket, so that within the space of ten strides it might be fetlock deep, then brushing the horse's belly. Willing and Tanathi trained, he floundered through, snorting, while she encouraged him onwards, dread sharpening her voice. Fess, light and swift, was bounding gracefully ahead of them over the crusty surface, an astonishingly brilliant yellow and black against the white.

The bottom of the valley was treacherous going, filled with drifts through which her horse waded bravely. In several places, it was up to Halthris's feet. She could see the grey more clearly now: he had noticed their approach and was watching them, ears pricked. Soon, he let out a hopeful and welcoming whinny, to which her mount responded eagerly.

But no sign of Ansaryon. The slope up became steeper, the snow shallower, and she dismounted: it would do no one any good if her labouring animal fell and hurt them both. She called Fess back to her side, and scrambled up towards the rocks where the grey stood, leaving her horse to pick its own way behind her.

His reins had been knotted, and trailed on the ground. Her fear subsided a little. Ansaryon surely knew that all Tanathi horses were trained to stand still if that was done: in rough ground, it was safer for the animal than hobbling it. He must have left the grey here deliberately, to await his return.

But the weather was changing rapidly. The wind had now risen to half a gale, and blown dry snow stung her cheeks when she turned northwards. There was some shelter, though, amongst the taller rocks, and the horses were hardy and sensible. She slipped the reins over the bay's head, and with a pat and a word of farewell, she left him to greet the grey. Then, with Fess alongside, she began the climb up through the rocks.

One thing was certain: if they did not find Ansaryon soon, the blizzard would descend on them all before they could reach the comparative safety of the pine forest, let alone return to Sar D'yenyi. And while she knew what to do in such conditions, and was quite capable of surviving them, she was certain that Ansaryon, still weak from his wounds and his long illness, and unused to such hardship and bitter cold, would not last very long without help.

The snow had been swept from many of the rocks, but here and there she found a footprint, already blurred by the gale. Grimly she struggled upwards, as fast as she dared. In the summer, it would have been an easy climb, but now, with wind, snow and ice to contend with, she was afraid of losing her footing on some frozen, slippery surface. And even if the fall did not kill her outright, injured, she would not last until dark in this cold.

Just as she had almost given up hope, she saw him. He was standing on the very pinnacle of the rocks, a bowshot above her, his back turned. He wore no cloak, and his hair blew out in a pale wild tangle. As she stared, the first real flakes of snow began to whip against her face, but he made no movement: he might have been one of those strange stone statues in Tsenit's courtyard in Zithirian, save for the mad, endless wind tugging at his hair and clothes.

He was right on the edge: if she shouted, he might fall. Halthris began to climb again, swiftly, silently, trying not to take risks. '*Keep with me*,' she told Fess urgently. '*Don't startle him.*'

'*I wouldn't dream of it*,' came the cat's indignant response, and she dropped back and waited until her partner came up level with her, so that they could continue together.

Suddenly, Halthris slipped, and her foot dislodged a sizeable chunk of rock which bounced downwards with a clatter, to land not far from the horses. She retrieved her balance, gasping, and looked up. The man above her had apparently not even noticed. As she scrambled breathlessly up the last crag, Ansaryon stretched out his hands.

Power thrummed in the air, and Fess snarled and cowered. The wind screamed across Halthris's face and then stopped, as abruptly as if an invisible wall had sprung up around her. Astonished, she stood on the rim of the cliff and stared at the blizzard sweeping down from Estray. The snow spun all around them and plunged onwards into the valley, but she and Ansaryon stood in a bubble made of sorcery, untouched by the storm.

He turned and smiled at her, with a delight that she had not seen in him since that night when she had saved him from Ayak's jaws. 'What are you doing here?'

'I followed you.' She looked up at the flakes streaming just over her head. Curious, wondering, she reached up her hand and felt the gale buffet her fingers, the icy wet touch of the snow. But down here, in their charmed sphere, there was stillness, peace, shelter.

Then she realized, with a sudden lurch of her heart, what this meant: and with the discovery, came understanding. She knew now why he had kept to his room, why he had locked himself away from her and from Kefiri, and why he had risked his life, here and now in the blizzard, to prove the impossible.

And the impossible had happened. She said slowly, 'You are still a sorcerer. You stopped taking Annatal – you should have died. But you did not, and you still have your power.'

'It seems so.' His eyes glittered with wild exultation. 'Stand still, Halthris of the Tanathi – watch!'

Again, he stretched out his arms. The protected sphere grew bigger, to embrace all the clifftop where they stood, an area some fifty paces across. Halthris studied him with newly observant eyes, seeing none of the weakness and exhaustion that had assailed him when he used his powers on the journey to Sar D'yenyi. There was no lightning, no sound, save that deep hum of sorcery, almost felt rather than heard, tingling in the air around them.

'How long can you go on?' she said after a while. Ansaryon did not seem to be doing anything: his hands had dropped to his sides, and yet the blizzard still avoided them.

'I don't know. As long as I have the strength, I suppose. And at this moment, I feel powerful enough to stand here all day.'

'I think that might be unwise,' Halthris said drily.

He glanced at her, and grinned like a boy. 'Do you? You don't have much faith in sorcery.'

'Not when the snow's certainly up to our waists in the valley, and Fess and the horses are loose in it, and Kefiri is probably organizing a search party even now.' She turned and peered down the rock face: the bubble moved with her. There was no sign of either mount, or of the cat, and the blizzard had blotted out everything beyond the tumbled boulders on the valley's floor. Even if Ansaryon were able to sustain this level of power until they reached Sar D'yenyi, it would not protect them from the cold, or from the increasing depth of the snow.

'Well, you've proved your point,' she said, turning back to him. 'Now can we get down off this eyrie and go home?'

For an answer he swung round, his hands sweeping up again into the empty air. For an instant the snow parted far above them, then the clouds, and she saw the blue sky between, sharp and pure as the promise of hope, and the swift flash of sunlight. Then he lowered his arms, and the blizzard closed in around them again, so that they seemed to be standing in an invisible cocoon.

'Come on,' he said briskly, as if she were the dawdler. 'Let's go. And stay close, or you'll force the power outwards, and I'm not sure how long I can hold it then.'

She followed him down the rocks within that miraculous calm, her mind struggling with the strangeness and the wonder of it. Such things were so alien to the Tanathi, whose only contact with the supernatural came in the rites and prophecies of their shamans, and in the myths and legends told around winter hearths.

And yet . . . and yet she could feel this power as strongly as she could feel the heat from the sun, it was real, it existed, and it all sprang from the mind of this man whom she had once feared and disliked, and whom she now called her friend.

But of whom, it seemed, she still had ample reason to be afraid.

CHAPTER
THIRTEEN

Although the great central tower of Zithirian's Royal Palace had survived the devastation of the Ska'i almost intact, the rooms within it had been despoiled and plundered. The great solid silver throne in which the King sat had been too heavy for Quenait's warriors to remove, but they had hacked pieces off it with their steel axes, and the once beautiful sweep of the firebirds' wings was now sadly irregular, the individual feathers raggedly broken off.

Even in such a sorry state, though, the throne was the symbolic heart of the kingdom, and Tsenit was relieved that it, and the tower, had survived the Ska'i sacrilege. He supposed that he should be thankful that he still at least had a throne and a tower left, let alone a city over which to rule.

The Ska'i had refused to go away. They had stayed, ensconced outside the Sunset Gate, eating, drinking, plundering, raping, killing, and he couldn't do anything about it because there were eight thousand of them and only thirteen hundred loyal members of the Royal Guard to oppose them. The rest had either been killed in the initial attack, or had leaked away from the city in dribs and drabs as Sundim approached. In any case, loath though he was to admit it, he needed Quenait and his bloodthirsty warriors far more than the chief, his tent crammed with looted goods and his men gorged on robbery and slaughter, needed him.

Ansaryon was alive. The news had appalled him, but there was no possible doubt about it: D'thliss had shown him. In that horrible reeking cavern under the Temple, he had peered into a silver bowl full of what looked and smelled like blood, and had seen his hated brother. True, he looked tired and ill, but it was unquestionably him. The scrying bowl never lied, in the hands of those who could unlock its powers.

Ansaryon's unexpected survival would not have been so dangerous if Tsenit had managed to keep it a secret. But within a month of the invasion, rumours were rife in Zithirian, and his Temple spies reported that many people believed them. He had already put the blame for the Ska'i attack on his brother, with what he had hoped had been total success, and now found that this official version of events was discussed with derision in every tavern in the city. And, most damaging of all, soldiers of the Royal Guard started to desert Zithirian, many of them men who, like Invan, he could not afford to lose.

So, Sar D'yenyi and all its occupants must be destroyed, and the citadel razed to the ground so that it would never again become a refuge for rebels and traitors. And he could not do it without Quenait's help.

Despite his repeated appeals to the Ska'i chief, the man refused to meet him. D'thliss, who was certainly in secret and sinister contact with his shaman, told Tsenit that there was no urgency. The bad weather would continue to Sundim, and until it cleared the Ska'i had no intention of leaving their camp and their supplies of food and plunder. Tsenit could see the sense of this, but still he fretted. The longer the barbarians remained outside Zithirian's walls, terrorizing the people, the greater the chance that the citizens would turn against their King, and begin to see Ansaryon as their saviour. Once Sar D'yenyi was taken, and his brother killed, he would be undisputed ruler: he could give Quenait his gold and the Ska'i would return to their homelands, leaving him free of them at last. And then, and only then, could he begin to wield the true power he had craved for so long.

D'thliss was right about the weather. Sundim passed in a blur of snow, with no public celebrations at all, and then the blizzards stopped, the skies cleared and the sun emerged, pale, weak, but a valid representation of hope. And when Tsenit next sent an invitation to Quenait, to discuss the attack on Sar D'yenyi, he was delighted to receive an acceptance.

Most of his father's courtiers had been slain by the Ska'i, and many of the servants too, but Tsenit had had no problems in recruiting others, mainly of the wealthy goldsmith and merchant classes, since the Descendants of Tayo and his Followers had become so few. He had abolished the ridiculous and restrictive Court Dress, and all the elaborate ceremonial which had so suffocated Varathand's court, but a little touch of pompous and imposing ritual should put the barbarian chief in his place.

He had never actually met Quenait before: he had purposefully kept his distance from the man who had slaughtered most of his family. He had seen him several times from a distance, though, and so when the chief strode into the Throne Room, quite unawed by the majesty and solemnity of the occasion, he recognized the squat body, the drooping moustaches and the swaggering arrogance immediately. True, almost every Ska'i warrior shared these characteristics, but Quenait seemed to take them to extremes: he was even smaller and even broader than his men, his moustaches reached his chest, and his bow-legged walk was grotesquely exaggerated.

He stood squarely in the centre of the wide circular room, his small eyes glancing everywhere with greedy curiosity. To Tsenit's surprise, he was obviously much younger than he had assumed, probably not even thirty. And certainly only a young man's energy and vision could have welded the diverse, ferocious and quarrelsome tribes and clans of the Ska'i and the Rerbresh into a cohesive and formidable fighting force.

Behind him crowded some dozen lesser warriors. They had evidently robbed corpses, for all were encased in the beautifully-made bronze armour of the Royal Guard. Since most Zithiriani were far taller than the Ska'i, the fish-scale tunics came down past their knees. It might have looked absurd, but somehow only added to their aura of menace.

And lurking amongst them was the most horrible, terrifying figure of all: Quenait's shaman, Br'nnayak, recognizable not only by his wolfskin cloak, his staff of power and the bones hung round neck and waist, but by the unmistakable stench of evil which surrounded him in a venomous cloud. In contrast to Quenait's comparative youth, the shaman was very ancient, far older even than D'thliss, although that might be due to the effects of Annatal.

After one appalled glance, Tsenit did not dare to look at Br'nnayak again. Those deep dark eyes seemed to be capable of sucking life, memories, personality, even his soul out of him, leaving a mere husk to be filled with abomination, vileness and despair. And just for a moment, as he sat on the silver throne which he had always coveted so desperately, he wished that he was still the youngest son, with his undistinguished future settled, his marriage to Kefiri, the eventual lordship of Sar D'yenyi, and a life of peaceful tedium untainted by the terrible corrosion of merciless ambition.

At last I have what I have always wanted, he reminded himself. The Ska'i, and D'thliss, are just means to the end. When I have no more need of them, I can get rid of them.

But that, a little voice whispered inside his head, would be much more easily said than done.

Quenait apparently knew only a few words of Zithiriani, and Tsenit had no intention of demeaning himself to learn Ska'i, a language as harsh, barbaric and ugly as its speakers. One of the chief's lieutenants, however, was moderately fluent in Tanathi, and as this was so similar to Zithiriani, he had been appointed interpreter. Tsenit had given up any attempt to discern individual faces: this man's distinguishing feature was a neck-ring of silver, mark of what passed for nobility among the Ska'i. Quenait's was of ornate twisted gold.

The Chief Minister, a tall middle-aged man overcome with self-importance by his newly exalted position, opened proceedings with pompous ceremony. 'His High Mightiness King Tsenit, Third of His Name, Descendant of the Divine Ancestor Tayo, Wielder of the Silver Spear, Incumbent of the Silver Throne, bids welcome to Quenait, leader of the Ska'i.'

The interpreter translated. Quenait's ferociously shaggy brows drew together, and he snapped something in his guttural tongue.

'I am not interested in empty titles. I demand to know your plans.'

Tsenit tried to conceal his anger: he did not want Quenait to realize just how easily the barbarian could annoy him. He smiled coldly. 'All in due course. You are aware that, due to a very unfortunate oversight by your warriors, my brother Ansaryon is still alive?'

Quenait knew more Zithiriani than Tsenit had been led to believe. He interrupted the interpreter. 'No oversight. Sorcery. Tanathi.'

'Perhaps,' said Tsenit. 'Whatever the reason, he was not killed as ordered, and he has fled to Sar D'yenyi.'

The chief's eyes lit up eagerly at the name. 'Ah. Gold. Silver.'

'Exactly. Even if he had not taken refuge there, the fortress must be seized as soon as possible. Until then, Zithirian has no control over the mines, or the supply route through the mountains. Since you have been promised a share of the gold, I ask you to join your men with my army, so that we may both attack in over-whelming numbers.'

'So, you need my help,' said the interpreter, translating Quenait's reply.

Tsenit had no intention of admitting the numerical weakness of his forces, however obvious it might be. 'It is not a difficult matter. The fortress can easily be stormed, if we act before the ice melts. I request your participation merely as a gesture of good will, between allies.'

Quenait said something brief and pungent, and spat. The interpreter glanced at his chief, and then at Tsenit. 'Rubbish. You need our help.'

'Will you give it?'

The Ska'i chieftain's eyes narrowed assessingly. He glanced around the still beautiful room, the nervous, richly-clad courtiers, and then addressed Tsenit directly. 'Yes. For all gold, half silver, for one year.'

It was outrageous. It was extortionate. But if it meant that he would be rid of Ansaryon, and the threat of Sar D'yenyi, and, eventually, the Ska'i, then he had no choice. 'Very well,' he said at last, grudgingly.

Quenait's mouth stretched into what passed for a smile, revealing several blackened and broken teeth. 'Good. We understand each other. You want brother for Ayak. Quenait wants gold. A bargain, huh?' And he held out his greasy, grimy, stinking hand, with that dreadful leer still on his face.

I will *not* take it, Tsenit thought, with revulsion. He said curtly, 'Agreed. A bargain. But I must see my brother's head before I hand over any gold.'

'You see many, many heads. Ska'i kill all, this time,' said Quenait gleefully. 'Ayak hungry again.'

Belatedly, Tsenit remembered that Sar D'yenyi also contained the girl whom he had promised to marry. Surely a sweet, pretty, sheltered seventeen-year-old was no threat to him. Perhaps her life could be spared?

A moment's thought convinced him that this would be unwise. He had, after all, ordered the murder of her father. And Ansaryon had doubtless been poisoning her mind against him for three months now. He did not want to risk her knifing him in his sleep: and besides, as King he was entitled to a more exalted bride. Temiltan of Minassa had a daughter, though she was quite young; the Prince of Lelyent, poor man, had seven. And he seemed to remember that the Emperor of Toktel'yi, whose mother had been Varathand's sister, was the father of several girls. Some were by concubines, but surely his official wife had given birth to at least one daughter. To have a Princess of Toktel'yi as his bride would enhance his prestige enormously.

'Yes,' he said, and smiled at Quenait. 'Your warriors may kill everyone. If Ayak wants blood, he can drink his fill at Sar D'yenyi.'

Kefiri had been sure that both Ansaryon and Halthris had perished in the blizzard. When they returned apparently safe and sound, and well after dark, she embraced them both with heartfelt relief, and then, unusually, lost her temper. 'What in Tayo's name were you *doing*, Ansary? You must be mad – you could have *died* out there! And don't just stand there grinning – you should be ashamed of yourself!'

Her cousin tried to look properly contrite, but it was a dismal failure: his smile kept breaking out again. Kefiri stamped her foot, her eyes glistening with tears of rage and fear. 'You fool, you *fool* – don't you understand? We *need* you here – we can't do without you!'

They were standing in the Hall, at the foot of the central tower, and there were at least a score of interested witnesses. Halthris said swiftly, 'I think this would be better discussed somewhere else. Your room perhaps, Ansaryon?'

He glanced at her, and nodded. His hair was wet and tangled from the snow and wind, his face flushed, his eyes brilliant with elation. He had only used his sorcery as far as the forest: after that, they had made their way unprotected through the blizzard and the rapidly encroaching darkness. But despite the terrible conditions, they had found Sar D'yenyi unerringly, following Fess, who had overcome her dislike of Ansaryon's sorcery and led them safely home. Halthris had wondered if he had somehow used his powers to guide the cat back to the citadel, but she still did not really know the full extent of his skills. He could control the weather, he could set an avalanche in motion, and he could link thoughts. What else could he do?

Anything, his appearance seemed to say. The subtle scent of power still clung to him, he was as wild, as dangerous, as exuberant as a lightning-bolt striking a blaze in summer grass. The contrast between this Ansaryon, intoxicated with his discovery, and the withdrawn, silent man who had brooded for months in his chamber, was astonishing.

Somehow, Halthris managed to steer him and Kefiri out of the Hall and up to his room without any further argument. A servant brought food and drink up to them, and with four braziers lit, it was comfortably warm. She stripped off her three outer tunics, removed her wet riding-boots, and stood steaming gently by the hottest fire, rubbing her hands above the glow.

Ansaryon had vanished into the inner half of the chamber, and reappeared a little later dressed in a long loose robe that looked like a more comfortable and informal version of Zithirian Court Dress. He said to Kefiri, 'We were never in any danger, you know – there was no need to be so worried.'

'But I *was*!' his cousin cried, still furious. She glared at him.

'How *can* you say there was no danger? You could both have died out there, quite easily.'

'No. We were quite safe.'

'You know that now,' Halthris reminded him sharply. 'But you didn't when you rode out, did you? You only suspected it.'

'Suspected what?' Kefiri stood between them, looking from one to the other, her face a mixture of anger, fright and bewilderment. 'Ansary, *tell* me – what are you talking about?'

And he said, his eyes glittering with triumph, 'I am still a sorcerer.'

Kefiri's blue eyes grew vast with astonishment. She said, stammering, 'I – I don't understand. It isn't possible, without Annatal.'

'It is. I don't know how, but it is.'

Halthris took pity on her. 'He kept the snow off us both. It *is* true, Hegeden alone knows how – he still has power.'

'More power,' Ansaryon said. He swung round, his face still alight with the memory of it. 'Kef, I can't explain it – I don't know how it has happened – but I can do things now that I never had the ability to do before, and do them easily.'

Kefiri was obviously remembering the lightning that had flashed round this room at the height of his illness. She said doubtfully, 'Can you control it?'

'Of course I can. I wouldn't be a Mazath if I couldn't harness and manipulate my own power. Watch,' Ansaryon said, and raised his right hand.

A servant had left a tray of food and a jug of warm spiced wine on a table against the wall. With fascinated awe, Kefiri and Halthris stared as the jug lifted, poured dark steaming liquid into three Minassan goblets, and set itself down again. One by one the cups, each painted with a delicate pattern of grape-hung vines, floated gently and steadily through the air towards them.

Kefiri took a deep breath, stretched out a hand and took hold of the nearest. Halthris did the same. It was real, certainly: the shiny pottery felt cool and hard in her grasp, and the rich fragrance of the wine crept into her nostrils. She took a sip. It was delicious, and untainted by magic. But Fess, lying by the largest brazier so close that she was surely in danger of singeing, was watching Ansaryon with her eyes slitted and a ridge of bristling fur along her back.

'Convinced?' he said, drinking the wine. 'Come on, Kef – I can tell that you're not. What else would you like me to do?'

He stood there in that strange loose robe, of a blue so deep that it was almost black, his eyes brilliantly silver. His cousin stared at him, and Halthris knew that the wonder, awe and admiration on Kefiri's face must be echoed in her own. She said in a whisper, 'I – I don't know, I can't think—'

'This, then.' He cupped his hands together. Within his long, slender, laced fingers something began to glow, a dark smouldering ruby at first, then growing lighter and lighter, changing from crimson to scarlet to gold to yellow. Suddenly he opened his hands and a white flame leapt up from his palms, searing their eyes with its brilliance.

Kefiri cried out, and covered her face. Halthris, dazzled but determined not to miss anything, watched as the flame changed, flickering, into a silver bird, with long, fringed wings and an extravagantly plumed tail. Ansaryon held out his arm, and the bird flew once round the room before alighting gently on his wrist.

'Is – is it *real*?' Kefiri had opened her eyes, and was staring at the bird. It sat quite still, but in its dark red eyes flickered the echo of the flame from which it had sprung.

'No,' Ansaryon told her softly. 'Sorcery can't create – it can fetch, and carry, and move, and show, but it can't create what isn't there, or anywhere.'

'But I've seen birds like that – they come from the Archipelago, they exist—'

'I can bring cups across the room, I can even fetch up more food from the kitchens, if someone didn't grab it on the way, but I'm not powerful enough to transport a firebird a thousand miles from its home. Sadly, this one is an illusion.' He stroked the creature's back with a delicate finger, and it faded away as gently and inexorably as a rainbow vanishes without sunlight.

'You see? Illusion,' he said again, smiling. 'I make you see it, in the form I wish it to take.'

Kefiri shivered. She said quietly, 'I'm sorry – I can't help it, but it frightens me. It isn't – it isn't *natural*.'

'Oh, but it is – as I said, it has its own laws, and its own limits. Strangely, I seem to have more power without Annatal than I did while I was using it. There's no hint of that in any Mazath book or teachings.'

'But if no one has survived withdrawal from the drug before, then there's hardly likely to be,' Halthris pointed out.

'And now I have – with extraordinary results.' Ansaryon crossed over to the table, and refilled his goblet in the conventional manner. 'I assumed that the power had left me, even though I was able to thought-link with you, that night. After all, you plainly have some untrained ability which doesn't depend on Annatal, so I supposed that I was the same. For a long time, while I was recovering, I had no inkling that there was any other power left in me. And I found the thought very dispiriting, for I knew we didn't have a chance of defeating Tsenit without sorcery. He has the witch priestess D'thliss to help him, as well as Quenait's shaman.'

'Couldn't you have *told* us?' Kefiri cried. 'I was so worried about you – I didn't know what was wrong—'

'I didn't want to raise or dash your hopes until I was certain. And now I am.' He smiled at her. 'Kef, I'm sorry – sorry for all the trouble and grief and anxiety I've caused you. I know it's been very difficult – I know I haven't been much help. But now, everything has changed. Tomorrow, we can start planning the retaking of Zithirian.'

In her lair under the Temple, D'thliss stared impatiently at her scrying bowl. The smooth surface reflected back only her withered face, the ragged strands of white hair, the deep and piercing eyes.

Seething with anger and frustration, she turned away at last. Magic had the potential to be all-powerful – she was sure of it, she could feel the omnipotence lurking there, almost within her grasp. Her certainty had led her to take greater and greater amounts of Annatal, so that now she was smoking four or five times the amount the other Priests used. It had shrivelled her body and her skin, withered her to a dry husk of the ambitious young girl who had entered the Temple with such boundless hopes, not forty years ago. But she had never been beautiful, or vain. Loveliness soon faded, but power did not: and D'thliss had always been hungry for power. She had studied intensively, her knowledge of sorcery was surely unrivalled anywhere in the known world, save on the remote, half-legendary island, far to the south, where it had all begun. And she had earned wealth and status – the first woman ever to be elected to the highest office in the Priesthood of Tayo. Even the King of Zithirian trembled before her.

Quenait was a different matter. Quenait feared nothing and nobody. She had plans for him, however. His shaman was, like her, a devotee of Ayak. But where she must keep her forbidden worship secret – all gods but Tayo were illegal in Zithirian, which was one reason why the Temple was so powerful – Br'nnayak revelled in his adherence to the Devourer. With him, she wielded the real power: Quenait and Tsenit might posture and strut like cockerels on a dung-heap, but they owed everything to the sorcery and cunning of

their respective priests. And both D'thliss and Br'nnayak desired
the same end – the undisputed reign of the Wolf God, through all
the northern lands.

But she was not yet all-powerful. There were, it seemed, still
limits to her abilities. No matter how much Annatal she smoked,
no matter how arcane her incantations, sometimes, as now, the
bowl remained obstinately uninformative, and she did not know
why.

Still, it was a comparatively trivial irritation. She knew perfectly
well what was happening in Sar D'yenyi, and that was something
which no other sorcerer, however powerful, could have achieved.

There was a hesitant scratch on the door. She had no need to
speak: after a while, it opened, and her two grandsons peered
round it. Lelya, as always, looked like a terrified rabbit. She could
not understand how her intelligent, gifted daughter Athayal could
have produced such an uninteresting child. He showed no talent for
sorcery – was terrified of it, in fact – and he had no desire to be
educated with the Temple scholars. She had tried, and it had been
a dismal failure: he hadn't even managed to learn how to write his
name. Soon she had given up on him, and now he ran wild, coming
and going as he pleased, and cherishing a desire to be a potter, of
all things. With the vindictiveness of disappointed hope, she had
told him that pottery was the one craft in all the world that she
would not allow him to pursue. He was too scared of her to argue,
which only increased her contempt for him. And once, she had had
such boundless aspirations . . .

Those hopes rested now on the narrow, frail shoulders of Bron.

'You sent for us, Grandmother?' Lelya enquired apprehensively.

'I sent for Bron. I don't need you. You may go.'

Without another word, the boy scuttled out. The door shut
behind him, and she could hear his footsteps rapidly receding up
the stairs, towards daylight and air. One day, Lelya would gather
up the courage to leave the Temple altogether: and good riddance
to the feeble, useless brat, thought D'thliss.

But the other . . . how she blessed the day when he had been
brought to her, a tiny new-born infant, Ayak's gift, and she had
looked into his eyes, dark and hazy, and seen the power lying there,
untapped, unknown, unimaginable, unfathomable. And hers to
command.

He stood in front of her, arms by his sides, in the filthy tunic
that was becoming too short for him, and a pair of torn woollen
trousers that were far too big, almost adult size. Eight years old,

but his eyes were still as ancient as the deep heart of the sea. He said nothing, nor did she, but the air between them shivered suddenly, and hummed, and then shook. And when it was still again, he was gone, and D'thliss sat staring into the foetid darkness, and looked through a child's eyes at the stone walls and bustling people of Sar D'yenyi.

A Council had been called. Everyone in the citadel knew of it, although comparatively few had been invited to attend, and excitement and expectation filled the air. True, it was only three days since the Sundim festivities had ended, but this feeling had nothing to do with the celebrations, which this year had been curtailed by the weather, and moreover had been undeniably shadowed by the dreadful events in Zithirian. Now, at last, things were moving, and people whispered in corners, engaged in heated debate, and went about their business with a new lightness of heart.

The Council Chamber lay immediately above the Hall, and was almost as large. Braziers had been placed all round the walls, and a long low table ran down the central axis of the room, with cushions along each side, in the Toktel'yan manner. This had been done more because of the numbers attending – there were fifty summoned, and not so many chairs in the whole fortress – than for reasons of fashion, although the Zithiriani were fond of copying Imperial ways.

Predictably, the conservative Ramath looked at these outlandish arrangements with an annoyance that might have had something to do with the fact that at his age he would find it more difficult to get up from a cushion than from a chair. Grumbling under his breath, he sat down near the top of the table, opposite Kefiri. Ansaryon's place was at the head, as befitted the rightful King of Zithirian: beyond Kefiri sat Abreth and Halthris, as acknowledged representatives of the Tanathi. Invan was placed beside Ramath, with several other officers of the Royal Guard beyond him. The remaining places, some two score, were occupied by soldiers and high-ranking officials from both Sar D'yenyi and Zithirian.

With such numbers, there was a great deal of hubbub. Ansaryon waited until everyone had found their places and sat down, and then lifted one hand.

Gradually, the noise dwindled into silence, and forty-nine faces, young, old, male, female, turned expectantly towards their leader.

'I have called this Council,' Ansaryon said, 'to discuss the retaking of Zithirian and the defeat of the murderer and usurper, my younger brother Tsenit. But before we begin, I intend to make several points quite clear.

'Firstly, although as the eldest surviving son of King Varathand, I am the rightful King of Zithirian, I have been neither Chosen nor Crowned. Accordingly, until we have overthrown Tsenit and established my sovereignty by the traditional and sacred rites enshrined in Zithirian law, I will accept neither the titles, the ceremony or the trappings of kingship.' He smiled wryly. 'I dislike counting my gold before it is mined – and in any case, the people of Zithirian, given the choice between a murderer and a sorcerer, might not want either of us.'

A low hum of comment whispered about the table. Never before had any Zithiriani not a priest of Tayo openly announced his magical powers. It was a thing forbidden, secret and greatly feared.

'And that is the second matter which I must raise,' Ansaryon said. His silver eyes glanced round the shocked, apprehensive faces. 'Many of you, over the years, have heard the rumours about me, and about my . . . practices. The wilder ones are untrue, and were spread by my brother and his accomplices, to enhance his own popularity and esteem. The fact remains, however, that for ten years I have been a Mazath – a secret sorcerer. I have never eaten babies, drunk virgins' blood or sacrificed children to savage gods. But I possess certain powers which may prove very useful. Tsenit has the benefit, if it can be called that, of the sorcery of his accomplice D'thliss, High Priestess of Tayo. He may also be able to call on the powers of Quenait's shaman, who is a man of extraordinary evil, as Invan will testify.

'You may find all this a terrifying prospect, and it might be a good moment to remind you of what sorcery can and cannot do. It is most important to remember that although our enemies are probably adept at making illusions, they are not gods – they cannot create. They may cause their warriors to appear in double their actual numbers to frighten us, but these will be harmless images. Only real soldiers can fight, and kill, and die. Touch an illusion, and it will vanish. Our enemies will also be able to control the weather, to a limited extent, to use projection to spy on us, and to influence us and our morale, although this cannot be done from a distance. If you are ever unfortunate enough to come face to face with D'thliss, or the shaman, do not look into their eyes. They are masters of despair. And finally, if this is making you downhearted – do not forget, whatever they can do, *so can I*.'

'But can you raise demons?' It was Invan, his likeable face creased with distaste. 'That foul shaman of Quenait's can do it, not a doubt of it.'

There was a mutter of fearful agreement around him. Ansaryon, smiling, shook his head. 'No. I can't raise demons – and since they're apparently uncontrollable and malevolent beings as dangerous to their friends as to their foes, I'm very glad of it. What's more to the point is that I'm certain that Quenait's shaman can't either, despite the stories you've heard. Various foolhardy Mazath have tried to summon demons in the past, and all have failed utterly. So I think you need have little fear of Quenait's shaman. Believe me, he and his methods are far more horrible and repulsive than his results.'

Some, but not all, of his listeners looked convinced or relieved. Ansaryon paused for a sip of water from the goblet at his elbow, and went on. 'I think that's enough of demons – if they exist at all, which I rather doubt. My third point concerns the future of Zithirian. It seems to me only fair to give you some picture of the type and style of government which I wish to introduce, if I am given the opportunity – and since it is your efforts, your loyalty which will elevate me to the throne, you deserve to be told about my intentions. If you do not think them right, or proper, you can raise your objections now. And if you can't bring yourselves to risk your lives fighting for something, or someone, to which you are opposed, I will not object if you withdraw your support. But if that is the case, for Tayo's sake do it now, and not later.'

'Well?' said Ramath, into the brief silence. 'What are you planning, Lord Ansaryon?'

'Probably the only matter on which my brother Tsenit and I appear to be in agreement is the manner in which the Court is conducted. Invan tells me that he has already reduced ceremonial to a minimum, abolished Court Dress, and introduced into his household people who in my father's day would never have been allowed to step inside the Palace, save in a subservient role. And although I loathe Tsenit and all his crimes, he does, I think, have right on his side in this. Lack of ceremony need not mean lack of respect. Recently, the Court has become too remote from the ordinary people of Zithirian, too exalted and incomprehensible. I propose that my brother's changes be continued. I also propose that a Council be formed to govern the city and its lands. And aristocrats, merchants, craftsmen, even labourers and peasants, will all find a place on it.'

This time, the sound of shocked gasps came from every part of the long table. Ansaryon laced his fingers together, and looked round at the appalled faces. Halthris, sitting between Kefiri and Abreth, caught a distinct gleam of mischief in his eyes.

'You can't, Lord Ansaryon – you can't do that!' It was a middle-aged courtier, one of those who had managed to escape the massacre in the Palace and make his way to Sar D'yenyi. 'Only the Children of Tayo are fit by birth or nature or ability to take any part in the government of Zithirian!'

'Why not? It is the work and skills of ordinary citizens which have made the city so prosperous, so famous and beautiful. They resent the Palace because they have no voice. I propose to give them that voice. I'm not denying that it will be difficult, if not dangerous, to do so. But I cannot defeat my brother without their help, and surely they deserve some incentive, and some reward, for the risks that I hope they will be taking on my behalf.'

He glanced directly at Halthris, and smiled at her. She wondered suddenly if her descriptions of Tanathi customs, the elected chiefs, the lack of formal ceremony, the right of every adult to take a full part in tribal affairs, had influenced his ideas. For surely no reforms as radical and drastic as these had ever been considered before, in all Zithirian's history.

The muttered comments were reaching a peak of astonishment. The man who had caused all this disturbance sat and watched them. He's enjoying this, Halthris thought. He relishes the idea of shocking them.

It was an unexpected quirk of his complicated personality, and one with which she was in sympathy. Even in her brief visits to Zithirian, she had realized the resentment and contempt with which the majority of citizens seemed to regard all the occupants of the Royal Palace, save only for Tsenit. By now, they must have realized what their hero had done. But would they rather have no king at all, than face the poor man's choice between the murderer and the sorcerer?

Or Kefiri, of course – she was the last heir. But would she wish to leave her beloved Sar D'yenyi to become the reigning Queen of Zithirian?

And far to the south, where the River Kefirinn flowed into the sea a thousand miles from its source in Lake Raiyis, the Emperor of Toktel'yi, son of a Princess of Zithirian, might well be casting covetous eyes on the city of his mother's family.

'Well?' Ansaryon said. He surveyed his Council, still with that enigmatic smile on his face. 'I don't wish to hurry you, but before we begin to discuss details of strategy, I would like to know how many of you are still prepared to support me. For whatever happens once we have defeated Tsenit, however I intend to distribute power in my future government, until Zithirian is regained we must present a strong and united front. Our enemies have a nose for weakness and dissent, and they will exploit any division in our ranks to the utmost. So, if you do not like me, or what I wish to do, leave us now, for during our campaign I will be your leader.'

Halthris glanced at the ranked faces. She knew the names and histories of many of them: others she had seen once or twice, vaguely, amongst the mass of refugees. Unintentionally, she caught Invan's eye, and he smiled at her warmly. Determined to give him no hint of encouragement, she looked away.

'I am with you, cousin.' Kefiri's voice rang out strongly, and she placed her hands, palm down, on the table.

'And so am I,' said Invan. 'You have been very honest with us, Lord Ansaryon, and I appreciate your candour. Besides, in view of the . . . special skills employed by our enemies, I am relieved to learn that your talents are equal to theirs. Usually I loathe and distrust sorcery, but these are extraordinary circumstances, and I'm with you, heart and soul.'

His statement was the turning point. All along the table, faces which had been doubtful and unhappy cleared, and grew positive. Halthris placed her palms firmly on the table, and her brother did likewise.

'I cannot serve you, Lord Ansaryon,' Ramath said heavily. 'I regret it deeply – I have served your grandmother, and your father, and your uncle, but I'll have nothing to do with sorcery. I won't betray you – your brother's far worse, to my mind – but I draw the line at doing a sorcerer's bidding. If the Lady Kefiri allows me, I will stay at Sar D'yenyi, as the Captain of her Guard.'

'Of course I allow it, Ramath,' she said, smiling at him with barely concealed relief. 'And I will continue to place absolute trust in you.'

'Then if you, Lady, and the Lord Ansaryon will excuse me, I will leave this Council.' The soldier struggled to his feet, ignoring the helping hand held out to him by Invan, thirty years his junior. With a curt nod to the rest of the company, he made his way stiffly to the door. Some followed him, mostly older courtiers, but when they had all gone there were still more than forty left.

'I thank you all, my friends,' said Ansaryon. 'And now, let us get down to our real business – the defeat of Tsenit and the Ska'i, and the recapture of Zithirian. I have had three long months in which to think about this, and I will share my plans with you. Then, you are welcome to make any suggestion you please – in turn, of course, not all at once. The fuller the discussion, the better – but I will remind you that in staying here, you have accepted me as your leader, and that I will have the final word. Agreed?'

A chorus of nods and murmurs, and a slap of hands on knees from the two Tanathi.

'Excellent. Now, the first and most obvious matter concerns our numbers, and for this I will turn to the Lady Kefiri, who has all such vital facts stored safely in her head. How many men of fighting age in Sar D'yenyi, cousin?'

'Eight hundred and seventy-nine. There are at least another thousand in the mining settlements at the head of the lake.'

'But they should be left there, I think, both to work in the mines and to protect them and Sar D'yenyi once we have gone. Of our eight hundred and seventy nine – plus, of course, the Tanathi – I would hope that at least eight hundred will join us. Have we enough weapons and armour in the stores to equip them all?'

'There's sufficient for a thousand, and it's all in good condition,' Kefiri told him, with satisfaction. 'Ramath has had the smiths working day and night.'

'Even better. But our putative eight hundred, however well armed and trained – and I know that Ramath has been working very hard on them – have no hope of defeating the Ska'i and Tsenit's soldiers. We shall have to ask for help – and I'm sure the gold in Sar D'yenyi's coffers will come in very useful here.'

'The Tanathi will help,' Abreth said. 'The Ska'i are our enemies too, and though we're not a warlike people, we will fight to defend ourselves. And if they are not driven back to their homeland, they will surely attack us next. If you wish, I will set out as soon as the weather clears, and organize assistance from our tribe.' He grinned disarmingly. 'And although I'm sure most will be glad to help you, some of that gold would be very welcome. It would certainly encourage volunteers.'

'As much as you want will be yours,' Ansaryon said. 'And I thank you and all your people for the gift of my life, and for your loyalty.'

Abreth looked slightly embarrassed. 'What numbers?' Invan asked him.

Halthris's brother shrugged. 'I don't know for certain. But I should think I could persuade several hundred Hunters, men and women, to join you. I can't promise anything, but it's certainly possible.'

'Good,' Ansaryon said. 'But we are unfortunately going to need many more. Temiltan of Minassa will help – not only is he my mother's brother, but his city is partly dependent on Zithirian for its prosperity. And he's not stupid – he must have realized by now that the Ska'i pose a serious threat to him as well. A fair number of refugees must have arrived at Minassa by now, so he should be well aware of what has happened. He ought to be able to give us at least a thousand men. Then there is Lelyent. Oh, I know it's a tiny place at the back of beyond, but they breed strong men in those hills and forests, and Prince Belerith is married to my father's sister. I should reckon five hundred Lelyentans at least.'

'It will take all year to collect your army, Lord,' said one of the Sar D'yenyi soldiers, doubtfully.

'I don't think so. I suggest that we decide on a rendezvous, probably near Minassa – it's easy to reach from all the cities, but far enough away from Zithirian to be out of danger from the Ska'i. If we leave as soon as the thaw begins, we should be able to visit both Minassa and Lelyent before Midsummer. And then . . .'

He paused significantly, and Invan said sharply, 'Toktel'yi?'

'Yes. The Emperor is my cousin, after all, and I'm sure I can offer him enough gold to tempt even his jaded appetite for wealth.'

A buzz of comment broke out. Halthris listened, feeling uneasy. The more she heard about the great southern Empire, the less she liked it. Once, a hundred and fifty years ago, it had turned its greedy eyes northwards to Zithirian's riches, and had been repulsed only after much bitter fighting and slaughter. It seemed unlikely that the Emperor, however strong his sense of obligation to his cousin, however tempting the golden bribe, would be able to resist such a splendid opportunity to get his hands on the city itself.

'You forget,' Ansaryon was saying. 'I know the Emperor. Oh, I'm well aware of the risks, but I think Djamal is safe. He's a fat, lecherous, indolent nonentity who likes the idea of reflected glory without having to exert himself. His son's another matter, but he's only a child. And remember, a hundred Toktel'yan soldiers are worth a thousand of anyone else's.'

'I still don't like it,' someone muttered.

'Neither do I, but I don't think we have any choice. Invan tells me that there are about eight thousand Ska'i. To have some chance of defeating them, and retaking the city, our army must at least approach those numbers. So unless we ask the Emperor for help, we haven't a hope.'

'The Ska'i are always raiding across the western borders of the Empire,' Abreth pointed out. 'I should think that the Emperor would jump at the chance to get rid of them.'

'I think he would – especially if someone else offers to do all the work for him, in one fell swoop. Well?' Ansaryon stared at his Council, eyebrows raised. 'Do you agree that we must ask Toktel'yi for help?'

One by one, with varying degrees of reluctance, they indicated their consent.

'Excellent,' Ansaryon said, and his warmest smile broke out on his face. 'Now that's settled, we can plan our strategy in detail.'

It took a very long time. The sun was sinking fast towards the early dusk of midwinter by the time everyone had had their say, and a more or less practical plan of campaign had been agreed. As soon as it became obvious that the Council was nearly over, Kefiri slipped unobtrusively from the room. The kitchens had been ordered to have food and wine ready at the end of the meeting, and she needed to find someone to take the message down.

There was someone outside, but not a servant. A small, familiar figure was sitting on the steps, his tangled, dirty head leaning against the wall. As she shut the door of the Council Chamber behind her, he jumped up so violently that he lost his balance and would have fallen had she not grabbed his arm. In her grasp, the frail bones felt as fragile as a bird's. She said gently, 'Bron! Be careful – you could have hurt yourself. Did I frighten you?'

Eyes vast, he stared up at her, and nodded.

'I'm sorry, I didn't mean to. Were you asleep?'

Another nod. She wasn't surprised: the blue-shadowed eyes, the wan pinched face, the thumb lingering near his mouth, all eloquently indicated his weariness.

'But you can't sleep here. Why don't you go to your bed? I know lots of people are sleeping on straw, but anything is more comfortable than a stone stairway.'

'I can't,' he said miserably. '*She* won't let me.'

'Oh, Bron! Who's "she"? Your grandmother?'

He nodded. 'I can't sleep until I do what she wants. And I haven't.' He gulped and then, defeated by wretchedness and exhaustion, buried his face in the soft woollen folds of her over-tunic, and sobbed brokenly.

Aware that at any moment someone might come out of the Council Chamber and stumble on this sad little scene, Kefiri pulled a handkerchief from her sleeve and gently wiped his face. Then she knelt down, smiling encouragingly. 'Come on, I'll take you to my own room. You can sleep there – your grandmother won't find you.'

'She will.' The boy's face was a mask of despair, appalling in such a young child. 'You don't understand. She can find me *anywhere.*'

'Even so, you can surely snatch a little sleep – and then you'll feel much better, and you can do whatever it is that she wants.' Kefiri's rare anger was beginning to simmer at the thought of this unknown woman who so obviously terrified her grandson. 'And I'll get you some food too. Would you like that?'

For the first time, his face livened, and he nodded. 'Oh, yes, please, Lady.'

Hand in hand, they walked up the stairs to her rooms above the Council Chamber. Like Ansaryon's, at the top of the tower, it was divided into two semi-circular halves. She guided him into the inner room, where her bed, low and heaped with furs and down-stuffed quilts, stood beside a glowing brazier. She tucked him under the bedclothes until only a crest of hair showed above a pair of lustreless dark eyes, drooping and glazed with tiredness. 'Warm enough? Cosy?'

He was already drifting into sleep, but managed a brief smile. Overcome by a sudden maternal impulse, Kefiri dropped a swift kiss on his dirty forehead, and tiptoed out. His breathing was even and regular before she reached the door.

Down in the hot, frantic kitchens, she told the servants to bring up the food for the Council members, and loaded a tray with bread, cheese, buttermilk and honey. They were too busy to ask her why she wanted it, and she hoped that they would assume that it was for her own consumption. It would not do to be seen to give one refugee special treatment, however neglected and deserving the child was.

She hurried back up the stairs, fortunately failing to meet anyone on the way: Ansaryon in particular would have been inconveniently curious. But she reached her rooms safely, put the tray down on the table, and peered very quietly round the door of her bedchamber.

The bed stood exactly where she had left it, but there was nothing under the covers. Suddenly anxious, Kefiri tiptoed up to it. He had been so tired: surely he must have burrowed further under the quilts . . .

There was nothing beneath them at all. Bron had vanished.

CHAPTER
FOURTEEN

The eagle soared high on air currents which, though still cold, were warmer than a week, a month ago. Below him, the signs of spring were already obvious. Icicles hung from trees; the surface of the snow, which had last fallen twenty days previously, was crusty and pitted; and small creatures were beginning to venture out of burrows and lairs to search for new green shoots, sprouting under the insulating blanket of white.

And larger, more predatory animals had come in search of them.

The eagle's sharp eyes spotted, far below, the shaggy, clumsy shape of a female grey bear, rearing up against a tree to gnaw the bark from it. She had emerged very early from her hibernation, but so was this thaw early, as if to compensate for the unprecedented arrival of the cold, three months before Sundim.

No small prey. He flapped his wings and changed direction, leaving the western banks of the lake and soaring south towards the pass and the river. It was a barren country, but he knew from past springs that the rocks and precipitous screes and crags harboured a surprising amount of life. And here, in contrast to the tree-crowded shores of the lake, there was little protective cover.

The sharp peak of Estray glittered grey and silver in the sunlight. On the lower slopes, where the sun had fallen all day, the first spears of young grass were beginning to poke through the melting snow. Here, surely, there would be hares, rock rabbits, or snow partridges: he would not even disdain a vole.

Movement caught his eye. The eagle turned and swooped down on broad wings to investigate.

Too much movement. He saw it all at once, the column of humans and horses, far below, toiling up the pass, scaring every living creature on the mountain back under cover. And surrounding them was the stink of sorcery that all animals recognized, and loathed, even if they had never encountered it before.

With a shrill, keening cry of frustration and disappointment, the eagle veered aside, and made for the emptier and perhaps more fruitful slopes of Mondir, to the east.

Up in their cave, on the eastern side of Estray, the ten soldiers on look-out duty were bored, disgruntled, and avidly counting the five days left until they would be relieved.

It was not that the cave was uncomfortable: far from it. A string of pack-horses had carried up enough burnstones to supply five braziers day and night until summer, and it was dry, sheltered, and equipped with plentiful food, bedding, cooking utensils. There was even a Sith, the native instrument of Zithirian, for anyone able to play it. A duty rota allotted each soldier four hours on look-out and four hours to patrol the narrow, difficult route, at times more of a scramble than a path, which zig-zagged south from the cave across Estray's eastern face. The rest of the day was their own. No strong drink was allowed, and the barrels of ale had been well watered. Dice and tenpegs, the soldiers' traditional games, had soon palled. All they wanted was to return to Sar D'yenyi. Ramath, Invan and the other officers were immersed in the detailed planning and organization of the force that would eventually lead the attack on Tsenit and the Ska'i. Seven hundred of the best fighters would be chosen, and the other hundred and seventy-nine must guard the citadel in their absence. No one wanted to be left behind in Sar D'yenyi, and they were all certain that out of sight of the generals also meant out of their thoughts.

Kazko, officer in charge, sat in his furs beside the outcrop of rock next to the cave, desultorily plucking at the Sith. It was an old instrument, and the wood had warped, making it almost impossible to tune the sixteen pairs of strings. Only Laydra, the youngest of his nine men, had the skill to make it sound as sweet as a Sith should, and his songs enlivened the long dark evenings.

The fourth pair were out again, and no matter how he adjusted the pegs, he could not bring them back into harmony with the rest. But at least it was warm enough to play bare-handed in the open. Up here, facing south-west, it was almost hot, and the snow was beginning to shrink quite noticeably in the afternoon sun. It'll soon be spring, Kazko thought happily, putting the Sith down. Green grass, young animals, warmth, rain, blue skies, birdsong, fresh food – and fighting.

He wanted the chance to avenge those who had died, in Zithirian and in the valley farms and in the mountains. They all did: everyone in Sar D'yenyi had heard the stories of slaughter, brutality and terrible privation. To an essentially peaceful, prosperous people, the appalling and apparently senseless savagery and destruction had been deeply shocking. Such things happened in other times, in other, barbaric places, not here and now in Zithirian. Some of the refugees had had their sanity as well as their lives ripped apart: the rest desired only vengeance, and the more swiftly and finally they could inflict it, the better. As far as he, and everyone else in Sar D'yenyi, was concerned, the only good Ska'i was a dead one. And as for Tsenit, no punishment could compensate for his terrible betrayal.

Fighting. Kazko's mouth watered at the prospect. He had seen all too little of it in his life: the most he had ever done, in ten years of service to Lord Tayma, had been to help suppress a riot of drunken miners up at Arket, one of the settlements at the other end of the lake. Since many of them had been relatives or friends (he was a native of Arket), he had had little taste for it. Killing Ska'i, on the other hand, was what he had been waiting to do all his life.

'Kazko!'

Annoyed at being roused from his thoughts, he turned. His deputy, Damresh, was scrambling along the path towards the cave, the three other men in his patrol stumbling and slipping in his wake. He waved his arms excitedly and shouted again. 'Ska'i! Fly the flag!'

Kazko sprang to his feet, all boredom and irritation forgotten. The other soldiers were tumbling out of the cave, their faces flushed with excitement. A moment of belated caution – Damresh was a good soldier, but impulsive and inclined to leap before he looked – made his commanding officer wait until the patrol had reached him. After all, if the Ska'i were coming, it was best not to let them know they had been seen by shouting the news all over Estray.

'Ska'i? Are you sure?'

'Course I'm sure,' Damresh gasped. He was scarlet in the face, and held aching sides. 'About three miles down the pass. Just like all the stories.'

'You can smell 'em from up on the mountain,' one of his men added, with a face of gleeful disgust. 'Horrible squat men on shaggy ponies, and they've got *heads* hanging off their lances!'

'How many?' Kazko demanded.

'Didn't stay to count them,' Damresh said in between gasps. 'Thousands, at least. You could see them from the Eagle Rock right back to Needle Crag and beyond. In single file. Two thousand, perhaps nearly three.'

Kazko turned, drawing himself up with dignity and pride to give what was probably the most important order of his life.

'Laydra. Fly the red flag.'

'They're coming,' Ansaryon had said, three days ago, to Halthris and Kefiri.

Halthris knew only that his information must have come from sorcery. Kefiri, who had spent five years of her childhood at the Temple school, and who had a surprisingly wide knowledge of the subject considering her dislike of such things, told her that he had probably looked into a silver bowl. The technique was called scrying, and was an important part of a sorcerer's practice. The bowl could be any size or shape, but it had to be made of silver, the metal of power.

'Not gold?' Halthris had asked, for that was far more highly prized by the Tanathi than silver, which tarnished.

'Silver is sacred to Tayo, and to all sorcerers,' Kefiri told her. 'The scrying doesn't work unless it's done in a silver bowl. The priests fill it with blood, and look into it. It shows you pictures – of what is, or has been, or will be. But it's not easy to interpret or control them. Sometimes you see nothing at all – and sometimes you see in it things you don't want to see. It's more difficult to scry than anything else, apparently.'

But evidently Ansaryon had mastered it. Halthris wondered whose, or what, blood had filled the bowl, but Kefiri assured her that the Mazath, who eschewed the more gruesome aspects of sorcery, usually employed ink, or dyed water. 'The liquid itself doesn't have any significance. The bowl reflects and magnifies the sorcerer's own power, and the pictures appear on the surface. Don't ask me exactly how it works – I'm not a Mazath, or a priestess, and in any case I don't think I'd know even if I was.'

It was now two months since Sundim, and everyone in Sar D'yenyi could feel the spring thaw beginning, much earlier than usual. For days now, the Ska'i had been expected, for if an attack on the citadel was to have any chance of success, it must be undertaken before the frozen lake melted. In summer, the fortress was impregnable.

The garrison had therefore been in a state of readiness for some time. Ramath, in his element, organized shooting practice, long morning runs, training in the subtle arts of combat with sword or spear. In their workshops in the rocks under Sar D'yenyi, the smiths toiled, making and repairing blades, turning out bronze-plated tunics and steel helmets. The soldiers had had all the long dark winter months to prepare their revenge, and they were desperate to put their training into practice.

So when the man posted on top of the soaring central tower turned his gaze to the slopes of Estray, and saw the tiny square of red cloth raised beside the jumble of rocks that hid the look-out cave, the three blasts of his signal horn were very welcome, but no surprise. And by the time Kazko and his nine men came scrambling down from the mountain, and ran across the mile of slippery, thaw-smoothed ice that separated the lake shore from Sar D'yenyi's rock, the great gate was barred shut, the ramparts and windows bristled with armed men, and there were heaps of wood and burstones piled up in the courtyard, waiting for the flame. Boiling water, resin and pitch were all excellent weapons against a besieging force.

Rather to Kazko's relief, there was very little banter – 'How do we know you're not the Ska'i? You look pretty hideous to us – and you smell far worse!' – before the gate opened to admit him and his men. It shut behind them with a heavy, comforting thud, and the three huge bars, each made of half a tree trunk and the length of three men, were hauled home by a dozen muscular soldiers.

'Well, Kazko?'

It was the Lord Ansaryon, as he continued to call himself. He was flanked by Ramath, whom Kazko privately considered a silly old fool, well past it, and Invan, who was exactly the sort of commander he liked: pleasant, friendly, knowledgeable about his men and a very popular officer. Kazko performed the palm-on-shoulder salute of soldier to superior, and made his report, trying not to sound too breathless after his breakneck descent down Estray's precipitous slopes.

'Nearly three thousand, you think?' Invan said, when he had finished. 'Not the whole army, then, by a long way. I expect they'll have left the rest of them back in Zithirian, in case of trouble. Tsenit's terrified of traitors.'

There were several sniggers from the soldiers jostling around them in the courtyard, and someone said loudly and caustically, 'Takes one to know one, doesn't it?'

'Are they all Ska'i?' Invan added.

Kazko glanced at Damresh, who shook his head. 'I think so, sir. All mounted, and armed to the teeth, and moving fast. They'll be here before sunset, I reckon. They haven't even got any baggage with them – just those cursed heads.'

A low mutter of disgust and revulsion rose from the throng. Ansaryon turned to survey them all. Like any ordinary member of the garrison, he wore a leather tunic plated with bronze fish-scale armour, and a workmanlike plain sword at his belt. Only his steel helmet, decorated with a blue plume, marked him out from the other soldiers. Halthris, watching him closely, remembered the sick, exhausted man who had arrived at Sar D'yenyi five months ago, thin and weakened by his wounds and the effects of withdrawal from Annatal. This confident and decisive leader, with an impressive air of casual strength, might have been a different person altogether. But since Sundim he had joined Ramath's training groups with all the other volunteers, and had practised his shooting and swordsmanship with vigorous determination, submitting with humorous good grace to the cheerful abuse of the sergeants. Although so tall, his lightness of bone meant that he would never be a broad man, but the hard exercise in the open air had made him almost as fit and tanned as a Tanathi. The transformation from the effete, pale and sinister scholar whom she had first met in Zithirian was complete.

It was just as well, she thought, as Ramath ordered them all to their posts. That earlier Ansaryon had lacked the determination and the will, never mind the physical presence, to make a military leader. But adversity and suffering had hardened and strengthened him. Tsenit, who had always despised his brother's supposedly weak and cowardly nature, would probably find it difficult to recognize him now.

Unlike those at Zithirian, the ramparts of Sar D'yenyi were made of stone, and were very narrow, with no railing on the inward side, so that a mis-step meant a plunge to the courtyard below. But Halthris, kneeling to string her bow with bustle and noise all around her, was reminded sharply of that day on the city's walls, the fear and the uncertainty. She no longer felt, however, that dreadful, lurking suspicion that something was not right. She was certain, as surely as she knew that the sun would set and rise again, that Ansaryon would resist the attackers until there was no one left alive to fight. He knew, they all knew, that this time the Ska'i had come to kill everyone in the citadel, and so ensure that Tsenit would be left with no possible rival to his throne.

She finished stringing her double-curved, composite bow, that had once belonged to poor Vondrak, and leaned it carefully against the battlement. It was a beautiful and effective weapon, and had taken a Tanathi craftsman all winter to make from wood and horn. Her quiver held sixty arrows, with barbed steel heads and fletched with a twist to improve their accuracy. Even if only half of them hit the mark, her dead comrades would be amply avenged.

Cautiously, she peered out through the aperture. She was facing
south, but the sun was temporarily hidden by high, puffy white
clouds that threatened only fine weather. No need today for fur
cloak or thick gauntlets: even in the shadows, it was warm enough
to melt ice, and all trace of snow had vanished from inside Sar
D'yenyi. Spring was here, the air reeked of it, especially when the
wind blew from the south as it did now, and you could imagine the
fragrance of mountain flowers on the breeze.

'There they are!' The cry went up, and Halthris saw the first,
distant black figures file between the last rocks guarding the pass.
They rode down to the edge of the lake, and everyone on the walls
longed for Tayo's legendary bow, that could shoot arrows over a
mile, with unerring accuracy.

The Ska'i made no attempt to ride onto the ice: they stayed on
the shore, while more and more of them appeared from the pass,
so that soon the wide snowy ground between rocks and lake was
dark with their massed ranks.

'Afraid of the ice, I reckon,' Abreth said, gazing keenly over
the wall, bow optimistically in hand. 'Wonder why they took this
long to come here? Even a week ago would have been safer for
them.'

'Just as well they didn't,' said Kettan, clashing his jewellery
with relish. 'Let's hope they fall through it and drown – slowly.'

'They won't,' said Inri. She had completely recovered from her
wound, and her fair, braided hair framed a face as flushed and
healthy as those of her companions. 'The ice is still pretty thick
almost everywhere – it's just melting on the top. It won't crack yet
– I should think we need several more days of warm weather like
this, at least.'

'Good,' Abreth said, with satisfaction. 'I'm longing for the
chance to kill some of them myself. We have our friends to avenge,
remember.'

'And all the other Tanathi the Ska'i have slaughtered down the
years,' Halthris pointed out.

'Bet His Lordship's plotting some sorcery,' Kettan muttered
darkly, with a sidelong glance at Sherren, and another for Halthris.
'You're very thick with him, aren't you, Hal, closer than grains on
a seedhead – what's he got in mind, eh?'

For months now, Kettan had been needling her about her
friendship with Ansaryon, and Halthris was getting sick of it. He
never said anything outright, it was all insinuation, and she had
long since decided that where Kettan was concerned, ignoring him
was the only possible strategy, however infuriating his sly digs and

innuendo. She hoped that he was only envious of the fact that she was on such friendly terms with their leader: Kettan had always been unduly impressed by power and status. But she had an uneasy feeling that it was for another reason. And if she was right, then he was labouring under a serious misapprehension. Did he really think that a six-month relationship with her, seven years ago, gave him some sort of authority over her for ever more?

Two serious misapprehensions, in fact, but she was not going to think about the second one just now. Halthris glared at him, pushed a stray strand of hair out of her eyes, and turned her full attention on the distant Ska'i, as if by doing so she could draw them within range of her bow.

Whatever Ansaryon's gifts, she herself possessed no powers of sorcery, for the barbarians stayed obstinately on the lake shore, despite the fact that as the numbers there grew and grew, the narrow strip between rocks and lake became more crowded, until it seemed that there must be no more room for them, and they would surely spill onto the frozen water. It was as if they did indeed fear that the ice would not bear them.

Or, as one of the garrison nearby pointed out, they were planning another surprise night attack.

But this time there would be no treachery, no one to open the gates or to tell them where those of Royal blood might be found, and slain. The disparate population of Sar D'yenyi, soldiers, miners, refugees from farm or city, peasants and aristocrats and six Tanathi, had been welded together by their common experience, their common hatred, into a remarkably cohesive unit. They wanted the Ska'i to attack, but only because they were desperate for the chance to avenge those friends, relatives and comrades whose heads might even now be adorning the Ska'i's grotesque trophy lances.

They watched until Estray's sharp blue shadow crept across the frozen lake to engulf them, and the air grew still and cold with the approach of nightfall. The moon would be half full tonight, and the order went round: no lights outside, no torches, and all lamps indoors to be extinguished at the first sign of any attack. If the unthinkable happened, and Sar D'yenyi was invaded, the Ska'i, blundering in darkness or the limited moonlight, would be at a considerable disadvantage compared to its defenders, who knew every corner, every step, every hiding place.

In relays, the garrison trooped in to enjoy a hearty supper of the thick fragrant stew, laden with beans and herbs, which was the most popular offering from the kitchens, accompanied by large wedges of fresh bread. Halthris found a corner of the main stairs on which to sit, hoping that she had given Kettan the slip, and she and her brother ate in a hungry and companionable silence, concentrating on the food to the exclusion of everything else, even the bustle and noise around them.

'Just the people I wanted to find.'

It was Ansaryon, still in his armoured tunic. He added, 'Come up to my room. Kef will be there soon, too. I want to talk to you before the attack comes.'

The two Tanathi put the remains of their bread into the almost empty bowls, and followed him up the stairs. Their feet, encased in soft leather boots, made almost no sound on the stone, but once or twice Halthris thought she heard the echo of footsteps behind them. When she turned, however, there was no one there.

The braziers gave Ansaryon's room a glowing and welcoming warmth, and there were rugs and cushions heaped on the floor, Toktel'yan style.

'Rather softer than a stone step,' Ansaryon pointed out. 'Don't worry – you won't be needed for an hour or two, at least. I don't think the Ska'i intend to attack tonight.'

Halthris wiped the bowl with the last of her bread, chewed and swallowed. She said sharply, 'How do you know?'

'I know.' He gave her one of his more enigmatic and annoying smiles. 'And that's all *you* need to know, at the moment.'

'Kefiri told me how you probably do it,' she said, refusing to give in. 'Scrying, isn't it? Do you use blood, or ink, or dyed water?'

Abreth was looking at her with some alarm. Ansaryon laughed. 'Ink – although the kitchens might be able to supply me with some blood, when they next kill a sheep. Very well, yes, I scry – and there are other ways, too, of spying on people.'

'I remember,' said Abreth, who had never really managed to overcome his initial suspicion of Ansaryon. 'The Priests of Tayo leave their bodies and float around Zithirian at night eavesdropping. Is that what you do?'

'I'm not going to give you a lesson in sorcery, if that's what you're hoping. But when Kef arrives – ah, here she is!'

His cousin hurried in, carrying a tray of steaming cups. 'I thought some kuldi might be nice. I think we need something to hearten us tonight.'

They all settled themselves comfortably on the cushions. Kefiri sat calmly sipping her drink as if she had never heard of the Ska'i, although Halthris noticed that she was rather pale. In contrast, Ansaryon's eyes were glittering with what she recognized, rather to her surprise, as barely-suppressed excitement. Once more, she remembered the world-weary, cynical Prince of Zithirian, and marvelled at the change in him.

Kefiri put her half-empty cup down on the low table in front of her, and turned an enquiring gaze upon him. 'Well, Ansary? You said you wanted to talk.'

'I do. And I included Abreth and Halthris because they understand a little of sorcery. Neither Invan nor Ramath, good men and soldiers though they are, would be sympathetic. Dubious and distasteful means to a worthwhile end, that's what they think. But to defeat the Ska'i tomorrow, I will have to use magic – because they will use it against us.'

'How do you know?' Abreth asked.

'They have Quenait's shaman with them. Quenait himself is still at Zithirian, but he's sent his younger brother, and his shaman. You remember Invan talking about him? His name is Br'nnayak, and Invan was quite right – he is a man of terrible evil, and great power. He makes most of the priests of Tayo – with one notable exception – look like little children playing games of magic. And I think he knows that someone in Sar D'yenyi is watching him. We can sense each other's power. He probably doesn't know that *I* am the watcher – but he does know that there is a sorcerer in the citadel. And he will be ready for me.'

Abreth was chewing on his lip, a habit Halthris remembered from his childhood. He said unhappily, 'So what will he do? Can you see that, in your scrying-bowl?'

'No. It has never shown me the future, which is probably just as well. But when it's in a good mood, I can see the present very clearly. The Ska'i, for instance, making camp for the night, which is why I'm almost certain that they're not going to attack until tomorrow morning. Probably Br'nnayak needs time to concentrate his power. Also, I have managed to overhear some of their plans.'

'How?' Abreth demanded. 'I didn't think you understood Ska'i.'

Fortunately, Ansaryon didn't seem to notice her brother's rudeness. He grinned. 'No, I don't. But thoughts can be understood, in any language. And Br'nnayak, being a sorcerer, is comparatively easy to overhear. He's not used to defending his mind – I think Ska'i shamans are so powerful and terrifying that he's never needed to. And before he realized what was happening, and shut me out, I was able to discover his intentions. Or some of them.'

'Which are?' Halthris prompted. She wanted to shiver, despite the warmth of the room, and there were goose-bumps all up her arms. Fess, however, lay curled on the cushions by her side, quite unaffected by this talk of sorcery: it was only the practice of it that she hated.

'To attack at first light. And to use sorcery to gain entrance to Sar D'yenyi. Fire is one of the elements that sorcerers can control most easily. I think Br'nnayak plans to set fire to the gate. Being witch-fire, it can't be put out by conventional means. Once it's destroyed, the Ska'i will be able to pour in and slaughter us all.'

'You say that very calmly,' Abreth commented, with a glance at Kefiri, who was sitting very still, white and silent amongst the luxurious cushions. 'But what do you plan to do about it?'

'Fight fire with fire,' Ansaryon said. He smiled brilliantly, and Halthris had the same overwhelming sense of his excitement and exultation as she had received on the mountain, when he had kept the blizzard from them both. 'Don't worry. I am at least his equal in power. I'm not going to tell you what I plan to do, because Halthris can use thought-link, so it's quite possible you can too – and neither of you have been trained to defend yourselves against mind invasion.' He grinned again. 'Anyway, why should I tell you everything? Sorcerers should be mysterious and enigmatic.'

'Downright annoying, you mean,' Halthris pointed out drily. 'If this fire – this witch-fire that may destroy the gate – is there *any* way it can be put out?'

'Yes – by sorcery, I'm afraid. And power has its limits. I may not be able to spare enough to save the gate. Whatever happens, it'll be a close-run battle tomorrow.'

Abreth's freckled, pleasant face was grim. 'Then if our lives depend on your sorcery, you'd better make sure you're not killed, my Lord Ansaryon – or we're all dead.'

'Oh, don't worry,' said the King of Zithirian, with that unearthly, brilliant smile. 'I shall take as good care of my life as if I were really the coward Tsenit thinks I am.'

The night passed quietly. The Great Hall was filled with soldiers, sleeping head to feet on a sea of mattresses, their weapons and armour by their sides. There was no room for braziers, but the packed bodies gave off their own heat, and the huge high chamber was comparatively warm. The men slept restlessly, their dreams full of attacking Ska'i, as they waited for the attack that did not, after all, disturb their slumbers.

Halthris and Sherren had spent the second part of the night

watching from the ramparts, along with a score or more of other volunteers. The sky was clear, the half-moon shining icily down upon the frozen lake, the bitter, beautiful mountains, the silent, vigilant citadel. On the shore, over a mile away, minute flickering sparks marked the location of the Ska'i camp. But the white expanse of ice remained empty and featureless, and the warning trumpet stayed silent.

It had been easy, given the cold and the general level of excitement, for those on the walls to stay awake, but as the eastern sky behind Mondir, away to their left, began to lighten, and the moon's radiance dwindled before the onset of day, the watchers moved, stretched, yawned, and became suddenly and acutely aware of weariness, hunger and frozen feet.

As if this were a signal, the rest of the garrison began to stream out of the central tower, many still swallowing the last mouthfuls of breakfast. With relief, the night guard stood up and straggled stiffly down the steps.

Something made Halthris, last on her particular section of the wall, turn to look over the ramparts. A light blazed suddenly in the Ska'i camp, far larger and brighter than any camp fire. As she watched, it coruscated, contracted, and then suddenly flared up into a vast blinding brilliance that made her cry out and cover her eyes. And as she did so, Ansaryon's voice echoed in her mind.

'Br'nnayak plans to set fire to the gate.'

She ran along the wall to the steps, screaming as she went. 'The gate! Get away! Get away from the gate!'

Two or three members of the night watch were drifting casually in front of it. She glanced back. The fireball hung in the sky, she could see its pulsating evil glare, like a dreadful parody of the sun, and an arching track of smoke behind it, springing from the Ska'i camp. Then, yelling her warning again, she leapt down the steps two at a time. 'Get away from the gate!'

Two men, misunderstanding, ran to it, and as if in the grip of the horses of the night, her voice failed her. Then she saw Abreth, and Invan, and opened her mouth to make one last despairing effort.

And the fireball struck. There was a huge explosion of sparks and flame, and a beautiful, horrible, dripping silver-gilt rain sprayed over the walls and stuck to whatever it touched.

Three men, including the two who had run to the gate, ignited and fell screaming to the ground. As the deadly shower diminished, several ran forward, ripping off their cloaks to smother the fires.

As they, too, exploded into flame, panic took hold of the garrison. Howling, terrified, they plunged towards anything that might offer shelter against this new and terrifying weapon.

Halthris, swept along with them into the Great Hall, had lost sight of Invan and her brother. It was as much as she could do to breathe in the crush, let alone fight against the tide of fear. Once inside the building, however, she managed to push her way over to the nearest wall. Outside, a rush, a roar and more screams announced the arrival of a second fireball.

A trumpet blew suddenly. In this high, echoing space it was shatteringly loud, even above all the shouting around her. As the splinters of sound died away, so did the rest of the noise. Men stood still, trembling like frightened horses, with sudden shame on their faces, and struggled to banish the uncontrolled panic that had flung them here.

'Thank you.'

It was Ansaryon's voice, pitched to carry all round the packed, gasping mass of soldiers. He was standing head and shoulders above the crowd, probably on a table, on the other side of the circular Hall. He held up his hands, and went on. 'That was the best thing you could have done. Witchfire sticks to wood, flesh, cloth. It can't penetrate stone. You're safe from it in here. Stay in here, *whatever* happens. Understand? The gate will be destroyed – we can't prevent that. But . . .' He grinned at them with that wild, untrustworthy exuberance. 'But believe me, we are not defenceless. At the moment, the Ska'i think they have us at their mercy – but they'll soon discover their mistake, I promise you. And if any do manage to get inside the citadel, then fight them. If they're illusion, they'll vanish. If they're flesh and blood, they can be killed. There'll be no demons, no foul beasts, no man-wolves.' He grinned again. 'If the Ska'i *were* invincible, they'd have defeated the Toktel'yans years ago. They *can* be beaten – and we'll do it!'

They cheered him then, with the wildness of relief, and before the shouting had diminished, he dropped down from the table and out of Halthris's sight. She had no intention of skulking safe under stone while the real struggle went on somewhere else. As a third fireball exploded outside, with a crash and a peculiar, throat-catching stink, she put her head down and with grim determination, and the ruthless employment of feet and elbows, fought her way to the door leading to the main stairs. As she did so, urgent scraps of talk eddied around her.

'I don't like it.'

'You can't trust *any* sorcerer, that's what I say.'

'Why can't we fight them properly like we've been trained to do?'

'We're done for if the gate's gone!'

Disregarding them, Halthris reached the doorway, squeezed through it, and took the stairs at a run.

Her instinct had been correct. As she climbed, that familiar, eerie tingling began to prickle her exposed skin, and her hair lifted. The air buzzed and hummed with power. She passed the Council Chamber, then the door that led to Ramath's rooms, Invan's above, and then Kefiri's. Her legs grew tired, her breath came in gasps. Just in case the witchfire was still spreading its beautiful destruction on anything combustible, she ducked swiftly past each south-facing window, glimpsing the evil glare of the fires that must surely by now have almost consumed the gate. And then there would be nothing to stand between them and the evil of Br'nnayak and the ferocity of the Ska'i.

Ansaryon's chamber was the highest, and smallest: the tower was tiered, unlike the slim straight pinnacled turrets of Zithirian. And above lay the roof, surely the only place in Sar D'yenyi which would give a good view of the enemy, and was yet comparatively safe from the fireballs bombarding the gate.

Always assuming, of course, that Br'nnayak's aim was accurate. If it was not, Ansaryon risked being immolated like those poor men in the courtyard. And if that happened, Sar D'yenyi and all within it were doomed.

The power thrummed in the air around her like a bowstring. She hauled herself panting up the last few steps, and opened the rough wooden door in front of her.

To her astonishment, the first person she saw was Kefiri, who was supposed to be hiding with the other non-combatants in the rocky labyrinth under the citadel. Her dark hair was bound into one fat braid, and she wore the felt cloak, leather bodice and thick, sludge-coloured skirts of a Zithiriani peasant. She turned as Halthris stepped out onto the roof, put her finger to her lips, and beckoned.

It was still very early in the morning. To the east, the sky was brilliant with the promise of sunrise: to the north and west, it glowed a deep, unfathomable blue that predicted a fine day. But to the south, in the direction of the gate and the Ska'i, thick clouds of billowing purple and grey, brown and black, obscured everything, and the reek of it caught at her throat.

The tower was topped by a slate-tiled pinnacle, from the summit of which a banner, in the silver and blue-green of Zithirian, hung feebly in the unmoving air. There was a waist-high, notched wall around the outer rim of the tower, and a narrow circular walkway between it and the conical roof. Beyond Kefiri, who was crouched in the lee of the rampart, Ansaryon stood staring southwards, unprotected even by a helmet. But power flowed from him in a torrent.

Halthris had considerable respect for Br'nnayak's sorcery, even if the King of Zithirian did not. She ducked down and crawled on hands and knees round the walkway until she reached Kefiri. Both spoke identically and simultaneously, in hissing whispers. 'What are you doing here?'

'I followed him.' Kefiri's round face was pale but determined. 'I *can't* skulk down in the caves – I *can't*. So I thought that if I dressed like a peasant, if the worst happened I'd have more chance than if I looked like a princess. What about you?'

'I wanted to find out what he was doing, of course.'

'I don't think he's aware of us,' Kefiri said, with a quick glance over her shoulder at the motionless figure of her cousin. 'He knows we're here, but all his attention is focused on *them*.'

Halthris raised herself a little, very slowly, until she could just see over the parapet. The gate was burning with a fierce, greedy blaze that was rapidly devouring the massive planks and bars. What she could see of the courtyard was deserted, save for the dozen or so black, contorted, still smouldering shapes that had so recently been living men. The heavy pall of foul-smelling smoke blotted out not only the sky, but all trace of the lake, the distant shore, and the enemy tribesmen gathered there. She wondered if they were even now approaching across the ice, to pour through the gate when it fell . . .

There were no more fireballs. Three had been enough to destroy the gate and panic the garrison. Presumably, Br'nnayak believed in conserving his power. Why indulge in a wasteful show of strength, when very soon Sar D'yenyi would lie open and defenceless?

As she turned to crouch down again, the great gate trembled, wavered, and crashed downwards with a wild uprush of leaping flame and boiling smoke. Distantly, but not as distant as the shore, a gloating and victorious cheer went up.

'They're on the ice!' Halthris cried. 'Look, Kefiri – you can see them now!'

Beyond the thinning smoke, they saw the Ska'i, like some vast flood of alien insects, half way between shore and fortress. Mounted on their galloping ponies, they brandished their weapons and yipped the war-cry that would always remind Halthris painfully of Urdray, and the manner of his death.

'Now,' Kefiri whispered, her hands clenched on the stone. 'Now – now – Ansary, *now*!'

And as if he had heard her, the air around them exploded asunder, and lightning leapt from the tower.

Transfixed with fear, and awe, and wonder, the Tanathi hunter and the Zithiriani princess watched as the streak of molten power flashed towards the Ska'i. It forked, and encircled them in flame: and then, as suddenly as it had sprung, it vanished.

And so did the ice.

Where, an instant before, had been two and a half thousand charging horses and their riders, there was now a great black hole in the frozen surface of the lake. Even at this distance, Halthris could see, or imagine she saw, the turmoil of splashing, floundering men and animals, clawing at the heat-smoothed edge of the ice, falling back into the deathly cold water, screaming in helpless rage and fear until their panic and exhaustion dragged them down into the darkness.

It did not take very long. And when the last of them had drowned, a vast and terrible silence hung over the void in the ice, like a shroud.

Halthris, straining her keen eyes, could see a tiny number of Ska'i, no more than five or six, still safe on the distant shore. As she watched, they turned their horses and disappeared southwards, on the long trail back to Zithirian.

But Sar D'yenyi, thanks to Ansaryon's sorcery, had survived.

With a sob of relief, Kefiri flung her arms round the Tanathi woman. 'Is it really true? Have they really all drowned?'

'It's true.'

Ansaryon's voice was a hoarse husk of its usual pleasant tones. There was no colour anywhere on his face at all, he was bloodless to the lips, utterly drained by the unleashing of so much power. He held onto the wall beside him, and tried to smile at them. 'They're dead. More than two thousand of them, including Quenait's brother. Not Br'nnayak – the cunning old fox stayed on the shore. But he's gone. And Quenait won't dare to attack us here again, now that he knows what I can do. If he wants to avenge his brother, he'll have to try something else next time.'

'Next time?' said Halthris.

But Ansaryon, clinging to the wall and obviously perilously close to collapse, was in no condition to answer her.

CHAPTER
FIFTEEN

The cemetery where the dead of Zithirian were buried lay on the eastern bank of the Kefirinn, opposite the city. The poor were commemorated by wooden or sometimes stone slabs laid over their graves, with names and dates scratched in the angular native script that was easier to carve than the curling extravagances of Tok-tel'yan, which was designed to be written on paper. The families of the rich erected statues and monuments, sparing no expense: marble, gilding, expensive and elaborate inscriptions in the Tok-tel'yan letters that, like almost everything to do with the Empire, were obligatory in wealthy and aristocratic circles.

In summer, the place was a popular resort: the Zithiriani, so fond of gardens, had planted trees and shrubs, laid out gravel walks, and installed fountains. There were kiosks selling refreshments, and even a guide on hand to show country bumpkins the sumptuous Royal Tombs and the last resting places of a variety of famous or notorious past Zithiriani: poets, musicians, sculptors, assassins, generals, rebels.

But in winter, the cemetery was desolate. The workmen always dug enough graves, before the ground froze too hard, to accommodate the corpses of those who died during the cold season. In any year, the bitter weather took its toll on the very old, the sick, and the very young, but unless it was a time of plague – and a really virulent epidemic had not struck the city for eighty-five years – the citizens were, on the whole, healthy and resilient, well-nourished and snug in their thick stone houses, cool in summer and warm in winter.

Until this year. Never before had the city been forced to act as unwilling host to a pack of ruthless, greedy parasites. The Ska'i, with the nervous assistance of the city officials and Tsenit's henchmen, had at first acted with some restraint, and the absolute terror which they inspired in the ordinary citizens had ensured that they got everything they wanted. But as winter progressed, Quenait's men became more savage and rapacious. There were eight thousand of them, and by Sundim there was not a farm left intact within twenty miles of Zithirian: the buildings burnt, stores pillaged, animals driven off for slaughter. The lucky farmers died in useless defence of their property: the less fortunate fled with their families into the snowy hills until they died a lingering death from cold or hunger.

Tsenit at last summoned the courage to protest at this wanton brutality and destruction. Quenait laughed in his face. He had his warriors to feed, while he was waiting for the gold and silver that was his due. It was no concern of his that the wasted farms would be barren for years to come. Next winter, he and his men would be back in their homelands, laden with plunder, so Zithirian's welfare was irrelevant. He had kept his part of the bargain: he had killed the Royal Family and put Tsenit on the throne. Now the new King must keep his, and supply him with the gold he demanded, while feeding his tribesmen in the meantime.

Tsenit was powerless, and he knew it. Nor was D'thliss inclined to be helpful. The Temple of Tayo was sacrosanct, protected by sorcery: even the dreadful Br'nnayak had some respect for the Priestess's skills, and besides, he and D'thliss worshipped the same god and had the same end in view. The citizens would have to look after themselves. In any case, to have them weak and hungry, with the more rebellious elements weeded out by the Ska'i, suited her long-term plans exactly. D'thliss was not interested in gold, or material wealth. Power was her obsession and her drug, and a cowed and starving population would be in no state to resist her.

So the people of Zithirian found themselves gradually abandoned to the untender mercies of the Ska'i. Families had to stand by while their vital winter stores were looted wholesale. Those who protested, even in the mildest terms, were killed with the utmost savagery. Every day, in the hour before sunset, pathetic processions stumbled across the frozen Kefirinn to the cemetery, bearing the headless bodies of those who had fallen foul of the Ska'i. And in the long, hungry months after Sundim, came the light, shrivelled remains of those who had succumbed to hunger and cold. Babies, children and the elderly died in droves, and soon the workmen were packing several corpses into each grave. And still it seemed certain that they would run out of space before the thaw.

No family, no household was immune, save for those directly under Tsenit's or Temple protection. Indeed, the rich often suffered more than the poor, for they were not so used to hardship, and their opulent houses had been the first targets of the plundering Ska'i. In desperation, people buried their food, hid it in lofts or under beds, and the more devious always kept a pot of honey or a jar of wine on open display for the Ska'i to remove. A secret, unofficial distribution network sprang up across the city, in streets,

squares, alleys. Neighbours helped the destitute, and the more
fortunate shared their hidden supplies with those who had lost
everything. Quarter officials were hated for their open support of
Tsenit, and suspected, usually with justice, of assisting the Ska'i in
return for the safety of their own lives and property.

And amongst the survivors, cold, hungry and frightened, a vast
and bitter anger was growing, directed not only at Tsenit, impotent
and guilty in his Palace, but at the well-fed, unmolested Priests of
Tayo, and all the others who collaborated in the brutal oppression
of the citizens.

Kaydi Gandar's Widow had never had much truck with officials
of any sort – nosy, two-faced, self-seeking nonentities the lot of
them, from the Court downwards. Marriage to a querulous and
domineering older man had failed to improve her attitude, and
she knew that her insult to Djembeth had alienated some of the
older people in the Embroiderers' Quarter, most of whom had
previously been inclined to ignore her outspoken views and robust
contempt for authority because they had been friendly with her
husband. She did not miss any of them, or their fishy-eyed, vacuous
wives, who spent all their time in spiteful gossip and thought
themselves superior to her because their houses were crammed with
lavish, expensive and quite useless fripperies.

So when life in Zithirian had deteriorated to such an extent that
few people trusted anyone in authority any more, the residents of
Snowbringer Street naturally turned to Kaydi, fiercely independent
and tied to nobody's belt. And despite her fiery tongue, she had
had the sense not to argue with the Ska'i. At least she was still
alive, but she and her family had suffered the same hardship as the
rest of the city.

Nearly three months after Sundim, Kaydi buried her beloved
elder son, Thobin. He had always been prone to winter illness, and
this year the cough had settled on his lungs and killed him. He was
sixteen, but the wooden coffin was so light that it might have
contained the bones of a child. And Herris, now the man of the
family, lifted a thin hand and dropped the symbolic ashes on the
remains of his brother, while the priest intoned the words of burial
that he must have uttered a thousand times and more, that terrible
winter.

The servant, Shilda, had stayed behind to mind the house: if
the Ska'i came calling, someone needed to be there to point out the
stale bread and mouldering dried meat, whilst ensuring that no one
thought of looking in the loft above the kitchens, where enough
food to last them for two more months, if they were very careful,

lay concealed. And Kaydi, cursed with a practical mind, could not help thinking that with one less mouth to feed, those supplies would now go a little further, and hated herself for it. Thobin, her pride and joy, her quiet, industrious, dutiful son, was dead. And all she had left was the scapegrace Herris.

Trouble he might be, but she did have a soft spot for him, and she would guard him more fiercely than a mountain tiger watched her cubs.

Herris, turning away from the grave, saw her dark eyes on him and felt acutely uncomfortable. He grieved for his brother's death – he had always got on well with Thobin, although they had absolutely nothing in common – and the prospect of being the head of the household, by Zithiriani custom, terrified him. He was thirteen, he had no interest in embroidery or business (if the Ska'i left them any). He hadn't much interest in anything at all, really, except roaming the streets and getting into mischief. The thought of all that responsibility settling leadenly on his frail shoulders appalled him. He sniffed, not just for Thobin's sake, and wiped a hand across his eyes.

'Home,' said his mother briefly. The tragedy of losing her son had aged her overnight: she looked gaunt, tough, bleak, not a person to be easily defied.

They turned and trudged through the wet, trampled snow. The thaw a month ago had proved to be only a temporary respite, and the weather had turned cold again quite quickly. All around them, the statues and sepulchres of departed citizens stood sadly amidst the fresh-falling flakes. Segris, a famous general from Queen Zathti's time, was concealed beneath a white helmet and cloak, and his wife Djumi, languishing at his feet in a tangle of ornate drapery, had almost disappeared under a thick pall of snow.

In past summers, Herris had used the cemetery as a playground, running from his friends down the labyrinth of paths, playing hiding games amongst the monuments, telling each other frightening stories of walking corpses as dusk fell, before catching the last ferry-boat back across the river. But in winter the frozen, eerie desolation, the silence, the grim heaps of snow over the dead, many of whom he knew, had an appallingly depressing effect. He could not imagine sunshine, or warmth, or summer, or laughter, ever coming to Zithirian again.

As was customary, burials were strictly private affairs, for the immediate family only. All Kaydi's surviving friends had already made their way to her house for the farewell feast, a wildly inaccurate word to describe the paltry spread laid out on her kitchen table. There was bread, cheese, olives in brine, a little wine and gellin, a few apples and apricots preserved in honey, and her last three jars of the compressed, shredded spiced meat that was a city delicacy.

To Herris's delight, Kenmet was there. His friend had been ill for a long time after their nocturnal escapade, and he still looked white and gaunt, his breathing accompanied by a nasty wheeze. Herris bore him off to his bedroom with a few titbits sneaked from the table, to exchange news and gossip.

Meanwhile, his mother stood bleak and still by her kitchen fire – at least they had managed to keep this lit, however cold the rest of the house got – and received the sympathy of her friends. Most of the guests were women, and at least half of them had been widowed, directly or indirectly, by the Ska'i, so their grief was shared, and heartfelt. There were few in Zithirian who had not lost parent or spouse or child this winter.

'It can't go on,' said Chameni, a once cheerful and stout woman whose bones now showed through her wasted flesh. 'It can't last for ever, dear Kaydi.' She glanced around, and then leaned towards her hostess's ear and whispered, 'I have some very important news!'

Kaydi's eyes did not flicker. She said softly, 'Tell me later. Wait behind.' Although everyone here was either friend, or relative, or both, they were not all to be trusted. Information was dangerous, and valuable. Almost anyone might be driven to sell a neighbour to the authorities in return for food and protection, and Chameni was a noted gossip.

But when most of her guests, warm and almost full-bellied for once, had hurried back in the snow to their homes before the dusk-to-dawn curfew was imposed, Kaydi settled herself on a stool by the fire, newly banked up by Shilda, and looked round at her five closest friends. Chameni; Stekketh, Gandar's cousin, but a much younger and nicer man, who kept a tavern in the Potters' Quarter and had been a tower of strength this winter; Tsari, who had the misfortune to be mother to Kenmet and his flighty, troublesome elder sister Djumi; Engris, Kaydi's brother's wife's cousin, another widow, from the Potters' Quarter, a tall thin woman with little to say, but a good mind; and Djalli, a near neighbour, who had lost husband and eldest son to the Ska'i, and her two youngest children to the winter.

No one here would sell information, or mention, with malicious envy, Gandar's Widow's generous funeral feast. Even Chameni, though fond of gossip, knew when to keep her mouth shut. Kaydi had known them all her life, and trusted them absolutely. 'Well?'

she said, looking at the dark-haired woman in the corner. 'What's this news that's so important, then?'

Chameni grinned gleefully. 'You remember all those Ska'i rode out nearly a month ago, across the river and into the mountains, and never came back? Well, I heard today what happened to them!'

'There must be a hundred different versions of that,' Djalli said dismissively. 'And no way of knowing which one is true – if any of them are.'

'But this *is* the truth,' Chameni said earnestly. 'I had it from Garsi, and she heard it from her cousin, the one who's having an affair with a Priest – oh, not a *real* Priest, of course, but a novice who hasn't taken his vows yet – and *he* told her that the Lord Ansaryon is alive, and hidden in Lord Tayma's secret fortress in the mountains, and the Ska'i attacked it and he killed them all with sorcery. Only a handful came home, so this Priest said.'

There was a brief, stunned silence. Then Stekketh said quietly, '*If* it's true, it's the best news we've had for six months. But personally, I wouldn't trust the word of a priest if he told me your name was Chameni.'

'There have been rumours for months that Ansaryon is alive,' Engris pointed out. 'No one ever saw his head, did they? And if he *is* still alive, then he's the rightful King, not Tsenit.'

'But we don't want a sorcerer for a King,' Tsari objected, looking dismayed.

'I'd rather have him than his brother, any day. The whole city knows Tsenit was the traitor who let the Ska'i in, despite all his attempts to put the blame on Ansaryon.' Kaydi put her hands on her hips and gazed solemnly round her friends. 'Chameni. *Do* you think this story's true?'

'Garsi was certain. Apparently this priest is quite a good man, for a Tayan. And his information's always been accurate, up to now.'

'Kaydi's right,' Stekketh said. 'If Ansaryon *is* alive – and I'd love to believe that he is – then he should be on the throne, not that treacherous conceited idiot up in the Palace. Sorcerer or not, at least Ansaryon isn't in league with the Ska'i, or the priests.'

'I don't like sorcery,' said Tsari unhappily. 'It's not right – not natural! The Divine Tayo knew what he was doing when he banned it.'

'But he allowed his own priests to practise it, didn't he?' Kaydi pointed out. 'And it's only forbidden in Zithirian. In the Empire, every town and village has its own wizard, and they have to train for ten years first, before they qualify.'

'Oh, the *Empire*,' said Engris caustically. 'If they all stood on their heads to piss in Toktel'yi, you'd have some fools here doing the same, because anything Toktel'yan is the fashion.'

'Some fools, perhaps – but not anyone we know,' Kaydi told her. 'We've rather strayed off the point, haven't we? Let's say that *if* the Lord Ansaryon is still alive – *if* he wants what's rightfully his rather than sitting in Sar D'yenyi for the rest of his days—'

'He wouldn't be allowed to,' Stekketh said. 'It guards the mines. If Tsenit wants gold, he needs to take Sar D'yenyi. And if that priest's information is right, the first attempt has already failed.'

'And Tsenit can't do it without the Ska'i's help. Sometimes,' said Kaydi, with malicious satisfaction, 'I feel almost sorry for him. I bet he didn't realize what a mess he'd get himself into, and all because he was too greedy to be satisfied with what he'd got. Well? If Ansaryon tried to get his kingdom back, kick out the Ska'i and give that treacherous no-good brother of his the come-uppance he deserves, are we for him or against him? And remember – according to that priest, his sorcery, like it or not, has already got rid of more than two thousand of those ugly little devils.'

Silence. The fire smoked sullenly. Something rustled and scratched outside. Kaydi's eyes widened in sudden alarm. Without a sound, she rose carefully from her stool, crept to the door, and flung it abruptly open.

On the other side, startled and cowering, stood Herris and Kenmet.

Kaydi grabbed an arm of each, hauled them inside the kitchen and kicked the door shut. She said roughly, 'How long have you two been skulking out there?'

'Not very long,' Herris said, trying to wriggle out of her grasp, without success: his mother had very strong hands. 'Honest, Ma – we didn't hear a thing!'

'And we won't tell anyone about the Lord Ansaryon and the Ska'i,' Kenmet added.

Herris glared at him. Since that strange night when they had first met the Temple boys, their relationship had undergone a change. Kenmet, once the reckless and daring leader, now deferred to Herris, who was physically much more fit, and more sensible too, though this was hardly difficult. Both children knew that they could very easily have been killed by the soldiers, and Kenmet in particular had been subdued by the experience, as well as his long period of subsequent illness.

'So you did hear everything. Well, you'd better go and sit down over there.' Kaydi let go of them and thrust her son and his friend towards the cold corner furthest away from the hearth, where children in disgrace were customarily placed. 'And understand this, you two. No chatter beyond these walls. It could mean all our deaths if you did. This talk is *dangerous*, Herris – *dangerous*. So keep your mouths shut, both of you.'

As if pulled by the same string, the boys nodded. Then the irrepressible Herris said, '*Is* the Lord Ansaryon really coming to kick Tsenit and the Ska'i out?'

'If he's any man at all under that la-di-da appearance, then he certainly will,' Stekketh said. He fixed the two boys with a grim and gimlet eye. 'You understand what your mother says, young man? Don't go gossiping to anyone – least of all those Temple brats I've seen you with a couple of times.'

Herris, to his discomfiture, went bright red. He had gone ice-sliding with Bron and Lelya quite often during Kenmet's illness, but he had kept even that casual friendship secret from his mother, who hated and feared anything to do with the Temple, and would surely forbid him to see them again. And he liked Lelya, who was streetwise and cheerful. Bron, though, still made him uneasy. He was small, dirty, malnourished like everyone else in Zithirian this winter, but there was something in his dark eyes, in his silences, in the way he watched you, that made the hairs rise on the back of Herris's neck. And then Lelya would say something, and he would smile and laugh, and be an ordinary boy again.

But Herris, afraid of Bron though he would never admit it, knew that he was far from ordinary.

'Temple brats? You mean scholars?' Kaydi asked sharply.

Herris shook his head. 'No, Ma. One of the Priestesses is their gran, I think. Anyway, I'm not really *friends* with them – I've just met them on the ice a few times.'

'Well, you won't meet them again. And a Priestess has no business having grandchildren. I thought they were all supposed to be celibate.'

'Rules are made to be broken, and the Tayans are better at it than most,' Engris observed cynically from her stool.

'Well, whatever the truth of it, you're not to speak to these two again, Herris, understand? However friendly you are with them. It's too dangerous.' Kaydi folded her arms and glared at her son. 'Promise me?'

'Yes, Ma, I promise.'

'Good. Now shut up the pair of you and listen, and keep it all to yourselves. Where was I?'

'For or against Ansaryon,' said Djalli helpfully.

'Well, I'm for, and any help he needs, I'll gladly give him. What about the rest of you?' Kaydi looked round at her husband's cousin. 'Stekketh?'

'If he'll get rid of his brother and the Ska'i, I'm all for him.'

'Tsari?'

'I don't like it,' said Kenmet's mother, who shared her son's dark red hair but not his tendency to rashness. 'Surely if we keep our heads down and do nothing, they'll go away in the end?'

'If they get the gold they're after. If Tsenit gives it to them. More likely he won't be able to get any because Ansaryon is holding Sar D'yenyi, so the Ska'i will be on our backs for ever until the city's ruined and all of us are dead, or reduced to living in mud-huts and eating grass. Do you want to see your children grow up like that? I know I don't.'

'Always assuming you live long enough, of course,' Engris added.

'Well . . .' Tsari hesitated, pleating a fold of her best blue woollen skirt between her rough hands. 'All right, Kaydi. I'm with you. But nothing too dangerous, please. Now that Rigan's dead, I'm all that Djumi and Kenmet have got.'

'It'll be dangerous all right,' Kaydi said. 'But not foolhardy. No gossip, no rushing in on impulse. We widen our band of supporters gradually, and make sure the ones we tell only know about those closest to them. That way, if they rumble us, they won't take all of us. Just ask people you know well, whom you're certain you can trust. They ask their friends, and so on. We don't need to do anything else at the moment – in fact, we can't. But if Ansaryon makes his move, we can be ready. Tsenit won't know what's hit him – and from two directions at once!'

'But how can we help?' Djalli asked. 'I'm not saying I don't want to – I'm behind you, Kaydi, all the way. But I don't see what a few poor widows and craftsmen can do against all the Ska'i and the Royal Guard.'

'Well, for a start I don't think we'll be only a few – I think we'll be nine-tenths of the city, from what I've heard people saying. And there's more ways of killing soldiers than running at them with a spear. Herris can tell you all about the roof-tops of Zithirian, can't you, my boy? He spends more time up there than a tom-cat. And soldiers, just like the rest of us, don't usually look upwards. With any luck, they'll never know what's hit them.'

Herris gave a cackle of glee. 'You mean, drop things on their heads, Ma?'

'That's exactly what I do mean. When the time comes, bricks, stones, tiles, arrows, maybe even a spear or two. Anything to dent their helmets and knock them over. And before they realize it, we'll have gone. Oh, no, Djalli, we're not helpless. And even if you or I can't go gallivanting about on the roof at our time of life, we know plenty of younger lads and girls who'll be delighted to oblige, eh, Herris?'

Her son grinned at her joyfully. 'Of course we will, Ma.'

'So – are you all with us?'

They all were, although the timid Tsari still looked rather doubtful. Kaydi glanced round at her five guests, and the two boys, with a broad and satisfied smile. 'So, you know what to do? Don't go rushing into it – take time to think of two or three friends you'd trust with your lives – and who have friends they'll trust with *their* lives. Seek 'em out singly, and drop a word in their ear when no one else can hear it. All we need at the moment is the promise of loyalty to the Lord Ansaryon, and utter secrecy. Nothing else until the time is ripe, and then we'll be ready and waiting for him. That puffed-up fool in the Palace won't stand a chance.'

She made it sound so easy. But it was not only Tsari who wondered just where all this impromptu conspiracy would lead them.

The Lady Kefiri stood on the roof of the central tower of Sar D'yenyi, where a month ago her cousin Ansaryon had used his sorcery to kill more than two thousand men in a few terrible moments, and stared enviously at the eastern shore of the lake.

The ice had all but gone now, and there were only a few floes left to mar the deep clear waters, smooth in the calm of early evening. The air smelt fresh and clean, and the setting sun still held the warmth of the day. Mondir, the long mountain, named for its resemblance to the ridged back of an ox, was almost free of snow save in sheltered gullies and upon the shallow hump of its summit. Behind her, Estray's lower slopes were covered in fresh green grass and bright starry flowers, and the dark pine-trees around the lake were fringed with new viridian growth.

Spring had come at last, and Sar D'yenyi was now safe from attack. No sorcerer living, so Ansaryon had assured her, possessed the power to bridge the waters from shore to island, and there weren't enough boats to transport large bodies of men. It had taken most of the day to ferry Sar D'yenyi's garrison across the two miles of water to the eastern bank, and the boats, a variety of craft large and small, from fishing vessels to the big square-sailed barges that plied to and from the mining settlements at the head of the lake, had for safety's sake been brought back to the citadel. They jostled along the jetty now, more than a score of them, as empty as the fortress rising above them.

Seven hundred men had embarked in those boats, and were now gathered on the distant shore. They included Ansaryon, Invan, now promoted to general of this small force, and three of the Tanathi: Halthris, Inri and Sherren. The other three, led by Abreth, had left Sar D'yenyi half a month ago, as soon as the thaw was established, to make the long and hazardous journey through the mountains to Lake Raiyis, to raise support for Ansaryon's army.

Kefiri had said goodbye to Halthris with sadness. She liked all the Tanathi, except possibly Kettan, but she had become particularly fond of Abreth's sister over the long months of winter. She had even managed to grow accustomed to the big spotted cat that followed her almost everywhere. And though she liked the girl immensely, her direct friendly manner, the way in which she stood up to everyone, her courage and determination, she valued her most because she had saved Ansaryon's life.

But she was also deeply, painfully envious. It was true that Sar D'yenyi was her home, and her responsibility, that she loved it and preferred it to anywhere else the known world might offer. Her five years in the Temple School in Zithirian had been mostly unhappy: she had been desperately homesick, and had only endured it because a Temple education was essential for any Zithirian princess.

She was not a schoolgirl now, but she felt that she had been treated like one. What could she do in Sar D'yenyi, save sit on a pile of gold and fret? The citadel was safe until the return of winter, nearly six months away, and besides, Ansaryon had left her a garrison of two hundred men, with Ramath in charge. And her Captain of the Guard, very conscious of his position and anxious to redeem some of the prestige he thought he had lost, had already wasted no time in making her feel superfluous.

She wanted to help, to *do* something, but Ansaryon had dismissed her pleas. If he were killed, she would be the last Descendant of the First Line of Tayo left to oppose Tsenit. Dead or alive, she would be extraordinarily valuable to her younger cousin. He might even want to marry her . . .

She shuddered at the very thought. The man on whom she had built her adolescent dreams had turned out to have feet of foul mud. She hated him for what he had done to his own family, and to Zithirian, once so peaceful and prosperous, now a cold, devastated, half-ruined city, filled with terrified and starving people. And above all she owed it to her murdered father, to avenge his death.

She brooded, her elbows on the parapet and her chin in her hands, gazing towards the eastern mountains. Soon Ansaryon and his tiny army would be gone, climbing the high pass between Mondir and Sargenn, then descending to the River Ger, on which the city of Lelyent stood amidst the pine forests. And after he had secured the assistance of his uncle by marriage, Prince Belerith, he and his men would take boats down the river to Minassa, built where the Ger joined the Kefirinn. Then south, to Toktel'yi, the huge and ancient city at the heart of its great Empire, a menace for generations to the peace and independence of Zithirian, and yet also, paradoxically, a civilization which all its wealthy citizens aspired to emulate.

Kefiri had never felt the slightest desire to visit Toktel'yi. She had heard too many disturbing stories about the squalor and desperate poverty in which many of its inhabitants lived. It was too far, too hot, too crowded, too frightening. But at least Ansaryon was *doing* something. She, being female, was forced to stay here and wait out events.

But she could help. She could go to Zithirian. Someone must, to tell the people that Ansaryon was alive, that he had not forgotten them, that he had gone to get help and would be at their gates before the summer's end. She took a deep breath as the idea filled her. Why shouldn't she go? Ramath didn't need her. Sar D'yenyi would be quite safe under his leadership: he was an excellent garrison commander, he had the attention to detail and the logical mind that his position required, as well as the dour obstinacy that would make him so good in a siege. Moreover, he had devoted his life to the service of Lord Tayma, who had raised him from humble origins – Ramath's father had been a mine labourer – and placed boundless trust in him. And on Tayma's death, she had inherited that loyalty. While there was breath in his body, Ramath would not surrender Sar D'yenyi. She need have no qualms about leaving her home.

She wouldn't tell him in advance – she would leave him a letter, and make sure he didn't find it until it was too late for anyone to catch up with her. She knew the trail along the D'yenn quite well, and at this time of year it was not difficult going, unless the spring rains were heavy. She would disguise herself as a peasant girl, she had suitable clothes, and she would take one of the pack-mules, with enough food for the journey. It should be only three or four days, at the most. And in Zithirian no one would recognize her; it was two years since she had left the Temple School, and then she had been even smaller, spotty, and round with puppy fat. The Ska'i had killed most of the courtiers, who might well know her again, so probably only two or three people in the whole city would remember what she looked like.

And I'll go alone, Kefiri thought. If it *is* dangerous, then I wouldn't want to risk anyone else's life.

The sun had disappeared behind Estray, although it still shone reddish gold on the rocky purple ridge of Mondir. With a new sense of purpose, she turned and made her way to the stairs.

A small, familiar figure lurked there in the gloom, making her jump. 'Bron! What are you doing up here?'

'I came to find you,' he said, after a pause. He looked like a wraith, so pale and thin that Kefiri had the uneasy feeling that under his patched tunic, his body would be transparent.

'To find me?' she said, frowning. She hadn't seen Bron for some time – indeed, she could not remember when she had last spoken to him.

'Yes, Lady.'

'Have you got a message for me, then? From your gran?'

The boy shook his head violently. 'No, no – she doesn't know I'm up here.'

'Then what do you want?' Kefiri spoke as kindly and gently as she could. She felt so sorry for this pathetic child, and she wondered, with sudden guilt, whether anyone else would take notice of him once she had left Sar D'yenyi.

Bron hesitated, his eyes enormous. Then he said, so low that she could barely hear him, 'I – I'm so hungry, Lady.'

'Hungry?' Kefiri stared at him in bewilderment. 'But there's plenty of food here. No one else goes without, I'm sure. Does your Gran keep you short?'

He nodded. 'She says there isn't enough for all of us.'

'Well, she's wrong – there is. Perhaps I ought to have a word with her.'

Once more, he shook his head. 'No – no, Lady, you shouldn't. She'd be so angry—'

'And take it out on you, I suppose,' said Kefiri, feeling angry herself on his behalf. 'All right, I won't say anything to her if you don't want me to. Listen, it must be nearly time for supper. I have it on a big tray in my room, and there's always more than I can eat. Would you like some?'

The pinched, wan face grew gloriously and vividly animated. 'Oh, yes, please, Lady – yes, *please!*'

It was waiting on the table in her outer room: bread, broth, three kinds of cheese, a cold roast chicken, spiced plums in honey, and wine. She heaped the plate, handed it to Bron, and watched him devour it as if he had not eaten for a month. In the face of such desperate need, her own hunger seemed trivial: she picked at the chicken and dipped a few pieces of bread into the rich broth.

At last he finished. There was colour in his face now, his dark eyes sparkled, he grinned and rubbed his distended stomach with profound appreciation. 'Oh, Lady, that was *wonderful*! Like a royal feast!'

With compassion, Kefiri regarded him in the soft golden light of the lamps. Cleaned up, well fed and well dressed, he would be a lovely-looking boy. That smile, though rare, was dazzling and delightful.

And yet . . . she remembered Halthris's doubts, and the growls and raised hackles of the cat Fess. There *was* something strange about him, about the way in which he appeared and disappeared, not seeming to belong anywhere or to anyone. And the 'gran' who seemed so unpleasant – what kind of woman would deprive her grandchild of food, or inspire such fear in an innocent child?

She said slowly, 'That time when you were here before – when I let you sleep in my bed – where did you go? I just popped down to the kitchens to get you some food, and when I came back you'd vanished into thin air.'

'I'm sorry,' he said. 'I had to go – Gran called me. But thank you, Lady – thank you for the food, and everything.'

He was getting up, sidling towards the door. She said quickly, 'Bron! Where are you going?'

'Back, Lady – I've got to get back – my gran doesn't know where I am and she'll be furious that I've given her the slip.'

'Wait!' Kefiri's voice was sharp with the inherited command of generations of aristocratic leaders. 'Bron, please wait – just a moment. I may not – I may not be able to do this again for you, but please don't think I'm deserting you—'

'Why not, Lady?'

His eyes had changed: suddenly, they were narrowed, staring at her in a most unchildlike way. Instinct, and a spasm of unaccountable fear, made her lie hastily. 'It's awkward, I'm afraid. People will think it odd. But ask at the kitchens – they're very kind down there, it's warm, and they'll gladly feed you if you say you're hungry.'

His face relaxed. 'Thank you, Lady!' he said happily. And with his usual brief, almost exuberant salute, he turned and ran out.

She sat there for a long time afterwards, while the maid cleared away the remains of the meal, trying to plan her escape to Zithirian in more detail. But Bron's face, gaunt and hungry, kept intruding on her thoughts. She would leave Sar D'yenyi to Ramath's guardianship without any doubts, but the thought of abandoning the boy to the apparent callousness and brutality of his grandmother caused her real pain and guilt.

Almost, she wavered in her resolve: almost, but not quite. For on what she did, or did not do, the fate of Zithirian and the remaining sons of Varathand might depend. And in the end, the plight of one small child meant little beside the chance to play a vital part in these momentous times.

PART
THREE

CHAPTER
SIXTEEN

Lelyent called itself the City in the Pines, and the last part of the description at least was accurate. It lay high in the foothills of the Northern Mountains, three hundred Toktel'yan miles east of Zithirian, sheltered in the valley of the River Ger. Everywhere the slopes above it were clothed in woodlands – not the dense, almost impenetrable forest on the western edge of the steppe, but groves of tall, slim, graceful pines, interspersed with glades and meadows where deer grazed, and the children of Lelyent herded flocks of mountain goats and sheep, and the small, large-eyed tawny and white cattle who, fed on the rich alpine grass, gave huge quantities of creamy milk in the warm summer months.

'City', Halthris thought, as they rode down through the trees towards it, was rather a misnomer. Zithirian had contained nearly ten thousand houses: Lelyent had perhaps eight hundred. And unlike the great mother city, it was built entirely of wood. Walls, gates, roofs – everything made from the ubiquitous pines, elaborately carved, decorated and gleaming with fresh paint and even gilding.

Only the chimneys were made of stone, which was just as well: Invan informed her as they passed through the entrance gate, with the flag of Prince Belerith, red with a green pine tree device, fluttering bravely above it, that even so, fires were regrettably common. The worst, in the time of Prince Belerith's father, had devastated the entire city, and killed hundreds of people.

The journey from Sar D'yenyi had taken twenty days. Despite their long and thorough winter training, for many of the soldiers it had been an arduous trek along rough mountain tracks that were at best difficult, at worst almost non-existent. Only after they had successfully negotiated the pass between Mount Sargenn, spiky, precipitous and still cloaked in snow, and the longer, lower but still rocky bulk of Mondir, did the way become easier. The weather, too, was kinder here, for spring was at its height, and the frozen rain, hail and even snow of the high passes vanished in warm breezes, cloudless skies and brilliant sunshine. The last hundred miles were accomplished in four days, in a mood of cheerful optimism. Men forgot their weariness, and the cuts, bruises and fractures which many of them had earned in scrambling up and down rocky screes and treacherous slopes. More than a score of their comrades had been killed in falls, or by descending boulders, and many times that number of pack-mules and horses. A man with a broken leg could be carried: an animal must be killed, hastily butchered for the best of its fresh meat, and the rest left to the kites and wolves.

It was on that pleasant last part of the march, when they seemed to be always travelling through fragrant fields of flowers, or amongst the rich sharp aroma of the pines, that Invan took to riding alongside Halthris. Previously, they had all been too intent on endurance and survival to have the leisure for idle chat: nor had it been possible to walk abreast, conversing pleasantly, on a ledge less than a pace wide, with a gale blowing and a sheer drop plummeting half a mountainside below. But now, with Lelyent almost in sight, and a temporary respite ahead, an air of light-hearted gaiety had infected the army, and its progress down the upper reaches of the Ger was marked by laughter, talk and bursts of more or less melodious song.

Halthris did not object to Invan's company. Inri and Sherren had been wrapped up in each other almost exclusively, ever since leaving Sar D'yenyi, and Ansaryon, the only other member of the force with whom she might have enjoyed casual small talk, was embedded in the duties of leadership. She had watched as he urged, persuaded and cajoled his men up the hazardous passes, made them laugh while negotiating appalling obstacles, and encouraged flagging morale every night as they shivered round meagre camp-fires in the inadequate shelter of a few rocks. By his own example, persistent, stubborn, undaunted, he had inspired them to follow him when, left to themselves, at least half would probably have returned to Sar D'yenyi, vowing to forget all about this lunatic plan to save Zithirian. It was a performance that had aroused her appreciative admiration: and no sorcery had been involved, save on one occasion when he had used his power to clear a rockfall which was completely blocking their path.

But although Ansaryon had shared the same hardships, sat by the same fires, endured the same weather, faced the same dangers, and eaten the same food – dried flat bread, meat half-raw, half-charred, water from the ice-cold streams – he had once more retreated into that unapproachable shell which she remembered from their flight to Sar D'yenyi, after Zithirian's fall. At the time, she had put it down to his injuries, and the shock of the disaster that had befallen them. Now, she knew that it must be his response to the demands of overwhelming responsibility. Every part of his mind was concentrated on the enormous task before him, and there was no room left for the trivial niceties of friendship. It made him a superb leader, and a very poor companion.

Invan, on the other hand, seemed to have plenty of time to engage her in conversation. She wished that his interest in her was not quite so obvious – even Inri had noticed, and teased her about it – but he was pleasant, friendly and usefully informative. Before they had arrived in Lelyent, she had learned the broad outlines of its history (it had been founded nearly two hundred years previously by a great-grandson of Tayo, ironically named Tsenit), its resources, its customs and its people, a mixture of Tayan descendants and native mountain-dwellers who lived together in apparent harmony.

'You know a lot about Lelyent,' Halthris commented.

Invan smiled. 'My mother came from the city. She always said it was the most beautiful place in the known world. I, of course, being Zithiriani, think *that* city is the most beautiful.' He glanced at her. 'And you, a nomad, have no such ties to any one place. It must be strange.'

'No stranger than wishing to spend all your life behind walls,' Halthris pointed out. 'In any case, we Tanathi are not true nomads. We spend every winter in our valleys around Lake Raiyis. And *there*, to our mind, is the most beautiful place in the world.'

Invan laughed. 'So you are not so unlike us, after all.'

'Of course not – for you are just Tanathi who chose to follow Tayo, and live in houses. We are the ones who stayed on the steppe, to follow the old ways and worship the old gods – the true gods.' She glanced at him wickedly. 'Not some self-important chieftain with unbelievable delusions of grandeur.'

If Invan was offended by this blasphemous description of the Divine Ancestor, he gave no indication of it. 'But nearly three hundred years of city life divide us now. You cannot accuse me of being a Tanathi under the skin.'

'I wasn't – I was just pointing out that our differences are not so great as some believe. We are all the children of Sarraliss.'

It was perhaps fortunate that at that moment a shout went up from the leaders of the column, and soon, in a gap between the pines, they could see Lelyent nestling in the valley below.

Though small, it had its own miniature charm, and the welcome the inhabitants gave to the army was exuberant, noisy and warm. An advance party had given warning of their arrival, and a field outside the walls had been allotted for their camp. There, a large troop of cheerful, industrious Lelyentans were busy making shelters and stockpiling heaps of wood for cooking fires.

Prince Belerith himself came out to greet them, riding in a litter supported by four very large black horses. He was a likeable man in late middle age, hugely fat, with tiny dark eyes almost lost in rolls of shiny glowing flesh. As well as being Ansaryon's distant cousin – the Tayan royal lines of Zithirian, Lelyent and Minassa had inter-married for centuries – his wife, Tesi, was King Vara-thand's younger sister. They had seven daughters, famous for their plainness, and one, much indulged son, Enkellis, who was still a child.

Belerith, with the irresistible force of an overwhelmingly good-natured host, insisted that Ansaryon and his senior officers should enjoy the hospitality of his own Palace. The Tanathi were included, rather to Halthris's surprise, and dismay, for Fess's sake. The cat had revelled in the freedom of the journey from Sar D'yenyi, and it seemed unkind to persuade her to accept, for the third time in half a year, a sojourn behind walls. She insisted on staying close to Halthris, however, and leapt onto her horse's crupper as they approached the gate.

It caused some comment amongst the onlookers, and even more when they reached the Palace. Over and over again, Halthris had to assure anxious enquirers that Fess was not dangerous, and could be trusted to behave herself within a building. But she was, nevertheless, glad of the cat's company. Sooner or later – in Lelyent, on a riverboat, in Minassa, in Toktel'yi – Invan would declare himself: she could read his feelings in his face. And it was very comforting to know that Fess was by her side, a deterrent and a protection. For Invan, though likeable, pleasant and friendly, was the kind of man who would not readily take 'no' for an answer.

And her answer would be no. She did not find him physically attractive: indeed, she positively disliked the symmetrical perfection of his features, his golden curls and warm blue eyes. She could not say why she was unaffected, when most of the women at Sar D'yenyi had thought he was wonderfully good-looking, but sus-pected that the apparent lack of any flaw was what made her so resistant to his very obvious appeal.

She tried to recall her lover, Vinnath, but his face, his voice, his mannerisms, were vague and shadowy in her mind. He had been brown-haired, darker than most Tanathi, and a friendly man with whom she had always felt at ease. But the events of this last year, and her extraordinary experiences, would lie like a gulf for ever between her and any Tanathi who had not shared them. She had gone too far to return, and had no idea what to do if she did not.

The Palace was tiny, just two storeys, and distinguished from the houses clustered around it only by the extravagant magnificence of its carvings, and the lavish use of costly scarlet and gold in the paintwork. She was given a small room on the ground floor to share with Inri, and they were led to the Bath House to wash away the dirt and sweat of the journey.

This was the greatest marvel of Lelyent, and one which Invan had described in lyrical terms. The hot waters bubbled up from the earth in an inexhaustible, steaming supply, and there were five such springs, situated all round the city. Over each one a Bath House had been built, four for the use of the citizens, and one in the Palace itself.

The water was a peculiar orangey colour, and smelt foul, but the warmth and power of the spring was a wonderful restorative. She and Inri had the women's bath to themselves, and thoroughly enjoyed rolling, splashing, swimming and diving in the warm deep pool, almost as large as Ansaryon's courtyard in the Palace at Zithirian. And when two solemn serving women appeared, laden with thick towels, it was extraordinarily difficult to abandon their shrieking games and return to being dignified and responsible members of Ansaryon's army.

'That was good – I haven't laughed so much in ages.' Inri squinted down at her lean, muscular body. 'At least I'm not flabby any more. All that good food and lazy living at Sar D'yenyi was making me as fat and sleepy as an old cow.' She stepped out of the water without a trace of embarrassment, ignoring the astonished stares of the servants, took a towel and wrapped herself in it. 'I don't know about you, Hal, but I could get too used to this decadent city life.'

She said it jokingly, but her green eyes were serious. Halthris joined her, squeezing the water from her red hair. She grinned at her friend, and nodded towards the Lelyentan women. 'I don't think they've ever seen tattoos before.'

'Oh.' Inri looked up, surprised. All Tanathi who had success-fully completed their Ordeal had the right to be marked with the representations of those animals with whom they felt a special affinity, or which they had slain with particular courage. Halthris bore a leopard on one upper arm and a wolf on the other, as well as the signs and symbols of the hunting cat Sayni, Guardian of her clan, across her breasts. Inri, almost as proficient a hunter, was tattooed with Emmesar, the hare, giver of speed, agility and intelligence, a wolf and a running stag.

'It doesn't matter whether we get used to city life or not,' Halthris said softly. 'To them, we'll always be barbarians. The tattoos brand us as outsiders, as well as Tanathi.'

'Ashamed of it?' Inri challenged, her eyes gleaming.

Halthris shook her head, spraying sulphurous water on the warm slatted wooden floor around the stone pool. 'Not in the least. Shall we go and put on enough finery to make an Emperor jealous?'

They dressed in their best tunics, braided each other's hair with cords and amulets of gold and silver, and adorned themselves with rings, bracelets, and strings of precious stones: amber, jade, lapis lazuli, amethyst and turquoise. Inri put on her spectacular gold neck-ring, in the shape of a ruby-eyed serpent eating its own tail, which had been acquired by her grandfather in western lands. Then, in this splendid array, they were escorted to the Council Chamber.

Belerith was there, exuding geniality so radiantly that Halthris began to wonder if he were in fact as benevolent as he appeared. But the people she had seen in the streets seemed healthy, happy and well-fed, Lelyent looked clean and prosperous, and there was no trace of the atmosphere of sullen suspicion and hidden resentment that had marred Zithirian's beauty. The Prince was apparently popular and respected, and had decreed that the priests of Tayo should enjoy no monopoly of worship. Invan had already told her that Hegeden and Sarraliss were openly venerated here, and indeed she had already seen enough eagles, suns, moons and horses carved on the houses they passed to be certain of it.

Beside Belerith, at the head of the table, sat a tall, slender, white-haired woman in loose embroidered robes. This was surely his wife, Tesi, a Princess of Zithirian and Ansaryon's aunt. On his other side was a much younger woman, large, hawk-nosed and keen-eyed, who must be Alayni, the third of the seven daughters, reputed to possess the best mind in her family, according to Invan. Half a dozen assorted officials and ministers made up the rest of the Lelyentan contingent.

Opposite Belerith sat Ansaryon, rightful King of Zithirian. He too had dressed magnificently for this occasion, in tunic and trousers of deep green, embroidered in gold and overlaid by a long furred gown in the most expensive colour, glowing scarlet, with golden fire-birds leaping across the fine Kerentan silk. As the three Tanathi entered, he glanced across and smiled.

Invan, with Kazko and three other senior officers, all men who had served in the garrisons of Zithirian or Sar D'yenyi, was the last to take his place at the long table, which was made of polished, honey-coloured pine, like most of the furniture in Lelyent. Belerith looked round at his Council, cleared his throat, and picked up a small hammer with which he knocked twice on the golden wood. 'In the name of the Divine Ancestor, I declare this Council Meeting to have begun. And I welcome my cousin and my wife's nephew, the Lord Ansaryon, and his councillors. Well, young man? You have a great deal to tell us, I understand, so you'd better get started.'

Once again, Ansaryon described the plotting of Tsenit, the attack of the Ska'i, and the treachery which had resulted in the capture of Zithirian and the murder of his family. The Princess Tesi, bereaved of both her brothers, bit her lip and stared at her hands, but Alayni's large blue eyes glittered with anger. On and on went the pleasant, even, unemotional voice, relating the flight to Sar D'yenyi, the loyalty and courage of the Tanathi and the others who had joined him there in exile, and the successful defeat of the Ska'i attempt on the fortress. He did not mention sorcery, but Halthris, watching Belerith's narrowed eyes, was certain that the Prince suspected that it had been used.

'And so I have come to Lelyent to request your help, Uncle.' Ansaryon had been speaking for a long time, but his voice was still clear. 'I do not demand the impossible, but a few hundred men, armed and willing, would make all the difference. Nor will you be the only one to be asked for assistance – we plan to visit Minassa next, and then Toktel'yi.'

'Is that wise, nephew?'

'Probably not,' Ansaryon said candidly. 'But we don't have any choice. Even after the loss of part of their army at Sar D'yenyi, the Ska'i must number five or six thousand, plus perhaps a thousand or more of the Zithiriani Royal Guard who are still loyal to Tsenit. Against them, my little army would stand no chance, even if you gave us five hundred men, and Minassa a thousand. But the Toktel'yans are so well trained and armed that a hundred of them are worth ten times that number of ordinary soldiers.'

'It is a risk, though.' Belerith stared at his cousin thoughtfully, his fat pale hands clasped together on the table. 'By asking for the Emperor's help, you admit your own weakness, and you place yourself under an obligation to him for evermore. That's why the Empire claimed Tamat, in Queen Zathti's time – because the last Lord of Tamat made the mistake of enlisting the Emperor Nekkat's help against Minassa, in some trivial boundary dispute. Next thing he knew, the Imperial army was tramping through his gates, and

Tamat's been part of Toktel'yi ever since, despite all Queen Zathti's efforts to dislodge them. It was only because Nekkat was assassinated halfway through the campaign that Zithirian and Minassa are still free. And don't forget, Emperor Djamal is your cousin. He may well think that because his mother was a Zithiriani Princess, he's entitled to claim the city for himself.'

'Djamal only cares about eating, drinking and visiting his concubines,' Ansaryon said. 'He has no ambitions to annex Zithirian. In the short term, at least, I am certain we are safe. And the Toktel'yans have much to gain from helping to defeat the Ska'i. They've been a menace on the Empire's western borders for centuries. And with a leader the calibre of Quenait to unite them, they'll pose a still greater threat in the future, if they're not stopped now.'

Belerith was still frowning. 'You're very persuasive, cousin. Are you sure you can't do without the Empire? What if they say no?'

'Then we shall have to think again. But to my mind it's worth taking the risk – and my friends agree with me.' He indicated Invan, Kazko, the three other officers, and the Tanathi. 'Without Imperial troops, we really don't stand much chance against Tsenit and the Ska'i. And since your people will be risking death in my cause, I feel it's only fair to you, and to them, to be honest. Tanathi, Lelyent, Minassa, we need help from all of them. But only with a strong force from the Empire can we have any hope of success, I think.'

'Unless you use your powers of sorcery, cousin.'

Silence dropped on the table like a shroud. Belerith's wife, daughter and councillors looked shocked and horrified, as if he had accused Ansaryon of some unspeakably foul crime. The eyes of the two leaders, dark brown and silver grey, met and locked together. Halthris found her hands clenched painfully in her lap, and slowly, deliberately, relaxed them. When she looked up, Ansaryon was smiling. 'There is that to fall back on, I suppose.'

Invan leaned forward. 'Believe me, Prince Belerith, I have seen Lord Ansaryon's powers with my own eyes. Two months ago, sorcery saved Sar D'yenyi, and everyone in it, men, women and children, from a hideous death. The Ska'i have a shaman of evil reputation and enormous power, and they will make full use of him. Lord Ansaryon's own gifts are essential for our struggle against the usurper Tsenit and his allies. I must admit to being doubtful, not to say frightened, of his powers – until I saw them in action. Prince, we owe our lives to him, and sorcery can never again seem the absolute horror which we have all been taught to hate and fear.'

'I disagree.' Tesi spoke for the first time, in a voice so quiet as to be barely audible. 'I was brought up to believe that it was a weapon of huge and dreadful potential, and safe only when used by those who had been properly taught and trained to employ magic for worthy purposes. In the wrong hands, it is a devastating evil.'

'As it is in the hands of Br'nnayak, Quenait's shaman,' Ansaryon pointed out. 'Are you saying, Aunt, that I am not a fit person to practise sorcery? A matter of certain defects in my character, perhaps?'

Tesi was not as fragile as she appeared. Her faded grey eyes gleamed. 'You must admit that your reputation has been rather dubious, recently. But better the lesser evil than the greater, I suppose – and there can certainly be no greater crimes than those which your brother Tsenit has committed. You have my reluctant blessing, nephew, if you wish to fry him in sorcery.'

Ansaryon smiled, and there was even a nervous titter from one of Belerith's councillors. 'I am a Mazath, and although our training and rituals are utterly secret, I can assure you that we are not unleashed irresponsibly upon the world. I know the extent of my powers, I know the limits of them, and I will not attempt to exceed them. Nor will I use them in anything other than the direct pursuit of my vengeance against Tsenit and the Ska'i. That is my vow, and I will swear it again in the Temple of the Ancestor if you wish.'

'No need,' said Belerith. 'You have my blessing, and my wife's, and that of all our council. You may also have five hundred men – three hundred of them will be fully trained troops from my army, the rest made up of militia men – part-time soldiers maybe, but fit, and armed, and willing. How will that suit you?'

'It will suit me very well, Uncle,' said Ansaryon. 'And I and all my men – and women – thank you, with all our hearts.'

'Family duty, my dear boy – think nothing of it,' said Belerith, waving a be-ringed hand, and once more the jovial host. 'But there is one thing you can do in return – also a family matter.'

Ansaryon's face had grown suddenly wary. Only those who knew him well would know that look, but Halthris recognized it. 'Of course, Uncle – anything within my power.'

'As you know, my dear wife and I have been blessed with many children. Young Tesi and Sedrano are married now, of course, with children of their own, and Alayni here has many times told me that she has no intention of marrying anyone less intelligent than herself – which in her view comprises the entire male population of the known world!'

Alayni smiled rather wryly at this, as if it were an old and familiar bone of contention between them.

'But my four younger daughters are all in hopes of a husband, one day soon. When you have retaken Zithirian and dealt your rogue brother his just deserts, you will need to marry and found a dynasty, or you'll find the Toktel'yans eager to stake their claim. So, cousin, when it's all done and finished, come back here and make your choice, eh? Anmari's a kind sensible girl who won't give anyone any trouble – Merrith is almost as clever as Alayni but doesn't give herself such airs – Djeyis sews the finest embroidery outside Zithirian – and Hathenas – well, you'll have to see Hathenas for yourself. Prettiest girl in all Lelyent, for my money. So there you are – what do you say?'

'Thank you very much, Uncle,' said Ansaryon solemnly, with the exact manner of a child receiving birthing-day gifts.

Belerith laughed and slapped his thigh. 'I promise you won't regret it! And where else would you find a wife worthy of you? My two nieces in Minassa are children – and so are most of the Emperor's daughters.'

There is Kefiri, Halthris thought, but knew even as the image of Ansaryon's cousin rose in her mind that she would not wish to become Queen of Zithirian. She hated the city, she wanted only to remain at Sar D'yenyi. And in any case, Kefiri seemed far too young. Tanathi women did not usually marry until they were well into their twenties.

If the Ska'i had not attacked Zithirian, she would now be Vinnath's wife, perhaps already carrying his child.

Significantly, she found the thought alarming, as if she had just managed to escape from great danger.

They stayed six days in Lelyent, long enough for the river boats which would take them three hundred and fifty miles down the Ger to Minassa to be prepared and provisioned. During that time, Ansaryon's army was treated like royalty: roast sheep every night, crowds of admiring children round them during the day, a ready audience for their hair-raising and not greatly exaggerated tales of battles and escapes and marches, and troops of giggling girls, pretty as flowers in the bright braided dresses traditional in Lelyent, all eager to claim a soldier for their own.

Aware that the most arduous part of their long journey was already over, the army revelled in all this luxury and attention, and took its leave of Lelyent with regret, but with considerable anticipation. Already, many of the former miners, shepherds, fishermen and so on, who comprised the bulk of Ansaryon's forces, had travelled five times further than ever in their lives before. Lelyent was a pretty place, but must pale before the prosperous craftsmen's city of Minassa, and the legendary wonders of Toktel'yi. Fifty of them, chosen by lot and deeply envious, were ordered to stay behind, to help organize the Lelyentan contingent. They would escort them to the meeting place near Minassa by summer's end, along with the horses which had carried many of the soldiers from Sar D'yenyi, and which would not now be needed until the final march on Zithirian. The rest of the army embarked on the river-boats with their leader.

The almond-trees in the orchards along the Ger were in full bloom as the two score of boats gathered by Prince Belerith moved ponderously into the current. They were quite unlike the graceful, swan-like craft seen on the Kefirinn, with their bright triangular sails and swooping lines. The River Ger was shallow and fast-moving, and the vessels which plied on it were correspondingly shallow-draughted, indeed little better than rafts, made of logs lashed together with a single low mast and square, ugly sail.

Apart from the crossing from Sar D'yenyi, Halthris had never been on a boat before, and the sight of these rudimentary examples, laden with stores and equipment, did not exactly fill her with pleasurable excitement. From their rather set, concentrated expressions, Inri and Sherren felt the same. And every hair on Fess's back was stark, her eyes narrowed, her tongue constantly licking her lips with fright. In the end, Halthris knelt beside her, and attempted to communicate, in simple mind-pictures, that there was absolutely nothing to fear. It wasn't easy, as she was not so sure of it herself. But at last Fess followed her on board with grudging reluctance, and stayed beside her, glued to her leg, all the way down the bright running river to Minassa.

Minassa was close to the steppe grassland that was Fess's natural home, and where, Halthris knew, with sorrow and also with acceptance, she would have to let her beloved cat free.

With the thaw, a little normality had returned to Zithirian. Since only six warriors out of two and a half thousand had survived the attack on Sar D'yenyi, the remaining Ska'i, though still rapacious and savage, were less of a burden on the unfortunate citizens. And the disappearance of the snow meant that the tribesmen could now hunt and raid across the edge of the steppe and along the valley of the Kefirinn, activities much more to their taste than robbing the people in the city. Those inhabitants who had come through the winter began to breathe a little easier, and to think that, possibly, their remaining life-spans might be measured in months or years rather than hours or days.

And spring in Zithirian was always a time of great beauty. Even now, when many of the trees and plants in their tubs and pots and boxes had died from the frost because no one had been able to bring them indoors or cover them with protective blankets, the city was bursting with fresh green leaves, flowers blazoned in strident shades of red and yellow, eager birdsong and heartening warmth. It was difficult to be miserable or terrified when all around the year's renewal symbolized hope, rebirth, regrowth. A lush forest of grass and trumpet vines spread over the devastated ruins of the Palace and its gardens, hiding the black fire scars and concealing overlooked corpses with vivid and kindly green.

Perhaps the only native of the city not to feel happier with the approach of summer was its Crowned and Chosen King. The return of Br'nnayak and his five companions from Sar D'yenyi, with a graphic and appalling account of the fate of Quenait's brother Oquargul and two and a half thousand Ska'i, had thrown him into a paroxysm of rage. Later, as he began to realize what this defeat meant, he had gazed into an abyss of despair.

Ansaryon was alive. Somehow, he had managed to conserve, even to improve, his powers of sorcery. How this could be when D'thliss, months ago, had assured him that Ansaryon had no Anna-tal with him, Tsenit could not imagine. By rights, the removal of the drug should have killed him outright, or at least left him an impotent, mindless husk. Instead, he had survived with his abilities unaffected, and had used them to defeat and destroy the Ska'i in less time and with less effort than it took to climb to the top of the central tower.

Bitterly, Tsenit had cursed his brother. He cursed Br'nnayak too (though only when alone), for the shaman's own much-vaunted powers had obviously been too feeble to withstand Ansaryon's. His own position, too, was beginning to seem more and more precarious. He depended on the Ska'i to keep the city in subjection, and to defend him from Ansaryon if – when – he came to claim the throne. But they were a hideous burden, always having to be fed, appeased, restrained. Without D'thliss's influence, he suspected that they would long ago have slain the entire population. Somehow, the priestess had managed to persuade Quenait and his shaman that wholesale destruction and slaughter would not bring them the mountain of gold which they craved.

But that strategy had one obvious disadvantage. The Ska'i had no intention of leaving until they got what was promised them.

Quenait was implacable, and since he was now ruler of Zithirian in all but name, Tsenit could do nothing. Sar D'yenyi was now safe until next winter, so he and the city must endure these violent and greedy invaders for at least six more months.

And what would Ansaryon do in the meantime? According to D'thliss, he was training an army of exiles. Their numbers were pathetic compared to the Ska'i, but they were still a threat. He wouldn't sit in Sar D'yenyi for ever: he would ask the neighbouring cities for help. Lelyent and Minassa would give it willingly – their rulers had already made it plain to Tsenit's ambassadors that they were appalled by events in Zithirian, and would not acknowledge him as its true King.

The help that such puny places could offer Ansaryon would not count for much against Quenait's warriors, still more than five thousand strong. But Tsenit sometimes had the despairing feeling, in the sleepless small hours of the night, that he was floundering powerless in a sticky, merciless morass, and that control of events had slid out of his hands. Quenait treated him with open contempt, all the more insulting because he was such a primitive and disgusting barbarian; Br'nnayak utterly terrified him; and D'thliss, once such a soothing, encouraging and flattering ally, was now brusque and impatient, scolding him as if he were a child. She fed him scraps of information, doubtless obtained by dark sorcery, and he suspected that he was only told what she wished him to know.

He had begun all this: it was his idea, his plan, his strategy. It had worked so well to start with. And only now was he beginning to see, dimly, that his three allies had trapped him: that he had been their willing and gullible tool all along.

But during the more cheerful hours of daylight, his natural optimism revived. Once the Ska'i were gone he could get rid of D'thliss, with the help of the other priests, who undoubtedly loathed her. And then he would be King in truth, and the Golden Age would begin, an age of beauty and prosperity that would cast long shadows down the ages, so that in centuries to come men would talk about the reign of Good King Tsenit, Third of His Name, with the same awe, reverence and wonder with which they spoke of the Divine Tayo.

And no one, *no one*, would remember how he had achieved the throne in the first place.

Some of the people who had fled from Zithirian during the attack and the terrible winter that followed it were beginning to trickle back to the city, drawn by hope or by the desire to discover what had happened to relatives and friends. Every day, a small number of travellers would approach the gates nervously, giving the Ska'i camp, sprawled along the river bank, a very wide berth, and glancing with sickened horror at the trophy lances, laden with withered heads and gorged crows, that bristled out of the green grass sward where the Gathering Fair had always been held. The tribesmen ignored those who carried pathetic bundles, but anyone rash enough to appear on horseback, or with any animal in tow, was instantly and brutally relieved of their livestock.

The peasant girl trudging towards the city on this particular afternoon, warm and pleasant after overnight rain, was just like all the others: weary, hungry, and apprehensive. Her face dirty, her hair tangled under the leather cap, her skirts ripped and the soles of her boots almost worn away with long walking, no one but her closest friends would have recognized in this bedraggled figure a Princess of Zithirian. And much to Kefiri's relief, everyone she had so far encountered had unquestioningly assumed that she was exactly what she appeared to be.

The journey from Sar D'yenyi had taken her seven days, and she was exhausted. The mule which she had taken to ride had proved to be a fatally clumsy beast, and had broken a leg early on, falling on rocky ground. Summoning up all her courage, Kefiri had cut its throat and left it to the kites. Her clothes had been spattered with its blood, but that no longer appalled her. After six more days tramping through the mountains and negotiating the river D'yenn, her skirt was so filthy, torn and caked with mud that its original colour was indiscernible.

She had met no one until her descent, nervous but grimly determined, into the greener valley of the D'yenn as it approached Zithirian. Here, she came upon a small band of ragged, hungry-looking young men and women, who had spent all winter sheltering in a remote farmstead that the Ska'i had failed to find. Now, emboldened by the arrival of spring, and also driven by the need to find food for other members of the group left at the farm, they were going to Zithirian to see what was there.

Kefiri told them that she had been a refugee at Sar D'yenyi, and was returning to search for her parents, and they accepted her story without question. None of them had lived in the city, so she could invent a home and family in the Potters' Quarter without fear of discovery. Her five new-found companions were all haggard and gaunt, with prominent bones and the blank, incurious looks of those who have endured months of semi-starvation. She suggested to them that they should go back to the farm if Zithirian proved too dangerous, collect the children and old people, and make their way to Sar D'yenyi, where there was food, shelter and safety for the summer at least.

Up nearer the mountains, some of the farmsteads had still been occupied, and looked unmolested, although those living in them were distinctly unfriendly. Kefiri's group was warned off with shouts, dogs and even, once, a volley of arrows, which fortunately fell well short. The others seemed unsurprised, but Kefiri was shocked and angry at first. Surely, in these desperate times, giving food and shelter to six hungry travellers was a natural act of kindness?

But then they began to pass farms that were blackened and ruined, the headless remains of their inhabitants often left to rot outside the buildings. And she realized that to those who had kept their homes and their lives, any passing stranger was a threat.

She was very glad to have company, even if it meant that she had to share out the food in her pack: her conscience would not allow her to keep the spiced dried meat, crisp-baked bread, raisins and kuldi all to herself. It certainly heartened her companions, and the last few days of the journey were accomplished quite quickly.

They came within sight of Zithirian, and Kefiri saw the distant shape of the city, hunched around the Kefirinn, and could not at first think what was so terribly different. Then she remembered that the Royal Palace had been largely destroyed. Only the great central tower, so Invan had said, still remained standing amongst the ruins.

And there it was, looking very tall and bulky without the slender satellite towers around it, all now vanished. From its topmost pinnacle a tiny pennant fluttered in the afternoon breeze. She wondered what Tsenit would have taken for his own device, as was the custom for each King. His father's banner had featured a vine, symbol of prosperity and loyalty. By rights, she thought, her usurping cousin should choose a kite, the archetypal greedy robber.

The River Kefirinn, of course, was no longer frozen. Swollen with melted snow, it was running high and swift through the rapids above its confluence with the D'yenn. The roar of the waters could be heard a long way off, while the spray hung above the low cliffs in a cloud of white spume. In normal times, there were ferries to transport travellers from the east across the river to the city, but Kefiri had no idea whether they still operated. At least one, however, must still be in use, and she led her five companions along the bank of the river until they came to the cemetery.

She had often strolled here with her friends from the Temple

School, under the shade of the tall trees: it was a popular place to walk on warm summer evenings. Now, it appeared to be at once neglected and well-used. Grass and weeds sprouted through the gravel, and trumpet vines, that could climb the highest tower between spring and autumn, were already enveloping some of the monuments. But every scrap of space seemed to be occupied by a fresh grave, often with no more than the bare name and dates of its occupant scratched on a piece of wood laid on the earth.

A place that had once been pleasant now wore a sinister, silent, menacing air. There was a strong smell of death and decay, and Kefiri glimpsed a pack of skeletal dogs fighting over something a little way off. With a shudder, she averted her eyes and hurried down to the river's edge.

Yes, there was a ferry there. Two of the long thin grave-boats, designed to carry a coffin and half-a-dozen mourners, were tied up to the wooden jetty. The fare had once been five of the tiny silver coins called chells, but Kefiri realized suddenly, with a sick feeling of dismay, that she had no money. It had never been necessary in Sar D'yenyi, and it had not crossed her mind to bring any with her.

Well, she still had a little food, and there were also the minute chips of adulterated silver sewn round her leather cap, peasant style. She walked down the ramp and along the jetty, her footsteps echoing dully off the rough brown water underneath.

'Ferry?' The man rose up from one of the boats almost at her feet, making her jump. 'Want a ferry, do you?' He looked her up and down, assessing her deplorable state, and grinned. 'It looks as if you've been walking a long way, darling.'

'I have,' said Kefiri briefly, with a sinking heart. 'How much, for me and my friends?'

'You want to get into Zithirian? That's funny, most sensible folk want to get out.'

'I need to find my parents,' Kefiri told him wearily. Suddenly, with the city so close, the ruined towers and heaps of rubble marking the Royal Palace only five hundred paces across the river, she wanted nothing more than to find a quiet place and sleep, sleep, sleep, until she was restored to her usual energy and strength.

'Well, good luck to you. It'll cost you ten chells, and another ten each for your friends. Got the money, darling?' He was quite young, well-muscled like all ferrymen, and he was eyeing her in a way that made her feel acutely uncomfortable.

To her shame, Kefiri's voice wobbled. 'I – I haven't. I've been in the mountains all winter, and so have they.'

'You've got that, though.' He was looking down at her hand.

She followed his gaze and realized that she was still wearing the small, plain gold ring that had been her mother's, and which she had worn since she was ten years old. She was so used to the feel of it that she had not even thought about taking it off, though it was hardly the sort of thing a peasant girl would wear.

'My ring?' she said, and her hand curled over it protectively. 'I can't give you that – it was my grandmother's! And it's worth far more than sixty chells.'

'Suit yourself, darling – unless you want to pay in kind, of course – know what I mean?' He leered up at her, his eyes now frankly lecherous.

Kefiri glanced back, and saw her companions standing uncertainly on the jetty. The three men were tired, weak and thin, and even together would be no match for the brawny ferryman.

Angrily, she hauled the ring off and thrust it into his hand. 'There you are. Now take us.'

For a nerve-wracking length of time, he examined it, held it up, bit it and eventually pushed it into his belt-purse. 'Come on then, darling, you and your band of scarecrows. Though you won't find much to fatten you up over there!'

They sat huddled in the stern of the boat, and watched as the ferryman put on his thick leather gauntlets and took hold of the oars. Although the current was flowing swiftly, he was strong enough to hold the craft steadily on its course, even in the middle of the stream, and guided it unerringly across the river to the corresponding jetty jutting out from the northern side of the docks.

There were soldiers waiting for them, in the round helmets and fishscale armour of the Royal Guard. Kefiri's heart lurched, but she tried to keep her face impassive. Surely, surely no one could possibly recognize her in this ragged and disreputable guise?

They did not. A cursory examination of her almost empty pack, a few brief questions, and they let her go. An argument broke out as she turned to see how her companions fared. One of the young men had a knife hidden in his tunic, and the soldiers obviously thought this was highly suspicious. Kefiri walked unobtrusively away along the dockside, not looking back. She didn't like to abandon them, but at all costs she must avoid any trouble that might increase her chances of being detected.

She listened for the shout, the running feet, but no one seemed to have noticed her departure. She slipped round the corner of the nearest warehouse, and let out a gusty sigh of relief. For the moment, she was safe. But what now?

It was late afternoon. She had no idea how or when the curfew now operated, but all the refugees had reported that it was strictly enforced. The docks were usually seething with activity at this time of year, but were now almost deserted, save for a few people desultorily picking through heaps of rubbish by a burnt-out building. She trudged past without glancing at them, hoping that she looked too poor and too purposeful to be worth robbing. There had been rough areas in the Potters' Quarter, where daring fellow-students had gone to slum it in dubious taverns, but she had never before seen poverty and devastation on this scale, and it frightened and horrified her.

And where was she to go? Foolishly, in her haste to escape Sar D'yenyi and do something useful, she had given absolutely no thought to what she would do once she reached the city. She could hardly go knocking on doors begging for a bed, and she had no money, so she couldn't buy a room in an inn. She knew no one here save her cousin Tsenit. And he, for very obvious reasons, would be more than delighted to find her at the Palace gate asking for help.

But she must find some shelter for the night, and quickly – it couldn't be long now till sunrise. She walked faster, ignoring the inviting calls of a pair of evil-looking men skulking by another looted warehouse, and on impulse swung right as she reached the end of the docks.

It brought her to the broad sweep of the Ceremonial Way, leading up to the Palace. And a group of Ska'i were riding down it.

Fighting panic, she stood still, clutching her bundle, eyes averted. They passed her in a waft of unwashed greasy bodies and reeking leather, and she sighed with relief. They obviously thought her not worth the trouble of robbing.

'Saw you swanning past so high and mighty – we not good enough for the likes of you, eh?'

It was one of the men who had called to her from the warehouse. As she whipped round with a gasp, he grabbed her hand and pulled her into his embrace. For an instant, frantic, she smelt his stinking breath, felt his hand clawing at her breast, his unshaven jaw rasping against her skin as he forced his mouth against hers.

Wild with terror, she bit him. He jerked back, blood pouring from his lip. She wrenched herself free and ran across the Way and into the streets of the Goldsmiths' Quarter on the other side.

They were wide, straight, and apparently completely lacking in hiding places. She glanced back and saw that he was coming after her. Panic spurred her on. She dodged down a sidestreet, up a narrow alley between the blank high walls of two wealthy houses, ran through a large and rather overgrown public garden and into another alley. He was still behind, though dropping back. She could hear him cursing her, and knew that if he caught her, rape would be the best she could expect.

Another garden, glimpsed green between tall pillars, plenty of shrubs and trees. Her breath tearing in her lungs, she looked behind. Her pursuer was not yet in view. Uttering a frantic prayer to Tayo, she plunged through the narrow gap and threw herself deep into the nearest tangle of bushes.

One of them was a firethorn. Ignoring the sharp needle-like pains in hands and arms, Kefiri wriggled deeper beneath it, curled herself up into a ball, and tried to control her sobbing breath. If he found her here, there would be no escape.

But from the sound of it, he had not even noticed this tiny refuge. The running footsteps hurried past, and the furious voice diminished into the distance. Sick and shaking with relief, she almost wept.

It was almost dark under the thick new leaves, and suddenly she heard the curfew horn, low and booming through the city. Even if she emerged now from her hiding place, she risked attracting the attention of any soldiers on patrol.

She extracted the worst of the thorns from her hands, and searched inside her pack. She found some raisins, a large piece of the flat, crisp-baked bread that was standard fare on long journeys, some dried meat and a few sips left in her water-skin. She ate and drank everything, and then pulled her torn and dirty cloak around her. The nights were still cold at this time of year, but the worn felt was sufficient protection. Exhausted, she fell asleep almost at once.

She woke to birdsong, to morning light, and to the eerie, alarming sensation that she was being watched. Suddenly afraid, she sat up, and saw two boys crouching beside her.

The elder one, dark-haired, she had never seen before. The other, terrifyingly, she knew very well.

'Hello, Lady,' said the child called Bron.

CHAPTER
SEVENTEEN

King Temiltan of Minassa was a lean, spare, balding man in his fifties, with an air of barely-contained energy that made him seem much younger than he actually was. He had married Tesi of Lelyent rather late in life – she was only forty-two now – and they had a teenage son and two younger daughters. Under his rule, Minassa had prospered. The King was keen to foster the city's principal industry, the production of a wide range of famous and very beautiful pottery, and was an enthusiastic amateur potter himself. He spent much of his limited spare time hobnobbing with masters of the craft, or buried in the superbly-equipped workshop he had set up for himself in the Palace, honing his skills and experimenting with new glazes and techniques.

As a result of his active encouragement, the Minassan styles, always lovely, had reached new heights of elegance and sophistication. There was no house with any pretensions to wealth and taste, anywhere in the known world, from the pirate city of Fabriz in the west to the matriarchal lands of Kerenth in the east, the Toktel'yan Empire in between, on the islands of the Archipelago or up the Kefirinn to Zithirian, that did not have at least one item of Minassan pottery proudly displayed. The rich possessed complete sets – goblets, jugs, plates, bowls – arrayed on shelves, and the wealthiest of all flaunted the fact that they could replace such expensive wares with ease by actually using them.

There were over a thousand potters in Minassa at the last count, each with their own subtle variations on the city style, and each the master of a workshop employing up to six apprentices, as well as the services of a skilled brush-artist. Many potters married their artists, and reared their children to follow the craft. Every night, Minassa glowed fiery red from all the kilns and furnaces across the city, and every day a pall of smoke hovered above the roofs, to be eventually dispersed by the wind. The place was bustling, dirty and unpretentious: a typical Minassan always boasted of his or her plain honest craftsmanship. All their sense of beauty was poured into the infinitely pliable clay, leaving none over for the city. Let Zithirian give itself airs, calling itself the Flower of the World, the Silver City

– Minassa was where true artistry flourished, and everlasting loveliness created. For pottery can be broken, but never utterly destroyed.

The riverboats slid gently down the Ger on the last stage of the journey, and tied up at the Minassan docks. They had to be lashed together because space at the quayside was very limited. There were many more Kefirinn boats tied up here than normal, for the Toktel'yan trading captains had no wish to risk their vessels and their cargoes by sailing on to Zithirian. One man had foolishly ignored the danger, and he and his ship had not returned, so the suspicious captains feared the worst. Accordingly, they had gone no further than Minassa, selling their wares at cut rates with the thought that a safe small profit was better than a larger but risky one, and those potters and their families with money to spend – the vast majority – had enjoyed themselves buying up the bargain luxuries that usually went straight on to Zithirian.

Once more, Ansaryon and his small army were fêted like conquering heroes. The Minassans had much more to fear from the Ska'i than Lelyent: they were only a few days' easy travel down the river valley from Zithirian, and their city was poorly defended and full of plunder. But they were used to living with dangerous neighbours: Toktel'yi had always cast covetous eyes northwards, and Temiltan, like his predecessors, paid a handsome yearly tribute to the Emperor for the privilege of not being attacked.

The possibility of invasion from two directions at once was not a pleasant one, and Temiltan, of necessity, had learned his statecraft in a wily and devious school. Anyone who wished to get rid of the Ska'i was his friend, and would earn his wholehearted support. Unlike Belerith, he had no qualms about the idea of asking the Emperor for help: indeed, he had suggestions of his own to make. 'If you can, see the boy, the Emperor-in-waiting, Ba'alekkt. He's a proper young firebrand, by all accounts – we'll have trouble from him in the years ahead, if he survives, but he's only thirteen or fourteen, so he can't expand the Empire on his own just yet. He'll be very keen to help you, I reckon, and his father dotes on him. Ba'alekkt is supposed to be the only one who can get him to take any action at all.'

Temiltan was also very helpful on practical matters. The army were given billets in the city, with Ansaryon and his chief officers in the Palace, and the King promised at least a thousand men in his support. He also suggested a suitable rendezvous at a place called Chearno, some ten miles south-west of Minassa. There, before the last dark moon of summer, the force sent from Lelyent would meet with the Tanathi, the men supplied by Minassa, and Ansaryon's army, hopefully enlarged by a substantial contingent of Imperial soldiers.

If the Emperor obliged. And if his help was not offered only in exchange for promises and obligations that would place Ansaryon and his people under an intolerable burden in years to come. But there was no way out: they needed Toktel'yan support. And the price of it might be too heavy to pay.

At Zithirian, the Kefirinn ran narrow and deep between low, rocky cliffs. By the time it reached Minassa, three hundred miles to the south, the land through which it flowed had become broader and flatter, with gentle hills descending gradually to a wide plain through which the river meandered lazily, flooding it every spring. The receding waters left a thick black soil, extremely fertile, in which Minassan farmers grew grains, flax, hemp, pulses, vines, fruit trees and above all vegetables. Aristocratic Zithiriani had always sneered at the hard-working peasants of Minassa, purveying pots and peas and cabbages, and in return the Minassans muttered darkly about snooty folk who couldn't produce anything more useful than a row of fancy stitching on someone else's silk.

This contrast in attitudes was nowhere more vividly ilustrated than in the palaces of the two cities. Zithirian's was built for show and display, to awe and intimidate the population: it was a fortress and refuge, as well as the Royal Family's home, and it turned its back on the river, preferring to glower at its subjects instead. But at Minassa, Temiltan's ancestors had constructed a low, modest, rambling, comfortable place, rather in the Toktel'yan style, but of white Annako stone. Its lovely terraced gardens, bursting with flowers in all the glory of early summer, descended in gentle steps to the northern bank of the Kefirinn. Here, there was a splendid view of the lovely, high-arched bridges, which joined the three parts of the river-sundered city together.

The Tanathi were herders, not growers, and Halthris had never been able to appreciate the Zithiriani passion for gardens. But in Minassa, the shrubs and trees and plants had not been forced to grow in tubs, nor had their branches been clipped into symmetrical and coldly formal shapes: and statues, fountains, arched walks, pools and other ornamental features were obviously not in fashion. Instead, the flowers here were allowed to grow to their natural height and spread, to mix with each other in joyous and unregulated profusion, and even to fall over to sprawl across the grass if their habit dictated. And the Palace Garden was not the exclusive preserve of the King, his family and Court: at certain hours, anyone in Minassa could stroll down to the river's edge to feed the swans, ducks and other waterfowl that congregated hopefully along the bank.

But at sunset, the place was almost deserted, save for the rightful King of Zithirian, leaning over the plain stone balustrade in the lowest terrace in the west-facing part of the garden.

Here, if he turned his head to look upstream, past the North Bridge, he could see, just, where the huddled houses and workshops of Minassa, crowding down to the huge oaken piles of the Flood Wall, gave way to the green fields that lined the banks of the Kefirinn, all the way to Zithirian. Three hundred miles: two hundred and ten to the border town of Hailyan, famous for its wines, and another ninety to the city of his birth.

Here all was peaceful and prosperous, just as Zithirian had appeared to be: but he knew, had known for a long time, that the wealth of Minassa was more securely based, more just, more equitable, than in his own land. The Zithiriani dismissed Temiltan and his subjects as mere craftsmen, and their city a dirty place of few wonders and less beauty. But although there were rich and poor in Minassa, and many worked hard while a few did not need to, no one starved, no one felt oppressed, and there were no hidden, savage undercurrents of resentment, hatred and fear.

And no priests of Tayo, either. Temiltan, an essentially practical man, made no secret of the fact that he did not worship any gods, and did not care who or what his subjects revered as long as their beliefs did not impinge on other people's lives. And since devotion to the Divine Tayo was essentially an artificial concept, alien to the industrious potters and farmers of Minassa, most of whom had no kinship with the founder of Zithirian or his followers, his veneration was confined to a very few aristocratic families who imported Zithiriani priests to serve their households. Everyone else, in common with the rest of the known world outside Zithirian and the Empire, adhered to Hegeden and Sarraliss and their satellite deities, and worshipped them in the age-old manner, in their own ways and in their own homes.

Like his uncle Temiltan, Ansaryon was a descendant of Tayo, but he felt no love for the Divine Ancestor, and only hatred for the powerful priests, their corruption, their wealth, their relentless ambition, the way they used fear and sorcery to assert their authority over the people. And above all he loathed D'thliss, supreme embodiment of all that was worst, most evil, in the Temple. She had played a major part in the plot to murder his family, he knew. She had hooked her claws into Tsenit some years ago, after her discovery that he, Ansaryon, was no longer a willing vessel for her aspirations. And Tsenit, himself ruthlessly ambitious for power, had been her eager tool.

He could not entirely blame his younger brother, for he knew how easy it was to become tangled in the High Priestess's web. Under her loathsome spell, he had done things that would lay a vast and terrible burden of guilt on his soul, for ever more. But at least he had found the courage, and the strength, to tear himself free. He was a Mazath, of course, which had helped him considerably. It seemed, though, that Tsenit must lack both the will and the power to escape. And Ansaryon did not have the murders of most of his family on his conscience.

He turned his mind away from his brother, and breathed deeply in the evening air. It was not so clean as Zithirian's: he smelt smoke, flowers, fumes from the pottery kilns, and, very faintly, freshly mown grass from the haymaking in distant fields. It was good to be alone for once, to have the leisure and space to think about the long, hard road he must travel, the dangers to be faced and the difficulties he must overcome, before he ever saw the silver city again.

And the loneliness . . .

He had had friends long ago, as a boy, before D'thliss changed him for ever. Now, the hideous secret memories of his past lay like a wall between him and anyone who might be tempted to overlook the inevitable gulf of rank, and approach him too close.

He thought of the two people, both women, who had in the past few months almost breached that wall. Kefiri, of course, had known him all her life, but there was a ten-year gap in their ages, and he still could not help thinking of her as a child. She was not, though: and if anything were to happen to him, the torch of opposition to Tsenit would pass into her reluctant hands. She certainly seemed to have matured a great deal from the shy, unhappy Temple schoolgirl who had always been homesick for the beauty of Sar D'yenyi.

Halthris, outspoken, infuriating, was so different from the delicately sophisticated women of the Zithiriani Court that they hardly seemed to be the same sex. Nevertheless, he had come to trust her honesty and to value her deflating sense of humour. No flattery, hypocrisy, pretension or even tact distorted her mind: she said what she thought, with refreshing and breathtaking candour. And he realized, with some regret, that he missed her company. At Lelyent, they had embarked on different boats, and when he had seen her, she had usually had Invan on one side and Fess on the other. It was a formidable combination, and he, preoccupied with a host of other tasks and problems, had not had either the time or the opportunity to speak.

Moreover, he thought, with a wry smile, any attempt at a quiet private chat would probably be misconstrued by his General, who seemed to regard the Tanathi woman as his private property – although Halthris did not appear to realize it, or was not averse to his company.

His mind drifted on to the four Lelyentan daughters. He had agreed to marry one of them, though it was not an inspiring prospect. He suspected that if Temiltan had had a girl old enough, he would have been offered her as well. And there were several Toktel'yan princesses who would probably be put forward as a bribe, a threat or a condition of help.

The woman whom he would eventually marry meant little to him. Whoever she might be, he could never allow her close enough to know his soul: and so any kind of love or affection between them would be out of the question. A matter of policy, no more: and whether she were young or old, beautiful or plain, kind or shrewish, Toktel'yan or Lelyentan or Minassan, mattered not at all.

The sun had set in a blaze of scarlet glory behind the smoking chimneys of Minassa. A stork flew lazily across the glowing sky, legs trailing, to some roost on roof-top or tree. Below him, the dark snow-swollen water of the Kefirinn whirled and eddied as the swifter, colder stream of the Ger poured into the flow. One or two night fishermen were out already, lanterns in the prow of each boat, the men poised with spear or trident to stab the fish as they came to investigate the light. It was a scene of humble peace, and profound ordinariness, and extraordinary beauty. No wonder Minassans loved their city with a passion bordering on ferocity. And because of the evening calm, and because he was utterly alone, he opened his mind to the air around him, and to the spirits of this place.

It enhanced the senses: he became slowly, then acutely aware of every nuance of sound, of scent, of vision. He could hear the rustlings of mice amongst the flowers, the minute hum of evening insects collecting pollen, and smell the astonishingly powerful fragrance of the insignificant little plant called the Night Rose. He could feel the tense breathing of the man in the nearest fishing boat, the ache in the muscles of his forearm as he stood motionless, spear poised, waiting for the first tiny movement of a rising fish. He could see the ducks paddling together in the shelter of the river-bank, the water rippling gently round them, and the ghostly, graceful swans sleeping, heads tucked under wings, on their ramshackle nests. If he wanted, he could send his soul soaring into the still air, to gaze down on rivers and city and all who dwelled in it, with unseen, all-seeing eyes.

Someone else was in the garden. He felt her presence, sensed that she was unaware of him, and withdrew his mind. But too late: even as he came back to his earthbound self, he knew that her footsteps had turned in his direction.

Halthris had no idea of why she had come to the garden, save that she liked the place, and wanted to be on her own for a while. Inri and Sherren were still so deep in the first throes of passion that they had only eyes for each other, and had gone off together without waiting for supper. She was uncomfortably aware that Invan's feelings for her were growing stronger, and it was becoming increasingly difficult to fend him off. Tonight, however, she had managed to slip out of a side door while he was talking to Queen Tesi. In these large gardens, he would never find her. And she wanted to prepare herself, and Fess, for what was to come.

She strolled down the meandering stone paths towards the quiet river, her cat padding softly at her side. The voyage down the river from Lelyent had been a nightmare for poor Fess, and Halthris knew, with resigned sadness, that it would be cruelty to subject her to another long boat trip. And how would she fare in the hot, humid, alien surroundings of Toktel'yi? She would be much happier in the familiar freedom of the steppe, which lay only twenty miles or so to the west of Minassa. And if she wanted to renew her companionship with Halthris, she could return at summer's end, and find her.

Knowing it was easy. Telling her, in simple mind-pictures, would be very much more difficult. And trying to explain that this parting was for Fess's benefit, and was therefore no betrayal, would be the hardest of all.

The cat stopped suddenly, and uttered a soft rumble of welcome. Abruptly snatched from her reverie, Halthris realized that she was not alone. Someone stood on the lowest terrace, watching her.

For the briefest instant, she felt the touch of his mind in greeting, and knew who it was. 'Good evening, Lord Ansaryon,' she said formally, and came down the last steps to join him.

'Lord?'

She recognized the tone of his voice, and grinned. 'We've become rather distant lately, haven't we? So I thought it was appropriate.'

'A hit. My apologies – I have had a great deal on my mind, as perhaps you'll understand.' He smiled in return. 'A definite mistake on my part, I think – I've rather missed our talks.'

'Did you bring me here?'

Her voice was suddenly suspicious. He shook his head. 'No – not intentionally, anyway. Why? Did it feel as though I did?'

'I wanted to come here, but I didn't know why. Perhaps our minds are still in touch, without us being aware of it.'

'That could be possible. But so little has been written about such things. The accepted doctrine of the Mazath, and the Priests of Tayo, states that sorcery, thought-link, all these things, are not innate, and must be taught and practised with the aid of Annatal. There's nothing about people who appear, like you, to have natural gifts. Or about people who successfully withdraw from Annatal, and find their skills and powers undiminished. That's one reason why I want to go to Toktel'yi.'

Halthris had a sudden memory of Kefiri telling her about the Empire's matter-of-fact attitude to sorcery. She said slowly, 'It's not forbidden there, is it?'

'The reverse. They have schools for wizards, every village has its magic-worker, and there's a Guild of Sorcery to organize it all. The Court Sorcerer has the respect of everyone in the Empire, including Djamal himself. I visited Toktel'yi when I was hardly more than a boy – I was training to be a Mazath, but in secret, of course. No one in my entourage knew about it, so I could hardly question the Court Sorcerer openly, or go to lectures at the Toktel'yi School of Wizardry. This time, everyone knows what I am, and if I can understand what has happened to me, and why it has happened, I may be able to use my powers more effectively. There's always the chance that the Emperor will refuse to help, in which case I'll need the strongest sorcery possible to have a hope of regaining Zithirian.'

'Is it likely that he'll refuse?'

'It's certainly a possibility. But putting me under an obligation to him is so full of potential advantage to the Empire that I'm fairly sure his advisers won't let him refuse. I know I'm sacrificing the long-term safety of Zithirian for my own short-term interests—'

'Really? Kicking the Ska'i out of Zithirian is just in *your* interests?' Halthris's voice was scathing. 'I don't think the citizens would agree, somehow.'

'You're right – they wouldn't. Whether they'd agree with what I want to do when – if – we do get rid of the Ska'i, is another matter.'

'Which is?'

'To make Zithirian less like Toktel'yi and more like Minassa.'

Out on the river, a splash and a yell of triumph came from one of the boats. The man in the bow waved his spear aloft, a fat flapping fish impaled on it.

'They train birds to fish for them, in Toktel'yi,' Ansaryon said softly. 'But the Kefirinn there is so poisoned with filth and rubbish that I wouldn't care to eat anything that came out of it. The greatest city in the world, the heart of the greatest empire ever known, and it stinks like a week-old carcass, and teems with as many maggots. You'll see for yourself, soon – it'll only take seven or eight days to get there, travelling downstream.'

Halthris was silent, looking out at the dimly shining river. At last she said reflectively, 'I never knew – when I agreed to warn Zithirian about the Ska'i, all those months ago – I never guessed where the journey would lead me. I don't think any Tanathi will ever have travelled so far as Inri and Sherren and I have, in all our history. And we will never be the same, we will never be able to drop back into our old lives as if nothing had happened.'

'Perhaps they will. But you – you have always been too restless, haven't you?'

She glanced at him, startled, and then smiled rather ruefully. 'You're right, I suppose I have. Stinking or not, I long to see Toktel'yi. And the only thing I really regret is that I must leave Fess behind.'

The cat, sensing that Halthris was talking about her, leaned her head against her leg. She reached down to stroke her, and went on sadly. 'She hated the boat so much, I can't force her to endure that again. So tomorrow, I am going to take her up to the steppe, and set her free. And although the parting will be painful for both of us, I think she will be glad to go.'

Ansaryon said nothing, but she sensed his sympathy. Determined not to let it affect her, she changed the subject. 'Look – the lamps are being lit.'

Every so often, all along the balustrade, a lantern hung from a plain iron stand set into the top of the stone. Palace servants lit them after sunset so that the gardens were illuminated for the benefit of evening strollers. The glass in the lamps was sometimes clear, sometimes red or blue, green or yellow, so that a hundred brilliantly coloured suns glowed spectacularly in the darkness, attracting hopeful insects from all over Minassa.

'They're beautiful,' Ansaryon said. 'That coloured glass is another of King Temiltan's inventions – it was used in some of the windows in the Palace at Zithirian. But don't go too close to them, unless you want to be eaten alive by mosquitoes.'

A man was moving slowly along the terrace where they stood, using a long-handled torch, made of oil-soaked rags wrapped round a pole, to set the lanterns alight. He was chatting to a companion, and as they approached Halthris saw that it was a child.

A small boy of eight or so, with a distinctive cap of ash-blond hair. Her heart clenched, and began to pound the rhythm of danger. Beside her, Fess growled softly in her throat.

'Good evening, Lord Ansaryon,' the servant said. He reached up, and the nearest lamp came to sudden, glorious life, a rich crimson even more vivid than the fading sunset. 'And another fine day to come tomorrow, by the look of it.'

'I hope so.' Ansaryon did not seem to have noticed the child, but she realized suddenly that he might not have encountered Bron.

What was he doing here? He should be in Sar D'yenyi. There was no way, no *possible* way that he could have been there when they left, and here now. Not unless sorcery was involved.

And to look at Fess, sorcery surely was. She took a deep breath, and said quietly, 'Hello, Bron. What are you doing here?'

He turned and stared at her. She had forgotten how dark, how impenetrable, how unchildlike his eyes were. He said calmly, 'I'm helping Lemarth to light the lamps. He told me I could.'

'He's a useful lad,' the servant said. 'He's been carrying my tinder and flint for me, and keeping me company. Looks as though you could do with a square meal, though, eh? Just two more lamps left, and then I'll take you in to supper. We'll soon put some flesh on you.'

'Stay here and talk to us for a moment, while he finishes the row,' Halthris said swiftly. She stepped forward, and took the boy by the hand before he could move away. He felt warm, bony and reassuringly solid. He pulled against her a little and then stood still, while Lemarth went on to complete his task.

'You know him?' Ansaryon asked her.

Bron turned his pale face towards him. He said, 'You're the Lord Ansaryon.'

'I have that misfortune.' The King of Zithirian stared down at the child. The flickering red light from the lantern reduced the contours of his lean face to stark absolutes of colour and shadow, and gave him an almost demonic look. The boy, gazing back at him, was fully lit, save for those unutterably dark eyes.

'How did you come here, Bron?' Halthris asked him gently.

The hairs on her neck were standing up, she could feel the sorcery emanating from him, and yet Ansaryon did not seem to sense anything wrong.

'My gran sent me,' the boy said. He tried to pull his hand out of her grasp. 'Please – *please*, Tanathi lady, let me go – she'll want me back any moment.'

'And where is your gran?' Halthris persisted, refusing to release him.

Bron's face crumpled with real, childish fear. 'I can't tell you!' he cried. 'Please let me go – *please!*'

'She's not here, is she? Is she in Zithirian?'

With a wild, desperate twist, Bron wrenched himself free of her and fled. She heard his frantic footsteps running back up the garden towards the Palace, and then, quite suddenly, silence.

Ansaryon was looking at her with astonishment, and curiosity, and something else that might have been anger. She turned to Lemarth as he came back, and said calmly, 'He's run off, I'm afraid. I think he was hungry – perhaps he couldn't wait for you.'

'I don't blame him, poor little lad,' said the servant. 'He's skin and bone – nothing to him at all. You know him, Lady?'

'A little, yes. Where did you find him?'

'Oh, he was hanging about by the Palace, looking lost. I've a boy of my own that age, so I stopped to talk. Don't know where he comes from, but I've never seen him before, and he doesn't talk like a Minassan. Is he from Zithirian?'

'I think so,' Halthris said. 'You'd better go after him, or he won't know where to find his supper.'

Once the kindly, talkative servant was out of ear-shot, she found her knees shaking. She wiped the sweat from her face, fighting to stay calm. He's only a child, she told herself urgently. An eight-year-old child – what harm can he possibly do?

But Fess knew he was dangerous. And seeing him here in Minassa was certain proof that he was not just a child, but something else as well.

What?

Even as she tried not to think about it, Ansaryon took her by the shoulder and turned her to face him. 'Who in the name of the Ancestor was that?'

Halthris stepped back out of his reach. She said, 'A boy called Bron. Kefiri and I used to talk to him in Sar D'yenyi.'

'In *Sar D'yenyi*? Then what's he doing here?'

'I don't know.' She stared at him grimly. 'But I do know that it has something to do with sorcery. Didn't you see how Fess reacted

to him? Didn't you smell it on him, feel the power in him? Even
now my hand's tingling where I touched him.'

'Yes, I felt it.' Ansaryon pushed his fringe out of his eyes. 'But
a child – a child that age, a sorcerer? It isn't possible, Halthris, it
really isn't.'

'It is if you're right and I do have natural power – if I can, why
not a child? But I'm sure it also has something to do with his
grandmother, whoever she is. He said that she sent him, and he's
obviously terrified of her. Who is she? And is she sending him to
spy on us?'

'I don't know – I really don't.' She had never seen him look
bewildered before. 'It's something that seems to be totally outside
all my experience, and all I've ever been taught. But if he *does*
have natural power, I don't think that he can be evil in himself.
How can he, a child of seven or eight years old? But someone – this
grandmother – may be using him for evil purposes.'

'It's a shame he ran away,' Halthris said slowly. 'If he appears
again, I shall try and find out more.'

'I wouldn't, if I were you. You might do more harm than good.'

The warning note in his voice surprised her. She stared at him,
frowning, trying to make out the expression on his face in the
gloom. 'Why? Is there something you aren't telling me?'

'Possibly.' There was a bleak sadness now as he spoke. 'I don't
know. But what I do know is this – that child is dangerous. And I
think he is also to be pitied, as well as feared – for he is only a
weapon, with no idea of the harm he may do.'

Kaydi Gandar's Widow was in her secret loft, inspecting what stores
she had left. The arrival of spring had seen little difference in their
situation, save that with the warmer weather they were using far
fewer burnstones. Once, in happier times, there had been a daily
market outside the Sunset Gate, crowded with farmers and peasants
selling their produce, and citizens eagerly buying. Now there were
only a few old women, daring or desperate enough to brave the
menacing presence of the sprawling, stinking Ska'i camp between
them and the river bank. Needless to say, the tribesmen took
whatever they fancied, mainly meat, wine, grain and honey. Fortunately, they believed that milk, vegetables, cheese and gellin were
beneath their dignity to eat, and quite possibly harmful to their
prowess as well, so these foodstuffs were always on sale, although
at vastly inflated prices, or bartered for jewellery, burnstones,
clothes, silks – anything of value which the hungry citizens had left.

Many cursed those old women, for taking advantage of the city's misfortune. Kaydi, a hard-headed businesswoman herself, could not blame the peasants. If she were in their position, risking life and livelihood to bring their scanty produce to the city, she would want a good price too.

She had bought eggs, milk, and winter cabbages, and paid for them with some warm clothes belonging to her dead husband. For honey, scarce because the Ska'i had taken most of it, she had given a gold ring that had belonged to his mother. But it was worth it, for at last Herris was beginning to look a little less gaunt, and he had grown – his blue tunic was too short at the wrists, and she lengthened it with bands of braid. Her greatest grief was that Thobin had died just before the spring came. Surely, given good food once again, he would have survived the lung fever that had killed him.

But her duty was now to her remaining son, and she would not fail him. She had bought grain, little by little, day by day, until they now had enough stored to last until the harvest – if there was a harvest. Mice and rats had been a problem until Herris had presented her with a cat, a lean and mangy striped grey tom with sinister green eyes, who had cleared the house, loft and yard of vermin within half a month of his arrival. He was sitting comfortably now on a pile of empty sacks, his eyes slitted, his tail curled round his paws. Officially, he had no name, but Herris had dubbed him Garool, which apparently meant 'king' in the ugly Ska'i language, and it had stuck.

'Ma!' She heard her son's voice below, in the kitchen. 'Ma, where are you?'

She cast a final eye over the pots, tubs and jars, and made her way carefully over the boards to the opening, where a ladder jutted up into the loft. With a soft yowl, Garool leapt lightly off the sacks and followed her. She hitched her skirt up at her belt and climbed down, closing the trap-door behind her and the cat. It was made of roughly nailed planks, and when shut it looked exactly like the rest of the kitchen ceiling, which was why the Ska'i had never discovered her secret hoard.

'Ma . . .' Herris hesitated, his earlier excitement evaporating now into uncertainty.

Kaydi eyed him with the suspicion of long experience. 'Now what have you done, boy?'

'Nothing, Ma – nothing!'

'Well, what is it, then?'

'Ma – do we need another servant?'

Astonished, Kaydi stared at him, hands on hips. 'What do you think we are, royalty? Poor Shilda hardly has enough to keep him busy as it is.'

'But, Ma . . .' Herris took a deep breath. 'She's very keen. She came back to Zithirian to look for her parents, and they've disappeared, and she's got nowhere to go.'

'Came *back* here? Where's she been all winter?'

Herris's hazel eyes gleamed. 'Sar D'yenyi!'

This, as he had expected, took his mother completely by surprise. She gaped at him, mouth open like a stranded fish. '*Sar D'yenyi?*'

'That's what I said. Still don't think you want another servant?'

Kaydi closed her mouth and tried to think. If the rumours were true, Lord Ansaryon was at Sar D'yenyi. It was also where those Ska'i had gone months ago, and failed to return – save for their shaman, a man so pickled in his own evil that probably only a direct blow from Hegeden's wing had the power to strike him down. Someone who had spent the winter at Sar D'yenyi would have news, if nothing else.

Or was there something more sinister behind this? She said to Herris, 'Where did you meet this woman? What's her name? What else do you know about her?'

Her son's face acquired that slightly shifty look which indicated that, even if he was not lying outright, he was certainly giving her an edited version of the truth. 'I met her in – in Antelope Street, Ma. Some friends of mine know her – they can't help her, but they thought we could.' He stared at Kaydi with fierce and spurious honesty, willing her to agree, praying that she would not suspect that the friends so casually mentioned were in fact the Temple boys she had forbidden him to have anything to do with. If she knew that, she wouldn't have anything to do with this girl from Sar D'yenyi, either. And he knew, he *knew* that she was no spy, even if her story didn't quite ring true.

'I don't like it,' said his mother at last. 'Something's not right. What aren't you telling me, Herris?'

'Nothing, Ma!' he said, self-righteously aggrieved. 'Look, she's waiting outside in the entrance. At least *see* her, please. I'm sure you'll like her.'

'Hmm,' said Kaydi, surveying him suspiciously. 'Pretty, is she? In need of a good meal, perhaps?'

'So's everyone in Zithirian, Ma – 'cept them in the Palace and them in the Temple.'

'Just as well there's no hostile ears lurking to hear that,' was

Kaydi's comment. 'All right, bring her in. There's only bread and broth for dinner, but she's welcome to a share – *if* she's no more than you say she is.'

'Thanks, Ma,' Herris said jubilantly, and ran out of the kitchen with relief. Once his mother had seen and spoken to Kefiri, it would be all right, he was sure of it. She was so small, so pretty, so quiet and unthreatening that no one could fail to like her, or want to help her.

But the fact remained that meeting her had left him disturbed, confused and perhaps a little frightened. He had been ambling up Sargenn Way on an errand, when suddenly he had found himself taking a right turn into the Goldsmiths' Quarter, an area where he had no business. It was as if someone had called him, and his feet had answered. Bewildered, he had arrived in a small enclosed public garden, much overgrown and neglected like all such in Zithirian now, and apparently deserted.

And then Lelya had appeared from behind the bushes, Bron beside him. Once more, the stare from those dense eyes had made Herris distinctly uneasy. He said nervously, 'What are you doing here?'

'We're looking after a friend,' Lelya said. He glanced at Bron. 'She needs help, and we thought of you.'

'A friend? What friend?' Herris had demanded suspiciously.

'She's got nowhere to go,' said Bron. 'Please can you help?'

And then the girl had emerged shyly from the undergrowth, in her filthy tattered clothes, leaves in her hair, looking like something that Garool would have disdained to bring into the house, and Herris was lost. He was only thirteen, and until recently the opposite sex hadn't interested him at all, not even Kenmet's sister Djumi, who was two years older and so pretty that she could already take her pick of boys. But Djumi, despite her beauty, had a loud intimidating laugh and a contemptuous stare. This girl was small, smaller than Herris, and she seemed very young, with that mass of dark hair escaping from its plait, and those huge blue eyes: very young, and very much in need of help and protection.

He swallowed, and said at once, 'I'll help. Anything – I'll do anything I can.'

'I just want somewhere to stay, that's all,' said the girl. She gave Herris an apologetic smile that further increased his adoration. 'I'll do whatever you want me to in return – cook, clean, fetch water, anything, I'm not afraid of hard work.'

Herris said helplessly, 'I'll take you home with me. But my Ma – she's a bit – a bit suspicious of strangers.'

'I think everyone is now,' said the girl. 'My name is Kefiri Sedren's Daughter. When the Ska'i came, I managed to flee to Sar D'yenyi. I came back to look for my parents, but their house has been burnt down, and no one can tell me what's happened to them.' For the first time, her voice lost its firmness. 'So – I need somewhere to live, until I can find them.'

What would once have been a tragic story was now only a sad commonplace in the city, for so many people had fled Zithirian, or died, or been killed. Herris was touched, though. He said, 'Of course you can come home with me. Don't worry about my Ma – I'll get round her somehow, I always do.'

He had escorted Kefiri back to Snowbringer Street, his errand forgotten. Whenever they approached other passers-by, he could feel her nervousness and tension. Poor girl, thought Herris, with almost paternal sympathy. She's obviously had a hard time of it. I just hope Ma doesn't turn her away.

Kaydi stood in her kitchen and waited for her son to return with his latest acquisition. She did not know what she had expected, but this tiny ragamuffin girl was a complete surprise. She took in the dreadful state of her clothes, her filthy face, her air of exhaustion, and said without thought, 'Oh, you poor child! What you need is a bath!'

'A *bath*, Ma?' Herris said in amazement.

'That's what I said – a bath. Go and get it, lad and put the kettle on the fire first – go on, don't stand there gawping, jump to it!'

After one last wild look, her son ran to find Shilda, who would help him move the big wooden bathtub from the storeroom to the kitchen.

'I'm sorry,' said Kefiri, with a rather helpless, weary gesture. 'I don't want to be any trouble – I'll work for my keep—'

'We'll discuss all that later. What you need now is a bath, food, and sleep, in that order,' Kaydi said firmly. All three of her daughters had died as babies, and she had always wanted a girl to mother – boys were so much more trouble (or at least Herris was). 'You spent the winter in Sar D'yenyi, my lad tells me.'

The girl nodded. 'Yes, I did. I – I ran away from Zithirian when the Ska'i invaded, and made my way there. There were lots of other refugees from the city, hundreds and hundreds of them, but not my parents. So when the thaw came, I thought I'd come back to look for them.'

'And no joy, eh? Well, it's hardly surprising – so many here have died or fled, I should think there's less than half of us left now.' Kaydi stared hard at the girl, wondering what was making her nervous. Perhaps she was a spy, though it didn't seem very likely.

Herris and Shilda arrived dragging the tub. It was a warm morning, so the water would not need to be too hot. She watched as her son and the servant filled it with buckets from the well and steaming jugfuls from the kettle, and then poured in a generous measure of her own herbal oils, sweet-smelling and refreshing.

Herris and Shilda were standing staring at the girl, who looked very white around the mouth, as if she would faint any minute. 'Right,' Kaydi said to them briskly. 'You two – out! And don't come back until I tell you.'

'But, Ma—' Herris began, in a voice regrettably tainted by a whine.

'No buts, young man. You can't watch a girl in her bath, and that's that – you should know better.' Kaydi noticed his betraying blush, and grinned at her son. 'Now go on – off with you! Did you ever take those onions over to Chameni Tegril's Widow? I thought not. Then go now, this instant, and no dawdling on the way, or there won't be any dinner left for you by the time you get back.'

'Yes, Ma,' said Herris meekly, and fled in Shilda's silent wake.

When they had gone, Kaydi gave the girl a rueful smile. 'He's a good-hearted boy, my Herris, but he doesn't always know when enough's enough. Well, the bath's ready and waiting for you, and soap if you need it, and towels over the chair. I'll go and look out some clothes for you. Those are fit only for burning.'

Left to herself, Kefiri began dazedly to strip off her garments. It had all happened so fast – waking, seeing Bron, trying to understand why he was in Zithirian when she had left him in Sar D'yenyi. He had looked so alarmed by her questions that she hadn't liked to press them further, and the other boy, Lelya, who was rather older and just as thin, though more sturdily built, had said seriously, 'Bron doesn't like it, Lady – it's upsetting him, please don't.'

So she had asked Lelya if he knew any friendly household which might take her in. Bron had obviously told his companion who she was, for he understood the danger she was in if her presence here was discovered. 'I know someone,' he had said at once. 'He doesn't like the Ska'i or the King either. He'll look after you. I'll get Bron to call him.'

And although Bron had apparently done nothing more than sit silently by the older boy's side, in a little while another child appeared, wearing an expression of uneasy bewilderment that probably matched her own. He was about Lelya's age, with a sharp, rather cunning face offset by warm hazel eyes, and his vivid blush when she stepped out of the undergrowth indicated that she had acquired an admirer.

Thinking about the three boys, she left her clothes in a festering heap on the floor, and climbed gingerly into the bathtub. The water was pleasantly warm and fragrant, and it was very tempting to lie back against the wooden head-rest and sink into a blissful soaking doze. But she couldn't afford to relax, not yet. She found a small block of creamy soap, and rubbed the dirt and sweat off her body with industrious hands. Then she unbound her hair and ducked her head under the surface, wondering what horrors would float away. She washed and rinsed it twice, and rose from the tub feeling delightfully clean and refreshed.

She was drying herself when Kaydi came back with an armful of clothes. The older woman grimaced at the scummy, now tepid water. 'You certainly needed that! Here, take these. They're mine, so they're bound to be too big and too long, but they're warm and clean and you're welcome to borrow them for as long as you want.'

'Thank you – you've been very kind,' Kefiri said shyly. She stood wrapped in the towel, looking very small and young and vulnerable, with her mass of wet dark hair dripping on her shoulders.

Kaydi stared at her with suddenly narrowed eyes. 'Haven't I seen you somewhere before? You look familiar, somehow.'

Kefiri hoped that her sudden panic didn't show on her face. She said casually, 'You probably have. I've lived in Zithirian for most of my life, after all, except for last winter. We must have passed each other in the street, or at the market, or the Gathering Fair.'

'Probably. What's your name?'

'Kefiri Sedren's Daughter. My father is – was – an ironsmith. We lived in Vine Street, in the Potters' Quarter.'

'Did you now? My husband's cousin Stekketh keeps a tavern in Hemp Street, just round the corner – the Flax Flower, it's called. Do you know it?'

Kefiri produced what she hoped was a rueful smile. 'Not myself, but my mother was always complaining that my father spent too much time in there.'

'Really?' Kaydi surveyed her guest, hands on hips. 'That does surprise me. Perhaps he had a sweetheart on the side. No, don't look so shocked, young lady – you can't fool me so easily. There isn't any such place as Hemp Street in the Potters' Quarter, let alone a tavern called the Flax Flower – though Stekketh's is in

Crooked Alley, the Two Crows. So, if you're not Kefiri Sedren's Daughter, who are you?'

Sick at heart, her innards churning, Kefiri stared at her. Could she trust this brusque, vigorous woman? Or would the truth lead her at once into captivity, or worse? She had been such a fool to come here, to risk her life and Ansary's cause for the sake of her own stupid, selfish plan. Why, why, *why*, hadn't she stayed safe in Sar D'yenyi?

'I think I know,' Kaydi said at last. 'Your name *is* Kefiri, isn't it? But you aren't Sedren's daughter – you're Lord Tayma's!'

Unable to deny it, the Lady of Sar D'yenyi nodded, her head held proudly high and her eyes filled with unshed tears.

'Then we'd better make sure that villain Tsenit doesn't find out you're here, hadn't we?' said Kaydi briskly. 'And we'll have to think up a better story for you than the one you've just told me. But don't worry, Lady, don't worry – we're all your friends here.'

And Kefiri, gazing with sudden hope at her firm, kindly face, knew that it was true.

CHAPTER
EIGHTEEN

The steppe in summer was hot, dry and dusty: the infrequent rain usually fell in brief but torrential thunderstorms and soaked swiftly into the parched earth, while the clouds soon cleared, leaving the sky a fresh and infinite blue. So Halthris had thought that she was used to warmth, indeed revelled in it: but the suffocating thick wet heat of Toktel'yi was very different, and almost impossible to bear.

It had taken ten days to ride the stream down the river from Minassa, including a short delay while repairs were made to a boat that had struck a rock. In contrast to the crude Lelyentan rafts, Ansaryon had hired a dozen of the lovely Kefirinn boats, built in Toktel'yi, brightly painted and supremely graceful, with coloured sails and resoundingly optimistic or poetic names: *Prosperity*, *Riches*, *Snow Flower*, *Windswift*. It had cost him a great deal of gold, but he had brought a vast amount with him. Some of it had been given to Belerith and Temiltan, to help pay and equip their soldiers, but there was plenty left.

The boats were quite roomy when empty of cargo, and had comfortable cabin accommodation in bow and stern. Sated with good food and easy living, the six hundred remaining soldiers of Ansaryon's army – he had left another fifty at Minassa to help organize their force – lay about on deck sipping fruit juices, gazing at the lush scenery as it sailed past, and wondering half-seriously, sometimes aloud, why they need ever go back to Zithirian at all.

Halthris missed Fess intensely. The day before their departure from Minassa, she had ridden with Inri and Sherren up to the edge of the steppe, and had offered the cat her freedom. And, more painful even than the parting, had been the very faint tinge of regret that touched her mind as Fess sniffed the dry warm air and then bounded away through the grass without a backward glance. Halthris knew that she would be happier in her natural habitat than on a boat or in Toktel'yi, and she was sure, too, that this moment would have come quite soon anyway: Fess was three years old, and ready for a mate and cubs. But the absence of that prickly, loving companionship was very hard to bear, almost as if she had lost a part of her skin.

She and the two other Tanathi were travelling on the *Windswift*. A striped yellow and red awning covered half of the deck, but it was still bakingly hot. Unwisely, she borrowed a short Toktel'yan tunic from the captain, and caught the sun on her arms, legs and face so painfully that for the next few days she skulked exclusively in the shade, liberally spread with an evil-smelling ointment which apparently contained rancid tallow. At least it kept the fastidious Invan away, for which she was guiltily grateful. And Inri and Sherren, who were at last becoming less exclusively besotted with each other, joined her under the awning, similarly anointed, and triumphantly produced a threadbare piece of old carpet. The captain had used it as a door mat, but Inri's sharp eyes had noticed that it was the sad but still useful remains of a genuine Tanathi tek mat.

The flotilla stopped for the night at Tamat, once an independent town of Tayan foundation, now the northern-most outpost of the Empire. It was a bustling, lively place, dedicated to that most Toktel'yan of obsessions, bureaucracy. Each boat was searched, and the names of everyone on board recorded, along with their ages and places of origin, on endless sheets of crisp yellowy charsh paper. The Tanathi, who had thought the Zithiriani's need to write everything down bad enough, gazed at the endless stream of nosy officials with bemused astonishment. 'Don't they have anything more useful to do?' Inri asked.

'I don't suppose they have – so they've invented all this to keep them busy,' Halthris told her, with some scorn.

As they drew ever closer to Toktel'yi, the air grew more and more humid, like a thick, hot, wet, invisible blanket tied over the face. Nor was there so much to see: after Sabrek, a city a hundred and seventy miles by road from Tamat, and more than three times that distance along the broad and meandering Kefirinn, the hills vanished altogether, and the view consisted mainly of flat square fields, groves of strange-looking trees with huge fat tufts of leaves bursting from thick, straight trunks, and endless reeds. Invan, conquering his aversion to the tallow ointment – though Halthris noticed that he did not sit too close – told her that these were beds of charsh, from which paper was made.

'No wonder there's so much of it – they must get through a mountain of it every day,' she said drily, and Invan solemnly agreed.

During the long sweltering days, when they were not playing tek or trying to sleep under the awning, he told the Tanathi much about the Empire, and Halthris began to realize why Ansaryon had spoken of making Zithirian more like Minassa and less like Tok-tel'yi. It was the greatest, richest and most powerful nation in all the history of the known world, but half its people lived in squalid, abject poverty, worn down by the necessity of scratching a living from land that was not theirs, and could be snatched away without warning by a capricious or spiteful owner, leaving them destitute. The back streets and slums of every city, and notably Toktel'yi itself, were crammed with such unfortunates, eking out a living from crime, begging, prostitution, anything to keep starvation at bay.

Many people in Zithirian were poor, but not as desperate as that. And to the Tanathi, whose tribal law did not allow one man to go hungry while others ate, it was appalling. Inri, white with anger, kept saying, 'Why don't they *do* something?'

'They do – sometimes,' Invan told her. 'There is frequently unrest in the Empire – either because of poverty, or because they don't want to be under Toktel'yan rule at all. Some of the islands in the Archipelago have only been annexed in the last twenty years or so, and they bitterly resent it. But the Imperial army is so overwhelmingly strong that rebels have no chance against it. And the punishment for revolt is so severe that you have to be very desperate, or very brave, or very foolish to try.'

'What punishment?' Sherren asked, his pleasant, sunburnt face creased with disapproval.

'The rebels themselves are publicly executed – usually by beheading. Then their families are killed too – everyone, parents, brothers, sisters, sons, daughters, cousins. Only children under the age of twelve years old are exempt, and they are taken into slavery.'

The bewildered, horrified expressions of the three Tanathi told him that further explanation was necessary. 'Slavery?' Inri asked.

'It's a Toktel'yan custom,' Invan said. 'Slaves are like servants, but they do not earn money, neither do they have any freedom. They are the property of their master, and he can do what he wants with them – he can even have them killed for no reason, if he wishes. He can buy or sell them, and pass them on to his heirs when he dies – although it is more usual for slaves to be set free with a small gift of money on their owner's death.'

'And they call us barbarians,' Halthris commented with disgust.

'It's better for men than for women, too,' Invan continued. 'Haven't you and Inri noticed the sailors staring at you? They didn't realize that you were female at first – and now they think you're freaks. In the Empire, a respectable woman has little more freedom than a slave. She can't appear in public without a veil to hide her

face, and until she marries she's her father's property. Then she
becomes her husband's. Only widows have any kind of liberty at
all. Women in Zithirian were in much the same position too, you
know, not so long ago, until Queen Tesi changed the laws. Now at
least they have some choice in whom they can marry, and they can
run businesses and own land. A Toktel'yan woman is little more
than the chattel of her father, or her husband.'

Inri and Halthris were looking at each other in astonishment.
Sherren grinned. 'From now on, you two, I should offer your
heartfelt thanks daily to Sarraliss, that you were not born a woman
in Toktel'yi!'

For two days after passing Sabrek, the boats swept down the
river, aided by both wind and current. They met many others
progressing rather more slowly upstream under oars, laden with the
produce of the lush Toktel'yan lowlands – cotton, silk, oil, kuldi,
charsh paper – and goods from far countries and the diverse and
wonderful islands of the Archipelago. And with every mile, every
curve of the bank, every village built of mud bricks or wood or
reeds, every group of waving naked brown-skinned children, every
clump of palm trees or ox-drawn plough, Halthris felt more and
more unreal, as if she were taking part in a dream, and that soon
she would wake up inside her true self on the wide, severe emptiness
of the steppe, with Fess by her side, and become just an ordinary
Tanathi Hunter once more.

To her relief, Bron had not appeared again: nor did she see
Ansaryon, save as a distant, silver-haired figure standing on the
bow of the leading boat, *Prosperity*. At the ship's masthead floated
a long, pointed pennant in the silver colour of Zithirian, embla-
zoned with his chosen device: a sky-flower, symbol of hope, renewal
and rebirth, in a deep and glorious blue.

At last, they had nearly reached Toktel'yi. The marshes around
the main channel of the river were thick and evil-smelling in the
summer heat, and alive with swarms of small, biting insects. The
foul ointment, smeared onto exposed skin after dark, proved an
invaluable repellent, but something in the thick air brought disease,
and several men went down with a sharp, feverish illness which, so
the sailors assured them, was very common here, and not usually
fatal.

This was the delta of the Kefirinn, and many side streams and
tributaries, some no more than a gap in the reeds, others the width
of a score of boats, branched off on each side. The *Windswift*
drifted on in the stupefying heat, her bright red and yellow sails
limp, and only a couple of oarsmen to keep her steady on her

course. Ahead, the glaring blue sky was tempered by an evil-looking brownish haze. 'Toktel'yi,' the captain said, with pride.

The greatest city in the known world had originally been built aeons ago on a large mud bank in the centre of the delta, and had spread bridges like tentacles to other islands, until the whole vast conglomeration sprawled over an area that would have comfortably contained Zithirian, Lelyent, Minassa, Tamat, and all the other towns and villages along the Kefirinn as well. As it was constructed beside, on and over water, traffic was largely by boat, and the canals and ditches dug as sewers and conduits also acted as lanes and streets. The stench was unbelievable: rotting corpses, both human and animal, mud, filth, and decaying rubbish all lurked beneath the scummy brown surfaces of the river and its innumerable natural and man-made tributaries. Twice a day the clean salt water rolled in on the tide from the sea, six miles away, but could make little impression on the accumulated refuse of nearly half a million people.

The Tanathi gazed in horrified fascination as the *Windswift* glided past the northern suburbs, her helmsman avoiding the smaller vessels which thronged the river with a skilful flick of the steering oar. Obviously, only the very poorest lived here, in rotting houses teetering on muddy banks where naked, filthy children played, or paddled makeshift craft, even logs, out to the boats to beg or to offer trinkets in fierce shrill voices. They stared at the pale-skinned northerners with unabashed curiosity, and at the two Tanathi women, trousered and unveiled, with bewilderment and laughter.

'They do think we're freaks,' Inri said, staring at the teeming squalid life on the banks with a mixture of astonishment and horror, while Halthris fended off a particularly persistent child who seemed to be trying to sell her a misshapen carving of some fantastic animal with a fifth leg apparently growing out of its head.

At last the shacks and huts gave way to rather more salubrious dwellings, made of baked mud-bricks, many elaborately carved and decorated, and all with an air of seedy and almost attractive decay. Invan told them that until two hundred years ago, this had been the wealthy centre of Toktel'yi, and that the particularly grand building over there, made of red and white bricks with square, squat corner turrets, had once been the Imperial Palace.

'I'm not surprised the emperors moved out,' Halthris said, a hand across her nose, as it had been ever since entering Toktel'yi. 'They probably couldn't stand the smell.'

'Who lives in it now?' Sherren asked, eyeing the former Palace, which seemed, on the river-ward side at any rate, to be gently crumbling back into the mud from which it had been built.

'It's the Imperial Heart – their administrative centre,' Invan said. 'Stuffed wall to wall and floor to ceiling with paper, I should imagine,' he added with a rather uncharacteristic smile: he was not a light-hearted man.

All these older buildings had been packed close together in the central island, jostling for space, but as the *Windswift* continued southwards, the houses began to change in character, becoming more spread out, newer looking, with many trees sprouting up behind high, whitewashed walls, dazzling in the afternoon light. Nor did they face the stinking river, but shrank away from it, leaving a broad area next to the channel which quickly turned into docks on both sides, bustling with activity. Halthris counted over fifty moored ships before she gave up, bored. Many were of the *Windswift*'s type, low and shallow-draughted, but there were others, much larger and sturdier of build, with two and even three masts, and banks of oars.

'Sea-going ships,' Invan said, smiling at her. 'And you have never seen the sea, have you, Halthris?'

Unobtrusively, she moved a little further along the rail. 'No. Have you?'

'Of course. I was in Lord Ansaryon's entourage when he visited Toktel'yi, ten years ago, and I have always wanted to return.'

'*Return*? To *this*?' Her astonished gesture took in the murky, reeking water, the polluted haze above the workshops and paper mills upstream, the squalor and decay and poverty that had appalled the Tanathi all afternoon. 'Why?'

'It is the greatest city in the known world,' Invan said patiently, as if explaining something very simple to a child. 'The view from the river gives you no idea of the wonders here, the sights – and the sea is the crown of it all! Imagine a lake so vast that you cannot see any bank save the one on which you are standing – imagine gentle ripples become waves ten, twenty times larger – imagine the sands sweeping along the shore, so white you're almost dazzled – and the creatures! Fish, dolphins, sea-serpents, whales – we went to Tekkt, which is the nearest island in the Archipelago, for a few days, and the dolphins led us all the way, leaping in the bow-wave and dancing in the water. Until you have seen the ocean, Halthris of the Tanathi, you are not complete.'

She resisted the temptation to tell him that she felt complete enough already. 'Perhaps we shall see it, if the Imperial Palace is near.'

'Undoubtedly we shall – and it will be my honour and privilege to show it to you,' Invan said. 'There is not far to go now – there is the Palace itself, look, that white building in the distance, surrounded by palm-trees.'

There was something different about it, Halthris thought, shading her eyes against the bright quivering air. In form it seemed to be just the same, though of course very much larger, as the other substantial houses they had already passed, with their high blank walls surrounding numerous courtyards, living quarters, store rooms, gardens, and elegant pavilions designed to be cool and airy on the hottest days. Rich Toktel'yans valued space and privacy, and their dwellings rambled over an area large enough to contain a small village. The poor, packed into their squalid rotting hovels and tenements, enjoyed no such luxury.

Word of their arrival had obviously gone ahead, for now the banks of the Kefirinn were lined with cheering, waving people. In the sluggish current, the flotilla had bunched together, and the *Windswift* was almost up level with *Prosperity*. Halthris, leaning on the rail between Inri and Invan, saw Ansaryon, wearing a long loose Toktel'yan robe, acknowledge the people's greetings with a smile and a gracious sweep of his hand. Above him, the great silver pennant, with its lovely optimistic flower, stirred gently in the rising breeze.

The same evil stench still accompanied them, but it was now diluted by their distance – some five or six miles – from the poorest suburbs, and a new, fresh, salty tang touched Halthris's nostrils. She inhaled deeply, relishing its savour, and the feel of the cooler air drifting past her sunburnt skin. She did not need Invan to tell her that this was the sign and smell of the sea.

As they drew close to the Palace, she saw that a channel had been dug to connect it to the river, the entrance marked by two tall stone pillars, intricately carved. Between them, barring the way, a huge chain hung suspended about a man's height above the surface of the water, each massive link larger than her hand. The crowds stopped abruptly here, kept at bay by a row of soldiers wearing elongated, conical helmets glittering in the sun, their spears meshed to form a barrier at once decorative and menacing.

Halthris, looking at them, remembered Invan telling her about the Imperial Army, how each man was by law required to serve at least five years in it, and paid so well that many stayed much longer than that. Every town had its garrison, in addition to the numerous forts and outposts along the borders of the Empire, to keep the population quiet. For an able poor boy, army service offered one of the few means of advancement (there was also the navy, sorcery, the priesthood, and, inevitably, the bureaucracy). The Emperor's General-in-Chief, a man possessing an enormous amount of power, prestige and wealth, had been born into a mill-worker's family, and had risen to the top entirely on his own merits.

Invan had spoken of such customs with open admiration. In his view, the rigid separation of peasant, artisan, merchant and aristocrat in Zithirian, with all the top positions going to the wealthy as of right with no regard for competence, had greatly contributed to the overthrow of King Varathand. It was, however, one very small point in the Empire's favour, as far as Halthris was concerned, and represented a tiny feather in the balance compared with the leaden weights of poverty, despair, squalor and brutal repression on the other side of the scale.

She watched as the chain was lowered with much clinking of unseen machinery, while a score of trumpets sounded a fanfare of welcome. One by one, the twelve beautiful river-boats glided gently between the pillars, and into the Imperial Canal.

The Palace was built of stone, she realized suddenly: and not just any stone, but white, glistening, neatly-dressed blocks from the heart of Annako. Unlike Zithirian, though, there were no towers, no pennants, just more high blank walls, blind to the world outside.

A broad quay opened out at the end of the channel, with several boats of widely varying sizes tied up, amongst them a fabulously ornate craft, glittering gold and with a striped awning over the stern. Invan told her that this was the Imperial Barge, used to transport the Emperor about the city, and rowed by twenty good-looking and muscular young men.

To the brazen blare of more trumpets, the flotilla docked. With so many boats mooring at once, there might have been considerable confusion, but the quayside swarmed with men wearing the skimpy short-sleeved tunics and sandals of Toktel'yan workers, all of whom seemed to know exactly what they were doing. Halthris watched fascinated as the *Windswift*'s prow was hooked by a docker wielding a long pole, brought gently against the wooden side of the quay, and swiftly secured by two more men who caught the ropes flung to them by the sailors. Almost immediately, the rail-gate was opened, the ridged gang-plank run out, and the inevitable official stepped aboard, escorted by a perspiring boy clutching writing implements and a huge sheaf of paper.

Only Ansaryon and half-a-dozen of his highest-ranking officers, Invan of course amongst them, were to enjoy the Emperor's hospitality. The official told the rest that they were allowed the freedom of the city during the hours of daylight, but were strongly advised to return to the boats at dusk. Toktel'yi, he said, in thick, strangely-accented Zithiriani, was a dangerous place for the unwary after dark. The wealthier areas, of course, were quite safe, but there were some poorer parts of the city where no sane man would venture even in daylight, unless well-armed and escorted by a troop of soldiers. However, the strip of land between the Palace and the sea was regularly patrolled by the Imperial Guard, and any dubious characters instantly arrested, so Ansaryon's men would be welcome to wander there. Food and drink would be supplied in generous quantity from the Palace kitchens, and in the Emperor's name he hoped that their stay would be a pleasant one.

'Impossible, in this heat,' Halthris said later. The sun was sinking down behind the Palace, and the heavy air was cooling down a little at last, but it was still uncomfortably warm. 'Isn't it *ever* cold here?'

'Doubt it.' Inri was sprawled under the awning, fanning herself with one of the strange, stiff, giant leaves which all ordinary Toktel'yans apparently used for that purpose. 'Shame Invan isn't around,' she added, with a sly glance at her friend. 'I'm sure he'd tell us. It's like being accompanied by a talking book.'

'And what would you know about books?'

'Even less than you,' Inri said, grinning. 'Well? As Sherren's fast asleep, I'll ask you now – and please don't throw me overboard – are you going to let Invan unbind your hair for you?'

Halthris swallowed her annoyance, and shook her head. 'No, definitely not. Oh, he's a nice man, and very handsome, but I don't want him as a lover. And can't you just see him, in a year or two, boring some poor woman with all the details of Tanathi bed customs?'

Inri snorted with laughter. 'You're right – he's just as bad as the Toktel'yans, but at least his knowledge can be useful – and it doesn't waste any paper.' She got up and walked over to the rail.

Halthris joined her, leaving Sherren sleeping peacefully in a heap of cushions. The quayside was quiet now, save for a scattering of soldiers, and a few Zithiriani strolling back from the city, where many had gone as soon as the boats docked. She said softly, 'Inri, shall we go down to the sea? Now, before it gets dark? I'd like to see it for myself, not as Invan's gift, if you see what I mean. And the official said it was quite safe.'

'I hope so – I don't speak a word of Toktel'yan.'

'I do. Invan taught me. "Brek" – the most important word of all.'

'It must mean "no".'

'It does.' Halthris grinned. 'And I'm sure he didn't tell me just so that I could fend off small boys trying to sell me things. He's altogether too possessive, is Invan. I like him, but I don't like the way he wants to own me.'

'Well, you can tell *him* "no" in three different languages now – Tanathi, Zithiriani and Toktel'yan.'

'Could be useful.' Halthris paused, and glanced back under the awning at Sherren's recumbent figure. 'Will he be all right?'

'Oh, he's not the sort to panic if he wakes up and we're not there. Anyway, we can tell the guard where we're going. Come on, Hal – I'm longing to see the sea, too.'

The two Tanathi women walked down the plank and onto dry land. At once, the nearest Toktel'yan soldier approached them. Like most of his countrymen, he was not particularly tall – perhaps that was why their helmets were so ridiculously high – but his brown face was young and pleasant. 'Where you go?' he demanded, in very bad Zithiriani.

'We are going down to the sea,' Halthris said, slowly and clearly.

The sound of her voice startled the soldier, who had evidently not realized that she was female. Inri gave him her most charming smile, and with a look of bewilderment he stood aside and waved them past, muttering, 'Sea – that way.'

'Can you swim in it?' Inri asked hopefully, a little while later. A well-defined track led from the Palace towards a hummock of dunes and a long thin band of palm-trees, but the thick sand, still hot, made progress difficult, particularly as they had not walked further than a boat's length since leaving Minassa. In consequence, both women were soaked in sweat, despite the increasing coolness and freshness of the air.

'I don't see why not – if it's as Invan said, and just like a very big lake, we should be able to.' Halthris thought longingly of the clear cold waters of the few steppe rivers in summer, and the wonderful sensation as the current rushed past her bare skin, washing away dust, grease and sweat. She quickened her stride eagerly, and Inri matched her.

At last they came to the end of the dunes. Ahead, the trees crowded across their path, black against the fading sky. And beyond them, something sighed and murmured rhythmically, like a vast living creature.

Without a word, Halthris and Inri began to run. They dodged through the palms, avoiding roots and fallen trunks purely by luck, and burst out into the open beyond them. There they stopped, staring in wonder.

The sun had set not long since, and the dark was coming down with the swiftness they were still not used to, so far south. But there was enough light yet to see the broad pale sweep of the beach, two hundred paces wide, receding into the distance on their right: the low bulk of land to their left, and the black, flame-topped shape of a beacon, presumably marking the mouth of the Kefirinn's main channel: and ahead, the gentle white waves showing where sea met shore.

There was a fire, with people around it, some way off, but the Tanathi women paid it no attention: they stared at the huge, softly undulating mass of water before them. Dim and distant, but still unmistakable against the southern sky, was more land on the horizon: Tekkt, perhaps, the nearest island of the K'tali Archipelago, and of which Invan had spoken in such lyrical terms.

'There are lights – look, over there.' Inri pointed, and Halthris peered through the gloom. Sure enough she could just make out two tiny sparks, somewhere ahead, almost lost in the immensity of sea and darkness.

'A ship,' she said, realizing that they were moving with infinitesimal speed. The *Windswift* and all the other river-boats carried lanterns at bow and stern, and sea-going craft doubtless did the same.

'It must be very far away,' Inri said softly, and the two were silent, both thinking of the strangeness of standing here, on the unseen edge of their world. Over the rim of that distant, dark horizon lay islands upon islands, ranging in size from rocks barely dry at high tide to huge chunks of land two hundred miles across. And beyond them – what? Invan had never said, and perhaps no one knew.

'How about that swim?' Inri said at last: and together, they walked across the smooth, firm sand to the water's edge.

It was near complete darkness now, but the moon had already risen above the haze of Toktel'yi behind them, and it was full. They stripped off tunics, trousers and sandals, and stepped rather cautiously into the water.

It was warm, and soft, and the white foam ran sparkling over their feet and washed against their ankles. They waded in further, enjoying the novel sensation of the waves pushing against them, and then plunged full-length into the sea.

For the rest of her life, Halthris would remember that magical swim: lying drifting on her back in the ocean (no one had mentioned that it was salty, and so buoyant), looking up at the stars, some familiar, but in new locations, some altogether different, and all in a myriad profusion that she had never seen, even on the steppe: the distant voices, singing and laughter of the men around the fire, unaware of their presence: and above all the sensation of being temporarily a part of something vast, and immeasurable, and utterly mysterious.

At last even the warmth of the water began to seep away, and Halthris realized that she was cold, and very hungry. She called to Inri, and they began to swim back to the shore. And now, most wonderful of all, the water was somehow charged with sorcery, and glowed eerily in the dark where they splashed.

They dressed, and then by mutual consent walked down the beach to the fire, where some largish animal, a deer or a goat, was roasting aromatically over the flames.

As Halthris had guesed from the songs, these were Zithiriani soldiers, many of whom they knew by name or by sight. They were greeted with cheerful camaraderie and invitations to share the feast. Except for Invan, the Zithiriani seemed to think of Halthris and Inri as fellow-soldiers and good comrades, rather than as women. After all, they were not used to females wearing trousers (save under a dress for extra warmth in winter), or fighting, hunting and carrying weapons. The two Tanathi welcomed this, for it certainly made their lives much simpler to be treated like men. Fortunately, so far the Toktel'yans, despite their bewilderment, seemed to be doing the same. It was certainly easier to cope with such an attitude, than to be the subject of intolerant and indignant outrage, or open lechery.

. They ate, and Halthris was asked to sing, and obliged with several lively tunes she had learned in Sar D'yenyi, accompanied by one of the men on an old but tuneful Sith. It was very late, and the ral was going round, by the time she and Inri tore themselves away, thinking rather guiltily of poor Sherren, left behind on the *Windswift*. They stumbled up through the palms by the inadequate light of the moon, found the track to the dock eventually, and plodded wearily along it.

From the Palace, only a short way off to their left, came the distant sounds of music, delicate and subtly elaborate shifts of tone and scale so that it seemed to be a tapestry rather than a thread of tune. Presumably, the rightful King of Zithirian was being feasted and entertained in lavish Imperial style.

There were lamps lit on poles along the quayside, and each vessel had coloured lanterns hung at stem, stern and masthead. Halthris looked for the *Windswift*'s red and yellow awning and gilded, bird-shaped prow, hoping that Sherren would not mind that they had gone off on their own. Like Invan, he was a little too possessive, and she knew that Inri had rather enjoyed this brief respite from his attentions.

There was their boat, tied up next to *Prosperity*, and a small group of soldiers were standing by the gangplank. By the look of their sprouting white plumes and splendidly gilded armour, they were members of the Imperial Guard. Was there something wrong?

Sherren was with them. As they walked up the quayside, his face cleared with relief, and he pointed. 'There you are! Thank Hegeden for it! Inri, where have you been? I was so worried—'

'Well, there wasn't any need for it,' said Halthris briskly, before Inri could apologize. 'We told the guard where we'd gone – didn't you ask him?'

'I've only just woken up,' Sherren said defensively. 'Listen, Hal – there's a summons for you, from the Palace. My Zithiriani isn't as good as yours, and I can hardly understand theirs, but I think that's what they said.' He turned to the Guard Captain, a man rather taller than most Toktel'yans, with brown hair and blue eyes: presumably he had some northern blood. 'Here is Halthris of the Tanathi,' he said in Zithiriani.

'Ah. Good. You come with me now,' said the Captain. He held out his hand, indicating that she walk beside him.

'Wait,' Halthris said quickly. Something was wrong, she could sense it. 'Who wants me? Why must I go now?'

'Lord Ansaryon of Zithirian wants you. Urgent. Come now please.'

If Ansaryon had indeed summoned her, then it was no trap, and she had nothing to fear. And a few heartbeats' thought convinced her that no purpose would be served by running away, or resisting. If the message was genuine, she would only make a fool of herself, and do irreparable damage to their mission. And if the Toktel'yans, for some obscure reason, did mean her harm, then she could do little in the face of such overwhelming strength. In this strange, dangerous land, ignorant of its language, customs and geography, she would not last a day, even if she did manage to escape them now.

'Very well,' she said at last. 'I will come with you.'

As she was escorted away towards the Palace, she looked back to see Inri and Sherren staring after her, their faces such twin pictures of alarm that she might have laughed, had she not felt exactly the same apprehension.

The main gates of the Palace were made of carved wood, inlaid with gold leaf and coloured stone. Three times the height of a man, they were surrounded by flickering torches, and guarded by a score of immaculate soldiers in the ceremonial posture of the Imperial Guard, legs firmly planted apart, holding their spears forward to menace anyone who might threaten the Emperor's private domain. As Halthris and her escort passed between them, a smaller door, set in the larger one, opened suddenly, and they stepped through it into a different world.

There were courtyards, fountains, plants heavy with night-scented blossom, filling the air with heady, intoxicating, unfamiliar fragrances. Everywhere lanterns, plain and coloured, had been lit. A group of women, veiled and clad in the loose, flowing robes that looked somehow so cool and graceful after the workaday garb of the Minassans or the stiff elaborate Zithiriani court dress, passed them in a cloud of scent and whispers and soft laughter. Her ears could distinguish at least three separate pieces of music being played in different places, one a sweet and hauntingly simple tune on some kind of flute. For the first time, Halthris began to understand Invan's admiration for the Empire. If you were wealthy, and a man, then it must indeed be a wonderful place to live.

At last they came to a courtyard filled with young palm-trees growing in huge pottery tubs, and in the centre, a simple fountain made beautiful by the lanterns, blue, red and green, placed around it to colour the falling streams of water. A group of men in Zithiriani clothes stood talking, and one of them detached himself from the rest and came over.

To her relief, it was Invan. He smiled at her warmly, but his eyes were anxious. 'Halthris! At last! I had almost given you up.'

'Inri and I went for a walk,' she said, wishing she did not feel obliged to explain herself to him. 'What's the matter? I understand Lord Ansaryon wants to see me.'

'Yes, he does – and urgently, though I don't know why. I'll take you to him.' He dismissed her escort with a few clattering words of Toktel'yan, and led her inside an arched doorway to the room beyond.

It was breathtakingly beautiful. The murals of Zithirian, lovely though they were, could not compare with the cool shining tiles, thousands of them, laid on floor and wall and ceiling. Each one was different, and abstract in itself, but when set in its proper place resolved into a part of a wonderful, glorious whole. The lamplight sparkled on the glossy raised edges of petal or leaf or feather, birds, trees, animals, flowers, all entwined in fabulous profusion. She could not help gasping at the scale of it: and there was another pattern on the floor, a sunburst of rich reds and yellows radiating from the centre and touching brilliant fingers of colour to the far corners of the room.

For once, Invan did not seem in the mood to impart information. His hand on her arm, he guided her across the vast space, ignoring her stares of wonder and her hesitant feet, and through a door, made of pierced and painted wood, at the further end.

The next room was much smaller, and also empty. It had the look of a lobby or ante-chamber, but even this was tiled on every surface, with a plainer, more abstract design of dark blues and greens in a tangle of interlaced shapes. She had time to wonder how many craftsmen had laboured on just these two rooms, and how long it had taken them, and on the scores, even hundreds of similar rooms throughout the Palace, and then Invan halted her in front of another door. This one was quite solid, with two strange gilded beasts, perhaps winged lions, snarling in a very lifelike way out of the wood. He knocked twice, and then twice again.

Ansaryon opened it. He was still wearing his Toktel'yan robe, and despite its outlandish appearance – no wonder the people of the Empire hardly ever rode horses, Halthris thought, if they always wore a gown that reached their ankles – its graceful simplicity suited him very well. But there was a tension about his eyes that made her uneasy. Her first instinct on the quayside had been right: something had happened, something was wrong.

'Thank you, Invan,' he said. 'You can go now.'

Invan was looking at the room beyond with deep suspicion on his face. Halthris had already caught a glimpse of opulent furnishings, cushions and draperies, a low couch swathed in soft pastel silk. Suddenly realizing what he must be thinking, she put a hand to her mouth, trying to hide her amusement. A Tanathi proverb spoke of thieves who think all men are thieves. Invan obviously thought that he had brought her here to be seduced. And, knowing Ansaryon as well as she did, she was certain that nothing, at this moment, could be further from his mind.

'It's quite all right, Invan,' she said, giving him her most cheerful smile. 'I'll see you later.'

'Are you sure—'

'You must have a very peculiar opinion of my habits if you aren't,' Ansaryon said drily. 'But then most of Zithirian has a peculiar opinion of my habits. Go on, Invan, before I lose my patience. I want to talk to Halthris in private, if you please.'

With a last, yearning glance at her, the General turned and walked reluctantly away. Ansaryon stood aside with a smile, and ushered her in.

Perhaps it was in luxury such as this that the Emperor's fifty famous concubines were kept. This chamber was almost as large as the sunburst room, but the floor area, tiled in a yellow and white chequered pattern, was divided into smaller areas with loosely-woven mesh screens. In the further corner, just visible, a large pool was sunk in the floor, a gently splashing fountain at its centre. There were shutters across all the windows, which seemed strange, especially as the room, lit by a myriad bright lanterns, mainly yellow and red, was stiflingly hot.

Halthris felt the first beads of sweat break out on her forehead, and wondered at this surely excessive need for privacy. Was Invan right after all? Why did Ansaryon want to keep their meeting secret from any curious eyes or ears in the courtyard outside?

A man walked out from behind one of the screens. He was very tall and massively built, and his robes were a deep crimson, with tastefully restrained gold braid round neck and sleeve and hem. He glanced at Ansaryon and then smiled at her, revealing perfect white teeth. His hair was grizzled and tightly curled, and his skin had the colour and texture of black-dyed leather.

'Halthris of the Tanathi – I have brought you here to speak with this man,' Ansaryon said quietly. 'His name is Al'Kalyek, and he is the Emperor's Court Sorcerer.'

CHAPTER
NINETEEN

'You feel the power, do you not, Halthris of the Tanathi?'

Al'Kalyek's voice was deep, strong and resonant. His dark eyes were friendly, and his manner pleasant and unthreatening, but she sensed, as she had sensed in Ansaryon, the hidden menace of sorcery, vibrating softly in the air around him. Her mouth suddenly dry, she nodded.

'And you have had no training? You take no drug?'

His Zithiriani was fluent and clear, though rather formal. She fought down her irrational sense of panic, and said firmly, 'No, I have never had either.'

'That is interesting – very interesting indeed. And the Lord Ansaryon tells me that until recently you kept a hunting-cat, and communicated with her in a particular way. Can you enlighten me?'

The sweat was pouring off her back, and the thin cotton tunic was sticking to her uncomfortably. Ansaryon said something in Toktel'yan, and the sorcerer smiled apologetically. 'Of course. How very remiss of me, Halthris of the Tanathi. Pray sit, and refresh yourself. There are fruit juices of several kinds, and ice to cool them. Then we can continue our conversation.'

Ice? she thought dazedly. In this furnace?

'It is brought from the mountains of Tulyet in the cold season by fast ship, packed in straw to keep it frozen,' Al'Kalyek said, bringing goose-bumps to her arms despite the heat. 'Then it is kept in stone underground pits, lined with rushes and felt, until required. The Palace ice-chambers can supply us all with cooling drinks and cold food throughout the hot season.'

She sat down amidst the cushions, and found herself staring at the rightful King of Zithirian, proffering a tray on which were several tall jugs, unmistakably Minassan, and a matching goblet decorated with yellow flowers. 'You have a choice – orange, lemon, peach or lime.' He smiled at her, and she saw the genuine warmth and encouragement in his eyes. 'They're all delicious. Don't be alarmed by Al'Kalyek. To him, sorcery is a skill like any other – although the highest of all arts – and has no special mystery or menace. Toktel'yans are very matter-of-fact about it.'

She chose the yellow juice, called lemon. It was wonderfully cold, sharp and refreshing, with a lingering scent of honey on the tongue. She swallowed it all, much more quickly than she had intended, and Ansaryon poured out another helping, before refilling both his own cup and the sorcerer's. Feeling a little more relaxed, a little less threatened, she sat cross-legged, Tanathi style, and sipped her second drink slowly, enjoying the flavour.

'I did not intend to alarm you,' Al'Kalyek said, sitting down in another pile of cushions opposite. He put his cup on a low bronze table, its legs cast in the form of sitting lions, and leaned forward. 'But I hope you understand my interest, my excitement. As the Lord Ansaryon has already said, here in Toktel'yi magic is admired as all skills are, from humble carpentry to the making of such gracious artefacts as you can see all around you. When every village has its own sorcerer, to influence the weather, heal minor wounds and illnesses, create illusions, find missing objects and people and brew potions for unrequited lovers, we could hardly take any other view. Most Toktel'yans see magic as a tool, useful as an axe or a spade is useful. Some, though, have studied more deeply, and sense that it has enormous potential, far greater than any power yet discovered, waiting for the right key to unlock the door. But although scholars have been searching for such a key for more than a thousand years, ever since the effects of the drug Annatal were first discovered, it has never been found. It will be one day – I am sure of it. And I have been wondering, after what the Lord Ansaryon has told me, whether you and he are not part of the puzzle.'

Halthris stared at him in bewilderment. 'How? How can I be?'

'You appear, Halthris of the Tanathi, to have a certain amount of natural ability. You are quite sure that you have never taken Annatal in your life?'

'Quite sure.'

'Then you must indeed be gifted. For instance, I believe that you could thought-link with your cat?'

'Yes – but I didn't know I was doing it until I found out that I could communicate with the Lord Ansaryon in the same way, by using words rather than pictures.'

'She saved my life,' Ansaryon said quietly, with the gratitude he had never really voiced to her before. She glanced at him, and surprised an expression on his face that she could not interpret.

'And does anyone else in your tribe possess such abilities? Other members of your family, for instance?'

She shook her head. 'No, not that I know of. If they do, they have never mentioned it to me, nor have I seen any signs. My brother and sister and I are close, and sometimes they can tell what I'm thinking, but I'm sure that's because we know each other so well, rather than any special power. I did meet an old man who had had a hunting-cat in his youth, and he used thought-link as well – pictures in the head, was how he described it. But that is all.'

'I suspect,' Al'Kalyek said slowly, 'that you might find many Tanathi who possess such gifts, although they do not acknowledge them as such. The situation may well be the same in Zithirian, where many have Tanathi blood, and have been taught to fear and shun magic – so if any have potential power, they will be very reluctant to recognize it. And now we come to you, Lord Ansaryon. For you undoubtedly possess more power than many Toktel'yan sorcerers – power that normally can only be attained after a score of years spent in study, practice and regular ingestion of Annatal.'

'And since I didn't become a sorcerer at the age of seven or eight, there must be some other explanation.'

'Precisely. Either you already had the power, untapped and unrecognized, before you ever became a Mazath – power that enabled you to survive withdrawal from Annatal and emerge with your gifts increased – or you lived by chance, and with the help of Halthris of the Tanathi, and found the drug's effects were still with you. Of course, since you are as far as I know the only person ever to recover after abandoning the drug, it is not a theory which is easy to prove or to disprove. For myself, I would incline to the view that your power is inborn. There is Jo'ami blood in you, is there not?'

Halthris, bewildered, looked at Ansaryon. He evidently understood what the sorcerer meant, for he said, 'Yes, there is. The second King Varathand married a woman from Jo'ami. But he lived nearly a hundred and fifty years ago. Six or seven generations separate me from her. How can it emerge in me now?'

'Bloodlines and inheritance are strange things, as anyone with experience of breeding animals will know – as you undoubtedly do, Halthris of the Tanathi. A particular characteristic, sometimes favourable, sometimes not, may lie dormant through successive generations and then reappear without warning. My brother, who lives on the island of Onnak, is trying to establish a superior breed of hound, combining keen sight with speed, intelligence and an excellent nose. He made the mistake of using a good but evil-tempered dog, many years ago, and even now puppies are occasionally born who are so savage that they are dangerous. Invariably the most promising animals in other ways, too. So, your ancestress

from Jo'ami may have implanted the seed of magic in her descendants, to be disclosed at last in you.'

'I'm sorry,' Halthris said, when he had paused. 'But what is
Jo'ami?'

'My apologies, Halthris of the Tanathi – I had forgotten that
you might not know. Jo'ami lies far, far to the south – the southern-
most island of all the Archipelago, and the only one that Toktel'yi
has not conquered. It is where the art of sorcery was born. There
are many stories about Jo'ami, for few of my people have ever been
there, and the legends say that it is hidden from all but wizards. I
do not believe that myself – but then I have never tried to find it.
Another story has it that Jo'ami sorcerers are born – not made with
drugs, but born. If that is true, then King Varathand's wife may
well have passed the gift down the generations to the Lord
Ansaryon.' His dark face was regretful. 'We know so little – so
much lies waiting for us to discover it, and I have only half my
lifetime left! But I am very grateful to you, Halthris of the Tanathi,
for speaking to me – you have provided perhaps a few more tiles in
the mosaic.'

'So what will you do now?' Ansaryon asked, his voice tinged
with dry amusement. 'Devise some test for natural ability, and then
examine children up and down the Empire for signs of it?'

'Quite possibly – quite possibly.' Al'Kalyek was beginning to
sound quite excited. 'If we could do that, it would transform the
magic arts. Just imagine – no need for Annatal any longer!'

Halthris remembered what Kefiri had told her about the drug's
disadvantages, and looked at the sorcerer. It was hard to tell his
age, but if his remark about half his lifetime left was true, he might
be fifty or sixty. The grey hair and deeply lined face, however, were
those of a man twenty or thirty years older than that. Not many
Tanathi lived to see their grandchildren, let alone achieve venerable
old age, so she could barely imagine the dilemma faced by those
who wished to practise sorcery. How had Ansaryon, possessing that
spare, delicately-sculptured face, ever made the choice that, after
ten years or so, would have precipitated him into a premature and
long-lasting old age?

He was looking at her. She saw his eyebrows lift slightly, and
knew what he wanted. She gave an imperceptible nod.

'*Don't worry,*' said his voice inside her head, full of gentle self-
mockery. '*I gave up Annatal soon enough. I'll be shrivelled up like
a winter leaf only when I'm in my dotage, and not before.*'

Al'Kalyek stared at them quizzically, and then smiled. 'A
perfect illustration,' he said. 'Have no fear, I did not listen – it is

the height of bad manners to eavesdrop on a thought-linked conversation, just as it is on an audible one. But even amongst experienced sorcerers, such a close and instinctive bond is rare.'

'We have shared a great deal in the last few months,' Ansaryon said, smiling at Halthris. 'And now there is something else that must be discussed with some urgency – indeed, that's why I wanted to see you both at such a late hour. You, Halthris, because you seem to know much more about this . . . apparition than I do – and you, honoured sorcerer, because you may be able to explain it.'

Suddenly, the air around her felt chilly, despite the stultifying closeness in the room. Aware that the colour must have left her face, she stared at him. 'Bron? Have you seen Bron again? Was he here?'

'Here in this room, not two hours ago. He didn't stay once I'd seen him, but I don't know how long he'd been lurking. He was over there, behind that screen in the corner.'

A cold weight seemed to have settled on her heart. Al'Kalyek was staring at them both with an expression of deep concern on his face. He said slowly, 'Bron? That is a form of a Ska'ian word meaning "servant", or more often "slave".'

'Is it?' Ansaryon said. 'I wondered what it meant. And that would tally with the little we know of him.'

Halthris thought of the small, thin child, the fear in his face, the unspeakable, unknowable depth of his eyes, and shivered. She said, 'If he has a Ska'i name . . . he *must* be evil.'

'No!' Ansaryon's voice was unusually sharp. He went on more quietly. 'No – I cannot believe that he is intrinsically evil. He may be used for evil purposes – but he is only a child.'

Al'Kalyek was looking from one to the other, a great ridged frown between his thick brows. 'My Lord Ansaryon, I think you had better explain. I do not like the sound of this.'

The younger man hesitated, and Halthris knew, as clearly as if he had told her, that there was something that he did not wish to reveal either to her or to Al'Kalyek. She felt a touch of anger. If Bron was dangerous and evil, then it was vital that all the facts about him were known, and suspicions fully discussed.

She gave Ansaryon a brief, frowning glance, and then turned to the sorcerer. 'I saw him first in Sar D'yenyi. It was just after we knew that the Lord Ansaryon might survive the withdrawal of Annatal. After that, I saw him again, several times, and so did the Lady Kefiri, and some of my Tanathi friends.'

'Describe him to me, if you would.'

She considered for a moment, seeing again the child who had

once seemed harmless, if a little strange, and who now appeared to be some kind of portent or agent of evil. She said at last, thoughtfully, 'He is small – about seven or eight years old. He's so thin and underfed, it's hard to tell his age. He has very fair hair, almost white, and a dirty face, pinched and hungry-looking. But above all I remember his eyes – they're so dark, so deep, that when you stare into them it's impossible to remember he's just a child. If he *is* just a child. Sometimes, his look makes me shiver. I can smell the sorcery in him, my flesh tingles with it. And so could Fess, my cat. Every time she saw him, she growled, and raised all her hackles.'

'And have you touched this child?'

'Yes, I did, at Minassa. The Lord Ansaryon and I were talking in the Palace gardens. Bron came down with the lamplighter, who'd befriended him. Ansaryon and I both spoke to him, and I took his hand. It was quite real, warm, living, you could feel it – he wasn't an illusion.'

'I see.' Al'Kalyek was chewing his lip thoughtfully. 'And have you ever seen this boy vanish or appear out of thin air?'

Halthris shook her head. 'No. If I had, I would have been suspicious of him earlier. But for a long time I just assumed that he was one of the refugees in Sar D'yenyi – the place was packed with them. He always seemed so lost, so hungry, and I felt sorry for him. So did the Lady Kefiri.'

'And what changed your attitude towards him?'

'Seeing him in Minassa – *knowing* that he must have come there through sorcery.' She paused, and then added, 'It did puzzle me, the way he just seemed to appear – I never *saw* him come or go, he was just *there* – in my room, on the stairs, hanging about outside Ansaryon's room or the Council Chamber, looking so lost. And there was Fess's response to him, too – that told me he was not just an ordinary child. So I suppose that I had been suspicious of him for some time. But not *certain* – not until Minassa.'

'And you, Lord Ansaryon? What are your thoughts on this child?'

Halthris had noticed that while he had been speaking, Al'Kalyek's attention had been divided between her and Ansaryon. As he was sitting to one side of her, half-reclining on the cushions, she could not study his face without making it obvious that she did. His voice, when it came, was even and controlled. 'Unlike Halthris, I had not encountered him in Sar D'yenyi, so at first I did not realize the significance of his appearance in Minassa.'

'And now that you have also seen him here, what do you think?'

Out of the corner of her eye, Halthris could see his hands, relaxed in his lap. She risked a glance, and noted that his face was calm, and quite empty of feeling. But a single, betraying nerve twitched in his cheek as she watched, and then was gone.

'I think,' Ansaryon said at last, 'that he has been sent to spy on us. I think I know who sends him – there is only one person in Zithirian who has anything approaching that level of power, and the knowledge to use it. But I cannot understand how it is done. I have never heard of any sorcery strong enough to transport another creature bodily over such a distance. Even those who can spirit-walk – a much less difficult skill – are very restricted in their range. They can go a mile or so, no more. In Tayo's name, what force must be necessary to send that child a thousand times further?'

'No power that we have yet discovered,' Al'Kalyek said grimly. 'But if what you say is true, then there is no other explanation for the child's appearances *except* such a power.'

'Unless he stowed away on one of the boats,' Halthris pointed out. 'But that would not explain the stink of sorcery, every time I see him – nor would it explain Fess's reaction to him. He is evil, through and through.'

'No!' Ansaryon said forcefully. She stared at him, seeing his hands locked together, the knuckles white. 'No – he is not. He is the helpless and unwilling tool of someone who is evil, to the core of her bones. She is using him, I am sure of it. But that does not make him evil too – he is not old enough to be anything other than her instrument.'

'And who is this person who controls him?'

'Her name is D'thliss, and she is the High Priestess of the Temple of Tayo in Zithirian.'

D'thliss, whom he had cursed in Ayak's name, with sorcery and hatred. Halthris shivered, sensing behind his bare words something vast, menacing, lurking with dreadful malevolence. She said, 'Why does D'thliss want to spy on us?'

Ansaryon's voice was suddenly raw with weary impatience. 'Why do you think? She is Tsenit's accomplice, after all. In fact, I wouldn't be surprised if she had not planned everything – the invasion of the Ska'i, the slaughter of my family, and his seizure of the throne. And Tsenit is as much her tool as Bron, with one crucial difference – he is willing, and knows exactly what he is doing, whereas the child does not.'

'I have heard of D'thliss, although I have never met her,' Al'Kalyek said. 'Some young Tayan Priests came here to Toktel'yi a few years ago, to study at the School of Wizardry here. She was not then their High Priestess, but they spoke of her with a mixture of awe, respect and terror. I should imagine she would make a formidable adversary.'

'She is more than that,' Ansaryon said. 'I do not wish to go into details, but when I was young, beginning my training as a Mazath, she and I . . . came into contact. For a while, I think she saw me as the means to the power she craves. When she realized her mistake, she abandoned me and turned instead to Tsenit.'

'Who is not a Mazath, and therefore can be more easily influenced and controlled,' Al'Kalyek said softly. 'There is much you are not telling me, Lord Ansaryon. Will you not be more open?'

'No,' he said. Halthris saw that his face, sheened thinly with sweat, was utterly determined. 'There is nothing I can tell you that would help you further.'

'A shame.' Al'Kalyek stroked his lined cheek with one large, bony finger. 'But as you wish. And perhaps you are right – between you both, you have given me the most essential facts, and I have already come to certain conclusions. I think that your instincts are right, Halthris of the Tanathi – I beg you, Lord Ansaryon, let me speak.'

The younger man had looked as if he would spring to his feet, but at the sorcerer's gently raised hand, fell back on the cushions.

'I feel that this child, Bron, is extremely dangerous, even if he is not actually evil. Dangerous because he is a vessel containing vast power – power which, up until now, we sorcerers have only contemplated in our wildest and most far-fetched dreams. How he came by it, whether he was born with it or whether D'thliss uses him as a channel or conduit for her own power, I do not really know. But in himself, he is deadly. That is the only explanation for his appearances at Sar D'yenyi, and Minassa, and now here. She would only be able to send him such vast distances if he himself also possessed power – and power, I suspect, very much greater than hers.'

There was a chill silence. Then Halthris said, 'If he is spying – *how* is it done? Does he see, and report? Or does she look through his eyes?'

'Since he is still a young child, I suspect she enters his mind. She might not be able to do it consistently – she might come and go inside his head. That would explain why you took so long to be suspicious of him – and also why his eyes seemed so strange, sometimes.'

Halthris remembered the despair she had once felt, looking into those eyes, and shivered despite the heat. The idea of the aged, evil priestess taking over the mind of a small boy was peculiarly horrible. She said, 'He sometimes spoke of his grandmother, and he seemed to be terrified of her. Was she D'thliss, then?'

'Undoubtedly.'

'He said she kept him hungry – he was so thin, dirty, dressed almost in rags – why is she so unkind to him, if he is so valuable to her?'

'She wishes to keep him in fear, in subjection,' Ansaryon told her, and there was a bitter, anguished loathing in his voice. 'She rules through terror. If I am ever granted the opportunity, I shall take the greatest pleasure in separating her spirit from her body – painfully, and permanently. She is Ayak's creature, and I shall force him to devour her in the end.'

'And Ayak is the chosen deity of the Ska'i, is he not?' said Al'Kalyek. 'It all fits. You have an enemy of enormous power, my Lord Ansaryon – you had better think long and hard how to defeat her. Bring her down, and your brother and the Ska'i, fearsome though they may be, will fall like overripe fruit under your feet.'

'Why not try to seize Bron, when he next appears?' Halthris suggested. 'He can be held, I've proved that.'

'D'thliss would bring him back – he would melt out of your hand and into nothingness like ice on a hot day,' Al'Kalyek told her. 'Perhaps if you took the time to befriend him, he would eventually prefer you rather than D'thliss – and perhaps, as he begins to think more for himself, he might be able to resist her. If he is as powerful as I suspect, he may – if he has the will. If you took him away from her now, or very soon, you might save him from evil. But the longer he stays in her clutches, the more likely it is that he will eventually succumb. And *then*, my Lord Ansaryon, you may find he is an adversary who cannot be defeated.'

'So surely it would be safest to kill him now,' Halthris said. She saw Ansaryon's face open, for an instant, to an intensity of emotion, and continued doggedly. 'If my Lord Sorcerer is right, then it would be best to kill him before D'thliss takes him over completely, and save much grief later.'

The King of Zithirian's silver eyes were glittering with wild anger. 'I thought the Tanathi loved children, and cherished them.'

'They do – but Bron isn't a child, is he? Not a true child. Soon D'thliss will have sucked all his life, all his character, all his self out of him, and left him just a husk, to be filled with unspeakable evil. Isn't it kinder to spare him that horror?'

'Kinder to get him away from her before that happens,' Ansaryon said. To her dismay, he was looking at her with something very like loathing in his face. He stood up in one swift, fluid movement and approached her: and for the first time since their earliest acquaintance, she felt afraid of him. 'Listen to me, Halthris of the Tanathi, and listen well. I swear, here and now, by the blood of the Divine Ancestor that runs in my veins, that I will do my utmost to save the child Bron from the fate that D'thliss has planned for him. And never, as long as there is breath in my body, will I do him harm – nor will I allow anyone else to hurt him. Do you understand me? If you lay a finger on him, Halthris of the Tanathi, I will defend him with all the power at my command – and I will kill *you*, if necessary.'

The silence was appalling. Al'Kalyek's black face wore a mixture of concern, bewilderment and suspicion. It restored some of her spirit. She forced herself to look Ansaryon in the eye without flinching, and calmed her shaken nerves. Then she said, with deceptive coolness, 'I think you might find that difficult.'

His eyes flickered: she wondered if he would strike her, and did not look away. Then, with a muttered exclamation, he turned and strode to the door. His fingers on the handle, he looked back at the Tanathi woman and the sorcerer. 'Go,' he said. 'Go, now. Both of you.'

'Of course, my Lord Ansaryon,' Al'Kalyek said. He rose to his feet with studied care, and adjusted the plain leather belt around his ample midriff. 'If that is what you wish. Are you leaving also, Halthris of the Tanathi? It might be wise.'

He moved with stately dignity to the door. Ansaryon opened it for him, and with a last, warning glance back at her, the sorcerer walked out. Halthris, her jaw set and her apparently casual pose held rigid to stop her trembling, stayed defiantly where she was.

The door shut. The King of Zithirian surveyed her, his arms folded, every taut line of his body betraying his hard-held rage. He said, 'I told you to go.'

'Not yet. I will, but not yet. Not until we have talked.'

'There is nothing more to say. Get out.' He walked over to where she still sat amongst the cushions and stood over her. Against the clusters of coloured lanterns glowing behind him, he was a dark, featureless, terrifying image of menace. 'Now, before I do something you'll regret. Get up and get out.'

'Not until we have talked,' Halthris repeated stubbornly. She heard his impatient intake of breath, and went on swiftly. 'If I have angered you, I am very sorry. I thought we were friends—'

'So did I – but you have just revealed your true nature.'

'*My* true nature?' She sprang up, driven by indignation, and also by fear. 'What of yours, my Lord Ansaryon? Why is this child so important to you? Is he himself so special? Or is it his power, perhaps? Do you want him for yourself, as *your* instrument?'

She knew she had gone too far, even as he raised his hands. She heard the crack of sorcery, saw the blue flash leap from his fingers, and then something picked her up and hurled her backwards, crashing into oblivion.

For a long, long time Ansaryon stood utterly motionless, staring at the Tanathi woman who had saved his life, with whom, once, he had shared a tiny part of the burden on his soul, and who now lay crumpled against the tiled wall, ten paces away, where his rage and his power had thrown her. Then he dropped to his knees and buried his face in his hands.

The door opened and closed, very softly. Al'Kalyek crossed the floor, and stood looking at the man and the woman. He said quietly, 'Have you killed her?'

There was no answer: it was as if Ansaryon had not heard him. The Emperor's sorcerer walked over to Halthris and knelt beside her, searching with gentle, skilful fingers. A lump on the back of her head was already prominent, but there seemed to be no bones broken, and she was breathing softly and evenly. He had no need to ask how she had been hurt: the room still reeked of sorcery, the brief explosion of power that had overwhelmed him before he had left the sunburst hall, and brought him hurrying back.

He laid her head carefully down on a cushion, made her more comfortable, and then turned back to Ansaryon, his expression stern. There were some things which etiquette demanded should never be said to potential kings, still less potential kings who were also sorcerers of considerable power, but Al'Kalyek had never minced his words when necessary.

'She is not dead,' he said. 'The damage would appear to be slight, thanks be to Kaylo the Life-Giver – and no thanks to you. What did she say, to deserve that?'

Silence. Ansaryon had dropped his hands, but his head was bowed: Al'Kalyek could not see his face, only the bright fall of his hair.

'Whatever she said, whatever the insult, surely it was not worth risking her death? Earlier this evening, you spoke of her most warmly, as a dear friend. Indeed, she once saved your life. Is *this* how you repay your debt?'

Still no response. Al'Kalyek said brutally, 'What kind of King are you? No explanation, no remorse, just the cowering of a sulky child.'

Ansaryon moved, perhaps involuntarily. He said softly, despairingly, 'Then perhaps I have been tried – and found wanting.'

'Perhaps you have.' Al'Kalyek's voice was hard, and singularly unsympathetic. 'I don't know what you Mazath teach each other, up in your cold northern city, but if you have any claim at all to be true sorcerers, the first lesson to be learned is responsibility. Unlike that waif, Bron, you are adult – you know what you are doing, you know your power, its extent and its limits. You have a gift that places you at a significant advantage, compared to ordinary people. The First Master of the High Art, Ai-Mayak of Jo'ami, laid down the Four Rules more than a thousand years ago. Sorcery should be used for the benefit of others, rather than selfishly; it should not be employed to work harm or damage; it should be used with forethought and restraint; and the sorcerer should accept full responsibility for the consequences if he should break any of the first three rules. Will you accept it, Ansaryon of Zithirian?'

'I accept.' His voice was bleak and bitter. 'All of it, the present and the past . . . and the future.' He gave a brief, mirthless laugh. 'Would killing more than two thousand Ska'i in order to save half that number of my own people break those rules, do you think?'

'You must examine your own mind, my Lord Ansaryon, and answer that for yourself. And I believe you already have.'

For the first time, the younger man looked up. Al'Kalyek caught a glimpse of glittering, haunted eyes, and felt suddenly uncomfortable, as if he had pried too close to a soul.

'I can still hear them screaming,' Ansaryon said at last. 'I loathe them, they and all their kind are evil, they would have slaughtered us all and only I could prevent it – but still I hear their cries in my dreams.'

'Then there is hope for you – but why show compassion for your enemy, and none whatsoever for your friend? What harm did she do to you? Or did she come too close to the truth?'

'No, she did not.' He sounded very weary. 'And I should not have used my power on her. She did not deserve it. She has always said what she thinks – I should have tolerated it, I always have done before.'

'And will you say that to her, when she comes to herself?'

'She probably won't listen,' said Ansaryon, with bitter amusement. 'And I couldn't really blame her.'

'Nor could I.' Al'Kalyek paused, looking down at the rightful

King of Zithirian. He did not need sorcery to detect the altered pattern of breathing, the sweat soaking the thin robe, the clenched hands and the thrumming tension emanating from the man kneeling before him, as if he were a sith-string wound too tight. He said very softly, 'That child means much more to you than any other, despite his menace. Why? Will you tell me?'

A slow, emphatic shake of the head.

'Then if you will not, perhaps I can guess. He is supposedly the grandson of your bitterest enemy. He is being used as a weapon against you, and he may well possess vast powers which might eventually destroy you. But in response to the obvious solution – callous, perhaps, but eminently practical – your reaction is disproportionately extreme. You swear to protect him, and the level of your anger with your friend was, to put it mildly, unreasonable. No, hear me out. What other explanation could there be, save that the child Bron is of your own blood? *Is* he your son?'

They were the first words that Halthris understood as full consciousness returned to her. She had vaguely heard their voices, Al'Kalyek's deep tones contrasting with the brief, lighter sound of Ansaryon, but they were competing on very unequal terms with the throbbing agony inside her skull. She lay on the cool hard floor and wondered, with remote interest, how she had come to be there, and why her head hurt so much. Was she dying?

And then the sorcerer demanded, '*Is* he your son?' And she remembered everything, with terrifying clarity, and waited, rigid and tense, for the answer.

It took a long time. 'I don't know,' Ansaryon said at last, his voice very low. 'Not for certain.'

'But you suspect that he is, do you not? I saw your reaction when I told you that your powers might be inherited – you looked as if you had been given a vital piece of a Kal-Gan puzzle. I will not ask all the other, obvious questions – who his mother is, why the child is in the hands of D'thliss, why you have made no attempt to rescue him before now. Those are for you to resolve, and they are not my business. But heed my warning, King of Zithirian, and heed it well. Do not let your concern for the child Bron blind you to the danger he presents. He is lethal, to you and to all your companions. And I am sure that D'thliss, who seems to be surpassingly cunning, will have realized that you are vulnerable to him. For he can destroy you – but you have sworn an oath never to harm him. And those unequal terms may yet prove to be your downfall.'

'*Unless I kill him.*'

Halthris did not realize that her thought had been picked up, until she heard swift footsteps. Someone knelt by her side, and the movement of his robes stirred the heavy air around her. She opened her eyes, and saw Ansaryon's face, looking down at her.

'*Unless I kill him*,' she repeated stubbornly. '*I won't slay him out of hand, I promise – but if his death is the only way to save us all from utter obliteration at the hands of D'thliss, and the Ska'i, then I shall not hesitate to kill him.*'

Faintly, she became aware of his reluctant and difficult acceptance. '*If he is mine, then I owe him a great deal, to make up for the nightmare of pain and suffering that my neglect and thoughtlessness have caused him.*' She saw, through a fog, his bitter smile. '*When I accused you of callousness, I was turning my own faults against you. Halthris, I am sorry – it was a despicable way to treat a friend. Will you forgive me?*'

She heard the genuine remorse in his silent words, and felt a surprising rush of anger. '*You could easily have killed me,*' she said to his mind, furiously. '*What gives you the right to treat anyone like that, never mind a friend? You will be King soon, if our plans succeed. I pity the people of Zithirian, if you let your emotions rule everything else – including your sorcery.*'

Once, she had thought him incapable of feeling. It was strange, now, to realize that he was probably far more vulnerable to it than she was. But being Zithiriani, and trained at that hideously formal court, he had been taught to hide emotions too well. Whereas she, schooled on the harsh steppe, had learned in early childhood the brutal lessons necessary for survival. Indulgence in inappropriate sentiment was a luxury that no Tanathi could afford.

And so, she had cut to the heart of the problem, and suggested Bron's death. She knew for certain that she could kill him, if necessary, although the deed would cause her considerable pain and grief. For all her tribe understood the necessity of sacrifice, the loss of the small, the old, the frail, the superfluous, whether stores or animals or people, so that the Tanathi as a whole might survive.

She had thought that her honesty would enrage him again, but his bleak, sad expression surprised her. In her mind, he said slowly, '*I have many hard lessons yet to learn. That is just one of them. I am not perfect, Halthris, and never will be – but if I have the grace to try to change myself, will you give me the chance to do it?*'

'Of course,' she said, aloud though it came out barely above a whisper. 'But please, is there something to take away my headache?'

'Allow me.' The avuncular tones of Al'Kalyek arrived with his face, dark and smiling behind Ansaryon's shoulder. 'This is a branch of the High Art that you Mazath do not teach, am I right? I thought not. Perhaps I can give you a few hints, before you return to the north. It is not difficult for anyone skilled in sorcery – it just requires a different kind of concentration, that is all.'

Ansaryon made way for him, and he knelt beside Halthris. The brief, intense thought-linked conversation had drained her: she felt sick, and exhausted, and the outside world had surrendered once more to the unbearable pain behind her eyes. She closed them, and felt the sorcerer's thick, smooth fingers touch her face with cool and surprising gentleness.

Inside her skull, the heavy throbbing beat began, mercifully, to lessen. Al'Kalyek stroked her forehead, and then laid his hand flat against her temple. She felt his presence enter her flesh, seeking out the sore muscles, the bruised bone, the shaken brain. He moved his fingers, and the pain coalesced fearfully for one last time. She gasped in agony, and then it was gone, leaving with his touch, and she was free.

The relief was astonishing. She lay, eyes still shut, and let other sensations creep back. The discomfort of the hard tiles under her body; the very distant sound of voices in the courtyard outside; the soft everlasting splash and trickle of the fountain; the all-enveloping heat.

'Halthris?'

It was Ansaryon's voice, aloud. She opened her eyes and smiled at him. 'It's all right. It's gone. I don't know what he did – it was as if he came into my head and drew the pain away.'

'A fair description of the technique,' Al'Kalyek observed. He rose to his feet. 'Well, I for one am weary, and wish for my bed. We will have ample opportunity, the three of us, to discuss all these matters more calmly at another time. Now, since I am tolerably certain that you have renewed your friendship, I will take the daring step of leaving you alone together. But be warned, my Lord Ansaryon – I am extremely sensitive to sorcery. If you use your power in such a manner again, I will know of it instantly.' He smiled. 'But on the whole, this evening has been very interesting indeed. And in case you were wondering, you can be sure that I will not discuss what has happened, and what has been said, with anyone – not even the Emperor himself. Goodnight, my Lord Ansaryon – good night, Halthris of the Tanathi.'

'Thank you, Lord Sorcerer,' she said.

The sorcerer's black eyes glinted. 'It was no trouble. I find myself continually having to rescue people from the fruits of their own folly. Unfortunately, not all the damage is so easily mended. Goodnight, and may Kaylo the Life-Giver keep you both.'

Footsteps, the door opening and closing, and he was gone. She closed her eyes again, wondering why she felt so tired, why even the faintest movement seemed to be beyond her.

'Halthris? Can you sit up?'

'I don't know,' she said helplessly.

'Well, you can't stay there all night.' There was a trace of the old dry amusement back in Ansaryon's voice. After the events of the past hour, it was like stepping onto firm ground from a quaking morass. 'Come on – I'll help you. Apart from anything else, Invan will be knocking on the door at any time, and I don't want to give him any more reason to doubt me.'

'He wants me all to himself,' Halthris said. She smiled, remembering her small act of rebellion, going with Inri down to the sea. 'I'm afraid he's not going to succeed.'

'I'm glad to hear it. You're worth twenty of Invan, good man though he is. Now, if I take your hands . . .'

Appearances were deceptive: she found movement quite possible. Helped and supported by Ansaryon, she struggled stubbornly to her feet, and managed to walk the five paces to the nearest cushions on her own. She sank down into their luxurious softness, the quilted, embroidered silk and smooth satin extraordinarily tactile and sensuous under her hands, and wondered how long she could keep awake.

'Sleep if you like – it doesn't matter,' Ansaryon told her. He crouched beside her, as she had seen Toktel'yan men do when they were discussing something. 'I'll send word to Inri and Sherren – they'll be worried if you don't come back.'

'Thank you,' Halthris said drowsily. It seemed a lifetime since she had left them on the quayside, but only an hour or two had elapsed since then. And in that time something had been apparently smashed beyond repair, and yet, strangely, seemed to be mended again.

She didn't want to risk a return of her headache, thinking about it, or any of the other things that had been revealed tonight. That could wait until morning. For now, sleep was claiming her. She smiled at him hazily, and then surrendered to its welcome oblivion.

Even after what he had done to her, she trusted him absolutely.

TWENTY

'In a garden in Zithirian
Sits a lady fine and fair,
Her eyes like cool green water,
Her smile as warm as sunlight,
And flowers in her hair.'

The notes of a Sith, plucked as gently and delicately as the ripples in a pond, drifted through the warm summer air, and a young girl's voice, making an endearing effort to reach the higher notes, sang the accompanying words.

It was a tune everyone in the city must know by heart, from potter to prince. Kefiri found herself humming alongside that unseen, charmingly gauche singer. It was so long since she had heard music: no one seemed to sing or play anything in Kaydi's household, and she had not felt the lack of it until now, when the song's hesitant, melancholy sweetness struck an answering chord of sadness in herself.

'In a garden in Zithirian,
The lady sits and waits.
The daylight turns to evening,
The sun is close to setting,
Soon it will be too late.'

Too late: the words had a fateful echo. It was past midsummer. In three months' time it would be a year since the Ska'i invasion, and Tsenit's usurpation of the throne. And then, if winter came early again, Sar D'yenyi and its people and its gold would once more be in danger.

Three months left. She wondered where Ansaryon was, and what he was doing. No word had come to the city, no rumours. He and his meagre army might have vanished off the rim of the world, and she would have no way of knowing it. If, if, *if* all had gone according to his plan, he should be in Toktel'yi by now, negotiating with the Emperor, trying to find a way of obtaining Djamal's help without putting himself under some onerous obligation to the most powerful city in the known world.

'In a garden in Zithirian,
Sits a lady fine and fair.
Her tears pour down like raindrops,
Her lips are pale and trembling,
Her sorrow fills the air.'

How long would it take, to return from Toktel'yi? She had
never been there, and knew only that it was a thousand miles, more
or less, to the south. The journey down river, going with the flow
of the Kefirinn, was swift and easy: much less so, by all accounts,
when struggling back against the current, even the sluggish stream
in high summer.

Oh, Tayo, she prayed softly, to the Ancestor whose name, now,
she hardly ever invoked. Keep them all safe, give them success –
and bring them back to face Tsenit and the Ska'i, and defeat them!

The unseen girl had finished her song, and had embarked on
the standard practice scales on the Sith, up and down, up and down,
played without flair and obviously a hated but necessary chore. It
was a soothing sound, and Kefiri leaned back against the warm
stone seat – all those made of wood had gone to feed hungry fires
during the dreadful months of winter – and closed her eyes,
enjoying these few brief moments of doing absolutely nothing.
Music; birdsong; the rustle of the leaves overhead; distant sounds
from the heart of the city, a few streets away; all noises quite
peaceful and ordinary, and utterly welcome.

She had been in Kaydi's house for a month and a half, and to
her surprise had discovered that she enjoyed living as a member of
this humble, hard-working, hand-to-mouth household. At Sar
D'yenyi, troops of servants had performed every task, but in
Snowbringer Street, she did her share of the chores and was treated
with no deference, although Kaydi, Herris and Shilda all knew who
she really was. She had learned of Kaydi's secret network of Tsenit's
opponents with delight, and her news of Ansaryon's plan to
overthrow his brother and obliterate the Ska'i had been spread all
over the city, giving the half-starved inhabitants some real hope for
the future, and greatly encouraging those who, up until now, had
seen no point to active resistance.

It was as if fate had brought her to Kaydi's house: fate, or
something else, in the shape of a small fair-haired Temple boy
called Bron.

She had had a long and whispered talk to Herris about Bron.
They had sat on the roof in the sunshine, teasing Garool with straw
stalks and aiming bits of moss at various targets in the courtyard

below. They had pooled their experiences of the child, and agreed
that sorcery must be involved: otherwise, as Herris pointed out,
how could Bron possibly be at Sar D'yenyi one day and Zithirian
the next? And Kefiri, who had seen the magic performed by
Ansaryon, and by the priests in the Temple, strongly suspected that
Bron was not just an unwilling tool: he must have some power of
his own. 'Because even the most important priests – that horrible
D'thliss, for instance – couldn't transport themselves bodily, let
alone someone else. They just haven't got the power. She must use
Bron because in some way he augments her. I could never feel it
myself, but Halthris used to say that he reeked of sorcery. A sort of
humming, apparently, like a Sith string vibrating very quietly.'

'He just makes me uneasy,' Herris confided, chewing on a
straw. 'I wonder if I can hit that dove.' He picked up a large piece
of moss, squinted, and threw it over the parapet. It landed to one
side, and the bird, one of the few that had survived the cold of
winter, the household's hunger, and Garool's hunting instincts,
bustled over to investigate. Its air of disgust when it found that the
missile wasn't edible was so comical that Kefiri laughed aloud.
Grinning, Herris aimed again, this time with more success: the dove
flew up with an indignant whirring of wings, and took refuge on the
roof on the opposite side of the courtyard.

'He makes me uneasy, too,' Kefiri said, hugging her knees. She
liked being with Herris: her own childhood was not so far behind
her that she did not welcome the occasional respite from adult
dangers and responsibilities. She was always careful, though, about
what she said or suggested to Herris, for his cheerful recklessness
worried her.

'I don't believe *he's* evil or wicked,' the boy said thoughtfully.
'But that foul witch might make him do *anything* – even things he
didn't want to do.'

'And he knows who I am, and where I am,' Kefiri said, her
heart chill within her. 'What if he tells D'thliss?'

'He won't. He hates her, and so does Lelya.'

'But what if she *makes* him tell her? He's only eight, and she's
the High Priestess.'

Herris thought about it. He said at last, his tone encouraging,
'But he can't have told her – or they'd have come for you by now.
And I think he's more or less independent of her, most of the time.
When she wants him to help her with her sorcery, she takes control
of him. The rest of the time she leaves Lelya to look after him, and
they just run wild.'

'Isn't she afraid something will happen to him? If he's vital to her, why not take more care of him? He always looks half-starved and ragged and dirty.'

'I've been thinking about that,' Herris said, with a certain pride, as if exercising his brain was something he did not often do. 'I think she must reckon it's a good disguise. If she kept him under lock and key, people would wonder why. But no one suspects anything of a dirty little Temple boy, do they?'

'Unless they happen to know he can be in two places almost at once.'

'Or unless they've seen him fool some soldiers by leaving no footprints in the snow,' Herris said. He shivered. 'That was when I first realized he wasn't just an ordinary boy. Kefiri, what are we going to do about him? We can't avoid him – if he wants to find us, he always seems to know where we are.'

'We must try to befriend him,' she said. 'He's already fond of me, I think, because I was kind to him in Sar D'yenyi. Befriend him, feed him, help him – win him away from D'thliss. And then perhaps we can persuade him to leave her.'

'But won't she know where he is?'

'Perhaps. We'll have to take the risk. But it's all we can do. If we're right, and he is the key to D'thliss's power, then when Ansaryon attacks we must find some way of making sure that Bron can't be used against him. And the best way of doing it is to make him our friend. We must be nearly there already – he likes you, and I'm sure he trusts me.'

It was a considerable risk, she thought now, daydreaming in the sun, to place so much reliance on the fragile friendship of one small child, in thrall to the most powerful sorcerer in Zithirian. But, like Herris, she had a strong, instinctive sense of Bron's inner strength, and his needs. Like a flower turning towards the sun, he would follow anyone who treated him kindly. D'thliss, ruthless and cruel, had obviously never regarded him as anything other than a weapon and a source of power.

But he was a child as well: a human child, with thoughts, feelings, and perhaps a core of rebelliousness and independence that he might, one day, assert against his evil grandmother. In that lay their greatest hope.

'Lady?'

A hand touched hers. She gasped, and opened her eyes. Bron stood beside her, his bright hair almost dazzling in the sunlight, and a shy smile on his thin face.

'You startled me,' she said, trying to smile in return. 'I was just thinking about you.'

'I know.'

It was said in such a matter-of-fact way that she almost missed the significance of his words. Then she said, trying to keep her voice gentle, 'You *know*? How do you know, Bron?'

He gave her a wry, apologetic smile that was suddenly and strangely familiar, and shrugged. 'I don't know how, Lady. I just *know*.'

'Oh.' Kefiri decided not to risk scaring him off. She shifted along the seat and patted the space beside her. 'Come and sit here. How are you?'

'All right, Lady.' Bron sat down, swinging his legs. Like all younger Zithiriani children at this time of year, he wore just a thin summer tunic of Toktel'yan cotton, dirty, rather threadbare, and much too short – it failed to reach his knees. He was still too pale, too thin, but there was a faint flush now in his cheeks, and he no longer looked as if a light breeze would knock him over. 'Do you like living in Kaydi's house?' he added.

'Very much, thank you.' Kefiri smiled down at him. There was nothing but innocent friendliness, she would swear to it, in those dark eyes, and no taint of sorcery about him.

And yet . . .

And yet he had *known* where she was, and that she was thinking about him.

'Where's Lelya?' she asked.

'He's gone to Bathra's house. Bathra is a potter, a very good one, he comes from Minassa. Lelya wants to be his apprentice, but Gran won't let him.'

'That seems very unfair. Why not?'

Bron shrugged. 'I don't know. She hasn't said anything much. I think she just doesn't like giving people what they want. If Lelya wanted to be a goldsmith, she'd say no.'

'I don't think I'd like your gran, if I met her.'

'You wouldn't,' said Bron, with a child's blistering candour. 'Nobody does. I don't.' He shivered suddenly, and a shadow passed over his face.

'Are you very frightened of her?' Kefiri said softly.

Mute, the boy nodded, and she saw his eyes fill with tears.

'Well, you don't have to stay with her. You could run away. Herris and I would help you. Anything would be better than her cruelty, surely.'

He shook his head. 'She'd find me. Wherever in the world I'd go, she'd find me. She said that once, when – when I didn't do what she wanted. She said she'd B-Bind me for ever.'

'Bind you?'

'Like a slave, but worse.' His face crumpled suddenly, and he turned and buried his head in her chest, his whole body shaking with sobs.

Kefiri felt close to tears herself. She held him, stroked him and whispered soft comforting words until at last, his emotions exhausted, he managed to calm himself. She fumbled in the pocket of her skirt and found an old handkerchief. 'Here. Dry your eyes and have a good blow of your nose.'

'Thank you, Lady.' Bron scrubbed haphazardly at his face, red and blotchy with weeping, its dirtiness emphasized by the clean pink marks left by his tears. 'I'm sorry. I shouldn't cry. Lelya says only little boys cry, and I'm nine now.'

'Crying's good for you,' said Kefiri briskly. She took back the sodden piece of linen and gave her own eyes a swift surreptitious wipe. 'Listen, Bron. I'm your friend, and so is Herris. Do you understand that?'

He nodded.

'And a friend is someone who will listen to you, and help you. Even if you can't escape your gran, you still have some freedom in the city. She doesn't know you're here, does she?'

'No, Lady. She never bothers with me unless she wants me to do something for her. Then she calls me, and I have to go.'

'Does she know about me?'

Bron's eyes grew wide with shock. 'Oh, no, Lady. I don't tell her about anything unless she asks me straight.'

'Even if she did, would you tell her about me?'

Once more, he looked surprised. 'Course I wouldn't. Or I'd tell her a lie. She can get inside my head, but only for a little while – when she wants to see things. The rest of the time, I can keep her out. She doesn't like it, she gets very angry, but she doesn't know it's *me* stopping her. She just thinks her power isn't strong enough.'

Kefiri drew a deep breath. 'Can't you stand up to her?'

He shook his head. 'No – no, I can't, I'm not strong enough yet. If she *knew* I was – was—'

'Defying her?'

'Yes – if she knew, she'd Bind me for ever, like she said. She can do it. She Bound Grandad. The only way he got free was by killing himself.'

Kefiri stared down at him in horror. 'He *killed* himself?'

'Yes. Lelya told me. It was years and years ago. He was the handsomest man in Zithirian, he could've had anyone to marry, but Gran wanted him – and when he said no, she Bound him. But it didn't quite work, and he jumped off the top of the Sunset Gate. Just after that, she had our mother, I think. She was a witch too, like Gran, but she's dead – she died having me, Lelya said.'

'At least Lelya is your friend too,' Kefiri said comfortingly, trying to hide her revulsion at this appalling story.

Bron nodded. 'And you, and Herris.' He squeezed her hand. 'I'm glad you're my friend, Lady.'

'And so am I,' Kefiri said, making a silent vow in her heart. If I can, whatever the risk, I will get you out of D'thliss's clutches. And I will do it for your sake, Bron, and not for the power you possess.

'The most high and favoured Prince Ba'alekkt, Emperor-in-Waiting, greets Ansaryon, King by right of the noble city of Zithirian, and in the name of Kaylo the Life-Giver offers him and his comrades welcome!'

The sun, streaming through windows obscured by intricate screens, laid similarly complicated shadows on the floor, made of cut and polished marble from the mountainous princedom of Tulyet. The great flattened disc of gold that was the ceremonial instrument of the Toktel'yan Court shivered resonantly under the impact of a cloth-muffled striker, wielded by a muscular young official. The deep, eerie sound reverberated round the tiled walls of the Presence Hall of the Palace, and died away into the comparative coolness of the morning air.

As the echoes faded, Ansaryon stepped forward, his retinue behind him, to face the fourteen-year-old boy who was his cousin, and who would one day inherit the vast wealth and absolute power of the greatest Empire the world had ever known.

Ba'alekkt in appearance was almost all Toktel'yan. He was stockily built, quite short, with dark curly hair cropped evenly all over his head in the fashionable Empire style, and a nose already jutting belligerently out of the still childish roundness of his face. His eyes were a light greenish brown, contrasting surprisingly and rather disturbingly with the smooth, tanned gold of his skin. He was dressed in the simple cotton robes that everyone, even the most conservative Zithiriani, was wearing in the heat of high summer, and only the exquisite gold embroidery at neck and sleeve and hem, and the gold and lapis pectoral in the shape of a hawk's outstretched wings, revealed his exalted status.

'Greetings, cousin,' said the boy, speaking perfect Zithiriani. He stepped down from the throne, carved in sparkling quartz, to embrace Ansaryon in Imperial style, as between equals, with the ritual kiss on each cheek. The top of his head hardly came up to the older man's shoulder, and he exuded an air of cheerful, almost naïve friendliness. But Halthris, watching him from her place beside Invan amongst the other Zithiriani, saw the sharpness of his gaze and knew that appearances were deceptive.

'*He is dangerous,*' she said to Ansaryon, silently. '*Be careful.*'

His reply came swiftly. '*Do you think I don't know? Be careful too – Toktel'yi is full of sorcerers, and they are not all as friendly as Al'Kalyek.*'

'We have never met, of course,' Ba'alekkt was saying. 'I was only a very young child, still in the nursery, when you last visited Toktel'yi. But I heard many tales of Zithirian from my grandmother, while she still lived, and so I feel I know your city very well.' He beamed up at his cousin, revealing pristine white teeth. 'And so, for the sake of our family ties, I felt I must give you my own special welcome.'

Halthris, watching, wondered who would be taken in by this spurious display of geniality. Not Ansaryon, for sure: he was too well versed in the devious ways of the Zithiriani Court, where nothing had been as it seemed, and every nuance of tone and behaviour had carried subtle messages at odds with what was actually being said. The boy was good, an accomplished performer, used to being the admired centre of attention, and revelling in it. But he was not yet entirely convincing.

He'd convinced Invan, though. Ansaryon's General wore an avuncular smile that made Halthris feel at once irritated and superior. She turned her eyes back to the Emperor-in-Waiting, and wondered if this child would be able to persuade his father that Ansaryon was deserving of Imperial help.

'I thank you, cousin,' Ansaryon said formally. 'I am grateful for your favour, in answering my request for a meeting so promptly.'

'I was going to arrange one anyway,' Ba'alekkt said, and grinned disarmingly. 'Al'Kalyek tells me that you are an accomplished sorcerer. Is that true?'

Halthris felt Zithiriani outrage simmer all around her. It was one thing for their leader to be a sorcerer, quite another for him to confess it in public before the Emperor-in-Waiting and a considerable proportion of the Imperial Court.

Ansaryon, with a wry, self-deprecating smile, admitted that indeed Al'Kalyek had not lied.

'It is true!' Ba'alekkt said eagerly. 'Come on, cousin – why don't you give us a demonstration of your skill?'

There were several clearly audible gasps, the loudest from

Invan. Ansaryon glanced at his scandalized entourage, who preferred all practice of magic to take place behind locked doors, and
smiled mischievously. 'Of course. If you will allow me a moment to
prepare myself?'

'Certainly,' said Ba'alekkt, with every appearance of lively
adolescent curiosity, and stepped back a little, his bright hazel eyes
fixed on his cousin.

Silence. Halthris found she was holding her breath, and tried to
release it slowly. She remembered the illusory silver firebird he had
created in his chamber at Sar D'yenyi, and wondered what he
would do this time. Knowing Ansaryon, she suspected that it would
be something spectacular.

She wasn't disappointed. He lifted up his clasped hands, and
once more the witch-light began to grow between his fingers,
illuminating his calm, intent face with an eerie pale blue glow. Then
suddenly he brought his hands down and flung them apart, and a
full-sized mountain tiger, grey-striped, huge and ferocious, sprang
from his palms and landed softly on the floor.

All the Zithiriani gasped, and took several involuntary paces
backwards. The Toktel'yans, used to displays of sorcery, remained
calm, their faces expressing polite interest. The tiger stood between
the two groups, his head swinging suspiciously from side to side, his
nose snuffling the air. Halthris was close enough to see the round
glinting eyes, the bristling white whiskers, the flash of pink tongue
as he licked his lips. The creature was so real that her hand crept of
its own accord to the space at her belt where her knife usually hung.

The beast turned towards the Toktel'yans, who were nearest to
him. Ansaryon stood quite still, smiling at his creation. And then
the tiger crouched, gathered itself and sprang into the air, straight
at Ba'alekkt.

The boy stood motionless, with commendable aplomb, as the
great animal launched itself at him, mouth agape, claws extended.
Then Ansaryon snapped his fingers, and between one heartbeat
and the next, the tiger vanished, leaving only the faint but distinctive tingle of sorcery in the air.

As one, the Zithiriani exhaled in a huge collective sigh of
shocked relief. Ba'alekkt clapped his hands in apparently genuine
appreciation. 'That was superb, cousin! I haven't seen such a
convincing illusion from any of our Court sorcerers. I had no idea
you were so accomplished.'

'I am but a humble amateur, compared to the noble Al'Kalyek
and his honoured colleagues,' Ansaryon said.

Ba'alekkt laughed. 'You're too modest, cousin! But now that

you have given us a taste of your skills, I find I'm eager for more. Will you dine with me in private, tonight? And then perhaps if you would be willing to favour me with some more of your wonderful illusions . . .'

Ansaryon inclined his head in assent, apparently oblivious to the shocked expressions on the faces of his comrades. 'I would be glad to, cousin.'

'Excellent! That's settled, then.' Ba'alekkt paused, his eyes searching the dozen or so Zithiriani behind Ansaryon. 'And I would like to beg another favour of you, cousin. I've been hearing some very interesting rumours. Is it really true that there is a female barbarian warrior amongst our soldiers?'

Ansaryon smiled. 'Indeed there is. In fact, there are two – Halthris and Inri, of the Tanathi tribe.'

Ba'alekkt's face was aflame with eagerness. '*Women* – dressed as warriors, and handling weapons! Are either of them by any chance here today?'

Halthris had already seen his eyes resting speculatively on her, and was ready. Ansaryon's expression held a certain wariness as he turned towards her, and she realized with sudden amusement that he was unsure of her reaction. He probably thought that she would say something unforgivable. She smiled to herself, and stepped out from amongst the Zithiriani soldiers and officials.

She had put on her best Tanathi clothes for this occasion, so she was well aware of the barbaric and exotic appearance she must present. Glittering with gold on tunic, boots and jewellery, the talismans in her six ceremonial braids chiming gently as she walked, she came to stand proudly by Ansaryon's side, feeling twelve pairs of Zithiriani eyes boring into her back. Even the most doubtful were no longer suspicious or fearful of her and the other Tanathi, but she knew that some, Invan in particular, were jealous of the closeness of her special friendship with their leader.

'The High and Mighty Prince Ba'alekkt, Emperor-in-Waiting, Most Favoured of Kaylo the Life Giver,' Ansaryon said. 'May I humbly present to you Halthris, daughter of Charnak, chief of the Sayni clan of the tribe called the Tanathi.'

He took her arm and led her forward. She had no idea what ritual might be required of her – he, of course, was of royal blood himself, so formal dignities between him and Ba'alekkt were largely irrelevant. But the boy did not seem to insist on slavish ceremony, so she stood very tall and straight before him, waiting for his word.

Ba'alekkt surveyed her in a manner suddenly and disturbingly adult. He said, 'So it *is* true. A remarkably fine-looking woman, is she not, cousin?'

Ansaryon's amazed expression was so convincing that in another, less formal situation she would have been tempted to kick him. 'Is she?' he said in apparent surprise. 'I must confess it hadn't occurred to me. Halthris and Inri are representative of our Tanathi allies, and valued members of my staff. They live and fight alongside us, and I think that most of us have all but forgotten that they are female.'

'Really?' Ba'alekkt's look of disbelief stopped just short of a sneer. 'Well, cousin, each to his own. And you, Halthris of the Tanathi? Do all women in your tribe fight alongside their menfolk?'

'No,' she said. 'Most of us enjoy just a few years as Hunters before we decide to settle down in one tent with our chosen man, and live as women do everywhere.'

'And have you chosen a man yet, Halthris of the Tanathi?'

'A man called Vinnath wishes to marry me,' she said, with perfect truth. The fact that she no longer wished to marry him was probably best not revealed here and now.

'A pity,' said Ba'alekkt, smiling. She saw the open desire in his eyes and hoped that Invan would be sensible. After all, this was a boy whose voice had hardly broken, and ten years and more younger than she was. Emperor-in-Waiting or not, she surely had nothing to fear from him.

'Will you not miss your freedom, when you marry?' he asked.

Halthris nodded. 'I expect I will. But it is the price to be paid for happiness, and a husband, and children.'

'And your men are allowed to take just one wife? Here in Toktel'yi, the law states that only three are permitted.' His tone was regretful. 'However, a man may keep all the concubines his wealth and desires allow him. Most men can only afford half a dozen, perhaps ten. My father can command fifty!'

'All at once?' Halthris said, before she could stop herself.

Ba'alekkt looked hard at her, and she could have bitten her tongue. Then thankfully, he laughed. 'No. My father's legendary appetites would hardly be equal to that task, even in his prime. Now, he restricts himself to a favoured few. The others live a life of pampered idleness – such a waste! Still,' he added, the lascivious expression back on his face, 'I may shortly be able to set them up in my own apartments, as befits the Emperor-in-Waiting.' And he gave her a sly, inviting glance that left her in absolutely no doubt that, given the opportunity, he would like to install her amongst his future concubines.

She did not know whether to be angry, or amused at the boy's absurd impertinence. Fortunately, Ba'alekkt turned back to Ansaryon, and she was able to retreat into the comparative safety of the Zithiriani soldiers, carefully avoiding anyone's eye.

The audience came to an end shortly after that, rather to her relief. Ba'alekkt had other official duties to perform that morning, and was full of regret that he could not show his cousin the sights of Toktel'yi that day, though it would probably be possible on another occasion.

As they were all escorted out of the Presence Hall by members of the Imperial Guard, deceptively tall in their elongated conical helmets, Halthris could sense the mingled relief and indignation amongst Ansaryon's companions. They had been in Toktel'yi for three days now, and so far this brief meeting with the Emperor-in-Waiting was the only occasion on which their presence had been formally acknowledged. Several high-ranking Court officials had visited Ansaryon's apartments, and Al'Kalyek, who was supposed to be one of the most powerful men in the Empire, had apparently spoken to him in private several times since that first night. But there had been no word whatsoever from Djamal, which boded ill for the success of their mission. If the notoriously idle and dissolute Emperor could not even be bothered to see them, what hope did they have of obtaining his help?

'Did you like my tiger?' Ansaryon asked her softly.

Halthris grinned. 'Very impressive. But I could tell you've never seen one at close quarters. Their eyes are slanted, and quite a light golden brown, and their nose-leather should be grey or black, not pink. Apart from that, though, it was a fairly good attempt.'

Invan, on her left, was stiff with disapproval. He had never become used to the casual banter which she quite often exchanged with Ansaryon.

'I haven't had your opportunity to meet one face to face – my experience of them is limited to books.' The King of Zithirian glanced at her, and gave a very slight nod of his head. She knew what the signal meant, and was ready for his silent communication. *'Ba'alekkt seems to have taken a fancy to you. Be careful. He may seem just a friendly and likable child, but he's old for his years in many ways. I'm told that one of the Emperor's concubines is already instructing him in the arts of love. They take such things very seriously here.'*

'I'm more than ten years older than he is. He wouldn't dare, surely.'

'I hope not. But be careful, just the same.'

'You're getting as bad as Invan,' Halthris said sharply, and turned her eyes to the garden through which they were walking back to Ansaryon's apartments.

His last, amused words echoed in her mind, and made her smile despite herself. *'Tayo forbid!'*

After that strange and terrible night, most of which she had spent in a bruised and exhausted sleep on the cushions in Ansaryon's Reception Chamber, Halthris had woken to find that she had been elevated to one of the highly favoured few to be accommodated within the Palace. She was given a very small room compared to most, but it was cool and comfortable, with a latticed window looking out onto the shady side of the garden, and a beautiful tiled frieze of running antelope around the walls. She would have preferred to return to the cheerful company of Inri and Sherren and the soldiers on board the *Windswift*, but Ansaryon had insisted that she stay in the Palace. He told her that Al'Kalyek had thought it was wise, but would not reveal any other reason, despite her indignant curiosity. And she could hardly tell him that she disliked being in such close and continuous proximity to Invan.

So for two nights now she had slept on that luxuriously draped couch. An explanatory message had been sent to the *Windswift*, and her belongings had been fetched, so she hoped that Inri and Sherren would not be too worried about her. Certainly, it looked as though the worst she had to face was boredom.

The afternoon heat, even here close to the sea, was such that everyone save the servants rested or slept after the midday meal. One advantage of living in the Palace was that the food was excellent, though the unfamiliar spices, hot and tingling on the tongue, were an acquired taste. Returning to her room after Ba'alekkt's audience, she found a tray, covered against insect marauders, laden with heaps of cold rice and vegetables, a mound of flimsy red and green leaves in a sharp oily dressing, that the Toktel'yans called katchek, and a whole chicken carcass, marinated and cooked in a pungent orange spice. She picked at it gingerly, then with increasing hunger, and managed to eat about half of it. Then, rather reluctantly, she lay down on the couch. She was not used to sleeping in the middle of the day, but the suffocating heat made any activity almost impossible, even for those who were used to the climate.

A rap on the door woke her. She stared at it stupidly until a second knock forced her to gather her wits together. She sat up and called out, 'K'tenn!', which meant 'enter', and was one of the dozen or so Toktel'yan words and phrases she had managed to pick up over the past three days.

A young man in the plain black tunic of a Palace servant came in, carrying a broad, shallow box. He put it down on the small brass table by the window, and made the sign of obeisance, bending almost double.

'What is it?' Halthris asked, in Zithiriani.

The servant could apparently understand her, although his accent, full of Toktel'yan clicks and consonants, was appalling. 'Gift for you, Tanathi lady. From Emperor-in-Waiting.'

'For *me*?' Halthris stared at him with a mixture of surprise and unease. 'Why? What is it?'

'Emperor-in-Waiting sends greetings. Asks for you at supper tonight. Requests that you wear his gift. A woman will arrive shortly to help you. I will come for you when it is time, Tanathi lady.' And he bowed to the ground again, and went out.

Bewildered, Halthris stared at the box. It appeared to be made of painted wood, but when she picked it up, proved to be so astonishingly light that it might have been paper, save for its rigidity. She put it down on the table, raised the lid and stared.

Within lay a neatly folded mass of flimsy fabric, coloured a rich dark green, the material shot through with innumerable frail threads that were undoubtedly gold. She took hold of it gingerly, and lifted it up.

It was a gown in the Toktel'yan style, as fine as those she had seen the Court ladies wearing. The low square neckline was thickly encrusted with embroidered leaves and flowers, studded with jewels, and the material fell from it to the floor in loose, billowing folds. The sleeves were long, full and flowing, and open along the upper length of the arm, the gap closed at frequent intervals with gold filigree clasps in the shape of a simple flower, a tiny emerald at the heart of each one.

Halthris stared at it in disbelief, anger and fear. She, a Tanathi who had never worn a skirt in her life, was expected by that over-sexed precocious brat to appear at his private supper tricked out in some concubine's finery for his own personal delectation. And she strongly suspected that she had no real choice in the matter. If she refused, she would offend him, and thereby, almost certainly, ruin any chance that the Emperor would help Ansaryon. She had learned enough of Palace politics over the past few days to know that Djamal doted on his only son and heir. Ba'alekkt could persuade his father to do whatever he wished, and if he told Djamal to ignore Ansaryon's request for soldiers, the Emperor would oblige his son, and their journey, and all their hopes, would be wasted.

Trapped, furious, she threw the garment down so hard that the jewels rattled on the tiled floor. Left in the box were a pair of ornate leather sandals, with gold chasing and buckles, and a gauzy semi-transparent piece of cloth in the same deep sea-green as the gown. With loathing, she recognized it as a veil, symbol of the oppression and subjection of Toktel'yan women.

I am *not* going to wear it, Halthris decided savagely, and flung herself down on the couch. And if he thinks he can persuade me to be one of his concubines, he's in for a nasty surprise.

But slowly, surely, as she lay rigid with rage, the cold voice of common sense trickled back into her mind. Ansaryon would be at that supper. Ansaryon would help her. And she could not jeopardize their mission by indulging in childish tantrums. Ba'alekkt was the child. She was an experienced and level-headed woman, free, confident and emphatically no man's plaything. Tactfully, humorously, the boy must be brought to realize that he was making a grievous error of judgement.

Another knock on the door interrupted her thoughts. It proved to be a woman servant, quite handsomely dressed and obviously of higher status than the man who had brought the clothes. She walked briskly in, put down the large bundle she was carrying, and made her bow. 'Worshipful Tanathi lady, I am Rolkenno. I have come to array you in your garments.'

For a last, brief, insane moment Halthris contemplated kicking her out and barring the door. Then, accepting the inevitable, she nodded and smiled through stiff lips. 'Thank you. I am ready.'

During her stay in the Palace at Zithirian, she had never become used to the presence of servants, and since then she had guarded her independence jealously. She stood in an uncomfortable silence as the Toktel'yan woman removed her tunic and trousers. She had expected some comment on the tattoos rioting over her body, but beyond a pursing of the lips and a slight indrawn breath, Rolkenno ignored them. Instead, she indicated the couch. 'Lie there, if it pleases your worship.'

Obediently, still inwardly seething, Halthris settled herself down on the cushions and waited. There was the sound of a jar being opened, and suddenly something glutinous and deliciously cold was slapped on her back. It smelt aromatic and refreshing. Slightly mollified, she lay still and allowed the servant to massage the ointment, or whatever it was, into her skin with soothing, capable fingers.

'Turn over, if it please your worship.'

Now, she could see that Rolkenno was holding a large glass jar, full of a rich yellow substance, about the colour and consistency of good fresh butter kept in a warm room. As the woman began on her shoulders, she said curiously, 'What is that stuff?'

'An unguent from the isle of Onnak, your worship. It restores life and vigour to weary bodies and minds. Do you find it pleasant?'

'Yes, I do,' Halthris said, and closed her eyes.

It did not take long for Rolkenno to rub the ointment in all over her chest, stomach and even her legs. Then, feeling slightly sticky, she obediently stood up and allowed her hair to be unbraided.

It felt very strange to have a stranger perform this intimate act, usually undertaken by a close friend, lover or husband. The mass of her curling red-gold hair, unbound, hung heavy and hot over her cool, scented skin. Rolkenno brushed it, with surprising gentleness, into a shining sweep of flame, and then stood back to assess the result with a dispassionate eye.

Halthris was beginning to be irritated by her lack of personal comments: she would have welcomed any criticism of her physical appearance, her tattoos, her freckles, even her sinewy body, so long as it opened some human contact between them. It was like being tended by an animated statue.

On impulse, she said, 'Rolkenno? In what styles do Toktel'yan women wear their hair? Like this, loose?'

The servant stared at her in surprise. 'No, worshipful lady. There are many, many ways of dressing the hair, and I am skilled at some. If you will permit me, I will demonstrate one or two, so you may see the effect – I have a mirror.' She looked rather wistfully at the flood of coppery gold. 'Although, if you will forgive my presumption, worshipful lady, your hair is shown to best advantage like this.'

'Perhaps,' Halthris said. 'But a Tanathi woman who appears in public with her hair unbound is as shocking as a Toktel'yan woman without her veil. Do you understand?'

Rolkenno's thin mouth was touched, briefly, by a half-smile. 'Yes, worshipful lady, I understand very well. Fear not, I will arrange your hair as you desire.'

For what seemed like an age, she combed and brushed, twisted and pinned, while Halthris sat quite still beneath her ministrations and allowed her mind to wander. She thought of her brother Abreth, a thousand miles or more to the north, and hoped he was safe, and had managed to recruit a sizeable Tanathi force to augment Ansaryon's army. And then, unwillingly, she returned to the problem of the child Bron. Could he be saved? Was it wise to save him? And if he were indeed Ansaryon's son, how had he come to be in the hands of D'thliss?

She could not ask him, for it was plainly obvious that Bron touched a raw place on his soul. And she did not wish to put their strange, erratic friendship in jeopardy again.

Rolkenno finished, and stepped back. She surveyed her handiwork, and smiled with broad satisfaction. 'Ah, yes, worshipful lady. What a transformation! Now, if we put on the gown, and the sandals, you will be able to see the effect in my mirror.'

The green dress slid over her head, and Rolkenno pulled her hair gently free. 'Now, worshipful lady, behold your new self!'

She picked up the polished steel mirror and held it some distance in front of Halthris. Through some cunning craft or magic, her image was smaller than life, and whole. She stared in astonishment at this alien creature. The curled, scented hair was piled high on her head, interwoven with glittering ribbons, with a few red-gold locks cascading down to its shoulders. The beautiful, sophisticated gown, apparently voluminous, clung to the slender contours of her body. And in the middle of all the finery was set her pale, freckled face, delicately painted, familiar and yet utterly strange. It was as if some sorcerer's spell had changed her into someone else. She shuddered suddenly, and shook her head in denial. 'No – no, Rolkenno, I can't. This isn't me.'

'Where the Emperor-in-Waiting commands, so all must obey, worshipful lady,' Rolkenno said. She began to pack away her boxes of pins, her jars of ointments and cosmetics and her bottles of scented oils. 'You are highly honoured, Tanathi lady. You should be proud to be called.' She gave her a last, critical survey, as if to check that nothing in Halthris's appearance would disgrace her handiwork. 'Genlak will come for you very soon. It is all but dark. May Kaylo the Life-Giver grant you his blessings, worshipful lady.'

'Thank you, Rolkenno,' Halthris said, without enthusiasm.

The servant made her obeisance, and turned to go. There was a brisk tap on the door. 'Ah, that will be Genlak now, worshipful lady.'

Halthris's heart began to thud sickeningly beneath the soft thin gown. What was she going to do? How could she tactfully prevent a fourteen-year-old Emperor-in-Waiting from raping her, without making an enemy of him for life?

Rolkenno had gone to open the door. A pace or two away, Halthris saw something glinting on the floor: a hairpin, needle sharp and the length of her index finger. In one fluid movement, she bent, picked it up, and jabbed it into the full folds of her left sleeve.

The door opened, but it was not the servant, Genlak, who stood there. Instead, she saw a tall Zithiriani in a rather crumpled cotton robe, his fair hair curling on his shoulders, and a look of utter horror and revulsion on his face.

It was Invan.

CHAPTER
TWENTY-ONE

At one savage gesture from the Zithiriani General, Rolkenno made herself scarce. As the door shut behind her, Invan said furiously, 'Take it off!'

Only moments before, Halthris had been desperately wanting to do exactly that. Now, the curt command raised her hackles. She said, 'No, I will not.'

'It's disgusting!' Invan passed a shaking hand across his face. 'Halthris, not *you* – it's revolting, dressing you up like some Toktel'yan concubine. Take it off, I beg you, and I'll go and tell him exactly what I think of him – taking advantage of you – I never believed all those rumours before, but by Tayo's bones I could smash his face in!'

Halthris's calm was in stark contrast to his incoherent and rising hysteria. She said drily, 'That might be unwise. After all, he *is* the Emperor-in-Waiting.'

'He – *what*?' Invan stared at her incredulously. 'This is Ba'alekkt's idea? But he's a child—'

'Oh, no, he isn't – and let me tell you, Invan, I dislike this as much as you do. But for all our sakes, I have to go along with it, and fend him off as tactfully as I can. So don't please do anything rash – it's not worth risking the future of Zithirian. And Ba'alekkt seems to be our only hope.' She grinned mischievously. 'So who did you think gave me the gown, then?'

Invan had the grace to blush. He muttered defensively, 'It doesn't matter now. But – but Halthris, you can't, you really can't, go to Ba'alekkt's private supper, especially dressed like that. In Zithirian a woman has more freedom, but here such an invitation means only one thing—'

'Are you implying that I don't *know* what it means? And I'm not going gladly, Invan, I'm doing this out of duty! What's more, I'm not some shy virgin, nor am I *anyone*'s concubine, or plaything, or chattel, and I don't intend to be. Surely you can trust me to deal with that big-headed, precocious young lecher? And besides, Ansaryon will be there.'

If anything, Invan looked even more unhappy. 'I know, and that worries me too. If he feels he has to protect you—'

'I have told you. I'm not a chattel, and I don't need protection, certainly not from Ba'alekkt. And Ansaryon relies on winning the boy to our side. He won't put all our plans in jeopardy by doing something stupid.'

'Even if Ba'alekkt tries to – tries something in front of him?' Invan's tone indicated that anyone who could calmly stand aside in such a situation was utterly despicable.

'He won't. He's curious, and reckless, and he enjoys manipulating and teasing people, that's obvious. But he's still only a boy, and he must surely have some sense of the responsibilities of his position. He wouldn't dare.'

'Wouldn't he? You don't know Toktel'yi. Here, women are the property of their fathers, or husbands, or lovers. If he wants you, he'll take you, and you'll be completely helpless.'

'No, I won't,' Halthris said, exasperated. 'Invan, can't you see that I *have* to do this? If I can manage to put him off with fine words and flattery, it will have been worth it – especially if he promises to use his influence with his father to help us.' She gave him her most reassuring smile. 'Don't worry – trust me. I can look after myself. And remember, I'm *no one*'s property. Not Ba'alekkt's, not Ansaryon's – and not yours, either.'

Invan flushed a dull red. He said at last, hesitantly, 'This man Vinnath, whom you mentioned this morning – you said he wanted to marry you. Is that true?'

'Yes. If I had not been caught up in all this, I would be married to him now, and probably already big with our first child.' She saw the crease between his brows, and knew she had hurt him. Better, though, to be cruel now, and dash all his false hopes and unwarranted assumptions before they could lead him further down the smiling path of illusion. She went on. 'When everything is over, and Tsenit and the Ska'i are defeated, I and my friends will return to our people. I'm not bred to live in cities, behind walls, never to ride fast horses or feel the steppe wind in my hair. I'm sorry, Invan. I value you as a friend, as I value Ansaryon, and Kazko and the other officers, and the Lady Kefiri too. But I am not one of you. I can't be confined in a stone cage. *Please* understand that. In another life, under other circumstances, things might have been different. But I am a Tanathi and you are a Zithiriani, and although our people were once the same, three hundred years ago, they are very different now.'

He stared at her in a miserable silence. It was broken by a soft tap on the door. Snatching at the opportunity to end this unhappy scene, she called, 'Come in!'

It was Genlak, obsequious in his dull black. He made his bow, and said in execrable Zithiriani, 'Time, Lady. Come now. Emperor-in-Waiting expects you.'

Invan gazed at her with mute appeal and adoration filling his eyes, like a particularly loving dog. It made her feel acutely uncomfortable. She gave him another heartening smile. 'Please, Invan – *don't worry!*'

'You look so beautiful,' he said suddenly, on what sounded dreadfully like a sob. Then he turned abruptly and pushed past the servant, out into the night.

She felt guiltily irritated. It was disturbing to see such a handsome, capable and confident man reduced to such a state. And surely there were women in plenty who would be only too glad to have him fall in love with them. Why, why, *why* had he picked on the one who was completely unattainable?

Genlak was looking at her. He said impatiently, 'Lady – not ready yet. Wear veil, please.'

She opened her mouth to refuse, and then thought better of it. Invan's reaction to her new and temporary appearance would probably be shared by all the other Zithiriani, Ansaryon included. If she slipped out now, veiled, they would hardly notice her in the darkness, and if they did, would with luck assume she was just another Palace lady or concubine. And it might prove extremely inconvenient and embarrassing to remind her friends so ostentatiously that she was not just their comrade in arms, as good a man as they were, but also an apparently beautiful and very desirable woman.

Invan was biased, of course, and she had seen nothing beautiful about the prinked-out stranger in Rolkenno's mirror. But the Tanathi were seldom vain. Perhaps others, especially men who had been lacking in female company for months, might see what she, in all honesty, could not.

With a sigh, she picked up the veil, and draped it over her head. It was long enough to cover her distinctive hair, and presumably the gauzy fabric concealed her face, for she found it difficult to see through it in the gloom. She said to Genlak, 'I'm ready now.'

'Good, Lady,' said the servant, and stood aside to let her leave the room.

He picked up a lantern standing outside the door, which was just as well. In the dark, and veiled, she would have fallen over a shrub or a flower pot within a few paces. There was no one in the garden, except for a solitary lamplighter. She thought of Bron standing on the terrace at Minassa, and shivered, despite the lingering warmth of the day. And then shivered again, at the thought of what was coming, and of how much depended on what she said and did in the next few hours.

The route to Ba'alekkt's apartments lay through gardens, courtyards, gateways, more gardens. She had not realized until now just how vast was the area the Palace covered. Several times she saw groups of women, all veiled, and noted how their loose light gowns flowed gracefully against their bodies as they walked. She felt clumsy and oversized by comparison, and her vigorous Tanathi stride was hampered by her unaccustomed skirts. After several near falls, she concentrated on adapting her pace to a more elegant stroll, and Genlak no longer had to hurry to keep up with her.

At last, they came to a doorway, set in yet another high blank stone wall. The two guards before it turned aside in answer to Genlak's request, and one opened the door.

Her heart thumping, her palms sweating and her head proudly high, Halthris stepped through, and stared in amazement.

The garden before her was so brilliantly lit, by a hundred or more lanterns, that night had been banished within it. A host of tiny birds and huge butterflies, all as bright as jewels, fluttered amongst the trees and shrubs. Everywhere gleamed the white waxy flowers of the plant that looked like a larger and more exotic version of the Zithiriani trumpet vine, and the heavy evening air was filled with its thick, cloying scent. Her dazed, dazzled eyes noted fountains, a pool filled with huge red flowers and coloured fish, and in the shadows a slender, naked girl that startled her, until she realized that it was only a statue, lifesize, and astonishingly natural.

'Come, Lady.' Genlak was urging her onwards. A stone path wound amongst the flowers, and ahead she heard voices, laughter, and music. Resolutely, Halthris walked forward to meet her fate.

In a corner of the garden, a pretty summer-house had been built. Its walls were painted white, and vines and creepers scrambled up to the curved, pointed roof. Behind the intricate pierced grilles covering the wide windows, she glimpsed more coloured lanterns, and heard Ba'alekkt's boyish, scarcely-broken voice telling a joke in Zithiriani.

Well, at least Ansaryon must be there already. She steadied herself, her mind repeating over and over again the meaningless syllables of an old Tanathi shaman's chant, originally intended to calm eager hunters before doing battle with lion or bear.

'Wait here, please, Lady.' Genlak gestured that she stay at the foot of the wide, shallow steps leading up to the pavilion. Feeling suddenly very alone, Halthris watched him disappear inside, and heard him announce something in Toktel'yan. A butterfly or moth brushed against her face, and she almost shied like a frightened mare.

Ba'alekkt's voice, speaking Zithiriani, rose suddenly above the splash of the fountain and the softly twittering birds. 'You'll enjoy this, cousin – a rare surprise for you. Just wait till you see her!'

And before she had time to be angry, Genlak reappeared at the top of the steps, and gestured urgently for her to come up.

She climbed two steps, trod on her gown and nearly fell over, hoisted it above her ankle, and reached the servant's side without further mishap. He nodded to her: he might only be a humble servant, but it seemed that his status as a male outweighed her rank in her own world. Here in Toktel'yi, she was just another chattel.

In a sudden surge of rebellion, she pulled the veil from her head, stuffed it into his astonished hands, and swept past him and into the pavilion.

It was furnished with an enormous quantity of piled cushions, and several low tables, laden with food. The spicy aroma filled the air, mingling uneasily with the flowers and the rather suffocating smell of perfumed candles. A low brazier occupied the centre of the room, the heavy perfume of incense coiling smokily upwards from the glowing burnstones. On one heap of cushions, Ba'alekkt was sprawling, sucking on a ripe round fruit, and opposite him, apparently equally relaxed, Ansaryon reclined with a fluted Minassan goblet of wonderful delicacy in his hand, and gazed with interest at his cousin's rare surprise.

For fully twenty heartbeats, he did not recognize her. Then Ba'alekkt said, with sly malice, 'Welcome to my pavilion, Halthris of the Tanathi.'

She saw Ansaryon's eyes widen, and his fingers clenched suddenly on the goblet's slender, twisted stem. There was a tiny crack, and after a pause he glanced down in surprise, as if he had been unaware of the strength of his reaction.

Halthris turned to Ba'alekkt, her voice cool and unsubmissive. 'I thank you for your gift, but it is surely a little unsuitable.'

The boy finished the fruit, and flicked the stone with his fingers to join a small, sticky pile on the floor in front of him. He grinned, his eyes unashamedly appraising her. 'Unsuitable? To dress a lovely woman in a way which displays and enhances her beauty? I hope you are not ungrateful, Halthris of the Tanathi.'

'Indeed I am not,' she said, belatedly trying to be tactful. 'I am truly appreciative of the honour you have shown to me, and the gown is very beautiful. But . . . I am not accustomed to wearing such garments, and I think it will take me a little while to adjust to it.'

'You appear to have adjusted yourself very well already,' Ba'alekkt observed. He leaned on his elbow and glanced at Ansaryon, who had drained his goblet and laid the separate stem and bowl unobtrusively on the floor beside him. 'Do you not agree, cousin? Your female Tanathi warrior would make a very decorative addition to any man's concubines.'

'Not for long,' Ansaryon said drily. 'She would knife anyone who attempted to force her. I wouldn't advise you to try, unless you're not particularly bothered about keeping your manhood.'

'Really?' Ba'alekkt stared at Halthris with interest. 'So you would geld me if I tried to take you?'

'If I had the means, undoubtedly I would,' she told him kindly. 'But the situation is hardly likely to occur, after all. I shouldn't worry about it too much.'

The boy shot her a sly, teasing smile. 'That's a pity. But you are a feast for the eyes, even so. Now you are here, Halthris of the Tanathi, would you care to partake of our supper?'

She found, suddenly, that she was ravenously hungry. She sat down on the cushions between them, rather nearer to Ansaryon than to Ba'alekkt, and a silent black-clad servant brought another loaded table, and a jug and goblet full of a light, fruity and refreshingly cool wine. She admired the workmanship of the pottery: it was Minassan, of course, but unlike most of that city's wares quite plain. The clay, though, was almost white, and so thin that when she held up the goblet she could see light through the bowl.

Using her fingers as all Toktel'yans seemed to do – certainly, there was neither knife nor spoon provided – she worked her way through the rice, spiced meat and savoury, delicious vegetables and pastries. In a corner, so dim it was a marvel that they could see their instruments, two musicians played a soft, lilting tune on an eight-stringed, swan-necked djarlek, and some kind of flute with an exquisitely liquid, melancholy sound.

She concentrated on eating, letting the music fill the silence. Ba'alekkt seemed utterly at ease, lounging amidst the silken draperies and feather-soft cushions, picking at a bunch of grapes. But from Ansaryon, to her right, she felt the tension flowing in waves.

She risked a glance at him, and saw him staring at her, a frown between his brows. The Emperor-in-Waiting was apparently absorbed in his bunch of grapes, although she knew already that he was keenly observant. She let her mind reach out, cautiously, to the man who was looking at her as if he had never seen her before. *'I'm sorry, Ansaryon. It was an invitation, and a gift, which I felt it would be very unwise to refuse.'*

His answer came immediately. *'You did the right thing. I'm not angry – with you. But I could cheerfully wring Ba'alekkt's neck.'*

'That certainly WOULD be unwise.'

'Don't worry – I intend to keep my temper with the poisonous little brat.' Ansaryon's tone was distinctly exasperated. *'Tayo help the Toktel'yans when he becomes Emperor.'*

'You are very quiet, cousin?' Ba'alekkt's voice cut across their silent conversation. Halthris swallowed a mouthful of meat and wondered uneasily if the boy had guessed what they were doing. After all, thought-linking was commonplace in Toktel'yi.

'I was enjoying the music,' Ansaryon told him. 'The flute-player is uncommonly skilful.'

'Akket is a master of his craft,' Ba'alekkt said, in a voice which indicated that the Emperor-in-Waiting was entitled to no less. 'The djarlek player is also very gifted, don't you think? I have asked them to play Zithiriani tunes, in your honour. Do you know this one?'

'Yes, I do,' said Ansaryon, with a rather amused smile. As Ba'alekkt continued to look at him expectantly, he elaborated. 'It's one of our story-songs – very popular in taverns and kuldi-houses. It's called "The Tale of Shabren".'

'Oh?' The boy was full of curiosity. 'What is the story, then? Who is Shabren?'

'Shabren,' Ansaryon said carefully, 'was the general whose superior tactics won the Battle of Umnath, a hundred and fifty years ago, although he himself was sadly slain at the moment of victory.'

'Slain? By whom, cousin?'

'By a Toktel'yan spear-caster,' said Ansaryon, his face expressionless. 'As I think you know full well, cousin.'

There was a tiny pause, and then the boy burst out laughing. 'You're quite right. I wanted to find out what you'd say. No hard feelings, eh?'

'None. It was a very long time ago, and Zithiriani and Toktel'yi are now on excellent terms – which is why my aunt married your grandfather.' He glanced at Ba'alekkt, who was watching, his gaze bright and mischievous. 'And I will not insult your intelligence by asking if you know why I and my small force have come to your city.'

'I know it's not a courtesy visit,' the boy said. He swallowed the last grape and flicked the pips neatly onto the pile of debris on the floor. 'Something to do with the wholesale slaughter of your family, the invasion of the Ska'i, and the usurpation of your brother Tsenit, perhaps?'

'Perhaps,' said Ansaryon.

'Did you know that Tsenit has formally requested the hand of my sister K'djelk in marriage?'

It was almost the first time since her dramatic entrance that Halthris had seen Ansaryon's façade of casual calm disrupted. 'He's done *what*?'

'My father is still debating the matter with his advisors,' said Ba'alekkt blithely. 'It involves a rather tricky question, after all. If he agrees to the union, he strengthens Imperial ties with Zithirian. But there is also a certain amount of danger involved. For instance, what would happen to K'djelk if Tsenit were to be overthrown?'

Ansaryon was staring at him. He said at last, 'She would be treated with the utmost courtesy and respect, and escorted back to her native land.'

'As a wife? Or a widow?'

The rightful King of Zithirian smiled thinly. 'I think you know the answer to that, cousin. Should I defeat Tsenit, his crimes both to his family and to the city and its people allow nothing less than the ultimate penalty. Indeed, if I am granted the opportunity, I intend to kill him myself.'

Ba'alekkt's eyes glistened avidly. 'I had no idea you were so bloodthirsty, cousin. I had thought—'

'That I was an effete scholar with a decadent reputation and a heart full of cowardice? You thought wrong. Tsenit has much the same misconceptions about me, and I fully intend to make him realize how wrong he was before meting out his punishment. Unfortunately, to make sure of it I shall need more soldiers. The King of Minassa and the Prince of Lelyent have been most generous, but their contributions are, alas, insufficient for my needs.'

'So you want our help?' Ba'alekkt was studying him thoughtfully. 'How many men do you require?'

'Even a thousand would be useful. Your soldiers are so well trained and armed that one is the equal of ten ordinary men. But ideally, I would like three, four or even five times that number, to be certain of victory.'

Ba'alekkt leaned back on the cushions. Halthris, glancing at him, was grateful that military talk seemed to interest him more than leering at her. But she wondered how far, if at all, he could be trusted. He had been reared as Emperor-in-Waiting, and the Imperial Court here was even more awash with intrigue, political squabbles, rivalry and machinations than at Zithirian under Vara-thand. He must surely be aware of all the implications of Ansaryon's request.

And if he was, he would see the advantage that the loan of Toktel'yan soldiers would give to the Emperor.

'They are not mine to give, of course, cousin,' Ba'alekkt said at last. 'My father the Emperor is Commander-in-Chief of all our armies – not that he's ever used a sword in anger, of course, but their disposition depends on his word. So you will have to speak to him about it.'

'If he will grant me an audience.'

'Oh, he will. He's probably wondering whether to see you in the morning or the afternoon. My father,' said Ba'alekkt, with spuriously affectionate contempt, 'has trouble making up his mind what to have for breakfast. Everyone else has to make his decisions for him.'

'Including you?'

'Especially me,' Ba'alekkt said, with pride. 'And if I tell him that the sun rises in the west, or that his cousin Ansaryon of Zithirian needs five thousand soldiers to win his city back, then he will listen.'

'And will you tell him, cousin?'

'That depends.' Ba'alekkt shot him a look of gleeful mischief. 'I might. Or I might not. Or, then again, I might demand certain conditions. Like the loan of your delightful lady here, for the night.'

Silence. Halthris, her heart thudding furiously, dared not look at Ansaryon: indeed, she did not need to. He said, his voice taut with controlled rage, 'If that were the case, a hundred thousand soldiers would not be a sufficient exchange. Halthris is not my lady, nor is she my possession. She is a free woman, and makes her own choices.'

The boy laughed. 'I know that, cousin. I meant it as a compli-ment to you, Halthris of the Tanathi. In Toktel'yi, it is a great honour for a woman – or a man – to be desired and coveted by the Emperor-in-Waiting.'

'I am aware of that,' Halthris said. 'I appreciate your admiration – and I thank you again for giving me the opportunity to wear this lovely garment.'

'I'm glad of that,' Ba'alekkt said, grinning at her. 'For you look as gorgeous as one of Kaylo's fifty thousand concubines, Halthris of the Tanathi, a vision straight from Paradise. Do you not agree, cousin?'

There was a fractional pause, before Ansaryon answered him. She glanced at the King of Zithirian curiously, and surprised a strange light in his eyes. 'Oh, yes, I agree whole-heartedly,' he said softly, at last.

'Then at least you have displayed yourself in a different light, Halthris,' Ba'alekkt said cheerfully. 'Now, cousin, to serious matters. I have a scheduled private session with my father and his advisors tomorrow. I will put forward your position, and I will do my utmost to persuade him to help you. After all, defeating the Ska'i is in his own best interests as well – they've been a menace on our north-western borders for centuries, and this Quenait sounds a formidable opponent. If he is capable of uniting all the separate tribes of the Ska'i under his banner, then it is surely only a matter of time before he turns his attention to the Empire.' He grinned. 'Anyway, I'm very fond of K'djelk, even though she's not nearly as pretty as Tsenit probably thinks she is – our ambassador is a little prone to exaggeration, I'm afraid. I wouldn't want to see my sweet little sister married to a murdering usurper. And if she *did* marry him, it would be much more difficult for my father to help Tsenit's enemies. So this idea of another union between our families must be abandoned, I fear.' He glanced slyly sideways. 'Unless *you* want her for a wife, cousin?'

Ansaryon laughed. 'I have been offered my pick of the daughters of Prince Belerith, and King Temiltan's cousin. Now the Princess K'djelk as well! Rest assured, noble cousin, if I *do* pick a wife from amongst them, your sister will undoubtedly be my preferred choice.'

'Excellent,' Ba'alekkt said gleefully. 'I shall be delighted to promote closer links between the Empire and Zithirian. We are cousins already – soon I hope we will be brothers.'

'I hope so too,' Ansaryon said, with apparent sincerity. '*If* I can overthrow Tsenit and defeat the Ska'i.'

'There is a Toktel'yan proverb – "It is easier to tame the wild bull in the tavern than in the field". But five thousand men should go a long way towards taming your wild brother and his wilder allies, and I will do my utmost to obtain them for you, I promise. By this time tomorrow, I should be able to give you good news. And I will ensure that my father demands no conditions or promises.'

Halthris could sense Ansaryon's relief and delight, tempered with some caution. After all, Ba'alekkt was only a fourteen-year-old boy, even if he was the Emperor-in-Waiting, and he held no actual formal power in Toktel'yi. He could only put forward his views, and hope that his father would take notice. But he had a very forceful and persuasive manner, and Djamal was notorious for his indolence and for his tendency to listen most closely to the loudest voice. It was certainly now possible that success was almost within their reach.

'Well, cousin?' Ba'alekkt said teasingly. 'You seem struck dumb with astonishment. Surely you knew that from family feeling alone, we were likely to help you?'

'There is always doubt,' Ansaryon said drily. 'And although I have great faith in your powers of persuasion, it is not only your father the Emperor who must be convinced. There are also his advisors.'

'Oh, they'll be on my side,' said Ba'alekkt cheerfully. 'They're looking to the future, aren't they? Once I'm Emperor, things will be very different, and they know it. Therefore, they flatter me now so that they can keep their heads later. I may only be fourteen years old, cousin Ansaryon, but already I command more power than you can possibly dream of. And it will not be long before I am the most mighty man in all the known world.'

It might have been a child's boast, but it was not. Halthris, looking at the strong, compact body, the curling dark hair, the air of vigour and confidence and purpose, knew that Ba'alekkt was very dangerous. He would help them now, but in the future he might well turn and rend anyone blocking his path to glory, despite family ties, with the unthinkingly savage ferocity of a tiger.

'In that case,' Ansaryon said, 'I shall be glad indeed to count you as my friend as well as my cousin. My heartfelt thanks to you, and I hope they do not prove premature.'

'I *know* that they will not,' Ba'alekkt told him, smiling. 'And now, since there is nothing more to discuss, I suggest that we spend the rest of the evening being entertained by the finest singers and dancers that Toktel'yi has to offer.'

He clapped his hands sharply, and the musicians in the background came to a swift and rather ragged halt. They bowed, and slipped out like shadows. For a moment there was silence, save for the endless singing and twittering of the birds outside. Ba'alekkt lounged back, snapping his fingers for the unobtrusive servant to refill their goblets.

Cymbals clashed suddenly, making Halthris jump. A troupe of

men and women ran in, their brief garments fluttering brilliantly in
the lamplight. They were black-skinned, like Al'Kalyek, and their
powerful, muscular bodies gleamed with oil and glittered with
silvery dust. One man held the cymbals, another a small hand-
drum, and a young woman had the reed-pipes that Halthris had
heard many times, wailing over the marshes and charsh-beds along
the banks of the Kefirinn. They began to play a swift, eerie,
rhythmic tune, and the others, three men and three women, whirled
and stamped and flung each other in the air with an abandon that
reminded Halthris irresistibly of the clan shaman Doresh, when he
particularly wanted to impress.

A slight movement in the shadows caught her eye. She glanced
over to her right, beyond Ansaryon's shoulder, and saw a small
figure almost lost in the murky shadows behind the door, where the
light from the lamps did not fall.

A child, with pale hair that no depth of darkness could disguise.

How long had he been there? What had he heard? Was D'thliss
watching through his eyes, or was there only Bron inside his head?

With a considerable effort, she managed to make no sudden
sound or movement that might indicate that she had seen him.
Instead, she stared at the frantic dancers – one of the women was
being tossed from man to man as if she were a gracefully animated
parcel – and sent her mind in search of Ansaryon's.

'*Don't move – don't look at the door, look at the dancers. Bron
is here.*'

'*I know. I saw him when they came in. I was hoping you
wouldn't notice him.*'

'Why?' she demanded, with some hostility. '*I'm hardly likely to
leap up now and stick a knife into him.*'

'*I know that – it would be difficult to hide a knife in those flimsy
clothes, anyway. But I didn't want you to betray that you had seen
him.*'

'*How long has he been here?*' Halthris said silently, repressing
her anger. They seemed always fated to quarrel over Bron.

'*Some time, I think. Long enough, perhaps, to hear what
Ba'alekkt said.*'

'*Then why is he still here? If D'thliss was watching through him,
she must know that the decision has been made. Why risk discovery,
and leave him here?*'

'Perhaps,' said Ansaryon's soft, uninflected voice in her mind,
'*he is more in control than we think. Perhaps he just wants to watch
the dancers.*'

Halthris risked a quick glance. The child did seem to be

fascinated by them. Between the shifting, athletic bodies, the flying garments and rippling hair, she could see his eyes, gleaming in the reflected light. He had come forward a little, and was therefore more visible. She wondered if Ba'alekkt had noticed him, and decided that he hadn't: he was gazing at the superb half-naked bodies of the female dancers with the avid stare of a child presented with a loaded tray of sweetmeats.

'*He's gone*,' Ansaryon said sharply. She looked back to where Bron had been. The shadows were once more innocent and empty, but the air tingled slightly with the after-effects of sorcery.

'*He vanished very suddenly*,' Ansaryon added. She could hear grim amusement in his thought-voice. '*Perhaps D'thliss doesn't appreciate Toktel'yan dancing*.'

The troupe came to a sudden and dramatic finish, with a flourish of clashing cymbals and a last wild shriek from the pipes, and stood panting, awash with sweat. Ba'alekkt nodded, smiling, and said something in Toktel'yan. At once the men filed out, leaving the three women. The pipes embarked on a different music, slow and achingly sad, and the remaining dancers began to move in an intricate, sensual pattern, weaving in and out of each other like a human tapestry.

Halthris felt a hand on her arm, and looked round. To her relief, it was Ansaryon. He smiled, significantly, and moved a little closer, so that they were almost touching. Realizing that this must be for Ba'alekkt's benefit, she relaxed into his embrace, hoping that the boy would not take offence. Perhaps if he thought that she was, or would soon become, Ansaryon's lover, he might be less likely to want her for himself.

She had not had a man in her bed for over a year, and the sensations beginning to wake inside her now were at once very pleasant, and very unwelcome. The Tanathi were an uninhibited people, and once a member of the tribe had successfully endured the Ordeal, he or she was free to experiment with the opposite (or sometimes the same) sex, until settling down into marriage, which was supposed to be faithful while it lasted. In the past seven or eight years, Halthris had taken several lovers, starting with Kettan and ending, so she had thought, with Vinnath.

So she had thought. But the warm, sensual delight of a man's arm around her was a reminder of how long she had been celibate, and also of how remote Vinnath now seemed, both in reality and in her mind. She could hardly remember his face, let alone why she had agreed to marry him. And Ansaryon was here beside her, and even if his touch was no more than a ploy to discourage Ba'alekkt, her starved senses thought otherwise. It was astonishingly difficult not to respond, to behave as if it were a cushion she leaned against, not a lean, masculine body. And she knew that if he were to kiss her, she would respond to him with passion.

Of course he would not. He was her friend, and even this diaphanous Toktel'yan gown could not conceal the honest, out-spoken, unfeminine Tanathi Hunter beneath. She imagined him undressing her, and his shocked astonishment when he saw the tattoos over her breasts and arms, indelible reminders that she was, after all, a barbarian, and smiled to herself. If that did not discourage him, nothing would. Their relationship was complicated enough without sex entering the game, and besides, she had no supplies of the dried herb called Engren, which all Tanathi women took when they wanted to prevent pregnancy.

Inri must have some, said the little voice of temptation at the back of her mind. Inri and Sherren have been love-making like rock rabbits ever since we left Sar D'yenyi, and before. Unless she's barren, or very lucky, she's surely got some with her.

If I ask her, Halthris thought wryly, she's bound to assume that I want it because of Invan. And just think of all the unpleasantness that particular misunderstanding could cause.

Ansaryon's free hand had begun to play idly with her hair. Halthris became aware of movement to her left, and glanced over. A woman, dressed in a blue gown that was almost transparent, was nestling next to Ba'alekkt, and the boy was fondling her in a manner that made Ansaryon's touch seem positively impersonal. The music ended: he snapped his fingers and beckoned, and the three dancing women came over to the cushions to join him.

Ansaryon slid forward, and stood up. The Emperor-in-Waiting looked at him, his eyes gleaming with lust and malice. 'Going so soon, cousin? I had thought we had all night ahead of us.'

'I'm sorry, but Zithiriani and Tanathi are more prudish and less broad-minded than you Toktel'yans,' Ansaryon said. He bent and reached his hand to Halthris: she took it, and was pulled effortlessly upright. 'I'm afraid that you will have to manage without us, cousin, but I see you have everything already in hand. Thank you for the superb entertainment, for the supper and above all for your help. I am forever in your debt, and so are all my people.'

'That is nothing,' Ba'alekkt said, with a negligent wave of his free hand. 'You are my beloved cousin – I could do no less. Good night, Ansaryon – good night, Halthris of the Tanathi. Sleep well – if you want to!' He chuckled, and turned his full attention to the woman in blue. Unnoticed, Ansaryon slipped his arm around Halthris, and led her from the pavilion.

Many of the lights had gone out, or been doused, and the noise of the birds was almost stilled, save for the occasional sleepy twitter from shrub or tree. Fortunately, there were lanterns set at intervals along the paths, near to the ground, so at least there was no danger of tripping over anything. Intensely aware of him, Halthris said quietly, 'Thank you. I thought I was going to be enrolled amongst his concubines.'

'I doubt he would dare. He needs my friendship – now. He knows that if he were to offend me by stealing my woman, I would not risk putting myself in his debt, whatever the cost to me. And that's what he wants – to have me and Zithirian under an obligation to him. One day, he will threaten us all.'

'Then why take his help?' Halthris halted. They were under a tall tree with twisted branches and huge, ragged leaves that drooped down like exhausted heads, nearly to the ground. There were no lanterns here, and she could see little more of his face than a pale, oval glimmer in the shadows.

'Because if I do not, Zithirian is lost to me for ever. Tsenit will marry K'djelk, and beget his dynasty, and I and all my companions will be doomed to roam the world in exile, homeless for the rest of our lives. To be honest, I would rather die in battle, fighting the Ska'i against insuperable odds.'

'And condemn your followers to the same fate?'

'Only those whose eyes are open, and are certain they wish to share it.' There was suddenly a terrible sadness in his words. 'Dear Hal, I know there is a choice. But it is not mine to take. I must win back Zithirian, or die in the attempt. I will not live out my days in shame and poverty.'

'If you return to Sar D'yenyi, you still have control of the gold mines,' Halthris reminded him.

'Until Tsenit sends sorcery against us again. Sar D'yenyi is vital to his survival, and it is not impregnable. Sooner or later, whatever Kefiri and Ramath might think, it will fall. Temiltan would like his son Cathallon to marry Kef, and if I fail, that is her only chance of survival. Tsenit hopes to marry K'djelk, so as long as Kefiri remains alive she will be a danger to him, as the only alternative to his rule. In Minassa, she will be safer than in Sar D'yenyi. And probably happier, too, in the long run. Cathallon is a nice boy.'

'Have you asked her?'

'No, of course not – I haven't had the chance.'

'I should, when you next see her. She might not like her future being discussed and arranged behind her back.'

Silence. At last he said, softly, 'You seem very angry tonight.'

'No, not angry – annoyed.' Halthris paused, determined not to let her tongue run away with her this time. 'Annoyed with Ba'alekkt – the conniving, precocious little brat. And annoyed with you, too. Whatever anyone likes to think or pretend, I am not a piece of property, to be owned or coveted or stolen.'

'I know.' His voice was unexpectedly gentle. 'I apologize. I couldn't think of any other way to deflect Ba'alekkt's intentions – and believe me, they were plain as sunrise even before you arrived. He was boasting to me about the delicious woman we were going to share. I had no idea, until you walked in, that it would be you.'

'And he changed his mind – just like that? When you let him think I was "your woman"?' She tried to keep the sneer out of her voice, failed, and wished the words unsaid.

'Yes. Aren't you glad he did? Although I suspect my mention of the possibility that you might geld him had some influence, as well. Ba'alekkt is very proud of his newly-acquired manhood.'

Despite her anger, she could not suppress a laugh. 'He's so *young*! Tanathi boys his age still think girls are just made to run and laugh with.'

'They mature fast in this hot climate. If he's not careful, he'll soon become overripe like his father, bloated with excess. Djamal will fall off the tree very soon, I suspect – or be pushed.'

Again, she could not hide a smile. 'I hope no one is listening to us.'

'I don't particularly mind if they are. In Toktel'yi, ambassadors are regarded as sacred to Kaylo, and cannot be molested, hurt or imprisoned. And that goes for their entourage as well. We are quite safe as long as we offer no harm to the Emperor or his family. And infuriating though Ba'alekkt is, I'm not yet provoked enough to attempt his murder.'

'I would have hurt him, if he had tried to force himself on me,' Halthris said. 'The servant who dressed me dropped a pin. It's tucked into my sleeve.'

Ansaryon laughed. 'Then I was right to warn Ba'alekkt in those blood-curdling terms! But I should have remembered that you are not a submissive Toktel'yan woman – despite that very beautiful disguise.'

'No, I am Tanathi still – I think.'

'I know you are.' He paused, and then added softly, 'Is that pin intended as a weapon against all-comers? Or just for Ba'alekkt?'

She peered through the gloom, trying in vain to see his face. But suddenly, with a lurch of her heart, she was certain that his caresses in the pavilion had not just been for Ba'alekkt's benefit. Torn between longing and unease, she said slowly, 'I had only intended it for the Emperor-in-Waiting. I thought he was all I had to fear.'

'To fear?'

Halthris hoped desperately that he would not touch her again. If he did, all her control would vanish, and she would forget everything in the face of her urgent hunger. And afterwards, she was sure that she would regret it most bitterly.

Something heavy and wet fell on her head, making her gasp. They had been so intent on each other that neither had noticed that the almost impenetrable darkness was caused by the swift arrival of a thick muffling of cloud, blotting out moon and stars. And that distant ominous muttering was surely thunder.

'It's raining,' she said, laughing with relief as more drops smacked onto the leaves above her. 'I didn't think it ever *did* rain, in Toktel'yi.'

'Rain? It's more like a flood here,' Ansaryon told her. He took her hand and pulled her out from the tree's inadequate shelter. Water exploded onto her head, her shoulders, her arms, warm and astonishingly welcome after the thick close heat of the night. Above the noise, he added, 'Come on, or we'll drown – *run!*'

Breathless, laughing, she hurried with him through rain that rapidly turned from a scattering of heavy drops to a downpour, and then to a drenching torrent that reminded her of the time she had stood under a waterfall on one of the steppe rivers. To a grassland nomad, such a rare soaking was a delight. Her gown flapped wetly round her ankles, her face streamed and her elaborate hairstyle was quite ruined, but she did not care. And Ansaryon laughed too, sounding younger and more light-hearted than she had ever heard him, as if the bitterness of the past, the problems of the present and the menace of the future had all been washed away with the rain.

She had no idea where they were going until he opened a door in a tree-shrouded wall, and swept her into a small, plain, empty room, through it and into another. It was furnished in the opulent Toktel'yan style, cushions and drapery everywhere, a low table spread with paper, and two small wall-lamps disseminating a low and friendly light.

Outside, thunder cracked and the rain hammered on the ground. Ansaryon went to the windows and pulled the shutters across. Halthris looked down at the spreading pool of water collecting on the floor around her feet, and realized that in this soaked, clinging, flimsy garment she might just as well not be wearing anything at all.

Ansaryon turned to face her, and she saw that he was aware of it too. He walked across the tiles, leaving a trail of drips, and stood in front of her, his eyes wide and dark with desire. He said very softly, 'I want you so much. Do you want me?'

Lies, excuses, evasions, flitted through her mind, and were discarded. Her eyes met his, and she said with honesty, 'Yes, I do.'

His hands had come up to embrace her: he dropped them suddenly to his sides, and said, his voice wry, 'But?'

'But I feel that matters between us are too complicated already. You are my friend, and I value that above anything else. If you were to become my lover as well . . .'

'I know.' He smiled at her, and she saw his acceptance of defeat and was suddenly and sharply disappointed. 'And I know too that if we were to start an affair, we would both lose a great deal of respect.' His smile became a grin, suddenly and heart-breakingly attractive. 'Besides, Invan would probably stick a knife into me.'

'You've noticed?' She was clenching her hands, so strong was the urge to touch him.

'When two men desire the same woman, they're bound to be aware of each other's feelings. Invan has suspected me of seducing you ever since I gave you your room here in the Palace. In fact, I have to confess to a kind of perverse pleasure in proving him wrong . . . Are you cold?'

She shook her head so violently that water scattered from her wet hair to join the pools on the floor. 'No. I think I'd better go.'

'Hal?' For the second time that night, he had addressed her by the affectionate diminutive which only her closest Tanathi friends used. Surprised, she looked into his eyes, and saw there a depth and strength of feeling that left her suddenly weak and shaking. 'Hal, I want our friendship to continue. *Whatever* happens.'

'Of course it will,' she said softly, hoping her longing did not show as nakedly on her face as it did in his. 'And perhaps one day, it will be different.'

'*It will.*' He spoke in her mind, where she knew already that there could be no deception, and no lies. '*One day, dear Hal – one day.*'

And before she could change her mind, she smiled, and turned, and left him.

PART
FOUR

TWENTY-TWO

As arranged months ago, the armies of Ansaryon's alliance began to gather before the last dark moon of summer. Although the days were shortening, the cold air had not yet begun to breathe down from the mountains, out of sight four hundred miles to the north, and it was still warm enough for the men to camp out of doors, without the protection of tents.

The contingent from Lelyent had been the first to arrive, more than four hundred of them, slightly less than Belerith had promised but still a good showing from such a small city. They had spent all summer training under the fifty Sar D'yenyi soldiers that Ansaryon had left behind for this purpose, and looked tanned, fit and confident. They marched past King Temiltan into the camp, singing a cheerful song echoed by drums and pipe, and with their arrival the King felt that his nephew's enterprise was truly begun.

The messenger pigeons had brought the news from Toktel'yi some time ago, winging their way straight and swift as an arrow northwards from the great city, across hundreds of miles of fields, villages and towns, and the sinuous windings of the Kefirinn. Through the good will and generosity of his cousin the Emperor (and the Emperor-in-Waiting), Ansaryon had obtained the five thousand men he needed. Because of their numbers, and the need for haste, they would make the journey on land rather than by river, struggling against the current. A good road ran north almost straight from Toktel'yi to Tamat on the Empire's border, and thence to Minassa. It was five hundred miles by that route, and it took them rather less than a month.

The rendezvous was at a town called Chearno, about ten miles south of Minassa. It was a prosperous place, given over to its market. Four days in five, the broad central square was filled with sheep, cattle, horses, and produce of every conceivable kind: great bunches of undried kuldi leaves, heaps of vegetables, conical piles of glowing orange and yellow fruit, like King Temiltan's lamps. Enthused by the prospect of feeding such a large army, it seemed that every farmer between Minassa and Tamat had transported his produce here in wagons, or on horse or mule back, in the hopes of obtaining a share of Ansaryon's gold in exchange.

Outriders had brought news of his approach, and when the King-in-exile rode into the camp at the head of his men, one warm evening just before the last dark moon of summer, the rest of his alliance was there waiting for him, cheering their leader and his army until their voices grew hoarse.

Ansaryon sat on the tall white stallion, half-bred Tanathi and a gift from the Emperor, and acknowledged them with a smile and a wave of his hand. Behind him, the men who had followed him all the way from Sar D'yenyi glittered erratically in their dusty armour, grins cracking their tired, sunburnt faces. And bringing up the rear came the five thousand Toktel'yan soldiers, tramping in terrifyingly perfect step.

The last time such troops had marched into Minassa, a hundred and fifty years ago, they had been hostile invaders, only repulsed with much difficulty and bloodshed. Many Minassans, eyeing them warily on the long march up from Tamat, had hoped fervently that it would be easier to get rid of these soldiers. Such men had made Toktel'yi the greatest power in the known world, and beside their well-drilled precision, their gleaming steel armour, and the razor-sharp efficiency of their weapons, even Ansaryon's entourage looked shabby and somehow unthreatening. Five thousand of them should be more than enough to defeat the barbarian Ska'i.

To Halthris, this return to a more temperate climate and congenial country had come as a considerable relief. After that momentous night when Ba'alekkt had entertained her and Ansaryon in his pavilion, events had moved very quickly. True to his word, the Emperor-in-Waiting had extracted a promise of help from his father the very next day, and within half a month the five thousand soldiers had been collected, equipped, provisioned and given their orders. Ansaryon had been furiously busy, occupied with plans and briefings until late each night, and Halthris had been grateful for this respite.

In her mind, she had relived over and over again the details of that night. Her response to him was by no means easy to analyse. Was it lust? Or friendship? Or love? Would she feel the same for any personable man who expressed his desire for her so openly?

No – for Invan had not aroused her desire, although his craving for her, albeit unspoken, was just as obvious as Ansaryon's. And now, with the climax to the campaign rushing ever closer, was not the time to subject her emotions, such as they were, to minute scrutiny. She would play her part once more as a trusted member of his staff, and try not to think about anything else until after they had won back Zithirian.

It was almost impossible, for her heart leapt whenever she saw him, even at a distance, but for the sake of her peace of mind, she would try.

She had not seen Bron again, and if he had appeared to anyone else, she had not heard of it. Perhaps his absence meant that something had befallen his mistress, but she doubted it. From all that she had heard of D'thliss, the priestess was a born survivor, and possessed of enough power to ensure it. Either she had learned enough, that night in Ba'alekkt's pavilion, or she was now much more careful where she sent Bron, and who saw him. Halthris was glad of it: the child was a disturbing reminder that the defeat of Tsenit and the Ska'i was by no means the certainty that everyone seemed to think it would be, now that they had Imperial help.

Now, riding her rangy Toktel'yan horse through the cheering soldiers, she was tense with anticipation and fear. The Lelyentans were here, recognized by their leather jerkins, and the Minassans too of course. But where, oh where, was her brother Abreth?

Even as she searched the crowd, she heard her name shouted, and out of the corner of her eye glimpsed frantic movement. Then Inri, beside her, laughed and pointed, and she saw Abreth and Chettay standing together, waving. It was impossible to stop there and hold up the procession, but she waved back, her grin stretching her face, and saw him jab his finger at an area of the camp behind him. Presumably, that was where the rest of the Tanathi were located.

The relief was overwhelming: she had not seen or heard from her brother for so long, and a nagging fear for him had always lurked unpleasantly at the back of her mind. Inri, well aware of how she felt, gave her a friendly clasp of the hand. 'Thanks be to Hegeden and Sarraliss – Abreth and Chettay at least are safe.'

At the centre of the camp the Minassan King had pitched a handsome tent in the Toktel'yan style, a cone of canvas pulled out from a central pole, and Temiltan stood before it, his staff beside him, to welcome his cousin. The cavalcade broke up in some confusion as each contingent began the task of finding somewhere to sleep before darkness fell: already, the sun had disappeared behind the rumpled, distant horizon of the steppes, and the broad plain to the west of Chearno was dotted with campfires and the tents being put up for the Toktel'yan officers.

Even in this huge area, locating the Tanathi was easy. With a shock of joyful recognition, Halthris saw the distinctive rounded shapes of a dozen 'mareks' grouped together, quite close to the river. Eagerly, she urged her narrow-chested dark bay horse through the dispersing crowds, Inri and Sherren just behind her.

'Hal!'

Abreth came running up, his braids flying and the four bracelets on his arm clashing with every stride. She had time to notice that he looked fit, and healthy, and happy, and then she leapt from the bay's uncomfortable back and flung herself into her brother's embrace.

The next few moments passed in a confused blur – everyone asking questions at once, and hardly listening to the answers – but at last the initial elation of their reunion diminished, and Abreth looked at his sister and his friends, grinning. 'There are fires lit, and meat roasting in your honour, and six hundred Tanathi waiting to hear all your news.'

'Six hundred?' Inri cried in astonishment. 'That's far more than you were hoping to bring.'

'I know.' Abreth grinned, very pleased with himself. 'Whether it was just my persuasive tongue, or the fact that a baby could see that the Ska'i are a menace to us all and have to be stopped no matter what the cost, I don't know. Anyway, there are Hunters from every clan here, and nearly fifty from ours.' He glanced significantly at Halthris. 'And quite a few from Djarna's.'

Vinnath was a member of Djarna's clan. Halthris felt suddenly both apprehensive and annoyed. What was he doing here? She didn't want to talk to him, even to see him. Too much had happened since they had last met, and she couldn't face the thought of complicating her confused emotions even more.

But of course that was hardly fair to Vinnath, who knew nothing of this, and probably thought that her feelings were unaltered. She said, trying to sound enthusiastic, 'Is he here, then?'

'Vinnath? Yes, of course. He's in the blue marek at the far end of our camp. He was very eager for news of you – I'm sure he's waiting for you now.'

'Thank you,' Halthris said, her heart sinking. But little as she liked the prospect, she could not avoid him for ever, and it would be best to get this difficult and unpleasant meeting over now.

Whatever would she say to him? She knew, without the least taint of doubt, that she did not want to marry him. But what were the alternatives? She was twenty-five now – she could not stay a Hunter for ever. And neither did she think that she could settle to Hearth life. She had seen Minassa and Lelyent and Toktel'yi, and Sar D'yenyi in the morning. She had tasted new lands and new customs, and she wanted more. To return to her tribe, circum-scribed by the ceaseless, monotonous rhythm of the steppe, was unthinkable.

And an Emperor-in-Waiting had desired her: and so had a King.

Face it, she thought angrily, as she urged her tired horse towards the Tanathi tents. It's Ansaryon who lures you away – nothing else. If he did not exist, you would still be happy with Vinnath – whatever else you had seen and done.

And that was the bitterest thing of all, that she, who had controlled her life so completely up until now, could not control this. She had felt considerable affection for all her lovers – even Kettan, seen with the blindness of extreme youth, had been dear to her once. But never, ever had she experienced this longing, this temptation, this feeling that nothing was worthwhile unless he was there to share it with her. On the march from Toktel'yi, she had missed his companionship terribly, even though she had tried to tell herself that they were both occupied with much more important matters than the mere slaking of desire.

But *was* it just desire? Would she feel like this if they had become lovers that night in Toktel'yi, however briefly? Single Tanathi men and women played no elaborate games of courtship: mutual desire, once acknowledged, was usually indulged immedi-ately. Never before had she wanted someone and been denied, even if she had done the denying. Was this why she felt such desperate yearning? Perhaps, if it was, she should allow her feelings free rein, in the hope that it was no more than a fire in summer grass, swift to flare up, just as swift to burn away into ashes.

She could not know. There was only one way to prove it, and that must wait until after Tsenit and the Ska'i had been defeated. She knew Ansaryon too well: he was very susceptible to emotion, and to embark on such an affair now would surely be a dangerous distraction from the vital task ahead of him.

She smiled wryly. In Toktel'yi, she had taken pride in her supposed invulnerability to the deep-buried feelings that ruled Ansaryon. And it was humiliating to realize that she herself was ruled by them too.

But now, there was Vinnath to be faced: and if he had indeed nursed a faithful devotion to her for a year and a half, she did not know how to let him down gently.

As she rode up to the blue tent, decorated with the running deer and stags that were the badges of Djarna's clan, the doorflap was pulled aside, and a man stepped out.

He was not as tall as she remembered. His dark hair was neatly bound into three braids, and he wore a bright red tunic that she knew was his best. His face, tanned, handsome, rather broad, gave nothing whatsoever away. Then he smiled, and walked towards her.

This was not going to be easy. Halthris dismounted, remembering not to drop the reins of her horse, who had not been Tanathi trained, and submitted to Vinnath's embrace. He smelt of leather, and smoke, and the aromatic ointments which the Tanathi used to protect their skin from the harsh weather of the steppe. He had obviously taken some trouble to get ready for her.

Her unenthusiastic response must have been obvious, for he drew away from her, frowning, his hands still on her shoulders. 'Hal? Hal, what's wrong?'

She gave a quick shake of her head. 'Vinnath, can we talk? Now?'

'Of course, but—' He stared at her, still plainly bewildered. Several avid Tanathi faces were peering out of his tent, and he waved them away with an impatient gesture, and the pungently-expressed hope that they would all fall into a pile of horse dung in the dark. 'Not here. We can walk down to the river, if you like. There are grey otters there – I saw one playing with her cubs yesterday.'

Usually, that information would have interested her. Now, she merely nodded. 'Yes, that would be best. Where shall I leave my horse?'

'We can go past the lines, and tie him up there.' Vinnath took her arm, and guided her between the blue tent and its neighbour, belonging to Umi's clan and covered in writhing red and purple snakes. 'You – you look very well, Hal. I've missed you – I've been thinking about you a lot. I'm very glad you're safe.'

'So am I,' she said drily. The next two mareks were her own clan's, and she saw Chettay, Grinya and Djekko tending the cooking fire, with what looked like a whole lamb or goat roasting fragrantly over it. Her mouth watered, but she waved to them and walked past to the horse lines beyond.

The bay gelding seemed quite happy to be tethered next to a smaller, steppe-hardened Tanathi black, and there was water and fodder for him. She removed his saddle and the hinged, ferocious-looking iron bit that seemed to be compulsory for all Toktel'yan horses, however docile, and left him to enjoy a well-earned rest.

The land sloped gently down to the broad Kefirinn, here fringed with trees and edged with spear-rushes, the tall plumes of their shaggy seed-heads a reminder that winter was coming. As Halthris and Vinnath approached, something entered the water with a soft plopping splash. She strained her eyes against the gathering gloom, but failed to see anything.

'Otter,' Vinnath said quietly. He stopped by a willow tree, and turned to face her. 'Hal, what's wrong? Why aren't you glad to see me?'

'I am.' She spoke honestly, aware that he deserved no less. 'But as a friend, no more than that. Vinnath, I may as well come straight to the point – I'm sorry, I hate to have to hurt you, but I can't marry you.'

'You *can't?*' He gripped her arm and she stood still, resisting the urge to twist out of his grasp. 'What do you mean, you can't? Hal, we promised each other—'

'I know. I'm sorry, I really am, but I can't keep that promise any longer.'

'Why not? Is there someone else?'

'No, I have no other lover.' She spoke only the truth, and was guiltily aware of the deception. 'I just – I don't – Vinnath, it's so difficult to explain, but I have changed. All the things that have happened to me over the past year have put a great gulf between us. I'm not even sure that I am a true Tanathi any more. It isn't your fault, there's nothing you could have done to alter it – I'm to blame, me, *I* have changed.'

'And so you don't want me any more,' he said, his voice dull and flat.

'I want you as a *friend* – yes, very much. But as a lover, a husband – I'm sorry, Vinnath, I hate to tell you this – but no, I don't.'

'Then that's it, as far as you're concerned.' He turned away, a dark defeated shape against the brighter expanse of the river. 'I should have expected it, I suppose. Abreth, Chettay, all of them have had such tales to tell of Zithirian and Sar D'yenyi – and you've seen far more even than they have, you've been to Toktel'yi.'

And in Toktel'yi, she had realized the full depth and strength of her feelings for Ansaryon. She said sadly, 'Yes. Oh, Vinnath, I know how I must be hurting you – I know how hard it must be to understand – but I want you to be happy too. And if I married you, we would only make each other miserable.'

'If you say so.' It was too dark now for her to see his face, but every drooping line of his body spoke of his wretchedness. 'I don't have a lot of choice, do I?'

Something perverse in her wished that he would shout, fight, argue, anything rather than accept defeat so tamely. And a serpent voice whispered in the back of her mind that marriage to Vinnath would have been a mistake, even if she had never set eyes on Ansaryon. She shook her head, annoyed with herself for finding him so irritating. 'No, I'm afraid you haven't. And I think one day you'll realize that it was for the best.'

'I doubt it,' said Vinnath, in tones of such abject despair that she longed to shake some sense into him. But she was being very unfair, she reminded herself sternly. If Ansaryon had rejected her, wouldn't she be just as miserable?

Yes, and she would hide it with fiery words and anger, not capitulate in this spineless manner.

'Come on,' she said briskly, and touched his arm. 'Let's go back, before they all put quite a different interpretation on our absence.' She knew she was being callous, but his feebleness was making her at once annoyed and relieved. No doubt of it, whatever might happen in the future between her and Ansaryon, she had made the right decision.

They returned to the Tanathi part of the camp in an unhappy and embarrassed silence. Halthris, ravenously hungry and exhausted by the long day's march, walked as quickly as she could, guided by the fires in front of them and the mouth-watering smell of roasting meat. Vinnath, just behind, radiated misery as the sun gave off warmth. She longed to tell him to pull himself together, that there were plenty of pretty young women eager for his attentions. It was not even as if they had ever been particularly loving or passionate – she had just felt comfortable in his company. And now there was not even that.

She paused a few paces from the mareks, and turned to face him. In the flickering firelight, his expression was utterly wretched. He had nourished his hopes and illusions for a year and a half, and now all had turned to dust in his mouth, at what should have been his moment of greatest happiness.

'Goodbye, Vinnath,' she said softly. And, feeling again that mixture of guilt and relief, left him to grieve alone.

She walked to the circle around her clan's fire. At her arrival there was a chorus of whistles and ribald comment, mostly concerning the allegedly perfunctory nature of Vinnath's love-making. And the first face she saw was Ansaryon's.

He was standing just beyond the circle of Tanathi, talking quietly to Abreth. There was no sign of Invan or any other members of his staff, and the rest of her clan, intent on giving her welcome, did not seem to be aware of his presence. But their eyes met, linked inexorably across the dancing wild flames and the grinning faces, and without conscious thought she spoke to him, mind to mind.

'*I have told Vinnath that I don't want to marry him.*'

'*Have you? Is that what you truly want?*'

'*Yes. It's not what HE wants, but it's for the best. We wouldn't have been happy together. I've changed too much.*'

'*What will you do?*'

'*I don't know. Inri and Sherren have seen what I have seen, but they have each other. Don't worry, I'll cope.*'

'Hal? Hal, are you all right?'

She started, and turned to see Chettay, her soft round face earnest and concerned. Halthris gave herself a mental shake and nodded, smiling. 'Yes, I am – thank you. But I could kill a dozen Ska'i bare-handed for a taste of that lamb.'

The Ska'i camp sprawled for nearly half a mile across the once green and pleasant triangle of land on the western side of Zithirian, between the banks of the Kefirinn and the city walls. They had no qualms about leaving their rubbish to fester in heaps outside their tents, which were low and round and looked from a distance not unlike those of the Tanathi. But the Ska'i, a more primitive people, had never mastered the art of curing leather, nor did they share the cleaner habits of their more fastidious neighbours. If you were moving on tomorrow, why worry about the mess around you? Just leave it behind for the scavengers to pick over, and if you came back after six months the site would be covered with fresh grass and bright, short-lived steppe flowers.

But Quenait and his tribe had now occupied this camp for nearly a year, and the whole area stank. When the warm summer wind called the Kedrin came drifting down from the steppe hills, the inhabitants of Zithirian had taken to closing their shutters and staying indoors, despite the heat. Their city had always been famous for its sparkling cleanliness, the purity, quantity and freshness of its water, and its comparative freedom from disease. Now bloated corpses, human and animal, jostled with Ska'i rubbish down the formerly unpolluted Kefirinn, and several alarming and mysterious cases of fever had appeared amongst the surviving population that summer.

It was now the start of the ninth month, and the nights were swiftly lengthening. If the snow came as early this year as the last, it would arrive before the next moon vanished. In the city, the people scratched an existence that was far from the life they had once known. There was some food, not abundant but just enough for survival. The fabric of the city had a shabby, neglected appearance, for there was no point in keeping the street clean, or tending the public gardens, when life was reduced to an all-day search for food and other necessities, barter had largely replaced money, and at any time the Ska'i could take your head, or you could succumb to one of those virulent fevers that obviously had something to do with the putrid squalor outside the walls.

Little work was done: no one had the energy, and there were no trading ships to carry goods down to Minassa and Toktel'yi. One had ventured up the river earlier in the summer, and a band of Ska'i had intercepted it just below the city, killed the crew, plundered it and set it on fire. The burned, beached wreck could still be seen from the wall-towers, a terrible reminder of the ever-present menace at the gates. While the Ska'i remained, the lucrative trade with the south could not exist, and without the Ska'i, Tsenit had no hope either of capturing Sar D'yenyi, with its hoard of mountain gold.

The King of Zithirian spent most of his time in his half-ruined palace. He had no spare money to rebuild what Quenait's men had destroyed, and in any case many of the craftsmen who had lavished their exquisite skills on the royal apartments were dead, or in exile. He had given up his Parades round the city, for the early adulation of the terrified people, convinced that he was their saviour, had rapidly given way to a sullen, malevolent silence.

The last time he had ridden down the Ceremonial Way in his finery, ignoring the pinched, resentful faces turned up to his, someone had shouted, 'Murderer!', and the cry had been taken up by many more. Of course, the Imperial Guard had tried to arrest the culprits, but for half-starved people they had proved surprisingly fleet of foot, and only one boy, a crippled lad who could barely walk, had been captured. General Seardrith had recommended that he be punished as an example to the citizens, and Tsenit, still smarting from the humiliation, had agreed with alacrity. The unfortunate captive was now imprisoned in the secret cells carved out of the rock below the central tower, along with others who had committed a variety of crimes, mostly involving some kind of resistance to authority.

At D'thliss's suggestion, Tsenit had expanded the network of spies set up by the Temple many years ago. Priests, Quarter officials and others who wished to curry royal favour, atone for misdeeds or just increase their household's food supply all reported back to the

Palace, and their information proved both discouraging and infuriating. It seemed that every tavern and kuldi-house was a hotbed of rumour, disrespect and sedition. Everywhere, men and women spoke of Tsenit and his government with contempt, and looked forward to the day when Ansaryon would lead an army to rescue them from the usurper and from the Ska'i.

No one could tell where these tales had come from, and however many announcements he made from the Palace, proclaiming that they were false, that Ansaryon was dead and that Tsenit was the only true King, they seemed to fall on deaf ears. In vain he denounced his brother as a sorcerer, a lover of sinister and evil rites, a necromancer and an effete weakling, incapable of the strong leadership which only he, Tsenit, could give to Zithirian. In vain, too, he pointed out that if Ansaryon attacked the city with an Imperial Army, the ensuing conquest and oppression would make the Ska'i look like those gentle, ascetic priests of Kaylo, the Toktel'yan Lord of Life, who had vowed to harm no living creature, whether man or insect.

It was no good. Bested by rumours far stronger than any of his official pronouncements, Tsenit gave up the struggle. In any case, D'thliss had her own sources of information, and her latest news was deeply unwelcome. Ansaryon had left Sar D'yenyi in the spring, and had taken a small army in turn to Lelyent, Minassa and Toktel'yi. And each of these cities had welcomed his brother with open arms, promising him help and soldiers for an attack on Zithirian. Even the Emperor, who had promised his own daughter for Tsenit's bride, had perfidiously changed his mind as soon as Ansaryon appeared, and offered her to him instead. And, more ominously, five thousand highly trained, superbly armed Toktel'yan soldiers as well.

Or so D'thliss had said, and Tsenit believed her. So did Quenait, but he was not alarmed at the prospect of fighting the finest and most feared soldiers in the known world. Why should he, when Ska'i tribesmen had been harrying the borders of the Empire, with considerable success, for countless years? He laughed at the King's fears, accused him of being a coward to his face, and demanded more 'tribute', as Zithirian's forced contribution to the Ska'i camp was euphemistically known. The complaints which Tsenit had intended to raise, mildly, about one or two rapes and murders, and the terrorizing of the few farming households left within twenty miles of the city, dried unspoken in his throat in the face of the Ska'i chief's open and humiliating contempt. He retreated from the stinking camp, handkerchief pressed against his flinching nostrils, and wished with passion and despair that he had never heard of the Ska'i, and never agreed to D'thliss's suggestion that he enlist Quenait as an ally.

The chief, with malicious satisfaction glinting in his narrow eyes, watched Tsenit go, and then ducked back into his tent. It was cluttered with the proceeds of plunder: silk embroidered hangings, Minassan pottery, gold and silver drinking vessels and bowls, beautifully carved and inlaid wooden furniture. In the middle of this chaotic splendour his shaman Br'nnayak sat like a wizened toad, smoking Annatal from a curved pipe made from a hollowed-out human rib-bone.

Quenait wrinkled his nose. Like all Ska'i, he was not personally fastidious – it was well-known that washing robbed a man of any fighting prowess he might possess – but he had never got used to the smell of the drug, at once pleasantly fragrant and sickeningly sweet.

Br'nnayak grinned at the chief's evident distaste and puffed harder. When the whole tent was full of the cloying smoke, and Quenait's eyes were watering, he removed the pipe and placed it carefully on a lovely inlaid table of Lelyentan workmanship, well aware that the hot bone would soon mark the pale, delicate yew-wood. 'A King of milk and water, that one,' he remarked. 'If the brother is the same, we'll have no worries.'

'From what I've heard, he's worse.' Quenait sat down cross-legged on the thickly-carpeted floor, trying not to cough. 'They're all rotten – soft, feeble, decayed with civilization – pah!' He spat with contempt. 'We'd be doing them all a favour, giving them to Ayak, from Tsenit down to the newest infant.'

'I know.' Br'nnayak picked up the pipe again. He knocked out the cooling ash onto the table, and took out the small leather pouch in which he kept his supplies of Annatal. 'Unfortunately, we need them to give us the gold. All we know is that the mines lie somewhere in the mountains. If we kill the people, Tsenit won't tell us how to find them – and he won't if you kill him, either.'

'I know that.' Quenait ruminated, his chin resting on one clenched fist. 'But nothing would give me more pleasure. Once the gold is safely in our hands, his life won't be worth *that*!'

Br'nnayak regarded his chief's snap of the fingers with a grim smile. He said softly, 'And after that? Will you become King of Zithirian in his place?'

Quenait laughed. 'You know me better than that. What would I want with walls and towers? I am sick of staying so long in the same camp – and so are my warriors. There are many other cities

that have never tasted Ayak's sacred terror. Minassa . . . Lelyent
. . . even Toktel'yi.'

'The Empire is full of soldiers and sorcerers. Magic alone will
not reduce it, and nor will the full might of the Ska'i.'

'Perhaps,' Quenait said impatiently, and his eyes shone with the
light of fanaticism. 'But you remember the prophecies made at my
birth. You pronounced them yourself, after all, and you ensured
that I would never be allowed to forget them. Because of me,
towers would crumble, cities die, empires fall. And there is only
one Empire in the known world – Toktel'yi.'

'You are right, of course,' Br'nnayak said, his voice soft and
sinister. 'Zithirian has already fallen to you – it lies grovelling at
your feet, begging for mercy. Lelyent and Minassa will be even
easier. What of the other lands? Gulkesh – Fabriz – even Kerenth?
And the deserts, far to the south? Do you wish to conquer those as
well?'

'If Ayak wishes it. I am his chosen instrument.' Quenait's eyes
glinted almost red in the dim light. 'As you are his chosen servant.
He is thirsty for blood. I have seen him in my dreams, howling for
it. And Toktel'yi will be the greatest of all gifts for him.'

'And if you offer him so much blood, it will be a very long time
before he demands yours,' Br'nnayak reminded him cunningly.
'Remember, Ayak grants long life to his most faithful followers. I
have seen over a hundred winters, I was shaman to your father,
your grandfather, and his father too. Ayak is pleased with what I
have brought him over the years – he is happy to let me live on, in
expectation of more. Give him Toktel'yi, and you and I may even
attain immortality.'

Quenait drew in his breath. 'Is that possible?'

'For the servant and the instrument of Ayak the Devourer, all
things are possible.' Br'nnayak smiled. 'But for reasons that are at
present obscure, he has given the weapon that will destroy the
Empire, and all the cities of the world, into the hands of his false
disciple D'thliss.'

'What?' Quenait stared at him in astonishment. 'What weapon?'

Br'nnayak was still filling the bone pipe with dried leaves of
Annatal, and did not answer. The chief watched the shaman with
desperate impatience as he rolled and inserted each brown flake
into the bowl with ostentatiously slow deliberation. At last, unable
to contain himself any longer, Quenait said urgently, 'What is it, in
Ayak's name? A spell? A talisman? A Stone of Power?'

'The Stones of Power no longer exist, in this world at least. No,
it is none of these things. D'thliss's power comes from a child.'

Beneath the straggling moustaches, Quenait's mouth dropped open. 'A *child*? You're lying!'

'I am not. A male child about eight or nine winters old, at a guess. D'thliss calls him Bron.'

'Bron? That's a Ska'i word—'

'As in my own name, "Br'nnayak", the Servant of the Devourer. This boy is no servant of Ayak, though. He is at present the tool of D'thliss. And in him lives a power so great that he could destroy us all – or all our enemies, if we were able to use him for our own purposes.'

Quenait was breathing hard. 'How do you know this? Why haven't you told me before? I knew the old witch was unusually powerful, but I never dreamed she had any weapon such as this.'

'I have suspected it for a long time.' Br'nnayak pulled a glowing tallow spill from the brazier and lit his pipe. In between puffs as the Annatal ignited, he went on. 'This drug bestows a certain level of power, and no more, to those who are trained to use it. My own superior abilities are a gift of Ayak. In D'thliss, I recognized a potency as great as my own – but although she professes to serve Ayak, she does so selfishly, for her own ends, to satisfy her desire to rule Zithirian. Her mind is too small to look further. And I have seen, in my dreams and trances, that the Devourer despises her. He knows what is in her heart, and he plans to destroy her.'

'Good,' Quenait commented vindictively. 'I never liked or trusted the old witch. So her death would be welcome to Ayak?'

'Supremely so. Worship purely for the sake of greed is repugnant to him. You will earn high favour from him if you kill her.'

'Excellent,' Quenait said softly. 'But you have still not told me about this child. How long have you known of him?'

'Just a day or so. For months now I have been attempting to spy on D'thliss, with little result – her defences are peculiarly strong, and resisted all my skills. But recently she has become more careless – or that feeble Tsenit has infected her with some of his own despair. Two nights ago, my spirit walked into her lair under the Temple. And I saw her with the child – only a glimpse, not enough to discover exactly how she used him, but enough to know what he is. He is very valuable to her. We enjoy Ayak's favour and good will, so he will be far more valuable to us.'

'I must have him.' Quenait leapt to his feet and prowled restlessly about the tent, one hand pulling at his moustache, as he always did when particularly excited. 'Once he is in my possession, all the prophecies will come true – I will destroy every soft, decaying, feeble city in all the known world – and the Empire of Toktel'yi will cease to exist. This I will do, in Ayak's holy name!'

'Then we shall seize the boy. It will not be difficult. D'thliss allows him to wander the streets like any other child.'

Quenait stopped his obsessive pacing and stared. 'The witch is mad! Why doesn't she keep him under guard, if he is so important to her?'

'I think she hopes to deflect any suspicion. But of course, this also makes him more vulnerable to us. A dozen soldiers will be more than sufficient, if I guide them.'

'But if the child is brim-full of sorcery, how will you catch him?'

'As any ordinary child can be caught. He is no more than nine years old – he is no sorcerer or shaman, merely a vessel, a tool used by D'thliss. Only when they are together is he dangerous.' Br'nnayak smiled, and the viciously gleeful twist in his mouth made even Quenait shiver suddenly. 'And once he is in my hands, that old witch's life will be Ayak's at last.'

CHAPTER
TWENTY-THREE

'Pigeons,' said Kefiri Tayma's Daughter, standing in Kaydi's courtyard.

The sun shone brilliantly down on the uneven stones, the lines of damp clothing strung out to dry, and the convex red tiles on the roof. Across them, three stout grey and white birds were pottering aimlessly. The cat Garool, sitting in a narrow strip of shade under Herris's bedroom window, fixed his sinister green eyes on them and chattered softly in his throat, his long whiplash tail twitching urgently.

'Pigeons?' Kaydi stared up at the plump objects of Garool's desire. 'Good in a pie, when there isn't much else, that's why we keep them. We had dozens last year – those are all that's left.'

'I picked them off with my sling.' Herris patted his belt proudly. 'I could get one of 'em now if you fancied it, Ma.'

'No!' Kefiri cried in alarm.

Kaydi and Herris looked round at her in some astonishment, and she hastened to explain. 'No – don't kill them. They could be very useful.'

'How?' Kaydi demanded, her hands on her hips and her face doubtful. 'I never heard they had any use other than eating.'

'Not here, they haven't. But in Sar D'yenyi, we use them to carry messages.'

Herris was looking at her as if she had suddenly gone mad. He giggled. 'No, Kef, you're joking. Pigeons can't take messages! You'd ask them what the news was, and they'd say, "Coo – coo-coo-coo!"'

'Yes, they can,' Kefiri told him patiently. 'You write it on a tiny piece of paper, and tie it to the pigeon's leg. Then you let it go, and it flies back to the place where it was bred. From Sar D'yenyi, they could reach the mining towns in less than an hour.'

'But that wouldn't be much good to us,' Kaydi pointed out. 'If we caught one of them and let it go again, it would just fly back here. And we need to get in touch with Minassa, to find out when the Lord Ansaryon is coming.'

'I know – so someone must take the pigeons to Minassa. And bring Minassan birds back to us in exchange!'

Kaydi stared at her with dawning and delighted understanding in her face. 'So – they'd have our pigeons, ready to send messages to us when it's needed. And we'll have theirs, all ready to take the answer back.'

'But there's only one problem,' Herris said thoughtfully. 'How do we get them out of the city? Surely *someone* will see, and realize what we're doing?'

'Will they?' Kefiri said. 'We use pigeons to communicate over long distances in Sar D'yenyi, true, but not in Zithirian. You didn't know about it, did you? And I don't think anyone else here would.'

Kaydi was frowning. 'But what about Minassa? Would they know what to do?'

'I'm sure they would – because it was a Minassan friend of my father's who first brought pigeons to Sar D'yenyi. My father was going to send them to Zithirian as well, but he didn't live long enough.' She swallowed, thinking of Tayma, whom she had loved and admired so much. 'They use pigeons in the Archipelago, I think, to communicate between the islands when the weather's too rough for boats. And they're quite common in Toktel'yi, too.' She glanced at Kaydi and her son. 'We need to know where Ansaryon is, how many men he has with him, and when and how he'll attack the Ska'i. Otherwise, how can we plan our uprising in his support? It's getting late in the year, and we've heard nothing certain all summer. *Someone* needs to go to Minassa with the pigeons, and tell him what's happening here.'

'They'll be running a huge risk,' Kaydi pointed out. 'It won't be easy getting the birds out of the city, for a start. I know people can come and go more or less as they please now, outside curfew hours, but anyone with any baggage is searched.'

'I'll go!'

Both women gazed at Herris as if he had announced he had three heads. 'Oh, no, you won't, lad,' said his mother briskly. 'I've plenty of work for you here. No, it needs a man. Stekketh perhaps – or, I know, his brother Kardan. His wife's people came from Hailyan down on the border, so he knows the way, and he's a wily young fox. If anyone can get past the Guard and the Ska'i with a sack full of pigeons, he can. I'll go and see him now.'

'But, Ma—' Herris stared at her in dismay, consumed by his longing for adventure. 'They wouldn't even think of searching me – I'm just a boy – I'd slip past 'em easy, I *know* I would! And Kardan's wife's just had a baby, he won't want to go.'

'Well, if he don't want to do it, that's fair enough – I'll find someone else.' Kaydi glared belligerently at her only surviving son. 'But you're staying here, and that's that – even if I have to lock you in your room. Understand?'

'Yes, Ma,' said Herris, his face meekly obedient, and rebellion seething unseen behind it.

'Good – I'm glad you've seen sense. Perhaps you're growing up at long last. Now, you and Kefiri can make yourself useful by catching those pigeons. I know Engris has a couple left too, so we can take them as well. You can give 'em a few scraps, even a handful of corn to lure 'em down, whatever you like. But I want them all safely caught by the time I get back from Kardan's. And if that sly cat takes one tail-feather off 'em, I'll wring your neck and his.'

'Yes, Ma,' Herris said, and risked a grin.

Kefiri could see that his mother was having trouble keeping her face suitably stern, and said quickly, 'They should come down if we offer them corn. All we need is a net.'

'A *net*? We've got nothing like that here. Gandar didn't like fishing.'

'Well, I'm sure I can improvise something.' Kefiri gave her a smile, woman-to-woman. 'Don't worry. I'll make sure he doesn't get into any mischief.'

Shortly afterwards, Kaydi set off for Kardan's house in the Potter's Quarter, leaving her son and her supposed female servant hunting through piles of scraps and remnants of material in the workroom, looking for something suitable for trapping pigeons. As soon as the street door had safely banged behind her, Herris sat back on his heels, wrinkling his nose at the dust, and said earnestly, 'Are you on her side, or mine?'

'Hers, of course,' Kefiri said promptly. 'This isn't a game, Herris. If they catch you, they'll kill you, *and* probably all the rest of us as well. Tsenit's tame priestess will rummage through your mind and remove all you know, so you won't have any choice but to betray us.'

Herris looked mutinous. 'But I've thought about how to get out without being searched. I'd just take a ferry over to the cemetery during daylight, and hide there until the curfew started. No one patrols there after dark. And then I'd steal a boat and ride down the river. It's easy, there are no rapids, or anything else dangerous, and I know how to handle a boat.'

'But all the ferry-boats tie up on the city side at night.'

'Then I'll just swim over and get one. I can swim, you know, and the current is slow at this time of year. Oh, Kef, I could do it, I *know* I could! And I'm sure Kardan won't want to go, not when the baby's only a few days old.' His eyes were huge with urgency. 'Please help me, Kef – *please*!'

'I can't,' she said, though she felt very sympathetic. After all, she herself had run away from Sar D'yenyi and her responsibilities because of a similarly desperate desire to help. But she had avoided disaster only with considerable good luck, and the thought of Herris, small, reckless, spuriously sharp, embarking on this dangerous mission that might bring a horrible death to them all, was terrifying.

She went on, before he could say any more. 'Herris, your mother is right. This isn't a job for a child. How could you row or even steer one of those big boats safely? You're about half the size of a ferryman.'

'I'd do it,' Herris said stubbornly. 'Better than most men, I'd do it.' He looked at her reproachfully, and she realized suddenly that by refusing to help him, she had forfeited much of his admiration.

'I'm very sorry,' she said softly. 'But we can't rush into this without any planning or forethought. If whoever takes the pigeons is caught, our whole network could be betrayed, and scores of people imprisoned, or worse. It could even wreck Ansaryon's chances of defeating Tsenit and the Ska'i. You do understand, don't you, Herris? We have to be so *careful*. Let's stick to catching those birds for now – our chances to make a real contribution will come when Ansaryon arrives.'

He looked as if he were about to cry, and abruptly turned away to sort through another heap of cloth. His muttered assent was so quiet and reluctant that she could hardly hear it. 'All right. Look – will this do?'

It was a large piece of loose, gauzy fabric, discoloured in several places by damp and mould, and marred by three holes which, although big enough to let a mouse escape, would probably stop a pigeon. Kefiri, determined to make amends if she could, said brightly, 'It looks perfect. Have you got a box for them?'

'Should be one in the storeroom.' The boy pushed the cloth roughly in her direction, got up and went out.

Kefiri sighed. To Herris, this conspiracy was indeed a game, a delightful adventure in which he saw the opportunity to prove his maturity and sense – and thereby, ironically, proved the exact opposite. Although she was only four or five years older, the gap between them in worldly wisdom seemed a century wide. Now, she

could look beyond the childish desire for excitement and discern
the wider implications. The fate of the city might well rest in the
hands of whoever undertook to carry those pigeons to Minassa –
always assuming she and Herris could catch them, of course – and
bring others back. Success was absolutely vital. And it was a task
much, much too important to be left solely in the hands of a
thirteen-year-old boy.

But oh, how acutely she could understand his longing to do it!

Sadly aware that their friendship was irrevocably altered, she
searched out a needle and thread, and swiftly cobbled the length of
fabric into something that, with a pole attached, might possibly trap
a particularly slow-witted pigeon. As she finished, Herris
reappeared, looking much brighter, and carrying a large-lidded
wicker basket. 'I found this. Will it do?'

'It looks perfect,' Kefiri assured him. 'Now all we need is a
handle and a framework for the net.'

It took some time to make, and when it was ready Herris
seemed almost his usual self. He could never be down-hearted for
long, and she had already noticed that planning new strategies or
solving problems was a good way to cheer him up. They collected
some scraps of bread and a handful of precious grain from the
kitchen, and crept out into the courtyard.

It was still warm, but the sharp edge had gone from the heat,
and the strip of shade had widened by four or five paces across the
worn, uneven flagstones. Fortunately, there was no sign of Garool.
Herris scattered the corn in the remaining sunlight, within reach of
the net, and they settled down to wait.

Rather to Kefiri's surprise, it did not take long. The pigeons,
although apparently quite plump, were obviously tempted by the
offer of real grain, and flew down together to take advantage of it.
She knew she had only one chance, for today at least, and took it
with a swift accuracy that left Herris gaping with delighted admiration. 'All three at once! Well *done*, Kef!'

'I used to catch them at Sar D'yenyi sometimes, so I've had
some practice,' she told him, modestly pleased. 'Let's be careful
getting them into the basket – I'd hate them to escape now.'

But soon the birds, struggling and cooing indignantly, were
safely imprisoned, and Herris tied the lid down with a triumphant
smile. 'Ma will be pleased! What about Engris's pigeons? We could
go and get those now – if they're as easy to catch as these ones
were, it won't take long.'

'We need another basket. Two baskets, in fact, because that

one isn't suitable to carry them to Minassa in. They'll need food and water, and if you open the lid they might fly out.'

'There's another one in the storeroom that'd be better, but it needs mending,' Herris told her. 'I'll do it now, if you like. You go over to Engris's house, you remember where it is? In Magpie Lane in the Potters' Quarter. She's bound to have a suitable box or basket, and you don't need my help to catch them.'

There was still an hour or so before curfew, so Kefiri reduced the net to a bundle of cloth and a handful of sticks, and left Herris in the storeroom, wrestling with recalcitrant canes, while the captured pigeons made muffled protest from their basket beside him.

She walked down Snowbringer Street with a new sense of purpose. Despite everything, the problems, the danger, the worry, she could not be unhappy on such a golden evening. She called out greetings to those whom she knew, and hummed one of the merry, bouncing tunes always popular in taverns and workrooms all over Zithirian. Once in Sunset Street, however, she was careful not to draw attention to herself, and walked casually across the thoroughfare between the milling people.

'Hello!'

The hand on her sleeve made her jump and gasp, even though she already knew who it was. Bron's small pale face smiled up at her, the dark eyes reassuringly childish. 'Where are you going?' he asked, omitting the 'Lady', much to her relief.

'I'm going to see a friend in the Potters' Quarter. Do you both want to come?'

Lelya, hovering just behind Bron, looked eager, and she remembered Bron saying that he wanted to be a potter. 'Yes, please,' he said.

'We'll be your escort,' Bron added, with a rather comical effort at adult gravity. 'You shouldn't be walking about on your own, you know.'

'Why not? I do it every day.'

'You still shouldn't,' said Bron softly. 'I can't see you all the time – I can't keep you safe and hidden everywhere you go.'

The goose-flesh rose on Kefiri's arms, but she refrained from asking him what he meant. 'Come on, then,' she said, holding out her hands. 'Engris makes very good honey cakes, and we haven't got much time before curfew.'

With a child on each side, laughing, she dodged through the crowds on Sunset Street and down Vine Alley, a narrow, twisting lane between the cramped, packed houses of the Potters' Quarter.

There was a general air of poverty and seedy neglect in this area, and almost as many taverns as around the docks, but Kefiri knew that most of the people living here were hard-working and respectable. There were exceptions, of course, but this tortuous labyrinth of tiny houses and workshops was much safer than it looked.

Then why was Bron glancing back, his face suddenly white with fear?

She said, 'What's wrong?' at the same moment as he cried suddenly, 'Ska'i! The Ska'i are coming for us!'

Kefiri looked back. Sunset Street was out of sight now, and the alley behind them was empty, save for a woman and a child just stepping into their house, and a couple of shabbily-dressed men strolling towards them, deep in conversation.

'The *Ska'i*? But I can't see them, Bron—'

With a blood-freezing screech, a small band of tribesmen erupted round the corner, mounted on their shaggy ponies and waving their double-headed axes. The woman screamed and dragged her dawdling child inside, shutting the door with a slam that could be heard above the Ska'i's yelps of triumph. The two men, taken completely by surprise, stood thunderstruck in the middle of the alley, blocking the way. Horrified, Kefiri saw one of the Ska'i swing his arm, the flash of metal, and one of the men crashed to the ground like a felled tree. It took her two or three heartbeats to realize that the round, leaking object rolling under the ponies' hooves was in fact his head.

'Run!' she screamed at the two boys, and they obeyed her. Hardly more than a short spear's cast ahead of the Ska'i, they sprinted along the dusty alley. Ahead there was a public garden, surprisingly well tended, more house walls and a tavern, unoriginally called The Vine. No hiding places anywhere – the Ska'i would just lop innocent heads like harvest wheat if they tried to take refuge in there –

But a cluster of empty barrels and jars stood outside it, waiting to be removed for refilling, and a couple of wooden benches. Kefiri yelled, dived across, and hurled a bulbous jar into the path of the Ska'i. With wild screeches, Bron and Lelya did the same. The coarse red pottery smashed into sharp shards, and the leading pony trod on one, stumbled and went down heavily on its knees, pitching its rider right over its head. She did not wait to see what happened next: she ran on, the children beside her, trying desperately to think amid her overwhelming panic, while the yells of fury behind them mingled with the screams of the injured horse.

Another, much narrower alley crossed their path. She remem-

bered suddenly where the boys would be safe, and pulled them
down the left-hand opening. It was so restricted that she doubted
the Ska'i could ride along it, and her flapping skirts almost brushed
the high, roughly plastered walls on either side.

Something clattered behind them. She glanced back and saw a
Ska'i standing in his stirrups at the entrance, and a double axe
skidding along the hard earth almost at her heels. He screeched in
thwarted rage and leapt from his pony, wrenching his knife from its
scabbard.

Throat rasping, heart thudding, she ran on, behind the two
boys. This alley, if it didn't run into a dead end, must come out on
Minassa Way, the broad street that led down to the river and
separated the Potters' Quarter from the Merchants'. She cried
frantically, 'The Temple! Go straight back to the Temple! You'll be
safe there!'

Lelya lifted a hand briefly as he ran. Bron did not seem to have
heard her. She could not risk another look behind, but the Ska'i
must surely be gaining on them. A woman unused to running and
softened by city life, and two malnourished boys – what chance did
they have against such ruthless and ferocious pursuers?

There was a kink in the alley. Bron stopped running so suddenly
that Lelya almost cannoned into him, and banged his elbow on the
left hand wall. Kefiri, immediately behind him, yelled, 'Go on – go
on! What are you doing?'

She did not move a muscle of her own volition, but suddenly
she was sprawling painfully in the dust. As she struggled to sit up,
Bron pushed past her and thrust out his hands.

There was no sound, no flash of light, none of the usual and
terrifying accompaniments of sorcery. She saw the Ska'i running
towards them, knife in hand, another behind him brandishing his
axe, their mouths open, howling in triumph –

And then the walls on either side of the alley fell down on top
of them.

The roar of collapsing masonry went on for quite a while. Dust
and debris belched into the air, and rained down on Kefiri and the
two boys. Lelya was crouched beside her, his hands laced over his
head. She could feel him shaking with terror, his breaths coming in
huge, shuddering gasps.

But Bron stood still until some of the dust had cleared, and the
noise had died away into tiny trickles of pulverized mortar and
fragments of stone. Then he said quite calmly, 'It's all right –
they're dead. And it'll take the others a long time to get over all
that, I think.'

Coughing, brushing the dirt and dust out of her hair, Kefiri pulled herself to her feet. The contrast between this awesomely self-possessed child and the frightened waif whom she had first befriended was appalling. She stared at the great heap of stones and rubble, at least twice Bron's height, with a mixture of terror and relief. He was right, the two Ska'i buried underneath that pile were surely dead, but there was no point in lingering here. At the very least, the owners of the fallen walls would have some awkward questions, and she didn't want to have to answer them.

She touched Bron's arm, not without some trepidation, and a certain amount of awed respect. 'Come on – let's go now, while we have the chance.'

Trying to shake and sweep the worst of the dust from their clothes, they hurried round the kink in the alley, out of sight of the debris. Ahead, there was space and sunlight opening between the walls. Minassa Way – and the Temple would be in sight to the left, three hundred paces distant.

She took the two boys by the hand, and they stepped together out into the sunshine. There was no sign of pursuit from the shadowed alley they had just left, but Kefiri wasn't taking any risks. She walked briskly up the street, ignoring the curious glances of passers-by at their dishevelled and dirty appearance.

'They wanted me,' Bron said suddenly. His fingers clutched at hers with painful force. 'They wanted me, didn't they?'

'I don't know, sweetheart,' Kefiri told him, although she was sure that he was right. 'They could just have been looking for someone to chase, for a bit of fun perhaps.'

The small, dusty blond head shook violently in denial. 'No, they didn't. They've found out about me. They want me.' He glanced up at her, and she saw the shock and fear in his white face. 'There's nowhere I can hide. I can't hide myself yet.'

'You'll be safe in the Temple,' Kefiri said robustly, with an encouraging cheerfulness that was entirely feigned. 'They wouldn't dare try and get you out of there. Your gran—'

'She'll keep me there for ever and ever now.' He shivered suddenly, and she saw tears in his eyes. 'She might even try to Bind me like she did Grandfather, and then I wouldn't be any use to anyone else. I don't want to, I don't want to stay there for ever and ever, it's so dark!'

The tragedy of it struck at her with sudden and heart-rending force. A child so full of sorcery that he could cause the deaths of two men with a single gesture, and remain apparently unmoved by their fate: and who yet was afraid of the dark.

'Oh, Bron,' she said on a sob, and in the middle of Minassa Way pulled him into her arms. 'Oh, Bron, you'll be safe there – you only have to bear it for just a little while longer, and then you'll be free.' When Ansaryon comes, and the Ska'i and Tsenit and D'thliss are all defeated or dead, she thought, with fierce and desperate hope.

'No,' said Bron. He had stopped crying, and his dark eyes stared up at her with terrible sadness. 'No – I don't think I shall ever be free.'

And she did not think that it was just freedom from D'thliss that he meant.

She walked with them right up to the Temple gate, and Lelya took Bron's hand and led him firmly within. She hovered under the frost-slain trees, watching until they were out of sight, with the memory of their thanks and of Bron's dirty, tear-streaked, desperate face still agonizingly clear in her mind. Then, her knees shaking and her heart still pounding erratically, she made her way slowly back to Snowbringer Street.

Kaydi opened the door before her hand had touched the latch, and stared at her, frowning anxiously. 'Where have you been? There are Ska'i all over the city, I was worried sick – something's upset 'em, the Potters' Quarter is all in uproar and they've killed someone just for getting in their way, Stekketh said—' She stopped, and said, as if she had only just noticed the girl's dishevelled appearance, 'What's happened? Are you all right? You look as if a house fell on you! And where's Herris?'

'*Herris?*' Kefiri stared at her in bewilderment. 'I went out on my own – I left him here, he was in the storeroom, mending a basket for the pigeons.'

'Oh, Sarraliss preserve him,' Kaydi whispered, her hands going to her face in horror. 'I thought he was with you – he isn't here – he's gone!'

Kefiri brushed past her, and ran for the storeroom, Kaydi at her heels. She peered into all the corners, behind jars and tubs and boxes, but it was obviously empty.

'He *was* in here,' she said despairingly at last. 'There's the cane he was using, and there's the basket he was going to mend – and the pigeons were in another basket, there.'

'Well, they've gone, and so has he.' Kaydi gave the cane a furious kick. 'You know what the stupid brat's gone and done, don't you?'

'I *told* him not to!' Kefiri cried, seeing distress and angry accusation mingled in the older woman's face. 'I *told* him, over and over again! I thought he'd seen sense – I'd never have left him if I'd thought he'd run away!'

'Well, he didn't, and you shouldn't,' Kaydi said bluntly. 'We'd better find him now, before the curfew. We haven't got long, but he can't have gone far. Hurry, girl!'

Her weariness forgotten in the desperate urgency of finding Herris, Kefiri ran out into Snowbringer Street. Kaydi was right, there was hardly any time left before curfew. The sun had dropped well below the level of the surrounding houses, and only the tall Palace tower, soaring above the roof-tops in front of her, was still flushed with a rich, red-gold light.

Without a thought in her head beyond finding Herris, she ran down the street, brushing heedlessly past people hurrying home, and out into the broad space of Sunset Street, still busy with passers-by. The docks, she thought, fighting panic. If he's going to carry out his plan, and hide in the cemetery, he'll have gone to the ferry at the docks.

The great white and gold bulk of the Temple, where she had left Bron and Lelya only a short while ago, loomed in front of her, blocking her path. With a sharp ache in her side, her breath rasping in her raw throat, she slowed to a walk and glanced behind. There was no sign of Kaydi – perhaps she'd better wait for her.

But if she did, there would be no chance of finding and stopping Herris. She drew a deep, ragged, despairing breath and broke once more into a run round the curved side of the great building, heart and centre, but not soul, of Zithirian.

Soldiers were coming the other way, not Ska'i, but Royal Guard. Consumed by the need to find the boy, she hardly noticed them. Ahead, an imposing inn called The Firebird, with a handsome sign in white and silver, marked the corner of the short wide thoroughfare leading down to the docks. Praying that she would catch him, she increased her pace, and found a line of soldiers suddenly blocking her way.

'Stop!'

Too late, she tried to dodge, felt her sleeve grabbed, wrenched it frantically free, managed two steps and found herself seized by a couple of huge guardsmen, one on either side. Struggling was utterly pointless; she hung in their grasp, sweat-soaked, gasping, and wondered in despair how Herris could possibly be stopped now.

'And where are you off to in such a hurry at this time of day, eh?'

The officer's voice was not unkind, and she did not recognize him. Perhaps there was still a chance. She said breathlessly, 'I'm looking – for my little brother – he's run off and I've *got* to find him before curfew – *please* let me go!'

There was no doubt of her sincerity, or her desperation. The tall guardsman looked down at her, fingering his lip, and she could see that he thought she was no more than a child herself. 'Where do you think he has gone?' he asked. 'What does he look like?'

'He often goes down by the docks – he's a bit younger than me, he's small and thin with light brown hair and he's wearing a blue tunic – oh, please, *please* let me go and look for him!'

The officer smiled. 'Very well. You'd better be quick, though. You haven't got much time. I'll keep a look out for him on patrol. What's his name?'

Before she could reply, a new voice cut like a knife between them. 'That's her! Don't let her go!'

The High Priestess of Tayo, in her white and silver robes, pushed through the soldiers. Although twice her size, they fell back, avoiding her eyes and her touch as though both carried poison.

Kefiri stared into the Annatal-ravaged face of D'thliss, on whom her cousin Ansaryon had laid the curse of Ayak, and who was the real ruler of Zithirian, and knew the true meaning of fear.

'Are you blind?' The Priestess's voice spat contempt. 'You were told what to look for – young, small, long dark hair, blue eyes, green dress. What's that standing in front of you, fool?'

The officer glanced apologetically down at Kefiri. The soldiers' grip had tightened convulsively and painfully on her arms, and she wondered remotely if she might faint. D'thliss came right up to her, so that she could smell the stale reek of the drug that gave her such power, and see the lined, shrivelled face surrounding the hideously impenetrable gaze that seemed to reach out and suck her soul away . . .

'Yes, it's her all right – I'd know her anywhere. And you've never seen her before?'

'N – no, Most Wise.'

'Blockhead. His High Mightiness has no use for idiots like you in his Guard, and I shall tell him so. What's your name?'

'Andrik, Most Wise.'

'I shall remember it. Well, now you have your prey, you can take her up to the Palace. They'll be expecting you. And if you let her go again, your life won't be worth a candle-stub. I shall follow shortly. Now go!'

It was not surprising that D'thliss had recognized her, for Kefiri had been a Temple student. But how had the High Priestess known what she was wearing, and that she would be here, now, by the Temple?

Sorcery, of course. Sorcery, through the medium of a child called Bron.

Kefiri managed to look round as she was hauled away. A crowd had gathered, at a respectful distance. She heard cries of 'Shame!' 'Pick on someone your own size!' 'What's she done?' 'Let her go, you brutes!'

Two of the younger soldiers turned on them threateningly, spears levelled, and the people backed away. Amongst the shifting, hostile faces she saw Kaydi's, so at least Herris's mother would know what had happened to her. For a wild moment, Kefiri thought of shouting out who she was. The crowd was sympathetic, and if they knew her identity they would surely come to her aid.

But the consequences might be tragic. Her vivid imagination pictured the sharp steel-tipped spears impaling the unarmed men, women and children, and then leapt on to the results of a premature uprising, all too likely given the mood of the citizens, and its brutal repression by the Royal Guard and the Ska'i before Ansaryon could even gather his army together . . .

So she kept her mouth shut, praying that Kaydi would do the same, and offered no resistance. They were not particularly gentle, despite the fact that she hardly came up to the shortest soldier's chin, and must have been half his weight. She could not see what was happening behind her, but she knew that an increasing crowd must be following them up the Ceremonial Way towards the Palace. She could hear the swelling chorus of disapproval, the insults and abuse shouted freely against the soldiers, Tsenit and the Temple: and the angry threats of the Captain in response. Please don't do anything stupid, she begged Kaydi and the citizens silently. Please don't, or all our plans will be ruined.

The Palace Gate had been roughly mended, but still showed the scars of the night of slaughter which had ended the lives of her father, her uncle and her cousins, as well as hundreds of their courtiers, guards and servants. She was pulled roughly through it, to a surging howl of rage from the crowd behind her. The great doors swung together, and the bar came down with an ominous crash.

Kefiri was in the Palace, and no doubt she would soon be facing her cousin Tsenit, whom she had once wanted to marry. And quite probably, this time tomorrow she would be dead.

It seemed curious that at this terrible moment, her main feeling should be not fear, but disappointed anger. Anger with herself, for being captured so easily: disappointment, that she would never know what would happen now, or how the events which she and Ansaryon, Kaydi and Herris had set in motion would turn out. Would the pigeons arrive safely at Minassa? Had the Toktel'yans agreed to help? Would Ansaryon's army come in time? And, most vital of all, would it defeat the Ska'i and free the city from Tsenit's oppressive rule?

She would never know, and she could have wept with frustration.

Despite the speed with which she was being rushed through the tortuous passages of the Palace, she was still able to notice the indelible signs of Ska'i violence: burn-marks, hacked and slashed plaster, defaced murals, bloodstains on the floor and walls. Once, too, these corridors had teemed with servants in livery, men and women rustling in their Court finery, going about their business or just passing the time of day. Now, the long echoing passages were almost empty. They encountered only two men, both in the bright blue tunics and gowns of upper servants, who stared curiously as Kefiri, filthy and bedraggled, was dragged past in the grip of the burly soldiers.

Only three years ago, of course, she had been familiar with this building, but somehow nothing looked the same now, and it all seemed so dark. None of the lamps had been lit, though the sun had set and the curfew horn had blared out just after they'd entered the Palace. But suddenly they came upon a place she did recognize, for the curved walls and arching staircase were unmistakable. Up there, in the great Central Tower, was Tsenit. And with him, her fate.

By now, she was exhausted both by the fear of what she faced, and by the terrible events of the afternoon. Was it really only a few hours since she and Kaydi and Herris had been discussing pigeons in the peaceful warmth of the courtyard in the house on Snow-bringer Street? The steep curling flight of steps, snaking up into the walls of the tower, was almost more than she could manage. She tripped, and nearly fell, and after that the soldiers were slower, and more gentle. She wondered if it was the thought of D'thliss that had earlier made them so frantic with haste.

They approached the door to the Council Chamber. She remembered the graceful dancing storks carved in its panels. Something, probably a Ska'i axe, had slashed across the delicately outlined legs. The officer opened it with a flourish, and she was pushed inside.

There were lamps lit here, and she blinked in the increased light. Around the long table were ranged perhaps a dozen men, only two of whom she recognized. One, Seardrith, was General of the Royal Guard, a man with an unpleasant reputation for ruthlessness and brutality.

And at the head of the table sat her cousin Tsenit, Third of His Name, King of Zithirian by right of treachery and murder.

The soldiers let her go, and she rubbed the tingling blood back into her bruised arms. Then they backed away to stand in ceremonial pose against the curved walls, leaving her alone in the middle of the chamber.

'At long last – my dear little cousin!' Tsenit rose to his feet with the athletic grace she remembered so well. His face, however, no longer wore that look of handsome smugness. To her considerable satisfaction, Kefiri saw printed on the regular, deceptively pleasant features the unmistakable marks of tiredness, anxiety and stress.

Good, she thought vindictively. I'm glad to see that he's not enjoying his ill-gotten gains.

As he approached, she stared at him with open contempt and hostility. 'I may be little, but I am certainly not dear to you – and I am shamed by the relationship between us, you murdering usurper.'

Tsenit stopped in his tracks, and she saw surprise and anger battling in his face. He said in bewilderment, 'Kef? Come on, now, Kef, we were friends – we were betrothed—'

'One of the bigger mistakes in my life,' she told him furiously. 'How dare you stand there and pretend to friendship? You had almost your whole family slaughtered – including my father.'

Tsenit's eyes shifted slightly. 'Believe me, Kef, that was not my doing. You know what the Ska'i are like – murder was no part of my plan—'

'If I'm expected to know what they're like, then so did you, you lying snake!' Possessed by a sudden surge of rage, she walked up to him and struck him as hard as she could across the face.

The sound echoed through the chamber. As two soldiers pulled her away from him, she had the vast satisfaction of seeing his split lip begin to well blood. He put a hand to the place and stared at the red mark on his fingers. With sudden fear, she saw his face flush with wild fury. 'You'll pay for this before you're done, you little bitch! Take her away, take her below, and give her nothing, d'you hear me? *Nothing*, no food, no water, no light, no bedding. Let her rot down there until she's more docile.'

Kefiri had heard terrible rumours of these prison cells, concealed deep beneath the central tower. She had never, even in her most dreadful nightmares, expected to occupy one of them herself. She was dragged down and down and down into the darkness, smelling of damp and decay and foulness, and thrust into a hole quarried out of the rock on which the Palace had been built. The floor was wet and uneven, and she fell, banging her knees and elbows painfully. A barrier clanged shut with the implacable ring of iron, and she was left alone.

Darkness, impenetrable, suffocating. A space hardly more than a crack between rocks, in which it was almost impossible to lie down. No straw, no bucket, no water, no food – nothing. And, worst of all, the distant and piteous cries of others who had been incarcerated here, perhaps for months.

She wanted to break, to weep, but she could not allow herself to give Tsenit and his guards the satisfaction. With difficulty, she pulled her underskirt off and wrapped it round her shoulders, both for extra warmth and to alleviate, a little, the bitter and unyielding discomfort of the rocks. Then she curled up on the cold hard floor and closed her eyes. And surprisingly soon, despite her discomfort and despair, she gave way to exhaustion, and slept.

TWENTY-FOUR

He had thought of everything, he was sure. The pigeons, quiet in their cloth-covered basket, slumbered peacefully beside him. He had a bag of grain, a water container – empty, there was no point in lugging it around full when the Kefirinn was only a few paces away – and some food for himself. He had even remembered to filch one of his mother's precious kitchen knives. Now all he needed was a boat.

The curfew horn had blasted out its message at sunset, echoing round the city. Well-hidden within a patch of bushes and thick scrub just by the river edge of the cemetery, Herris knew he was quite safe. He had watched, rather wistfully, as the last boat left with its cargo of mourners, and rowed across the sluggish, summer-low Kefirinn to the docks on the other side. He heard distant voices, dogs barking, someone playing a Sith. As darkness fell, lights began to appear in the remaining tower of the Royal Palace, but in the city, where all windows looked inwards into courtyards, there seemed to be no illumination at all.

'Hegeden curse him,' Herris muttered, with a rude gesture at the distant tower and its royal occupant. He waited until darkness was complete, and then picked up his few belongings and crept down to the jetty.

And encountered his first real stroke of luck – there was a boat still there. He could see it plainly, a rounded darker shape against the pale, star-lit river. Probably its owner, for reasons best known to himself, was still somewhere in the cemetery. It had always been a popular place for young men to take their girls, away from disapproving parental eyes, and although there weren't many young men left now in Zithirian, Herris knew some still came there for that purpose. He listened intently. Was that a giggle he heard, very distantly amongst the furthest tombs?

If it was, the boat's owner was hardly likely to have his attention focused on his craft. Herris slunk down the jetty, peering intently into the darkness. The starlight was quite adequate for one whose eyes were used to it, and he was less likely to be seen.

He found where the boat was tied up, and pulled it gently in. It wasn't a ferry, being much fatter and shorter than those slender craft, and probably only meant to carry two people. To his relief, its owner had left the oars in it. He dropped the water bottle and the bags of food and grain down into the bow, and followed them carefully. The little vessel rocked under his weight, and the slap of wood on water sounded fearfully loud in the night stillness.

No going back now. He lifted the basket of pigeons into the boat, placing it with great care in the stern. Then, with trembling hands, he unknotted the rope and pushed off.

As he had expected, once out into the stream it was easy. The current took his humble vessel into its graceful grasp, and swept it downstream with surprising speed. He glanced back. The walls and towers of Zithirian lay dense and black against the stars. There were no yells of rage from the bank. He had done it: he was free.

Too exhilarated to feel tired, Herris took up an oar and sat in the stern, letting the river do the work, steering the single blade when necessary. Zithirian was rapidly receding behind him. By morning, he would be far enough away from it to be quite safe, even from marauding bands of Ska'i.

Eyes bright and a huge joyful excitement filling his heart, Herris stared eagerly into the gloom ahead, where Minassa lay, three hundred miles to the south.

'I say she stays there – for ever, if need be!'

'And I say let her out. Now.'

The King of Zithirian glared at his High Priestess. D'thliss, unmoved, glared back. 'If you leave her there out of sheer spite, that thick lip will cost you the throne.'

'She insulted me – she *hit* me, for Tayo's sake, in front of all my Council! I can't let that go unpunished, I'd be a laughing stock – and I'd have no authority left at all.'

'Have you any now?' asked D'thliss nastily. 'Listen to me, your High Mightiness, and listen well. Your rule is crumbling. When Ansaryon's army arrives, you'll be in real danger of defeat. And I have no intention of letting you go down, and dragging me with you. I have delivered Kefiri into your hands. Now make use of her.'

'How?' Tsenit cried in exasperation.

'Ayak give me strength!' The witch beat the table between them with her fist. 'You marry her, of course, you fool!'

Tsenit's mouth dropped. '*Marry* her? But I've asked for the Emperor's daughter—'

'He won't give her to you – not until you've defeated Ansaryon, anyway. But marrying your cousin Kefiri will be much more advantageous, at present.'

'How? She's turned into a proper little shrew, and I don't want her. She isn't even pretty any more.'

'Pretty? K'djelk isn't pretty either, I can assure you. You blockhead, haven't you the mind you were born with? After Ansaryon, Kefiri is your only, your *only* heir. Kill him, and she is left to carry on resistance – which by the look of her, she'll be only too willing to do.'

'So I kill her.'

'And make yourself even more unpopular? It won't be long before word gets out of who she is. If the people discover you've slain Tayma's seventeen-year-old daughter in cold blood, your name will be reviled for ever more, and you'll never win back that popularity you crave so desperately. Like as not, you'll be assassinated sooner or later, and the First Line of the Children of Tayo will end with you. Is *that* what you want, your High Mightiness?'

Tsenit flushed at her sneering contempt. He muttered resentfully, 'No, it isn't.'

'Didn't think it was,' D'thliss said. 'But if you marry her . . . all Zithiriani love a good wedding.' The derision in her voice deepened. 'Give 'em a nice romantic tale of true love against all the odds, a bit of spectacle to lighten their days, and they'll be eating out of your hand. Marry her, and get a child on her as soon as possible to make your dynasty certain. *Then*, if you like, you can kill her – easy enough to make it look as if she died in childbirth, or of a summer fever. And if K'djelk still appeals to you, you can make her your second wife. Or have one of Belerith's daughters, or Temiltan's. They're all descended from Tayo, you can pick and choose at your leisure. But I'm telling you to marry Kefiri *now*. After all, the Emperor has already promised K'djelk to Ansaryon. He's given him five thousand soldiers, so why not his daughter as well?'

'And you really think that marrying that little bitch of a cousin will help me?'

'Her blow really rankles, doesn't it?' D'thliss observed spitefully. 'Well, it's in your hands, boy. I've set out the advantages and disadvantages clearly enough. And think about it in another way. If you don't want to marry her, you can be pretty sure she doesn't want to marry *you*. You'll get the chance for some sweet revenge on the wedding night, don't you think? And she'll be as much your prisoner, as much at your mercy, as she is now in that stinking hole under the rocks.'

Reluctantly, Tsenit did think about it. He had to admit that the prospect of Kefiri, defiant, angry, dragged into a marriage utterly repugnant to her, was an enticing one. He liked the idea of forcing a woman who screamed and struggled but still had to submit to his superior strength and power. And with a wife who hated him, who had plotted against him and who could be expected to betray him at the first opportunity, he would be perfectly justified in venting on her helpless body and mind all the pent-up anger, frustration and bitterness that had built up inside him ever since his rule had begun to turn sour. He needed his Councillors, he needed the citizens, he needed D'thliss – the good will and support of all of them were essential if he wanted to keep the throne and defeat Ansaryon. But a wife whom he disliked, a wife thrust on him by circumstance and expediency, was quite a different matter.

Yes, he would enjoy making Kefiri's life a misery.

'Very well,' he said at last, his tone of grudging and reluctant consent belying the eager anticipation in his eyes. 'I'll marry her. It seems there's little to lose, and much to gain.'

'Excellent,' D'thliss said with satisfaction. 'I knew you'd see sense.' She smiled mockingly. 'I congratulate you on your impending nuptials, your High Mightiness. When are the celebrations to take place? Soon, I trust.'

'There will be a great many things to organize,' Tsenit said, thinking of the pageantry, the spectacle and above all the expense of a royal wedding in the expectedly lavish style. And a great deal of money to be spent, he added to himself. Money which he did not have: gold which was still sitting in Sar D'yenyi and in the mountain mines, and the missing proceeds from the trade with Minassa and Toktel'yi which had dried up once the depredations of the Ska'i became notorious.

But of course, he remembered, Kefiri was the Lady of Sar D'yenyi – and once he married her, all that gold would legally become his by right.

Until then, though, he would have to improvise, somehow. If this marriage was to achieve its principal aim, and win over the hearts of the citizens, it must not be some mean, hole-in-the-corner affair undertaken only grudgingly. He must play his part, the part of a happy and loving bridegroom. And Kefiri must be persuaded into at least the semblance of consent.

'Don't worry,' D'thliss said, with one of her most unpleasant cackles. 'There are drugs that will ensure she complies in public – and they'll wear off before nightfall, so you'll have that to look forward to.'

Tsenit regarded her with a mixture of awe and horror. The ease with which she seemed to peer inside the murkier depths of his soul had never ceased to terrify him. He might make a pretence of defying her, but he was her tool, her creature, and at the dark base of his heart he knew it. There was, however, some consolation in store for him. He would be able to inflict on Kefiri some of the feelings of powerlessness and humiliation that D'thliss aroused in him.

'How about the full moon after next?' he suggested tentatively.

'Too late,' D'thliss said. 'Don't you listen? Ansaryon's army is coming. In less than half a month they'll be here. It has to be before this full moon – six or seven days, your High Mightiness, to plan a sumptuous celebration that will remain in the happy memories of your citizens for the rest of their lives. Well, you'd better hurry up. I suggest you tell the lucky bride of her destiny, and her good fortune. I shall see you again soon. Goodbye.'

With the complete lack of ceremony that had always annoyed him so much, she turned and strode across his private chamber to the door. It opened at a peremptory tap of her bone and silver staff, and she disappeared through it.

As always, once out of her presence Tsenit felt bigger, taller, stronger. He took several deep breaths, and then called for his Chamberlain.

After a slight but irritating interval, Sathen appeared. He was a wealthy merchant who had long nursed ambitions of power, and lacked the aristocratic breeding to obtain it. Tsenit's seizure of the throne had given him his opportunity, and he had grasped it eagerly. He made his obeisance. 'Your High Mightiness commands?'

'The Lady Kefiri – I have new plans for her.' Tsenit licked his lips, thinking of those plans. Already, his resentment was evaporating, and he was looking forward to forcing himself on his cousin. 'I want her taken out of the cell now. Have her cleaned up and made presentable – there must be a gown somewhere that she can wear. Then have her brought to me in the Council Chamber.'

The Chamberlain had been present at the Council meeting earlier, and his eyebrows rose in surprise. However, he clasped his hands to his breast and bowed. 'As your High Mightiness wishes it, so it shall be done.'

Kefiri was roused from her exhausted, uncomfortable sleep by the tramp of feet and the rattling of metal. She sat up too suddenly, and banged her head on a lump of rock above her. As she gasped, her eyes watering in pain, a lantern dazzled her, and a voice said brusquely, 'Come on, out.'

She crawled, because the cell was too low to stand, and was hauled roughly upright as she emerged. 'What's happening?' she demanded. 'Where are you taking me?'

'You'll see soon enough,' said the guard, in a voice not intended to encourage further questions.

Dazed, her head ringing from the encounter with the rock, she stumbled back up the steep, uneven, slippery steps that led back to sanity, and the light. Behind her, she could hear the wails and protests of the other prisoners.

When Ansaryon becomes King, I'll tell him to fill that hole with rubble and rocks so that no one ever rots down there again, she thought furiously. She tripped over the last step, and the guards wrenched her upright with a curse. They pulled her through an arched doorway at the top, and into the civilized part of the Palace.

At last, when she thought that her arms would soon be pulled from their sockets, they arrived in front of a plain door. She had no idea where she was: it could have been anywhere on the ground floor of the Palace, but from the absence of elaborate decoration, it was probably in the servants' quarters. All the royal apartments, apart from the central tower, had been devastated by the Ska'i.

This room had not. This room, though small, had a bed, and a chair, and best and most astonishing of all, a round wooden bath-tub full of steaming aromatic water.

Kefiri could not think what this meant: she could not think at all. Completely bewildered, she stood and stared at the comfort and warmth laid out for her benefit, and felt dangerously close to tears.

A girl in servant's blue stepped forward, smiling kindly. The guards left, with much tramping of feet and jingling of armour, but she knew they would be standing outside to prevent any escape.

And there was no escape. Where could she go, in this confusing labyrinth? Where could she hide? And who, here in Tsenit's lair, would help her?

She would not break – she would not. Kefiri held her head proudly high, and allowed herself to be divested of her filthy, ragged clothes and helped into the bath.

The blissful feel of the warm water was almost as welcome as it had been on that first day in Kaydi's house, months ago. But here there was the quiet, smiling maid to wash her, and dry her, and array her clean fresh body in garments finer than any she had worn, even in Sar D'yenyi. An under-robe of softest, lightest cream silk;

a gown to go over it, in a glorious vivid blue, heavily embroidered over the skirt with a pattern of flowers in gold thread; and finally, rather drowning her scanty figure, a stiffly boned silk bodice, encrusted with jewels.

By now, an awful suspicion was beginning to dawn on Kefiri, but she had no intention of disclosing her fear to the girl beside her. Her wet hair was combed, twisted, pulled and dressed into an elaborate style very different from the simple ribbon with which it had been bound at Kaydi's house. Then, her heart pounding and her knees still weak beneath the heavy blue folds of silk, she was ushered from the room and given into the custody of the guards again.

This time, they treated her with more respect, and did not touch her. In their midst, she walked down more corridors, endless, in the flickering light of the lamps, so that she began to feel that she was adrift in some terrible nightmare, or that she had died unawares and was doomed henceforth to wander the bowels of the Palace, forever guarded, forever fated never to reach her destination.

But arrive she did, at last, at the foot of the stairs in the central tower. Almost too tired to move, she toiled upwards, feeling no urge to climb any faster. For she knew who was waiting for her: and she knew, too, what he must want of her.

But it was to the Council Chamber that she was led, and brought inside with rather more deference than a few hours ago. And there at the table sat all the men who had faced her before: and, rising to greet her, the man whom she hated above all others. For Quenait had never pretended to be anything other than a brutal savage, whereas her false cousin had turned on his own family and friends, and betrayed them.

'Ah, Kefiri,' said Tsenit, smiling. She saw the spark of greed in his eyes, and managed to hide her fear. 'The rest has done you good. You look so much better than you did earlier – and very beautiful. Servants and members of my Council, may I present to you Kefiri, daughter of the late and lamented Lord Tayma, and Lady of Sar D'yenyi. Gentlemen, this is the future Queen of Zithirian.'

The Lord Ansaryon, with his army of Zithiriani, Toktel'yans, Lelyentans, Tanathi and Minassans, had set out from their camp at Chearno some days after his arrival. The force, nearly eight thousand men in all, had been carefully deployed. Half the Toktel'yans marched in perfect step in the van, and the other half brought up the rear. The rest, most of them soldiers who had only received their military training that summer, made up the centre of the army. The six hundred Tanathi, well-mounted, fast and courageous, were given scout duties, riding along the steppe's edge several miles in advance of the main body, to guard against a surprise attack.

But there had been no sign of the Ska'i, although Temiltan had warned Ansaryon that Quenait had sent patrols and raiding parties almost as far south as the border with Minassa, earlier in the year. At the town of Hailyan, marking where the two states met, they were told that there had been no sign of the barbarians now for two or three months. The terraced vineyards on the south-facing slopes above the town were groaning with fat purple and golden grapes, and the inhabitants, greeting the army with uninhibited joy, looked well-fed and prosperous. They camped beside the river, and the town's Governor, a local wine-merchant, offered the army the best food that Hailyan could provide, plus unlimited quantities of last year's vintage, a good one despite the early onset of winter.

Ansaryon accepted most of the gift, but regretfully declined the wine: speed on this march was of the utmost importance, and his men wouldn't be able to manage thirty miles tomorrow after a night spent enjoying the potent product of those famous grapes. And even if the Ska'i hadn't come this far south for some time, there was still a good chance that they might attack tomorrow, or the next day. Clear heads would be essential, despite the Governor's generosity.

The tent he shared with Invan and Temiltan was pitched at the centre of the camp, and the disparate forces of the Alliance settled themselves around it. The Governor of Hailyan, a fat and fussy little man, had expressed a desire to inspect the liberating soldiers for himself, and Ansaryon, mindful of the need to reassure his subjects, had taken him across to see the Toktel'yans, leaving his uncle and his general deep in strategic conversation in their tent.

'Sir – Sir! Someone from Zithirian to see you, Sir!'

Temiltan broke off his discussion with Invan and looked enquiringly at the young messenger standing in the tent doorway. 'From *Zithirian*? An ambassador from Tsenit?'

'No, Sir – at least, I don't think so, Sir. To be honest, Sir, I don't know much about him.' The boy looked rather sheepish, and shuffled his feet. 'He's just arrived at Hailyan in a boat. Do you want to see him now, Sir?'

Temiltan glanced at Invan, whose fair and handsome face was showing signs of considerable interest. 'Yes, indeed, Dirdjen. But if he has any news, the Lord Ansaryon should hear it too. I think he went over to the Toktel'yan part of the camp. Find him, and tell him that this man's arrived.'

'Yes, Sir.' The messenger hesitated. 'But – it isn't a man, Sir, it's a boy. I think he must be younger than I am.'

'Younger than you? Hegeden's wings!' Temiltan said in astonishment. 'And came all the way from Zithirian – in a *boat*? On his own?'

'I think so, Sir.'

'A brave, determined and capable boy, obviously,' Temiltan said, leaning back. 'Well, let's hope he has interesting news. I should find the Lord Ansaryon as soon as possible, Dirdjen – go on, don't stand there gawping, look sharp!'

'Yes, Sir,' the boy said, and ran out.

'He must have some very pressing reason for coming here,' Invan said thoughtfully. 'Let's hope it's not just a boyish desire for adventure.'

'Even if it is, he must be able to tell us a great deal about the present situation in Zithirian,' Temiltan pointed out. 'Most of our information is stale. The main flood of refugees stopped once winter ended – there haven't been more than a dozen since High Summer. The Ska'i patrols pick them off, coming south.'

'Why? Surely a few fugitives can't do them any harm.'

'Not to our mind, no. But the Ska'i are savages, remember. Their favourite game is man-hunting. Those who were lucky enough to escape them had some very unpleasant stories to tell, believe me. I'm a peaceable man, Invan, willing to live and let live, but there's no doubt the world would be a better place without the Ska'i in it. Brutal, ugly, bloodthirsty, cruel, utterly callous and ruthless – as far as I can make out, they haven't got a single redeeming feature. Pity Ayak can't be persuaded to take the lot of them now. It would certainly save us the trouble.'

'I couldn't agree more.' Invan's face was grim. 'Though I must say, it cheers me to think of the dance they must be leading Tsenit. He took the wolf by the tail with a vengeance. I'll wager you he's been regretting it bitterly for months, and even that is far better than the man deserves.'

'I trust you're not referring to me?' Ansaryon, his eyes bright with mischief and elation, ducked into the tent and grinned at his uncle and his General. 'If you are, I shall just have to pretend I didn't hear anything.'

'Of course not.' Temiltan waved a hand at the vacant chair, a folding one with stamped leather seat and back, its uncomfortable design barely disguised by several soft cushions. 'No, we were talking about your delightful younger brother, and the problems he must be having with the Ska'i. I'd be tempted to send them packing, if I were him.'

'He can't. He hasn't got the military strength to eject them – and besides, he needs them to fight us, and to take Sar D'yenyi this winter. *If* he gets the opportunity, of course.' Ansaryon flung himself down in the chair and rested his feet on an upholstered stool. The long march had burned away the effects of soft and idle living in Toktel'yi: to Temiltan's shrewdly observant eyes, he looked hard, fit and formidable. 'Well?' he added. 'Where's this boy your messenger was telling me about?'

He arrived a little later, looking weary and rather bewildered. He was indeed very young, no more than thirteen or fourteen, with a shock of ragged light-brown hair and a thin, sharp face, at once reckless and intelligent. His narrow hazel eyes darted round the tent and its occupants, taking everything in, before resting finally and intently upon Ansaryon. Then he went down on one knee, hands clasped to his chest in the Zithiriani posture of obeisance to royalty.

No one had knelt to Ansaryon for nearly a year. He glanced at Invan, and then got up and touched the boy's shoulder. 'There's no need for that. I'm neither Chosen nor Crowned, yet. And even when I am, there will be changes. Sit down on that stool.'

His eyes wide with awe and surprise, the boy obeyed. 'Thank you, your High – thank you very much.'

'That's better.' Ansaryon returned to his chair, forsaking his previous relaxed posture for one of alert interest. 'First of all, what's your name, and where do you live?'

'Herris Gandar's Son, sir, of Snowbringer Street in the Embroiderers' Quarter.'

Only the night before last, he had left Zithirian, embarking on his greatest adventure with high hope, but also considerable trepidation. And it had gone better than he could possibly have dreamed. No Ska'i had appeared, and his little craft had avoided all hazards. The pigeons too had all survived the indignities of their basket, and were being cared for by one of Temiltan's soldiers, who had worked in the Royal Pigeon House in Minassa.

And now he was sitting in the Lord Ansaryon's own tent, with two kings and a General hanging on his words as if he were an Imperial Ambassador instead of a runaway boy.

'Why did you come here, Herris?'

'I brought some pigeons, Sir.'

The three men facing him registered varying degrees of surprise. '*Pigeons?*' Ansaryon said. 'Live ones?'

'Yes, Sir. You see, we thought – well, Kefiri thought – they could carry messages in and out of the city. And I was going to take some birds from Minassa back with me—'

'And who is Kefiri? Your sister?'

'Oh, no, Sir – sorry, the *Lady* Kefiri. Of Sar D'yenyi,' he added helpfully.

There was a brief, stunned silence. Then the big solid blond man, the General, whom Herris thought he recognized as a former officer in the Royal Guard, said carefully, 'But the Lady Kefiri – Lord Tayma's daughter – we left her in Sar D'yenyi.'

'I know, Sir – but she's in Zithirian now, she's been staying with me and my Ma since before High Summer.'

Ansaryon let out his breath in an explosive rush. 'She shouldn't be in Zithirian at all. What in Tayo's name possessed her to go there? She couldn't have chosen anywhere in the known world more dangerous.'

'She came to tell us about you, Sir,' Herris said. 'And I found her – well, Bron found her – I didn't know who she was then—'

'*Bron?*'

Ansaryon was staring at him with such appalled horror on his face that Herris shrank. 'Yes, Sir – Bron. I know he lives in the Temple, but he's all right really. He and Lelya are friends of mine. Why? Do you know him, Sir?'

'You could say that we're acquainted,' Ansaryon told him. He rose and walked over to the boy's stool. 'Stand up, Herris Gandar's Son, and look at me.'

Obeying him took more courage than Herris had known he possessed. His knees suddenly shaking, he lifted his head and stared into the King's eyes. They were a strange colour, a pale glittering silver-grey, and eerily compelling. Too late, he remembered that the Lord Ansaryon had possessed an evil reputation for sorcery.

He could not move, or look away: it was as if he hung there on an invisible hook, bereft of strength and speech. Images raced through his mind: of Bron in the snow, and the footprints that should have followed him, and didn't; of Kefiri in the garden, filthy and exhausted; and then a more vivid picture of her, kneeling in his mother's courtyard, the westering sun turning her dark hair to fire, catching pigeons to send to Minassa.

Only two days ago. He thought of his river-voyage, a blur of confused memories, and then Hailyan, homely, welcoming and somehow very comforting after the austere, half-ruined grandeur of Zithirian.

'You can sit down again now.'

Ansaryon's voice was quiet, and quite kind. Herris needed no second bidding: he didn't think his knees would support him a heartbeat longer. Breathless, frightened and yet relieved, he stared up at the King of Zithirian, and was astonished, and greatly heartened, to receive the full benefit of his smile before Ansaryon turned back to his chair.

'He's telling the truth. Kefiri, Tayo knows how or why, is in Zithirian. At least she was still safe when he left two days ago. As for Bron . . .'

Ansaryon looked round at the other adult occupants of the tent, both of whom were, quite obviously, trying to disguise their rampant curiosity. He added quietly, 'Bron is a child of the Temple. He is also apparently the grandson of the High Priestess D'thliss. She uses him in some sinister way as her minion, to spy on us and also, I suspect, to augment her powers. He is about eight or nine years old, with fair hair and dark eyes – am I right, Herris Gandar's Son?'

'That sounds like Bron, Sir.'

'It's very important to understand that he himself is an innocent child. He is D'thliss's weapon, her slave in a sense. Any evil he does is at her command, and he cannot disobey her. Once she is slain, as I have sworn to do, he will be quite harmless.'

Herris looked at the Lord Ansaryon. He wanted to say that this optimistic opinion did not quite coincide with his own experience of Bron, who had the ability, as he had once confided to Kefiri, to give him the shivers. Somehow, though, the words died in his throat.

The King of Zithirian added quietly, 'So, he is not to be hurt or killed. I wish only the most guilty to be punished – D'thliss, Tsenit, and those who have helped them in the full knowledge of the consequences. I'm not interested in venting retribution on children, or upon anyone too frightened for themselves or their families to resist Tsenit.'

'But we *are* resisting him, Sir!' Herris cried, jumping up. 'My Ma – she's organized it all – that's why I brought the pigeons, so that when you're ready you can send word to Zithirian and all the people will rise up against Tsenit and the Ska'i.'

'Will they?' Ansaryon said. 'Tell me all about your mother and her plans – and for Tayo's sake, if not mine, start at the beginning and make it simple.'

So Herris explained. He told the three men about Kaydi, and her secret network of Tsenit's opponents whose exact ramifications no one knew; about Kefiri, who was to be the focus of the rising once it had begun; and again about the pigeons, vital messengers.

They listened in a flatteringly attentive silence, and when the boy's voice had trailed at last to an exhausted halt, Ansaryon said softly, 'This conspiracy is all very well, but it seems remarkably vague. What are your mother and the other leaders actually planning to *do*?'

'I'm not really sure, Sir,' Herris confessed rather resentfully. 'They wouldn't tell me very much, but I managed to pick up a few bits here and there. My Ma's cousin's son's nephew is a servant in the Temple, and I think he's going to set fire to it.' He grinned. 'Hope you don't mind that, Sir.'

'On the contrary, Herris Gandar's Son – that particular strategy has my whole-hearted approval.' Ansaryon smiled as the boy stifled a yawn, not for the first time. 'I think that's enough for tonight. We'll talk again in the morning. Invan and I will want to know everything you can tell us about Zithirian, the state of the walls, the mood of the citizens, the Royal Guard – everything you can remember. In the mean time, get a good night's sleep – you look as if you could do with it, and we'll be on the march at sunrise tomorrow. There's a bed waiting for you in one of the tents nearby – Dirdjen outside will show you where.'

'Thank you, Sir.' Herris struggled to his feet, his head whirling with dazed delight at his importance. The fate of Zithirian was being decided, and he, Herris Gandar's Son, was to be consulted! He made the obeisance before he remembered, and saw the three men smiling at him.

'Good night, Herris,' said the King of Zithirian. 'And I thank you. It was very brave, to set out on that journey alone. Well done.'

And with that royal praise ringing triumphantly in his mind, Herris stumbled sleepily to his bed.

CHAPTER
TWENTY-FIVE

'You have no choice.'

Her cousin's angry words were brutally uncompromising. They were also tediously familiar. If I had a chell for every time I'd heard him say that over the last few days, Kefiri thought wearily, I'd have emptied the gold from Sar D'yenyi by now.

'Don't be stupid, of course I have a choice,' she said, turning away from the window to face him. 'You can hardly parade me on a horse down the Ceremonial Way to the Temple and expect me to do and say all the right things during the ritual if I *don't* want to marry you, can you?'

'Believe me, Kefiri, I can.'

She glared at Tsenit with all the contempt and derision she could muster. '*You!* What are you, a sorcerer? And I know from what Ansaryon has told me that even a sorcerer finds it difficult, if not impossible, to control someone who isn't. You have to marry me in the most public celebration you can devise, or there's no point in it. And I will *not* co-operate.'

In the three days since her capture, Tsenit's face, already showing clear signs of strain, had become increasingly hag-ridden. He said urgently, 'It would be better for everyone, Kefiri, if you do as you are told. Better for everyone – better for me, better for the citizens, and especially better for you.'

'Why? What are you going to do? Torture me? Maim me? Kill me? This is Zithirian, not Toktel'yi or Fabriz. You can hardly show off your beloved Queen with half her fingers missing, can you?'

Tsenit's face twisted savagely. He strode forward and gripped her painfully by the shoulders. 'You'll do as I say! Listen to me! I *am* going to marry you, and that's that! D'you hear me, you little bitch?' He shook her violently with each word, and then pushed her away from him. She lost her balance and fell painfully against the wooden frame of the bed.

It was the first time that he had really lost control of himself. Dazed, rubbing her bruised arm, she pulled herself upright and stood with proud defiance, determined not to reveal the fear that flooded her. If she once disclosed to him the extent of her terror, she was lost. She knew instinctively that dignity and derision were the weapons that would serve her best. She watched him approach, his blue eyes wild with rage, and said, 'You can smash my face to a pulp if you like. It won't make any difference to what I think, and it might give the citizens something to talk about when they see me next.'

Tsenit paused, his hand already raised. She added scornfully, 'A fine King you are! You're at the beck and call of the Ska'i and that foul witch, so you take it out on me! Do you honestly believe I'd tamely give in and marry the man who had my father murdered? What do you think I am? Now get out!'

For a moment longer he stared at her, and for the briefest heartbeat she almost felt sorry for him. Then he turned and left, slamming the door with a furious crash that seemed to shake the whole Palace.

For a moment Kefiri stood in her crumpled silk, staring at the empty space he had left. Then, rather helplessly, she sank down onto the bed, put her head in her hands, and began to laugh.

If she had gone to the window of her guarded room, on the topmost floor of the central tower, she would have seen a grey and white pigeon, its outstretched wings tipped with gold from the setting sun, circling above the city before diving spear-straight down through the air, to land on the roof of an ordinary house on Snowbringer Street.

In her dark chamber under the Temple, D'thliss stared into her scrying bowl, her eyes narrowed as she tried to interpret what she saw beneath the gleaming surface of the blood.

An army, marching in sunlight, their trampling feet raising a huge pall of dust that hung around the soldiers and obscured her vision. She cursed, but the image remained obstinately cloudy for a few heartbeats longer. Then, it faded.

'Bron!'

The child drooping beside her jerked upright suddenly and rubbed his eyes. He looked very pale and exhausted, but D'thliss ignored this. She said sharply, 'Look at me. What did you see?'

Gradually the expression of childish bewilderment faded. His eyes stared back into hers, dark, dense and blank. He spoke tonelessly. 'An army. Many men. From Minassa, and Lelyent, and Sar D'yenyi, and Toktel'yi. And Tanathi, too.'

'Where?'

'I couldn't see.'

D'thliss gave an exclamation of fury, but the boy did not flinch. 'What do you mean, you couldn't see? Answer me!'

'I couldn't see,' Bron repeated, in that dead voice. 'Too much dust.'

The High Priestess picked up her staff and cracked it down on his thin shoulders. 'I don't believe you! You're lying, you misbegotten little wretch! Where were they? For the last time, if you know what's good for you – *answer me!*'

Bron had not moved, although the blow must have been very painful. He gazed impassively at his grandmother for a long time: then, as she raised the staff again, spoke suddenly. 'I told you. I couldn't see.'

'If you are deceiving me – if you are lying to me—' The old woman leaned over and cuffed him across the face. 'Is that the truth?'

'Yes, Grandmother.' He still had not moved, and the mark of her hand stood out starkly red against the pallor of his cheek.

D'thliss regarded him pitilessly for a moment longer, and then jerked her head towards the door. 'You may go.'

At once Bron turned and went out. She watched until the door had shut behind him, and then uttered a long and bitter curse.

The boy was defying her, there was no doubt of it. All the care she had taken with his training, all the years of planning and effort which she had poured into this, the source of her great power, and he, a child nine years old, thought he could obstruct her. Well, D'thliss decided grimly, she would stand none of that nonsense. He was her creation: he must be forced to acquiescence, made to do her bidding as abjectly as any slave.

And she needed him. Without him to focus and enhance her skills, she would no longer be able to control Tsenit, or keep the rapacious Ska'i in check. Her power depended on Bron's compliance and her long-cherished ambition to rule Zithirian would crumble to dust if she did not have the child to help her.

She had so nearly lost him, too. Lelya, in the grip of shock, had told her how the two boys had almost been captured by the Ska'i, and how they had been saved by Kefiri and by Bron's sorcery. Curious, she had looked inside Bron's mind and realized that the girl was in fact Lord Tayma's daughter, an invaluable prize. With the information the child had unwittingly given her, she had been able to have Kefiri seized.

But that was the only good result of the boys' escapade. She had been forced to admit that Bron was already able to use and control his power independently of her, and without her knowledge. She had known it would happen eventually, of course, but not so soon, not when he was so young. It revealed the astonishing extent of his abilities, but it had also served as a timely warning. If she wanted continued access to his power, she would have to Bind him utterly to her will. She had hoped to avoid it – who would have thought the brat would have proved so rebellious, so soon? But it looked now as if there would be no alternative, and his defiance this afternoon confirmed it.

And deep in what passed for her heart, another nagging serpent of doubt and alarm had uncoiled itself. The Ska'i had tried to capture Bron. That meant that Br'nnayak, once her ally, had discovered the child's true significance, and wished to seize him for his own nefarious ends. And now she could see, with hideous clarity, that the complicated structure of all her careful, devious plans was beginning to crumble.

The Ska'i knew about Bron, and wanted him for themselves. Therefore, Br'nnayak, through power, skill or even luck, must have managed to penetrate her defences. If he ever got his hands on the boy, he would become invincible, and the fragile, delicately balanced alliance between Tsenit, D'thliss and the Ska'i, mutually dependent on each other to realize their separate ambitions, would collapse. She would be in mortal danger: and Quenait's warriors would obliterate Tsenit and Zithirian with an inferno of destruction in Ayak's name.

D'thliss had no intention of ruling, if she survived, over a heap of rubble and a pile of bones. And so, she must Bind Bron to her for ever, and thereby ensure he was useless to the Ska'i.

It was a process that would stretch the limits of her power, perhaps to the breaking-point. And it had several disadvantages, which was why she had not seriously considered it until this dire necessity forced her to do so. The Binding, which stripped its victim of all independent thought and action, would also by its very nature diminish the child's integral power. By how much, D'thliss had no idea: there had never, in all the history of sorcery, been anyone with such extraordinary natural ability, and so she would be entering entirely uncharted seas.

Moreover, the ritual was long, complicated, and would advertise what she was doing, and the nature of Bron's power, as plainly as if she had shouted it from the topmost tower of the Temple. She would have no sorcery left over to maintain her defences until the Binding was complete, and the process might take many more hours, during which she would be hideously vulnerable.

But it must be done, and soon, or Bron would no longer be sufficiently docile to submit. She could feel a deep inner core of resistance within him now. Despite her domination of him, he had turned against her, and before long he would begin to understand and use his powers to the full.

The thought terrified her. That a child so young could be in command of sorcery as awesome, destructive and uncontrollable as a forest fire was unthinkable.

Her mind made up, D'thliss took a handful of dried Annatal leaves from the pouch she always carried. It was several times the normal daily dose, but she would need all her strength for the task ahead, and her powers must be at their highest possible level. She pushed the drug into a little brass brazier, and lit it with a taper from one of the candles burning before Ayak's head. Then she flung an old cloth over her head and began to breathe the fumes deeply and regularly, feeling the familiar soaring sense of omnipotence that was part of Annatal's gift.

Not long now: not long, a few hours, a day, until she had Bound him to her. And then she, not Br'nnayak, would become invincible.

In the Ska'i camp, the tribesmen were restless. Obedient to their chief, a man charismatic enough to do the unprecedented, and unite all the clans under his wolf's head banner, they had at first been content to stay here in this alien place, with the memory of great bloodshed to enliven them, and the promise of much more, and gold and plunder besides, lying encouragingly in the future. They ate, drank, raided and killed in the linked names of Ayak and Quenait, and had asked for no more.

But they had camped here for nearly a year now. The last full moon of summer was approaching, and ahead lay the chillier days of autumn, shading into another icy winter. The Ska'i homelands lay far to the south, on the borders of the Empire. It could be bitterly cold there too, but these northern lands, so close to the mountains, possessed a bleak dark savagery during the Sundim months that filled many of the warriors with dismay. They began to grumble, and the muttering grew around the fires and within the stinking stuffy darkness of their tents. What were they doing sitting here in idleness? Why not seize the city, plunder it and kill all its inhabitants, and return to their own country ahead of the winter storms, to the women and children and old men they had left behind them, almost unprotected?

Quenait was well aware of these stirrings of discontent. Even if Br'nnayak had not told him about them in graphic detail, he would have guessed long ago from the sidelong glances, the sullen conversations that always broke off as he approached, and the manic eagerness with which his bored men embarked on every raid. He made sure that they were reminded frequently of the fabulous wealth within Sar D'yenyi, theirs for the taking once the lake froze: and he also promised that as soon as the gold had been seized, his warriors would be allowed to sack Zithirian as their just reward for their loyalty and patience.

But Quenait had no real fear that his army would begin to disintegrate. They were still too much in awe of him, too enslaved by the fear and worship of Ayak, to desert him. He had already decided, though, that with the first sign of winter, they would march on Sar D'yenyi.

If Ansaryon, of course, did not stop them: and Ansaryon was coming. Quenait had little fear of him, however. Even if he proved to have twice the spirit of his spineless brother Tsenit, he would still be easy prey. And Quenait looked forward to his destruction with relish. Oquargul had been a fool, and had made grievous and fatal errors – for which Quenait in his darkest heart held Br'nnayak to be partly responsible – but he was his brother, his own blood, and must be avenged.

On the sixth day before full moon, Quenait scanned the northern sky eagerly, as he did every morning, but there was no sign of any storm-cloud, and the air was warm and mild. With a curse, the chief turned his horse and urged it back to the camp. D'thliss, for whose powers he still had a healthy respect despite Br'nnayak's confident superiority, had brought winter early last year. If they could only get hold of the child who was her weapon, surely his shaman would be able to do the same now.

Br'nnayak was waiting for him when he returned. The old man's lined, shrunken face was more grim than Quenait had ever seen it, and he wasted no time on courtesies. 'I have news for you. We must act at once, or we are all lost.'

Quenait stared at him in angry surprise. 'What news?' Is Ansaryon here already? I'll have the scouts disembowelled if he's taken us by surprise!'

'He is indeed approaching, but he is still a couple of days' march away. No, he'll be easy enough to deal with in good time. This is a far more desperate matter, and if it cannot be stopped then we are as good as dead – you, me and all your warriors.'

And in a harsh, urgent whisper he explained to Quenait the

exact details of the mortal peril which now faced the Ska'i, and how they could be saved from destruction.

The light from the candles glittered on the wet, uneven rock walls of D'thliss's chamber under the Temple. There were twenty-seven of them, a ritually important number, three times three times three, and the majority of them burned before the mad, glaring wolf's head that represented Ayak the Devourer of Blood, Lord of Death. The others, smelling sickly and evilly sweet, were grouped around the still, recumbent figure of the child Bron, lying on the floor.

All night, D'thliss had gathered the material for the Binding, with care and secrecy. Nothing must go wrong – nothing. The minutest error in the ritual, the smallest deviation from the prescribed instruments and accessories, might spell disaster. The only other time she had tried to Bind someone, the young man who had been father to her only child, he had somehow retained a tiny fragment of free will, and had used it to kill himself rather than submit to his fate. And her one mistake then had been to use a golden bowl for the blood, rather than silver, thinking with the arrogance of youth that it would not matter.

So this time, she had taken enormous pains to ensure that all went well. The number and positions of the candles; the colour of her robes and of the tunic which Bron wore; the drugs she had administered to ensure his compliance; the potions and words she would use to empty his mind of all independent thought, will or personality. Then only the power which she craved would be left, to be wielded at her command.

All had gone smoothly so far. The only problem had been Lelya, who had been fiercely protective of the younger boy since their narrow escape from the Ska'i, refusing to let him out of his sight. Lacking Bron's inner resources, he was far more frightened of his grandmother, but obstinately stuck close to his brother, despite her threats. And in the end, D'thliss had been forced, reluctantly, to the conclusion that she must Bind Lelya too. He might be useful, there was no denying it: and if she left him free, there was now the very considerable danger that, despite his fear, he would betray her.

So Lelya lay on the floor beside Bron, dressed in a plain white tunic exactly like the other boy's, and sharing the same drugged oblivion. D'thliss stared down at him for a last long moment, her face almost soft. He was so like his dead mother, her only child:

and so like, too, the beautiful young man whom she had Bound to her, long ago, because she was ageing fast from the effects of Annatal, and she feared to lose him. And like that long-dead lover, Lelya was a handsome boy, but stupid.

She turned abruptly away, and stood before the wolf's head. The empty eye-sockets had each been filled with a faceted red crystal, and they glowed evilly in the flickering light. She took a long, deep breath of the drug-laden air, and began the Invocation.

Invocation, Blood Sacrifice, Terror, Madness, Binding: the Five Parts of the ritual. First Ayak's presence must be requested, and his blessing sought by presenting to him the silver bowl, filled with the mingled blood of D'thliss and the children whom she wished to Bind. Then she would sprinkle a different drug over the candles. Bron and Lelya would wake to terrifying and hideous visions, intended to empty the mind of all rational and coherent thought. The hallucinations would continue until the flames burned out, and all the while D'thliss would chant the words of the Binding, over and over again, until the two boys were utterly consumed by her will. She had already taken the antidote to the vision drug, so it would have no effect on her. Throughout the whole process, which would probably take many hours, she would remain in complete control.

Everything was ready. Her eyes gleaming with greed for the absolute power which now lay within her grasp at last, D'thliss summoned the Presence of Ayak to witness the sacred ritual.

It was only when she had almost ended, when the sense of the Devourer filled her nostrils and her mind with the glorious and intoxicating stench of evil, that she realized that something was wrong.

The wolf had been so close that she could almost see his flaming eyes, and the savage fangs dripping with the blood she had promised to give him. Suddenly, however, this image wavered, and began to fade. D'thliss fought down her alarm and continued with the chant, her arms rising and falling with the intonation.

> 'Blood offering,
> Blood flowing,
> Blood gift,
> I prepare for thee!
> Draw near,
> Supreme Lord,
> Master of Death,
> Devourer of Souls!

Take my blood,
Grant me life,
Grant them death-in-life,
Accept my offering –
Ayak, come!'

She dropped her hands. The candle flames guttered and sighed all at once, as if a wind had passed amongst them, but she felt nothing. The room was empty.

Save for two eyes, dark and unfathomable as the depths of the Abyss, staring at her.

D'thliss shrieked in fury: and at the same moment something smashed into the door. The timbers, softened by long neglected years of duty in the damp atmosphere underground, shuddered under the impact and gave way.

Cursing, she flung her hands in the air. Blue lightning poured from her fingers and engulfed the man who pushed his way into her sanctum. He fell smoking, with a reek of charred flesh, and she screeched in savage triumph.

The sound curdled in her throat. Something invisible wound itself about her, freezing movement, pinioning every muscle, leaving only her mind free, incandescent with helpless fury. She saw with dreadful clarity the tribesmen pouring into her sacred chamber, overturning the candles, flinging aside all the precious paraphernalia of her trade, gathered over the long years. Even the wolf's head did not deter them, though one made a hasty sign of respect at the snarling face.

Behind her eyes, she cursed them, she called up every spell, every incantation she could remember. But nothing obeyed her, and her outstretched hands were as powerless and immobile as a statue's.

Br'nnayak stood before her, the man with whom she had once allied herself in common worship of Ayak, and whom she had thought to deceive. In a paroxysm of despairing fury, D'thliss wrenched herself free of the invisible bonds that held her, and spat the first words of the Curse of Ayak.

The shaman smiled, and raised his staff.

She never saw the axe which sliced through flesh and sinew and bone with contemptuous ease. But certainly Ayak, if his presence lingered within the room, would have been pleased with the bright fountains of blood that sprayed from her headless corpse, the instant before it fell to the floor.

'Killing witches is not so difficult,' said Br'nnayak, smiling, and bent to retrieve D'thliss's head, which had rolled in a track of blood almost to the wolf's altar. Gripping it by ragged strands of white hair, he raised it up. The eyes glared hideously at the half-dozen tribesmen who filled the room. For a last brief moment, the wildly leaping candle flames gave the twisted face a horrible illusion of continuing life, and more than one of the Ska'i made the sign against evil.

Br'nnayak laughed, and gleefully shook the gruesome object so that blood spattered. 'Take the child, and go. Soon the whole Temple will be ablaze.'

'Child? Master, which child?'

For the first time, the shaman saw that there was not one boy lying surrounded by candles, but two. Both dressed in the ritual white tunic, both in a drugged sleep, and both, obviously, intended for Binding. He knew from his spirit-walking which of them had the power, but it seemed that D'thliss must also have found the older one useful, or why go to the trouble and risk of Binding him as well?

Already his keen nostrils could detect smoke from the burning Temple above them, filtering through the stench of burnt flesh from the slain Ska'i. There was no time to be lost.

'Take them both,' he said. 'And set fire to this – make sure it burns well. I myself will carry the witch's head to Quenait.'

Impotent and terrified, Tsenit watched the Ska'i's destruction of the Ancestor's Temple from the ramparts of the Palace Gate.

From here, the Ceremonial Way stretched broad and straight down to the heart of the city, and he had an excellent view. Ignorant of the reason for this raid, he was certain that it must be the prelude to a more general onslaught, and had ordered the gates to be closed and every soldier of the Guard to appear on the walls, armed and ready. Strangely, though, the Ska'i did not seem to be interested in anything other than the Temple.

Its walls and towers might be built of white Annako stone, which was proof against fire, but the floors were made of wood, and the whole building was stuffed full of precious and inflammable objects, carpets, hangings, furniture, books and papers. There was a dry westerly breeze off the steppe, and soon every one of the Temple's nine towers was trailing sheets of flame, while a vast plume of black smoke billowed briskly over the eastern side of the city. Ash and debris dropped over Tsenit as he stood helplessly on the walls of the Palace, and listened to the distant screams and cries as the Priests and Priestesses of Tayo died trying to defend their sacred place.

He did not see the grey and white bird plunging down through the smoky air to land with unerring accuracy on the roof of a house in Snowbringer Street. But the cat Garool, lurking watchfully in the courtyard below, narrowed his green eyes and twitched his tail eagerly. He was hungry, and the first pigeon, who had arrived the previous day, had made a fine feast.

The bird walked down the tiles, with a weary, rolling gait. There was a shallow trough in the far corner of the yard, with a little water in the bottom, and he was very thirsty after his long flight. Abandoning his usual caution, he spread his wings and sailed downwards.

Garool crouched, waiting: slunk closer, crouched again. The pigeon, intent on its drinking, did not see him until the moment when the cat sprang, claws ready for the kill.

And by then it was too late.

The sun had sunk scarlet behind that obliterating cloud before a terrible quiet at last descended on the burning building. Only the roar and crackle of the flames could now be heard. Several hundred Ska'i, burdened with heads and plunder, gold and silver and precious jewels worked into boxes, caskets, staffs of office, plates and goblets, even robes and vestments, streamed jubilantly from the Temple, their hands and their axes liberally dabbled with blood. As dusk fell, they swaggered back to the camp singing songs of triumph and slaughtering any unfortunate citizen who happened to get in their way.

No curfew would sound that night, or any other now: the great sacred horn of Tayo, bound with gold and silver and needing the strength of two men to lift it, lay twisted and unrecognizable amidst the white-hot flames filling the central tower. And the men and women who had served the Ancestor, and been hated for it, burned incandescently along with their Temple.

When it was certain that the Ska'i had all left the city, for the moment at least, a few brave men crept out from their houses and shut the Sunset Gate, an hour after sunset. Others gathered up the mostly headless bodies of the dead, two score or more of the slow or the foolhardy or the unlucky, who littered the gracious tree-lined avenue of Sunset Street. Then, those who were bold enough to leave the shelter of their houses congregated round the Temple, to watch the final destruction of the symbol of their oppression.

Long after dark they watched, cheering each falling stone, each crashing roof-beam as if another enemy had been slain. And when at last, under the pale eye of a moon five days from full, the flames began to die down into a sullen, evil glow, they dispersed with reluctance and returned to their homes, yawning, exhausted, but filled with a strange mixture of hope, and joy, and fear.

And in the morning, the Ska'i had gone.

'I don't believe it!' Kaydi cried. 'They can't have upped and gone just like that! You're fooling me, Engris!'

'You know I wouldn't do that,' said her cousin. She lived in the Potters' Quarter, in Magpie Lane not far from the Sunset Gate, and had come hammering on Kaydi's door with the news, just before sunrise. 'Come on, woman – if you don't believe me, come and see for yourself.'

So Kaydi put a cloak over her old gown, for last night had been clear and cold, and called to Shilda. Then the two women and the limping servant hurried through the twisting alleys of the Embroiderers' Quarter to the Sunset Gate.

It must be true. The gates were flung wide, and the people, a great throng even at this early hour, were pouring out, laughing, crying, singing. Kaydi jerked her head up at the double towers soaring above them. 'Any chance of getting up there for a better view, d'you reckon?'

'I should think so,' Engris said. 'I haven't seen any sign of the Guard at all this morning.'

Together, with Shilda labouring behind them, they climbed up the wooden steps to the rampart beside the gate. The eastern sky at their backs was brightening fast, with a flare of light beyond the low, far-distant bulk of Mondir to show where the sun would soon rise, but the wind had gone round to the north, and there was no warmth in it. Kaydi took a deep breath, smelling winter in the air, and looked over the wall.

It was true. For whatever reason, the Ska'i had gone. There was the sprawling empty wreckage of their camp, the piles of rubbish, the bare dusty trampled earth, the stumps of trees cut down for firewood all along the river: and there, plain as day, leading north-west along the valley of the Kefirinn, the trail they had left.

Beside her, Engris began to whisper the Thanksgiving Prayer to Sarraliss, only uttered after a life had been saved, or great danger averted. For a few heartbeats longer, Kaydi savoured the derelict emptiness between the walls and the river, and then turned to look at the city.

The Temple still smouldered, with a pall of dense smoke shrouding the ruins. Two of the outer towers had fallen, leaving a ragged pile of precarious stones like broken fangs. Beyond it, she could see the outline of the Royal Palace wavering in the hot air rising from the burning building.

Kefiri, whom she had grown to love like a daughter, was somewhere in there – if she was still alive, which Kaydi somehow doubted. And Herris, her last surviving child, had vanished as if he had stepped off the rim of the earth. He had been gone five days now, and no pigeons had returned to her courtyard. Sooner or later, she would have to face the terrible fact that he was probably dead.

But she was still here, and would carry on the fight until the last breath left her body, if necessary. She would not allow them to die in vain.

She turned to Engris, a smile of satisfaction hiding her grief. 'Well, we've got rid of two or our burdens within the same day. Now, we ought to be thinking about disposing of the third.'

'Your High Mightiness . . .'

Sathen, the Royal Chamberlain, hovered apprehensively in the outer doorway of the King's apartment. He had no idea what Tsenit's mood would be this morning, but was fairly certain that it would not be pleasant. The destruction the previous day had been bad enough, although the Ska'i had miraculously restricted their predatory activities to the Temple. Now, this latest news would be an even more bitter blow.

'What is it, Sathen?'

Tsenit did not appear to have been to bed, although his fine embroidered tunic and silk gown certainly looked as if he had slept in them. He stood glowering at his Chamberlain, his darkly unshaven jaw giving him an alarmingly villainous appearance. Then he strode aggressively forward and thrust his nose within a hand's breadth of Sathen's quailing and indignant face. 'Come on, out with it – I can tell it's bad news. *What is it?*'

The older man took a deep breath, and plunged into the abyss. 'Your High Mightiness – the Ska'i have gone.'

Tsenit's jaw dropped. He stared in horror at the unfortunate Chamberlain. 'Gone? *Gone?*' What d'you mean, gone? They can't have – you're lying!'

'No, your High Mightiness.' Sathen stepped unobtrusively backwards, alarmed at the expression in the King's eyes. 'They must have broken camp some time in the night. They've gone – up the valley, by the look of it. And no one knows why.'

'Ayak curse them – may their flesh rot on their bones before they die in agony!'

Sathen looked at Tsenit in dismay. 'Your High Mightiness – surely this is not a complete disaster—'

'Of course it is, you fool!' The King rounded savagely on his Chamberlain. 'How in Ayak's name am I going to take Sar D'yenyi now? And even more important, how can we defeat Ansaryon? In a few days' time, perhaps even less, he'll be here! He has five thousand Toktel'yans, as well as all his other allies – and what have I got left? Less than twelve hundred poxy Royal Guards!'

Sathen said soothingly, 'But the Palace is a great fortress, your High Mightiness. The Ska'i were only able to break into it because . . .' He paused, on the brink of mentioning the forbidden word 'treachery', and went on, 'Because they were helped from within. Adequately provisioned, and with nearly twelve hundred loyal soldiers, you could hold Ansaryon at bay for days, perhaps months. And as long as you have the person of the Lady Kefiri in your hands, you are in possession of a bargaining counter of great price.'

Tsenit stared at him. Gradually the look of blind rage faded from his eyes, to be replaced by a calculating expression which Sathen recognized with relief. He said slowly, 'I have not announced our wedding yet. Surely once I do, the people will be on my side, and they will see Ansaryon for what he is – a noxious sorcerer who will do nothing but harm if he is allowed to take the throne.'

'An excellent idea, your High Mightiness,' Sathen said, with well-concealed relief.

'I shall proclaim it today.' Tsenit smacked a fist into his palm. 'The wedding shall take place tomorrow. Not as much ceremony as I had been planning, of course, but that can't be helped. And the important thing is to marry her before my brother turns up.'

Sathen had suddenly remembered something, and it drove the blood from his face. He stared at his revitalized monarch, wondering whether he should point out the considerable obstacle blocking Tsenit's plans. If he didn't, someone else surely would, but he didn't relish, either, the prospect of being beaten senseless or pushed down the stairs. And when the King was in the throes of one of his increasingly frequent rages, he was undoubtedly strong enough to kill with his bare hands.

It was at times like these that Sathen felt most nostalgia for his boring, humdrum, restricted but above all secure life in the Merchants' Quarter, where the most important decision he had ever had to make concerned the best prices to charge for Kerentan silk.

'What is it, man? Now what's wrong?' Tsenit was staring at him suspiciously.

That settled it. Sathen assessed the distance between them – some six strides, far enough to give him some warning – and then said carefully, 'Your High Mightiness – who will perform the marriage ritual?'

Tsenit gaped at him as if he had been struck by lightning. Committed, Sathen continued doggedly. 'Under Zithiriani law, only marriages performed by a Priest or Priestess of Tayo are valid. And of course the Ska'i—'

'I know what the law says, Ayak damn you! They can't have killed them *all*, can they? Send someone out to find one – I don't care if it's a novice or a senile old greybeard – find me one live priest of Tayo, or I'll have you suffocated in your own silk, you whining low-born fool – go on, go, before I—'

Sathen needed no further encouragement. He turned tail and fled, his ornate blue robe whisking down the stairs of the central tower. Behind him, Tsenit slammed the door so hard the wood shivered, and then turned and strode to the window which faced westwards, over the city.

He was alone – utterly alone. The Ska'i had deserted him. Had they grown impatient, and gone to attack Sar D'yenyi without waiting for the lake to freeze? If so, they'd gone in the wrong direction – unless, of course, they were looking for a safe place to cross the Kefirinn. The nearest point was some eighty miles upstream, where the waters ran fast and shallow over rocks, and a causeway had been built between two settlements on opposite banks.

And without his presence, they would lay claim to all the gold. Of course, hope was not yet lost. With Sar D'yenyi destroyed and its wealth plundered, the Ska'i would go back to their homeland, and he would then be able to control the mountain mines and take their vast riches for himself – and for rebuilding Zithirian. But that did not solve his most pressing problem. How was he to defeat Ansaryon with that pitiful remnant of soldiers? Especially since many of them might be tempted to desert him as soon as they saw the overwhelming force that faced them.

And his other ally, D'thliss, was dead: the Ska'i had carried her severed head before them in triumph as they left the blazing

Temple. Part of him, the part that had quailed before her evil, her contempt, her terrifying power, was glad of his new freedom. But she had helped him and encouraged his ambitions, she had planned every detail of his seizure of the throne. Now, he was utterly alone. Henceforward, the decisions, the strategies, the orders must come from him. And only he would be responsible if it all went wrong.

Smoke still glowered over the Temple. Sathen was right – who could have survived both the Ska'i and the flames? Perhaps one or two priests might have been in the city, running errands or undertaking private tuition, but he doubted it. Yesterday had been one of the Contemplation Days, when the acolytes of Tayo were supposed to spend their time in quiet prayer and study. More than likely, none would be found alive.

Filled with raging despair, Tsenit bowed his head in his hands and screamed his frustration and bitterness at the cruelty of fate.

CHAPTER
TWENTY-SIX

There were several traditional ways of announcing Palace news in Zithirian. It could be imparted to the officials of each Quarter, to be disseminated amongst the citizens individually; a notice might be nailed to the Palace gates, a tactic of dubious value for a population in which, even now, many adults could not read the Toktel'yan script used by the Court; or it could be proclaimed, with escort and trumpeter, at the key points of the city – Palace Gate, docks, Temple and Sunset Gate.

To broadcast tidings as important as the King's imminent marriage, only the latter method would suffice. The wedding should be announced with all possible ceremony. Similarly, there must be no hole-in-the-corner air about the ritual itself.

If it took place. Sathen, gathered with General Seardrith and half a hundred soldiers around the smoking ruins of the Temple, stared gloomily at the blackened stones and knew that their chances of finding a living Priest or Priestess were slender. But still the attempt must be made.

The main gate was blocked by a heap of charred rubble from one of the collapsed flanking towers. The soldiers peered at it, muttering, and Sathen despaired silently. How was the King to marry if they could not find a priest? And where was the wedding to take place? The Memorial, the sacred hall in the central tower where the relics of Tayo were kept and all rituals solemnized, would surely be filled with more smouldering wreckage. And the more Sathen thought about it, the worse his dilemma grew. For if any urgent public search for a living Priest was mounted, Tsenit would be a laughing stock. He could see it all too clearly. The King of Zithirian, unable to find anyone to officiate at his own marriage!

Still, he had to do something, or risk Tsenit's wrath. He turned unhappily to Seardrith, who stood waiting with the grim impassivity that always hid his thoughts. 'There can't be anyone left alive in there. You'd better start a search. After all, the Temple is one of the twin pillars of authority in Zithirian. Who will continue the worship of Tayo, if there are no priests left?'

'No one, with any luck!'

It must have been one of the soldiers who had spoken, but when Seardrith turned to confront them, he saw only fifty blank, expressionless faces. He stared at them menacingly for a few heartbeats, then swung round to face Sathen again. 'You can report to His High Mightiness that I am undertaking a search immediately. Somewhere, we will find one.' And he added, so low that only the Chamberlain could hear him, 'Or if we can't, we can always dress someone up. It's all empty foolishness anyway, so who'll know the difference?'

With reluctant feet, Sathen made his way back to the Palace, his escort of half-a-dozen Guards tramping behind him. At least the streets were almost empty: everyone, it seemed, had gone to dance for joy on the abandoned Ska'i camp. He felt conspicuous and vulnerable in his distinctive blue livery. He almost turned aside to the comfortable house in the Merchants' Quarter, where his wife and children still lived: almost, but not quite. For whatever his other faults, at least Sathen was loyal to his master.

The Lady Kefiri had seen the smoke and flames that announced the end of the hated Temple, and her young maid, M'yani, had told her about its complete destruction by the Ska'i, and of the slaughter of all its inhabitants, including the High Priestess, D'thliss. And when the girl had left her locked in for the night, with everything but freedom for her comfort, she had wept long and bitterly for the children who might have died brutally in the attack, or, worse, might have been taken into hideous slavery.

'You'll be safe in the Temple,' she had told Bron and Lelya, and she had watched them, two dear and vulnerable figures, running through the great gate. But it seemed that the Ska'i had been so desperate to seize Bron – or to kill him – that they had wreaked wholesale and savage destruction to achieve their ends. And she would probably never know whether the two boys had survived as prisoners, or had perished in the flames.

But she must try to find out, if she could. And the next morning she would ask M'yani for news when the maid came up with her breakfast.

M'yani, however, had momentous news of her own. The Ska'i had gone in the night, tidings which did not really surprise Kefiri when she thought about it. And, unpleasantly closer to home, the date for her wedding to Tsenit had been brought forward, and would now take place tomorrow.

She stared at the servant girl's sympathetic face, and shook her head. 'No. He can't. I won't agree. And anyway, how can he marry me if the Temple's burnt down and all the Priests are dead?'

'I hadn't thought of that one, Lady,' said M'yani. 'But everyone's talking as if it's a certainty. And you don't want to be Queen?'

'Of course I don't!' Kefiri said angrily. 'I have *never* wanted to be Queen of Zithirian. I am the Lady of Sar D'yenyi – that is my home and my responsibility, and I want to return there when all this is over. And besides, how can I possibly marry my father's murderer? Oh, if only I could get *out* of here! Ansaryon must be coming, or why else would Tsenit want to marry me in such a hurry? And while I'm locked up and in his power, he can use me as a hostage, to bargain for his own life and freedom.'

'And the Lord Ansaryon *will* come, lady. Everyone in the city is sure of it. Soon we'll all be free.' M'yani put the tray down and came close to Kefiri. 'Listen, lady,' she went on, very quietly. 'I've been thinking a lot, in the last few days. I know a way to get you out of here.'

Kefiri stared at her in astonishment. She had assumed that M'yani, being a Palace servant, would naturally be loyal to Tsenit. She said in disbelief, 'Why? Why would you want to help me?'

'Because I'm on the Lord Ansaryon's side, of course,' M'yani told her, as if this was something that Kefiri should have instinctively recognized. 'Most of us servants are, and some of the soldiers too. We're all citizens, after all, not courtiers. My Da's a potter, and my Ma and two of my little brothers died of hunger last winter. Why should I want Tsenit for King? I'd much rather have his brother, sorcerer or not – at least he wasn't a traitor, nor did he have his own family murdered.'

'I'm sorry about your family,' Kefiri said softly. On impulse, she clasped the maid-servant's hands in the universal sign of friendship and equality. 'Do you *really* think you can get me away from here? If I can be free and in hiding in the city before Ansaryon arrives, then Tsenit's last hope is gone.'

'Of course I can.' M'yani grinned at her. 'Just you sit tight here, Lady – I'll soon be back.'

The door closed behind her. Kefiri sank down on the bed, her knees suddenly weak. The tray of food lay within easy reach, but she found that she wasn't in the least hungry, though she normally ate a good breakfast. She thought of the five days she had spent cooped up here as Tsenit's prisoner, subject to his increasingly violent attempts at persuasion, and then of his face when he discovered she had escaped. For without her, he had nothing left to bargain with, and if M'yani was right, he wouldn't even be able to rely on the loyalty of many of his own Royal Guard, let alone the Palace servants.

Too excited to sit still, she got up and paced round the circular room, pausing at every one of the four windows to look out. Northwards, to the clear snow-tipped peaks of Annako, Estray and Sargenn, the guardians of her heart and her home. East, into the rising sun, symbol of promises and hope. South, down the shining ribbon of the Kefirinn, the snow-water for which she had been named, her narrowed blue eyes seeking a distant glitter, a far-off smudge of dust, which might herald the arrival of Ansaryon's army. And finally west, across the city, still shaded by smoke from the burnt Temple, where she would find refuge with her friends until the appointed hour when they would rise up against Tsenit, and help to destroy him.

M'yani's brisk double-single tap sounded at the door, and she entered, carrying a bundle of what looked like green linen, rather creased and dirty. She glanced significantly behind her, and said loudly, 'His High Mightiness commands your presence in his chamber, Lady. Shall I make you ready?'

'Of course,' said Kefiri, trying to make her voice sound natural. It was difficult to prevent excitement and apprehension colouring her tones: as it was, she could not stop herself grinning at M'yani like an eager child.

The girl grinned back. She shook the cloth out onto the bed. From within the green linen tumbled a tunic and skirt of the familiar bright blue that all the servants wore. 'Put it on *under* your gown,' she hissed. 'Once we're past the soldiers, you can take the gown off and you'll be just like any of us – especially with your hair tied back.'

Kefiri looked at her doubtfully. 'Where will I take the gown off?'

'Once we get past the turn in the stairs. It'll have to be done very quickly and quietly.'

'It's too risky – it won't work!'

'Oh, yes, it will.' M'yani stared at her with a challenge in her face. 'You can't tell me you're *scared* now, Lady, after all you've done and all that's happened?'

'No – no, I'm not.' Kefiri took a deep and rather shaky breath. 'But if something goes wrong, there'll be no second chance. He'll chain me to the wall rather than risk me escaping again.'

'Then we just can't get caught, can we?' M'yani said. 'And pray to Sarraliss, Mother of all, to help us.'

Swiftly, with fumbling nervous fingers, Kefiri removed her

bodice and gown and slipped the blue tunic over her head. The skirt was much too long, so she rolled it up around its waistband until it was clear of her ankles, fastened the broad leather belt over the tunic, and then pulled the loose silk gown back on over the top. It was also blue, though of a darker, richer hue than the sharp colour of the Palace livery, so perhaps anything that showed underneath would not be too conspicuous.

She had a jewelled bodice which laced up the front. Like all the clothes that had been given to her, it had originally been made for someone much broader and taller, so it was quite loose, and would be easy to slip off in a hurry. M'yani helped her to put it on, and then surveyed her critically. 'That's not too bad, Lady. Nothing shows, and it doesn't look too bulky. I've got a ribbon to tie your hair back – that should do the trick.'

The two girls stared at each other, on the brink of danger. Then Kefiri smiled. 'Whatever happens, M'yani – thank you, from the well of my heart, for giving me this chance. I won't forget it.'

They clasped hands in friendship once more, and then moved to the door. A last exchange of glances, a last silent prayer for success and good luck, and then M'yani ushered her mistress out.

The guards outside hardly gave her a glance. They were sitting in the corner under the window, playing skrath, a quicker and simpler version of the Tanathi game of tek. The stairs to freedom wound downwards into the heart of the tower. Kefiri, her heart pounding under the silk bodice, began to descend.

Twelve steps, and they were out of sight of the men above, and also of the door to the Chief Minister's chamber below. Kefiri loosened the laces of her bodice undone and tugged it silently over her head. The gown followed, to be pushed into M'yani's bundle. The maid, standing on the step above, gathered up her mass of dark hair and tied it up, dragging it back off her face in the practical fashion of every servant girl. The transformation was complete, and had taken no more than two score heartbeats.

They hurried down the stairs. Past the Chief Minister's door, past the Chamberlain's, then that of Tsenit himself, fortunately closed; below, the Council Chamber, and after that the Throne Room. The only person they saw was a male servant, sweeping the steps, and he did not even look up as they passed.

'Follow me,' M'yani whispered when they reached the bottom, and her warm hand touched Kefiri's arm beneath the short, braid-edged sleeve of her tunic. And the Lady of Sar D'yenyi, with no choice but to put herself, and her fate, and perhaps the future of Zithirian too, into the maid-servant's hands, did as she was told.

The passage snaked in a spiral round the ground floor of the central tower, with others radiating off it. Most of these, Kefiri knew, led to what had been, a year ago, the Royal Apartments, each with its own courtyard and tower, each now destroyed or derelict after the Ska'i attack. One entrance was still blocked by a heap of fallen plaster and roof-beams. At last they came to a tall wooden door. M'yani turned the handle, and daylight, dazzling sunlight, flooded into Kefiri's eyes.

This was the entrance courtyard, through which she had been dragged as a prisoner, five days ago. Blinking, she saw the maid's frown, and her unobtrusive but urgent gestures, and hurried along in her wake, head bent. Ahead lay the huge double towers of the Palace Gate, and between them a solid wall of wood. She was wondering how M'yani proposed to bluff her way past the guards when she realized that the other girl had turned aside to a small door set in the base of one of the high flanking towers. Acutely conscious that there were many people in the courtyard, servants, soldiers, even a well-dressed clutch of courtiers, all of whom might recognize her at any moment, she followed M'yani through the door, and into the servants' quarters.

It was almost dark inside the tower. Steps climbed upwards, and a doorway beckoned on the other side. M'yani grasped her arm and pulled her towards it.

A man appeared, so abruptly that Kefiri almost flinched. He was young, broadly built, and likewise clad in blue livery. He stopped when he saw them, and smiled. 'Hello, M'yani – I thought you were on duty.'

'So I am, but Amethi isn't very well – I should stand aside unless you want her to be sick all over you.'

The young servant stepped smartly out of their path, and Kefiri made a gulping noise in her throat and put her hand over her mouth. M'yani whisked her through the further door, along a brief passage, and suddenly into a wide courtyard, warm, sunlit, the walls laden with bright green fronded leaves and scented white and yellow flowers of the ubiquitous trumpet vine. The fragrance hung deliciously in the air, birds sang, the sky overhead was still the clear, infinite blue of summer. Astonished and delighted – she had somehow never realized that even the servants' quarters in the Palace could be so beautiful – Kefiri paused, and M'yani pulled her forward impatiently. 'Come on – please, hurry!'

The courtyard was empty, and the big central fountain silent, its bowl filled with green scummy water. But there was a broom propped up against a pillar, and damp washing piled up in a basket next to it, so they could not afford to linger. An arcade ran round the big square space, and M'yani scurried across the expanse of smooth flagstones, between two pillars and through an entrance beyond. She shut the door behind her and Kefiri, and let out a gusty sigh of relief. 'That's it! Done it!'

Kefiri looked around. The chamber was obviously a dormitory: six or seven low wooden beds, neatly made, were ranged round the room, each with a small chest for personal possessions at the foot. An empty brazier stood in one corner, and in another there was a small table and a chair. Nothing else: it was all clean and tidy, but the walls were bare, and the atmosphere was somehow cheerless.

'Right.' M'yani went over to one of the chests, presumably her own, and began rummaging inside. 'These should fit you. Take your livery off now, and put them on. Come *on*, Lady – it won't be long before they realize you've gone, and start a search.'

Kefiri unbuckled the belt, hauled the tunic over her head and divested herself of the skirt. In exchange, she received a rather old thin woollen gown, unobtrusively patched and of a faded sludge green colour, and a stamped leather bodice, the sort worn by peasants or poor citizens when they wanted to look their best. Kefiri had seen a hundred women dressed like this in Zithirian, so she would be quite inconspicuous – and with D'thliss dead in the ruins of the Temple, there was no one left with the abnormal powers necessary to find her in such an anonymous disguise.

The bodice had cheap clasps of adulterated silver, and like everything else was much too big, but it would have to do. She fastened it, hitched up the skirt, and looked at M'yani. 'Does that look all right?'

'Perfect.' The maid was obviously becoming increasingly apprehensive. 'Now to get you out.'

'But surely there's no way out except through the gate?'

'Oh, yes, there is.' M'yani jumped onto one of the beds. Above it, quite high in the wall, there was a window. Kefiri realized suddenly that as the other one was opposite and gave onto the courtyard, this one must surely look out over the city.

But of course it was blocked by an ornate iron grille, presumably to allow a defender to fire arrows out while preventing an attacker from climbing in. The maid had hold of the central bar and was tugging at it fiercely, muttering under her breath. One last frantic pull, and it came away in her hands.

'Several of us have sweethearts in the city – it comes in handy,' she explained, dropping the grille on the bed. 'It's a tight squeeze for some of us, and quite a longish drop too – more than your height, probably.'

'I don't mind.' Kefiri scrambled up onto the bed beside M'yani, and peered out. Below, the Palace wall fell to a grassy bank, gently sloping down to a defensive ditch, and up the other side. Once, this area had been kept tidy by an army of servants. Now, the grass and weeds were thick and neglected, promising not only a soft landing, but plenty of cover.

A quick glance to her right showed that the bulk of the double tower blocked the view of any soldiers guarding the Palace Gate. Unless someone happened to be looking out of a window or over a wall at the wrong moment, her escape would not be seen.

'The Merchants' Quarter is just the other side of the ditch,' said M'yani urgently. 'Keep low and go down it as far as the River Tower on the left, then work your way round by the docks.' She gave the Lady of Sar D'yenyi a brief, encouraging grin. 'You've got friends to go to, of course? Don't tell me who or where – it's best for me not to know. Go now – and good luck!'

With her help, Kefiri managed to wriggle through the narrow aperture and slithered painfully down the wall, scraping arms and legs and landing with a bone-shaking jar. She looked up to thank M'yani, and say goodbye, but the grille was already back in place over the window, and there was no sign of her unlooked-for and invaluable friend.

Outside the Palace Gate, trumpets sounded, startlingly harsh and abrupt. Instinctively Kefiri ducked down into the tangled grass, wondering if this meant that her absence had already been discovered. Then, her keen ears picked out the words that the King's Chamberlain was declaiming.

With unconsciously splendid timing, he was announcing her imminent marriage.

It was too much. Weak with silent laughter, Kefiri lay on her stomach in the ditch and stuffed her hand into her mouth to stifle the noise. For the first and only time in her life, she was envious of sorcerers. Oh, to be able to spy on Tsenit, and to see his face when he realized that his bride had escaped!

But of course, if she stayed here much longer, she might well be caught. Managing to keep her amusement under control, she crawled through the thick undergrowth, ignoring her bleeding arms and ripped skirt. When she reached the huge mass of the River Tower, she stood up cautiously in the deep shadow where it joined the wall. With a quick glance round, she took in the houses of the

Merchants' Quarter, spacious and comfortable, stretching down the hill to the docks; the neglected and overgrown strip of grass, scrub and rocks between Palace and houses; and the little gathering of people, some two hundred paces away, standing at a respectful distance before the Palace Gate, listening to the announcement of the King's marriage to the Lady Kefiri.

Unobtrusively, the Lady Kefiri climbed out of the ditch, shook the grass-seeds and earth from M'yani's old gown, and walked briskly down the hill to the secluded lanes and alleys separating the houses of the Merchants' Quarter.

Tsenit had resolved to tell Kefiri himself that the marriage was to be tomorrow. He wanted no one else to savour that moment when his cousin finally realized the folly of resistance and the complete absence of choice. She could agree to do as she was told: or he would rape her, then and there.

She was probably still a virgin. Tsenit, his desire stirring at the thought of it, rather hoped that she would continue defiant. In any case, she was his whatever happened. Even if he did not marry her, even if he was killed, no one else would have her after she had been defiled. And once he had stormed her fortress, there were any number of loyal Guards willing and eager to follow him in.

Faced with that fate, even Kefiri's proud obstinacy would falter. Almost a pity, Tsenit thought, and took the last steps to her high chamber at a run. Still, there was the wedding night to look forward to.

The two soldiers outside her door were playing skrath. He wondered why they were looking at him in some surprise. Then, they hastily scrambled to their feet and gave him the Royal Salute.

'Announce me to the Lady Kefiri,' he said briskly.

The guards exchanged horrified glances. The younger one went white to the lips, his eyes wide with fear. The other swallowed and said, his voice shaking, 'Your High Mightiness – you summoned her this morning, after breakfast.'

'I did *what*?' Tsenit stared at the two men. A dreadful suspicion was waking in his mind, and he thrust it away. 'I did not. You are lying.'

'No, your High Mightiness, I heard the servant tell the Lady herself. You had asked to speak to her in your chamber. And a few moments later, the Lady and the servant left.'

Blind, terrible rage was beginning to afflict him. Tsenit turned and flung the door open. Kefiri's room lay beyond, finely furnished, with clothes strewn across the bed, her untouched breakfast stale on the tray, and the sun striking warmly through the southern window. And completely, damningly empty.

She had gone. She had escaped him. And it was all the fault of these blind, negligent, treacherous, *stupid* fools who had sat there and watched her go.

He swung round. The younger guard, standing by the head of the stairs, saw the King's intention too late. Tsenit's hands clasped round his throat, choking him, and then suddenly released him. For a brief, wild instant of relief, the guard thought that was all. And then the hands hurled him with terrible force backwards down the stairs.

There was a cry, abruptly cut off. Tsenit wheeled round, his hands raised like claws, to find the other sentry staring at him in horrified disbelief. He had not even drawn his sword. With a quick, vicious movement Tsenit dragged it from the soldier's scabbard, and plunged it savagely into the man's chest.

Bronze armour had never turned steel aside. The guard screamed and fell, blood spilling profusely. Tsenit wrenched the blade out of his body and ran down the stairs, avoiding the twisted corpse of the younger soldier a dozen steps down.

The Palace must be searched. She can't have got out. She must still be here. He repeated it to himself over and over like a prayer, amid the uproar as guards and servants scoured every room, every chamber, every courtyard. Seardrith arrived back after his fruitless search for a surviving priest, and took command at once. Tsenit was strangely sorry for it. He had never killed anyone himself before, and in his present mood of savage fury, found that he was looking forward to doing it again. To strangling Kefiri, if they found her, with his bare hands.

Not immediately, though. Afterwards.

She was not in the barracks. Not in the stables, or the servants' quarters. One by one the officers came back to report to Tsenit in the Council Chamber, where Seardrith had persuaded him to go. Not in the tower, nor on the ramparts, nor in the garden or the ruined Royal Apartments. Nor was she in that grim, dank hole in the rock where he had imprisoned her, and where, now, he wished bitterly that he had left her.

Seardrith had suggested that Kefiri's maid-servant be sought as well. Tsenit occupied some of the long time of waiting by considering, in lurid and unpleasant detail, the exact fate he would design for her. But M'yani Agar's Daughter had gone out of the Palace

Gate an hour or so ago, alone and talking of some errand, and had failed to return.

It was the final proof, if proof were needed. And Tsenit, grinding his teeth in rage, had at last to acknowledge the awful and humiliating truth. Even as his Chamberlain was publicly announcing his wedding, his bride had escaped him.

If she was no longer within the Palace, she must be in the city. He would burn Zithirian down if he had to, in order to flush her out. He found he was shouting, and that all the men sitting around the Council table were staring at him with shocked and disapproving faces. And Seardrith's expression was the most hostile of all.

'Your High Mightiness, pray control yourself,' said his General icily. 'This outburst helps no one, and does nothing to find her.'

Tsenit struggled for calm against the suffocating rage which threatened to overwhelm him entirely. At last he said, through clenched jaws, 'Well, what do you suggest we do about it? Just let her go?'

'We can hardly do anything else.' Seardrith stared at him, contempt plain in his light blue eyes. 'What are the options? We can proclaim her defection, and offer a reward for her capture, with death for anyone who harbours her. That will only make you ridiculous, as well as announcing to all and sundry that she was being forced into marriage. Or, we can search the city. But that would take too long, leave the Palace dangerously unprotected, and probably arouse great hostility amongst the people. In any case, she may well have left Zithirian already, and be on her way to join your brother's army. If you still have any desire at all to win the citizens to your side, that is not a course I would advise.'

Belatedly, some sense was beginning to penetrate Tsenit's wrath. He said tightly, 'Or?'

'Or we say nothing. Ignore it. Concentrate on devising our strategy for the conflict to come. We have lost one part of our advantage, true, but we have others. And one, I may suggest, is you, your High Mightiness.'

And to Tsenit's growing interest, he outlined a plan that might yet ensure that he remained a King in Zithirian.

In every tavern in Zithirian, they were celebrating the departure of the Ska'i. Never mind that a very uncertain future lay ahead. Whichever prevailed, Tsenit or Ansaryon, the coming winter was likely to be almost as harsh as the last. But in every drinking den, low or high, landlords brought out a barrel or two of wine, carefully hoarded against just such a miracle, and invited passers-by, neighbours and regular customers to drink in thanksgiving for the freedom of the city from two of the three burdens under which it had groaned for almost a year.

The Two Crows, in Crooked Alley in the heart of the Potters' Quarter, was no exception. Its keeper, one Stekketh, had loathed the priests of Tayo, and worshipped Hegeden in his heart all his life. He had danced around the warm ashes of the Temple, he had walked across the Ska'i's deserted camp with triumphant delight, and he was in a mood to be generous. Three barrels of fine Hailyan wine – a good red vintage, strong and smooth – had been hidden in his cellar for months behind a false wall, waiting for this moment. He had his serving-men demolish the cunningly-painted wood and plaster, and carry the barrels up to the courtyard, where Stekketh himself offered brimming cups free of charge to everyone who came in. The tapsters helped him, and they were soon joined by his cousin Kaydi Gandar's Widow, and her kinswoman Engris.

'Drink?' Stekketh said happily, proffering a cheap pottery cup overflowing with wine.

Kaydi nodded. 'Only the one, though. I reckon someone needs to keep a clear head in all this, even if it's only me.'

Stekketh gestured round at the laughing, riotous people pouring into the courtyard. 'Quite a few are more than merry already. But it ain't every day we get our freedom back – and on two counts. Let's drink to the downfall of our last enemy!' He turned and raised his own cup. 'To the defeat of His Low Feebleness King Tsenit – may his death come soon, but not soon enough for his liking!'

There was a roar of appreciative laughter from those close enough to hear him, and Kaydi laughed too. What did it matter who spied on them now? Tsenit and his remaining supporters were holed up behind the Palace walls, rats in a trap, and soon, with luck, Ansaryon might be here. Perhaps the first pigeon would be waiting at the house in Snowbringer Street, bearing the message that would announce his arrival, and the fact that Herris was safe.

And when Ansaryon and his army did arrive at Zithirian, they would find no opposition, no Ska'i, no resistance at all save what his treacherous, cowardly younger brother might be able to offer from the shelter of the Palace. Tsenit was doomed, and the departure of Quenait and his warriors had sealed his fate.

But despite the jubilation of those around her, the horrible worm of fear continued to gnaw at her mind. Herris had been gone five days. Why hadn't they heard anything? The conclusion was inescapable. Either he had met with some terrible misfortune on the journey to Minassa, or there was no returning pigeon because Ansaryon wasn't coming after all.

Her worries were obviously not shared by the crowd. They had begun to sing a tavern song, which was, like all such, subtly subversive. Now, however, the impromptu chorus had changed the apparently innocent words for something much more openly derisive. Amid cheers and laughter, they shouted it again, for good measure.

'The King sits in Zithirian,
He wears a paper crown,
And soon the people will rise up
And tear his Palace down!

The King sits in Zithirian,
So sad, he's all alone,
And soon his brother will return
To take back what's his own.

The King sits in Zithirian,
He hasn't got a chance!
So eat and drink and celebrate,
And on his grave we'll dance!'

Out of the corner of her eye, Kaydi saw an eddy in the pack. Someone who wasn't too bothered about the means was struggling through it relentlessly. As the singing died raggedly away with sporadic shouts and whistles, the source of the disturbance forced her way to the space where Kaydi, Engris and Stekketh stood beside the barrels.

It was their friend and fellow conspirator Chameni. She spoke breathlessly, her rather high voice pitched to carry all round the courtyard.

'Have you heard what that misbegotten usurper is doing now? They've announced it all round the city—' She stopped for breath, her bosom heaving under her coloured leather bodice. She was still an attractive woman, and there were several ribald comments and suggestions from the more inebriated members of the crowd. Chameni folded her arms and glared at them. 'Shut up, or I won't tell you!'

At once there was a chorus of mock-grovelling pleas, and one man rolled over on his back like a dog at her feet, limbs waving in the air. 'Oh, please, Chameni, I'll be good if you tell us!'

'Shut *up*!' Kaydi yelled, above the laughter. 'She don't look as if the news is good, so it's no joking matter, is it?' Something to do with Kefiri, she was thinking, sick with apprehension. Has he had her killed? Is it her death they've proclaimed with such ceremony all over Zithirian?

But of course murdering her, though entirely characteristic of Tsenit's spiteful and vindictive nature, would make absolutely no sense now. If Ansaryon turned up, he would need every possible bargaining counter he could lay his hands on.

'He's going to marry the Lady Kefiri tomorrow!' Chameni said hoarsely.

The people gaped at her. Someone, drunkenly stupid, spoke blearily into the silence. 'What? Who? Who's going to marry her?'

'Tsenit, you stupid peasant. The King's going to marry the Lady Kefiri tomorrow – *that's* the news Chameni's brought!'

Uproar broke out. Kaydi offered a swift prayer to Sarraliss, both of thanksgiving and entreaty. At least she's still alive. But guard her, Lady of love and marriage and delights. If half the tales I've heard about the King are true, she'd probably prefer death to becoming his Queen.

From the comments around her, a good proportion of the crowd, mostly women, felt the same. Close by, two men were arguing furiously: one thought that the impending marriage strengthened Tsenit's hold on the throne, the other was scornful. 'He could marry the Emperor's daughter and he'd still be a traitor and a murderer! This doesn't change a thing!'

Stekketh grinned at his cousin's widow, and offered her another cup of wine. 'Take this – you look as if you need it. Now what are we going to do?'

In the middle of this yelling, half-drunk, disputatious throng, they might have been standing alone on Mount Annako and enjoyed less privacy. Even Engris was engaged in hot debate with Chameni. Kaydi said urgently, 'I don't know. All I do know is that she wouldn't agree to marry him unless she was forced into it. And while he's got her as a hostage up in the Palace, married or not, he's got a hold over us and over Ansaryon – when he comes. But why? Why announce the marriage now?' She chewed her lip, thinking furiously. 'Unless he thinks the citizens are more likely to support him if he marries her? After all, without the Ska'i to protect him, he'll need all the help he can get against Ansaryon.'

'He might be right.' Stekketh gestured at the turbulent mass jostling around them. Several, wine-cups in hand, were toasting the wedding. Others were jeering them for traitors, and the mood of the crowd was rapidly turning ugly. One of Tsenit's supporters reeled against Kaydi, spilling a good part of his wine onto her skirt, and bawled, 'Let's drink to the King and his new Queen!'

'Not if I have any say in the matter!' she said, her irascible temper beginning to get the better of her. She knocked the cup out of his hand, and it smashed on the flagstoned courtyard.

All around them, the noise stopped abruptly. Into the brief, blessed silence, Kaydi cried urgently, 'You fools – do you really think the Lady Kefiri would willingly marry her father's murderer? This won't be a true marriage – she wouldn't give her consent, she'd die first! She's being forced into it!'

'How do you know?' The man whose cup she had broken thrust his face belligerently close to hers. 'When did you last go up to the Palace, Kaydi Gandar's Widow? How do you know what the Lady Kefiri wants?'

'*I* know.'

It was a girl's voice, young, clear, and loud. Kaydi whipped round, staring.

A few paces away, flushed, disreputable, clad in old torn clothes and her hair a tangled and unruly mass of dark curls, the King's bride stood amongst the crowd.

She sent a swift smile to Kaydi, and then spoke again. 'I know because I *am* the Lady Kefiri. I've just managed to escape from the Palace. Believe me, I wouldn't marry Tsenit if he were the last man in the known world. And perhaps when he finds out I've gone, he'll realize it!'

There was a brief, astonished silence, and then the cheering began. Windows rattled, panic-stricken sparrows and pigeons shot into the air, and Kaydi, tears in her eyes, put her hands over her ears. Kefiri, looking dazed, was suddenly the centre of a wild mass of gesticulating, shouting, exultant people. Within a few heartbeats they were hoisting her upwards onto the broad shoulders of one of Stekketh's tapsters, as if she were a gardener whose work had won the Green Crown, or a successful competitor in the Bridal Race. Someone was shouting, 'To the Palace! We'll show him what we think of him, eh, boys?'

Suddenly, Kaydi saw what would happen next with awful clarity. They would pour out of the Potters' Quarter with their Princess at their head, and sweep like an avalanche up the Ceremonial Way, drawing all the other citizens with them, to roar their hatred and defiance at the Palace Gate.

And then?

She could imagine the men on the walls, all loyal to Tsenit, and equipped with bows and arrows and throwing-spears. And against even a few score soldiers, the unarmed, headstrong, valiant people of Zithirian would have little chance.

And neither would Kefiri. If the archers had any sense, she would be one of the first to die, bargaining counter or not.

Kaydi picked up the big mallet which Stekketh had used to tap the wine, and swung it against one of the iron staves binding the cask. It must have been almost empty, for it gave off a hollow, resonant sound. No wonder they're so riotous, part of her mind thought drily. Even two or three cups of strong Hailyan wine goes a long way on half-starved stomachs.

The deep boom of the blow turned heads and brought a slight diminution of the rumpus. She thumped the mallet twice more, harder, and was rewarded by something approaching silence. Kefiri, precariously perched on the tapster's shoulders, looked rather astonished, and a little frightened as well, as if she had underestimated the scale and strength of the welcome she had received.

'Listen to me, all of you!' Kaydi shouted at the sea of faces filling the courtyard. She glanced at Stekketh, standing there with Landaya, his largest tapster, and added swiftly, 'Get me up onto the barrel. I need to be heard, and seen.'

She had half imagined that Stekketh might argue, he hadn't her quickness of thought and would probably have gone rushing off to the Palace with the rest without reckoning the consequences. But to his credit he nodded to Landaya, and the two men hoisted her up onto the top of the cask. Being nearly empty, it wobbled a bit on the uneven stones, but they steadied it.

Kaydi stared down at the people clustered round her, people she had known all her life, friends, cousins, husband's kin, customers or acquaintances, women she had gossiped with, men who had sold her pots, cloth, provisions, and for a moment her sense of certainty wavered. What was she, Kaydi Gandar's Widow, doing up here? What right had she to tell the citizens what to do?

Into the expectant silence, a hoarse voice cried her name. She stared at the entrance to the courtyard, where there seemed to be some sort of struggle going on. A hand gestured frantically above the crowd, and the voice shouted again. 'Kaydi! It's come! At last, it's come!'

And she realized that it was her servant, Shilda, who had gone back to her house after they had looked at the deserted Ska'i camp from the walls.

'Let him through!' someone yelled, and with reluctance the people made way for him. Scarlet with excitement and exertion, her lame servant emerged from the crowd at her feet, and thrust something up at her. 'Here you are, Kaydi – the message has come!'

It was a tiny piece of paper, tightly folded and worn at the edges. With extreme care, she unrolled it and stared at what was written inside.

'If all goes well, we will be in sight of the city this afternoon, five days before the full moon. Have the people ready.' And the Lord Ansaryon's own sign was below, the symbol for each of the four syllables of his name, in the old, angular Zithiriani script.

They were all looking at her expectantly, in utter silence. With sudden wild jubilation bubbling up inside her, Kaydi waved the paper in the air. 'A message – from the Lord Ansaryon! He and his army are coming – they'll be here today!'

The barrel beneath her feet swayed alarmingly. As the screams and shouts of joy erupted all around her, Kaydi finally lost her balance and tumbled sideways, the precious paper still clutched in her hand. Her landing on the hard stones was painful, and would have hurt even worse if poor Stekketh hadn't unwittingly broken her fall.

But it didn't matter. Herris was safe, and Ansaryon was only a few hours away. At last, at long long last, it seemed as if Zithirian's troubles were truly over.

CHAPTER
TWENTY-SEVEN

The grey pigeon, her neck handsomely collared with jewelled feathers in green and gold, launched herself from Herris's hands and rose into the air on a clatter of wings. As the boy and the army watched, she circled high above them, twice, three times, and then abruptly changed direction and flew unerringly north, towards Zithirian.

They had halted some ten miles from the city, a distance that would take a man on horseback a couple of hours to accomplish, if he were not in too much of a hurry. As the pigeon flew, with the hope of home-coming to spur her on, she would reach the city before the trampling army could travel a mile further.

Herris, his duty done, climbed back onto the wagon with the empty basket, and the driver urged the horses on again. Home. He craved it even more than the pigeon did, despite the fact that his mother's welcome would probably include a blistering tirade about his stupidity and disobedience. And if it was only ten miles away, they would reach the city well before sunset.

The first pigeon had been sent as the army left Hailyan, and the second had been flown the following morning. Now that his mission had been successfully accomplished, Herris was secretly rather relieved that he was evidently not expected to fight. He had played his part, and been commended for it by the Lord Ansaryon himself. He'd had enough of adventure. All he really wanted was to be home again.

A few miles north of Hailyan, they had come upon the first burnt-out village. Either someone had buried the bodies, or the people had managed to escape in time: anyway, it was utterly deserted, the fields full of tangled weeds, and not an animal in sight. It was the first of many: over the next three days, the army saw sickening evidence, along the road, of the Ska'i's lust for wanton destruction and slaughter. They did not stop to bury the headless, decaying corpses scattered around the ruins, but with every new horror, each fresh atrocity, the mood of the army grew darker and grimmer. Even the Toktel'yans, hardened soldiers who had a reputation for brutality themselves, seemed appalled by this dreadful display of barbarity and cruelty. In some places, it appeared that no one had been spared, not even the tiniest baby.

'And whatever you may say of us,' remarked General Sekkenet, surveying one particularly ghastly scene of slaughter at a small farmstead, 'we Toktel'yans do not make a practice of maiming and murdering young children for amusement.'

From time to time, the boldest of those who had escaped the Ska'i came down from their refuges in the hills. Most of them were a pathetic sight, half-starved, ragged and fearful. To each of them, Ansaryon spoke in person: they were given food, money and clothes, and told to return to their homes, for their long nightmare was ended at last.

And finally, three days after leaving Hailyan, the first of the Tanathi outriders breasted a low hill to the west of the river road, and saw, very far in the distance, something sparkling fitfully in the morning sun.

'Zithirian!' Abreth cried, reining in his horse and pointing.

His sister, sitting beside him, shaded her hand over her eyes, and nodded. 'Yes, those are the gold banners on top of the towers.' She paused for a moment, and then said, in a different voice, 'I think some part of it is burning.'

There was indeed a smudge of smoke against the distant sky. They stared at it for a few heartbeats longer, and then Abreth turned to beckon Sherren, urging his horse up the hill. 'Go back to Ansaryon, tell him Zirithian's in sight. And there's no sign of the Ska'i between us and the city – no movement at all, as far as we can see. And tell him too that something seems to be on fire within the city – although as it must be a dozen miles away as Hegeden flies, it's hard to be sure.'

Sherren raised his hand in acknowledgement, and wheeled his black gelding round. They watched him gallop back down the hill and set off towards the long, heavy pall of dust, some two or three miles away in the valley of the Kefirinn, that marked the progress of the main army. Then Halthris turned again to look at the city which she had last seen burning, on the night of the Ska'i attack, and where fire seemed to be raging again.

'We could be there before nightfall,' Abreth said softly. 'I wonder what's waiting for us?'

'Ansaryon might know.' Halthris stood in her stirrups, flexing tired muscles, and glanced at her brother. 'Sorcery can be useful, sometimes.'

'After he saved us at Sar D'yenyi, I wouldn't argue with that.' Abreth paused, his eyes still on that distant blur and glitter, and then added, 'Have you and he fallen out?'

Halthris gave him a startled glance. 'What do you mean?'

'When we were all cooped up in Sar D'yenyi last winter, you two were very friendly, as I remember. But now I haven't seen you exchange so much as a glance, let alone speak to each other.'

'He's had rather a lot on his mind recently – or hadn't you noticed?' Halthris narrowed her eyes. 'Anyway, what business is it of yours?'

'I'm your brother. I have a right to know. Also, Tarli asked me to find out what you were going to do about Vinnath. You know she's never liked him – she thinks he isn't good enough for you.'

'And elder sisters are worst of all! Just because Tarli has been happily wed to her Hearth for eight years, she thinks I should be too. I wish all of you would stop speculating, just for once, and leave my affairs out of your morbid obsession with gossip.'

'There's no need to be nasty about it.' Abreth checked his horse, which was shifting restlessly, and gave his sister a mischievous grin. 'Anyway, it all goes to prove what Inri was saying yesterday. A lover can pretend anything except indifference. And you, little sister, are certainly not indifferent.'

And before she could retaliate, he had urged his horse forward, out of her reach, and down the long smooth hill towards the river.

Sometimes, Halthris thought angrily, her family could be so infuriating that she almost wished she'd been born an orphan.

She turned her mount to look over the wide empty steppe, stretching for hundreds of miles to the west. Somewhere perhaps, among those moors and hills, rocks and valleys, Fess roamed wild and free at last. She sent out her silent call, as she had done ever since leaving Minassa, but there was no reply. There never had been any, and nor, in her heart, did she expect it. The cat had left her, and would not return. She had always known it would happen one day, but even now, months after their parting, she missed Fess more intensely than she had ever dreamed possible.

Only the wind stirred in the dry dun grass of late summer. She sighed, and sent her dark bay Toktel'yan horse down the hill after her brother.

The miles reeled on, under the Toktel'yans' booted steady feet. Ten to go: then seven: then five. The Tanathi, ranging ahead, sent back regular reports, and each messenger said the same. Zithirian, or something within it, is burning. And there is no sign, anywhere, of the Ska'i.

Three miles from the city, Ansaryon halted his army again. It was two hours until sunset, and they had no idea of what awaited them. Surely by now Quenait's warriors would have attacked them, or at the very least watched their progress from the hills. And yet there had been nothing.

It was then that the first farmer, an old woman with almost no teeth left, came out of a house they had assumed to be a deserted ruin, and approached them. Her news proved to be so astounding that cheers broke out spontaneously amongst the Zithiriani soldiers who spoke to her first. They hoisted her onto an officer's horse and led her back to where the Lord Ansaryon stood with his generals, waiting for more Tanathi reports, and discussing their next move.

The Ska'i had left, the previous night. They had raided the Temple, slaughtered every last man and woman in it from the High Priestess downwards, and were gone this morning. The man calling himself King was making a proper fool of himself scouring the city for a living priest so that he could marry the Lady Kefiri –

'*What* did you say?' demanded the Lord Ansaryon, and the old woman, who'd killed two Ska'i with a pitchfork and survived the hardships of winter and the raids of summer undaunted, stared up at him, refusing to be cowed.

'What I said, Sir. Your brother's going to marry the Lady Kefiri tomorrow, though how he can do it without a priest I'm sure I don't know. My cousin came out this morning to tell me the Ska'i had gone, and that's what he said, anyway. Everyone's been hoping you were coming, sir, but we never expected you this quick – and neither will Tsenit. He's in the Palace with his Guard, hiding from the people – they keep shouting and throwing things at him when he goes out, and he don't like it.'

'You surprise me,' Ansaryon said drily. 'So – the citizens will welcome me?'

'With open arms, Sir. We've been waiting so long – you be sure and kill that wicked treacherous usurper for all our sakes, won't you!'

'I'll do my best,' he promised her solemnly, and watched as she was led away, her lined brown face crackling with joyful glee.

She had told him exactly what he had most hoped to hear. He was sorry, though, that the Ska'i had apparently saved him the duty of killing D'thliss. And there was no word of Bron's fate. Had his son died too, in the burning Temple?

He had sworn a sacred oath to protect him. And if it still lay in his power to do so, he would.

He looked up at the ring of expectant faces around him: Invan; Sekkenet; King Temiltan; Halmon, who led the men of Lelyent.

'It seems the people are with us. Also, by now the pigeon should have brought its message to Kaydi Gandar's Widow, so they should know that we are almost at the gates. I propose we march on to Zithirian now, make our camp outside the walls and send a force within the city to secure it. Then we can extract Tsenit from the Palace at our leisure.'

The men were tired: they had marched nearly thirty miles that day, and the same the day before. But the news that Zithirian lay open to them put a smile on every face, and renewed vigour in every step. The last three miles swept by, to the beat of drums and the cheerful songs of five different armies, in three contrasting languages. And as the sun at last began to drop into a low band of cloud on the farthest horizon above the steppes, the advanced guard appeared before the gates of Zithirian.

Ansaryon had rearranged the order of march, and it was now his own men, from Sar D'yenyi and the city itself, who led the column with himself, Invan and his other chief officers at their head, the Lelyentans and Minassans behind them, and the Imperial soldiers, the traditional enemy, discreetly in the rear.

It was just as the old woman had said. There were no Ska'i on what had obviously been the site of their camp. But the huge Sunset Gate was firmly shut, and the high ramparts to either side were thronged with curious heads.

'Don't approach within bowshot,' Invan said urgently to his leader. 'Send a herald, I beg you – it only takes one traitor with a bow, and our cause is lost.'

Ansaryon did not appear to be listening. His eyes were shut, and his face, turned towards the city, was remote, closed, and totally without expression. Invan reached out to touch him, and Sekkenet swiftly stopped him, with a significant shake of his head.

Of course, the Toktel'yans understood sorcery. Invan, the hairs prickling on his arms, had to wait impatiently until Ansaryon came back to himself. Magic still made him thoroughly uneasy, and his fingers itched to make the warding sign.

It didn't take more than a few heartbeats longer. Suddenly, his leader's eyes were open, and he was smiling. 'Your concern for me is very touching, Invan – but misplaced. And I've had enough of being called a coward. Come with me.'

They had halted perhaps three bowshots to the south of the city, fairly close to the river. Ansaryon twitched the reins of his white Toktel'yan horse, and rode forward alone, to the cheers of the men behind him. Hastily, his generals glanced at each other and then followed with considerable apprehension.

As they drew closer to the city, the applause behind them diminished, and Invan heard at last the cries of joyous welcome from the citizens gathered on the walls. Someone leaned over and threw something, and Halmon swore and clapped a hand pointlessly to his sword. But it was only a branch of trumpet vine, descending lazily in the cooling evening air to lie on the trampled earth in front of the gate.

Ansaryon halted his horse, and as he did so a last spear of sunlight leapt out from the clouds behind him, striking sparks of silver from his pale hair and gold from his bronze tunic, and casting a long purple shadow right up to the two double towers flanking the gate. A murmur rose from the walls, as if people saw an omen or a portent in the sight. Still desperately worried, Invan reined in his own horse a couple of paces behind his leader's, and felt his heart thud sickeningly beneath his scaled armour. One man with a bow . . .

'Citizens of Zithirian!'

Ansaryon had pitched his voice to carry right along the walls. Suddenly there was utter quiet, as if those on the ramparts were holding their breath. In the hush, Invan heard the distant sighing of the breeze in the rushes along the river, and then, far and high and keen, the cry of an eagle. But the sky, luminously blue, was quite empty.

'Citizens of Zithirian, I am Ansaryon, second son of Varathand, Fourth of His Name. I ask for your help to overthrow my brother Tsenit, who holds the throne illegally by right of murder and treachery, and to restore rightful rule to our city. And in return I promise you truth, and freedom, and justice, for everyone in all the lands of Zithirian, from the poorest to the most wealthy. And this I swear to you on my blood, in the name of my Ancestor Tayo, and also in the sacred names of Hegeden, Lord of Sky and Air, and of Sarraliss, Lady of Horse and Earth and Harvest, that I may suffer their everlasting hatred if I break my oath!'

He had a dagger in his grasp, gold-hilted and studded with gems: as Invan drew in his breath at the invocation of the forbidden deities, Ansaryon stroked the blade lightly across the back of each hand, three times, making a star of blood. Then he sheathed the knife and held them up, palms inwards, so that the people on the walls could see.

For a heartbeat longer, there was silence, until the wild cheering began. Invan, moved despite himself, swallowed convulsively. And then the two huge gates, three times the height of a tall man, swung ponderously inwards with a groan of welcome, and Ansaryon, alone, bareheaded, walked his horse towards the city he had come to set free.

Invan had initially feared and mistrusted his leader, and respect, let alone liking, had come slowly and grudgingly. But at that moment all his doubts finally vanished, and he saw at last the marks of true greatness in the man he served.

'He's mad!' Halmon was saying in his rustic Zithiriani. 'What does he think he's doing? They could tear him in pieces!'

'No, they won't,' Invan said, a smile curving his mouth. 'I think you'll find he knows exactly what he's doing. But you're right, he shouldn't go in there entirely alone.' He turned and snapped his fingers at one of the younger officers, sitting his horse just behind them. 'Go and order the Zithiriani contingent up to escort the Lord Ansaryon into the city. Go on – hurry!'

The man sketched a salute, wheeled his mount and set off at a gallop back to the waiting army. Invan waited until the first ranks of men began to move, and then he urged his own horse forward, under the deep shadowed arch beneath the Sunset Gate.

Up in the Palace, they had been aware for some time that Ansaryon was approaching. The news brought by the last pigeon – saved by Shilda in the nick of time from Garool's eager jaws – had spread round the city like a summer grass fire. The more equivocal of Tsenit's supporters hurried home to their houses, and hoped that their neighbours' memories would prove short. Those who were still loyal made their way to the Palace, to give the King the dreadful tidings. The day of reckoning had arrived: his brother was almost at the gates, with an army inflated by rumour and terrified exaggeration to twenty thousand men. What hope did they have, against such an enemy?

Tsenit, however, did not despair. Seardrith had shown him a possible way out. If it worked, he would become the undisputed ruler of Zithirian. And if it didn't . . . well, with the odds so greatly stacked against him, he had nothing left to lose.

So he ordered the Palace Gate to be barred and the Guard to man the walls, and went up to the ramparts of the central tower, the highest point in the city. He stood there for a long time, watching the southern road. At last, he saw the first signs of Ansaryon's

approach. And with a gambler's hope lightening his heart, he ran
down the stairs to make ready for the confrontation to come.

The crowds lined Sunset Street five, six deep, cheering, throwing
flowers and greenery into the path of Ansaryon's horse. His cousin
Kefiri stood in the open space in front of the smouldering Temple,
her heart banging against her ribs and her palms sweating despite
the autumnal chill in the evening air. She wore the best gown that
Kaydi had been able to find, a gorgeously embroidered crimson silk
with a bodice of gilded leather, and in her arms she carried a
hastily-woven garland of white trumpet flowers. For, as Kaydi had
pointed out, the rightful King needed a crown of some sorts until
he could lay his hands on the real one, and what better than the
flowers which were one of the symbols of Zithirian?

He was nearly here. People were surging forward, showering
him with blossoms and petals, kissing his horse, shouting their
overwhelming joy and relief, so his progress was very slow. But at
last he emerged into the space where she stood alone, and halted
his white stallion. All around him, the jostling crowds paused too,
waiting expectantly for Kefiri to speak.

She met her cousin's eyes. They were brilliant with barely-
contained emotion, and he looked dazed, wondering, as if the
exultation and acclaim of his people had been far beyond all hope.
She sent him a small, private smile, and then walked forward until
she was only a pace of two from the white horse's nose. Making her
voice loud and clear, she spoke the words she had been rehearsing
to herself for hours, though they still came from her heart.

'My Lord Ansaryon, rightful heir to the rule and kingship of
this city – I bid you joyfully welcome in the name of all the people.
And I give you this crown of flowers as a symbol and promise of
the sacred silver crown of Tayo, which will soon be yours.' And she
held out the intricate garland which Tsari's nimble fingers had
woven together from the flowers in Kaydi's courtyard, white and
fragrant in her hands.

Gravely he accepted it, and placed it on his head. At once, a
huge roar of approval erupted around them, and the horse, who
had been quite steady up until now, flung up its fine head and side-
stepped nervously. Ansaryon bent and calmed it with a few words
and a soothing pat, and then turned to look at his people, his hand
upraised. As silence fell again, he spoke to them: and perhaps only
Kefiri, who knew him so well, could discern the depths of feeling
disguised by his composed manner and level voice.

'I thank you all from my heart for this welcome, citizens of Zithirian. I come to claim what is mine by right of birth, and to overthrow the murderer and usurper, my brother Tsenit. Have I your consent?'

Their shout of fervent agreement might have been heard on Estray, fifty miles away.

'Then with your permission I will go now to confront my brother, and demand that he surrender his wrongful and unlawful rule over you. Will you follow me?'

Again, the yell of assent that sent Kefiri's ears ringing. Ansaryon leaned down and said to her, 'You have earned this as much as I have – more, perhaps. Will you ride with me?'

And so, when the Guard waiting on the Palace walls saw the procession, approaching up the Ceremonial Way, it was led by a man and a woman sitting together on a tall white horse, richly caparisoned in red and gold. A great seething mass of people crowded behind them, soldiers, citizens, men, women and children all mixed in together, in such vast numbers that almost every house in Zithirian must have lain empty.

At the broad open space before the Palace Gate, Ansaryon stopped his horse and turned to indicate to the people that they should halt too. Invan, fighting his way through the packed, joyful mass with a few of his men panting in his wake, felt an awful apprehension clenching his bowels. It had been foolhardy enough for his leader to ride alone into Zithirian, when only his life stood between Tsenit and almost total victory. True, sorcery had ensured that he was certain of his welcome. But here in the Palace lurked the brother and enemy who had gained the throne by deceit and treachery, and who would surely not hesitate to use such methods again. And yet he was once more going to ride up to the Gate as if protected by a sorcerer's rumoured invulnerability. What was the legend? That a man who had sold his soul to demons and evil spirits could only be slain by a silver-tipped arrow?

Invan prayed to Tayo, as he had never prayed before, that the weapons of the men gazing down from the walls were made of ordinary wood and steel.

He struggled out of the confines of the crowd. Ansaryon had put Kefiri down, and she stood beside him, her hand on the horse's reins, talking urgently. Invan could guess what she was saying, and was proved right when the girl turned to him, desperate appeal in her face. '*You* try and persuade him, Invan – I can't. He wants to speak to Tsenit face to face. And we're almost within bowshot now – he can't go any closer, or they'll surely shoot him down!'

'They won't,' Ansaryon said. His eyes were fixed on the walls of the Palace, and in his face was still the light of purpose, the spirit of destiny, that had led him into the city and brought him the passionate acclaim of the people. 'Tsenit knows there is no further advantage in treachery. He must behave with honour now. And if he kills me in full view of the people of Zithirian, he forfeits their support and their affection for ever more. As soon as they get the chance, they will have their revenge – and he knows it.' He glanced round at Invan and Kefiri, and his voice was suddenly and unexpectedly bitter. 'Besides, I will give him no further opportunity to call me a coward.' And he flicked the reins out of his cousin's grasp and urged the horse forward, up the slope towards the Palace.

'He mustn't go on his own,' Kefiri said fiercely, and began to walk after him. Invan looked round, saw a group of his soldiers hovering at the front of the crowd, and beckoned urgently. They came running up at once, and he ordered them into a Toktel'yan column, in five rows of three.

Ansaryon said, without looking back, 'Keep them there, Invan. This is for me alone.'

'No, it's not.' Kefiri came up beside him. 'If I can share the glory with you, then I can certainly share the danger.'

For a long moment their eyes met, blue and silver, but no silent speech passed between them. Then Ansaryon laughed suddenly. 'Very well, Kef – I've said it isn't dangerous, so you may accompany me. I just hope that Tsenit's love of power hasn't corrupted all his common sense.'

And Kefiri, who had good reason to suspect that it had, smiled bravely back, and once more took the reins of his horse.

They walked together up to the Gate. Behind them, the vast crowd swayed and muttered and pushed each other, frantic for a better view. Up on the walls, the archers of the Royal Guard, famous for their ability to hit a target at a hundred paces, not once but twenty times in succession, bent their bows and waited for the order.

'I am Ansaryon, rightful King of Zithirian – and I come to you in peace, with the support of all the people of this city who are standing now behind me, to demand the surrender of my brother Tsenit, usurper of the Crown, so that he may be properly called to account for his crimes.'

Silence fell. The sun had set, and the high, light clouds above them were delicately tinged with dove grey and apricot. The steady, brilliant beacon of Issir already glowed bright against the deepening blue of the evening sky. Northwards, the clouds were massing, grey and ominous, and the air felt cold and damp: there would be rain tonight.

Kefiri, watching, saw a sudden shuffle of heads on the walls, and then, appearing amongst them, a man whom she recognized immediately, with a piercing, visceral stab of loathing and disgust. He wore Tayo's sacred Crown, a narrow band of silver, and his voice was friendly and reasonable.

'Good evening to you, brother. What can I do for you?'

Nausea swept over Kefiri, so strong that she nearly vomited. How could she ever have been deceived by that pleasant, plausible mask?

'You know very well what you can do for me,' Ansaryon said. 'You can return to me my rightful inheritance. Unfortunately, those innocents whom you had murdered to obtain it cannot have their lives restored to them so easily. As you can see, I have the support of the citizens of Zithirian, who have come to despise and loathe you for the suffering they have endured because of what you have done. Also, I think it's only fair to warn you that I have an army of eight thousand men outside the gates of the city. As your repulsive allies seem to have deserted you, you must be heavily outnumbered. Are you going to hide in the Palace until we break the door down, or will you take the path of courage and honour, and surrender to me now? That way, no one else need die.'

Kefiri, her knees shaking with cold and fear beneath the thin silk of her gown, saw with astonishment a smile break out on Tsenit's face. He leaned over the rampart, his dark hair blowing around the narrow, gleaming Crown. 'I can tell you now, my feeble, necromantic brother – I will never willingly surrender what is mine by right of possession. I have the Crown, the Guard, the Palace. What are you going to do? Throw men against the walls like rocks? They will only break. And the Ska'i will be back.'

'Even if they do return, my army is more than a match for that barbarian rabble.' Ansaryon's voice was quiet, but the hush was so absolute that most of the people could hear him quite clearly. 'However, the point is this, Tsenit – I will no longer call you "brother", for you forfeited that title when you ordered me and all our family killed, because we stood in the way of your greed and your ambition. The point is this. I have eight thousand soldiers, I have the overwhelming support of the citizens, and I have right and justice on my side. What do you have? A thousand or so of the Royal Guard at a guess, no more, a high wall to hide behind, and a huge amount of bravado. You made a great show of your courage, when you ran the Bridal Race four times. Will you deploy it now, and come down, and surrender to me, or will you compel me to use force? You have no hope, Tsenit – you cannot possibly win.'

The man on the walls laughed. The shocking, ugly sound crashed against Kefiri's ears, and she shivered. 'I challenge you!' he shouted, in a great voice that reverberated all down the Ceremonial Way. 'I challenge you, Ansaryon, to a fight to the death. To the survivor will go the Kingdom, without further dispute. That seems fair, doesn't it? And since you are so keen to avoid bloodshed, it's only right that it should be restricted to the two of us. No one else need suffer, or die. What do you say, brother? Will you prove yourself a man, and accept? Or will you waste more lives, or use your filthy sorcery to bring me to my knees? For I can assure you, dear brother, that I will not surrender to you while there is any breath left in my body!'

His last words bounced and echoed over the heads of the crowd. Kefiri looked up at Ansaryon and felt sick. Tsenit was fit, hardy, well practised with sword and knife and spear, skilled in the fighting arts since childhood, while his brother, immersed in learning and sorcery, had always scorned such pursuits. The hardships and experiences of the past year had wrought a considerable change in him, and he had put in many hours of weapons training at Sar D'yenyi. But he could not possibly have acquired the instinctive reflexes and intuitive gifts of an athletic and natural fighter like Tsenit.

You have the choice, she thought, willing him to hear her unspoken words: never had her desire for the ability to thought-link been more urgent. To fight Tsenit in this ludicrous challenge, in hand-to-hand combat, will surely risk your death. It's obvious why he has chosen to do this – he has nothing to lose. But you have all the winning counters, Ansary. For all our sakes, for Zithirian, for everything we have worked for over the past year – give his suggestion the contempt it deserves.

The silence stretched out interminably. The white stallion shifted his weight from one hind leg to the other, and blew softly down his nose. Automatically Kefiri stroked his neck, and glanced up at her cousin's face. He was staring at his brother on the ramparts, and there was a look of such naked hatred in his eyes that she flinched.

'Well?' Tsenit's voice boomed mockingly down. 'I'm surprised you even have to think about it, *brother*. After all, a proven coward who hasn't even got the guts to enter the Bridal Race isn't going to take the opportunity to fight like a true man for what he wants. Come on, Ansaryon, admit it – you're just a miserable faint-heart

who's only capable of being brave with an army to do your fighting
for you. You're frightened, aren't you? Frightened of losing?
Frightened of pain? That doesn't surprise me. Anyone who uses
sorcery likes life comfortable, easy and *safe*. You're so sure you've
got justice on your side – well, let Tayo be the judge of that. Or are
you too scared to put it to the test?'

His jeering tone must have been clear to all the crowd, even
those who were too far away to hear the actual words. Kefiri was
trembling so violently that she had to cling to the horse's mane for
support. No man with any vestige of pride or self-respect could
listen to those derisive taunts without rising to the bait. And she
knew that the popular, sneering assumption of his supposed weakness and cowardice had cut Ansaryon very deep.

'I am not frightened of you, Tsenit,' he said. 'I am not even
frightened of your deviousness, or your treachery. I accept your
challenge.'

Silence, brief and astounded; and then a great howl arose from
the ranks of the citizens. Protest? Anger? Support? Approval?
Kefiri could not tell. Her eyes were filling fast with tears: she tore
her hand impatiently across her face, and hissed furiously, 'Ansary,
listen to me! You don't have to do this – you don't have to respond
to his horrible insults. He's goaded you into it, you've done just
what he wants, and you'll throw your life away because he's bound
to win, and for what? To satisfy your stupid ideas of pride and
honour!'

She might as well not have spoken. His gaze did not flicker
from that dark, jubilant figure on the ramparts. Tsenit laughed
again, like a prisoner unexpectedly released. 'Well, *brother*, I didn't
believe you had it in you! So you accept! Tomorrow, outside the
Sunset Gate, an hour after sunrise?'

'I accept.' Ansaryon paused, and then added, 'As the person
challenged, by custom I may propose the weapons. One sword and
one dagger each, no more – no shields, no spears, no bows, no
axes. No poison, either – and no sorcery. Do you agree to these
conditions?'

'I agree,' Tsenit said eagerly. 'And the fight will be to the death.
No quarter to be asked, or given.'

'Agreed.' Ansaryon smiled, and raised his hand. 'May the
Ancestor choose which of us has the right, and guide our hearts,
our hands and our weapons accordingly. Until tomorrow, Tsenit –
and I will not wish you a good night, or pleasant dreams.'

'Until tomorrow, brother.' Tsenit dropped his voice so that only
those closest could still hear. 'And I am glad to discover that you

are after all not such a coward – even if you are still a fool. Sleep well, on your last night of life.'

And to Kefiri, his mocking words seemed like a certain portent of doom.

CHAPTER
TWENTY-EIGHT

'Hal! I've been looking for you everywhere!' Inri came running up to her friend's horse. 'Where have you been?'

'On patrol,' Abreth said, halting his own mount next to his sister's. 'We've found the Ska'i's track – it leads northwards, along the river. And they've left no one to cover their retreat, by the look of it. So – what's been happening here?'

He gestured round at the camp, which had been pitched just south of Zithirian, on overgrown fields that last year had been rich and yellow with grain. The Tanathi mareks, large and round, were easy to spot amongst the pointed white canvas tents of the Tok-tel'yans, and the open fires of everyone else, and Halthris and Abreth had made for them first, threading their way through the confusion and gathering dusk, and wondering, with increasing alarm, why the army seemed to be in such an uproar.

'The city's for us, and the gates are open,' Inri said breathlessly. 'But Tsenit is still in the Palace – Ansaryon rode up with all the citizens to demand his surrender. Tsenit refused – I suppose you wouldn't expect him to do anything else, really. But then he challenged Ansaryon to a single combat – a fight to the death, with the winner getting the crown. *And Ansaryon accepted!'*

Aware of Halthris's sudden stillness beside him, Abreth said in astonishment, 'He must be mad!'

'I know. Whatever else Tsenit is, or has done, he's surely a much better fighter than his brother. Until last year, I don't think Ansaryon knew whether to hold a sword by the blade or the hilt.' Inri's voice cracked suddenly with the force of her feeling. 'We've spent a year – a *whole year* – helping him. Why does he have to go and throw it all away now, when we must outnumber Tsenit and his Guard by nearly ten to one?'

'Perhaps Tsenit called him a coward,' Halthris said suddenly. 'He's very sensitive to that accusation.'

'He can't be!' Inri cried in exasperation. 'He's *proved* he isn't – on that retreat to Sar D'yenyi, if nothing else! And the way he rode into the city today, alone – you should have seen it, you really should, it was magnificent – he might have been killed, and still he went in on his own. That's not the action of a coward.'

'I know.' Halthris was glad that the encroaching dusk would make it hard to read the expression on her face. 'But he still feels the need to prove it to himself, if not to anyone else.'

'And so he risks his life tomorrow,' Inri said. She looked up at her friend, her hands spread in appeal. 'You're closer to him than anyone else, Hal. Couldn't *you* do something? Persuade him not to throw everything away for the sake of a stupid gesture?'

'What could I do?' Halthris asked bleakly. In her mind, suddenly sharp, were images of Ansaryon commanding the avalanche; keeping the snow from them on the slopes of Estray; practising with his sword, doggedly determined, on the frozen lake around Sar D'yenyi; and in his room in the Imperial Palace in Toktel'yi, his clothes dripping wet, his eyes dark and desperate with desire, saying, 'I want you so much. Do you want me?'

Yes, she would try to speak to him. Not to persuade him – she knew him well enough to be certain that he could not, now, be deflected from his chosen course. But to offer him some hope for the future, even if that future did not contain him.

'You could do *something*,' Abreth was saying earnestly. 'I know you could. He'd listen to you.'

Halthris was tempted to point out that if Ansaryon were to withdraw from Tsenit's challenge now, hours after accepting it, that would brand him a coward far more completely and damningly than any malicious rumour or gossip had done. Rightly or wrongly, he had made his free choice: what possible justification did she have to try and persuade him to change his mind? He would not listen to her, and their friendship would be destroyed.

And on what might be the last night of his life, she could not do it.

She would reveal nothing of this, however, to her dear brother and her closest friend, or the real reason why she would try to speak to Ansaryon. She said slowly, feigning reluctance, 'I can try . . .'

Inri's face cleared magically. 'Oh, thank you, Hal – I knew you would, and no one else has a chance of succeeding. Half the army are furious, and the other half are laying bets.'

'Including all the Tanathi, I expect,' Halthris said drily. 'Where is he? In his tent?'

'His tent? Oh, sorry, he isn't in the camp – he's in the city, with Kefiri, at the house of one of the leaders of the resistance. I don't know where it is exactly, but the gates are still open, and I'm sure anyone will be able to tell you.'

'I'd better go now, then,' Halthris said. She smiled rather bleakly at them. 'Please don't expect me to work a miracle. He can be very stubborn, as you know. But at least I can say I've tried.'

'And you never know,' said Abreth, with a rather half-hearted attempt at optimism. 'He might even win tomorrow.'

'Only if he uses sorcery,' Inri said. 'And the conditions of the combat are clear – he laid them down himself. No sorcery. And no quarter asked or given, either.'

To the death. But Halthris had already resolved that whatever might happen in that fight tomorrow, Tsenit would never walk away from it alive, and victorious.

She said goodbye to Inri and Abreth, and they wished her luck. Then she turned her tired horse and rode away through the camp towards the dim, pale walls of the silver city.

For a year of her life she had striven to save it, for reasons which had been confused and obscure to her, and were only now becoming clear in her mind, along with a great deal else.

Today, as on other days, she had ridden along the borders of the steppe, the great undulating hills of grass that were her home. And she had looked into the land west and north, Tanathi country, known, loved, familiar, and found it alien and empty. Her heart had moved, and she was adrift like a boat without sails or steering oar, controlled only by the inexorable sweep of events. She could no longer look beyond what might happen tomorrow morning: but the fate of Zithirian, and of the man who should be its King, meant more to her now than anything else.

The men on duty at the Sunset Gate were Zithiriani, and knew her. She told them she had a message for the Lord Ansaryon, and they gave her directions to the house of Kaydi Gandar's Widow. His banner would be outside, one of them added, but there'd be no mistaking the place anyway – half of Zithirian would probably be outside it as well.

The stars above her were cold and clear, and set once more in the familiar patterns of the north. Their myriad, glittering brilliance was reflected in the lights burning at every door. The entire city seemed to be celebrating, somewhat prematurely, the restoration of their rightful King. The taverns lining Sunset Street were bursting with song. She heard over and over again snatches of verses beginning, 'The King sits in Zithirian', each one more mocking and derisive than the last. Revellers spilled out into the streets, blocking her path, pressing her to share a drink, to toast Ansaryon's health, to rejoice in Tsenit's downfall. She excused herself, saying she had an important message to deliver, and urged her horse onwards.

Once she had turned off the main street, progress was much easier, although this route was considerably narrower, and there were a lot of people hurrying past, obviously intent on joining those in the taverns and kuldi-houses on Sunset Street. In the flaring, intermittent light thrown by torches and lanterns, their faces looked exultantly happy, though everyone seemed much thinner and more shabby than she remembered.

As the guard had said, there was no mistaking the house where Ansaryon was staying. There must have been at least a hundred people milling around in the street outside, singing, cheering, passing bottles, jugs and flasks from hand to hand. When they saw her approaching, there was a chorus of questions, applause and cheerful welcome. She guided her mount carefully between the eager citizens, repeating that she had a message for the Lord Ansaryon. They made way for her with laughter and good humour. She wondered whether they would be so light-hearted tomorrow, if the man they hailed as their deliverer was killed.

But of course, it was not certain that he would be. She had seen Ansaryon triumph over apparently insuperable odds before. There was no real reason for her feeling of utter despair. Hegeden guide his hand, she prayed silently. And Sarraliss, Mother of Horses and of us all, keep him safe.

There were more soldiers at the entrance, men who had been her comrades all through that long journey down to Toktel'yi and back. She knew they would let her in, and they did. One led away her horse, and another opened the door with an exuberant flourish and escorted her inside.

She had never entered an ordinary house in Zithirian before. Her experience up until now had been limited to one tavern, visited two years ago, and to the Palace. She was led through a dark passage and into a small, pleasant courtyard, festooned with trumpet vines and filled with the sweet heavy fragrance of their flowers, always much stronger in the evening. It was packed with people, laughing, talking, eating: there was a board set out on trestles, just by the entrance, and laden with food. Her mouth watered – apart from some dry bread and meat at noon, she had eaten nothing since dawn.

'Halthris!'

For an instant she did not recognize the girl standing in front of her: taller, prettier and far more confident than she remembered, and dressed in a beautiful gown and bodice in the most fashionable Zithiriani style. Then Kefiri took her hands, and they embraced.

'I was wondering where you were,' the Princess said, looking up at her. 'Ansaryon didn't seem to know, which puzzled me.'

'Out on scouting duty, with Abreth and Sherren,' Halthris told her. 'Is Ansaryon here? Is it possible to talk to him?'

'I don't know if it is. He's surrounded by people. Half the Goldsmiths' Quarter seem to have come to ensure him of their undying loyalty, which is strange, given that they were all delighted to be given posts in Tsenit's Court.' Kefiri made a face of disgust. 'Time-serving creeps! The real contribution to his cause has been made by the ordinary people of the city, and I shall make sure he knows it. People like Kaydi, over there – this is her house, I've been staying here all summer and she's been like a mother to me. And this is Herris, her son.'

'I know you,' Halthris said, looking at the sharp-faced boy with the mischievous grin. 'You're the pigeon carrier!'

'Yes,' Herris said, licking the grease off his lips and dropping a chicken bone on the ground, where it was instantly retrieved by a grey cat with the speed and subtlety of a shadow. 'And that animal down there is Garool, the pigeon slayer.'

'Herris sent three pigeons back to us,' Kefiri explained. 'One from Hailyan, two days ago, one yesterday, and one this morning. Garool ate the first two, and Shilda – Kaydi's servant – only just managed to rescue the third. And when he was sweeping up this afternoon for the party, he found the first messages, and some feathers and feet that Garool hadn't eaten, in a corner by the water-trough. So that's why we didn't know Ansaryon was coming until today. Kaydi was terribly worried, because she thought that as we hadn't heard anything, something awful had happened to Herris.'

'But it hadn't,' the boy said, taking another chicken leg from the pile on the table. 'Ma gave me a real telling-off when I came home, though.'

'That was because you ran away without saying where you were going,' Kefiri pointed out. 'Admittedly, it wasn't hard to guess, but you'd been told not to do it.'

Herris looked completely unrepentant. 'The Lord Ansaryon himself told me how well I'd done, you know. Where's Kenmet? He wanted some chicken too.' And he grabbed several more legs from the table and vanished into the crowded courtyard.

'I should have something to eat yourself, before he and his

friends scoff the lot,' Kefiri said. She handed Halthris an earthenware plate. 'And we can talk. Have you heard the news?'

'About the combat tomorrow? Yes, Inri told me.' Halthris paused, searching for the right words. 'Why did he do it? Why did he accept?'

'Because Tsenit, may Tayo curse his black and rotten soul for ever, taunted him, told him he was a coward if he didn't, insulted him – I don't think any man would have done otherwise, under that sort of abuse.' Kefiri shivered suddenly. 'I'm frightened, Halthris. I know he won't be persuaded to withdraw – that would be worse than refusing the challenge in the first place. Tsenit is a born fighter, with years of training behind him, and he has nothing to lose. Ansaryon has too much.'

Halthris was piling her plate with whatever came nearest to hand: hunks of roast lamb, the chicken legs, bread, cheese, an apple and a few plums. She took a mouthful of meat, and said round it, 'I'm not here to change his mind. I'm here to suggest something to him. Something that will ensure that, whatever happens tomorrow, Tsenit will never claim victory.'

In the light of the lantern hung above the table, the other girl's eyes were wide with understanding. She said, 'He was going to marry me. Until this morning, I was his prisoner, in the Palace. One of the servants helped me to escape, or I'd be his hostage still.' She paused: that frantic episode seemed to be days, not hours, in the past now. 'And if – *if* he defeats Ansaryon tomorrow, he will claim me for his wife. I think I'd rather throw myself in the Kefirinn.'

'So have you thought what you're going to do?'

'Oh, yes – Ansaryon has worked it all out. As soon as the fight is over, the news will be signalled to me. I'm to wait in the cemetery, on the other side of the river, with an armed escort. If Ansaryon – loses, a white flag will be flown from the southern tower at the entrance to the docks. And then I must ride back to Sar D'yenyi, and take refuge there. If the Ska'i haven't got there first, of course.'

'Is that where they're going? To seize the gold?'

'I think so. And there's something else.' Kefiri glanced around, and though no one was near them, dropped her voice right down to a whisper. 'Have you heard about what has happened to the Temple?'

Halthris shook her head.

'The Ska'i came and burnt it yesterday. All the priests and priestesses are dead, as far as anyone knows.'

'Including D'thliss?'

'Including D'thliss. They were carrying her head on a spear when they went back to the camp, apparently. But that wasn't what they came for. I think they came for Bron.'

Halthris felt the prickle of remembered sorcery on her arms. 'Did they kill him? Or did they take him with them?'

'They took him away, with another boy who's D'thliss's grandson.' Kefiri paused, and stared at the food as if seeking inspiration. 'I don't know how much you know about him – about what he can do. But he has incredible power – I saw him demolish a high wall just by looking at it. And yet he's also an ordinary small boy.' Her voice wobbled with compassion. 'He told me he was frightened of the dark in the Temple.'

Halthris thought of the child she had last seen in Ba'alekkt's pavilion, watching the dancers. 'But he is dangerous, Kefiri – very dangerous.'

'And even more so if the Ska'i have captured him. If – if all goes well tomorrow, Ansaryon plans to lead his army in pursuit. The Ska'i shaman will use Bron even more ruthlessly than D'thliss ever did – they will employ his power to shatter Sar D'yenyi, and probably to destroy Zithirian and everyone in it as well. For that reason, as well as for his own sake, he has to be rescued. Ansaryon *has* to win tomorrow – he *has* to. Why, of why, did he ever accept that challenge?'

'We both know why.' Halthris thought of the years when the sorcerer Prince had been the subject of evil rumour, malicious gossip, and open slights on his honour and his courage. He had been given the chance to redeem himself, with stunningly impressive results. No wonder that he had refused to abandon his new-made reputation and popularity, and back away from his brother's cunning taunts.

'I swear to you,' she said softly to Kefiri, 'that if the fight goes against him tomorrow, I shall kill Tsenit myself. It would leave you the last true heir of Zithirian – do you want that?'

Slowly, Kefiri nodded, her face very pale. 'Yes. Yes, given the alternative, I certainly do. Don't worry, Halthris. Even if it would mean leaving Sar D'yenyi, I would do so gladly, if the city needed me.' She essayed a rather weak smile. 'I hope and pray to Tayo and all the forbidden gods that it won't come to that – but I will do what is necessary, if I am called.'

A large and familiar figure loomed up beside them, and Invan said heartily, 'Halthris! I'm glad to see you back. Any news of the Ska'i?'

'They've gone north along the river valley,' she told him, naggingly aware that she should have made her report before doing anything else. 'No sign of any rearguard. Kefiri says they may be going to attack Sar D'yenyi.'

'Yes, so Ansaryon thinks.' Invan was smiling down at Halthris. His blue eyes shone warmly in the lamplight, reminding her that his feelings had never changed. 'He knows you're here, by the way, and he wants to speak to you. Will you excuse us for a moment, Lady Kefiri?'

He steered Halthris gently but firmly through the mass of people. Ansaryon stood in the centre of the courtyard, the heart of the crowd. Taller than many of those around him, his cap of pale bright hair was immediately noticeable. The air around him had a feverish, almost frenetic quality: the laughter was too loud, the gaiety too forced. The thought of what might happen tomorrow was being hidden with desperate determination.

As so often before, his eyes sought hers. '*You know,*' said the familiar voice in her head. '*Don't say anything – you don't have to.*'

'*I would like to speak to you. Please. Alone.*' She smiled at him, as if that was her first greeting, and gave him the soldiers' salute. '*It doesn't matter when, so long as it is tonight.*'

'*Before Tsenit kills me, you mean?*' His eyes flashed sudden amusement. '*Of course. There is a room off the courtyard – the door's just by the water trough. Wait for me there. I won't be long. Invan tells me I ought to have an early night.*'

She said aloud, 'General Invan bids me make my report, Lord Ansaryon.'

'Excellent. What have you found?'

Once more, she told of the Ska'i, and heard his speaking voice, as light and pleasant as if almost certain death did not await him tomorrow, commending her for her efforts. She thanked him and withdrew, relieved that Invan's attention had been snared by an overdressed merchant in silk and fur.

In this company, with even the humblest clad in their celebratory best, her plain leather tunic and trousers made Halthris feel curiously out of place, a brutal intrusion of the truth amidst a sea of lies. A terrible sensation of coming grief seized her suddenly. Where was she to go? What was she to do? The steppe was no longer her life, nor, lacking Ansaryon, was this beautiful city. She had no place, no future – except the destiny that had already crept like a thief of peace into her dreams, a vision of her fate that might, if the worst happened, yet give victory, and peace, to all in Zithirian, and amongst the Tanathi too. And if the price to be paid was her life, then, like Kefiri, she would do what was asked of her, what was necessary, for the sake of freedom.

She went back to the table. Kefiri had vanished into the crowd. Halthris picked up her plate of food, filled a cup with wine, and went unobtrusively over to the door that Ansaryon had indicated. No one noticed as she slipped inside, shutting it behind her.

There was one small window, grilled and high in the wall. In the dim light, she could make out a bed, a table and chair, and a heap of what might have been cushions, or cloth, or clothes. It was not a King's chamber. She sat down on the mound of textiles, listening to the noise outside. Amid roars of laughter and shouts of approval, someone was singing a verse of the song that had poured out of every tavern courtyard that evening.

> 'Two Kings sit in Zithirian,
> The right one and the wrong.
> And Tsenit will be wishing soon
> He'd never heard this song!'

Halthris, sitting alone in the dark, suddenly remembered another, much older verse. She could not now recall where she had heard it, but its meaning, once obscure, was now becoming terrifyingly clear.

> 'A King sits in Zithirian,
> He wears a silver Crown.
> Until the child of evil born,
> Shall come to strike him down.'

She knew who the child must be. But which King? Ansaryon? Or Tsenit?

Halthris shivered, and swallowed the wine. Then she set the cup and plate carefully down on the floor beside her, and settled down to wait.

She was tired, the room was dark and warm, and the unpromising heap beneath her surprisingly comfortable. Sleep crept up on her unawares, and her eyes closed.

She woke to a hand on her shoulder, and a voice saying softly, 'Hal?'

The noise outside had died down, and it was utterly dark. She could see nothing of him at all. She lay still for a moment, letting her sleepy mind wake up properly. Then she said, 'Yes?'

'It's very late. What do you want to talk to me about?'

'Tomorrow.' She sat up, feeling very thirsty. 'Is there some water?'

'Plenty. I'll make a light.'

She waited, eyes open to the dark, listening to his soft movements, and wondering how, unseeing, he could be so deft. Was it sorcery?

A flame burst into sudden life, and she blinked. The window was shuttered and the door firmly closed. Their privacy was assured, and she was glad, for no one else should hear what she was going to offer him.

Ansaryon set the glass back into the lamp, and the uneasy flame settled into steady brightness. There was a jug on the table, and he poured out water into an ancient and precious Minassan goblet, chipped on the base. Around the bowl was painted a design of leaping, graceful fish in a shade of turquoise that was achingly, desperately pure. 'Here you are. As you can see, Kaydi has given me her best cup. This style is at least a hundred years old. Temiltan spent a whole year trying to recreate that exact blue, and failed.'

'It's beautiful.' Halthris gulped the cool water, and felt the last rags of sleep washing away. She handed it back to him with a smile, and stood up. 'Thank you. That's much better.'

He was leaning against the table, his arms folded, regarding her with an enigmatic smile. He was wearing full Zithiriani dress: trousers and tunic of richly embroidered deep blue silk, overlaid with a long gown in a more brilliant shade that was nearly, but not quite, the same as that on the goblet. And her breath caught suddenly in her throat, for now at last, in this small bare room, she could sense the greatness in him.

She put the lovely cup down on the table beside him, and said bluntly, 'I have not come to persuade you to change your mind about tomorrow. That would be pointless, as well as astonishingly presumptuous and arrogant. I have come to make a suggestion to you.'

His eyebrows rose. 'What is it?'

'If Tsenit wins tomorrow – will you let me kill him?'

He stared at her for a brief, shocked moment, and then laughed suddenly, a sound of genuine amusement. 'Why?'

'You know why. For Kefiri, above all. And for Zithirian.' She smiled rather grimly. 'Don't look so surprised. Remember, I am Tanathi.'

'How could I ever forget? Yes, you can kill him if you wish. After all, if it comes to that point, I shall be past caring.'

'So you do not object?' she said, in some surprise. 'I thought it would be against the rules.'

He smiled. 'It probably is. But if the worst happens, at least he will not enjoy his victory for long.'

'I swear to you,' Halthris said softly and intensely, 'by Hegeden's wings, that if you die tomorrow, Tsenit's life will last only a few heartbeats longer than yours.'

'Does Kefiri know anything about this?'

'Yes, I have already told her.' She smiled. 'Of course, you'll probably beat him – in which case no one save the three of us will know what I would have done.'

'But I probably won't. Ansaryon looked at her fully, and she saw the tiredness in his face, the grief he could no longer hide for the fate which almost certainly awaited him tomorrow. 'I'm sorry, Hal. I couldn't do anything else. And my excess of pride may well cost me my life – and Zithirian its freedom.'

'Not if I kill Tsenit,' Halthris said. She knew what else she must do, if he died under Tsenit's sword, but she would never ever tell him, least of all tonight, that for the sake of his people, and for the peace and safety of the known world, she planned to slay his son as well as his brother.

'Thank you,' Ansaryon said, and smiled, brilliant and shadowed in the lamplight. 'Oh, dear Hal, you are the truest of friends – and I love you.'

The quiet, passionate words dropped into the stillness like stones into water. She felt the ripples widen inside her heart, and knew what gift she could bring him, on this night of triumph and dread.

They were very close. She could have reached out to touch him, but did not. Instead, she said softly, 'Will you unbind my hair for me?'

He stared at her as if he could not believe what he had heard. Smiling, Halthris lifted one of her long, thick braids, woven with strips of red leather, and tipped with the tiny golden figure of Djarna, the deer, symbol of love and pleasure. 'Must I ask you twice?'

'No,' said Ansaryon, suddenly laughing with shaken and amazed delight. 'No, you may not.'

Seven men, all Tanathi, had performed this office for her, many other times in the past. She could not now remember their faces, nor did she want to. All she knew was that none of her previous lovers had roused in her such a hunger of expectation, or such a certainty of passion.

Clumsy at first, though gentle, his touch grew increasingly sure as he unwrapped the four intricate braids one by one, laying the coloured thongs and golden talismans on the table beside him. When he had done, she shook her hair out, combing it swiftly loose with her fingers, and then turned to face him. 'As far as I know, that is the only custom which is different. What follows is the same.'

'Oh, no,' he said, a smile curving his mouth, all the dread vanished from his eyes. 'Not the same – never the same.'

And it was not.

Afterwards, she lay in his arms, breathless and shaken with the memory of extreme delight. He ran his hands through her tangled flood of red-gold hair, and then traced the whirling tattoos on her body, marks of a Hunter, with gentle, curious fingers. 'These must have hurt you, when they were done.'

'No one thinks about the pain – just as no one thinks about the Ordeal all Tanathi must face. We pay the necessary price, and do it gladly.'

'I never thought I would ever lie with a woman who has a hunting-cat on her breasts.' His touch followed the curling line of the animal's tail, and she shivered, but not from the cold. Then he bent his mouth to hers, with sudden urgency, and she lost herself once more amid the overwhelming strength of her response.

At last they slept, her head on his shoulder, her flame-coloured hair trailed across his face and her body, his arm gathering her close even in oblivion. Then the flame within the lamp trembled and smoked, and Halthris woke suddenly, with the glow of another, brighter flame still sweet and fresh in her mind.

He was deeply asleep, his face open, vulnerable, utterly at peace. Whatever happens tomorrow, she thought, with sudden and tearing grief, at least I have given him this – and I have given him hope, too, for Zithirian and Kefiri if not for him.

Very slowly and carefully, she disentangled her body from his. He stirred, and drowsily spoke her name. She touched her lips to his, and whispered the words she had not said to him, despite the urgings of her heart. 'Ansary – I love you.'

Smiling, he drifted back into slumber. Halthris dressed swiftly and silently, tying back her hair with one strip of leather. The four golden talismans she left for a token, lying on the table: Djarna the deer; Sayni the cat; Immith the leopard, bestower of power and fighting skills; and Emmesar, the hare, to give speed, agility and intelligence.

Together, the four beasts were a formidable combination. She laid her hand over them, and whispered a prayer to Sarraliss, to guard and guide the man she loved. And then, with one last glance at the King of Zithirian, she slipped silently from his room into the cold soft rain falling on the dark courtyard outside.

Tsenit, also King of Zithirian, slept long and well, with no unpleasant dreams to disturb his rest, and woke refreshed and eager for the task ahead. He ate a good breakfast, and then called for his personal servant to array him in the armour befitting his royal blood.

The bronze thigh-length tunic, with its hundreds of overlapping pieces resembling the scales of a fish, or a monster, gleamed richly in the morning light. Under it, he wore fine dark linen trousers, tucked into soft leather ankle-boots. His lower legs were protected by bronze shin-guards. The helmet was close-fitting and round, with an arrogant plume of white feathers, Tayo's sacred colour. It was made of hard steel, still a rare and precious metal, but gilded to match the colour of the bronze.

Last of all, the servant brought his sword-belt, and buckled it round his lean waist. The weapon, heavy in its jewel-studded leather scabbard, felt reassuringly heavy and solid against his leg. In common with all aristocratic Zithiriani boys, he had been given that sword by his father at the age of sixteen. Smiling contemptuously, he wondered what had happened to Ansaryon's, and decided that it had probably rusted away from lack of use.

He unsheathed the dagger, the length of a man's hand from wrist to fingertip, and almost as thin and sharp as an embroidery needle. He tested the point, and watched the track of blood it left across his forearm with satisfaction. Still smiling in anticipatory relish, he replaced the deadly knife in its scabbard, strapped to the right side of his sword-belt. Then he tucked his helmet into the crook of his arm, and strode from his chamber.

Down in the Palace courtyard, everyone was waiting for him. The soldiers of the Royal Guard lined the walls, and his ministers and courtiers stood in a large group in front of the outer gate. Their cheers at his appearance were loud, and reassuringly sincere. Tsenit stood smiling, acknowledging their support with a gracious wave of his hand, until the last shout had died away into echoes. Then, he walked forward to General Seardrith, who held the reins of the tall, dapple-grey Tanathi-bred gelding which he had picked out yesterday in the Palace stables.

Last night's rain had stopped, leaving the morning shining, fresh and full of good omen. Tsenit swung up into the saddle, settled the horse, which was sidling restively, and turned it to address his household. He had always possessed the knack of making rousing speeches – to those who were already on his side – and the ability had not deserted him now. He thanked them all for their loyalty and support, spoke contemptuously of the opponent he was about to face, and ended with a glowing, wonderful description of the Golden Age that was about to dawn in Zithirian. With all its enemies fled or defeated, under his benevolent and enlightened rule the city would enter a new and glorious era of peace, prosperity and fame.

It sounded superb, and they cheered him again until the walls rang. A small escort of mounted soldiers, led by Seardrith, formed up behind him, and he gave the order to open the outer gates.

He was not quite sure what he had expected – another applauding crowd, perhaps – but not this silence, this emptiness. A scattered handful of people waited on the fringes of the open space before the Palace, but the Ceremonial Way, normally busy, stretched deserted in front of him, all the way down to the ruined Temple. Disconcerted, Tsenit checked his horse for a moment, and then smiled to himself. Of course, everyone in the city would be packing the walls and thronging around the field marked off for the combat. They would not want to miss the spectacle of his glorious victory, after all.

But it was still very unnerving to parade through the empty, silent city, with only a few children and old people to watch him ride to his triumph. Tsenit held his head high, ignoring them, thinking about the moment when his sword would enter Ansaryon's body, and his right to the throne of Zithirian would at last become undisputed and absolute.

The ramparts and walkways around the Sunset Gate were groaning with people. There must have been thousands of them, jostling for the best view, small children perched on adults' shoulders, and all of them come to see him defeat his brother. He smiled, and waved his hand, but no applause rose from the massed faces looking down at him. Instead, faintly at first and then with increasing fervour, the hissing and jeering began.

It was then that the first worms of doubt and fear at last began to enter Tsenit's mind, along with the brutally emphasized realization that not one of these people supported him. But he continued to smile and wave as he and his escort rode under the huge, deep arch of the Sunset Gate, between the great double towers.

On the other side, the crowd was vast, and there were one or two cheers, which he acknowledged with pleasure until he caught

their derisive note. A way had been cleared through the mass of
people, leading to a more or less square arena, perhaps fifty paces
in each direction, marked out with rope tied between spears thrust
point-down into the soft earth. This was part of the area where the
Gathering Fair was usually held, and the ground was level but
covered in rough, unkempt grass. Tsenit thought of objecting, and
then decided against it. He was too keen to see this business
completed, once and for all: his blood was singing, his sword-hand
tingled with eager anticipation. Any delay now would be
intolerable.

The combat space was guarded by soldiers standing two paces
apart, all round the perimeter. Most were Zithiriani, but he saw
some from Minassa and Lelyent as well, and, to his surprise, several
Tanathi. He recognized the red-haired girl who had brought the
news of the Ska'i advance on Zithirian, a year ago, and almost
wrecked his plans. Her gaze was cold and hostile, and he decided
that she would never have the chance to return to her homeland.

He dismounted in the centre of the arena, and handed the reins
of his horse to one of his Royal Guard. A small group of men were
standing there to greet him. He saw the renegade Guards officer,
Invan, two more soldiers, one Lelyentan and the other in the
unmistakable armour of Toktel'yi, and King Temiltan of Minassa,
his mother's brother. All of them were staring at him with grim
faces. They expect me to win, Tsenit thought exultantly. They
know Ansaryon doesn't stand a chance.

He looked around as his horse was led out of the arena, and
laughed. 'I see no sign of my brother. Where is he? Skulking
cowardly still in his tent?'

'He is coming,' said King Temiltan, his normally pleasant face
full of forbidding animosity. 'There – can you not hear it?'

And he realized that the distant sound, like wind in trees or
waves on shore, was the applause of the people of Zithirian,
cheering the man who had come to claim the throne. In a furious
silence, Tsenit stood and listened to that approaching noise. Fools,
he thought savagely. They can't see how unfit he is for kingship.
They'll shout for me just as loudly, once I've killed him.

On and on, the rapturous acclaim swept nearer, louder. He
could see people on the ramparts waving, and the eddying disturbance, like a rock beneath fast water, that marked Ansaryon's slow
progress through the adoring crowd. By the time he reached the
arena, Tsenit was sick with waiting, and jealous resentment, and
the cheers and shouts had reached a deafening level.

The soldiers parted to let him enter, and Tsenit set eyes on his brother at close quarters for the first time since before the Ska'i attack, a year ago.

It was not a pleasant surprise. Gone was the slender, exquisite figure with languid movements and that general air of effete and rather sinister decadence which he had once held in such contempt. The man dismounting from his white horse, wearing bronze armour almost identical to Tsenit's, was muscular and broad-shouldered, with a look of calm confidence that must, surely, be completely false. Or he was not Ansaryon at all.

But the face was still the same, although more resolute by far than before, a grim sense of purpose overlaying the delicate, beautiful features, the silvery eyes and pale, straight hair. Ansaryon walked up to Temiltan, who as King of Minassa and uncle of the combatants had obviously appointed himself as the referee for the contest, and made the soldiers' salute. And all around them, the screams and shouts of the crowd went on and on and on, until Tsenit could hardly keep his hands from his ears.

Temiltan turned and beckoned to a Minassan standing just behind him, a big hairy bear of a man. Obediently, the soldier lifted a curved ox horn to his mouth and blew. The raucous blast was barely audible, and he had to repeat it four times before the noise at last began to die down into an expectant murmur.

Temiltan stepped forward, and raised his hands in the air. There was one last distant cry of 'An-sary-on!' and then, almost, silence.

The King of Minassa had a strong voice, and needed it. Even so, the people on the walls of the city could not conceivably have heard his individual words: even those around the arena must have had to strain their ears. Tsenit stood in a dignified silence, ignoring his brother, as Temiltan announced the rules of formal challenge, accepted by all the lands in the known world. The custom had originated in Toktel'yi, where single combat had been used in early times to settle claims between rivals for the Imperial Throne, and was still in use, though rarely, to avenge insults or to decide disputes between bitter enemies. But never before, to anyone's knowledge, had the prize for the winner of such a fight to the death been the city of Zithirian.

'And I ask all citizens here present to agree to the judgement of Tayo, who will decide which of these men, the last two male children of his Royal Line of Zithirian, carries right and justice in his blade!' Temiltan faced each side of the arena in turn, and shouted, 'Will you give your consent to this combat?'

The crowd's response was thunderously loud, and died away raggedly into comparative quiet.

'When the horn gives the signal, the fight will commence.' Temiltan's voice was beginning to sound strained. 'It will end only in death. May Tayo's will prevail – may his favoured child win the contest, and the throne of Zithirian!'

The shouting exploded around them. They were chanting Ansaryon's name over and over again, like an incantation. Tsenit pulled on his helmet, adjusting the cheek and nose guards for a perfect fit. His brother did likewise: in contrast to Tsenit's white plume, his was blue, the deep rich shade of the flower on the banners carried by his entourage. It symbolized hope: and hope, Tsenit thought contemptuously, was all that Ansaryon had in his favour.

The other men in the arena were moving back to give a broad clear space for the combat. Tsenit stood ready, his fingers on the hilt of his sword, staring at the still figure of his elder brother, the stipulated ten paces away, while the silence seemed to go on for ever.

And then Temiltan raised his hand, and the horn howled again.

CHAPTER
TWENTY-NINE

As the sound of the horn blasted his ears, Tsenit slid his sword from the scabbard and sprang forward with a yell. His first down-stroke met Ansaryon's blade with an arm-jarring clang. He with-drew, side-stepped in the classic manner, and struck again. Once more, the blow was parried. Belatedly, Tsenit realized that this wasn't going to be as easy as he'd thought.

For quite a long time after that, the fighting was cautious and wary, as each man sought to expose and test the other's weaknesses. The roughness of the ground was a handicap to both of them, but the sun had not yet risen above the walls of Zithirian, and the morning air was cool and fresh. Nevertheless, they were soon sweating inside their close-fitting armoured tunics and steel helmets, and Tsenit's grasp on his sword-hilt felt wet and slippery.

Blow, parry; blow, parry; sooner or later, Ansaryon must crack. Already, he had lasted far longer than his brother's worst imagin-ings, although his face was shiny with perspiration, and his breath was beginning to come in gasps. Sensing the beginnings of an advantage, Tsenit began a renewed onslaught. He pressed forward, his blade rising and falling with aggressive strength, and was rewarded by the satisfying sight of his opponent giving ground. Ansaryon's silver eyes were fixed, intent on his task and on his brother: but as he warded off a particularly heavy blow with some difficulty, Tsenit saw his gaze flicker, and knew that he was afraid.

He gave a wild exultant yell, and lunged. Ansaryon was not quite quick enough: the blade ripped through the thick leather sleeve of his tunic, and into his left arm. A look of shock and surprise on his face, he stumbled back, and nearly fell. Tsenit, his heart filled with savage and triumphant glee, brought his sword down two-handed for the final stroke.

It fell upon empty air. Somehow, his opponent had moved with astonishing speed. Unbalanced, Tsenit struggled wildly to stay upright, and found his weapon almost torn from his hands by Ansaryon's sword, engaging against it. For a few desperate heart-beats, the brothers wrestled together, blade to blade, and then, with one final agonising twist, Tsenit found the hilt wrenched out of his grasp.

For a brief instant, he could not believe it. He stood empty-handed, gulping air, and stared at Ansaryon in dumbfounded horror.

His brother did not quite seem to believe it either. He glanced sideways to where Tsenit's sword lay a couple of paces away in the grass, and then raised the point of his own weapon until it was levelled at the younger man's heart. He could not quite keep it steady, and his left arm was pouring blood. He said softly, 'Are you ready to die, Tsenit?'

Don't just stand there, you fool, said an inner voice: you have another weapon! As the thought crashed through his mind, Tsenit pulled the dagger from its sheath and hurled it at Ansaryon.

It was a long time since he had thrown a knife, and his aim was poor. The point hit his brother's armoured helmet and rebounded into the grass. But Tsenit, with the courage of desperation, had already launched himself at his mortal enemy. He crashed into Ansaryon, who staggered backwards and fell, the sword flying from his hand and Tsenit's considerable weight on top of him. They grappled together, rolling over and over on the rough ground. Tsenit knew he must have the advantage: his opponent had lost a lot of blood, his left arm was effectively useless, and though taller than his brother, Ansaryon was lighter and not so strong. Snarling, Tsenit managed to get his hands round the other man's throat at last. He saw his brother's eyes widen as he choked, and lifted himself up to put all his weight behind his stranglehold.

It was an old trick, and he had forgotten that his effeminate opponent might know it. With failing but still effective strength, Ansaryon brought his feet up and kicked his brother in the groin.

Tsenit fell backwards, to land with a jarring thud on the trampled ground. Winded and gasping with pain, he stared blankly up at his brother looming above him, his retrieved sword once more pointing at Tsenit's heart. And this time, he had nothing left to fight with.

Ansaryon struggled for breath. His arm was still dripping blood, and his face was absolutely white beneath the steel helmet. He swallowed, and attempted to speak: it came out as a croak, and he tried again. 'Tsenit, falsely calling yourself King of Zithirian – do you accept defeat in fair and honest combat?'

Amidst the fog of pain and fear and rage, Tsenit had no option. He nodded, and then said grudgingly, 'Yes. I do.'

'Then I will accept your surrender, but I will not slay you here and now, richly though you deserve it.' Ansaryon paused, and then resumed, his voice slightly stronger. 'For the deaths of your father, your brother, your sister and your uncle, and for all the other people of Zithirian who suffered and died because of your treachery, your life must be forfeit – but you are my brother, my own flesh, and for the sake of what you have left of our family I will not stain my hands with your blood. I therefore now order that you be taken back to the Palace as a criminal, and kept there in confinement, as you kept our cousin the Lady Kefiri: and that in due course you be given up to the judgement of the people of Zithirian, so that they can decide upon your fate.' He turned to address the packed, now silent crowd. 'I give him to you. Do you accept that the punishment is rightfully yours?'

Tsenit raised his head. Ansaryon was standing with his back to him, sword in hand. All around the arena, the shouts and cheers of rapturous assent crashed into the air, and he knew that if they had their way, his death at the command of the citizens would be neither swift nor merciful.

A glint of metal caught his eye: it was his fallen dagger, just out of reach. Ignoring pain, ignoring everything save the desperate necessity of victory, no matter how it was achieved, he scrambled to his feet and snatched up the weapon. Then he hurled himself at his brother's unsuspecting back, and with all his strength plunged the knife into Ansaryon's body.

His enemy staggered two steps and fell face down into the grass, his sword slipping from lifeless fingers. Tsenit bent and picked it up.

The cheers had changed to a terrible howl of rage and despair. Ignoring them, he brandished the weapon triumphantly above his head and turned to face Temiltan, smiling in glee at his victory.

He saw the Tanathi woman standing beside the King of Minassa, but he did not realize what she was doing until the arrow was already in the air – and by then, it was too late.

The steel point took Tsenit in the throat, the bare unprotected gap between helmet and armoured tunic. The force of its impact sent him reeling back, his hands clawing frantically at the shaft as his mouth filled with blood. He had time to be angry, to rage against the barbarian woman who had snatched his victory from him at the very moment of his triumph: time, too, to understand that it had all been an illusion, a mockery, and that fate, or Tayo, or Halthris of the Tanathi, had never intended him to preside over a Golden Age in Zithirian.

He fell backwards onto the still body of his brother, his sworn and bitter enemy: and by the time Temiltan reached him, he was dead.

It had been the shot of a lifetime, the shot that had saved the silver city from Tsenit's tyranny. But as Halthris stared down at the snarling face and blank, glaring blue eyes of the slain King, she felt only a sick and empty despair. '*Oh, Ansary*,' she cried silently to the empty morning air. '*I have done as I promised, I have killed him, but too late to save you.*'

Against all hope, all belief, an answering voice whispered in her mind. '*Not too late.*'

Astounded, she dropped to her knees by the bodies of the two brothers. Invan, Temiltan and Sekkenet were beside her: amid the wild turmoil in her mind, she had time to notice that the Zithiriani General's handsome face was streaked with tears. As they dragged Tsenit's corpse away, she laid her hand against the pulse-point on Ansaryon's neck.

There was a heartbeat there, fast, but surprisingly strong. The voice in her mind said, '*Pull the knife out.*'

'*I can't*,' she cried in anguished silence. '*You'll die if I do.*'

'*No, I won't.*' With joy, she heard his dry amusement, far more reassuring than his words. '*Despite Tsenit's efforts, I think I stand a good chance of surviving this.*'

Invan crouched beside her. She said breathlessly, 'He's alive. He told me to pull the knife out.'

'What?' The General's grief-stricken face was suddenly lit with a mixture of delight and astonished disbelief. 'He can't be!'

'Oh, yes, I am,' Ansaryon said aloud, though his voice was no more than a hoarse whisper. 'Get the knife out, one of you, and then I can sit up.'

More than anything else, it was his tone of honest exasperation that finally persuaded Halthris. Ignoring Invan's cry of horror, Halthris grasped the dagger's intricate gold-plated hilt and pulled.

It came out so easily that she almost fell backwards. She stared at it in bewilderment, and then realized the reason. More than half of the slender blade had broken off, leaving a ragged-tipped weapon barely the length of her middle finger.

'Here's the rest of it.' Invan picked up something from the grass a pace or so distant, and showed it to her. The two pieces fitted exactly. 'Tsenit probably didn't even notice.'

'It broke against my helmet when he threw it at me,' Ansaryon said. 'Help me up, Hal – now, before the people run riot.'

With gentle care, she and Invan supported him as he struggled to sit, and then to stand. The crowd realized that he was alive after all, and their wails of grief and anger turned suddenly to a huge, deafening wave of applause that was echoed again and again from the walls of the city.

Painfully, his injured arm still streaming blood, Ansaryon walked between his General and his lover to face Temiltan. The King of Minassa stood a few paces away, his shrewd features transformed with honest delight. As the citizens roared their approval, their King gave the soldiers' salute to his uncle, and then shrugged himself free of supporting hands, and stood alone.

'Ruler of Minassa, and judge of this combat, I present myself as the survivor of the contest, though the death of my opponent was none of my doing – and I humbly crave your decision.'

'There is no decision to make,' Temiltan said briskly. 'Tsenit had accepted defeat, and then treacherously rose up and attacked you from behind. Such conduct is forbidden by all the rules of challenge, in any land. I hereby declare you the victor of the combat, and by the will of our Divine Ancestor Tayo, and of all the peoples of Zithirian, I proclaim you the rightful and undisputed King of this city, and of all the lands under its rule.' His face broke into a broad, friendly smile. 'And speaking for myself, may I say, well done, my boy – well done indeed.'

He gave his nephew a genial, fatherly clap on the shoulders, and then stared in consternation as Ansaryon's face suddenly turned to a corpse-like pallor, and he fell in a dead faint at Temiltan's feet.

Since before dawn, Kefiri had sat on the east bank of the river for which she had been named, waiting for the news which would decide her future. Behind her waited twenty armed men and twenty-one fast horses, to escort her to the safety of Sar D'yenyi if the worst happened.

She had not allowed herself to imagine anything other than the certainty of Tsenit's victory. Instead, she had occupied the time planning for her grim future. The Ska'i, with Bron as their prisoner, were probably also heading for Sar D'yenyi. With the child's incredible power to help them, the citadel would be defenceless, whether the lake was frozen or not. Therefore, she must lead all its inhabitants into the comparative safety of the mountains, perhaps to Lelyent. The gold did not matter: if that was all the Ska'i wanted from Sar D'yenyi, they could have it and welcome. It meant nothing beside the terrible picture of Ramath and the other people she had known all her life, men, women and children, hideously slain by sorcery or by the barbarians. And there was plenty more gold unmined under Sargenn and Annako.

The thought of Bron and Lelya in the Ska'i camp also caused her much anguish, but she knew that there was nothing she could do now to save them. At least Bron's power was so valuable that they would not be harmed – physically, at any rate. But she shed tears now for the terror both children must be feeling, alone with those ruthless, brutal men, and for the dreadful future that awaited Bron, as the tool of an evil far more unspeakable than anything at D'thliss's command.

The sun rose at last, and she sat on the cold, damp ground and felt its rays warming her back. Across the brown, gently flowing river, the two towers that guarded the entrance to the docks remained innocent of any signal. Very distantly, she heard cheering, then a long pause, and then, chillingly, the unmistakable mass wail of grief.

And they would not be weeping for Tsenit.

Almost, then, she was tempted to leave. But something made her wait, her eyes fixed on the left-hand tower, where soon, surely, the white flag announcing Tsenit's victory would be raised.

Behind her, the captain of her escort was saying something in an undertone to one of his men. A horse stamped and whinnied: another answered. Her attention had been momentarily distracted, and she looked again at the tower.

A man was standing at the top, something in his hands. As the tears of bitter grief rushed to her eyes, he held up his arms, and a broad triangular banner, of the type used by soldiers, whipped out in the breeze.

It was blue.

For a heartbeat, two, she did not believe what she was seeing. And then the men behind her broke into spontaneous cheers, and it was as if a huge and terrible weight had lifted from her mind. It was all right. Ansaryon had triumphed. Tsenit was dead. And suddenly, despite the Ska'i, the future was full of hope rather than dread.

She leapt up and turned to the men, her face shining, and tears of joy replacing sorrow. 'Let's return to the city at once. I would like to welcome the new King of Zithirian to his throne.'

The captain tried to say something about the need for caution, the possibility of treachery or deceit. But now, clear on the westerly wind, came the sound of rapturous and triumphant acclaim.

'They would not shout like that if Tsenit had won,' Kefiri said exultantly. 'Come on – or do I have to row the boat myself and leave you all here to make up your minds?'

And she led them, rejoicing, down to the ferry that would take them back to Zithirian, free at last of oppression and fear.

'Lord Ansaryon, this is madness – lunacy – you *cannot* go now, not today! Tomorrow, perhaps, when you have had time to recover – but not *now*!'

Invan stopped, words failing him, and wiped his sweating brow. The mid-morning sun was shining strongly outside, and it was much too hot inside the tent. Ansaryon sat on a folding leather chair, wearing only a thin linen shirt over his trousers, the heavy bandaging around his left arm and right shoulder clearly visible through the flimsy fabric. His face was still very pale, but implacably determined. As soon as he had recovered consciousness, while Temiltan's Healer was still binding his wounds, he had announced his immediate intention of leading the army in pursuit of the Ska'i. And nothing that his uncle, or Sekkenet, or now Invan could say seemed to have the power to deflect him from his course.

Halthris sat cross-legged and almost unnoticed in the corner, listening to the raging argument, but knew better than to join in. She was well aware of the reason for his decision, and had no intention of mentioning it. Invan, in particular, would not understand the necessity of capturing Bron before his powers could be turned against Sar D'yenyi, and then Zithirian. And he would certainly wonder why Ansaryon was so desperate to retrieve a small boy who might, or might not, be his son.

And if Bron *was* his son, who had his mother been? Halthris could not imagine Ansaryon linked to any daughter of D'thliss, and yet, if the child was indeed the witch's grandson, as she had apparently claimed, there could be no other explanation.

'Listen.' The King of Zithirian's voice was still strained, his larynx bruised by Tsenit's attempt to strangle him, but the words were perfectly clear. 'The Ska'i are marching against Sar D'yenyi. Winter is not yet upon us, but the citadel is in great danger, for I have reason to believe that their shaman's powers of sorcery have recently been considerably increased. If we can attack them, take them by surprise before they can cross the Kefirinn, then we have an excellent chance of defeating them. They won't be expecting us – they'll think that we'll be tied up here for days, trying to extract Tsenit from the Palace.'

'But you just said their Shaman is even more powerful than

before,' Invan objected. 'Surely he'll see us coming, in his scrying-bowl or whatever it is?'

'Not necessarily. I am a sorcerer too, don't forget. And there are several ways of ensuring that they don't realize where we are and what we're doing, until it's too late.' Ansaryon stared up at his General and his uncle, his mouth set in an uncompromising line. 'Make no mistake – I am going to ride out this afternoon at the head of the army. You may come or not, as you choose. But short of sticking another knife into my back, you will not stop me.'

The silence was brief, and pungent. Then Temiltan gave a snort of unwilling laughter. 'Very well. You've made your point, and you are our leader. Come on, Invan, look lively. If we're to get these men on the move before midday, there's a great deal to do.'

It was much to the General's credit that he barely hesitated before saluting both Kings, and leaving the tent. With a knowing wink at his nephew, Temiltan followed him.

For a brief, precious moment, Ansaryon and Halthris were alone in this small, over-hot island of calm amidst the noisy turmoil of the camp outside the tent. He smiled at her, and said softly, 'I haven't had the chance yet, to thank you. Once again, you've saved my life.'

'I promised you I would kill Tsenit,' Halthris reminded him. She rose from the floor and came to stand a pace or so in front of him. Here, where anyone might come in, they could not embrace, but she saw his love for her plain on his face, and it was very hard not to reach out and touch him. 'And I keep my promises.'

'I'm very glad of it.' He smiled again, his expression utterly unreserved, and her heart turned over. 'I dreamed last night that you said you loved me.'

'That was no dream,' she told him, very softly. 'That was, and is, no more than the truth.'

'Then when the Ska'i have been wiped clean from the face of the earth, we must think about what will happen to us.' He stared up at her thoughtfully. 'I have no desire for a future which does not have you at my side. But you are a Tanathi, you are not made to live in cities.'

'I am not a creature of the steppe now, either,' Halthris said, after a pause. 'I do not seem to belong there anymore – I have seen too much, done too much. What use is freedom, if it means nothing? And I would not be the first Tanathi woman to forsake her tent for stone walls and star-painted ceilings.'

'I am not asking you to be my lover,' he said. 'I am asking you to be my Queen.'

Halthris gazed at him, astounded. 'Your *Queen*? Your *wife*?'

'Yes. It would be an insult to you, and the love I have for you, to offer you anything less. Never mind the scandal, or the offence I would cause to whichever of all those princesses I might have to take for a wife instead of you. And the last King of Zithirian who followed his heart, married a Tanathi woman – my great-grand-mother Djerrin. So there are precedents. And such is the mood of hope and joy that I don't think anyone, soldiers or citizens, would object.'

'I'm glad to hear it.' Halthris stood still, while her mind whirled in frantic tumult. 'Was she happy, Queen Djerrin?'

'She and her husband and her two eldest children were mur-dered by the last Usurper, Ansarit. But her youngest child survived – and she was the great Queen Tesi, my grandmother, who overthrew the Usurper when she was nineteen years old, and reigned for another fifty-seven years. I can remember her well – she died when I was six. And according to her, Queen Djerrin was loving, and much loved.'

'And would it be acceptable for a Queen of Zithirian to ride, and to hunt?'

'Certainly. Except when carrying the King's children, of course.' Ansaryon reached out his right hand, rather stiffly, and touched her fingers. 'As you may already be carrying mine.' He grinned sud-denly. 'I'll let you ride with us today, though.'

'Thank you,' she said drily, all her senses roused by his brief caress. She paused, and then added, uncharacteristically hesitant, 'Do you want an answer now?'

'Not necessarily. I am quite happy to wait. And I will under-stand if you decide to choose freedom, after all. Whatever happens to us, I will love you for ever.'

For ever. The words seemed suddenly heavy with significance. And she thought of Vinnath, of how she had agreed to share her life with him without loving him, without even really knowing him properly, because it was time for her to settle down, and she had always felt at ease with him.

But then, she had never experienced the depth of companion-ship, of closeness, of friendship, that she had enjoyed with the man in front of her. And he was trying not to put pressure on her, trying not to disclose how much her answer mattered to him.

'*There is something else*,' he said in her mind, before she could speak. '*Something you should know. Something that no one else in the world now knows, save me. If you are to lie beside me, and listen to my dreams, and share my soul, you have the right. And . . . and yet, it is not pleasant. You will not like it – and it may affect your decision.'*

Halthris felt her heart beginning to thud dangerously. She sank to her knees before him, and gripped his hands with hers, not caring who might come in and see them thus. She said slowly, silently, *'Is it to do with Bron?'*

He nodded, his eyes very wide and dark with the memory of terrible anguish. *'Yes. He is my son, as Al'Kalyek suspected. But he is not D'thliss's grandson.'*

She swallowed, and silently uttered the words he wanted her to ask. *'Who is his mother, then?'*

For a long, long space he did not give her an answer, and she knew that he, who had shown such courage, was desperately afraid of her reaction to it. Cold sweat broke out on her skin, despite the heat, and she shivered. Outside, men were shouting orders, and the camp was being broken up. Soon, someone would come in, and this terrible, ominous moment would be lost.

'He is the child in the prophecy, the child of evil born,' Ansaryon said bleakly. *'His mother is dead. She was the Lady Zathti, my sister.'*

A tide of nausea surged in Halthris's throat, and she desperately fought it back. She thought of that pale, wraith-like, beautiful girl, her mind indelibly damaged by what had been done to her, and of the mad, grateful eagerness with which she had gone to her death under the axes of the Ska'i.

Entangled in her memory, he was still speaking. *'I raped her. I was drawn into D'thliss's web, and entangled Zathti with me. She was my twin, she worshipped me, followed me wherever she could. We were eighteen years old. I think D'thliss must have seen the hidden power in us, and hoped that she could breed a child from us who would inherit that power a thousand-fold. She devised some ritual nonsense that she said would enhance my own skills of sorcery. She drugged Zathti, so that she was completely helpless, yet she still knew what was happening to her. Needless cruelty was in D'thliss's nature.'*

'And you?' Halthris spoke aloud, in a hoarse whisper.

'When she realized that I did not want to rape my own sister, she used sorcery to compel me. It was as if I was forced to stand aside from my body, and watch what I did. I could do nothing to stop myself.' He shuddered, and his hands clenched on hers. *'I still dream of it – almost every night. And the most dreadful, sickening thing was that part of me enjoyed it.'*

I don't want to hear this, Halthris thought despairingly: but I must, for his sake I must. She said to his mind, with forced calm, *'What happened then?'*

'No one else knew save the three of us. Zathti kept it all inside herself, saying nothing to anyone, not even to me. I don't think – I don't think she ever realized that I had been as powerless as she was. She thought I was as evil and cruel as D'thliss. And I hated myself so much, I would have agreed with her. I tried to break free of D'thliss, but it was not easy – I was very young, and my knowledge of sorcery was still inadequate. I could be controlled and manipulated, but I did not have the power to escape her. Then D'thliss told me that Zathti was pregnant. It was simple to arrange for her to go into seclusion in the Temple, before her condition became obvious. Girls thinking of entering the priesthood often spent a year or more there, in study and contemplation. Zathti was behaving so strangely, I don't think anyone doubted her reasons. Our mother might have done, if she had not died when we were fifteen. So Zathti gave birth to a child, a boy, in the Temple nine years ago, and D'thliss took him away at once, to be fostered – presumably with her own grandson. Zathti didn't want him – she tried to smother him when he was born. Then she tried to kill herself, and nearly succeeded.' His face twisted in anguish. *'That was when she went truly mad. D'thliss looked after her until she'd recovered from the physical effects of the birth, and then I took her back to the Palace. Eventually, the Royal Healer managed to restore her to some semblance of sanity. After that, D'thliss lost interest in us. She had what she really wanted, the baby, and besides, I was at last beginning to break away from her. Two or three years later, she began to lure Tsenit into her web.'*

'And the baby? Didn't you ever wonder what had happened to him? Didn't you want to take him away from D'thliss when you knew full well how evil she was?'

'No.' His voice carried its own condemnation. *'I pretended that I did not care – I told myself he had probably died. He was a terrible reminder of my guilt, of the harm I had done to my own sister. It was easier to forget him. And besides, I did not then know what he was.'*

'Then why do you want him now?' she cried.

'Because he is my son. Because he is only nine years old, and alone, and frightened, and in great danger. And because if I do not take him now, and teach him how to use his power wisely and well, he has the potential to destroy us all.'

Halthris was weeping, she who never cried, the tears pouring down her face. He said aloud, gently, 'I will understand if you want to go now.'

'I don't know. I don't know what I want.' Halthris withdrew her hands and stood up, frantically wiping her eyes. 'Let me think, Ansary – please, give me time to think.'

And as she stumbled blindly from the tent, she glanced back and saw him still sitting there, his face remote, his eyes closed, as if no description of those terrible things had ever passed between them at all.

It was surprisingly easy, even for an army of nearly eight thousand men, to break camp and march onwards in pursuit of their last remaining enemy. By midday, the first Tanathi scouts were already several miles ahead of the main body, following the Ska'i's trail. They rode along the steppe ridge or in the valley in groups of four, two to watch, two to report back with any news. And the vanguard of the army, a solid wedge of dour Toktel'yans, tramped purposefully in their wake.

Quenait and his warriors had more than a day's start, but must be encumbered by all the paraphernalia of their camp: tents, wagons, plunder. Ansaryon had given orders that his men must travel light, with no superfluous baggage to slow their progress. It should not take long to catch the Ska'i, and the sweet prospect of vengeance quickened every step.

Halthris rode with Djekko, Grinya, and Chettay's older brother Ormeth. They all knew her well, but not so well as to ask awkward questions, particularly concerning her relationship with Ansaryon. And now, with her mind recoiling in horror from what he had told her, she wanted to control her instinctive revulsion, and to think rationally about her dilemma.

Easy enough – too easy, perhaps – to make excuses, to say that it was not his fault, that D'thliss had manipulated him and his sister for her own hideous ends, and that he had only been her tool. But he had admitted enjoying the rape: and that, clearly, had caused him more grief and guilt than anything else in the whole ghastly tale.

And yet, last night in his room at Kaydi's house, he had joined her in love, in desire and pleasure and delight, as if that dreadful and incestuous violation had never happened.

For a brief while, when he had asked her to be his Queen, her destiny had lain clear and glorious before her, as if she had been born for this, and never known it until this moment. And then he had told her about Zathti, and now she did not know what to do.

Why, oh why did he have to tell me? she asked herself over and over again. But the answer was plain enough. Because he would speak of it in his dreams; because sooner or later, she was bound to find out; because he wanted to share the burden with her; and above all, perhaps, because there should be no deception between them, nothing hidden or disguised.

And he did love her: his feelings were in no doubt. But Halthris had always been cautious, careful with her emotions. It had taken her a year to admit that her response to him encompassed rather more than mere lust, or even friendship. And now, faced with the dreadful truth about his past, her first instinct was to run.

For a while, she managed to leave her tumultuous thoughts behind in the exhilaration of a wild gallop along the hills above the Kefirinn, racing the other three until their horses were tired and sweating, before a belated sense of duty returned to her. But once they were moving northwards again, keeping prudently below the skyline, her mind returned once more to the stark choice before her.

Ansaryon. Not an ordinary man with ordinary strengths and vices, but a King, possessed of a unique and terrible gift. She remembered how she had been afraid of him, at their first encounter. And even later, when they had come to know each other so well, when they had discovered that their minds could be linked, when they had become lovers, she had still felt as if there was a part of his soul that was too deep and dark to penetrate.

Well, now she knew what lay there. And she could accept his past, ignoring what had happened ten years ago for the sake of their future together. Or she could run away from that horror, back to the steppe, back to those who knew and loved her, back to the world where in the end she must surely belong, despite the momentous events and changes of the past year.

'Hal! Hal, what are you *doing*?' Ormeth had ridden up alongside her to grab her mount's reins. 'Look – stop *now*, and look!'

She stared past his pointing finger. Below them, the rough rocky hillside fell away quite steeply into the valley of the Kefirinn. She saw overgrown fields, and a herd of steppe deer grazing on the remains of someone's neglected harvest. Beyond them, the burnt-out ruins of a farmstead showed black and grim amidst groves of orchards, woodland and pasture, stretching into the distance along the gently curving river.

And just visible, a dark and smoking smudge three or four miles away beyond the most distant trees, was what could only be the Ska'i camp.

'They didn't get very far, did they?' said Djekko dismissively. 'Looks as though they've settled down for the night already.'

Ormeth, who was the eldest, and famous for his slow but steady common sense, glanced round at the sun, already close to disappearing behind the hillside on which they stood. 'It will be nearly dark before we get back to the army. Too dangerous to investigate closer – I suggest we all return now, and make our report. With any luck, the Ska'i won't even know they've been seen.'

'I want a better look,' said Djekko, who had always had a tendency to rashness. 'Come with me, Hal?'

She shook her head firmly. 'No. Ormeth's right. We've found them, and we know already how many they are. If they *are* camped for the night – and it looks as though they are, judging by those fires – then they'll still be there in the morning. And the army's coming up fast.'

'Perhaps a night attack, then,' Grinya said, his face gleaming with anticipation. 'That'd take them completely by surprise. Come on, Djekko, don't look so glum – you'll have your chance to avenge Iriyan and the others soon enough. Let's go back!'

Reluctantly, Djekko nodded. 'All right. Do you think they *can* see us from there?'

'If they've posted scouts or look-outs, perhaps,' Halthris told him. 'But the Ska'i aren't like the Toktel'yans – strategy doesn't seem to be their strong point. They're probably relying on that horrible old shaman and his scrying bowl. And A – the Lord Ansaryon is a powerful enough sorcerer to be able to hide the army from prying eyes.'

'I sincerely hope so,' Ormeth said. 'Are we decided then? Very well – let's go!'

And the four Tanathi turned their horses and rode back along their own trail, towards the approaching army.

'They are coming.'

Quenait strode over to his shaman, who was peering into his silver bowl. The liquid, fresh blood from a sacrificed prisoner, was rapidly congealing, and as he approached the shiny surface dulled and grew dark. With an exclamation of fury, Br'nnayak whirled round and poked the end of his staff angrily at his chief's chest. 'You fool! Now look what you've done!'

'Who are coming?' Quenait demanded, stepping adroitly sideways. 'That pathetic bird-brain who calls himself King of Zithirian?'

'No. He's dead. It's his brother, the sorcerer.'

Quenait stared at him. 'He can't be on our trail already. You're lying – or the brat is.'

Br'nnayak smiled contemptuously. 'A child? He can't change the pictures in the bowl – his presence just gives them more clarity.' He stabbed his staff in the direction of the two boys, huddled together at the edge of the tent. 'Look at him. You wouldn't imagine he has the potential to destroy cities, would you? But believe me, Ansaryon has killed Tsenit and is marching towards us. He'll be here tomorrow, unless we can cross the river first.'

'Get your brat to whisk us all over it, then,' Quenait said. 'Or bring winter early, so we can cross on the ice, or roll the waters back. If he's as powerful as you say he is, any of those should be easy for him.'

'It's not as simple as that,' Br'nnayak said, with the air of an impatient teacher explaining something to a particularly stupid child. 'The witch has controlled him all his life. She knew how to do it, how to make use of him. I don't – yet. And I don't speak his language, either.'

'Are you sure he's not defying you?'

'I told you, that's impossible.' Br'nnayak's shrivelled face was livid with fury. 'But there's a way to tap his power – there must be. Give me time, and I'll find it.'

'If you're right, we don't have any time.' Quenait swung round and approached the two children. They stared up at him with round, terrified dark eyes, and the elder one, the useless one, put his arms protectively round the younger boy.

The Ska'i chief groped through his scant knowledge of Zithiri-ani, and then shouted, 'You! Do as he says, understand? Obey, or you die. Horribly. Understand me?'

Mutely, they nodded. Both were crying. Quenait spat contemp-tuously. Ska'i children did not weep: these boys were weaklings, unworthy of any respect. And he still could not quite believe that the undersized, frail-looking blond one possessed the terrifying power that Br'nnayak claimed he did.

But his shaman should know. Cursing, the chief turned away from the sobbing children and addressed the old man. 'How many in Ansaryon's army? Could you see?'

'No. You disturbed the blood before I had the chance. Nor do I know exactly where they are. They could be anywhere between here and Zithirian.'

'Then we must cross the river!' Quenait smacked his fist into his other palm. 'Once in the mountains, we can lay traps and ambushes for them as we please. But here, with the river at our backs . . .

Make that brat work for us tonight, or we may lose everything.'
And with a final, menacing glance shared between the shaman and
the two boys, he turned and went out.

Br'nnayak stared in fury at the spoiled bowl of blood. Another
sacrifice would be needed now, and they were running short of
prisoners. But if the child could not be controlled, all the scrying in
the world would be useless.

Muttering a savage prayer to Ayak, he began again to consider
his options. He could Bind the boy, of course, as D'thliss had
attempted to do, but that course was a dangerous one, and had led
directly to her death. The child's power would be permanently
reduced: his own power, for the duration of the process and for
some time afterwards, considerably diminished or even exhausted.
Above all it required time – and time they did not have. If Ansaryon
attacked before the Binding was complete, Br'nnayak would be
virtually defenceless.

There must be other ways of coercion. He paced the tent,
thinking furiously. D'thliss had evidently known the secret. There
was a key to that boy, somewhere there must be a key: he had to
find it, and unlock the power within him. And then Ansaryon, and
his army, and his city, and all those who claimed allegiance to the
King of Zithirian, would be given to Ayak, and their blood would
wipe clean the insult of their defiance of the Devourer's Holy Will.

Other ways. Coercion. Outside in the darkness, the Ska'i
warriors gathered round their fires, ignorant of their enemy's
approach. Tomorrow, they must cross the river, or turn and give
battle. But whatever happened, by whatever means, he must force
the child called Bron to use his power to destroy Ansaryon's army.

And Ayak must have been listening, for suddenly he realized
how it might be done.

The four Tanathi met the army some twenty miles north of
Zithirian, fifteen from the Ska'i camp. Like the enemy, they were
following the rough road that wound between farmsteads and
settlements along the west bank of the river, and extended nearly
two hundred miles further, to the borders of Zithirian at Lake
Raiyis. On the other side of the Kefirinn, the valley was narrower,
and edged by the rapidly rising foothills of Estray. The mountain
itself stood clear, right up to its distinctive symmetrical summit, but
the more distant peaks were hidden in cloud, and the wind now
blew cold and fresh from the north.

Ormeth led the other Tanathi past the tramping, orderly ranks of the Toktel'yan vanguard, marching as tirelessly as though they had rested for a week rather than a night, to the Zithiriani force in the centre of the column. The recent rain had dampened the earth, so that there was no betraying cloud of dust hanging above the army to mark its inexorable progress, or to choke the soldiers' throats. Halthris saw Ansaryon, flanked on one side by Invan and on the other by King Temiltan. He rode stiffly and awkwardly, his reins in his right hand, and he still looked very white around the mouth, but there were no other signs of weakness. With sudden fear for him, she wondered how he would fare when battle was joined. The injury to his left arm meant that he would be unable to use a shield, or to control his horse while wielding his sword. And she could not imagine that he would want to stand in the rearmost rank while other men fought and died on his behalf.

Wearily, she supposed that such acute concern for his safety meant that despite everything, her feelings for him had not changed.

Ormeth urged his horse up to Invan's, and made his report. 'We've found the Ska'i camp, General – it's not more than fifteen miles from here!'

Halthris saw Ansaryon's head turn. His blue-plumed helmet was strapped to his saddle, so his expression was quite plain: from his remote, slightly dazed look, she guessed that he had been practising sorcery, perhaps hiding the army from the Ska'i shaman. He said, after a pause, 'Yes, I can see it. Not very clearly, but it's there – just past the Lion Rock. We can reach it in a few hours, and attack them as they sleep – take advantage of darkness, and surprise.'

Invan looked as if he might object, and then, obviously, changed his mind. 'Surely the men should have some rest, before giving battle.'

'There should still be time for that. It's nearly sunset – we should reach Lanyai settlement soon after nightfall. That's only five miles from their camp. We can rest, eat, and then strike at them before they even know we're coming.' He paused, and glanced at Halthris. In her mind, she heard his voice. *They have sorcery planned. They are trying to hide it, but I can feel it in my blood. We outnumber them, but they have more power. Are you ready for what must come?*'

'*I am,*' she said grimly. '*I too have my revenge to take, remember.*'

'*And remember too – I am yours for ever – no matter what may befall us tonight.*'

With his words haunting her soul, she rode alongside him and watched as men were despatched up and down the marching ranks, to deliver his message. Two more hours or so – then rest, food, and a surprise night attack. And from the buzz of excited comment, even a sprinkling of cheers, she knew that the soldiers were all relishing this early opportunity to tackle the hated Ska'i.

But she was not. For she could not rid herself of the feeling that somehow, in some way, the coming night would see destruction and slaughter on a scale so monstrous, so appalling, that nothing could withstand it.

THIRTY

Bron woke from an exhausted sleep that had been full of hideous dreams. In his nightmare, the severed, bodiless head of his grandmother D'thliss had loomed over him, her eyes mad with evil, her mouth dripping blood and curses . . .

He gave a sob of terror, and then stuffed his hand into his mouth to stifle the sound. She was dead, D'thliss was *dead* – her decaying head topped the trophy lance outside Br'nnayak's tent, the eyes already taken by the crows, and she had no power to hurt or frighten him any more.

But Br'nnayak now threatened him in her place. And he knew, in the way that he knew such things, without question or discovery, that the shaman was infinitely more evil, more dangerous, than ever D'thliss had been. For the High Priestess of Tayo had only wanted to rule a city, whereas Br'nnayak wanted to destroy all of civilization in Ayak's name, and would gleefully wade through an ocean of blood to achieve his ambition.

Bron knew what else Br'nnayak wanted. The shaman wanted him, Bron, his heart and soul and mind and above all his power, to use in furtherance of his dream. And although the boy had managed so far to keep him at bay, he knew his covert defiance could not withstand the old man much longer. Sooner or later, the shaman would lose patience. And Bron knew, none better, that sorcerers were at their most dangerous when the power within them was unleashed by rage or fear, and allowed to rampage uncontrolled by the usual precise and limiting practices of magic.

Lelya lay beside him, his body warm under the rough scratchy felt blanket. At least Br'nnayak had given them food, and had not yet resorted to physical cruelty. But Bron knew that this would not last long, for the shaman was desperate to unlock his power. And although he and Lelya had both endured beatings, hardship and abuse from D'thliss, and had grown almost accustomed to such treatment, Bron was certain that anything Br'nnayak could do to him would be far worse than his grandmother's spiteful malevolence.

But he was not in danger of death. He was their prize, the

reason the Ska'i had attacked the Temple, the reason they had left the city so suddenly. Lelya, though, was useless to them, although it had taken Br'nnayak almost a day, until the boys had recovered from the Binding drugs given to them by D'thliss, to discover it. And Bron was certain that if he had not clung so tightly to Lelya, and screamed so loud, his foster-brother would have been slain then and there.

So for as long as they remained prisoners, Lelya was at risk. Bron breathed the thick, stinking air of Br'nnayak's tent, wondering if he could somehow help Lelya to escape. But the older boy's habit of protectiveness was impossible to break. He would never believe that he might be in danger, and he would certainly refuse to leave his foster-brother behind.

And Bron still lacked the strength to defy Br'nnayak openly. He had been able to spoil D'thliss's scrying, and to hide himself and others from her, but only very subtly, so that she did not realize, until the end, what he was doing. The shaman, though, would be very difficult to deceive.

Lying in the dark, he became aware of a low mutter of voices, speaking in the ugly, staccato Ska'i language. He could not understand what was being said, and their thoughts were strongly defended, but he could sense their anger, their ruthlessness and their desperation. A sudden and terrible premonition gripped him, and he rolled over and touched Lelya's face.

His foster-brother came awake with a grunt, and a whimper of fear. Bron put a hand over his mouth, but too late. The voices stopped at once, and footsteps approached the dark edge of the tent where the boys lay. Bron opened his eyes, flinching, and saw light, smoke, and the shaman's terrible face, saturated in evil, staring down at him. Beside him stood the chief, younger but no less threatening. 'Awake, I see,' said Quenait, in his harshly-accented Zithiriani. 'Both of you – up!'

Lelya rubbed his eyes and wearily obeyed, though he was still half asleep. He stood in front of the younger boy, in a pathetic attempt to protect him, and said, 'What do you want?'

'You'll see,' said Quenait, as Br'nnayak lifted his staff threateningly. 'Now walk!'

Lelya did not move. With a sudden shriek of rage, the shaman whirled and shouted something. Four Ska'i pushed into the tent and grabbed the two boys with rough and painful hands. Bron, his arms almost wrenched from their sockets, was treated no more gently than his foster-brother. Too frightened to struggle, the children were dragged out of the foetid tent to stand pinioned in the open air.

It was late in the night, and the chilly stars shone impassively down: the moon, nearly full, sailed high above them. Bron shivered uncontrollably, from the sharp cold and from fear. A huge fire glowed red in front of him, and around it he saw the avid, cruel faces of many Ska'i, watching them.

Br'nnayak strode up to the sullen blaze. He cast a handful of powder on the dying flames, muttering some spell. At once, they leapt up at his command, a brilliant and dazzling flare of light.

Lelya sobbed, and turned his face away. Bron stood quite still, staring into the heart of the fire, trying desperately not to panic, struggling to gather his strength.

The shaman, followed by half a dozen younger acolytes, walked three times round the blaze, chanting. At every sound of Ayak's name, the watching tribesmen shouted a response, and the flames sprang higher still, as if in homage. At the end of the ritual, he stopped, turned and walked over to the two boys. Still chanting in an incessant, malevolent undertone, he thrust his staff suddenly at Lelya's face. As the boy flinched, he laughed, and said something to the men holding him. At once, they hauled Lelya roughly forward until he was almost within reach of the flames, and then forced him to his knees.

Bron, his eyes very dark, saw the shaman and the chief turn to him. Br'nnayak's face was twisted and glittering with unspeakable rage and evil. He said something in Ska'i, the spittle flying from his mouth with every word, and Quenait translated. 'You listen, boy, listen well. You help us. Zithirian army close. You help shaman destroy them, or he dies.'

Despite all his desperate attempts to be brave, Bron could not stop the tears. He said frantically, sobbing, 'No – don't – he's my brother – don't kill him, please don't kill him!'

'Then help Br'nnayak.' Quenait thrust his face very close to the child's. His breath stank, and his teeth were rotten. 'Help him now. Destroy Ansaryon's army. It is easy, for one of your power. Kill them all, and your brother lives.'

So D'thliss's ally Tsenit must be dead. Bron hardly cared, in the face of the terrible choice forced upon him. For how could he willingly help Br'nnayak to slaughter thousands of men by sorcery?

But if he did not, then Lelya, his one friend, his foster-brother, who had loved and protected him all his life, would be brutally murdered.

'Choose. Now. Or he dies.' Quenait turned and gestured at the tribesmen holding Lelya down. One of them raised his double axe high above the boy's bent neck, ready for the fatal blow.

'No!' Bron screamed. 'No – no!' He pushed the tears from his eyes and cried in despair, 'No – don't kill him – please don't – I'll help you, I promise it.'

Br'nnayak smiled, showing fangs as menacing as the Devourer he worshipped. He said something to the tribesmen, and the painful grip on Bron's arms was released. Quenait smiled too. 'Take his hand, boy. Let his mind reach yours. Then you may look in the bowl together.'

Br'nnayak extended his bony fingers to the quailing child. They touched, and Bron felt the power of evil pulse through him suddenly, tingling in his hand as if he had been bitten by a poisonous snake. The shaman smiled, sensing his ultimate victory, and his grip tightened.

A malevolent grin appeared on Quenait's face. He turned and gestured quite casually to the men holding Lelya. Br'nnayak saw him, and shouted something frantically, but too late. The fire-lit axe, still poised above the child, fell with a flash of flame. There was a dull, sickening thud, and Bron's beloved foster-brother toppled forward, blood spurting from his severed neck, while one of the acolytes ran up with a silver bowl to catch the precious liquid.

With a screech of savage protest, Br'nnayak flung Bron aside and lashed out at his chief with his staff. Quenait stepped back out of reach, laughing with malicious glee at this petty victory over the shaman who had ruled his life, and whom he had always secretly feared, and loathed.

And at the sound, a huge, overpowering rage flooded Bron. He raised his hands, and the bright flames roared suddenly, and leapt from the fire. The Ska'i who had killed Lelya screamed hoarsely as his body was engulfed: the acolyte turned to run, dropping the bowl of blood, and his long robes flared up like a pitch-soaked torch.

It was so easy. He was Master of the Fire, and death was his to command. Bron howled with grief and rage as the flames leapt to consume all the men around him. Before Quenait could pull his axe from his belt, he was enveloped in a gown of witch-fire, brilliant and terrible, and his screeches of agony mingled with the cries of his burning warriors.

Br'nnayak, still untouched, was staring at Bron as though transfixed with horror. Then the greedy flame grasped his staff, his garments, his hair, and roared up in a great sheet of blue-white fire.

He backed away, screaming and cursing, his hands outstretched as if to ward off this final, terrible vengeance.

And smiling, without moving or touching him, Bron flung him into the heart of the furnace.

Along with the rest of the army, Halthris had tried to snatch an hour or so of sleep before the final attack, that might bring a horrible death to them all. It proved impossible: the ground was hard and damp, her cloak inadequate against the cold, and her horse had an annoying habit of snuffling and clinking its bit as it moved in its hobbles. After a while, she gave up, and sat against the wall of the burnt-out barn where most of the Tanathi were camped, looking up at the glittering stars, and thinking of Ansaryon, and of the answer she would give him, if they both survived.

If. Already, they had overcome impossible odds, but she could not believe that now, with the last battle imminent, and all the advantage apparently on their side, they might actually succeed. For the Ska'i had Bron: and Bron, it seemed, had the power to destroy everything, and everyone, in his path.

A star-streak shot across the northern sky. She watched the place for a long time, but there were no more. To see one was supposed to be a sign of ambiguous but significant portent. Two were the unmistakable harbingers of great good fortune.

Dawn must be approaching already, for there was a definite lightening of the sky above the shoulder of the hill lying between them and the Ska'i camp. She stared at it stupidly for several heartbeats before she realized that she was looking north-west. And in all the history of the known world, the sun had never risen there before.

Cold and discomfort forgotten, Halthris jumped to her feet. She stood still, straining her eyes, until she was certain of what she saw. Then she turned, and ran through the ruined village, dodging sleeping or resting soldiers, their armour and horses, until she came to the wrecked house where Ansaryon had set up his headquarters.

There was no light within: they had been forbidden to make fires or to show any other signs of their presence that might warn a watching Ska'i. Two guards stood on duty at the entrance: she whispered to them, and they let her through.

The place had no roof, and the moonlight showed her Invan, sitting on the floor, sharpening his sword with slow, careful strokes of the whetstone. Beside him, Temiltan was talking softly to the other Generals, Sekkenet and Halmon. More men, officers and messengers, slept in dark corners. She could not see Ansaryon.

'Invan?' she said quietly, and he looked up. 'Invan, there's something strange in the sky – I think you ought to see it.'

At once, the General got to his feet and moved to the doorway with a caution that might, at another time, have seemed absurdly exaggerated. Temiltan and the other Generals followed.

Outside, the camp was still quiet, although everywhere Halthris could hear the soft, betraying sounds of tense, wakeful men and horses. She turned to the north-west, ready to describe what she had seen in case there was nothing there any more, and gasped.

The hill between was edged like a blade, flat and black against the blinding light behind it. A light that possessed the flickering, sinister brilliance of sorcery, and also a wonderful, terrible beauty.

Halmon muttered a prayer, and made the warding sign. Temiltan, more down-to-earth, said sharply, 'What in Hegeden's name is that?'

'The Ska'i camp, I think.' Halthris shivered, wishing she hadn't left her cloak beside her horse. 'It looks like sorcery, doesn't it? Are they going to attack us?'

'If they are, we're done for,' Invan said bluntly. 'Not even Ansaryon could defend us against that sort of power.'

'I don't have to.'

They turned, and saw the King of Zithirian standing at the entrance to the ruined house. The witch-light in the distant sky was so strong that his features were quite distinct, although his eyes were shadowed. He added in explanation, 'That is not directed against us. We are in no danger from it – and the Ska'i will not threaten us any more.'

They stared at him in bewilderment. Finally, Sekkenet said urgently, 'What do you mean? What is happening over there?'

'I don't know exactly,' Ansaryon said. 'But we shall see in the morning, when it's all over. For now, I think we'd best leave well alone. I can tell you, though, that it'll be quite safe to relax and get some rest. There must be four hours at least till dawn. I'm going back to sleep.' And he disappeared into the house, leaving his Generals staring after him in amazement.

'He's right,' Invan said, after a stark pause. 'That kind of power is not to be meddled with, even if you know what you're doing. I thought I'd seen it all at Sar D'yenyi, but that's beyond my worst dreams.'

Halthris said nothing, but shivered. She knew in her bones that whatever was happening on the other side of that distant hill was evil, terrible, an eruption of enormous power. The Devourer would be bloated tonight – but not with the army's blood.

They stayed, watching with strained eyes and faces, until that dreadful glare had at last diminished. Then, still in an appalled silence, they turned away.

At long last, the clear, cold night gave way to a clear, cold morning. Those men who had managed to sleep all through the hours of darkness, too exhausted to stay awake even in the tension before imminent battle, woke bewildered at dawn, wondering why they had not been roused as promised for the surprise attack on the Ska'i. Those who had sat restlessly wakeful, and wondered at the unearthly light in the north-western sky, had already heard the news, flown like sorcerer's fire around the camp. Something terrible had happened to their enemies. And at sunrise they were to march on again, with caution, but not prepared for battle.

Once more, the army broke camp with varying degrees of competence – the Toktel'yans brisk and speedy, the Lelyentans slow and thorough, the Minassans slapdash and already inclined to argue with their officers – and marched onwards. This time, though, their generals led them away from the Kefirinn valley, up onto the edge of the bordering steppe. It added extra hours and miles to the distance they must travel, but no one grumbled. No one knew exactly what horror lay waiting for them beyond that hill, but at least they would be able to see it from a safe distance.

The sun was quite high, and the birds singing sweet and oblivious overhead, when the vanguard came within sight of the Ska'i camp. There were some wisps of smoke rising, but no other sign of life at all. The Toktel'yan soldiers halted on the ridge above it. And even they, accustomed to sorcery, smelt the faint stench of roasted flesh wafting up to them on the wind, and by tacit consent, went no further.

All along the crest of the hill, the rest of the army gathered and stared at what lay below them. The coils of evil-looking, oily smoke plumed lazily from charred heaps that might once have been wagons, or camp fires, or tents. Scattered amongst them, as if some giant hand had flung down a bowlful of crushed charcoal, were thousands of smaller, darker pieces. And in all that vile desolation, nothing moved save what could be blown by the wind.

Halthris, looking down, felt tears prick her eyes: not from pity for the Ska'i, who had met an end as hideous and cruel as they were themselves, but in fear and wonder at the awesome power that had wreaked such total devastation.

Someone rode up beside her. She turned her head, and saw Ansaryon. No trace of the horror she felt showed on his face: it was pale, as always, and quite without expression. But she knew, without having to listen to his thoughts, that this was a mask disguising emotions which, at this moment, would be inappropriate to reveal. For somewhere down there in that vast pyre was the son he had sworn to protect, the child of evil born who had caused a King's downfall. And whether Bron was dead or alive, both he and Halthris knew that the boy must in some way have been the cause of this destruction.

'I'm going down,' Ansaryon said aloud. 'I've told Invan and Temiltan to stay up here. Will you come with me?'

She did not want to. She was not afraid for herself: there was no peril lurking in the Ska'i camp, not any more. But the horrors below would be quite outside her experience, and the thought of viewing them at close quarters filled her with dread.

Ansaryon was still looking at her. She saw the appeal in his eyes, and swallowed her fear and nausea. 'Yes. If you want me to, I will come.'

With eight thousand Toktel'yans, Lelyentans, Zithiriani and Minassans watching them, they urged their horses down the long slope. The camp was perhaps a mile away, sprawled across the abandoned pasture and meadow land beside the river. The valley of the Kefirinn narrowed here, with the shoulders of the steppe hills thrusting into the lower ground.

As they drew nearer, riding at a slow and cautious canter, the wind blew in their faces, and the nauseous reek of burnt meat clogged their nostrils. A hundred paces or so from the edge of the camp, both horses refused to go any closer. In the end, they gave up the fruitless attempts at persuasion, dismounted and tied their mounts' reins to a bush.

Ansaryon turned to face her. He said, his voice oddly strained and hesitant, 'Hal – I'm glad you're here. I must see what – if he is there. I couldn't just turn away without knowng what had happened to him. And whatever it is that I have to confront here, whatever I must bear – I can only bear it with you.'

Their eyes met. Halthris looked away first. She did not want to lay herself open to him again, not now. She would need all her defences for what lay ahead. She gave him a brief, sliding smile, and they walked forward, in silence.

She made herself look at the first tangle of twisted, blackened corpses. After that, she just stared straight ahead, trying not to breathe the tainted air too deeply, trying not to remember that these had once been men: ugly, repulsive, cruel and brutal men, admittedly, who would kill children and babies without compunction, but still men, who had lived, and breathed, and then suffered this hideous and agonizing death.

'Listen!'

She stopped as Ansaryon raised his hand. They had penetrated almost to the heart of the camp, and so far the only sound had been made by the wind blowing briskly against them, stirring ashes and moving the branches of the trees down by the river. Not even the kites had come to this place of slaughter: but something here still lived, for now she could hear the exhausted, desolate sobbing of a child.

Ansaryon began to run. She followed, dodging between debris and corpses. Suddenly he halted, and she came to a breathless stop beside him.

That heap of blackened, smoking felt must be the remains of a tent. The trophy lance still stood sentinel outside it, untouched, the heads in varying stages of gruesome decay. But Ansaryon was not looking at them: he was staring at the two children, one dead, one living, huddled together on the ground beside the ashen remains of a huge fire.

Once, she had thought of that small, weeping figure as a threat. Once, she had wanted to kill him. It was not possible now. Abandoning all her past thoughts and beliefs, Halthris walked forward, and knelt beside him. She said softly, 'Bron?'

There was no response save that eternal, dreadful sobbing. She touched him, and he did not move. With gentle hands, she prised him away from the headless corpse of the other boy, and gathered his shaking body close to hers, murmuring words of comfort in Tanathi and in Zithiriani, until at last his broken weeping died away into soft, hiccuping breaths, warm against her shoulder.

Then she looked up, her face wet with tears, and saw that Ansaryon was kneeling beside her, his own expression full of terrible anguish. And finally she realized that he had been right all along: that Bron himself, for his own sake and not because of his awesome power, was more important than anything else. They could not abandon him here, amidst the death and destruction he had caused. And neither could she run away from Ansaryon, or his love, or the destiny awaiting them as rulers of Zithirian.

'Let me hold him,' he said, and she transferred Bron to his father's arms. Ansaryon stood up, and the boy stirred, muttering something. The King of Zithirian smiled, with extraordinary tenderness, and stroked the pale head resting against his shoulder.

'Come on,' said Halthris softly. 'Let's take him home – home to Zithirian.'

And together, they turned and walked out of the Ska'i camp, back towards the watching soldiers on the hill.